Robert Burns, Peter Hately Waddell

Life and works of Robert Burns

Volume Second

Robert Burns, Peter Hately Waddell

Life and works of Robert Burns
Volume Second

ISBN/EAN: 9783337056452

Printed in Europe, USA, Canada, Australia, Japan

Cover: Foto ©Raphael Reischuk / pixelio.de

More available books at **www.hansebooks.com**

LIFE AND WORKS

OF

ROBERT BURNS.

BY

P. HATELY WADDELL,

MINISTER OF THE GOSPEL.

ENRICHED WITH PORTRAITS, AND NUMEROUS ILLUSTRATIONS IN COLOUR,
FROM ORIGINAL DESIGNS, IN THE HIGHEST STYLE OF THE ART.

VOLUME SECOND.

GLASGOW:
PRINTED AND PUBLISHED BY DAVID WILSON, 14 MAXWELL STREET.
1867.

PROSE WORKS:

BEING CHIEFLY

CORRESPONDENCE.

WITH

BIOGRAPHICAL REMARKS

BY EDITOR.

CONTENTS.

SPECIAL CORRESPONDENCE.

BIOGRAPHICAL REMARKS.

BURNS'S LETTER-WRITING TO WOMEN.

READERS who refer to our Biography will be reminded that, on the authority of the shrewdest and most accomplished critics of the time, Burns's gift of speech was equal—in the opinion of many superior—to his gift of poetry. In argument or in conversation he was alike fascinating and instructive, and in the peculiar gift of imaginative story-telling, he was altogether unrivalled. Had the conversation, or most eloquent colloquial oratory, with which he thus entertained and delighted society for the time, been recorded or even epitomised, like Coleridge's or Johnson's, the world might now have been in possession of an invaluable legacy of wisdom, or of fiction, as worthy of preservation in many respects as the memorabilia of Socrates by Xenophon, or the eloquent fabrications of Plato. But such speech never can be recorded. It belongs essentially to the lips and air; and, when once delivered, will brook no tarrying, but passes on with the atmosphere, enriching its echoes by reverberation only, never to return. All, therefore, that can be said to remain of the Prose Works of Robert Burns, is to be found in his Epistolary Correspondence; on which, fortunately for the world, he bestowed both enthusiasm and care, and of which, although much has been lost or destroyed, much yet survives to attest sufficiently the variety and beauty of the whole.

The value and prospective interest of this correspondence seems to have been suggested to him by friends; for towards the close of his life he had already commenced a revision of all the rough-draft letters in his own hands, and had even proceeded to some length in their transcription in a volume prepared expressly for their preservation. This work, we presume, was delayed by sickness, and finally interrupted by death. All we know, therefore, of this most extraordinary outpouring of epistolary eloquence has been from the gradually increasing accumulation of originals, where they have been scattered by friendship or by chance over the world. Not a few, we believe, remain yet to be discovered, and of those which are already known to the public the most careful study and redistribution is required, to illustrate the writer's character and elucidate their own perfection.

The arrangement of this rich and varied material in the mere order of time, although it has advantages in a statistical point of view, is most unsatisfactory in other respects. To every correspondent and to every subject, as well as to every epoch and day of his life, these letters have an especial and instructive relation of their own, which is absolutely lost, or immensely impaired, by the intrusion of other dates, interests, or individuals on a sphere with which they have no such relation. The continuity of the writer's thoughts and sentiments is thus broken, and his idea of the individual addressed is hopelessly entangled with that of others, with whom for the moment he has no concern, and of whom we do not care to hear or think whilst he is earnestly or affectionately addressing another in our presence. Subjects, also, that should appear in their entirety to be understood with advantage, or understood at all, are thus disintegrated or marred; and finally, which is most to be lamented, the grand characteristic aspects of the man's own intellectual or moral nature are completely obliterated, a confused, although delightful medley of thought and speech being all that remains—like a landscape seen through a continual shower or waterfall of indiscriminate commingled radiance—hills, woods, valley-tracts, and rivers swimming all together in perpetual maze before us. To remedy these defects of mere chronological arrangement, some new principle of classification was desirable; some method of presenting the whole in such groups or masses as should present the man himself most clearly in distinguishable characteristic phases, and preserve at the same time, as far as possible, the chronological order also. With this double object in view, we have arranged the whole, as already intimated, under four distinct but by no means opposing heads, each having some natural and instructive affinity to the other; whilst the various contents of each have in like manner been subdivided and arranged independently, yet harmoniously: all the letters, for example, addressed to any one person being grouped together as much in consecutive order of their own dates as possible, that the extent and character of correspondence with the individual may be ascertained at a glance, and the relation of that individual, as a correspondent at least, to the writer's whole life, in time or in importance, determined accordingly.

In such arrangement of our Author's Correspondence as was thus suggested, we had very little hesitation as to which particular portion should have bulk and precedence of its own; and in assigning that precedence exclusively to his epistolary correspondence with women, much more than mere deference to their sex was implied. There is, indeed, a considerable number of letters addressed to persons of the other sex—sometimes of rank, sometimes of influence—that have manifestly been written with the utmost care, and on topics of the highest special importance, which might also have been admitted on such grounds in this department; but as some of these relate to literary subjects, and others are almost isolated in their individual references, we felt as if it would be a sort of intrusion on this peculiar region to allow them to appear. Whatever else of special interest these may have in the way of careful composition or peculiar theme, they lack the special and peculiar tone which distinguished every epistolary communication addressed by him to women; and would only distract the attention of the reader from the strange and interesting study of so wonderful a nature in correspondence more immediately with them. In writing to men (with most of whom naturally he might be on more familiar relations), he was whatever the theme suggested, and often more; but the variety of the topics necessarily arising in course of such correspondence with them, although it did not alter, to a certain extent obscured the moral aspect of the writer himself. He was the same in all, but not so distinctly seen through the multiplicity of topics. His correspondence with persons of his own sex, therefore, or with the world at large, required considerably more analysis and subdivision to make it entirely appreciable. What was purely literary must be relegated to the region of literature; what was general or indifferent, or even special and ceremonious, but on trivial or on strictly business subjects, might be grouped together, and allowed to illustrate itself; what was chiefly or altogether domestic should have a sacred column of its own, however brief or humble: and so, it seemed most advantageous to arrange it all.

In writing to women, on the other hand (with whom he was necessarily to some extent on ceremony), whatever variety of subject might occur, he was always and conspicuously the same—man proper, in his highest intellectual attitudes. No theme whatever could come amiss to him in their presence, or was ever treated otherwise than with propriety, originality, elegance, and ease. Religion, morality, philosophy, the highest literature; friendship, love, life, death, courtship, marriage, grief, or joy; gloves, ribbons, fashions, travels, politics, theatres; music, versification, criticism, printing, penmanship itself, and poetry—are all themes of deferential solicitude, or of fascinating talk, before them; whilst the sentiment, the tone, and very diction of his letters corresponds. In the course of this wonderful special epistolary authorship, we have every phase of masculine regard by turns—courtly independence, romantic gratitude, respectful devotion, chivalrous consideration; gallantry, raillery, obeisance—nay, absolute prostration; imperious passion, and occasionally wrath itself—from a man like him, not always unacceptable; with a profusion of complimentary homage interwoven or implied, the manliest and sincerest ever offered for womanly recognition or acceptance. On this correspondence, to whomsoever addressed, we have the best authority for believing also that the writer bestowed the utmost care and expended his utmost brilliancy. Every letter might not be formally prepared (we have his own express declaration that only one letter to Mrs. Dunlop was transcribed; in which, however, we are much inclined to believe his memory deceived him), but every letter certainly was studied; and some of the most important, on difficult or painful topics, were probably revised, if not re-written, before being despatched to their destinations. He revels in them all with the grace of freedom, with the licence of decorum, with the ease of absolute self-control, and with the fascination of conspicuous idolatry in presence of these privileged divinities—who certainly, on their part, were far from being either averse or insensible to his worship. Such correspondence, therefore, for a thousand reasons, had prominent claims to precedence as special; with this additional recommendation, that it extends, in one form or another, throughout the Author's entire literary life—from the earliest dawn of love and poetry in his bosom, to the last sad hours of sorrow and decay; and is the best unbroken, many-sided, varied mirror of the man's personal existence extant.

Besides all which, in a literary point of view, there is much also of the highest personal interest pervading the whole of this special correspondence with women. The confidence he reposes in them, and the conscious assurance of their sympathetic interest in him and in his most intimate concerns, are remarkable features throughout. The whole truth in every case he does not divulge to them all, and was not expected to communicate perhaps

even to the most matronly or confidential among them; but the delicate boldness with which he makes many an avowal at which most ordinary letter-writers so highly privileged would either stumble and fall, or outrage with senseless impertinence the taste and good-nature of their correspondents, bespeaks the innate sense of propriety that was one of his highest characteristics, and the extent of honourable reliance he could exercise on the sympathy and admiration of the best and most accomplished of their sex. In the course of such revelations, also, we have numerous individual topics of health, of fortune, of domestic satisfactions or domestic trials, of the difficulties and triumphs of authorship, of social relations and of personal feelings, and of the general onward progress of his life and literary labours, all incidentally introduced, and slightly or more seriously, sometimes impatiently, discussed, after such a peculiar fashion as would only be attended to, or cared for, by women; and which, from this very fact, may be accepted as indicating the purer and higher action of his soul, at least in its meditative moods, when called on to discourse, in loving freedom, on such subjects, with listeners of unquestionable purity: which thus accumulated and examined, and impartially weighed, afford perhaps as true an average revelation also of his moral or religious state, as could be hoped for through any other sort of medium; whilst those letters of a peculiarly ardent or even questionable character, indited without consideration of consequences, and without reserve, during the same period, touching on whatever topic might be most conducive to his own object at the moment, unfold such an extraordinary underlying depth of passionate existence as to constitute the man himself, with all that appertained to him in thought or life, a theme of astonishment and wonder.

Minuter treatment in detail is here, perhaps, unnecessary; but it may be remarked, that the correspondence with Mrs. Dunlop—the realest, the most important, and dignified of its kind; and the selected correspondence with 'Clarinda'—approaching more nearly to the region of purely fictitious epistolary work than anything absolutely real ever did, are doubtless in many ways the most conspicuous portions of the whole. But the rest have a peculiar although subordinate interest of their own.

We place foremost, however, as in point of time and therefore of inexperience they precede the rest, a short series of formal letters addressed to some now only half-recognisable correspondent; whose ideas on the tender topic the writer seems to have been anxious to educate after a most serious, and, as he no doubt at the time believed, most exemplary fashion. The fair one thus solemnly approached was presumably Ellison Begbie—a sweet, unaffected girl then domiciled in the neighbourhood of Lochlea, and for whom the Poet long after entertained undoubtedly a genuine and devout affection. But the letters themselves, in which assurance of this regard was so unsuccessfully attempted to be conveyed, can hardly, we should think, at this date be read, even by the most inexperienced lover, with gravity. How laughable, in a few years after, would the whole affair seem to be to the half-awakened writer himself!

Under same head of early, perhaps rather elaborate, epistolary efforts, but on the topic of religion, a most valuable collection of letters never published has also by some untoward accident been now irretrievably lost. The particulars of this misfortune will be detailed hereafter in our Appendix.* In the meantime, we can but deplore, whilst we thus incidentally announce it as one of the greatest losses of its kind, both to his religious reputation and for the satisfaction of the world, that could well be imagined. The correspondence with Mrs. Dunlop, which dates from the commencement of his authorship and continues till the very close of his life, was reciprocated and sustained by that admirable woman, it may be said without interruption; but was obtained from her for publication, on the express condition only, that her own letters to the Poet should be surrendered to herself again in exchange for his. The letters to 'Clarinda' likewise date from a very early period in his authorship, and continue, with some characteristic passionate interruptions, till near the end of his career. By their fervid eloquence, as well as by their peculiar and in some respects their questionable character in the circumstances, these letters have attained a wide celebrity; although it would have been better, perhaps, had most of them remained unknown. They may be said to have been

anonymous, having only a fictitious signature, although undoubtedly authentic, and were manifestly never intended to be seen by any-one but the person to whom they were addressed. But their piecemeal publication rendered concealment ultimately impossible; and it was therefore better upon the whole, that they should be known and judged of entire as they were, than condemned on conjecture as being more reprehensible than they are.* It is something astonishing, however, to reflect that two such series of letters should have been proceeding together during such a number of years, as those to Mrs. Dunlop and the others to 'Clarinda,' each to the respective correspondent perfect in their way, yet with such vast dissimilarity of tone and tendency. That another series, so bright, natural, half-passionate and beautiful, as the letters to Miss Chalmers, should have been interwoven in point of time with the others, or at least running side by side with them both so long; whilst not a single word in any of them seems to be misplaced, nor a topic misapplied; is perhaps not less astonishing—numerous special letters to individual indifferent, or rival parties, in the meantime, being all equally appropriate, characteristic, and perfect in their way.

The letters to Mrs. Walter Riddel, which date all from and after the year 1792—the latest epoch of his life—as they embody an extravagant friendship and relate to a distressing feud, and are throughout characterised by the greatest brilliancy and point, have a corresponding attractive interest, although comparatively few in number. The published collection of letters to this lady, however, we may mention, has hitherto been by no means complete—some of the most perfect being as yet publicly unknown. Our own best endeavours, we rejoice to say, have been to some extent successful in obtaining access to these interesting documents, several of which will now be added, in their place, to the already existing collection. The utmost we can do with respect to others, is to present fragments of those which are still beyond our reach; and which we now refer to thus prominently in the hope that the fortunate possessors of the originals, wherever they exist, may be induced hereafter, perhaps, to communicate them to the public.

CORRESPONDENCE.

(1.)

To Miss E.

[Supposed by Mr. Chambers to have been Ellison Begbie. Date of entire series, Lochlea, 1780-81. Letters first published by Currie, afterwards omitted.]

I VERILY believe, my dear E., that the pure, genuine feelings of love are as rare in the world as the pure, genuine principles of virtue and piety. This I hope will account for the uncommon style of all my letters to you. By uncommon, I mean their being written in such a serious manner, which to tell you the truth, has made me often afraid lest you should take me for some zealous bigot, who conversed with his mistress as he would converse with his minister. I don't know how it is, my dear, for though, except your company, there is nothing on earth gives me so much pleasure as writing to you, yet it never gives me those giddy raptures so much talked of among lovers. I have often thought that if a well-grounded affection be not really a part of virtue, 'tis something extremely akin to it. Whenever the thought of my E. warms my heart, every feeling of humanity, every principle of generosity kindles in my breast. It extinguishes every dirty spark of malice and envy which are but too apt to infest me. I grasp every creature in the arms of universal benevolence, and equally participate in the pleasures of the happy, and sympathize with the miseries of the unfortunate. I assure you, my dear, I often look up to the Divine Disposer of events with an eye of gratitude for the blessing which I hope he intends to bestow on me in bestowing you. I sincerely wish that he may bless my endeavours to make your life as comfortable and happy as possible, both in sweetening the rougher parts of my natural temper, and bettering the unkindly circumstances of my fortune. This, my dear, is a passion, at least in my view, worthy of a man, and I will add worthy of a Christian. The sordid earth-worm may profess love to a woman's person, whilst in reality his affection is centered in her pocket; and the slavish drudge may go a-wooing as he goes to the horse-market to choose one who is stout and firm, and as we may say of an old horse, one who will be a good drudge and draw kindly. I disdain their dirty, puny ideas. I would be heartily out of humour with myself if I thought I were capable of having so poor a notion of the sex, which were designed to crown the pleasures of society. Poor devils! I don't envy them their happiness who have such notions. For my part, I propose quite other pleasures with my dear partner.

R. B.

(2.)

TO MISS E.

MY DEAR E. :

I DO not remember in the course of your acquaintance and mine, ever to have heard your opinion on the ordinary way of falling in love, amongst people of our station of life: I do not mean the persons who proceed in the way of bargain, but those whose affection is really placed on the person.

Though I be, as you very well know, but a very awkward lover myself, yet as I have some opportunities of observing the conduct of others who are much better skilled in the affair of courtship than I am, I often think it is owing to lucky chance more than to good management, that there are not more unhappy marriages than usually are.

It is natural for a young fellow to like the acquaintance of the females, and customary for him to keep them company when occasion serves: some one of them is more agreeable to him than the rest; there is something, he knows not what, pleases him, he knows not how, in her company. This I take to be what is called love with the greater part of us; and I must own, dear E., it is a hard game such a one as you have to play, when you meet with such a lover. You cannot refuse but he is sincere, and yet though you use him over so favourably, perhaps in a few months, or at farthest in a year or two, the same unaccountable fancy may make him as distractedly fond of another, whilst you are quite forgot. I am aware that perhaps the next time I have the pleasure of seeing you, you may bid me take my own lesson home, and tell me that the passion I have professed for you is perhaps one of those transient flashes I have been describing; but I hope, my dear E., you will do me the justice to believe me, when I assure you that the love I have for you is founded on the sacred principles of virtue and honour, and by consequence so long as you continue possessed of those amiable qualities which first inspired my passion for you, so long must I continue to love you. Believe me, my dear, it is love like this alone which can render the marriage state happy. People may talk of flames and raptures as long as they please, and a warm fancy with a flow of youthful spirits, may make them feel something like what they describe; but sure I am the nobler faculties of the mind, with kindred feelings of the heart, can only be the foundation of friendship, and it has always been my opinion that the married life was only friendship in a more exalted degree. If you will be so good as to grant my wishes, and it should please Providence to spare us to the latest periods of life, I can look forward and see that even then, though bent down with wrinkled age; even then, when all other worldly circumstances will be indifferent to me, I will regard my E. with the tenderest affection, and for this plain reason, because she is still possessed of those noble qualities, improved to a much higher degree, which first inspired my affection for her.

> "O! happy state when souls each other draw,
> When love is liberty, and nature law." *

I know were I to speak in such a style to many a girl, who thinks herself possessed of no small share of sense, she would think it ridiculous; but the language of the heart is, my dear E., the only courtship I shall ever use to you.

When I look over what I have written, I am sensible it is vastly different from the ordinary style of courtship, but I shall make no apology—I know your good nature will excuse what your good sense may see amiss.

R. B.

[Pope: Eloisa to Abelard.]

(3.)   **TO MISS E.**

I HAVE often thought it a peculiarly unlucky circumstance in love, that though in every other situation in life, telling the truth is not only the safest, but actually by far the easiest way of proceeding, a lover is never under greater difficulty in acting, or more puzzled for expression, than when his passion is sincere, and his intentions are honourable. I do not think that it is very difficult for a person of ordinary capacity to talk of love and fondness which are not felt, and to make vows of constancy and fidelity which are never intended to be performed, if he be villain enough to practise such detestable conduct: but to a man whose heart glows with the principle of integrity and truth, and who sincerely loves a woman of amiable person, uncommon refinement of sentiment and purity of manners—to such a one, in such circumstances, I can assure you, my dear, from my own feelings at this present moment, courtship is a task indeed. There is such a number of foreboding fears, and distrustful anxieties crowd into my mind when I am in your company, or when I sit down to write to you, that what to speak, or what to write I am altogether at a loss.

There is one rule which I have hitherto practised, and which I shall invariably keep with you, and that is honestly to tell you the plain truth. There is something so mean and unmanly in the arts of dissimulation and falsehood, that I am surprised they can be acted by any one in so noble, so generous a passion, as virtuous love. No, my dear E., I shall never endeavour to gain your favour by such detestable practices. If you will be so good and so generous as to admit me for your partner, your companion, your bosom friend through life, there is nothing on this side of eternity shall give me greater transport; but I shall never think of purchasing your hand by any arts unworthy of a man, and I will add of a Christian. There is one thing, my dear, which I earnestly request of you, and it is this; that you would soon either put an end to my hopes by a peremptory refusal, or cure me of my fears by a generous consent.

It would oblige me much if you would send me a line or two when convenient. I shall only add further that, if a behaviour regulated (though perhaps but very imperfectly) by the rules of honour and virtue, if a heart devoted to love and esteem you, and an earnest endeavour to promote you happiness; if these are qualities you would wish in a friend, in a husband, I hope you shall ever find them in your real friend, and sincere lover.

R. B.

(4.)   **TO MISS E.**

I OUGHT, in good manners, to have acknowledged the receipt of your letter before this time, but my heart was so shocked with the contents of it, that I can scarcely yet collect my thoughts so as to write you on the subject. I will not attempt to describe what I felt on receiving your letter. I read it over and over, again and again, and though it was in the politest language of refusal, still it was peremptory; "you were sorry you could not make me a return, but you wish me," what without you I never can obtain, "you wish me all kind of happiness." It would be weak and unmanly to say that without you I never can be happy; but sure I am, that sharing life with you would have given it a relish, that, wanting you, I can never taste.

Your uncommon personal advantages, and your superior good sense, do not so much strike me; these, possibly in a few instances may be met with in others; but that amiable goodness, that tender feminine softness, that endearing sweetness of disposition, with all the charming offspring of a warm feeling heart—these I never again expect to meet with, in such a degree, in this world. All these charming qualities, heightened by an education much beyond any thing I have ever met in any woman I ever dared to approach, have made an impression on my heart that I do not think the world can ever efface. My imagination had fondly fluttered myself with a wish, I dare not say it ever reached a hope, that possibly I might one day call you mine. I had formed the most delightful images, and my fancy fondly brooded over them; but now I am wretched for the loss of what I really had no right to expect. I must now think no more of you as a mistress; still I presume to ask to be admitted as a friend. As such I wish to be allowed to wait on you, and as I expect to remove in a few days a little further off, and you, I suppose, will perhaps soon leave this place, I wish to see or hear from you soon; and if an expression should perhaps escape me, rather too warm for friendship, I hope you will pardon it in, my dear Miss—(pardon me the dear expression for once) * * * *

R. B.

[After such sermonising, the result was by no means wonderful.]

To Miss ——.

[Date and person unknown.]

MY DEAR COUNTRYWOMAN,

I AM so impatient to show you that I am once more at peace with you, that I send you the book I mentioned directly, rather than wait the uncertain time of my seeing you. I am afraid I have mislaid or lost Collins' Poems, which I promised to Miss Irvin. If I can find them, I will forward them by you; if not, you must apologize for me.

I know you will laugh at it when I tell you that your piano and you together have played the deuce somehow about my heart. My breast has been widowed these many months, and I thought myself proof against the fascinating witchcraft; but I am afraid you will "feelingly convince me what I am." I say, I am afraid, because I am not sure what is the matter with me. I have one miserable bad symptom; when you whisper, or look kindly to another, it gives me a draught of damnation. I have a kind of wayward wish to be with you ten minutes by yourself, though what I would say, Heaven above knows, for I am sure I know not. I have no formed design in all this; but just in the nakedness of my heart, write you down a mere matter-of-fact story. You may perhaps give yourself airs of distance on this, and that will completely cure me; but I wish you would not: just let us meet, if you please, in the old beaten way of friendship.

I will not subscribe myself your humble servant, for that is a phrase, I think, at least fifty miles off from the heart; but I will conclude with sincerely wishing that the Great Protector of innocence may shield you from the barbed dart of calumny, and hand you by the covert snare of deceit.

R. B.

To Miss I——.

[See song—"Young Peggy blooms our bonniest Lass."]

MADAM,

PERMIT me to present you with the enclosed song as a small though grateful tribute for the honor of your acquaintance. I have, in those verses, attempted some faint sketches of your portrait in the unembellished simple manner of descriptive TRUTH.—Flattery, I leave to your LOVERS, whose exaggerating fancies may make them imagine you still nearer perfection than you really are.

Poets, Madam, of all mankind, feel most forcibly the powers of BEAUTY; as, if they are really POETS of nature's making, their feelings must be finer, and their taste more delicate than most of the world. In the cheerful bloom of SPRING, or the pensive mildness of AUTUMN; the grandeur of SUMMER, or the hoary majesty of WINTER; the poet feels a charm unknown to the rest of his species. Even the sight of a fine flower, or the company of a fine woman (by far the finest part of God's works below), have sensations for the poetic heart that the herd of man are strangers to.—On this last account, Madam, I am, as in many other things, indebted to Mr. Hamilton's kindness in introducing me to you. Your lovers may view you with a wish, I look on you with pleasure; their hearts, in your presence, may glow with desire, mine rises with admiration.

That the arrows of misfortune, however they should, as incident to humanity, glance a slight wound, may never reach your heart—that the snares of Villainy may never beset you in the road of life—that INNOCENCE may hand you by the path of HONOR to the dwelling of PEACE, is the sincere wish of him who has the honor to be, &c.

R. B.

To Miss Alexander.

[Rough-draft letter.]

Mossgiel, 18th Nov., 1786.

MADAM,

POETS are such outré beings, so much the children of wayward fancy and capricious whim, that I believe the world generally allows them a larger latitude in the laws of propriety, than the sober sons of judgment and prudence. I mention this as an apology for the liberties that a nameless stranger has taken with you in the enclosed poem, which he begs leave to present you with. Whether it has poetical merit any way worthy of the theme, I am not the proper judge; but it is the best my abilities can produce; and what to a good heart will, perhaps, be a superior grace, it is equally sincere as fervent.

The scenery was nearly taken from real life, though I dare say, Madam, you do not recollect it, as I believe you scarcely noticed the poetic rover as he wandered by you. I had roved out as chance directed, in the favourite haunts of my muse on the banks of the Ayr, to view nature in all the gaiety of the vernal year. The evening sun was flaming over the distant western hills; not a breath stirred the crimson opening blossom, or the verdant spreading leaf. It was a golden moment for a poetic heart. I listened to the feathered warblers, pouring their harmony on every hand, with a congenial kindred regard, and frequently turned out of my path, lest I should disturb their little songs, or frighten them to another station. Surely, said I to myself, he must be a wretch indeed, who, regardless of your harmonious endeavour to please him, can eye your elusive flights to discover your secret recesses, and to rob you of all the property nature gives you—your dearest comforts, your helpless nestlings. Even the hoary hawthorn twig that shot across the way, what heart at such a time but must have been interested in its welfare, and wished it preserved from the rudely-browsing cattle, or the withering eastern blast? Such was the scene,—and such the hour, when, in a corner of my prospect, I spied one of the fairest pieces of nature's workmanship that ever crowned a poetic landscape or met a poet's eye, those visionary bards excepted, who hold commerce with aërial beings! Had Calumny and Villainy taken my walk, they had at that moment sworn eternal peace with such an object.

What an hour of inspiration for a poet! It would have raised plain dull historic prose into metaphor and measure.

The enclosed song was the work of my return home: and perhaps it but poorly answers what might have been expected from such a scene.

I have the honor to be,
Madam,
Your most obedient and very humble Servant,
R. B.

To Mrs. Stewart,

OF STAIR AND AFTON.

(Compare Notes on Various Readings, also foregoing letter.)

[1786.]

MADAM,

THE hurry of my preparations for going abroad has hindered me from performing my promise so soon as I intended. I have here sent you a parcel of songs, &c., which never made their appearance, except to a friend or two at most. Perhaps some of them may be no great entertainment to you, but of that I am far from being an adequate judge. The song to the tune of "Ettrick Banks" [*The Bonnie Lass of Ballochmyle*] you will easily see the impropriety of exposing much, even in manuscript. I think, myself, it has some merit: both as a tolerable description of one of nature's sweetest scenes, a July evening, and one of the finest pieces of nature's workmanship, the finest indeed we know anything of, an amiable, beautiful young woman; but I have no common friend to procure me that permission, without which I would not dare to spread the copy.

I am quite aware, Madam, what task the world would assign me in this letter. The obscure bard, when any of the great condescend to take notice of him, should heap the altar with the incense of flattery. Their high ancestry, their own great and god-like qualities and actions, should be recounted with the most exaggerated description. This, Madam, is a task for which I am altogether unfit. Besides a certain disqualifying pride of heart, I know nothing of your connexions in life, and have no access to where your real character is to be found—the company of your compeers: and more, I am afraid that even the most refined adulation is by no means the road to your good opinion.

One feature of your character I shall ever with grateful pleasure remember;—the reception I got when I had the honor of waiting on you at Stair. I am little acquainted with politeness, but I know a good deal of benevolence of temper and goodness of heart. Surely, did those in exalted stations know how happy they could make some classes of their inferiors by condescension and affability, they would never stand so high, measuring out with every look the height of their elevation, but condescend as sweetly as did Mrs Stewart of Stair.

R. B.

(1.)

To Mrs. Dunlop,

OF DUNLOP.

Ayrshire, 1786.

MADAM,

I AM truly sorry I was not at home yesterday, when I was so much honor'd with your order for my copies, and incomparably more by the handsome compliments you are pleased to pay my poetic abilities. I am fully persuaded that there is not any class of mankind so feelingly alive to the titillations of applause as the sons of Parnassus: nor is it easy to conceive how the heart of the poor bard dances with rapture, when those, whose character in life gives them a right to be polite judges, honor him with their approbation. Had you been thoroughly acquainted with me, Madam, you could not have touched my darling heart-chord more sweetly than by noticing my attempts to celebrate your illustrious ancestor, the Saviour of his Country.

"Great patriot hero! ill-requited chief!"

The first book I met with in my early years, which I perused with pleasure, was "The Life of Hannibal;" the next was "The History of Sir William Wallace;" for several of my earlier years I had few other authors; and many a solitary hour have I stole out, after the laborious vocations of the day, to shed a tear over their glorious, but unfortunate stories. In those boyish days I remember, in particular, being struck with that part of Wallace's story where these lines occur—

"Syne to the Leglen wood, when it was late,
To make a silent and a safe retreat."

I chose a fine summer Sunday, the only day my line of life allowed, and walked half a dozen of miles to pay my respects to the Leglen wood, with as much devout enthusiasm as ever pilgrim did to Loretto; and, as I explored every den and dell where I could suppose my heroic countryman to have lodged, I recollect (for even then I was a rhymer) that my heart glowed with a wish to be able to make a song on him in some measure equal to his merits.

R. B.

(2.)

TO MRS. DUNLOP.

Edinburgh, 15th *January*, 1787.

MADAM,

YOURS of the 9th current, which I am this moment honor'd with, is a deep reproach to me for ungrateful neglect. I will tell you the real truth, for I am miserably awkward at a fib. I wished to have written to Dr. Moore before I wrote to you; but though every day since I received yours of December 30th, the idea, the wish to write to him has constantly pressed on my thoughts, yet I could not for my soul set about it. I know his fame and character, and I am one of "the sons of little men." To write him a more matter-of-fact affair, like a merchant's order, would be disgracing the little character I have; and to write the author of "The View of Society and Manners" a letter of sentiment—I declare every artery runs cold at the thought. I shall try, however, to write to him to-morrow or next day. His kind interposition in my behalf I have already experienced, as a gentleman waited on me the other day, on the part of Lord Eglintoun, with ten guineas, by way of subscription for two copies of my next edition.

The word you object to in the mention I have made of my glorious countryman and your immortal ancestor, is indeed borrowed from Thomson; but it does not strike me as an improper epithet. I distrusted my own judgment on your finding fault with it, and applied for the opinion of some of the literati here, who honor me with their critical strictures, and they all allow it to be proper. The song you ask I cannot recollect, and I have not a copy of it. I have not composed anything on the great Wallace, except what you have seen in print; and the enclosed, which I will print in this edition. You will see I have mentioned some others of the name. When I composed my "Vision" long ago, I had attempted a description of Koyle, of which the additional stanzas are a part, as it originally stood. My heart glows with a wish to do justice to the merits of the "Saviour of his Country," which sooner or later I shall at least attempt.

You are afraid I shall grow intoxicated with my prosperity as a poet: alas! Madam, I know myself and the world too well. I do not mean any airs of affected modesty; I am willing to believe that my abilities deserve some notice; but in a most enlightened, informed age and nation, when poetry is and has been the study of men of the first natural genius, aided with all the powers of polite learning, polite books, and polite company—to be dragged forth to the full glare of learned and polite observation, with all my imperfections of awkward rusticity and crude unpolished ideas on my head— I assure you, Madam, I do not dissemble when I tell you I tremble for the consequences. The novelty of a poet in my obscure situation, without any of those advantages which are reckoned necessary for that character, at least at this time of day, has raised a partial tide of public notice which has borne me to a height, where I am absolutely, feelingly certain, my abilities are inadequate to support me; and too surely do I see that time when the same tide will leave me, and recede perhaps as far below the mark of truth. I do not say this in the ridiculous affectation of self-abasement and modesty. I have studied myself, and know what ground I occupy; and, however a friend or the world may differ from me in that particular, I stand for my own opinion, in silent resolve, with all the tenaciousness of property. I mention this to you once for all to disburthen my mind, and I do not wish to hear or say more about it.—But,

> "When proud fortune's ebbing tide recedes,"

you will bear me witness, that when my bubble of fame was at the highest, I stood unintoxicated with the inebriating cup in my hand, looking forward with rueful resolve to the hastening time, when the blow of Calumny should dash it to the ground, with all the eagerness of vengeful triumph.

Your patronizing me and interesting yourself in my fame and character as a poet, I rejoice in; it exalts me in my own idea; and whether you can or cannot aid me in my subscription is a trifle. Has a paltry subscription-bill any charms to the heart of a bard, compared with the patronage of the descendant of the immortal Wallace?

R. B.

(3.)   TO MRS. DUNLOP.

Edinburgh, 22nd March, 1787.

MADAM,

I READ your letter with watery eyes. A little, very little while ago, I had scarce a friend but the stubborn pride of my own bosom; now I am distinguished, patronized, befriended by you. Your friendly advices, I will not give them the cold name of criticisms, I receive with reverence. I have made some small alterations in what I before had printed. I have the advice of some very judicious friends among the literati here, but with them I sometimes find it necessary to claim the privilege of thinking for myself. The noble Earl of Glencairn, to whom I owe more than to any man, does me the honor of giving me his strictures: his hints, with respect to impropriety or indelicacy, I follow implicitly.

You kindly interest yourself in my future views and prospects; there I can give you no light. It is all

> "Dark as was Chaos ere the infant sun
> Was roll'd together, or had tried his beams
> Athwart the gloom profound."

The appellation of a Scottish bard, is by far my highest pride; to continue to deserve it is my most exalted ambition. Scottish scenes and Scottish story are the themes I could wish to sing. I have no dearer aim than to have it in my power, unplagued with the routine of business—for which heaven knows I am unfit enough—to make leisurely pilgrimages through Caledonia; to sit on the fields of her battles; to wander on the romantic banks of her rivers; and to muse by the stately towers or venerable ruins, once the honored abodes of her heroes.

But these are all Utopian thoughts: I have dallied long enough with life; 'tis time to be in earnest. I have a fond, an aged mother to care for: and some other bosom-ties perhaps equally tender. Where the individual only suffers by the consequences of his own thoughtlessness, indolence, or folly, he may be excusable; nay, shining abilities, and some of the nobler virtues, may half sanctify a heedless character; but where God and nature have entrusted the welfare of others to his care; where the trust is sacred, and the ties are dear, that man must be far gone in selfishness, or strangely lost to reflection, whom these connexions will not rouse to exertion.

I guess that I shall clear between two and three hundred pounds by my authorship; with that sum I intend, so far as I may be said to have any intention, to return to my old acquaintance, the plough, and, if I can meet with a lease by which I can live, to commence farmer. I do not intend to give up poetry; being bred to labour, secures me independence, and the Muses are my chief, sometimes have been my only enjoyment. If my practice second my resolution, I shall have principally at heart the serious business of life; but while following my plough, or building up my shocks, I shall cast a leisure glance to that dear, that only feature of my character, which gave me the notice of my country, and the patronage of a Wallace.

Thus, honored Madam, I have given you the bard, his situation, and his views, native as they are in his own bosom.

R. B.

(4.)   TO MRS. DUNLOP.

Edinburgh, 15th April, 1787.

MADAM,

THERE is an affectation of gratitude which I dislike. The periods of Johnson, and the pauses of Sterne, may hide a selfish heart. For my part, Madam, I trust I have too much pride for servility, and too little prudence for selfishness. I have this moment broken open your letter, but

> "Rude am I in speech,
> And therefore little can I grace my cause
> In speaking for myself—"

so I shall not trouble you with any fine speeches and hunted figures. I shall just lay my hand on my heart and say, I hope I shall ever have the truest, the warmest sense of your goodness.

I come abroad in print, for certain on Wednesday. Your orders I shall punctually attend to; only, by the way, I must tell you that I was paid before for Dr. Moore's and Miss Williams' copies, through the medium of Commissioner Cochrane in this place, but that we can settle when I have the honor of waiting on you.

Dr. Smith* was just gone to London the morning before I received your letter to him.

R. B.

* [Dr. Adam Smith, author of the *Wealth of Nations*.]

(5.)

TO MRS. DUNLOP.

[Extract by Currie.]

Edinburgh, 30th April, 1787.

————Your criticisms, Madam, I understand very well, and could have wished to have pleased you better. You are right in your guess that I am not very amenable to counsel. Poets, much my superiors, have so flattered those who possessed the adventitious qualities of wealth and power, that I am determined to flatter no created being, either in prose or verse.

I set as little by princes, lords, clergy, critics, &c., as all those respective gentry do by my bardship. I know what I may expect from the world by and by—illiberal abuse, and perhaps contemptuous neglect.

I am happy, Madam, that some of my own favourite pieces are distinguished by your particular approbation. For my "Dream," which has unfortunately incurred your loyal displeasure, I hope in four weeks, or less, to have the honor of appearing at Dunlop, in its defence in person.

R. B.

(6.)

TO MRS. DUNLOP.

Edinburgh, 21st January, 1788.

After six weeks' confinement, I am beginning to walk across the room. They have been six horrible weeks; anguish and low spirits made me unfit to read, write, or think.

I have a hundred times wished that one could resign life as an officer resigns a commission: for I would not take in any poor ignorant wretch, by selling out. Lately I was a sixpenny private: and, God knows, a miserable soldier enough; now I march to the campaign, a starving cadet: a little more conspicuously wretched.

I am ashamed of all this; for though I do want bravery for the warfare of life, I could wish, like some other soldiers, to have as much fortitude or cunning as to dissemble or conceal my cowardice.

As soon as I can bear the journey, which will be, I suppose, about the middle of next week, I leave Edinburgh: and soon after I shall pay my grateful duty at Dunlop-House.

R. B.

(7.)

TO MRS. DUNLOP.

[Extract by Currie.]

Edinburgh, 12th February, 1788.

Some things in your late letters hurt me: not that *you say them*, but that *you mistake me*. Religion, my honored Madam, has not only been all my life my chief dependence, but my dearest enjoyment. I have, indeed, been the luckless victim of wayward follies; but, alas! I have ever been "more fool than knave." A mathematician without religion is a probable character; an irreligious poet is a monster.

*   *   *   *   *   *   *   *   *

R. B.

(8.)

TO MRS. DUNLOP.

Mossgiel, 7th March, 1788.

Madam,

The last paragraph in yours of the 30th February affected me most, so I shall begin my answer where you ended your letter. That I am often a sinner with any little wit I have, I do confess: but I have taxed my recollection to no purpose, to find out when it was employed against you. I hate an ungenerous sarcasm a great deal worse than I do the devil; at least as Milton describes him; and though I may be rascally enough to be sometimes guilty of it myself, I cannot endure it in others. You, my honored friend, who cannot appear in any light but you are sure of being respectable—you can afford to pass by an occasion to display your wit, because you may depend for fame on your sense; or, if you choose to be silent, you know you can rely on the gratitude of many, and the esteem of all; but, God help us who are wits or witlings by profession: if we stand not for fame there, we sink unsupported!

I am highly flattered by the news you tell me of Coila.* I may say to the fair painter who does me so much honor, as Dr. Beattie says to Ross the poet of his muse Scota, from which, by the by, I took the idea of Coila ('tis a poem of Beattie's in the Scottish dialect, which perhaps you have never seen):—

> "Ye shake your head, but o' my fegs,
> Ye've set auld Scota on her legs:
> Lang had she lien wi' beffs and flegs,
>> Bumbaz'd and dizzie,
> Her fiddle wanted strings and pegs.
>> Wae's me, poor hizzie."†

* [A lady (daughter of Mrs. Dunlop) was making a picture from the description of Coila in the "Vision."—*Currie.*]

† [Lines quoted are from Beattie; poem referred to is by Ross.]

R. B.

(9.)　　　　TO MRS. DUNLOP.

Mauchline, 28th April, 1788.

MADAM,

YOUR powers of reprehension must be great indeed, as I assure you they made my heart ache with penitential pangs, even though I was really not guilty. As I commence farmer at Whitsunday, you will easily guess I must be pretty busy; but that is not all. As I got the offer of the excise business without solicitation, and as it costs me only six months'' attendance for instructions, to entitle me to a commission—which commission lies by me, and at any future period, on my simple petition, can be resumed—I thought five-and-thirty-pounds a-year was no bad *dernier ressort* for a poor poet, if Fortune in her jade tricks should kick him down from the little eminence to which she has lately helped him up.

For this reason, I am at present attending these instructions, to have them completed before Whitsunday. Still, Madam, I prepared with the sincerest pleasure to meet you at the Mount, and came to my brother's on Saturday night, to set out on Sunday; but for some nights preceding I had slept in an apartment, where the force of the winds and rains was only mitigated by being sifted through numberless apertures in the windows, walls, &c. In consequence, I was on Sunday, Monday, and part of Tuesday, unable to stir out of bed, with all the miserable effects of a violent cold.

You see, Madam, the truth of the French maxim, *Le vrai n'est pas toujours le vrai-semblable.* Your last was so full of expostulation, and was something so like the language of an offended friend, that I began to tremble for a correspondence, which I had with grateful pleasure set down as one of the greatest enjoyments of my future life. * * * *

Your books have delighted me: Virgil, Dryden, and Tasso, were all equally strangers to me; but of this more at large in my next.

R. B.

*[Should of course be words'.]

(10.)　　　　TO MRS. DUNLOP.

[Extract by Currie.]

Mauchline, 4th May, 1788.

MADAM,

DRYDEN's Virgil has delighted me. I do not know whether the critics will agree with me, but the Georgics are to me by far the best of Virgil. It is indeed a species of writing entirely new to me; and has filled my head with a thousand fancies of emulation: but, alas! when I read the Georgics, and then survey my own powers, 'tis like the idea of a Shetland pony drawn up by the side of a thorough-bred hunter, to start for the plate. I own I am disappointed in the Æneid. Faultless correctness may please, and does highly please, the lettered critic: but to that awful character I have not the most distant pretensions. I do not know whether I do not hazard my pretensions to be a critic of any kind, when I say that I think

Virgil, in many instances, a servile copier of Homer. If I had the Odyssey by me, I could parallel many passages where Virgil has evidently copied, but by no means improved, Homer. Nor can I think there is anything of this owing to the translators; for, from every thing I have seen of Dryden, I think him in genius and fluency of language, Pope's master. I have not perused Tasso enough to form an opinion: in some future letter, you shall have my ideas of him; though I am conscious my criticisms must be very inaccurate and imperfect, as there I have ever felt and lamented my want of learning most.

R. B.

(11.)　　　　TO MRS. DUNLOP.

27th May, 1788.

MADAM,

I HAVE been torturing my philosophy to no purpose, to account for that kind partiality of yours, which unlike * * * * has followed me, in my return to the shade of life, with assiduous benevolence. Often did I regret, in the fleeting hours of my late will-o'-wisp appearance, that "here I had no continuing city;" and, but for the consolation of a few solid guineas, could almost lament the time that a momentary acquaintance with wealth and splendour put me so much out of conceit with the sworn companions of my road through life—insignificance and poverty. * * * *

There are few circumstances relating to the unequal distribution of the good things of this life that give me more vexation (I mean in what I see around me) than the importance the opulent bestow on their trifling family affairs, compared with the very same things on the contracted scale of a cottage. Last afternoon I had the honor to spend an hour or two at a good woman's fire-side, where the planks that composed the floor were decorated with a splendid carpet, and the gay table sparkled with silver and china. 'Tis now about term-day, and there has been a revolution among those creatures, who though in appearance partakers, and equally noble partakers, of the same nature with Madame, are from time to time—their nerves, their sinows, their health, strength, wisdom, experience, genius, time, nay a good part of their very thoughts—sold for months and years, not only to the necessities, the conveniences, but, the caprices of the important few.* We talked of the insignificant creatures; nay, notwithstanding their general stupidity and rascality, did some of the poor devils the honor to commend them. But light be the turf upon his breast who taught "Reverence thyself!" We looked down on the unpolished wretches, their impertinent wives and clouterly brats, as the lordly bull does on the little dirty ant-hill, whose puny inhabitants he crushes in the carelessness of his ramble, or tosses in the air in the wantonness of his pride.

R. B.

* [Hiring terms for domestic servants—Whitsunday and Martinmas.]

(12.)   TO MRS. DUNLOP,
            AT MR. DUNLOP'S, HADDINGTON.

Ellisland, 13th June, 1788.

> "Where'er I roam, whatever realms I see,
> My heart, untravell'd, fondly turns to thee:
> Still to my *friend* it turns with ceaseless pain,
> And drags at each remove a lengthen'd chain."
>   GOLDSMITH.

THIS is the second day, my honored friend, that I have been on my farm. A solitary inmate of an old smoky spence; far from every object I love, or by whom I am beloved; nor any acquaintance older than yesterday, except Jenny Geddes, the old mare I ride on; while uncouth cares and novel plans hourly insult my awkward ignorance and bashful inexperience. There is a foggy atmosphere native to my soul in the hour of care; consequently the dreary objects seem larger than the life. Extreme sensibility, irritated and prejudiced on the gloomy side by a series of misfortunes and disappointments, at that period of my existence when the soul is laying in her cargo of ideas for the voyage of life, is, I believe, the principal cause of this unhappy frame of mind.

> "The valiant, in himself, what can he suffer?
> Or what need he regard his single woes?" &c.

Your surmise, Madam, is just; I am indeed a husband.

*   *   *   *

To jealousy or infidelity I am an equal stranger. My preservative from the first is the most thorough consciousness of her sentiments of honor, and her attachment to me; my antidote against the last is my deep-rooted affection for her.

In housewife matters, of aptness to learn and activity to execute, she is eminently mistress; and during my absence in Nithsdale, she is regularly and constantly apprentice to my mother and sisters in their dairy and other rural business.

The Muses must not be offended when I tell them, the concerns of my wife and family will, in my mind, always take the *pas;* but I assure them, their ladyships will ever come next in place.

You are right that a bachelor state would have ensured me more friends; but, from a cause you will easily guess, conscious peace in the enjoyment of my own mind, and unmistrusting confidence in approaching my God, would seldom have been of the number.

I found a once much-loved and still much-loved female, literally and truly cast out to the mercy of the naked elements, but as I enabled her to *purchase* a shelter;—and there is no sporting with a fellow-creature's happiness or misery.

The most placid good-nature and sweetness of disposition; a warm heart, gratefully devoted with all its powers to love me; vigorous health and sprightly cheerfulness, set off to the best advantage by a more than commonly handsome figure; these, I think, in a woman, may make a good wife, though she should never have read a page but the Scriptures of the Old and New Testament, nor have danced in a brighter assembly than a penny pay-wedding.

                                        R. B.

(13.)   TO MRS. DUNLOP.

Mauchline, 2nd August, 1788.

HONORED MADAM,

YOUR kind letter welcomed me, yesternight, to Ayrshire. I am, indeed, seriously angry with you at the quantum of your luckpenny; but, vexed and hurt as I was, I could not help laughing very heartily at the noble lord's apology for the missed napkin.

I would write you from Nithsdale, and give you my direction there, but I have scarce an opportunity of calling at a post-office once in a fortnight. I am six miles from Dumfries, am scarcely ever in it myself, and, as yet, have little acquaintance in the neighbourhood. Besides, I am now very busy on my farm, building a dwelling house; as at present I am almost an evangelical man in Nithsdale, for I have scarce "where to lay my head."

There are some passages in your last that brought tears in my eyes, "The heart knoweth its own sorrows, and a stranger intermeddleth not therewith." The repository of these "sorrows of the heart" is a kind of *sanctum sanctorum:* and 'tis only a chosen friend, and that, too, at particular, sacred times, who dares enter into them:—

> "Heaven oft tears the bosom-chords
> That nature finest strung."

You will excuse this quotation for the sake the author. Instead of entering on this subject farther, I shall transcribe you a few lines I wrote in a hermitage, belonging to a gentleman in my Nithsdale neighbourhood. They are almost the only favours the Muses have conferred on me in that country.

[Lines in Friars-Carse Hermitage, here transcribed.]

Since I am in the way of transcribing, the following were the production of yesterday as I jogged through the wild hills of New Cumnock. I intend inserting them, or something like them, in an epistle I am going to write to the gentleman on whose friendship my Excise hopes depend, Mr. Graham, of Fintry; one of the worthiest and most accomplished gentlemen, not only of this country, but, I will dare to say it, of this age. The following are just the first crude thoughts "unhousel'd, unanointed, unaneal'd:"—

*   *   *   *

> Pity the tuneful Muses' helpless train;
> Weak, timid landsmen on life's stormy main:
> The world were blest, did bliss on them depend;
> Ah, that "the friendly e'er should want a friend!"
> The little fate bestows they share as soon;
> Unlike sage, proverb'd, Wisdom's hard-wrung boon.
> Let Prudence number o'er each sturdy son,
> Who life and wisdom at one race begun;
> Who feel by reason and who give by rule;
> Instinct's a brute and Sentiment a fool!
> Who make poor *will* do wait upon *I should;*
> We own they're prudent, but who owns they're good?
> Ye wise ones, hence! ye hurt the social eye;
> God's image rudely etch'd on base alloy!
> But come   *   *   *   *   *

Here the Muse left me. I am astonished at what you tell me of Anthony's writing me. I never received it. Poor fellow! you vex me much by telling me that he is unfortunate. I shall be in Ayrshire ten days from this date. I have just room for an old Roman farewell.

R. B.

(14.)   TO MRS. DUNLOP.

Mauchline, 10th August, 1788.

MY MUCH HONORED FRIEND,

Yours of the 24th June is before me. I found it, as well as another valued friend—my wife, waiting to welcome me to Ayrshire: I met both with the sincerest pleasure.

When I write you, Madam, I do not sit down to answer every paragraph of yours, by echoing every sentiment, like the faithful Commons of Great Britain in Parliament assembled, answering a speech from the best of kings! I express myself in the fulness of my heart, and may, perhaps, be guilty of neglecting some of your kind inquiries; but not from your very odd reason, that I do not read your letters. All your epistles for several months have cost me nothing, except a swelling throb of gratitude, or a deep-felt sentiment of veneration.

Mrs. Burns, Madam, is the identical woman · · ·

When she first found herself "as women wish to be who love their lords," as I loved her nearly to distraction, we took steps for a private marriage. Her parents got the hint: and not only forbade me her company and their house, but, on my rumoured West Indian voyage, got a warrant to put me in jail, till I should find security in my about-to-be paternal relation. You know my lucky reverse of fortune. On my *éclatant* return to Mauchline, I was made very welcome to visit my girl. The usual consequences began to betray her; and, as I was at that time laid up a cripple in Edinburgh, she was turned, literally turned out of doors, and I wrote to a friend to shelter her till my return, when our marriage was declared. Her happiness or misery were in my hands, and who could trifle with such a deposit? · · ·

I can easily fancy a more agreeable companion for my journey of life; but, upon my honor, I have never seen the individual instance. · · ·

Circumstanced as I am, I could never have got a female partner for life, who could have entered into my favourite studies, relished my favourite authors, &c., without probably entailing on me at the same time expensive living, fantastic caprice, perhaps apish affectation, with all the other blessed boarding-school acquirements, which (*pardonnez moi, Madame*) are sometimes to be found among females of the upper ranks, but almost universally pervade the misses of the would-be gentry. · · ·

I like your way in your church-yard lucubrations. Thoughts that are the spontaneous result of accidental situations, either respecting health, place, or company, have often a strength, and always an originality, that would in vain be looked for in fancied circumstances and studied paragraphs. For me, I

have often thought of keeping a letter in progression by me, to send you when the sheet was written out. Now I talk of sheets, I must tell you my reason for writing to you on paper of this kind is my pruriency of writing to you at large. A page of post is on such a dis-social, narrow-minded scale, that I cannot abide it; and double letters, at least in my miscellaneous reverie manner, are a monstrous tax in a close correspondence.

R. B.

(15.)   TO MRS. DUNLOP.

Ellisland, 16th August, 1788.

I AM in a fine disposition, my honored friend, to send you an elegiac epistle; and want only genius to make it quite Shenstonian:—

> "Why droops my heart with fancied woes forlorn?
> Why sinks my soul beneath each wintry sky?"

My increasing cares in this, as yet strange country—gloomy conjectures in the dark vista of futurity—consciousness of my own inability for the struggle of the world—my broadened mark to misfortune in a wife and children:—I could indulge these reflections, till my humor should ferment into the most acid chagrin, that would corrode the very thread of life.

To counterwork these baneful feelings, I have sat down to write to you; as I declare upon my soul I always find *that* the most sovereign balm for my wounded spirit.

I was yesterday at Mr. Miller's to dinner for the first time. My reception was quite to my mind: from the lady of the house quite flattering. She sometimes hits on a couplet or two *impromptu*. She repeated one or two to the admiration of all present. My suffrage, as a professional man, was expected: I for once went agonizing over the belly of my conscience. Pardon me, ye my adored household gods, independence of spirit, and integrity of soul! In the course of conversation, "Johnson's Musical Museum," a collection of Scottish songs with the music, was talked of. We got a song on the harpsichord, beginning,

> "Raving winds around her blowing."

The air was much admired: the lady of the house asked me whose were the words. "Mine, Madam—they are indeed my very best verses;" she took not the smallest notice of them! The old Scottish proverb says well, "king's caff is better than ither folks' corn." I was going to make a New Testament quotation about "casting pearls," but that would be too virulent, for the lady is actually a woman of sense and taste.

After all that has been said on the other side of the question, man is by no means a happy creature. I do not speak of the selected few, favoured by partial heaven, whose souls are tuned to gladness amid riches and honors, and prudence and wisdom. I speak of the neglected many, whose nerves, whose sinews, whose days are sold to the minions of fortune.

If I thought you had never seen it, I would transcribe for you a stanza of an old Scottish ballad, called, "The Life and Age of Man;" beginning thus:

> "'Twas in the sixteenth hunder year
> Of God and fifty-three,
> Frae Christ was born, that bought us dear,
> As writings testifie."

I had an old grand-uncle, with whom my mother lived awhile in her girlish years: the good old man, for such he was, was long blind ere he died; during which time his highest enjoyment was to sit down and cry, while my mother would sing the simple old song of "the Life and Age of Man."

It is this way of thinking; it is these melancholy truths, that make religion so precious to the poor, miserable children of men.—If it is a mere phantom, existing only in the heated imagination of enthusiasm,

> "What truth on earth so precious as the lie!"

My idle reasonings sometimes make me a little sceptical, but the necessities of my heart always give the cold philosophisings the lie. Who looks for the heart weaned from earth; the soul affianced to her God; the correspondence fixed with heaven; the pious supplication and devout thanksgiving, constant as the vicissitudes of even and morn; who thinks to meet with these in the court, the palace, in the glare of public life? No: to find them in their precious importance and divine efficacy, we must search among the obscure recesses of disappointment, affliction, poverty, and distress.

I am sure, dear Madam, you are now more than pleased with the length of my letters. I return to Ayrshire middle of next week; and it quickens my pace to think that there will be a letter from you waiting me there. I must be here again very soon for my harvest.

R. B.

(16.)

TO MRS. DUNLOP.

Mauchline, 27th Sept. 1788.

I HAVE received twins, dear Madam, more than once; but scarcely ever with more pleasure than when I received yours of the 12th instant. To make myself understood: I had wrote to Mr. Graham, enclosing my poem addressed to him, and the same post which favoured me with yours brought me an answer from him. It was dated the very day he had received mine; and I am quite at a loss to say whether it was most polite or kind.

Your criticisms, my honored benefactress, are truly the work of a friend. They are not the blasting depredations of a canker-toothed, caterpillar critic; nor are they the fair statement of cold impartiality, balancing with unfeeling exactitude the *pro* and *con* of an author's merits; they are the judicious observations of animated friendship, selecting the beauties of the piece. I am just arrived from Nithsdale, and will be here a fortnight. I was on horseback this morning by three o'clock; for between my wife and my farm is just forty-six miles. As I jogged on in the dark, I was taken with a poetic fit as follows:

"Mrs. Ferguson of Craigdarroch's lamentation for the death of her son; an uncommonly promising youth of eighteen or nineteen years of age.

> "Fate gave the word—the arrow sped,
> And pierced my darling's heart."

You will not send me your poetic rambles, but, you see, I am no niggard of mine. I am sure your impromptus give me double pleasure; what falls from your pen can neither be unentertaining in itself, nor indifferent to me.

The one fault you found, is just; but I cannot please myself in an emendation.

What a life of solicitude is the life of a parent! You interested me much in your young couple.

I would not take my folio paper for this epistle, and now I repent it. I am so jaded with my dirty long journey that I was afraid to drawl into the essence of dulness with any thing larger than a quarto, and so I must leave out another rhyme of this morning's manufacture.

I will pay the sapientipotent George most chearfully, to hear from you ere I leave Ayrshire.

R. B.

(17.)

TO MRS. DUNLOP,
AT MOREHAM MAINS.

Mauchline, 13th November, 1788.

MADAM,

I HAD the very great pleasure of dining at Dunlop yesterday. Men are said to flatter women because they are weak; if it is so, poets must be weaker still; for Misses R. and K. and Miss G. M'K. with their flattering attentions, and artful compliments, absolutely turned my head. I own they did not lard me over as many a poet does his patron, but they so intoxicated me with their sly insinuations and delicate inuendos of compliment, that if it had not been for a lucky recollection, how much additional weight and lustre your good opinion and friendship must give me in that circle, I had certainly looked upon myself as a person of no small consequence. I dare not say one word how much I was charmed with the Major's friendly welcome, elegant manner, and acute remark, lest I should be thought to balance my Orientalisms of applause over-against the finest quey in Ayrshire, which he made me a present of to help and adorn my farm-stock. As it was on Hallow-day, I am determined annually, as that day returns, to decorate her horns with an ode of gratitude to the family of Dunlop.

*   *   *   *   *

So soon as I know of your arrival at Dunlop, I will take the first conveniency to dedicate a day, or perhaps two, to you and friendship, under the guarantee of the Major's hospitality. There will soon be threescore-and-ten miles of permanent distance between us; and now that your friendship and friendly correspondence is entwisted with the heart-strings of my enjoyment of life, I must indulge myself in a happy day of "The feast of reason and the flow of soul."

R. B.

(18.)　　　TO MRS. DUNLOP.

Ellisland, 17th December, 1788.

MY DEAR HONORED FRIEND,

YOURS, dated Edinburgh, which I have just read, makes me very unhappy. "Almost blind and wholly deaf," are melancholy news of human nature; but when told of a much-loved and honored friend, they carry misery in the sound. Goodness on your part, and gratitude on mine, began a tie which has gradually entwisted itself among the dearest chords of my bosom, and I tremble at the omens of your late and present ailing habit and shattered health. You miscalculate matters widely, when you forbid my writing on you, lest it should hurt my worldly concerns. My small scale of farming is exceedingly more simple and easy, than what you have lately seen at Moreham Mains. But, be that as it may, the heart of the man and the fancy of the poet are the two grand considerations for which I live: if miry ridges and dirty dunghills are to engross the best part of the functions of my soul immortal, I had better been a rook or a magpie at once, and then I should not have been plagued with any ideas superior to breaking of clods and picking up grubs; not to mention barn-door cocks or mallards, creatures with which I could almost exchange lives at any time. If you continue so deaf, I am afraid a visit will be no great pleasure to either of us; but if I hear you are got so well again as to be able to relish conversation, look you to it, Madam, for I will make my threatening good. I am to be at the New-year-day fair of Ayr; and, by all that is sacred in the world, friend, I will come and see you.

Your meeting, which you so well describe, with your old schoolfellow and friend, was truly interesting. Out upon the ways of the world!—They spoil those "social offspring of the heart." Two veterans of the "men of the world" would have met with little more heart-workings than two old hacks worn out on the road. Apropos, is not the Scotch phrase, "Auld lang syne," exceedingly expressive? There is an old song and tune which has often thrilled through my soul. You know I am an enthusiast in old Scotch songs. I shall give you the verses on the other sheet, as I suppose Mr. Ker* will save you the postage.

[Should auld acquaintance be forgot?]

Light be the turf on the breast of the Heaven-inspired poet who composed this glorious fragment! There is more of the fire of native genius in it than in half-a-dozen of modern English Bacchanalians! Now I am on my hobby-horse, I cannot help inserting two other old stanzas, which please me mightily :—

[Go fetch to me a pint of wine.]

R. B.

* [Mr. Ker was the postmaster in Edinburgh—a very different kind of official from what have since ruled in the same chair. This worthy man was always ready to frank a letter for a friend. Strange stories are told of weighty packets—one, it is said, containing a pair of buckskin breeches for a sportsman in the Highlands—passing free through the post-office in his day.—Chambers.]

[The reader will observe that the "old stanzas" here spoken of, as of unknown authorship, and associated as such with 'Auld Lang Syne,' are all, except the first four lines, by Burns himself: which may be considered conclusive evidence on the subject of Auld Lang Syne itself. See Notes—p. 201.]

(19.)　　　TO MRS. DUNLOP.

Ellisland, New-year's-day Morning, 1789.

THIS, dear Madam, is a morning of wishes, and would to God that I came under the apostle James's description!—*the prayer of a righteous man availeth much.* In that case, Madam, you should welcome in a year full of blessings; every thing that obstructs or disturbs tranquillity and self-enjoyment should be removed, and every pleasure that frail humanity can taste should be yours. I own myself so little a Presbyterian, that I approve of set times and seasons of more than ordinary acts of devotion, for breaking in on that habituated routine of life and thought, which is so apt to reduce our existence to a kind of instinct, or even sometimes, and with some minds, to a state very little superior to mere machinery.

This day, the first Sunday of May, a breezy, blue-skyed noon some time about the beginning, and a hoary morning and calm sunny day about the end, of autumn! these, time out of mind, have been with me a kind of holiday.

I believe I owe this to that glorious paper in the Spectator, "The Vision of Mirza," a piece that struck my young fancy before I was capable of fixing an idea to a word of three syllables: "On the 5th day of the moon, which, according to the custom of my forefathers, I always *keep holy*, after having washed myself, and offered up my morning devotions, I ascended the high hill of Bagdad, in order to pass the rest of the day in meditation and prayer."

We know nothing, or next to nothing, of the substance or structure of our souls, so cannot account for those seeming caprices in them, that one should be particularly pleased with this thing, or struck with that, which, on minds of a different cast, makes no extraordinary impression. I have some favourite flowers in spring, among which are the mountain-daisy, the hare-bell, the fox-glove, the wild brier-rose, the budding birch, and the hoary hawthorn, that I view and hang over with particular delight. I never hear the loud solitary whistle of the curlew in a summer noon, or the wild mixing cadence of a troop of grey plovers in an autumnal morning, without feeling an elevation of soul like the enthusiasm of devotion or poetry. Tell me, my dear friend, to what can this be owing? Are we a piece of machinery, which, like the Æolian harp, passive, takes the impression of the passing accident? Or do these workings argue something within us above the trodden clod? I own myself partial to such proofs of those awful and important realities—a God that made all things—man's immaterial and immortal nature—and a world of weal or woe beyond death and the grave.

R. B.

[Let reader compare this beautiful letter with "Elegy on Captain Matthew Henderson," p. 114, Poetical Works. By 'spring' we must here understand early summer.]

(20.)   TO MRS. DUNLOP.

Ellisland, 4th March, 1789.

HERE am I, my honored friend, returned safe from the capital. To a man who has a home, however humble or remote—if that home is like mine, the scene of domestic comfort—the bustle of Edinburgh will soon be a business of sickening disgust.

"Vain pomp and glory of this world, I hate you!"

When I must skulk into a corner, lest the rattling equipage of some gaping blockhead should mangle me in the mire, I am tempted to exclaim—"What merits has he had, or what demerit have I had, in some state of pre-existence, that he is ushered into this state of being with the sceptre of rule, and the key of riches in his puny fist, and I am kicked into the world, the sport of folly, or the victim of pride?" I have read somewhere of a monarch (in Spain I think it was), who was so out of humour with the Ptolemean system of astronomy, that he said had he been of the Creator's council, he could have saved him a great deal of labour and absurdity. I will not defend this blasphemous speech; but often, as I have glided with humble stealth through the pomp of Prince's Street, it has suggested itself to me, as an improvement on the present human figure, that a man in proportion to his own conceit of his consequence in the world, could have pushed out the longitude of his common size, as a snail pushes out his horns, or, as we draw out a perspective. This trifling alteration, not to mention the prodigious saving it would be in the tear and wear of the neck and limb-sinews of many of his majesty's liege subjects, in the way of tossing the head and tiptoe strutting, would evidently turn out a vast advantage, in enabling us at once to adjust the ceremonials in making a bow, or making way to a great man; and that too within a second of the precise spherical angle of reverence, or an inch of the particular point of respectful distance, which the important creature itself requires; as a measuring-glance at its towering altitude, would determine the affair like instinct.

Your are right, Madam, in your idea of poor Mylne's poem, which he has addressed to me. The piece has a good deal of merit, but it has one great fault—it is, by far, too long. Besides, my success has encouraged such a shoal of ill-spawned monsters to crawl into public notice, under the title of Scottish Poets, that the very term Scottish Poetry borders on the burlesque. When I write to Mr. Curfrue, I shall advise him rather to try one of his deceased friend's English pieces. I am prodigiously hurried with my own matters, else I would have requested a perusal of all Mylne's poetic performances; and would have offered his friends my assistance in either selecting or correcting what would be proper for the press. What it is that occupies me so much, and perhaps a little oppresses my present spirits, shall fill up a paragraph in some future letter. In the mean time, allow me to close this epistle with a few lines done by a friend of mine * * * * *. I give you them, that as you have seen the original, you may guess whether one or two alterations I have ventured to make in them be any real improvement.

"Like the fair plant that from our touch withdraws,
Shrink, mildly fearful, even from applause;

Be all a mother's fondest hope can dream,
And all you are, my charming . . . ., seem
Straight as the fox-glove, ere her bells disclose,
Mild as the maiden-blushing hawthorn **blows,**
Fair as the fairest of each lovely kind,
Your form shall be the image of your **mind;**
Your manners shall so true your soul express,
That all shall long to know the worth they guess;
Congenial hearts shall greet with kindred love,
And even sick'ning envy must approve."

R. B.

[These beautiful lines, we have reason to believe, are the production of the lady to whom this letter is addressed.—*Currie.*]

(21.   TO MRS. DUNLOP.

[**This** singular letter is now for the first time printed in full, from original document in possession of George Manners, Esq., F.A.S., Fleet Street, London; to whom, for this, and **similar favours,** hereafter to be acknowledged, we are under the highest obligations. **Words and** passages, including the strange place of "psalmody" originally **omitted by Dr.** Currie, and hitherto unknown, are enclosed by us in brackets; that **their relation to** the other parts, and unity of the whole, may be seen. Much has **been said of Dr.** Currie's editorship. We rejoice to do honour **to one who so well deserves it.** It is manifest from this solitary instance, **that Dr.** Currie was both **a discriminating,** an affectionate, and a **very** able editor. **To have printed this letter in full,** at the moment, would **have seriously compromised the prospects of the Poet's fatherless family; but to cut the letter down without betraying so large a gap, required the greatest consideration and skill. As** Currie *prints* it, the letter **begins abruptly; but the first sentence of the** original, containing the word *folio* where no folio was required, would have discovered the deficiency; it was therefore struck out; and all other words referring to the subject were omitted, to prevent the possibility of suspicion and avert inquiry into the matter; yet the letter, as edited by him, with all these deductions, reads perfectly enough. "The most blasphemous party London Newspaper" alluded to by Burns was probably the *Star,* then edited or published by his friend Stuart; in which we are curious to learn whether the "new psalmody," under any signature, or any other anonymous pieces by Burns, ever appeared. Farther remarks we reserve for a place among Notes on Posthumous Works of our Author.]

Ellisland, 4th April, 1789.

[YOU see, Madam, that I am returned to my folio epistles again.] I no sooner hit on any poetic plan or fancy, but I wish to send it to you; and if knowing and reading them gives half the pleasure to you, that communicating them to you gives to me, I am satisfied.

[As I am not devoutly attached to a certain monarch, I cannot say that my heart run any risk of bursting, on Thursday was se'ennight, with the struggling emotions of gratitude.—O—forgive me for speaking evil of dignities! but I must say, that I look on the whole business as a solemn farce of pageant mummery.—The following are a few stanzas of new Psalmody for that "joyful solemnity," which I sent to a London newspaper, with the date and preface following:—

Kilmarnock, 25th April.

MR. PRINTER,

IN a certain chapel not fifty leagues from the market cross of this good town, the following Stanzas of Psalmody, it is said, were composed for, and devoutly sung on, the late joyful solemnity of the 23rd.

O sing a new song to the L——,
Make, all and every one,
A joyful noise, even for the king
His restoration.

The sons of Belial in the land
  Did set their heads together;
Come, let us sweep them off, said they,
  Like an o'erflowing river.

They set their heads together, I say,
  They set their heads together;
On right, on left, and every hand,
  We saw none to deliver.

Thou raisedst strong two chosen ones,
  To quell the Wicked's pride;
That Young Man great in Issachar,
  The burden-bearing tribe.

And him, among the Princes chief
  In our Jerusalem,
The Judge that's mighty in thy law,
  The man that fears thy name.

Yet they, even they, with all their strength,
  Began to faint and fail;
Even as two howling, ravening wolves
  To dogs do turn their tail.

Th' ungodly o'er the just prevailed,
  For so thou hadst appointed;
That thou might'st greater glory give
  Unto thine own anointed.

And now thou hast restored our State,
  Pity our Kirk also;
For she by tribulations
  Is now brought very low.

Consume that high-place, Patronage,
  From off thy holy hill;
And in thy fury burn the book
  Even of that man M'Gill.

Now hear our pray'r, accept our song,
  And fight thy chosen's battle:
We seek but little, L——, from thee;
  Thou kens we get as little.

So much for Psalmody.—You must know that the publisher of one of the most blasphemous party London newspapers is an acquaintance of mine, and as I am a little tinctured with Buff and Blue myself, I now and then help him to a stanza.]

I have [another] poetic whim in my head, which I at present dedicate, or rather inscribe, to The Rt. Honble. Ch. J. Fox, [Esquire]; but how long that fancy may hold, I can't say.—A few of the first lines I have just rough-sketched as follows:

SKETCH.

How Wisdom and Folly meet, mix, and unite;
How Virtue and Vice blend their black and their white;

How Genius, the illustrious father of Fiction,
Confounds Rule and Law, reconciles Contradiction—
I sing: If these mortals, the critics, should bustle,
I care not, not I, let the critics go whistle.

But now for a Patron, whose name and whose glory,
At once may illustrate and honor my story.

Thou first of our orators, first of our wits;
Yet whose parts and acquirements seem just lucky hits:
With knowledge so vast, and with judgment so strong,
No man with the half of 'em e'er could go wrong;
With passions so potent, and fancies so bright,
No man with the half of 'em e'er could go right;
A sorry, poor misbegot son of the Muses,
For using thy name, offers fifty excuses.

   *   *   *   *   *

[I beg your pardon for troubling you with the inclosed to the Major's tenant before the gate—it is to request him to look me out two milk cows; one for myself, and another for Captain Riddel of Glenriddel, a very obliding neighbor of mine.—John very oblidgingly offered to do so for me; and I will either serve myself that way, or at Mauchline fair.—It happens on the 20th curt., and the Sunday preceding it I hope to have the honor of assuring you in person how sincerely I am, Madam, your highly oblidged and most obedient humble servt.,]

ROBT. BURNS.

[Concluding sentence is printed by Currie with unnecessary abridgment, all reference to the Mauchline Fair being omitted, thus—
"On the 20th current I hope to have the honor of assuring you in person, how sincerely I am—" &c.
Two slight verbal alterations on the text of 'Sketch' have also been made, presumably by him: which liberty we cannot justify. They will be seen by comparing the above with his own, or common editions of poem. (See Notes on Posthumous Works.) The entire document has been endorsed by him thus—
"Psalm on the King's Restoration not to be printed. 9th April, 1789. Poem to Fox to be printed. Good Fragments."
Such glimpses into the editorial liberties and arrangements of a very able and judicious man, intrusted with a most laborious and difficult task, are to ourselves extremely interesting.]

——

(22.)   TO MRS. DUNLOP.

Ellisland, 21st June, 1789.

DEAR MADAM,

WILL you take the effusions, the miserable effusions of low spirits, just as they flow from their bitter spring? I know not of any particular cause for this worst of all my foes besetting me; but for some time my soul has been beclouded with a thickening atmosphere of evil imaginations and gloomy presages.

Monday Evening.

I have just heard Mr. Kirkpatrick give a sermon. He is a man famous for his benevolence, and I revere him; but from such ideas of my Creator, good Lord deliver me! Religion, my honored friend, is surely a simple business, as it equally concerns the ignorant and the learned, the poor and the rich. That there is an incomprehensibly Great Being, to whom I owe my existence, and that he must be intimately acquainted with the operations and progress of the internal machinery, and consequent outward deportment of this creature which he has made; these are, I think, self-evident propositions. That there is a real and eternal distinction between virtue and vice, and consequently, that I am an accountable creature; that from the seeming nature of the human mind, as well as from the evident imperfection, nay, positive injustice, in the administration of affairs, both in the natural and moral worlds, there must be a retributive scene of existence beyond the grave; must, I think, be allowed by every one who will give himself a moment's reflection. I will go farther, and affirm, that from the sublimity, excellence, and purity of his doctrine and precepts, unparalleled by all the aggregated wisdom and learning of many preceding ages, though, *to appearance*, he himself was the obscurest and most illiterate of our species; therefore, Jesus Christ was from God. * * * *

Whatever mitigates the woes, or increases the happiness of others, this is my criterion of goodness; and whatever injures society at large, or any individual in it, this is my measure of iniquity.

What think you, Madam, of my creed? I trust that I have said nothing that will lessen me in the eye of one, whose good opinion I value almost next to the approbation of my own mind.

R. B.

(23.)   TO MRS. DUNLOP.

Ellisland, 6th Sept. 1789.

DEAR MADAM,

I HAVE mentioned in my last my appointment to the Excise, and the birth of little Frank; who, by the bye, I trust will be no discredit to the honorable name of Wallace, as he has a fine manly countenance, and a figure that might do credit to a little fellow two months older; and likewise an excellent good temper, though when he pleases he has a pipe, only not quite so loud as the horn that his immortal namesake blew as a signal to take out the pin of Stirling bridge.

I had some time ago an epistle, part poetic, and part prosaic, from your poetess, Mrs. J. Little, a very ingenious, but modest composition.* I should have written her as she requested, but for the hurry of this new business. I have heard of her and her compositions in this country; and I am happy to add, always to the honor of her character. The fact is, I know not well how to write to her: I should sit down to a sheet of paper that I know not how to stain. I am no dab at fine-drawn letter-writing; and, except when prompted by friendship or gratitude, or, which happens extremely rarely, inspired by the Muse (I know not her name) that presides over epistolary writing, I sit down, when necessitated to write, as I would sit down to beat hemp.

Some parts of your letter of the 20th August, struck me with the most melancholy concern for the state of your mind at present. * * *

Would I could write you a letter of comfort! I would sit down to it with as much pleasure, as I would to write an epic poem of my own composition that should equal the *Iliad*. Religion, my dear friend, is the true comfort! A strong persuasion in a future state of existence; a proposition so obviously probable, that, setting revelation aside, every nation and people, so far as investigation has reached, for at least near four thousand years, have, in some mode or other, firmly believed it. In vain would we reason and pretend to doubt. I have myself done so to a very daring pitch; but, when I reflected, that I was opposing the most ardent wishes, and the most darling hopes of good men, and flying in the face of all human belief, in all ages, I was shocked at my own conduct.

I know not whether I have ever sent you the following lines, or if you have ever seen them; but it is one of my favorite quotations, which I keep constantly by me in my progress through life, in the language of the book of Job,

" Against the day of battle and of war"—

spoken of religion :

> "'Tis this, my friend, that streaks our morning bright,
> 'Tis this that gilds the horror of our night.
> When wealth forsakes us, and when friends are few,
> When friends are faithless, or when foes pursue;
> 'Tis this that wards the blow, or stills the smart,
> Disarms affliction, or repels his dart;
> Within the breast bids purest raptures rise,
> Bids smiling conscience spread her cloudless skies."

I have been very busy with *Zeluco*. The Doctor is so obliging as to request my opinion of it; and I have been revolving in my mind some kind of criticisms on novel-writing, but it is a depth beyond my research. I shall however digest my thoughts on the subject as well as I can. *Zeluco* is a most sterling performance.

Farewell! *A Dieu, le bon Dieu, je vous commende.*

R. B.

* [See conclusion of Special Correspondence.]

(24.)   TO MRS. DUNLOP.

Ellisland, 13th December, 1789.

MANY thanks, dear Madam, for your sheet-full of rhymes. Though at present I am below the veriest prose, yet from you every thing pleases. I am groaning under the miseries of a diseased nervous system; a system, the state of which is most conducive to our happiness—or the most productive of our misery. For now near three weeks I have been so ill with a nervous head-ache, that I have been obliged to give up for a time my Excise-books, being scarce able to lift my head, much less to ride once a week over ten muir parishes. What is man!—To-day in the luxuriance of health, exulting in the enjoyment of existence; in a few days, perhaps in a few hours, loaded with conscious painful being, counting the tardy pace of the lingering moments by the repercussions of anguish, and refusing or denied a comforter. Day follows night, and night comes after day, only to curse him with life which gives him no pleasure; and yet the awful, dark termination of that life is a something at which he recoils.

> "Tell us, ye dead; will none of you in pity
> Declose the secret————————————
> What 'tis you are, and we must shortly be?
> ————————————— 'tis no matter;
> A little time will make us learn'd as you are."

Can it be possible, that when I resign this frail, feverish being, I shall still find myself in conscious existence! When the last gasp of agony has announced that I am no more to those that knew me, and the few who loved me; when the cold, stiffened, unconscious, ghastly corse is resigned into the earth, to be the prey of unsightly reptiles, and to become in time a trodden clod, shall I yet be warm in life, seeing and seen, enjoying and enjoyed? Ye venerable sages and holy flamens, is there probability in your conjectures, truth in your stories, of another world beyond death; or are they all alike, baseless visions, and fabricated fables? If there is another life, it must only be for the just, the benevolent, the amiable, and the humane; what a flattering idea, then, is a world to come! Would to God I as firmly believed it, as I ardently wish it! There I should meet an aged parent, now at rest from the many buffetings of an evil world, against which he so long and so bravely struggled. There should I meet the friend, the disinterested friend of my early life; the man who rejoiced to see me, because he loved me and could serve me.—Muir, thy weaknesses were the aberrations of human nature, but thy heart glowed with every thing generous, manly and noble; and if ever emanation from the All-good Being animated a human form, it was thine! There should I, with speechless agony of rapture, again recognize my lost, my ever dear Mary! whose bosom was fraught with truth, honor, constancy, and love.

> My Mary, dear departed shade!
> Where is thy place of heavenly rest?
> Seest thou thy lover lowly laid?
> Hear'st thou the groans that rend his breast?

Jesus Christ, thou amiablest of characters! I trust thou art no impostor, and that thy revelation of blissful scenes of existence beyond death and the grave, is not one of the many impositions which time after time have been palmed on credulous mankind. I trust that in thee "shall all the families of the earth be blessed," by being yet connected together in a better world, where every tie that bound heart to heart, in this state of existence, shall be, far beyond our present conceptions, more endearing.

I am a good deal inclined to think with those who maintain, that what are called nervous affections are in fact diseases of the mind. I cannot reason, I cannot think; and but to you I would not venture to write any thing above an order to a cobbler. You have felt too much of the ills of life not to sympathize with a diseased wretch, who is* impaired more than half of any faculties he possessed. Your goodness will excuse this distracted scrawl, which the writer dare scarcely read, and which he would throw into the fire, were he able to write any thing better, or indeed any thing at all.

Rumour told me something of a son of yours, who was returned from the East or West Indies. If you have gotten news of James or Anthony, it was cruel in you not to let me know; as I promise you on the sincerity of a man, who is weary of one world, and anxious about another, that scarce any thing could give me so much pleasure as to hear of any good thing befalling my honored friend.

If you have a minute's leisure, take up your pen in pity to *le pauvre miserable.*

R. B.

*[Thus distinctly in Currie. In all other editions we have seen, the phrase has been altered, on what authority we know not, to 'has impaired,' which gives an entirely different and self-criminating sense to the whole passage; for which there is no justification, moral or circumstantial, that we are aware of, and which we have no right, therefore, to assume the writer intended to convey.]

(25.)   TO MRS. DUNLOP.

Ellisland, 25th January, 1790.

It has been owing to unremitting hurry of business that I have not written to you, Madam, long ere now. My health is greatly better, and I now begin once more to share in satisfaction and enjoyment with the rest of my fellow-creatures.

Many thanks, my much-esteemed friend, for your kind letters; but why will you make me run the risk of being contemptible and mercenary in my own eyes? When I pique myself on my independent spirit, I hope it is neither poetic licence, nor poetic rant; and I am so flattered with the honor you have done me, in making me your compeer in friendship and friendly correspondence, that I cannot without pain, and a degree of mortification, be reminded of the real inequality between our situations.

Most sincerely do I rejoice with you, dear Madam, in the good news of Anthony. Not only your anxiety about his fate, but my own esteem for such a noble, warm-hearted, manly young fellow, in the little I had of his acquaintance, has interested me deeply in his fortunes.

Falconer, the unfortunate author of the "Shipwreck," which you so much admire, is no more. After weathering the dreadful catastrophe he so feelingly describes in his poem, and after weathering many hard gales of fortune, he went to the bottom with the Aurora frigate!

I forget what part of Scotland had the honor of giving him birth; but he was the son of obscurity and misfortune.* He was one of those daring adventurous spirits which Scotland, beyond any other country, is remarkable for producing. Little does the fond mother think, as she hangs delighted over the sweet little leech at her bosom, where the poor fellow may hereafter wander, and what may be his fate. I remember a stanza in an old Scottish ballad, which, notwithstanding its rude simplicity, speaks feelingly to the heart:

> "Little did my mother think,
> That day she cradled me,
> What land I was to travel in,
> Or what death I should die!"

Old Scottish songs are, you know, a favourite study and pursuit of mine, and now I am on that subject, allow me to give you two stanzas of another old simple ballad, which I am sure will please you. The catastrophe of the piece is a poor ruined female, lamenting her fate. She concludes with this pathetic wish :—

> "O that my father had ne'er on me smil'd ;
> O that my mother had ne'er to me sang !
> O that my cradle had never been rock'd ;
> But that I had died when I was young !
>
> O that the grave it were my bed ;
> My blankets were my winding sheet ;
> The clocks and the worms my bedfellows a' ;
> And O sae sound as I should sleep !'"

I do not remember in all my reading, to have met with any thing more truly the language of misery, than the exclamation in the last line. Misery is like love ; to speak its language truly, the author must have felt it.

I am every day expecting the doctor to give your little godson† the small-pox. They are *rife* in the country, and I tremble for his fate. By the way, I cannot help congratulating you on his looks and spirit. Every person who sees him acknowledges him to be the finest, handsomest child he has ever seen. I am myself delighted with the manly swell of his little chest, and a certain miniature dignity in the carriage of his head, and the glance of his fine black eye, which promise the undaunted gallantry of an independent mind.

I thought to have sent you some rhymes, but time forbids. I promise you poetry until you are tired of it, next time I have the honor of assuring you how truly I am, &c.

R. B.

*[It may be mentioned, that he was a native of one of the towns on the coast of Fife; and that his parents, who had suffered some misfortunes, removed to one of the sea-ports of England, where they hath died soon after of an epidemic fever, leaving poor Falconer, then a boy, forlorn and destitute. In consequence of which he entered on board a man-of-war. The last circumstances are, however, less certain.—Currie.)

†[Francis Wallace, second son of Poet.]

(26.)   TO MRS. DUNLOP.

Ellisland, 10th April, 1790.

I HAVE just now, my over honored friend, enjoyed a very high luxury, in reading a paper of the Lounger. You know my national prejudices. I had often read and admired the Spectator, Adventurer, Rambler, and World; but still with a certain regret, that they were so thoroughly and entirely English. Alas! have I often said to myself, what are all the boasted advantages which my country reaps from the Union, that can counterbalance the annihilation of her independence, and even her very name! I often repeat that couplet of my favourite poet, Goldsmith—

> "————States of native liberty possest,
> Tho' very poor, may yet be very blest.'"

Nothing can reconcile me to the common terms, "English ambassador, English court," &c. And I am out of all patience to see that equivocal character, Hastings, impeached by "the Commons of England." Tell me, my friend, is this weak prejudice? I believe in my conscience such ideas as "my country; her independence ; her honor ; the illustrious names that mark the history of my native land ;" &c.—I believe these, among your *men of the world*, men who in fact guide for the most part and govern our world, are looked on as so many modifications of wrongheadedness. They know the use of bawling out such terms, to rouse or lead THE RABBLE ; but for their own private use, with almost all the *able statesmen* that ever existed, or now exist, when they talk of right and wrong, they only mean proper and improper; and their measure of conduct is, not what they OUGHT, but what they DARE. For the truth of this I shall not ransack the history of nations, but appeal to one of the ablest judges of men, and himself one of the ablest men, that ever lived—the celebrated Earl of Chesterfield. In fact, a man who could thoroughly control his vices whenever they interfered with his interests, and who could completely put on the appearance of every virtue as often as it suited his purposes, is, on the Stanhopean plan, the *perfect man* ; a man to lead nations. But are great abilities, complete without a flaw, and polished without a blemish, the standard of human excellence? This is certainly the staunch opinion of *men of the world*; but I call on honor, virtue, and worth, to give the stygian doctrine a loud negative! However, this must be allowed, that, if you abstract from man the idea of an existence beyond the grave, *then*, the true measure of human conduct is, *proper* and *improper*: virtue and vice, as dispositions of the heart, are, in that case, of scarcely the same import and value to the world at large, as harmony and discord in the modifications of sound; and a delicate sense of honor, like a nice ear for music, though it may sometimes give the possessor an ecstacy unknown to the coarser organs of the herd, yet, considering the harsh gratings, and inharmonic jars, in this ill-tuned state of being, it is odds but the individual would be as happy, and certainly would be as much respected by the true judges of society as it would then stand, without either a good ear or a good heart.

You must know I have just met with the Mirror and Lounger for the first time, and I am quite in raptures with them ; I should be glad to have your opinion of some of the papers. The one I have just read, Lounger, No. 61, has cost me more honest tears than any thing I have read of a long time. Mackenzie has been called the Addison of the Scots, and in my opinion, Addison would not be hurt at the comparison. If he has not Addison's exquisite humour, he as certainly outdoes him in the tender and the pathetic. His Man of Feeling (but I am not counsel learned in the laws of criticism) I estimate as the first performance in its kind I ever saw. From what book, moral or even pious, will the susceptible young mind receive impressions more congenial to humanity and kindness, generosity and benevolence ; in short, more of all that ennobles the soul to herself, or endears her to others— than from the simple affecting tale of poor Harley.

Still, with all my admiration of Mackenzie's writings, I do not know if they are the fittest reading for a young man who is about to set out, as the phrase is, to make his way into life. Do not you think, Madam, that among the few favoured of heaven in the structure of their minds (for such there certainly are), there may be a purity, a tenderness, a dignity, an elegance of soul, which are of no use, nay, in some degree, absolutely disqualifying for the truly important business of making a man's way into life? If I am not much mistaken, my gallant young friend, A * * * * * *, is very much under these disqualifications; and for the young females of a family I could mention, well may they excite parental solicitude, for I, a common acquaintance, or as my vanity will have it, an humble friend, have often trembled for a turn of mind which may render them eminently happy—or peculiarly miserable.

I have been manufacturing some verses lately; but as I have got the most hurried season of excise business over, I hope to have more leisure to transcribe any thing that may show how much I have the honor to be, Madam,

Yours, &c.

R. B.

(27.)   TO MRS. DUNLOP.

8th August, 1790.

DEAR MADAM,

AFTER a long day's toil, plague, and care, I sit down to write to you. Ask me not why I have delayed it so long? It was owing to hurry, indolence, and fifty other things; in short to anything—but forgetfulness of *la plus aimable de son sexe*. By the bye, you are indebted your best courtesy to me for this last compliment; as I pay it from my sincere conviction of its truth—a quality rather rare in compliments of these grinning, bowing, scraping times.

Well, I hope writing to *you* will ease a little my troubled soul. Sorely has it been bruised to-day! A ci-devant friend of mine, and an intimate acquaintance of yours, has given my feelings a wound that I perceive will gangrene dangerously ere it cure. He has wounded my pride!

* * * *

R. B.

(28.)   TO MRS. DUNLOP.

Ellisland, November, 1790.

" As cold waters to a thirsty soul, so is good news from a far country."

Fate has long owed me a letter of good news from you, in return for the many tidings of sorrow which I have received. In this instance I most cordially obey the apostle—" Rejoice with them that do rejoice"—for me, *to sing for joy*, is no new thing; but *to preach* for joy, as I have done in the commencement of this epistle, is a pitch of extravagant rapture to which I never rose before.

I read your letter—I literally jumped for joy—How could such a mercurial creature as a poet lumpishly keep his seat on the receipt of the best news from his best friend? I seized my gilt-headed Wangee rod, an instrument indispensably necessary in my left hand, in the moment of inspiration and rapture; and stride, stride—quick and quicker—out skipt I among the broomy banks of Nith to muse over my joy by retail. To keep within the bounds of prose was impossible. Mrs. Little's is a more elegant, but not a more sincere compliment to the sweet little fellow, than I, extempore almost, poured out to him in the following verses:—

> Sweet flow'ret, pledge o' meikle love
> And ward o' mony a prayer,
> What heart o' stane wad thou na move,
> Sae helpless, sweet, an' fair.
> November hirples o'er the lea
> Chill on thy lovely form;
> But gane, alas! the shelt'ring tree
> Should shield thee frae the storm.

* * * * *

I am much flattered by your approbation of my *Tam o' Shanter*, which you express in your former letter; though, by the bye, you load me in that said letter with accusations heavy and many; to all of which I plead, *not guilty!* Your book is, I hear, on the road to reach me. As to printing of poetry, when you prepare it for the press, you have only to spell it right, and place the capital letters properly: as to the punctuation, the printers do that themselves.

I have a copy of *Tam o' Shanter* ready to send you by the first opportunity; it is too heavy to send by post.

I heard of Mr. Corbet lately. He, in consequence of your recommendation, is most zealous to serve me. Please favour me soon with an account of your good folks; if Mrs. H. is recovering, and the young gentleman doing well.

R. B.

(29.)   TO MRS. DUNLOP.

Ellisland, 7th [April], 1791.

WHEN I tell you, Madam, that by a fall, not from my horse, but with my horse, I have been a cripple some time, and that this is the first day my arm and hand have been able to serve me in writing; you will allow that it is too good an apology for my seemingly ungrateful silence. I am now getting better, and am able to rhyme a little, which implies some tolerable ease; as I cannot think that the most poetic genius is able to compose on the rack.

I do not remember if ever I mentioned to you my having an idea of composing an elegy on the late Miss Burnet, of Monboddo. I had the honor of being pretty well acquainted with her, and have seldom felt so much at the loss of an acquaintance, as when I heard that so amiable and accomplished a piece of God's works was no more. I have, as yet, gone no farther than the following fragment, of which please let me have your opinion. You know that elegy is a subject so much exhausted, that any new idea on the business is not to be expected: 'tis well if we can place an old idea in a new light. How far I have succeeded as to this last, you will judge from what follows.

[Here follows the Elegy, for which see Posthumous Works.]

I have proceeded no further.

Your kind letter, with your kind *remembrance* of your godson, came safe. This last, Madam, is scarcely what my pride can bear. As to the little fellow, he is, partiality apart, the finest boy I have of a long time seen. He is now seventeen months old, has the small pox and measles over, has cut several teeth, and never yet had a grain of doctor's drugs in his bowels.

I am truly happy to hear the "little floweret" is blooming so fresh and fair, and that the "mother plant" is rather recovering her drooping head. Soon and well may her "cruel wounds" be healed! I have written thus far with a good deal of difficulty. When I get a little abler you shall hear farther from,

Madam, yours,

R. B.

(30.)   TO MRS. DUNLOP.

Ellisland, 11th April, 1791.

I AM once more able, my honored friend, to return you, with my own hand, thanks for the many instances of your friendship, and particularly for your kind anxiety in this last disaster that my evil genius had in store for me. However, life is chequered—joy and sorrow—for on Saturday morning last, Mrs. Burns made me a present of a fine boy; rather stouter, but not so handsome as your godson was at his time of life. Indeed I look on your little namesake to be my *chef d'œuvre* in that species of manufacture, as I look on Tam o' Shanter to be my standard performance in the poetical line. 'Tis true, both the one and the other discover a spice of roguish waggery, that might perhaps be as well spared; but then they also show, in my opinion, a force of genius and a finishing polish, that I despair of ever excelling. Mrs. Burns is getting stout again, and laid as lustily about her to-day at breakfast, as a reaper from the corn-ridge. That is the peculiar privilege and blessing of our hale, sprightly damsels, that are bred among the *hay and heather.* We cannot hope for that highly polished mind, that charming delicacy of soul, which is found among the female world in the more elevated stations of life, and which is certainly by far the most bewitching charm in the famous cestus of Venus. It is indeed such an inestimable treasure, that where it can be had in its native heavenly purity, unstained by some one or other of the many shades of affectation, and unalloyed by some one or other of the many species of caprice, I declare to Heaven, I should think it cheaply purchased at the expense of every other earthly good! But as this angelic creature is, I am afraid, extremely rare in any station and rank of life, and totally denied to such a humble one as mine, we meaner mortals must put up with the next rank of female excellence—as fine a figure and face we can produce as any rank of life whatever; rustic, native grace; unaffected modesty, and unsullied purity; nature's mother-wit, and the rudiments of taste; a simplicity of soul, unsuspicious of, because unacquainted with, the

crooked ways of a selfish, interested, disingenuous world; and the dearest charm of all the rest, a yielding sweetness of disposition, and a generous warmth of heart, grateful for love on our part, and ardently glowing with a more than equal return: these, with a healthy frame, a sound, vigorous constitution, which your higher ranks can scarcely ever hope to enjoy, are the charms of lovely woman in my humble walk of life.

This is the greatest effort my broken arm has yet made. Do let me hear, by first post, how *cher petit Monsieur*[*] comes on with his small-pox. May almighty goodness preserve and restore him!

R. B.

[*] [The 'little floweret'—Madame Henri's son, and grandson of Mrs. Dunlop.]

(31.)   TO MRS. DUNLOP.

Ellisland, 17th December, 1791.

MANY thanks to you, Madam, for your good news respecting the little floweret and the mother-plant. I hope my poetic prayers have been heard, and will be answered up to the warmest sincerity of their fullest extent; and then Mrs. Henri will find her little darling the representative of his late parent, in everything but his abridged existence.

I have just finished the following song, which to a lady the descendant of Wallace—and many heroes of his truly illustrious line—and herself the mother of several soldiers, needs neither preface nor apology.

Scene—A field of battle—time of the day, evening: the wounded and dying of the victorious army are supposed to join in the following

SONG OF DEATH.

Farewell, thou fair day, thou green earth, and ye skies
 Now gay with the bright setting sun;
Farewell, loves and friendships, ye dear, tender ties—
 Our race of existence is run!

* * * * * *

The circumstance that gave rise to the foregoing verses was, looking over with a musical friend M'Donald's collection of Highland airs, I was struck with one, an Isle of Skye tune, entitled "Oran an Aoig," or "The Song of Death," to the measure of which I have adapted my stanzas. I have of late composed two or three other little pieces, which, ere yon full-orbed moon, whose broad impudent face now stares at old mother earth all night, shall have shrunk into a modest crescent, just peeping forth at dewy dawn, I shall find an hour to transcribe for you. *A Dieu je vous commende.*

R. B.

(32.)   TO MRS. DUNLOP.

Annan Water Foot, 22nd August, 1792.

Do not blame me for it, Madam;—my own conscience, hacknied and weatherbeaten as it is, in watching and reproving my vagaries, follies, indolence, &c., has continued to blame and punish me sufficiently.

*   *   *   *   *   *

Do you think it possible, my dear and honored friend, that I could be so lost to gratitude for many favors, to esteem for much worth, and to the honest, kind, pleasurable tie of, now, old acquaintance, and I hope and am sure, of progressive, increasing friendship—as, for a single day, not to think of you —to ask the Fates what they are doing and about to do with my much-loved friend and her wide-scattered connexions, and to beg of them to be as kind to you and yours as they possibly can?

Apropos (though how it is apropos, I have not leisure to explain), do you not know that I am almost in love with an acquaintance of yours?—Almost! said I—I am in love, souse! over head and ears, deep as the most unfathomable abyss of the boundless ocean; but the word Love, owing to the *interminglements* of the good and the bad, the pure and the impure, in this world, being rather an equivocal term for expressing one's sentiments and sensations, I must do justice to the sacred purity of my attachment. Know, then, that the heart-struck awe; the distant humble approach; the delight we should have in gazing upon and listening to a Messenger of Heaven, appearing in all the unspotted purity of his celestial home, among the coarse, polluted, far inferior sons of men, to deliver to them tidings that make their hearts swim in joy, and their imaginations soar in transport—such, so delighting, and so pure, were the emotions of my soul on meeting the other day with Miss Lesley Baillie, your neighbour, at M——. Mr. B. with his two daughters, accompanied by Mr. H. of G., passing through Dumfries a few days ago, on their way to England, did me the honor of calling on me; on which I took my horse (though God knows I could ill spare the time), and accompanied them fourteen or fifteen miles, and dined and spent the day with them. 'Twas about nine, I think, when I left them; and, riding home, I composed the following ballad, of which you will probably think you have a dear bargain, as it will cost you another groat of postage. You must know that there is an old ballad beginning with—

> "My bonie Lizie Baillie
> I'll rowe thee in my plaidie," &c.

So I parodied it as follows, which is literally the first copy, "unanointed, unannoal'd," as Hamlet says.—

> O saw ye bonie Lesley
>   As she gaed o'er the border?
> She's gane like Alexander,
>   To spread her conquests farther.
>
> *   *   *   *

So much for ballads. I regret that you are gone to the east country, as I am to be in Ayrshire in about a fortnight. This world of ours, notwithstanding it has many good things in it, yet it has ever had this curse, that two or three people who would be the happier the oftener they met together, are, almost without exception, always so placed as never to meet but once or twice a-year; which, considering the few years of a man's life, is a very great "evil under the sun," which I do not recollect that Solomon has mentioned in his catalogue of the miseries of man. I hope and believe that there is a state of existence beyond the grave, where the worthy of this life will renew their former intimacies, with this endearing addition, that, "we meet to part no more."

*   *   *   *

> "Tell us, ye dead,
> Will none of you in pity disclose the secret,
> What 'tis you are, and we must shortly be?" *

A thousand times have I made this apostrophe to the departed sons of men, but not one of them has ever thought fit to answer the question. "O that some courteous ghost would blab it out!" but it cannot be: you and I, my friend, must make the experiment by ourselves and for ourselves. However, I am so convinced that an unshaken faith in the doctrines of religion is not only necessary by making us better men, but also by making us happier men, that I shall take every care that your little godson, and every little creature that shall call me father, shall be taught them.

So ends this heterogeneous letter, written at this wild place of the world, in the intervals of my labour of discharging a vessel of rum from Antigua.

R. B.

* [Blair's "Grave"—already quoted by our Author, in slightly different form, Letter (28).]

(33.)   TO MRS. DUNLOP.

Dumfries, 24th September, 1792.

I HAVE this moment, my dear Madam, yours of the twenty-third. All your other kind reproaches, your news, &c., are out of my head when I read and think on Mrs. H[enri]'s situation. Good God! a heart-wounded helpless young woman —in a strange, foreign land, and that land convulsed with every horror that can harrow the human feelings—sick—looking, longing for a comforter, but finding none—a mother's feelings, too:—but it is too much: he who wounded (he only can) may He heal!

*   *   *   *   *   *

I wish the Farmer great joy of his new acquisition to his family. *   *   *   *   *   * I cannot say that I give him joy of his life as a farmer. 'Tis, as a farmer paying a dear, unconscionable rent, a *cursed life!* As to a laird farming his own property; sowing his own corn in hope; and reaping it, in spite of brittle weather, in gladness; knowing that none can say unto him, "what dost thou?"—fattening his herds; shearing his flocks; rejoicing at Christmas; and begetting sons and daughters, until he be the venerated, grey-haired leader of a little tribe—'tis a heavenly life! but Devil take the life of reaping the fruits that another must eat.

Well, your kind wishes will be gratified, as to seeing me when I make my Ayrshire visit. I cannot leave Mrs. B. until her nine months' race is run, which may perhaps be in three or four weeks. She, too, seems determined to make me the patriarchal leader of a band. However, if Heaven will

* D

be so obliging as let me have them in the proportion of three boys to one girl, I shall be so much the more pleased. I hope, if I am spared with them, to show a set of boys that will do honor to my cares and name; but I am not equal to the task of rearing girls. Besides, I am too poor; a girl should always have a fortune. Apropos, your little godson is thriving charmingly, but is a very devil. He, though two years younger, has completely mastered his brother. Robert is indeed the mildest, gentlest creature I ever saw. He has a most surprising memory, and is quite the pride of his school-master.

You know how readily we got into prattle upon a subject dear to our heart: you can excuse it. God bless you and yours!

R. B.

(34.)   TO MRS. DUNLOP.

Dumfries, October, 1792.

[Supposed to have been written on death of Madame Henri, her daughter, who died at Muges, Alguillon, South of France, Sep. 15th, 1792. See foregoing Letter.]

I HAD been from home, and did not receive your letter until my return the other day. What shall I say to comfort you, my much-valued, much-afflicted friend! I can but grieve with you; consolation I have none to offer, except that which religion holds out to the children of affliction—*children of affliction!*—how just the expression! and like every other family, they have matters among them which they hear, see, and feel in a serious, all-important manner, of which the world has not, nor cares to have, any idea. The world looks indifferently on, makes the passing remark, and proceeds to the next novel occurrence.

Alas, Madam! who would wish for many years! What is it but to drag existence until our joys gradually expire, and leave us in a night of misery: like the gloom which blots out the stars one by one, from the face of night, and leaves us, without a ray of comfort, in the howling waste!*

I am interrupted, and must leave off. You shall soon hear from me again.

R. B.

*[When true hearts lie wither'd,
And fond ones are flown,
Oh! who would inhabit
This bleak world alone!—*Moore.*]

(35.)   TO MRS. DUNLOP.

Dumfries, 6th December, 1792.

I SHALL be in Ayrshire, I think, next week; and, if at all possible, I shall certainly, my much-esteemed friend, have the pleasure of visiting at Dunlop-house.

Alas, Madam! how seldom do we meet in this world, that we have reason to congratulate ourselves on accessions of happiness! I have not passed half the ordinary term of an old man's life, and yet I scarcely look over the obituary of a newspaper, that I do not see some names that I have known, and which I, and other acquaintances, little thought to meet with there so soon. Every other instance of the mortality of our kind makes us cast an anxious look into the dreadful abyss of uncertainty, and shudder with apprehension for our own fate. But of how different an importance are the lives of different individuals? Nay, of what importance is one period of the same life, more than another? A few years ago, I could have lain down in the dust, "careless of the voice of the morning;" and now not a few, and those most helpless individuals, would, on losing me and my exertions, lose both their "staff and shield." By the way, these helpless ones have lately got an addition; Mrs. B. having given me a fine girl since I wrote you. There is a charming passage in Thomson's "Edward and Eleanora:"

> "The valiant in himself, what can he suffer?
> Or what need he regard his single woes?" &c.

As I am got in the way of quotations, I shall give you another from the same piece, peculiarly, alas! too peculiarly apposite, my dear Madam, to your present frame of mind:

> "Who so unworthy but may proudly deck him
> With his fair-weather virtue, that exults
> Glad o'er the summer main! The tempest comes,
> The rough winds rage aloud; when from the helm
> This virtue shrinks, and in a corner lies
> Lamenting—Heavens! if privileged from trial,
> How cheap a thing were virtue!"

I do not remember to have heard you mention Thomson's dramas. I pick up favourite quotations and store them in my mind as ready armour, offensive or defensive, amid the struggle of this turbulent existence. Of these is one, a very favourite one, from his "Alfred:"

> "Attach thee firmly to the virtuous deeds
> And offices of life; to life itself,
> With all its vain and transient joys, sit loose."

Probably I have quoted some of those to you formerly, as indeed when I write from the heart, I am apt to be guilty of such repetitions. The compass of the heart, in the musical style of expression, is much more bounded than that of the imagination; so the notes of the former are extremely apt to run into one another; but in return for the paucity of its compass, its few notes are much more sweet. I must still give you another quotation, which I am almost sure I have given you before, but I cannot resist the temptation. The subject is religion—speaking of its importance to mankind, the author says,

> "'Tis this, my friend, that streaks our morning bright,"
> [&c., as in Letter (25.)]

I see you are in for double postage, so I shall e'en scribble out t'other sheet. We, in this country here, have many alarms of the reforming, or rather the republican spirit, of your part of the kingdom. Indeed we are a good deal in commotion ourselves. For me, I am a placeman, you know; a very humble one indeed, Heaven knows, but still so much so as to gag me. What my private sentiments are, you will find out without an interpreter.

*   *   *   *   *

I have taken up the subject in another view, and the other day, for a pretty actress's benefit-night, I wrote an Address, which I will give on the other page, called "The Rights of Woman:"

> While Europe's eye is fixed on mighty things,
>
> [See Posthumous Works.]

I shall have the honor of receiving your criticisms in person at Dunlop.

R. B.

(36.)   TO MRS. DUNLOP.
                         [FIRST HALF.]

[*Dumfries,*] *Dec.* 31, 1792.

DEAR MADAM,

A HURRY of business, thrown in heaps by my absence, has until now prevented my returning my grateful acknowledgments to the good family of Dunlop, and you in particular, for that hospitable kindness which rendered the four days I spent under that genial roof, four of the pleasantest I ever enjoyed.—Alas, my dearest friend! how few and fleeting are those things we call pleasures! On my road to Ayrshire, I spent a night with a friend whom I much valued; a man whose days promised to be many; and on Saturday last we laid him in the dust!

Jan. 2, 1793.

I HAVE just received yours of the 30th, and feel much for your situation. However, I heartily rejoice in your prospect of recovery from that vile jaundice. As to myself, I am better, though not quite free of my complaint.—You must not think, as you seem to insinuate, that in my way of life I want exercise. Of that I have enough; but occasional hard drinking is the devil to me. Against this I have again and again bent my resolution, and have greatly succeeded. Taverns I have totally abandoned: it is the private parties in the family way, among the hard-drinking gentlemen of this country, that do me the mischief—but even this I have more than half given over.

Mr. Corbet can be of little service to me at present; at least I should be shy of applying. I cannot possibly be settled as a supervisor, for several years. I must wait the rotation of the list, and there are twenty names before mine.—I might indeed get a job of officiating, where a settled supervisor was ill, or aged; but that hauls me from my family, as I could not remove them on such an uncertainty. Besides, some envious, malicious devil has raised a little demur on my political principles, and I wish to let that matter settle before I offer myself too much in the eye of my supervisors. I have set, henceforth, a seal on my lips, as to these unlucky politics; but to you, I must breathe my sentiments. In this, as in every thing else, I shall shew the undisguised emotions of my soul. War I deprecate: misery and ruin to thousands are in the blast that announces the destructive demon. But

* * * * *

[The remainder of this letter has been torn away by some barbarous hand.—*Cromek.* I can have no doubt that it was torn away by one of the kindest hands in the world—that of Mrs. Dunlop herself.—*Lockhart.* For explanation of difficulty see following note.]

[SECOND HALF.]

5th January, 179[3].*

YOU see my hurried life, Madam: I can only command starts of time; however, I am glad of one thing; since I finished the other sheet, the political blast that threatened my welfare is overblown. I have corresponded with Commissioner Graham, for the board had made me the subject of their animadversions; and now I have the pleasure of informing you, that all is set to rights in that quarter. Now as to these informers, may the devil be let loose to —— but hold! I was praying most fervently in my last sheet, and I must not so soon fall a-swearing in this.

Alas! how little do the wantonly or idly officious think what mischief they do by their malicious insinuations, indirect impertinence, or thoughtless blabbings. What a difference there is in intrinsic worth, candor, benevolence, generosity, kindness,—in all the charities and all the virtues, between one class of human beings and another. For instance, the amiable circle I so lately mixed with in the hospitable hall of Dunlop, their generous hearts—their uncontaminated dignified minds—their informed and polished understandings—what a contrast, when compared—if such comparing were not downright sacrilege—with the soul of the miscreant who can deliberately plot the destruction of an honest man that never offended him, and with a grin of satisfaction see the unfortunate being, his faithful wife, and prattling innocents, turned over to beggary and ruin!

Your cup, my dear Madam, arrived safe. I had two worthy fellows dining with me the other day, when I, with great formality, produced my whigmeleerie cup, and told them that it had been a family-piece among the descendants of Sir William Wallace. This roused such an enthusiasm that they insisted on bumpering the punch round in it; and by and by, never did your great ancestor lay a Suthron more completely to rest, than for a time did your cup my two friends. Apropos, this is the season of wishing. May God bless you, my dear friend, and bless me, the humblest and sincerest of your friends, by granting you yet many returns of the season! May all good things attend you and yours, wherever they are scattered over the earth!

R. B.

* [This letter is given by Currie as of date 1793, which was possibly the actual date in manuscript; but we entirely concur with Mr. Chambers, who was the first, so far as we are aware, to point out the fact—that it must be a mistake. The letter obviously refers to what took place of a painful character in December 1792, and therefore could not have been written a year before; but in the haste and excitement of the writer, thinking of what had just occurred in the end of —92, a wrong figure might easily be put down at the beginning of next year. But there is another fact, of curious interest, which seems entirely to have escaped Mr. Chambers—viz.: that this so-called letter is but the *second half* of another letter, and that the *first half* is the letter which goes immediately before. A very slight comparison of the two fragments will demonstrate this. The first half begins but does not end, the second half ends but does not begin; the dates are continuous at short intervals (too short to allow another letter to the same person to be written between them), and the subject of both is the same, with a little additional satisfactory news obtained in the meantime; the second half refers to a "last sheet" which has never elsewhere been seen, unless the sheet that goes before is the sheet in question; and finally, the tenor, the topics, and very terms—the reiteration of haste and hurry—in both fragments, are the same. The history of both is natural and consistent: The second sheet, having a subordinate date of its own, with Mrs. Dunlop's address on the outside, was so far perfect, and, above all, having no treason, would be handed without commentary to Mr. Currie, and printed accordingly. But the first sheet (what the writer calls "the other sheet," or "my last sheet," in relation to this) had most probably

some dangerous political complaints or condemnations of his own, or strange enough prayers by him about the issue of the war, at the end of it. These the affectionate lady would cautiously tear off, and hide the rest of the sheet, to prevent mischief. This mutilated sheet, with a beginning but no end, falls by and by into Cromek's hands, who cannot comprehend the deficiency—and it also gets printed in its own time and way. From which date till the present moment these fragments have been regarded as two distinct letters, being in reality but the first and second parts of one.

Mr. Chambers seems to have been misled by the formal signature in Cunningham's Edition, of " R. B." to the first fragment. This, we need hardly state, is a mere fabrication of Cunningham's, who supplied deficiencies of that kind without distress. There is no signature at all in Cromek, who first printed the letter; and there could not be; for even if the letter had been an independent document, the conclusion, according to his own account, had been "barbarously" torn away. The whole document, in short, has been one of those "progressive" letters which our Author kept lying before him, to eke out and fill up by degrees for Mrs. Dunlop's amusement or consolation, as opportunity occurred; and we have great pleasure now in presenting it for the first time, as far as circumstances will permit, in its own entirety. (Similar Letters (34.) and (39.), with corresponding dates, occur at same period in 1791, and 1795.) What the political sentiments or prayers were, which he "breathed" in his correspondent's ear, we can only now conjecture; nor will it be very difficult, in part; but absolute certainty on the subject she has herself removed for ever. Compare Letter (35.) at * * * * , also "The Rights of Woman"!

(37.) ### TO MRS. DUNLOP.

Castle Douglas, 25th June, 1794.

HERE in a solitary inn, in a solitary village, am I set by myself, to amuse my brooding fancy as I may.—Solitary confinement, you know, is Howard's favourite idea of reclaiming sinners; so let me consider by what fatality it happens that I have so long been [so] exceeding sinful as to neglect the correspondence of the most valued friend I have on earth. To tell you that I have been in poor health will not be excuse enough, though it is true. I am afraid that I am about to suffer for the follies of my youth. My medical friends threaten me with a flying gout; but I trust they are mistaken.

I am just going to trouble your critical patience with the first sketch of a stanza I have been framing as I passed along the road. The subject is *Liberty.* You know, my honored friend, how dear the theme is to me. I design it an irregular Ode for General Washington's birth-day. After having mentioned the degeneracy of other kingdoms I come to Scotland thus:

> Thee, Caledonia, thy wild heaths among,
> Thee, famed for martial deed, and sacred song,

[See *Posthumous Works*—as in Cromek.]

You will probably have another scrawl from me in a stage or two.

R. B.

(38.) ### TO MRS. DUNLOP,
IN LONDON.

Dumfries, 20th December, 1794.

I HAVE been prodigiously disappointed in this London journey of yours. In the first place, when your last to me reached Dumfries, I was in the country, and did not return until too late to answer your letter; in the next place, I thought you would certainly take this route; and now I know not what is become of you, or whether this may reach you at all. God grant that it may find you and yours in prospering health and good spirits! Do let me hear from you the soonest possible.

As I hope to get a frank from my friend Captain Miller, I shall, every leisure hour, take up the pen, and gossip away whatever comes first, prose or poesy, sermon or song. In this last article I have abounded of late. I have often mentioned to you a superb publication of Scottish songs which is making its appearance in your great metropolis, and where I have the honor to preside over the Scottish verse, as no less a personage than Peter Pindar does over the English. I wrote the following for a favorite air.

[This letter having been misplaced by Dr. Currie as of 1795, the song here referred to cannot now be easily identified—unless it be " My Nanie's awa."]

December 29th.

Since I began this letter, I have been appointed to act in the capacity of supervisor here, and I assure you, what with the load of business, and what with that business being now to me, I could scarcely have commanded ten minutes to have spoken to you, had you been in town, much less to have written you an epistle. This appointment is only temporary, and during the illness of the present incumbent; but I look forward to an early period when I shall be appointed in full form: a consummation devoutly to be wished! My political sins seem to be forgiven me.

This is the season (New-year's-day is now my date) of wishing; and mine are most fervently offered up for you! May life to you be a positive blessing while it lasts, for your own sake; and that it may yet be greatly prolonged, is my wish for my own sake, and for the sake of the rest of your friends! What a transient business is life! Very lately I was a boy; but t'other day I was a young man; and I already begin to feel the rigid fibre and stiffening joints of old age coming fast o'er my frame. With all my follies of youth, and I fear, a few vices of manhood, still I congratulate myself on having had, in early days, religion strongly impressed on my mind. I have nothing to say to any one as to which sect he belongs to, or what creed he believes; but I look on the man, who is firmly persuaded of infinite wisdom and goodness superintending and directing every circumstance that can happen in his lot—I felicitate such a man as having a solid foundation for his mental enjoyment; a firm prop and sure stay, in the hour of difficulty, trouble, and distress; and a never-failing anchor of hope, when he looks beyond the grave.

January 12th.

You will have seen our worthy and ingenious friend, the Doctor, long ere this. I hope he is well, and beg to be remembered to him. I have just been reading over again, I dare say for the hundred and fiftieth time, his "View of Society and Manners;" and still I read it with delight. His humour is perfectly original—it is neither the humour of Addison, nor Swift, nor Sterne, nor of any body but Dr. Moore. By the bye, you have deprived me of "Zeluco;" remember that, when you are disposed to rake up the sins of my neglect from among the ashes of my laziness.

He has paid me a pretty compliment, by quoting me in his last publication.*

   *   *   *   *   *

R. B.

* ["Edward"—*Currie*.]

(39.)   TO MRS. DUNLOP.

15th December, 1795.

MY DEAR FRIEND,

As I am in a complete Decemberish humour, gloomy, sullen, stupid, as even the deity of Dulness herself could wish, I shall not drawl out a heavy letter with a number of heavier apologies for my late silence. Only one I shall mention, because I I know you will sympathise in it: these four months, a sweet little girl, my youngest child, has been so ill, that every day, a week or less, threatened to terminate her existence. There had much need be many pleasures annexed to the states of husband and father, for God knows, they have many peculiar cares. I cannot describe to you the anxious, sleepless hours these ties frequently give me. I see a train of helpless little folks; me and my exertions all their stay; and on what a brittle thread does the life of man hang! If I am nipt off at the command of fate; even in all the vigour of manhood as I am—such things happen every day—gracious God! what would become of my little flock! 'Tis here that I envy your people of fortune.—A father on his death-bed, taking an everlasting leave of his children, has indeed woe enough; but the man of competent fortune leaves his sons and daughters independency and friends; while I—but I shall run distracted if I think any longer on the subject!

To leave talking of the matter so gravely, I shall sing with the old Scots ballad:

"O that I had never been married,
  I would never had nae care;
Now I've gotten wife and bairns,
  They cry crowdie! evermair.

Crowdie! ance; crowdie! twice;
  Crowdie! three times in a day;
An ye crowdie ony mair,
  Ye'll crowdie a' my meal away?"—

   *   *   *   *   *   *

December 24th.

We have had a brilliant theatre here this season; only, as all other business does, it experiences a stagnation of trade from the epidemical complaint of the country, *want of cash*. I mention our theatre merely to lug in an occasional Address which I wrote for the benefit-night of one of the actresses, and which is as follows:—

ADDRESS,

SPOKEN BY MISS FONTENELLE ON HER BENEFIT-NIGHT, DECEMBER 4TH, 1795, AT THE THEATRE, DUMFRIES.

Still anxious to secure your partial favour,

[*See Posthumous Works.*]

25th: Christmas Morning.

This, my much-loved friend, is a morning of wishes, accept mine—so Heaven hear me as they are sincere! that blessings may attend your steps, and affliction know you not! In the charming words of my favourite author, "The Man of Feeling," "May the Great Spirit bear up the weight of thy grey hairs; and blunt the arrow that brings them rest!"

Now that I talk of authors, how do you like Cowper? Is not the "Task" a glorious poem? The religion of the "Task," bating a few scraps of Calvinistic divinity, is the religion of God and nature; the religion that exalts, that ennobles man. Were not you to send me your "Zeluco" in return for mine? Tell me how you like my marks and notes through the book. I would not give a farthing for a book, unless I were at liberty to blot it with my criticisms.

I have lately collected, for a friend's perusal, all my letters; I mean those which I first sketched, in a rough draught, and afterwards wrote out fair. On looking over some old musty papers, which, from time to time, I had parcelled by, as trash that were scarce worth preserving, and which yet at the same time I did not care to destroy; I discovered many of those rude sketches, and have written, and am writing them out, in a bound MS. for my friend's library. As I wrote always to you the rhapsody of the moment, I cannot find a single scroll to you, except one, about the commencement of our acquaintance. If there were any possible conveyance, I would send you a perusal of my book,

R. B.

(40.)   TO MRS. DUNLOP.

[*Dumfries,*] 31st January, 1796.

THESE many months you have been two packets in my debt—what sin of ignorance I have committed against so highly-valued a friend I am utterly at a loss to guess. Alas! Madam, ill can I afford, at this time, to be deprived of any of the small remnant of my pleasures. I have lately drunk deep of the cup of affliction. The autumn robbed me of my only daughter and darling child, and that at a distance too, and so rapidly, as to put it out of my power to pay the last duties to her. I had scarcely begun to recover from that shock, when I became myself the victim of a most severe rheumatic fever, and long the die spun doubtful; until after many weeks of a sick bed, it seems to have turned up life, and I am beginning to crawl across my room, and once indeed have been before my own door in the street.

" When pleasure fascinates the mental sight,
  Affliction purifies the visual ray,
Religion hails the drear, the untried night,
  And shuts, for ever shuts! life's doubtful day."

R. B.

(41.)   TO MRS. DUNLOP.

Brow [*Saturday*], 12th July, 1796.

MADAM,

I HAVE written you so often, without receiving any answer, that I would not trouble you again, but for the circumstances in which I am. An illness which has long hung about me, in all probability will speedily send me beyond that *bourne whence no traveller returns.* Your friendship, with which for many years you honored me, was a friendship dearest to my soul. Your conversation, and especially your correspondence, were at once highly entertaining and instructive. With what pleasure did I use to break up the seal! The remembrance yet adds one pulse more to my poor palpitating heart.

Farewell!!!

R. B.

(1.) To Miss Margaret Chalmers.

(AFTERWARDS MRS. LEWIS HAY.)

[The following Fragments are all that now exist of twelve or fourteen of the finest Letters that Burns ever wrote. In an evil hour, the originals were thrown into the fire by the late Mrs. Adair of Scarborough; the "Charlotte" so often mentioned in this correspondence, and the lady to whom "The Banks of the Devon" is addressed.—*Cromek.*]

Sept. 26, 1787.

I SEND Charlotte the first number of the songs; I would not wait for the second number; I hate delays in little marks of friendship, as I hate dissimulation in the language of the heart. I am determined to pay Charlotte a poetic compliment, if I could hit on some glorious old Scotch air, in number second.* You will see a small attempt on a shred of paper in the book; but though Dr. Blacklock commended it very highly, I am not just satisfied with it myself. I intend to make it description of some kind: the whining cant of love, except in real passion, and by a masterly hand, is to me as insufferable as the preaching cant of old Father Smeaton, Whig-minister at Kilmaurs. Darts, flames, cupids, loves, graces, and all that farrago, are just a Mauchline * * * * —a senseless rabble.

I got an excellent poetic epistle yesternight from the old, venerable author of Tullochgorum, John of Badenyon, &c. I suppose you know he is a clergyman. It is by far the finest poetic compliment I ever got. I will send you a copy of it.

I go on Thursday or Friday to Dumfries to wait on Mr. Miller about his farms.—Do tell that to Lady Mackenzie, that she may give me credit for a little wisdom. "I Wisdom dwell with Prudence." What a blessed fire-side! How happy should I be to pass a winter evening under their venerable roof! and smoke a pipe of tobacco, or drink water-gruel with them! What solemn, lengthened, laughter-quashing gravity of phiz! What sage remarks on the good-for-nothing sons and daughters of indiscretion and folly! And what frugal lessons, as we straitened the fire-side circle, on the uses of the poker and tongs!

Miss N. is very well, and begs to be remembered in the old way to you. I used all my eloquence, all the persuasive flourishes of the hand, and heart-melting modulation of periods in my power, to urge her out to Hervieston, but all in vain. My rhetoric seems quite to have lost its effect on the lovely half of mankind. I have seen the day—but that is a "tale of other years."—In my conscience I believe that my heart has been so oft on fire that it is absolutely vitrified. I look on the sex with something like the admira-

tion with which I regard the starry sky in a frosty December night. I admire the beauty of the Creator's workmanship; I am charmed with the wild but graceful eccentricity of their motions, and—wish them good night. I mean this with respect to a certain passion *dont j'ai eu l'honneur d'être un misérable esclave:* as for friendship, you and Charlotte have given me pleasure, permanent pleasure, "which the world cannot give, nor take away," I hope; and which will outlast the heavens and the earth.

R. B.

* [Of the Scots Musical Museum—*Cromek.*]

(2.) TO MISS CHALMERS.

[*Without date.*]

I HAVE been at Dumfries, and at one visit more shall be decided about a farm in that country. I am rather hopeless in it; but as my brother is an excellent farmer, and is, besides, an exceedingly prudent, sober man (qualities which are only a younger brother's fortune in our family), I am determined, if my Dumfries business fail me, to return into partnership with him, and at our leisure take another farm in the neighbourhood. I assure you I look for high compliments from you and Charlotte on this very sage instance of my unfathomable, incomprehensible wisdom. Talking of Charlotte, I must tell her that I have, to the best of my power, paid her a poetic compliment, now completed. The air is admirable: true old Highland. It was the tune of a Gaelic song which an Inverness lady sung me when I was there; and I was so charmed with it that I begged her to write me a set of it from her singing; for it had never been set before. I am fixed that it shall go in Johnson's next number; so Charlotte and you need not spend your precious time in contradicting me. I won't say the poetry is first-rate; though I am convinced it is very well: and, what is not always the case with compliments to ladies, it is not only *sincere,* but *just.*

[Here follows the song "The Banks of the Devon."]

R. B.

(3.) TO MISS CHALMERS.

Edinburgh, Nov. 21, 1787.

I HAVE one vexatious fault to the kindly-welcome, well-filled sheet which I owe to your and Charlotte's goodness—it contains too much sense, sentiment, and good-spelling. It is impossible that even you two, whom I declare to my God I will give credit for any degree of excellence the sex are capable of attaining, it is impossible you can go on to correspond at that rate; so like those who, Shenstone says, retire because they have made a good speech, I shall, after a few letters, hear no more of you. I insist that you shall write whatever comes first: what you see, what you read, what you hear, what you admire, what you dislike, trifles, bagatelles, nonsense; or to fill up a corner, e'en put down a laugh at full length. Now none of your polite hints about flattery; I leave that to your lovers, if you have or shall have any; though, thank heaven,

I have found at last two girls who can be luxuriantly happy in their own minds and with one another, without that commonly necessary appendage to female bliss, A LOVER.

Charlotte and you are just two favourite resting-places for my soul in her wanderings through the weary, thorny wilderness of this world—God knows I am ill-fitted for the struggle: I glory in being a Poet, and I want to be thought a wise man—I would fondly be generous, and I wish to be rich. After all, I am afraid I am a lost subject. "Some folk hae a hantle o' fauts, an' I'm but a ne'er-do-weel."

Afternoon.—To close the melancholy reflections at the end of last sheet, I shall just add a piece of devotion commonly known in Carrick by the title of the "Wabster's grace:"

> "Some say we're thieves, and e'en sae are we!
> Some say we lie, and e'en sae do we!
> Gude forgie us, and I hope sae will he!
> ——Up and to your looms, lads."

R. B.

(4.)

TO MISS CHALMERS.

Edinburgh, Dec. 12, 1787.

I AM here under the care of a surgeon, with a bruised limb extended on a cushion; and the tints of my mind vying with the livid horror preceding a midnight thunder-storm. A drunken coachman was the cause of the first, and incomparably the lightest evil; misfortune, bodily constitution, hell and myself, have formed a "Quadruple Alliance" to guarantee the other. I got my fall on Saturday, and am getting slowly better.

I have taken tooth and nail to the Bible, and am got through the five books of Moses, and half way in Joshua. It is really a glorious book. I sent for my book-binder to-day, and ordered him to get me an octavo Bible in sheets, the best paper and print in town; and bind it with all the elegance of his craft.

I would give my best song to my worst enemy, I mean the merit of making it, to have you and Charlotte by me. You are angelic creatures, and would pour oil and wine into my wounded spirit.

I inclose you a proof copy of the "Banks of the Devon," which present with my best wishes to Charlotte. The "Ochelhills" you shall probably have next week for yourself. None of your fine speeches!

R. B.

(5.)

TO MISS CHALMERS.

Edinburgh, Dec. 19, 1787.

I BEGIN this letter in answer to yours of the 17th current, which is not yet cold since I read it. The atmosphere of my soul is vastly clearer than when I wrote you last. For the first time, yesterday I crossed the room on crutches. It would do your heart good to see my hardship, not on my poetic, but on my oaken stilts; throwing my best leg with an air! and with as much hilarity in my gait and countenance, as a May frog leaping across the newly harrowed ridge, enjoying the fragrance of the refreshed earth after the long-expected shower!

*   *   *   *   *   *   *

I can't say I am altogether at my ease when I see anywhere in my path that meagre, squalid, famine-faced spectre, poverty; attended, as he always is, by iron-fisted oppression, and leering contempt; but I have sturdily withstood his buffetings many a hard-laboured day already, and still my motto is—I DARE! My worst enemy is *Moi-même*. I lie so miserably open to the inroads and incursions of a mischievous, light-armed, well-mounted banditti, under the banners of imagination, whim, caprice, and passion; and the heavy-armed veteran regulars of wisdom, prudence, and forethought, move so very, very slow, that I am almost in a state of perpetual warfare, and, alas! frequent defeat. There are just two creatures that I would envy; a horse in his wild state traversing the forests of Asia, or an oyster on some of the desert shores of Europe. The one has not a wish without enjoyment, the other has neither wish nor fear.

R. B.

(6.)

TO MISS CHALMERS.

Edinburgh, Dec., 1787.

MY DEAR MADAM,

I JUST now have read yours. The poetic compliments I pay cannot be misunderstood. They are neither of them so particular as to point you out to the world at large; and the circle of your acquaintances will allow all I have said. Besides, I have complimented you chiefly, almost solely, on your mental charms. Shall I be plain with you? I will; so look to it. Personal attractions, Madam, you have much above par; wit, understanding, and worth, you possess in the first class. This is a cursed flat way of telling you these truths, but let me hear no more of your sheepish timidity. I know the world a little. I know what they will say of my poems; by second sight, I suppose; for I am seldom out in my conjectures; and you may believe me, my dear Madam, I would not run any risk of hurting you by an ill-judged compliment. I wish to show to the world, the odds between a poet's friends and those of simple prosemen. More for your information, *both* the pieces go in. One of them, "Where braving angry winter's storms," is already set—the tune is Neil Gow's lamentation for Abercarny; the other is to be set to an old Highland air in Daniel Dow's "Collection of antient Scots music;" the name is *Ha a Chaillich air mo Dheidh.* My treacherous memory has forgot every circumstance about *Les Incas,* only I think you mentioned them as being in Crooch's possession. I shall ask him about it. I am afraid the song of "Somebody" will come too late—as I shall, for certain, leave town in a week for Ayrshire, and from that to Dumfries, but there may hopes are slender. I leave my direction in town, so any thing, wherever I am, will reach me.

I saw your's to ——; it is not too severe, nor did he take it amiss. On the contrary, like a whipt spaniel, he talks of being with you in the Christmas days. Mr. —— has given him the invitation, and he is determined to accept of it. O selfishness! he owns in his sober moments, that from his own volatility of inclination, the circumstances in which he is situated, and his knowledge of his father's disposition,—the whole affair is chimerical—yet he *will* gratify an idle *penchant* at the enormous, cruel expense of perhaps ruining the peace of the very woman for whom he professes the generous passion of love! He is a gentleman in his mind and manners—*tant pis!* He is a volatile school-boy: the heir of a man's fortune who well knows the value of two times two!

Perdition seize them and their fortunes, before they should make the amiable, the lovely —— the derided object of their purse-proud contempt.

I am doubly happy to hear of Mrs. ——'s recovery, because I really thought all was over with her. There are days of pleasure yet awaiting her.

> " As I cam in by Glenap
> I met with an aged woman;
> She bade me cheer up my heart,
> For the best o' my days was comin."

This day will decide my affairs with Creech. Things are, like myself, not what they ought to be; yet better than what they appear to be.

> " Heaven's sovereign saves all beings but himself
> That hideous sight—a naked human heart."

Farewell! Remember me to Charlotte.

R. B.

(7.)   TO MISS CHALMERS.

Edinburgh, March 14, 1788.

I KNOW, my ever dear friend, that you will be pleased with the news when I tell you, I have at last taken a lease of a farm. Yesternight I completed a bargain with Mr. Miller, of Dalswinton, for the farm of Ellisland, on the banks of the Nith, between five and six miles above Dumfries. I begin at Whitsunday to build a house, drive lime, &c.; and heaven be my help! for it will take a strong effort to bring my mind into the routine of business. I have discharged all the army of my former pursuits, fancies, and pleasures; a motley host! and have literally and strictly retained only the ideas of a few friends, which I have incorporated into a life-guard. I trust in Dr. Johnson's observation, "Where much is attempted, something is done." Firmness, both in sufferance and exertion, is a character I would wish to be thought to possess; and have always despised the whining yelp of complaint, and the cowardly, feeble resolve.

    *   *   *   *   *

Poor Miss K. is ailing a good deal this winter, and begged me to remember her to you the first time I wrote you. Surely woman, amiable woman, is often made in vain! Too delicately formed for the rougher pursuits of ambition; too noble for the dirt of avarice, and even too gentle for the rage of pleasure: formed indeed for, and highly susceptible of enjoyment and rapture; but that enjoyment, alas! almost wholly at the mercy of the caprice, malevolence, stupidity, or wickedness of an animal at all times comparatively unfeeling, and often brutal.

R. B.

(8.)   TO MISS CHALMERS.

Mauchline, 7th April, 1788.

I AM indebted to you and Miss Nimmo for letting me know Miss Kennedy. Strange! how apt we are to indulge prejudices in our judgments of one another! Even I, who pique myself on my skill in marking characters; because I am too proud of my character as a man, to be dazzled in my judgment *for* glaring wealth; and too proud of my situation as a poor man to be biassed *against* squalid poverty; I was unacquainted with Miss K.'s very uncommon worth.

I am going on a good deal progressive in *mon grand but*, the sober science of life. I have lately made some sacrifices for which, were I *vini voce* with you to paint the situation and recount the circumstances, you would applaud me.

R. B.

(9.)   TO MISS CHALMERS.

[*No date.*]

Now for that wayward, unfortunate thing, myself. I have broke measures with Creech, and last week I wrote him a frosty, keen letter. He replied in terms of chastisement, and promised me upon his honor that I should have the account on Monday; but this is Tuesday, and yet I have not heard a word from him. God have mercy on me! a poor d-mned, incautious, duped, unfortunate fool! The sport, the miserable victim, of rebellious pride, hypochondriac imagination, agonizing sensibility, and bedlam passions!

"I wish that I were dead, but I'm no like to die!" I had lately "a hairbreadth 'scape, in th' imminent deadly breach" of love too. Thank my stars I got off heart-whole, "waur fley'd than hurt."—Interruption.

I have this moment got a hint * * * * I fear I am something like—undone—but I hope for the best. Come, stubborn pride and unshrinking resolution! accompany me through this, to me, miserable world! You must not desert me! Your friendship I think I can count on, though I should date my letters from a marching regiment. Early in life, and all my life, I reckoned on a recruiting drum as my forlorn hope. Seriously though, life at present presents me with but a melancholy path: but—my limb will soon be sound, and I shall struggle on.

R. B.

(10.)   TO MISS CHALMERS.

Edinburgh, Sunday [*February* 17].

TO-MORROW, my dear Madam, I leave Edinburgh. * * * * * * I have altered all my plans of future life. A farm that I could live in, I could not find; and indeed, after the necessary support my brother and the rest of the family required, I could not venture on farming in that style suitable to my feelings. You will condemn me for the next step I have taken. I have entered into the Excise. I stay in the west about three weeks, and then return to Edinburgh for six weeks' instructions; afterwards, for I get employ instantly, I go où *il plait à Dieu,—et mon Roi*. I have chosen this, my dear friend, after mature deliberation. The question is not at what door of fortune's palace shall we enter in; but what doors does she open to us? I was not likely to get anything to do. I wanted *un bût*, which is a dangerous, an unhappy situation. I got this without any hanging on, or mortifying solicitation; it is immediate bread, and though poor in comparison of the last eighteen months of my existence, 'tis luxury in comparison of all my preceding life: besides, the commissioners are some of them my acquaintances, and all of them my firm friends.

R. B.

(11.)   TO MISS CHALMERS,
                            EDINBURGH.

Ellisland, near Dumfries, Sept. 16, 1788.

WHERE are you? and how are you? and is Lady Mackenzie recovering her health? for I have had but one solitary letter from you. I will not think you have forgot me, Madam; and for my part—

> "When thee, Jerusalem, I forget,
> Skill part from my right hand!"

"My heart is not of that rock, nor my soul careless as that sea." I do not make my progress among mankind as a bowl does among its fellows—rolling through the crowd without bearing away any mark or impression, except where they hit in hostile collision.

I am here, driven in with my harvest-folks by bad weather; and as you and your sister once did me the honor of interesting yourselves much *à l'egard de moi*, I sit down to beg the continuation of your goodness.—I can truly say that, all the exterior of life apart, I never saw two, whose esteem flattered the nobler feelings of my soul—I will not say, more, but, so much as Lady Mackenzie and Miss Chalmers. When I think of you—hearts the best, minds the noblest of human kind—unfortunate, even in the shades of life—when I think I have met with you, and have lived more of real life with you in eight days than I can do with almost any body I meet with in eight years—when I think on the improbability of meeting you in this world again—I could sit down and cry like a child!—If ever you honored me with a place in your esteem, I trust I can now plead more desert.—I am secure against that crushing grip of iron poverty, which, alas! is less or more fatal to the native worth and purity of, I fear, the noblest souls; and a late important step in my life has kindly taken me out of the way of those ungrateful iniquities, which, however overlooked in fashionable licence, or varnished in fashionable phrase, are indeed but lighter and deeper shades of VILLAINY.

Shortly after my last return to Ayrshire, I married "my Jean." This was not in consequence of the attachment of romance, perhaps; but I had a long and much loved fellow-creature's happiness or misery in my determination, and I durst not trifle with so important a deposit. Nor have I any cause to repent it. If I have not got polite tattle, modish manners, and fashionable dress, I am not sickened and disgusted with the multiform curse of boarding-school affectation;

and I have got the handsomest figure, the sweetest temper, the soundest constitution, and the kindest heart in the county. Mrs. Burns believes, as firmly as her creed, that I am *le plus bel esprit, et le plus honnête homme* in the universe; although she scarcely ever in her life, except the Scriptures of the Old and New Testament, and the Psalms of David in metre, spent five minutes together on either prose or verse.—I must except also from this last, a certain late publication of Scots poems, which she has perused very devoutly; and all the ballads in the country, as she has (O the partial lover! you will cry) the finest "wood note wild" I ever heard.—I am the more particular in this lady's character, as I know she will henceforth have the honor of a share in your best wishes. She is still at Mauchline, as I am building my house; for this hovel that I shelter in, while occasionally here, is pervious to every blast that blows, and every shower that falls; and I am only preserved from being chilled to death, by being suffocated with smoke. I do not find my farm that pennyworth I was taught to expect, but I believe, in time, it may be a saving bargain. You will be pleased to hear that I have laid aside idle *éclat*, and bind every day after my reapers.

To save me from that horrid situation of at any time going down, in a losing bargain of a farm, to misery, I have taken my Excise instructions, and have my commission in my pocket for any emergency of fortune. If I could set *all* before your view, whatever disrespect you, in common with the world, have for this business, I know you would approve of my idea.

I will make no apology, dear Madam, for this egotistic detail: I know you and your sister will be interested in every circumstance of it. What signify the silly, idle gewgaws of wealth, or the ideal trumpery of greatness! When fellow-partakers of the same nature fear the same God, have the same benevolence of heart, the same nobleness of soul, the same detestation at every thing dishonest, and the same scorn at every thing unworthy—if they are not in the dependance of absolute beggary, in the name of common sense are they not EQUALS? And if the bias, the instinctive bias, of their souls run the same way, why may they not be FRIENDS?

When I may have an opportunity of sending you this, Heaven only knows. Shenstone says, "When one is confined idle within doors by bad weather, the best antidote against *ennui* is to read the letters of, or write to, one's friends;" in that case then, if the weather continues thus, I may scrawl you half a quire.

I very lately, to wit, since harvest began, wrote a poem, not in imitation, but in the manner, of Pope's Moral Epistles. It is only a short essay, just to try the strength of my Muse's pinion in that way. I will send you a copy of it, when once I have heard from you. I have likewise been laying the foundation of some pretty large poetic works: how the super-structure will come on, I leave to that great maker and marrer of projects—TIME. Johnson's collection of Scots songs is going on in the third volume; and, of consequence, finds me a consumpt for a great deal of idle metre.—One of the most tolerable things I have done in that way is two stanzas that I made to an air, a musical gentleman* of my acquaintance composed for the anniversary of his wedding-day, which happens on the seventh of November. Take it as follows:

* E

> The day returns—my bosom burns,
> The blissful day we twa did meet,
>
> [See Poetical Works.]

I shall give over this letter for shame. If I should be seized with a scribbling fit, before this goes away, I shall make it another letter; and then you may allow your patience a week's respite between the two. I have not room for more than the old, kind, hearty, FAREWELL!

———

To make some amends, *mes chères Mesdames*, for dragging you on to this second sheet, and to relieve a little the tiresomeness of my unstudied and uncorrectible prose, I shall transcribe you some of my late poetic bagatelles; though I have, these eight or ten months, done very little that way. One day, in a Hermitage on the banks of Nith, belonging to a gentleman* in my neighbourhood, who is so good as give me a key at pleasure, I wrote as follows; supposing myself the sequestered, venerable inhabitant of the lonely mansion.

LINES WRITTEN IN FRIARS-CARSE HERMITAGE.

> Thou whom chance may hither lead,
> Be thou clad in russet weed;
>
> [See Poetical Works.]

R. B.

* [Capt. Riddel of Glenriddel.—*Cromek.*]

———

To Miss Mabane.

[AFTERWARDS MRS. COLONEL WRIGHT.]

Saturday Noon, No. 2, St. James's Sqr.
Newtown, Edinburgh.

HERE have I sat, my dear Madam, in the stony attitude of perplexed study for fifteen vexatious minutes, my head askew, bending over the intended card; my fixed eye insensible to the very light of day poured around; my pendulous goose-feather, loaded with ink, hanging over the future letter; all for the important purpose of writing a complimentary card to accompany your trinket.

Compliment is such a miserable Greenland expression; lies at such a chilly polar distance from the torrid zone of my constitution, that I cannot, for the very soul of me, use it to any person for whom I have the twentieth part of the esteem every one must have for you who knows you.

As I leave town in three or four days, I can give myself the pleasure of calling for you only for a minute. Tuesday evening, some time about seven, or after, I shall wait on you, for your farewell commands.

The hinge of your box I put into the hands of the proper Connoisseur. The broken glass, likewise, went under review; but deliberative wisdom thought it would too much endanger the whole fabric.

I am, dear Madam,

> With all sincerity of Enthusiasm,
> Your very humble Servant,
>
> R. B.

To Mrs. M'Lehose.

(1.)   (CLARINDA.)

[The remarkable correspondence between our Author and Mrs. M'Lehose—"Clarinda"—was originally published in an imperfect, apparently surreptitious, way, as an appendix to an edition of the Poet's works, by Stewart and M'Gown of Glasgow, 1802. Notwithstanding the lady's remonstrance, who perhaps justly considered herself aggrieved, no fewer than six separate editions of this imperfect work succeeded in Scotland, England, or Ireland, down to the year 1831. To prevent further misapprehensions from this source, and also to render his own edition of the Poet's works as complete as possible, Allan Cunningham appealed earnestly to Mrs. M'Lehose for permission to make a selection at least from the entire correspondence, which he promised to do with "all due tenderness," &c. This application was refused; and strangely enough we find Mr. Cunningham, in one of his notes, depreciating the whole subject as "a sort of Corydon and Phillis affair" which had been "speedily suppressed." Finally, after the lady's own death and the death also of her son, into whose hands the documents had fallen, the question of a perfect edition was revived. This, after some delay in obtaining the originals, was undertaken by W. C. M'Lehose, Esq., grandson of "Clarinda;" who, with Mr. Chambers's valuable editorial assistance, brought out a reliable version of the entire correspondence, in 1843, with an interesting memoir of the lady. From that edition, the following letters by our Author have been selected, and carefully collated, as far as possible, with corresponding letters in original edition. There seems, indeed, to be very little difference between them as to text—the only remarkable difference being in the number of the letters themselves, which is very considerable, and in their consecutive arrangement, which is entirely different. The blanks which occasionally occur in final edition are to be accounted for by the circumstance, that many of the letters, having been preserved and frequently opened during a period of fifty years at least, had been torn or wasted, whilst from a few of them signatures and detached sentences had been clipt off, to gratify collectors of autographs.]

[December 6, 1787.]

MADAM,

I HAD set no small store by my tea-drinking to-night, and have not often been so disappointed. Saturday evening I shall embrace the opportunity with the greatest pleasure. I leave this town this day se'ennight, and probably I shall not return for a couple of twelvemonths; but I must ever regret that I so lately got an acquaintance I shall ever highly esteem, and in whose welfare I shall ever be warmly interested.

Our worthy common friend Miss Nimmo, in her usual pleasant way, rallied me a good deal on my new acquaintance; and, in the humour of her ideas, I wrote some lines, which I enclose you, as I think they have a good deal of poetic merit; and Miss Nimmo tells me you are not only a critic but a poetess. Fiction, you know, is the native region of poetry; and I hope you will pardon my vanity in sending you the bagatelle as a tolerable off-hand *jeu d'esprit*. I have several poetic trifles, which I shall gladly leave with Miss Nimmo or you, if they were worth house-room; as there are scarcely two people on earth by whom it would mortify me more to be forgotten, though at the distance of nine score miles.—I am, Madam, with the highest respect, your very humble servant,

ROBERT BURNS.

Thursday Even.

———

(2.)   TO MRS. M'LEHOSE.

[December 8.]

I CAN say with truth, Madam, that I never met with a person in my life whom I more anxiously wished to meet again than yourself. To-night I was to have had that very great pleasure—I was intoxicated with the idea; but an unlucky fall from a coach has so bruised one of my knees, that I can't stir my leg off the cushion. So, if I don't see you again, I shall not rest in my grave for chagrin. I was vexed to the soul I had not seen you sooner. I determined to cultivate your friendship with the enthusiasm of religion; but thus has Fortune ever served me. I cannot bear the idea of leaving Edinburgh without seeing you. I know not how to account for it—I am strangely taken with some people, nor am I often mistaken. You are a stranger to me—but I am an odd being. Some yet unnamed feelings—things, not principles, but better than whims—carry me farther than boasted reason ever did a philosopher. Farewell! every happiness be yours.

ROBERT BURNS.

Saturday Even., St. James' Sqr., No. 2.

(3.)　　　TO MRS. M'LEHOSE.

[*December* 12.]

I STRETCH a point, indeed, my dearest Madam, when I answer your card on the rack of my present agony. Your friendship, Madam! By heavens, I was never proud before. Your lines, I maintain it, are poetry, and good poetry; mine were, indeed, partly a fiction, and partly a friendship which, had I been so blest as to have met with you *in time*, might have led me—God of love only knows where. Time is too short for ceremonies.

I swear solemnly (in all the tenor of my former oath) to remember you in all the pride and warmth of friendship until —I cease to be!

To-morrow, and every day, till I see you, you shall hear from me.

Farewell! May you enjoy a better night's repose than I am likely to have.

[R. B.]

(4.)　　　TO MRS. M'LEHOSE.

[*December* 20.]

YOUR last, my dear Madam, had the effect on me that Job's situation had on his friends, when "they sat down seven days and seven nights astonied, and spake not a word."—"Pay my addresses to a married woman!" I started as if I had seen the ghost of him I had injured. I recollected my expressions; some of them indeed were, in the law phrase, "habit and repute," which is being half guilty. I cannot positively say, Madam, whether my heart might not have gone astray a little; but I can declare, upon the honour of a poet, that the vagrant has wandered unknown to me. I have a pretty handsome troop of follies of my own; and like some other people's, they are but undisciplined blackguards: but the luckless rascals have something of honour in them; they would not do a dishonest thing.

To meet with an unfortunate woman, amiable and young, deserted and widowed by those who were bound by every

tie of duty, nature, and gratitude, to protect, comfort, and cherish her; add to all, when she is perhaps one of the first of lovely forms and noble minds, the mind, too, that hits one's tastes as the joys of Heaven do a saint—should a vague infant idea, the natural child of imagination, thoughtlessly peep over the fence—were you, my friend, to sit in judgment, and the poor, airy straggler brought before you, trembling, self-condemned, with artless eyes, brimful of contrition, looking wistfully on its judge,—you could not, my dear Madam, condemn the hapless wretch to death "without benefit of clergy!"

I won't tell you what reply my heart made to your raillery of "seven years;" but I will give you what a brother of my trade says on the same allusion :—

> The Patriarch to gain a wife,
> Chaste, beautiful, and young,
> Served fourteen years a painful life,
> And never thought it long.
>
> Oh were you to reward such cares,
> And life so long would stay,
> Not fourteen but four hundred years
> Would seem but as one day!

I have written you this scrawl because I have nothing else to do, and you may sit down and find fault with it, if you have no better way of consuming your time; but finding fault with the vagaries of a poet's fancy is much such another business as Xerxes chastising the waves of Hellespont.

My limb now allows me to sit in some peace; to walk I have yet no prospect of, as I can't mark it to the ground.

I have just now looked over what I have written, and it is such a chaos of nonsense that I daresay you will throw it into the fire, and call me an idle, stupid fellow; but whatever you think of my brains, believe me to be, with the most sacred respect, and heartfelt esteem,

My dear Madam,

Your humble servant,

ROBERT BURNS.

To Clarinda.

(1.)　　　(MRS. M'LEHOSE.)

[At this date, Mrs. M'Lehose herself having assumed the name of 'Clarinda,' our Author, following suit, adopted that of 'Sylvander,' and correspondence was continued under these fictitious signatures—a fact which explains much extravagance that would have been otherwise inexcusable.]

Friday Evening.

I BEG your pardon, my dear "Clarinda," for the fragment scrawl I sent you yesterday. I really don't know what I wrote. A gentleman, for whose character, abilities, and critical knowledge, I have the highest veneration, called in just as I had begun the second sentence, and I would not make the porter wait. I read to my much-respected friend several of my own bagatelles, and, among others, your lines, which I had copied out. He began some criticism on them as on the other pieces, when I informed him they were the work of a young lady in this town; which, I assure you, made him stare. My learned friend seriously protested, that he did not believe any young woman in Edinburgh was capable of such lines; and, if you know anything of Professor Gregory, you will neither doubt of his abilities nor his sincerity. I do love you, if possible, still better for having so fine a taste and turn for poesy. I have again gone wrong in my usual unguarded way, but you may erase the word, and put esteem, respect, or any other tame Dutch expression you please, in its place. I believe there is no holding converse, or carrying on correspondence, with an amiable woman, much less a *gloriously amiable fine woman*, without some mixture of that delicious passion, whose most devoted slave I have more than once had the honour of being—But why be hurt or offended on that account? Can no honest man have a prepossession for a fine woman, but he must run his head against an intrigue? Take a little of the tender witchcraft of love, and add it to the generous, the honourable sentiments of manly friendship; and I know but one more delightful morsel, which few, few in any rank ever taste. Such a composition is like adding cream to strawberries: it not only gives the fruit a more elegant richness, but has a peculiar deliciousness of its own.

I enclose you a few lines I composed on a late melancholy occasion. I will not give above five or six copies of it at all; and I would be hurt if any friend should give any copies without my consent.

You cannot imagine, Clarinda (I like the idea of Arcadian names in a commerce of this kind), how much store I have set by the hopes of your future friendship. I don't know if you have a just idea of my character, but I wish you to see me as *I am*. I am, as most people of my trade are, a strange Will-o'-wisp being; the victim, too frequently, of much imprudence and many follies. My great constituent elements are *pride* and *passion*: the first I have endeavoured to humanize into integrity and honour; the last makes me a devotee, to the warmest degree of enthusiasm, in love, religion, or friendship —either of them, or all together, as I happen to be inspired. 'Tis true I never saw you but once; but how much acquaintance did I form with you in that once! Do not think I flatter you, or have a design upon you, Clarinda: I have too much pride for the one, and too little cold contrivance for the other; but of all God's creatures I ever could approach in the beaten way of acquaintance, you struck me with the deepest, the strongest, the most permanent impression. I say the most permanent, because I know myself well, and how far I can promise either on my prepossessions or powers. Why are you unhappy?—and why are so many of our fellow-creatures, unworthy to belong to the same species with you, blest with all they can wish? You have a hand all benevolent to give—why were you denied the pleasure? You have a heart formed, gloriously formed, for all the most refined luxuries of love—why was that heart ever wrung? O Clarinda! shall we not meet in a state, some yet unknown state of being, where the lavish hand of plenty shall minister to the highest wish of benevolence; and where the chill northwind of prudence shall never blow over the flowery fields of enjoyment? If we do not, man was made in vain! I deserved most of the unhappy hours that have lingered over my head; they were the wages of my labour. But what unprovoked demon, malignant as hell, stole upon the confidence

of unmistrusting busy Fate, and dashed your cup of life with undeserved sorrow?

Let me know how long your stay will be out of town: I shall count the hours till you inform me of your return. Cursed *etiquette* forbids your seeing me just now; and so soon as I can walk I must bid Edinburgh adieu. Lord, why was I born to see misery which I cannot relieve, and to meet with friends whom I can't enjoy! I look back with the pangs of unavailing avarice on my loss in not knowing you sooner: all last winter—these three months past—what luxury of intercourse have I not lost! Perhaps, though, 'twas better for my peace. You see I am either above, or incapable of dissimulation. I believe it is want of that particular genius. I despise design, because I want either coolness or wisdom to be capable of it. I am interrupted.—Adieu! my dear Clarinda!

SYLVANDER.

(2.)

TO CLARINDA.

[January 3d.]

MY DEAR CLARINDA,

Your last verses have so delighted me, that I have copied them in among some of my own most valued pieces, which I keep sacred for my own use. Do let me have a few now and then.

Did you, Madam, know what I feel when you talk of your sorrows!

Good God! that one, who has so much worth in the sight of heaven, and is so amiable to her fellow-creatures, should be so unhappy! I can't venture out for cold. My limb is vastly better; but I have not any use of it without my crutches. Monday, for the first time, I dine in a neighbour's, next door. As soon as I can go so far, *even in a coach*, my first visit shall be to you. Write me when you leave town, and immediately when you return; and I earnestly pray your stay may be short. You can't imagine how miserable you made me when you hinted to me not to write. Farewell.

SYLVANDER.

(3.)

TO CLARINDA.

[January 4th.]

You are right, my dear Clarinda: a friendly correspondence goes for nothing, except one write their undisguised sentiments. Yours please me for their intrinsic merit, as well as because they are yours; which, I assure you, is to me a high recommendation. Your religious sentiments, Madam, I revere. If you have, on some suspicious evidence, from some lying oracle, learnt that I despise or ridicule so sacredly-important a matter as real religion, you have, my Clarinda, much misconstrued your friend. "I am not mad, most noble Festus!" Have you ever met a perfect character? Do we not sometimes rather exchange faults than get rid of them? For instance, I am perhaps tired with, and shocked at a life too much the prey of giddy inconsistencies and thoughtless follies. By degrees I grow sober, prudent, and statedly pious. I say statedly; because the most unaffected devotion is not at all inconsistent with my first character. I join the world in congratulating myself on the happy change. But let me pry more narrowly into this affair. Have I, at bottom, any thing of a secret pride in these endowments and emendations? Have I nothing of a presbyterian sourness, an hypercritical severity, when I survey my less regular neighbours? In a word, have I missed all those nameless and numberless modifications of indistinct selfishness, which are so near our own eyes that we can scarce bring them within our sphere of vision, and which the known spotless cambric of our character hides from the ordinary observer?

My definition of worth is short: truth and humanity respecting our fellow-creatures; reverence and humility in the presence of that Being, my Creator and Preserver, and who, I have every reason to believe, will one day be my Judge. The first part of my definition is the creature of unbiassed instinct; the last is the child of after-reflection. Where I found these two essentials, I would gently note, and slightly mention, any attendant flaws—flaws, the marks, the consequences of human nature.

I can easily enter into the sublime pleasures that your strong imagination and keen sensibility must derive from religion, particularly if a little in the shade of misfortune; but I own I cannot, without a marked grudge, see Heaven totally engross so amiable, so charming a woman, as my friend Clarinda; and should be very well pleased at a *circumstance* that would put it in the power of somebody (happy somebody!) to divide her attention, with all the delicacy and tenderness of an earthly attachment.

You will not easily persuade me that you have not a grammatical knowledge of the English language.—So far from being inaccurate, you are elegant beyond any woman of my acquaintance, except one, whom I wish you knew.

Your last verses to me have so delighted me, that I have got an excellent old Scots air that suits the measure, and you shall see them in print in the Scots Musical Museum, a work publishing by a friend of mine in this town. I want four stanzas; you gave me but three, and one of them alluded to an expression in my former letter; so I have taken your two first verses, with a slight alteration in the second, and have added a third; but you must help me to a fourth. Here they are; the latter half of the first stanza would have been worthy of Sappho. I am in raptures with it.

> "Talk not of Love, it gives me pain,
>   For Love has been my foe;
> He bound me with an iron chain,
>   And sunk me deep in woe.
>
> "But Friendship's pure and lasting joys
>   My heart was formed to prove;
> There, welcome, win and wear the prize,
>   But never talk of Love.
>
> "Your friendship much can make me blest,
>   O why that bliss destroy!
> Why urge the [odious] one request,   [only]
>   You know I [must] deny!"   [will]

The alteration in the second stanza is no improvement, but there was a slight inaccuracy in your rhyme. The third I only offer to your choice, and have left two words for your determination. The air is "The Banks of Spey," and is most beautiful.

To-morrow evening I intend taking a chair, and paying a visit at Park Place to a much-valued old friend. If I could be sure of finding you at home (and I will send one of the chairmen to call), I would spend from five to six o'clock with you, as I go past. I cannot do more at this time, as I have something on my hand that hurries me much. I propose giving you the first call, my old friend the second, and Miss Nimmo as I return home. Do not break any engagement for me, as I will spend another evening with you at any rate before I leave town.

Do not tell me that you are pleased when your friends inform you of your faults. I am ignorant what they are; but I am sure they must be such evanescent trifles, compared with your personal and mental accomplishments, that I would despise the ungenerous, narrow soul, who would notice any shadow of imperfections you may seem to have, any other way than in the most delicate agreeable raillery. Coarse minds are not aware how much they injure the keenly-feeling tie of bosom-friendship, when, in their foolish officiousness, they mention what nobody cares for recollecting. People of nice sensibility and generous minds have a certain intrinsic dignity, that fires at being trifled with, or lowered, or even too nearly approached.

You need make no apology for long letters: I am even with you. Many happy New Years to you, charming Clarinda! I can't dissemble, were it to shun perdition. He who sees you as I have done, and does not love you, deserves to be damn'd for his stupidity! He who loves you, and would injure you, deserves to be doubly damn'd for his villainy! Adieu.

SYLVANDER.

P.S.—What would you think of this for a fourth stanza?

> ["Your thought, if love must harbour there,
>   Conceal it in that thought,
> Nor ease me from my bosom tear
>   The very friend I sought."]

(4.)   TO CLARINDA.

Saturday Noon.

SOME days, some nights, nay, some *hours*, like the "ten righteous persons in Sodom," save the rest of the vapid, tiresome, miserable months and years of life. One of these hours my dear Clarinda blest me with yesternight.

> ——"One well spent hour,
> In such a tender circumstance for friends,
> Is better than an age of common time."
>
>   THOMSON.

My favourite feature in Milton's Satan is his manly fortitude in supporting what cannot be remedied—in short, the wild broken fragments of a noble exalted mind in ruins. I meant no more by saying he was a favourite hero of mine.

I mentioned to you my letter to Dr. Moore, giving an account of my life; it is truth, every word of it; and will give you the just idea of a man whom you have honoured with your friendship. I am afraid you will hardly be able to make sense of so torn a piece.—Your verses I shall muse on deliciously, as I gaze on your image in my mind's eye, in my heart's core; they will be in time enough for a week to come. I am truly happy your head-ache is better.—O, how can pain or evil be so daringly, unfeelingly, cruelly savage, as to wound so noble a mind, so lovely a form!

My little fellow is all my name-sake.—Write me soon. My every, strongest good wish attend you, Clarinda!

SYLVANDER.

I know not what I have written—I am pestered with people around me.

(5.)   TO CLARINDA.

Tuesday Night.

I AM delighted, charming Clarinda, with your honest enthusiasm for religion. Those of either sex, but particularly the female, who are lukewarm in that most important of all things, "O my soul, come not thou into their secrets!"

I feel myself deeply interested in your good opinion, and will lay before you the outlines of my belief. He who is our Author and Preserver, and will one day be our Judge, must be (not for his sake in the way of duty, but from the native impulse of our hearts) the object of our reverential awe and grateful adoration. He is almighty and all-bounteous, we are weak and dependent; hence prayer and every other sort of devotion. "He is not willing that any should perish, but that all should come to everlasting life;" consequently it must be in every one's power to embrace his offer of "everlasting life;" otherwise he could not, in justice, condemn those who did not. A mind pervaded, actuated, and governed by purity, truth, and charity, though it does not merit heaven, yet is an absolutely-necessary pre-requisite, without which heaven can neither be obtained nor enjoyed; and, by divine promise, such a mind shall never fail of attaining "everlasting life;" hence the impure, the deceiving, and the uncharitable, exclude themselves from eternal bliss, by their unfitness for enjoying it. The Supreme Being has put the immediate administration of all this, for wise and good ends known to himself, into the hands of Jesus Christ, a great personage, whose relation to him we cannot comprehend, but whose relation to us is a Guide and Saviour; and who, except for our own obstinacy and misconduct, will bring us all, through various ways, and by various means, to bliss at last.

These are my tenets, my lovely friend; and which, I think, cannot be well disputed. My creed is pretty nearly expressed in the last clause of Jamie Dean's grace, an honest weaver in Ayrshire: "Lord, grant that we may lead a gude life! for a gude life maks a gude end; at least it helps weel."

I am flattered by the entertainment you tell me you have found in my packet. You see me as I have been, you know me as I am, and may guess at what I am likely to be. I too may say, "Talk not of love," &c., for indeed he has "plunged me deep in woe!" Not that I ever saw a woman who pleased unexceptionably, as my Clarinda elegantly says, "in the companion, the friend, and the mistress." One indeed I could except—One, before passion threw its mists over my discern-

ment, I know—the first of women! Her name is indelibly written in my heart's core—but I dare not look in on it; a degree of agony would be the consequence. Oh! thou perfidious, cruel, mischief-making demon, who presidest over that frantic passion—thou mayest, thou dost poison my peace, but shalt not taint my honour! I would not, for a single moment, give an asylum to the most distant imagination, that would shadow the faintest outline of a selfish gratification, at the expense of her whose happiness is twisted with the threads of my existence. May she be happy as she deserves! And if my tenderest, faithfulest friendship can add to her bliss, I shall at least have one solid mine of enjoyment in my bosom! Don't guess at these ravings!

I watched at our front window to-day, but was disappointed. It has been a day of disappointments. I am just risen from a two-hours' bout after supper, with silly or sordid souls, who could relish nothing in common with me but the Port. One! 'Tis now the "witching time of night;" and whatever is out of joint in the foregoing scrawl, impute it to enchantments and spells; for I can't look over it, but will seal it up directly, as I don't care for to-morrow's criticisms on it.

You are by this time fast asleep, Clarinda; may good angels attend and guard you as constantly and faithfully as my good wishes do!

> "Beauty, which, whether waking or asleep,
> Shot forth peculiar graces."

John Milton, I wish thy soul better rest than I expect on my pillow to-night! O for a little of the cart-horse part of human nature! Good night, my dearest Clarinda!

SYLVANDER.

(6.)   TO CLARINDA.

Thursday Noon.

I AM certain I saw you, Clarinda; but you don't look to the proper story for a poet's lodging—

> "Where Speculation roosted near the sky."

I could almost have thrown myself over for very vexation. Why didn't you look higher? It has spoiled my peace for this day. To be so near my charming Clarinda; to miss her look while it was searching for me. I am sure the soul is capable of disease, for mine has convulsed itself into an inflammatory fever. I am sorry for your little boy; do let me know to-morrow how he is.

You have converted me, Clarinda (I shall love that name while I live: there is heavenly music in it). Booth and Amelia I know well.* Your sentiments on that subject, as they are on every subject, are just and noble. "To be foolishly alive to kindness, and to unkindness," is a charming female character.

What I said in my last letter, the powers of fuddling sociality only know for me. By yours, I understand my good star has been partly in my horizon, when I got wild in my roveries. Had that evil planet, which has almost all my life shed its baleful rays on my devoted head, been, as usual, in its zenith, I had certainly blabbed something that would have pointed out to you the dear object of my tenderest friendship, and, in spite of me, something more. Had that fatal information escaped me, and it was merely chance, or kind stars, that it did not, I had been undone! You would never have written me, except perhaps once more! O, I could curse circumstances, and the coarse tie of human laws, which keeps fast what common sense would loose, and which bars that happiness itself cannot give—happiness which otherwise Love and Honor would warrant! But hold—I shall make no more "hair-breadth 'scapes."

My friendship, Clarinda, is a life-rent business. My likings are both strong and eternal. I told you I had but one male friend: I have but two female. I should have a third, but she is surrounded by the blandishments of flattery and courtship. Her I register in my heart's core by Peggy Chalmers. Miss Nimmo can tell you how divine she is. She is worthy of a place in the same bosom with my Clarinda. That is the highest compliment I can pay her.

Farewell, Clarinda! Remember

SYLVANDER.

* [Fielding's novel.]

(7.)   TO CLARINDA.

Saturday Morning [January 12].

YOUR thoughts on religion, Clarinda, shall be welcome. You may perhaps distrust me, when I say 'tis also my favourite topic; but mine is the religion of the bosom. I hate the very idea of a controversial divinity; as I firmly believe that every honest, upright man, of whatever sect, will be accepted of the Deity. If your verses, as you seem to hint, contain censure, except you want an occasion to break with me, don't send them. I have a little infirmity in my disposition, that where I fondly love or highly esteem I cannot bear reproach.

"Reverence thyself" is a sacred maxim, and I wish to cherish it. I think I told you Lord Bolingbroke's saying to Swift—"Adieu, dear Swift! with all thy faults I love thee entirely; make an effort to love me with all mine." A glorious sentiment, and without which there can be no friendship! I do highly, very highly esteem you indeed, Clarinda—you merit it all! Perhaps, too, I scorn dissimulation! I could fondly love you: judge then, what a maddening sting your reproach would be. "Oh, I have sins to *Heaven*, but none to *you!*" With what pleasure would I meet you to-day, but I cannot walk to meet the Fly. I hope to be able to see you, on *foot*, about the middle of next week.

I am interrupted—perhaps you are not sorry for it, you will tell me; but I won't anticipate blame. O Clarinda! did you know how dear to me is your look of kindness, your smile of approbation, you would not, either in prose or verse, risk a censorious remark.

> "Curst be the verse, how well soe'er it flow,
> That tends to make one worthy man my foe!"

SYLVANDER.

(8.)   TO CLARINDA.

[January 12.]

YOU talk of weeping, Clarinda: some involuntary drops wet your lines as I read them. Offend me, my dearest angel! You cannot offend me,—you never offended me. If you had ever given me the least shadow of offence, so pardon me my God as I forgive Clarinda. I have read yours again; it has blotted my paper. Though I find your letter has agitated me into a violent headache, I shall take a chair and be with you about eight. A friend is to be with us at tea, on my account, which hinders me from coming sooner. Forgive, my dearest Clarinda, my unguarded expressions! For Heaven's sake, forgive me, or I shall never be able to bear my own mind.

Your unhappy

SYLVANDER.

(9.)   TO CLARINDA.

Monday Evening, 11 o'clock [Jan. 14th].

WHY have I not heard from you, Clarinda? To-day I expected it; and before supper, when a letter to me was announced, my heart danced with rapture; but behold, 'twas some fool, who had taken into his head to turn poet, and made me an offering of the first-fruits of his nonsense. "It is not poetry, but prose run mad." Did I ever repeat to you an epigram I made on a Mr. Elphinstone, who has given a translation of Martial, a famous Latin poet? The poetry of Elphinstone can only equal his prose notes. I was sitting in a merchant's shop of my acquaintance, waiting somebody; he put Elphinstone into my hand, and asked my opinion of it. I begged leave to write it on a blank leaf, which I did.

TO MR. ELPHINSTONE, &c.

> "O thou whom poesy abhors,
> Whom prose has turned out of doors,
> Heard'st thou yon groan! proceed no further!
> 'Twas laurell'd Martial calling murther!"

I am determined to see you, if at all possible, on Saturday evening. Next week I must sing—

> "The night is my departing night,
>   The morn's the day I maun awa:
> There's neither friend nor foe o' mine
>   But wishes that I were awa!
>
> What I hae done for lack o' wit,
>   I never, never can reca';
> I hope ye're o' my friends as yet,
>   Gude night, and joy be wi' you a'!"

If I could see you sooner, I would be so much the happier; but I would not purchase the dearest gratification on earth, if it must be at your expense in worldly censure, far less inward peace!

I shall certainly be ashamed of thus scrawling whole sheets of incoherence. The only unity (a sad word with poets and critics!) in my ideas is CLARINDA. There my heart "reigns and revels."

> "What art thou, Love! whence are those charms,
>   That thus thou bear'st an universal rule?
> For thee the soldier quits his arms,
>   The king turns slave, the wise man fool.

> In vain we chase thee from the field,
>   And with cool thoughts resist thy yoke;
> Next tide of blood, alas! we yield,
>   And all those high resolves are broke!"

I like to have quotations ready for every occasion. They give one's ideas so pat, and save one the trouble of finding expression adequate to one's feelings. I think it is one of the greatest pleasures attending a poetic genius, that we can give our woes, cares, joys, loves, &c., an embodied form in verse, which, to me, is ever immediate ease. Goldsmith says finely of his muse—

> "Thou source of all my bliss and all my woe;
> Who found me poor at first, and keep'st me so."

My limb has been so well to-day, that I have gone up and down stairs often without my staff. To-morrow I hope to walk once again on my own legs to dinner. It is only next street. Adieu!

Sylvander.

(10.)

TO CLARINDA.

Tuesday Evening [Jan. 15].

That you have faults, my Clarinda, I never doubted; but I know not where they existed, and Saturday night made me more in the dark than ever. O Clarinda! why would you wound my soul, by hinting that last night must have lessened my opinion of you! True, I was "behind the scenes with you;" but what did I see? A bosom glowing with honor and benevolence; a mind ennobled by genius, informed and refined by education and reflection, and exalted by native religion, genuine as in the climes of heaven; a heart formed for all the glorious meltings of friendship, love, and pity. These I saw. I saw the noblest immortal soul creation ever showed me.

I looked long, my dear Clarinda, for your letter; and am vexed that you are complaining. I have not caught you so far wrong as in your idea, that the commerce you have with one friend hurts you, if you cannot tell every tittle of it to another. Why have so injurious a suspicion of a good God, Clarinda, as to think that Friendship and Love, on the sacred inviolate principles of Truth, Honor, and Religion, can be any thing else than an object of his divine approbation?

I have mentioned, in some of my former scrawls, Saturday evening next. Do allow me to wait on you that evening. Oh, my angel! how soon must we part!—and when can we meet again? I look forward on the horrid interval with tearful eyes! What have I not lost by not knowing you sooner? I fear, I fear my acquaintance with you is too short, to make that lasting impression on your heart I could wish.

Sylvander.

(11.)

TO CLARINDA.

Sunday Night [Jan. 20th].

The impertinence of fools has joined with a return of an old indisposition, to make me good for nothing to-day. The paper has lain before me all this evening to write to my dear Clarinda, but—

> "Fools rush'd on fools, as waves succeed to waves."

I cursed them in my soul: they sacrilegiously disturbed my meditations on her who holds my heart. What a creature is man! A little alarm last night and to-day, that I am mortal, has made such a revolution on my spirits! There is no philosophy, no divinity, comes half so home to the mind. I have no idea of courage that braves Heaven. 'Tis the wild ravings of an imaginary hero in bedlam. I can no more, Clarinda; I can scarcely hold up my head; but I am happy you don't know it, you would be so uneasy.

Sylvander.

Monday Morning.

I am, my lovely friend, much better this morning on the whole; but I have a horrid languor on my spirits.

> "Sick of the world and all its joy,
> My soul in pining sadness mourns;
> Dark scenes of woe my mind employ,
> The past and present in their turns."

Have you ever met with a saying of the great and likewise good Mr. Locke, author of the famous Essay on the Human Understanding? He wrote a letter to a friend, directing it " Not to be delivered till after my decease." It ended thus,— "I know you loved me when living, and will preserve my memory now I am dead. All the use to be made of it is, that this life affords no solid satisfaction, but in the consciousness of having done well, and the hopes of another life. Adieu! I leave my best wishes with you.—J. Locke."

Clarinda, may I reckon on your friendship for life? I think I may. Thou Almighty Preserver of men! Thy friendship, which hitherto I have too much neglected, to secure it shall, all the future days and nights of my life, be my steady care. The idea of my Clarinda follows :—

> "Hide it, my heart, within that close disguise,
> Where, mix'd with God's, her loved idea lies.'"

But I fear inconstancy, the consequent imperfection of human weakness. Shall I meet with a friendship that defies years of absence and the chances and changes of fortune! Perhaps "such things are." One honest man I have great hopes from that way; but who, except a romance writer, would think on a love that could promise for life, in spite of distance, absence, chance, and change, and that, too, with slender hopes of fruition?

For my own part, I can say to myself in both requisitions—"Thou art the man." I dare, in cool resolve, I dare declare myself that friend and that lover. If womankind is capable of such things, Clarinda is. I trust that she is; and feel I shall be miserable if she is not. There is not one virtue which gives worth, or one sentiment which does honour to the sex, that she does not possess superior to any woman I ever saw: her exalted mind, aided a little, perhaps, by her situation, is, I think, capable of that nobly-romantic love-enthusiasm. May I see you on Wednesday evening, my dear angel? The next Wednesday again, will, I conjecture, be a hated day to us both. I tremble for censorious remarks, for your sake; but in extraordinary cases, may not usual and useful precaution be a little dispensed with! Three evenings, three swift-winged evenings, with pinions of down, are all the past—I dare not calculate the future. I shall call at Miss Nimmo to-morrow evening; 'twill be a farewell call.

I have written out my last sheet of paper, so I am reduced to my last half sheet. What a strange, mysterious faculty is that thing called imagination! We have no ideas almost at all of another world; but I have often amused myself with visionary schemes of what happiness might be enjoyed by small alterations, alterations that we can fully enter to in this present state of existence. For instance: suppose you and I just as we are at present; the same reasoning powers, sentiments, and even desires; the same fond curiosity for knowledge and remarking observation in our minds; and imagine our bodies free from pain, and the necessary supplies for the wants of nature at all times and easily within our reach. Imagine, further, that we were set free from the laws of gravitation, which bind us to this globe, and could at pleasure fly, without inconvenience, through all the yet unconjectured bounds of creation; what a life of bliss should we lead in our mutual pursuit of virtue and knowledge, and our mutual enjoyment of friendship and love!

I see you laughing at my fairy fancies, and calling me a voluptuous Mahometan; but I am certain I should be a happy creature, beyond anything we call bliss here below: nay, it would be a paradise congenial to you too. Don't you see us hand in hand, or rather my arm about your lovely waist, making our remarks on Sirius, the nearest of the fixed stars; or surveying a comet flaming innoxious by us, as we just now would mark the passing pomp of a travelling monarch; or, in a shady bower of Mercury or Venus, dedicating the hour to love, in mutual converse, relying honour, and revelling endearment, while the most exalted strains of poesy and harmony would be the ready, spontaneous language of our souls! Devotion is the favourite employment of your heart; so is it of mine: what incentives then to, and powers for reverence, gratitude, faith, and hope, in all the fervour of adoration and praise to that Being, whose unsearchable wisdom, power, and goodness, so pervaded, so inspired, every sense and feeling! By this time, I daresay, you will be blessing the neglect of the maid that leaves me destitute of paper.

SYLVANDER.

(12.)　　　TO CLARINDA.

Thursday Morning [Jan. 24th].

"Unlavish Wisdom never works in vain."

I HAVE been tasking my reason, Clarinda, why a woman, who, for native genius, poignant wit, strength of mind, generous sincerity of soul, and the sweetest female tenderness, is without a peer; and whose personal charms have few, very few parallels among her sex; why, or how, she should fall to the blessed lot of a poor harum-scarum poet, whom Fortune had kept for her particular use to wreak her temper on, whenever she was in ill-humour.

One time I conjectured that, as Fortune is the most capricious jade ever known, she may have taken, not a fit of remorse, but a paroxysm of whim, to raise the poor devil out of the mire where he had so often and so conveniently served her as a stepping-stone, and given him the most glorious boon she ever had in her gift, merely for the maggot's sake, to see how his fool head and his fool heart will bear it.

At other times, I was vain enough to think that Nature, who has a great deal to say with Fortune, had given the coquettish goddess some such hint as—"Here is a paragon of female excellence, whose equal, in all my former compositions, I never was lucky enough to hit on, and despair of ever doing so again: you have cast her rather in the shades of life. There is a certain poet of my making: among your frolics, it would not be amiss to attach him to this masterpiece of my hand, to give her that immortality among mankind which no woman of any age ever more deserved, and which few rhymesters of this age are better able to confer."

Evening, Nine o'clock.

I AM here—absolutely unfit to finish my letter—pretty hearty, after a bowl which has been constantly plied since dinner till this moment. I have been with Mr. Schetki the musician, and he has set the song* finely. I have no distinct ideas of anything, but that I have drunk your health twice to-night, and that you are all my soul holds dear in this world.

SYLVANDER.

*["Clorinda, mistress of my soul."]

(13.)　　　TO CLARINDA.

[January 25th.]

CLARINDA, my life, you have wounded my soul. Can I think of your being unhappy, even though it be not described in your pathetic elegance of language, without being miserable? Clarinda, can I bear to be told from you that "you will not see me to-morrow night—that you wish the hour of parting were come:" Do not let us impose on ourselves by sounds. If, in the moment of fond endearment and tender dalliance, I perhaps trespassed against the *letter* of Decorum's law, I appeal, even to you, whether I ever sinned, in the very least degree, against the *spirit* of her strictest statute? But why, my love, talk to me in such strong terms; every word of which cuts me to the very soul? You know a hint, the slightest signification of your wish, is to me a sacred command.

Be reconciled, my angel, to your God, yourself, and me; and I pledge you Sylvander's honour—an oath, I daresay, you will trust without reserve, that you shall never more have reason to complain of his conduct. Now, my love, do not wound our next meeting with any averted looks or restrained caresses. I have marked the line of conduct—a line, I know, exactly to your taste—and which I will inviolably keep; but do not you show the least inclination to make boundaries. Seeming distrust, where you know you may confide, is a cruel sin against sensibility.

"Delicacy, you know, it was which won me to you at once: take care you do not loosen the dearest, most sacred tie that

* v

unites us." Clarinda, I would not have stung *your* soul—I would not have bruised *your* spirit, as that harsh crucifying "Take care" did *mine*; no, not to have gained heaven! Let me again appeal to your dear self, if Sylvander, even when he seemingly half transgressed the laws of decorum, if he did not show more chastised, trembling, faltering delicacy, than the many of the world do in keeping these laws?

Oh Love and Sensibility, ye have conspired against my Peace! I love to madness, and I feel to torture! Clarinda, how can I forgive myself, that I have ever touched a single chord in your bosom with pain! would I do it willingly? Would any consideration, any gratification, make me do so? Oh, did you love like me, you would not, you could not, deny or put off a meeting with the man who adores you;—who would die a thousand deaths before he would injure you; and who must soon bid you a long farewell!

I had proposed bringing my bosom friend, Mr. Ainslie, to-morrow evening, at his strong request, to see you; as he has only time to stay with us about ten minutes, for an engagement. But I shall hear from you: this afternoon, for mercy's sake!—for, till I hear from you, I am wretched. O Clarinda, the tie that binds me to thee is intwisted, incorporated with my dearest threads of life!

SYLVANDER.

(14.)   TO CLARINDA.

[January 26th.]

I WAS on the way, my *Love*, to meet you (I never do things by halves), when I got your card. Mr. Ainslie goes out of town to-morrow morning, to see a brother of his who is newly arrived from France. I am determined that he and I shall call on you together. So, look you, lest I should never see to-morrow, we will call on you to-night. Mary and you may put off tea till about seven; at which time, in the Galloway phrase, "an the beast be to the fore, and the branks bide hale," expect the humblest of your humble servants, and his dearest friend. We only propose staying half an hour—"for ought we ken." I could suffer the lash of misery eleven months in the year, were the twelfth to be composed of hours like yesternight. You are the soul of my enjoyment; all else is of the stuff of stocks and stones.

SYLVANDER.

(15.)   TO CLARINDA.

Sunday, Noon [Jan. 27th].

I HAVE almost given up the Excise idea. I have been just now to wait on a great person, Miss ——'s friend, ——. Why will great people not only deafen us with the din of their equipage, and dazzle us with their fastidious pomp, but they must also be so very dictatorially wise? I have been questioned like a child about my matters, and blamed and schooled for my Inscription on Stirling window. Come, Clarinda!—"Come, curse me, Jacob; come, defy me, Israel!"

I have been with Miss Nimmo. She is, indeed, "a good soul," as my Clarinda finely says. She has reconciled me, in a good measure, to the world with her friendly prattle.

Schetki has sent me the song, set to a fine air of his composing. I have called the song Clarinda: I have carried it about in my pocket, and thumbed it over all day.

Monday Morning.

If my prayers have any weight in heaven, this morning looks in on you and finds you in the arms of peace, except where it is charmingly interrupted by the ardours of devotion. I find so much serenity of mind, so much positive pleasure, so much fearless daring toward the world, when I warm in devotion, or feel the glorious sensation—a consciousness of Almighty friendship—that I am sure I shall soon be an honest enthusiast.

> " How are thy servants blest, O Lord !
> How sure is their defence!
> Eternal Wisdom is their guide,
> Their help, Omnipotence."

I am, my dear Madam, yours,

SYLVANDER.

(16.)   TO CLARINDA.

Sunday Morning [January 27th].

I HAVE just been before the throne of my God, Clarinda. According to my association of ideas, my sentiments of love and friendship, I next devote myself to you. Yesternight I was happy—happiness "that the world cannot give." I kindle at the recollection; but it is a flame where Innocence looks smiling on, and Honour stands by a sacred guard. Your heart, your fondest wishes, your dearest thoughts, these are yours to bestow: your person is unapproachable, by the laws of your country; and he loves not as I do who would make you miserable.

You are an angel, Clarinda: you are surely no mortal that "the earth owns."—To kiss your hand, to live on your smile, is to me far more exquisite bliss than any the dearest favours that the fairest of the sex, yourself excepted, can bestow.

Sunday Evening.

You are the constant companion of my thoughts. How wretched is the condition of one who is haunted with conscious guilt, and trembling under the idea of dreaded vengeance! And what a placid calm, what a charming secret enjoyment is given to one's bosom by the kind feelings of friendship, and the fond throes of love! Out upon the tempest of Anger, the acrimonious gall of fretful Impatience, the sullen frost of louring Resentment, or the corroding poison of withered Envy! They eat up the immortal part of man! If they spent their fury only on the unfortunate objects of them, it would be something in their favour; but these miserable passions, like traitor Iscariot, betray their Lord and Master.

Thou Almighty Author of peace, and goodness, and love! do Thou give me the social heart that kindly tastes of every man's cup! Is it a draught of joy?—warm and open my heart, to share it with cordial unenvying rejoicing! Is it the bitter potion of sorrow?—melt my heart with sincerely sympathetic woe! Above all, do Thou give me the manly mind, that resolutely exemplifies, in life and manners, those sentiments which I would wish to be thought to possess! The friend of my soul—there may I never deviate from the firmest fidelity and most active kindness! Clarinda, the dear object of my fondest love; there, may the most sacred inviolate honour, the most faithful kindling constancy, ever watch and animate my every thought and imagination!

Did you ever meet with the following lines spoken of Religion, your darling topic?

> "Tis this, my friend, that streaks our morning bright
> 'Tis this that gilds the horrors of our night;
> When wealth forsakes us, and when friends are few,
> When friends are faithless, or when foes pursue;
> 'Tis this that wards the blow, or stills the smart,
> Disarms affliction, or repels its dart;
> Within the breast bids purest rapture rise,
> Bids smiling Conscience spread her cloudless skies.

I met with these verses very early in life, and was so delighted with them, that I have them by me, copied at school. Good night and sound rest, my dearest Clarinda!

SYLVANDER.

(17.)

TO CLARINDA.

Thursday Night [January 31st].

I CANNOT be easy, my Clarinda, while any sentiment respecting me in your bosom gives you pain. If there is no man on earth to whom your heart and affections are justly due, it may savour of imprudence, but never of criminality, to bestow that heart and those affections where you please. The God of love meant and made these delicious attachments to be bestowed on somebody; and even all the imprudence lies in bestowing them on an unworthy object. If this reasoning is conclusive, as it certainly is, I must be allowed to "talk of Love."

It is, perhaps, rather wrong to speak highly to a friend of his letter; it is apt to lay one under a little restraint in their future letters, and restraint is the death of a friendly epistle; but there is one passage in your last charming letter, Thomson nor Shenstone never exceeded it, nor often came up to it. I shall certainly steal it, and set it in some future poetic production, and get immortal fame by it. 'Tis when you bid the scenes of nature remind me of Clarinda. Can I forget you, Clarinda? I would detest myself as a tasteless, unfeeling, insipid, infamous blockhead! I have loved women of ordinary merit, whom I could have loved for ever. You are the first, the only unexceptionable individual of the beauteous sex that I ever met with; and never woman more entirely possessed my soul. I know myself, and how far I can depend on passions, well. It has been my peculiar study.

I thank you for going to Miers.* Urge him, for necessity calls, to have it done by the middle of next week: Wednesday the latest day. I want it for a breast pin, to wear next my heart. I propose to keep sacred set times, to wander in the woods and wilds for meditation on you. Then, and only then, your lovely image shall be produced to the day, with a reverence akin to devotion.

*　　*　　*　　*　　*　　*

To-morrow night shall not be the last. Good night! I am perfectly stupid, as I supped late yesternight.

SYLVANDER.

* [A celebrated miniature painter of that time. A profile of Burns by him appears in Hogg and Motherwell's edition; and a profile of Clarinda, we presume by him also, appears in frontispiece to the Correspondence with her.]

(18.)

TO CLARINDA.

Saturday Morning [Feb. 2d].

THERE is no time, my Clarinda, when the conscious thrilling chords of Love and Friendship give such delight, as in the pensive hours of what our favourite Thomson calls, "philosophic melancholy." The sportive insects, who bask in the sunshine of Prosperity, or the worms that luxuriant crawl amid their ample wealth of earth; they need no Clarinda—they would despise Sylvander, if they dared. The family of Misfortune, a numerous group of brothers and sisters!—they need a resting-place to their souls. Unnoticed, often condemned by the world—in some degree, perhaps, condemned by themselves—they feel the full enjoyment of ardent love, delicate tender endearments, mutual esteem and mutual reliance.

In this light I have often admired religion. In proportion as we are wrung with grief, or distracted with anxiety, the ideas of a compassionate Deity, an Almighty Protector, are doubly dear.

> "'Tis this, my friend, that streaks our morning bright;
> 'Tis this that gilds the horrors of our night."

I have been this morning taking a peep through, as Young finely says, "the dark postern of time long elapsed;" and you will easily guess 'twas a rueful prospect: what a tissue of thoughtlessness, weakness, and folly! My life reminded me of a ruined temple: what strength, what proportion in some parts!—what unsightly gaps, what prostrate ruins in others! I kneeled down before the Father of Mercies, and said, "Father, I have sinned against Heaven, and in thy sight, and am no more worthy to be called thy son!" I rose eased and strengthened. I despise the superstition of a fanatic; but I love the religion of a man. "The future," said I to myself, "is still before me· there let me

> 'On reason build resolve—
> That column of true majesty in man!'

I have difficulties many to encounter," said I; "but they are not absolutely insuperable:—and where is firmness of mind shown, but in exertion? Mere declamation is bombast rant. Besides, wherever I am, or in whatever situation I may be,

> ———— "'Tis nought to me,
> Since God is ever present, ever felt,
> In the void waste as in the city full;
> And where he vital breathes, there must be joy.'"

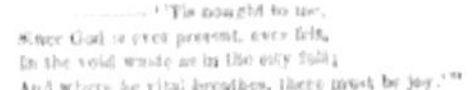

Saturday Night, Half after Ten.

WHAT luxury of bliss I was enjoying this time yesternight! My ever dearest Clarinda, you have stolen away my soul; but you have refined, you have exalted it; you have given it a stronger sense of virtue, and a stronger relish for piety. Clarinda, first of your sex! if ever I am the veriest wretch on earth to forget you; if ever your lovely image is effaced from my soul,

> "May I be lost, no eye to weep my end,
> And find no earth that's base enough to bury me!"

What trifling silliness is the childish fondness of the every-day children of the world! 'Tis the unmeaning toying of the younglings of the fields and forests; but, where Sentiment and Fancy unite their sweets, where Taste and Delicacy refine, where Wit adds the flavour, and Good Sense gives strength and spirit to all; what a delicious draught is the hour of tender endearment! Beauty and Grace in the arms of Truth and Honour, in all the luxury of mutual love.

Clarinda, have you ever seen the picture realised? not in all its very richest colouring, but

> "Hope, thou nurse of young Desire,
> Fair promiser of Joy."—

Last night, Clarinda, but for one slight shade, was the glorious picture—

> ———— "Innocence
> Look'd gaily smiling on; while rosy Pleasure
> Hid young Desire amid her flowery wreath,
> And pour'd her cup luxuriant, mantling high,
> The sparkling, Heavenly vintage—Love and Bliss!"

Clarinda, when a poet and poetess of Nature's making—two of Nature's noblest productions!—when they drink together of the same cup of Love and Bliss, attempt not, ye coarser stuff of human nature! profanely to measure enjoyment ye never can know.

Good Night, my dear Clarinda!

SYLVANDER.

(19.)   TO CLARINDA.

[February 4th, 1788.]

•   •   •   I am a discontented ghost, a perturbed spirit. Clarinda, if ever you forget Sylvander, may you be happy, but he will be miserable.

O, what a fool I am in love!—what an extravagant prodigal of affection! Why are your sex called the tender sex, when I never have met with one who can repay me in passion? They are either not so rich in love as I am, or they are niggards where I am lavish.

O Thou, whose I am, and whose are all my ways! Thou see'st me here, the hapless wreck of tides and tempests in my own bosom; do Thou direct to thyself that ardent love, for which I have so often sought a return, in vain, from my fellow-creatures! If thy goodness has yet such a gift in store for me, as an equal return of affection from her who, Thou knowest, is dearer to me than life, do Thou bless and hallow our band of love and friendship; watch over us, in all our outgoings and incomings, for good; and may the tie that unites our hearts be strong and indissoluble as the thread of man's immortal life!

I am just going to take your Blackbird,* the sweetest, I am sure, that ever sung, and prune its wings a little.

SYLVANDER.

*[song by Clarinda.]

(20.)   TO CLARINDA.

[February 5th.]

I CANNOT go out to-day, my dearest Love, without sending you half a line, by way of a sin-offering; but, believe me, 'twas the sin of ignorance. Could you think that I intended to hurt you by any thing I said yesternight? Nature has been too kind to you for your happiness, your delicacy, your sensibility. O why should such glorious qualifications be the fruitful source of woe! You have "murdered sleep" to me last night. I went to bed, impressed with an idea that you were unhappy; and every start I closed my eyes, busy Fancy painted you in such scenes of romantic misery, that I would almost be persuaded you were not well this morning.

> ———— "If I unwitting have offended,
> Impute it not,"
> ———— "But while we live
> But one short hour, perhaps, between us two
> Let there be peace."

If Mary is not gone by the time this reaches you, give her my best compliments. She is a charming girl, and highly worthy of the noblest love.

I send you a poem to read till I call on you this night, which will be about nine. I wish I could procure some potent spell, some fairy charm, that would protect from injury, or restore to rest that bosom chord, "tremblingly alive all o'er," on which hangs your peace of mind. I thought, vainly I fear thought, that the devotion of love, love strong as even you can feel, love guarded, invulnerably guarded by all the purity of virtue, and all the pride of honour,—I thought such a love might make you happy. Shall I be mistaken? I can no more, for hurry.

Tuesday Morning.

(21.)   TO CLARINDA.

Friday Morning, 7 o'Clock [February 8th].

YOUR fears for Mary are truly laughable. I suppose, my love, you and I showed her a scene which, perhaps, made her wish that she had a swain, and one who could love like me; and 'tis a thousand pities that so good a heart as hers should want an aim, an object. I am miserably stupid this morning. Yesterday I dined with a Baronet, and sat pretty late over the bottle. And "who hath wo—who hath sorrow? they that tarry long at the wine; they that go to seek mixed wine." Forgive me, likewise, a quotation from my favourite author. Solomon's knowledge of the world is very great. He may be looked on as the "Spectator" or "Adventurer" of his day: and it is, indeed, surprising what a sameness has ever been in human nature. The broken, but strongly characterizing hints, that the royal author gives us of the manners of the court of Jerusalem and country of Israel are, in their great outlines, the same pictures that London and England, Versailles and France exhibit some three thousand years later. The loves in the "Song of songs" are all in the spirit of Lady M. W. Montague, or Madame Ninon de l'Enclos; though, for my part, I dislike both the ancient and modern voluptuaries; and will dare to affirm, that such an attachment as mine to Clarinda, and such evenings as she and I have spent, are what these greatly respectable and deeply experienced Judges of Life and Love never dreamed of.

I shall be with you this evening between eight and nine, and shall keep as sober hours as you could wish. I am over, my dear Madam, yours,

SYLVANDER.

(22.)   TO CLARINDA.

[February 13th.]

MY EVER DEAREST CLARINDA,—I make a numerous dinner-party wait me while I read yours and write this. Do not require that I should cease to love you, to adore you in my soul; 'tis to me impossible: your peace and happiness are to me dearer than my soul. Name the terms on which you wish to see me, to correspond with me, and you have them. I must love, pine, mourn, and adore in secret: this you must not deny me. You will ever be to me

> "Dear as the light that visits these sad eyes,
> Dear as the ruddy drops that warm my heart."

I have not patience to read the Puritanic scrawl. Damned sophistry. Ye heavens, thou God of nature, thou Redeemer of mankind! ye look down with approving eyes on a passion inspired by the purest flame, and guarded by truth, delicacy, and honour; but the half-inch soul of an unfeeling, cold-blooded, pitiful Presbyterian bigot cannot forgive anything above his dungeon-bosom and foggy head.

Farewell! I'll be with you to-morrow evening; and be at rest in your mind. I will be yours in the way you think most to your happiness. I dare not proceed. I love, and will love you; and will, with joyous confidence, approach the throne of the Almighty Judge of men with your dear idea; and will despise the scum of sentiment, and the mist of sophistry.

SYLVANDER.

(23.)   TO CLARINDA.

Wednesday, Midnight [February 13th].

MADAM,—After a wretched day, I am preparing for a sleepless night. I am going to address myself to the Almighty Witness of my actions—some time, perhaps very soon, my Almighty Judge. I am not going to be the advocate of Passion: be Thou my inspirer and testimony, O God, as I plead the cause of truth!

I have read over your friend's haughty dictatorial letter: you are only answerable to your God in such a matter. Who gave any fellow-creature of yours (a fellow-creature incapable of being your judge, because not your peer), a right to catechise, scold, undervalue, abuse, and insult, wantonly and unhumanly to insult you thus? I don't wish, not even wish to deceive you, Madam. The Searcher of hearts is my witness how dear you are to me; but though it were possible you could be still dearer to me, I would not even kiss your hand, at the expense of your conscience. Away with declamation! let us appeal to the bar of common sense. It is not mouthing everything sacred; it is not vague ranting assertions; it is not assuming, haughtily and insultingly assuming, the dictatorial language of a Roman Pontiff, that must dissolve a union like ours. Tell me, Madam, are you under the least shadow of an obligation to bestow your love, tenderness, caresses, affections, heart and soul, on Mr. M'Lehose—the man who has repeatedly, habitually, and barbarously broken through every tie of duty, nature, or gratitude to you? The laws of your country indeed, for the most useful reasons of policy and sound government, have made your person inviolate; but are your heart and affections bound to one who gives not the least return of either to you? You cannot do it; it is not in the nature of things that you are bound to do it; the common feelings of humanity forbid it. Have you, then, a heart and affections which are no man's right? You have. It would be highly, ridiculously absurd to suppose the contrary. Tell me then, in the name of common sense, can it be wrong, is such a supposition compatible with the plainest ideas of right and wrong, that it is improper to bestow the heart and these affections on another —while that bestowing is not in the smallest degree hurtful to your duty to God, to your children, to yourself, or to society at large?

This is the great test; the consequences: let us see them. In a widowed, forlorn, lonely situation, with a bosom glowing with love and tenderness, yet so delicately situated that you cannot indulge these nobler feelings except you meet with a man who has a soul capable   *   *   *   *   *

(24.)   TO CLARINDA.

[February 14th.]

"I am distressed for thee, my brother Jonathan." I have suffered, Clarinda, from your letter. My soul was in arms at the sad perusal. I dreaded that I had acted wrong. If I have wronged you, God forgive me. But, Clarinda, be comforted. Let us raise the tone of our feelings a little higher and bolder. A fellow-creature who leaves us—who spurns us without just cause, though once our bosom friend—up with a little honest pride: let them go. How shall I comfort you, who am the cause of the injury? Can I wish that I had never seen you— that we had never met? No, I never will. But have I thrown you friendless?—there is almost distraction in the thought. Father of mercies! against Thee often have I sinned; through Thy grace I will endeavour to do so no more. She who, Thou knowest, is dearer to me than myself—pour Thou the balm of peace into her past wounds, and hedge her about with Thy peculiar care, all her future days and nights. Strengthen her tender noble mind, firmly to suffer and magnanimously to bear. Make me worthy of that friendship, that love she honours me with. May my attachment to her be pure as devotion, and lasting as immortal life. O Almighty Goodness, hear me! Be to her at all times, particularly in the hour of distress or trial, a friend and comforter, a guide and guard.

> "How are thy servants blest, O Lord,
> How sure is their defence!
> Eternal Wisdom is their guide,
> Their help, Omnipotence!"

Forgive me, Clarinda, the injury I have done you. To-night I shall be with you, as indeed I shall be ill at ease till I see you.

SYLVANDER.

(25.)   TO CLARINDA.

Two o'clock [February 14th].

I JUST now received your first letter of yesterday, by the careless negligence of the penny-post. Clarinda, matters are grown very serious with us: then seriously hear me, and hear me, Heaven!

I met you, my dear [Clarinda], by far the first of woman kind, at least to me. I esteemed, I loved you at first sight: both of which attachments you have done me the honour to return. The longer I am acquainted with you, the more innate amiableness and worth I discover in you. You have suffered a loss, I confess, for my sake; but if the firmest, steadiest, warmest friend-ship; if every endeavour to be worthy of your friendship; if a love, strong as the ties of nature, and holy as the duties of religion; if all these can make any thing like a compensation for the evil I have occasioned you; if they be worth your acceptance, or can in the least add to your enjoyments—so help Sylvander, ye Powers above, in his hour of need, as he freely gives these all to Clarinda!

I esteem you, I love you as a friend; I admire you, I love you as a woman, beyond any one in all the circle of creation. I know I shall continue to esteem you, to love you, to pray for you, nay, to pray for myself for your sake.

Expect me at eight; and believe me to be ever, my dearest Madam, yours most entirely,

SYLVANDER.

(26.)   TO CLARINDA.

[February 15th.]

WHEN matters, my love, are desperate, we must put on a desperate face—

> —"On reason build resolve,
> That column of true majesty in man"—

or, as the same author finely says in another place,

> —"Let the soul spring up,
> And lay strong hold for help on Him that made thee."

I am yours, Clarinda, for life. Never be discouraged at all this. Look forward: in a few weeks I shall be somewhere or other out of the possibility of seeing you: till then, I shall write you often, but visit you seldom. Your fame, your welfare, your happiness, are dearer to me than any gratification whatever. Be comforted, my love! the present moment is the worst; the lenient hand of Time is daily and hourly either lightening the burden, or making us insensible to the weight. None of these friends—I mean Mr. ———— and the other gentleman—can hurt your worldly support; and of their friendship, in a little time you will learn to be easy and, by and by, to be happy without it. A decent means of livelihood in the world, an approving God, a peaceful conscience, and one firm trusty friend—can any body that has these be said to be unhappy? These are yours.

To-morrow evening I shall be with you about eight; probably for the last time till I return to Edinburgh. In the meantime, should any of these two unlucky friends question you respecting me, whether I am the man, I do not think they are entitled to any information. As to their jealousy and spying, I despise them.

Adieu, my dearest Madam!

SYLVANDER.

(27.)   TO CLARINDA.

Glasgow, Monday Evening, Nine o'clock
[February 18th].

THE attraction of Love, I find, is in an inverse proportion to the attraction of the Newtonian philosophy. In the system of Sir Isaac, the nearer objects were to one another, the stronger was the attractive force. In my system, every mile-stone that marked my progress from Clarinda awakened a keener pang of attachment to her. How do you feel, my love? Is your heart ill at ease? I fear it. God forbid that these persecutors should harass that peace, which is more precious to me than my own. Be assured I shall ever think on you, muse on you, and in my moments of devotion, pray for you. The hour that you are not in all my thoughts, "be that hour darkness; let the shadows of death cover it; let it not be numbered in the hours of the day!"

> —"When I forget the darling theme,
> Be my tongue mute! my fancy paint no more!
> And, dead to joy, forget my heart to beat!"

I have just met with my old friend, the ship Captain*—guess my pleasure; to meet you could alone have given me more. My brother William, too, the young saddler, has come to Glasgow to meet me; and here are we three spending the evening.

I arrived here too late to write by post; but I'll wrap half a dozen sheets of blank paper together, and send it by the Fly, under the name of a parcel. You shall hear from me next post town. I would write you a longer letter, but for the present circumstances of my friend.

Adieu, my Clarinda! I am just going to propose your health by way of grace-drink.

SYLVANDER.

* [Mr. Richard Brown, alluded to in the Poet's autobiography as "a very noble character, but a hapless son of Misfortune," whose acquaintance he had formed at Irvine.]

(28.) TO CLARINDA.

Kilmarnock, Friday [February 22d].

I WROTE you, my dear Madam, the moment I alighted in Glasgow. Since then I have not had opportunity: for in Paisley, where I arrived next day, my worthy, wise friend, Mr. Pattison, did not allow me a moment's respite. I was there ten hours; during which time I was introduced to nine men worth six thousands; five men worth ten thousands; his brother, richly worth twenty thousands; and a young weaver, who will have thirty thousands good when his father, who has no more children than the said weaver, and a Whig-kirk, dies. Mr. P. was bred a zealous Antiburgher; but, during his widowerhood, he has found their strictness incompatible with certain compromises he is often obliged to make with these Powers of darkness—the devil, the world, and the flesh: so he, good, merciful man! talked privately to me of the absurdity of eternal torments; the liberality of sentiment in indulging the honest instincts of nature; the mysteries of * * * &c. He has a son, however, that, at sixteen, has repeatedly minted* at certain privileges, only proper for sober, staid men, who can use the good things of this life without abusing them; but the father's parental vigilance has hitherto hedged him in, amid a corrupt and evil world.

His only daughter, who, "if the beast be to the fore, and the branks bide hale," will have seven thousand pounds when her old father steps into the dark Factory-office of Eternity with his well-thummed web of life, has put him again and again in a commendable fit of indignation, by requesting a harpsichord. "O! these boarding-schools!" exclaims my prudent friend. "She was a good spinner and sewer, till I was advised by her foes and mine to give her a year of Edinburgh!"

After two bottles more, my much-respected friend opened up to me a project, a legitimate child of Wisdom and Good Sense; 'twas no less than a long thought-on and deeply-matured design to marry a girl, fully as elegant in her form as the famous priestess whom Saul consulted in his last hours, and who had been second maid of honour to his deceased wife. This, you may be sure, I highly applauded, so I hope for a pair of gloves by and by. I spent the two bypast days at Dunlop House with that worthy family to whom I was deeply indebted early in my poetic career; and in about two hours I shall present your "twa wee sarkies" to the little fellow.† My dearest Clarinda, you are ever present with me; and these hours, that drawl by among the fools and rascals of this world, are only supportable in the idea,

that they are the forerunners of that happy hour that ushers me to "the mistress of my soul." Next week I shall visit Dumfries, and next again return to Edinburgh. My letters, in these hurrying dissipated hours, will be heavy trash; but you know the writer.

God bless you.

SYLVANDER.

* [Anglice—Aimed at, attempted.]
† [Some little gift to the Poet's eldest son, then an infant, and of whose birth Clarinda was already informed (4.), is here referred to. She sent kisses also to "the little cherub," and speaks of him afterwards as "your little lamb."]

(29.) TO CLARINDA.

Cumnock, 2d March, 1788.

I HOPE, and am certain, that my generous Clarinda will not think my silence, for now a long week, has been in any degree owing to my forgetfulness. I have been tossed about through the country ever since I wrote you; and am here returning from Dumfries-shire, at an inn, the post-office of the place, with just so long time as my horse eats his corn, to write you. I have been hurried with business and dissipation, almost equal to the insidious degree of the Persian monarch's mandate, when he forbade asking petition of God or man for forty days. Had the venerable prophet been as strong as I, he had not broken the decree; at least not thrice a day.

I am thinking my farming scheme will yet hold. A worthy intelligent farmer, my father's friend and my own, has been with me on the spot: he thinks the bargain practicable. I am myself, on a more serious review of the lands, much better pleased with them. I won't mention this in writing to any-body but you and Mr. Ainslie. Don't accuse me of being fickle; I have the two plans of life before me, and I wish to adopt the one most likely to procure me independence.

I shall be in Edinburgh next week. I long to see you; your image is omnipresent to me; nay, I am convinced I would soon idolatrize it most seriously; so much do absence and memory improve the medium through which one sees the much-loved object. To-night, at the sacred hour of eight, I expect to meet you, at the Throne of Grace. I hope as I go home to-night, to find a letter from you at the post-office in Mauchline; I have just once seen that dear hand since I left Edinburgh; a letter, indeed, which much affected me. Tell me, first of womankind, will my warmest attachment, my sincerest friendship, my correspondence,—will they be any compensation for the sacrifices you make for my sake? If they will, they are yours. If I settle on the farm I propose, I am just a day and a half's ride from Edinburgh. We shall meet; don't you say, "Perhaps, too often!"

Farewell, my fair, my charming Poetess! May all good things ever attend you.

I am ever, my dearest Madam,

Yours,

SYLVANDER.

(30.) TO CLARINDA.

[March 6th.]

I OWN myself guilty, Clarinda: I should have written you last week. But when you recollect, my dearest Madam, that yours of this night's post is only the third I have from you, and that this is the fifth or sixth I have sent to you, you will not reproach me, with a good grace, for unkindness. I have always some kind of idea, not to sit down to write a letter, except I have time and possession of my faculties, so as to do some justice to my letter; which at present is rarely my situation. For instance, yesterday I dined at a friend's at some distance; the savage hospitality of this country spent me the most part of the night over the nauseous potion in the bowl. This day—sick—headache—low spirits—miserable—fasting, except for a draught of water or small beer. Now eight o'clock at night; only able to crawl ten minutes' walk into Mauchline to wait the post, in the pleasurable hope of hearing from the mistress of my soul.

But truce with all this. When I sit down to write to you, all is happiness and peace. A hundred times a-day do I figure you before your taper,—your book or work laid aside as I get within the room. How happy have I been! and how little of that scantling portion of time, called the life of man, is sacred to happiness, much less transport.

I could moralize to-night, like a death's head.

> "O what is life, that thoughtless wish of all!
> A drop of honey in a draught of gall."

Nothing astonishes me more, when a little sickness clogs the wheels of life, than the thoughtless career we run in the hour of health. "None saith, Where is God, my Maker, that giveth songs in the night; who teacheth us more knowledge than the beasts of the field, and more understanding than the fowls of the air?"

Give me, my Maker, to remember thee! Give me to act up to the dignity of my nature! Give me to feel "another's wo;" and continue with me that dear-lov'd friend that feels with mine!

The dignifying and dignified consciousness of an honest man, and the well-grounded trust in approving Heaven, are two most substantial foundations of happiness.

* * * * * *

I could not have written a page to any mortal, except yourself. I'll write you by Sunday's post. Adieu. Good night.

SYLVANDER.

(31.) TO CLARINDA.

Mossgiel, 7th March, 1788.

CLARINDA, I have been so stung with your reproach for unkindness—a sin so unlike me, a sin I detest more than a breach of the whole Decalogue, fifth, sixth, seventh, and ninth articles excepted—that I believe I shall not rest in my grave about it, if I die before I see you. You have often allowed me the head to judge, and the heart to feel the influence of female excellence: was it not blasphemy, then, against your own charms, and against my feelings, to suppose that a short

fortnight could abate my passion? You, my love, may have your cares and anxieties to disturb you; but they are the usual occurrences of life: your future views are fixed, and your mind in a settled routine. Could not you, my ever dearest Madam, make a little allowance for a man, after long absence, paying a short visit to a country full of friends, relations, and early intimates? Cannot you guess, my Clarinda, what thoughts, what cares, what anxious forebodings, hopes and fears, must crowd the breast of the man of keen sensibility, when no less is on the tapis than his aim, his employment, his very existence through future life?

To be overtopped in any thing else, I can bear; but in the tests of generous love, I defy all mankind! not even the tender, the fond, the loving Clarinda—she whose strength of attachment, whose melting soul, may vie with Eloisa and Sappho, not even she can overpay the affection she owes me!

Now that, not my apology, but my defence, is made, I feel my soul respire more easily. I know you will go along with me in my justification: would to Heaven you could in my adoption too! I mean an adoption beneath the stars—an adoption where I might revel in the immediate beams of

> "She, the bright sun of all her sex."

I would not have you, my dear Madam, so much hurt at Miss N[immo]'s coldness. 'Tis placing yourself below her, an honour she by no means deserves. We ought, when we wish to be economists in happiness,—we ought, in the first place, to fix the standard of our own character; and when, on full examination, we know where we stand, and how much ground we occupy, let us contend for it as property; and those who seem to doubt, or deny us what is justly ours, let us either pity their prejudices, or despise their judgment. I know, my dear, you will say this is self-conceit; but I call it self-knowledge. The one is the overweening opinion of a fool, who fancies himself to be what he wishes himself to be thought; the other is the honest justice that a man of sense, who has thoroughly examined the subject, owes to himself. Without this standard, this column in our own mind, we are perpetually at the mercy of the petulance, the mistakes, the prejudices, nay, the very weakness and wickedness of our fellow-creatures.

I urge this, my dear, both to confirm myself in the doctrine, which, I assure you, I sometimes need; and because I know that this causes you often much disquiet. To return to Miss N——. She is most certainly a worthy soul; and equalled by very, very few, in goodness of heart. But can she boast more goodness of heart than Clarinda? Not even prejudice will dare to say so. For penetration and discernment, Clarinda sees far beyond her. To wit, Miss N—— dare make no pretence: to Clarinda's wit, scarce any of her sex dare make pretence. Personal charms, it would be ridiculous to run the parallel: and for conduct in life, Miss N—— was never called out, either much to do, or to suffer. Clarinda has been both; and has performed her part, where Miss N—— would have sunk at the bare idea.

Away, then, with these disquietudes! Let us pray with the honest weaver of Kilbarchan, "Lord, send us a gude conceit o' oursel!" or, in the words of the auld sang,

" Who does me disdain, I can scorn them again,
And I'll never mind any such foes."

There is an error in the commerce of intimacy. . .

. . . .

way of exchange, have not an equivalent to give us; and, what is still worse, have no idea of the value of our goods. Happy is our lot, indeed, when we meet with an honest merchant, who is qualified to deal with us on our own terms; but that is a rarity: with almost every body we must pocket our pearls, less or more; and learn, in the old Scots phrase, "To gie sic like as we get." For this reason, we should try to erect a kind of bank or storehouse in our own mind; or, as the Psalmist says, "We should commune with our own hearts, and be still." This is exactly . . .

. . . .

I wrote you yesternight, which will meet you long before this can. I may write Mr. Ainslie before I see him, but I am not sure.

Farewell! and remember

SYLVANDER.

(32.) TO CLARINDA.

[31st March.]

I will meet you to-morrow, Clarinda, as you appoint. My Excise affair is just concluded, and I have got my order for instructions: so far good. Wednesday night I am engaged to sup among some of the principals of the Excise: so can only make a call for you that evening; but next day, I stay to dine with one of the Commissioners, so cannot go till Friday morning.

Your hopes, your fears, your cares, my love, are mine; so don't mind them. I will take you in my hand through the dreary wilds of this world, and scare away the ravening bird or beast that would annoy you. I saw Mary in town to-day, and asked her if she had seen you. I shall certainly bespeak Mr. Ainslie as you desire.

Excuse me, my dearest angel, this hurried scrawl and miserable paper; circumstances make both. Farewell till to-morrow.

SYLVANDER.

Monday, Noon.

(33.) TO CLARINDA.

[8th April.]

I am just hurrying away to wait on the Great Man, Clarinda; but I have more respect to my own peace and happiness, than to set out without waiting on you; for my imagination, like a child's favourite bird, will fondly flutter along with this scrawl, till it perch on your bosom. I thank you for all the happiness you bestowed on me yesterday. The walk—delightful; the evening—rapture. Do not be uneasy to-day, Clarinda; forgive me. I am in rather better spirits to-day, though I had but an indifferent night. Care, anxiety, sat on my spirits; and all the cheerfulness of this morning is the fruit of some serious, important ideas that lie, in their

realities, beyond " the dark and the narrow house," as Ossian, prince of poets, says. The Father of Mercies be with you, Clarinda! and every good thing attend you!

SYLVANDER.

Tuesday Morning.

(34.) TO CLARINDA.

[This letter is printed from copy of original in possession of George Manners, Esq., F.S.A., Croydon, to whom we are indebted for other similar favours (see letter to Mrs. Dunlop (21).]

Wednesday Morning [9th April].

Clarinda, will that envious night-cap hinder you from appearing at the window as I pass? "Who is she that looketh forth as the morning; fair as the sun, clear as the moon, terrible as an army with banners?"

Do not accuse me of fond folly for this line; you know I am a cool lover. I mean by these presents greeting, to let you to wit, that arch-rasc—, Cr—ch, has not done my business yesternight, which has put off my leaving town till Monday morning. To-morrow, at eleven, I meet with him for the last time; just the hour I should have met far more agreeable company.

You will tell me this evening, whether you cannot make our hour of meeting to-morrow one o'clock. I have just now written Creech such a letter, that the very goose-feather in my hand shrunk back from the line, and seemed to say, "I exceedingly fear and quake!" I am forming ideal schemes of vengeance. O for a little of my will on him! I just wished that he loved as I do—as glorious an object as Clarinda—and that he were doomed . . . . .

Adieu, and think on

SYLVANDER.

(35.) TO CLARINDA.

Friday, Nine o'clock, Night [11th April].

I am just now come in, and have read your letter. The first thing I did was to thank the Divine Disposer of events, that he has had such happiness in store for me as the connexion I have with you. Life, my Clarinda, is a weary, barren path; and wo be to him or her that ventures on it alone! For me, I have my dearest partner of my soul: Clarinda and I will make out our pilgrimage together. Wherever I am, I shall constantly let her know how I go on, what I observe in the world around me, and what adventures I meet with. Will it please you, my love, to get, every week, or, at least, every fortnight, a packet, two or three sheets, full of remarks, nonsense, news, rhymes, and old songs?

Will you open, with satisfaction and delight, a letter from a man who loves you, who has loved you, and who will love you to death, through death, and for ever? Oh Clarinda! what do I owe to Heaven for blessing me with such a piece of exalted excellence as you! I call over your idea, as a miser counts over his treasure! Tell me, were you studious to

* G

please me last night? I am sure you did it to transport. How rich am I who have such a treasure as you! You know me; you know how to make me happy, and you do it most effectually. God bless you with

> "Long life, long youth, long pleasure, and a friend!"

To-morrow night, according to your own direction, I shall watch the window: 'tis the star that guides me to paradise. The great relish to all is, that Honour, that Innocence, that Religion, are the witnesses and guarantees of our happiness. "The Lord God knoweth," and, perhaps, "Israel he shall know," my love and your merit. Adieu, Clarinda! I am going to remember you in my prayers.

SYLVANDER.

(36.) TO CLARINDA.

March 9th, 1789.

MADAM,—The letter you wrote me to Heron's carried its own answer in its bosom; you forbade me to write you, unless I was willing to plead guilty to a certain indictment that you were pleased to bring against me. As I am convinced of my own innocence, and, though conscious of high imprudence and egregious folly, can lay my hand on my breast and attest the rectitude of my heart, you will pardon me, Madam, if I do not carry my complaisance so far, as humbly to acquiesce in the name of Villain, merely out of compliment to your opinion; much as I esteem your judgment, and warmly as I regard your worth.

I have already told you, and I again aver it, that, at the period of time alluded to, I was not under the smallest moral tie to Mrs. B——; nor did I, nor could I then know, all the powerful circumstances that omnipotent necessity was busy laying in wait for me. When you call over the scenes that have passed between us, you will survey the conduct of an honest man, struggling successfully with temptations, the most powerful that ever beset humanity, and preserving untainted honour, in situations where the austerest virtue would have forgiven a fall: situations that, I will dare to say, not a single individual of all his kind, even with half his sensibility and passion, could have encountered without ruin; and I leave you to guess, Madam, how such a man is likely to digest an accusation of perfidious treachery.

Was I to blame, Madam, in being the distracted victim of charms which, I affirm it, no man ever approached with impunity? Had I seen the least glimmering of hope that these charms could ever have been mine; or even had not iron necessity——But these are unavailing words.

I would have called on you when I was in town, indeed I could not have resisted it, but that Mr. Ainslie told me that you were determined to avoid your windows while I was in town, lest even a glance of me should occur in the street.

When I shall have regained your good opinion, perhaps I may venture to solicit your friendship; but, be that as it may, the first of her sex I ever knew shall always be the object of my warmest good wishes.

(37.) TO CLARINDA.

[Spring of 1791.]

I HAVE, indeed, been ill, Madam, this whole winter. An incessant headache, depression of spirits, and all the truly miserable consequences of a deranged nervous system, have made dreadful havoc of my health and peace. Add to all this, a line of life, into which I have lately entered, obliges me to ride, upon an average, at least two hundred miles every week. However, thank heaven I am now greatly better in my health.

 * * * * *

I cannot, will not, enter into extenuatory circumstances; else I could show you how my precipitate, headlong, unthinking conduct leagued with a conjuncture of unlucky events, to thrust me out of a possibility of keeping the path of rectitude; to curse me, by an irreconcileable war between my duty and my nearest wishes, and to damn me with a choice only of different species of error and misconduct.

I dare not trust myself further with this subject. The following song is one of my latest productions; and I send it you as I would do anything else, because it pleases myself.

[Song enclosed—"My Lovely Nancy."]

(38.) TO CLARINDA.

[Autumn of 1791.]

I HAVE received both your last letters, Madam, and ought, and would have answered the first, long ago. But on what subject shall I write you? How can you expect a correspondent should write you, when you declare that you mean to preserve his letters, with a view, sooner or later, to expose them on the pillory of derision, and the rack of criticism? This is gagging me completely, as to speaking the sentiments of my bosom, else, Madam, I could, perhaps, too truly

> "Join grief with grief, and echo sighs to thine!"

I have perused your most beautiful, but most pathetic Poem: do not ask me how often, or with what emotions. You know that "I dare to *sin*, but not to *lie!*" Your verses wring the confession from my inmost soul, that—I will say it, expose it if you please—that I have, more than once in my life, been the victim of a damning conjuncture of circumstances; and that to me you must be ever

> "Dear as the light that visits these sad eyes."

I have just, since I had yours, composed the following stanzas. Let me know your opinion of them.

> "Sweet Sensibility, how charming,
> Thou, my Friend, canst truly tell;
> But how Distress, with horrors arming,
> Thou, alas! hast known too well!
>
> Fairest Flower, behold the lily,
> Blooming in the sunny ray;
> Let the blast sweep o'er the valley,
> See it prostrate on the clay.

Hear the wood-lark charm the forest,
   Telling o'er his little joys;
But, alas! a prey the surest
   To each pirate of the skies.

Dearly bought the hidden treasure
   Finer feelings can bestow;
Cords that vibrate sweetest pleasure
   Thrill the deepest notes of wo."

I have one other piece in your taste; but I have just a snatch of time.

(39.)   TO CLARINDA.

ENCLOSING "LAMENT OF MARY, QUEEN OF SCOTS."

SUCH, my dearest Clarinda, were the words of the amiable but unfortunate Mary. Misfortune seems to take a peculiar pleasure in darting her arrows against "honest men and bonny lasses." Of this, you are too, too just a proof; but may your future fate be a bright exception to the remark! In the words of Hamlet,

   "Adieu, adieu, adieu! Remember me."

                                                SYLVANDER.

Leadhills, Thursday, Noon [11th December, 1791].

(40.)   TO CLARINDA.

Dumfries [15th December, 1791].

I HAVE some merit, my ever dearest of women, in attracting and securing the heart of Clarinda. In her I met with the most accomplished of all womankind, the first of all God's works; and yet I, even I, had the good fortune to appear amiable in her sight.

By the by, this is the sixth letter that I have written you since I left you; and if you were an ordinary being, as you are a creature very extraordinary—an instance of what God Almighty in the plenitude of his power, and the fulness of his goodness, can make!—I would never forgive you for not answering my letters.

I have sent in your hair, a part of the parcel you gave me, with a measure, to Mr Bruce the jeweller in Prince's Street, to get a ring done for me. I have likewise sent in the verses On Sensibility altered to

   "Sensibility how charming,
   Dearest Nancy, thou canst tell," &c.,

to the Editor of the Scots Songs, of which you have three volumes, to set to a most beautiful air; out of compliment to the first of women, my ever-beloved, my ever-sacred Clarinda. I shall probably write you to-morrow. In the meantime, from a man who is literally drunk, accept and forgive!

                                                R. B.

(41.)   TO CLARINDA.

Dumfries, 27th December, 1791.

I HAVE yours, my ever dearest Madam, this moment. I have just ten minutes before the post goes; and these I shall employ in sending you some songs I have just been composing to different tunes, for the Collection of Songs, of which you have three volumes, and of which you shall have the fourth.

The rest of this song is on the wheels.

                              Adieu.   Adieu.
                                                SYLVANDER.

Songs enclosed—" Ae fond kiss," " Behold the hour," " Ance mair, I hail thee."

(42.)   TO CLARINDA.

[Autumn of 1792.]

I SUPPOSE, my dear Madam, that by your neglecting to inform me of your arrival in Europe—a circumstance that could not be indifferent to me, as, indeed, no occurrence relating to you can—you meant to leave me to guess and gather that a correspondence I once had the honour and felicity to enjoy, is to be no more. Alas! what heavy-laden sounds are these—"No more!" The wretch who has never tasted pleasure, has never known wo; what drives the soul to madness, is the recollection of joys that are "no more!" But this is not language to the world: they do not understand it. But come, ye few—the children of Feeling and Sentiment!—ye whose trembling bosom-chords ache to unutterable anguish, as recollection gushes on the heart! —ye who are capable of an attachment, keen as the arrow of Death, and strong as the vigour of immortal being—come! and your ears shall drink a tale——But, hush! I must not, can not tell it; agony is in the recollection, and frenzy in the recital!

But, Madam—to leave the paths that lead to madness—I congratulate your friends on your return; and I hope that the precious health, which Miss P. tells me is so much injured, is restored, or restoring. There is a fatality attends Miss Peacock's correspondence and mine. Two of my letters, it seems, she never received; and her last came while I was in Ayrshire, was unfortunately mislaid, and only found about ten days or a fortnight ago, on removing a desk of drawers.

I present you a book: may I hope you will accept of it. I daresay you will have brought your books with you. The fourth volume of the Scots Songs is published; I will presume to send it you. Shall I hear from you? But first hear me. No cold language—no prudential documents: I despise advice, and scorn control. If you are not to write such language, such sentiments as you know I shall wish, shall delight to receive, I conjure you, by wounded pride! by ruined peace! by frantic, disappointed passion! by all the many ills that constitute that sum of human woes, a broken heart!!!—to me be silent for ever.

(13.)   TO CLARINDA.

[1793.]

BEFORE you ask me why I have not written you, first let me be informed by you, *how* I shall write you? " In friendship," you say; and I have many a time taken up my pen to try an epistle of " friendship " to you; but it will not do: 'tis like Jove grasping a pop-gun, after having wielded his thunder. When I take up the pen, recollection ruins me. Ah! my ever dearest Clarinda! Clarinda! What a host of memory's tenderest offspring crowd on my fancy at that sound! But I must not indulge that subject.—You have forbid it.

I am extremely happy to learn that your precious health is re-established, and that you are once more fit to enjoy that satisfaction in existence, which health alone can give us. My old friend Ainslie has indeed been kind to you. Tell him that I envy him the power of serving you. I had a letter from him a while ago, but it was so dry, so distant, so like a card to one of his clients, that I could scarce bear to read it, and have not yet answered it. He is a good honest fellow, and can write a friendly letter, which would do equal honour to his head and his heart, as a whole sheaf of his letters which I have by me will witness; and though Fame does not blow her trumpet at my approach now, as she did *then*, when he first honoured me with his friendship, yet I am as proud as ever; and when I am laid in my grave, I wish to be stretched at my full length, that I may occupy every inch of ground I have a right to.

You would laugh were you to see me where I am just now. Would to Heaven you were here to laugh with me, though I am afraid that crying would be our first employment. Here am I set, a solitary hermit, in the solitary room of a solitary inn, with a solitary bottle of wine by me, as grave and as stupid as an owl, but like that owl, still faithful to my old song; in confirmation of which, my dear Mrs Mac, here is your good health. May the hand-maid bonisons o' Heaven bless your bonnie face; and the wratch wha skellies at your welfare, may the auld tinkler deil get him to clout his rotten heart! Amen.

You must know, my dearest Madam, that these now many years, wherever I am, in whatever company, when a married lady is called as a toast, I constantly give you; but, as your name has never passed my lips, even to my most intimate friend, I give you by the name of Mrs Mac. This is so well known among my acquaintances, that when any married lady is called for, the toastmaster will say—" O, we need not ask him who it is: here's Mrs. Mac!" I have also, among my convivial friends, set on foot a round of toasts, which I call a round of Arcadian Shepherdesses; that is a round of favourite ladies, under female names celebrated in ancient song; and then you are my Clarinda. So, my lovely Clarinda, I devote this glass of wine to a most ardent wish for your happiness.

> In vain would Prudence, with decorous sneer,
> Point out a censuring world, and bid me fear;
> Above that world on wings of love I rise,
> I know its worst, and can that worst despise.

> " Wrong'd, injured, shunned, unpitied, unredrest;
> The mock'd quotation of the scorner's jest "—
> Let Prudence' direst bodements on me fall,
> Clarinda, rich reward! o'erpays them all.

I have been rhyming a little of late, but I do not know if they are worth postage.

Tell me what you think of the following monody.

*   *   *   *   *

The subject of the foregoing is a woman of fashion in this country, with whom at one period I was well acquainted. By some scandalous conduct to me, and two or three other gentlemen here as well as me, she steered so far to the north of my good opinion, that I have made her the theme of several ill-natured things. The following epigram struck me the other day as I passed her carriage.   *   *   *

[For Monody, Epitaph, Epigram, &c., see Posthumous Works, p. 341, &c.]

[Although we can hardly read the entire correspondence, of which the foregoing letters constitute but one side, without some qualms of apprehension for the moral rectitude of both parties concerned, the final conviction is that there was really no actual guilt between them; yet it was a narrow escape; and as Mrs. Jamieson remarks, applying the expressive words of Scripture to their situation, "they are saved, yet so as by fire." That such a correspondence should terminate without reproaches on both sides, was perhaps impossible; but no permanent unkindness seems to have been the result, nor perhaps any real mischief intended. Clarinda must have been blind indeed, if she did not see how it would all end. Her own sentiments of regard, however, for the gifted man by whom she had been so highly distinguished, seem to have continued undiminished during life, as the following words recorded in her diary, and published by her grandson, prove!

" *6th Dec.*, 1831.—This day I never can forget. Parted with Burns in the year 1791, never more to meet in this world.—Oh, may we meet in Heaven!"

And that Burns's regard for her was compatible, at least for a while, with genuine convictions both of religion and morality on his part, may be fairly enough inferred from such an inscription as the following in his own handwriting, on a copy of such a book as ' Young's Night Thoughts,' presented by himself to her.

To Mrs. M'Ilhose* this Poem, the sentiments of the heirs of immortality, told in the numbers of Paradise, is respectfully presented by   ROBT. BURNS.

* [So spelt.]

The date of this inscription cannot be exactly ascertained. It must have been sometime after the commencement of their acquaintance, however, for the date of the edition is 1788. Below the inscription the following note occurs, in the lady's own hand—

" Mrs. M'Lehose presents this Book to Mr. Kilpatrick Sharp as a small return for all his kindness."

This volume was sold along with the rest of Mr. Kirkpatrick Sharpe's books at Edinburgh in 1852, and is now the property of C. G. Clark, Esq., Dumfriesshire; by whose courtesy, through Dr. Grierson of Thornhill, we have a photograph of the inscription. The above writing in Mrs. M'Lehose's hand, bequeathing the volume to Mr. Sharpe, is marked with much trepidation and excitement. The syllables of the gentleman's first name, in fact, are completely transposed. The word stands actually thus—Mr. Calpitrick Sharp; being a strange accumulation of all his names at once, which were Charles Kirkpatrick Sharpe.]

To Miss Mary Peacock.

Dec. 6, 1792.

DEAR MADAM,

I HAVE written so often to you and have got no answer, that I had resolved never to lift up a pen to you again; but this eventful day, *the sixth of December*, recalls to my memory such a scene! Heaven and earth! when I remember a far-distant person!—but no more of this until I learn from you a proper address, and why my letters have lain by you unanswered, as this is the third I have sent you. The opportunities will be all gone now, I fear, of sending over the book I mentioned in my last. Do not write me for a week, as I shall not be at home, but as soon after that as possible.

> Ance mair I hail thee, thou gloomy December,
> Ance mair I hail thee wi' sorrow and care;
> Sdre was the parting thou bids me remember,
> Parting wi' Nancy, oh, ne'er to meet mair!

Yours,

R. B.

To Miss Williams,

ON READING HER POEM OF THE SLAVE-TRADE.

Ellisland [August], 1789.

MADAM,

Of the many problems in the nature of that wonderful creature, Man, this is one of the most extraordinary—that he shall go on from day to day, from week to week, from month to month, or perhaps from year to year, suffering a hundred times more in an hour from the impotent consciousness of neglecting what he ought to do, than the very doing of it would cost him. I am deeply indebted to you—first, for a most elegant poetic compliment; then for a polite, obliging letter; and, lastly, for your excellent poem on the Slave-Trade; and yet, wretch that I am! though the debts were debts of honour, and the creditor a lady, I have put off and put off even the very acknowledgment of the obligation, until you must indeed be the very angel I take you for if you can forgive me.

Your poem I have read with the highest pleasure. I have a way whenever I read a book—I mean a book in our own trade, Madam, a poetic one—and when it is my own property, that I take a pencil and mark at the ends of verses, or note on margins and odd paper, little criticisms of approbation or disapprobation as I peruse along. I will make no apology for presenting you with a few unconnected thoughts that occurred to me in my repeated perusals of your poem. I want to show you that I have honesty enough to tell you what I take to be truths, even when they are not quite on the side of approbation; and I do it in the firm faith that you have equal greatness of mind to hear them with pleasure.

I know very little of scientific criticism, so all I can pretend to in that intricate art is merely to note, as I read along, what passages strike me as being uncommonly beautiful, and where the expression seems to be perplexed or faulty.

The poem opens finely. There are none of those idle prefatory lines which one may skip over before one comes to the subject. Verses 9th and 10th in particular,

> "Where ocean's unseen bound
> Leaves a drear world of waters round."

are truly beautiful. The simile of the hurricane is likewise fine; and, indeed, beautiful as the poem is, almost all the similes rise decidedly above it. From verse 31st to verse 50th is a pretty eulogy on Britain. Verse 36th, "That foul drama deep with wrong," is nobly expressive. Verse 46th, I am afraid, is rather unworthy of the rest; "to dare to feel" is an idea that I do not altogether like. The contrast of valour and mercy, from the 46th verse to the 50th, is admirable.

Either my apprehension is dull, or there is something a little confused in the apostrophe to Mr. Pitt. Verse 55th is the antecedent to verses 57th and 58th, but in verse 58th the connexion seems ungrammatical:—

> "Powers . . . . .
> With no gradations mark'd their flight,
> But rose at once to glory's height."

Ris'n should be the word instead of rose. Try it in prose. Powers,—their flight mark'd by no gradations, but [the same powers] risen at once to the height of glory. Likewise, verse 53rd, "For this," is evidently meant to lead on the sense of the verses 59th, 60th, 61st, and 62nd; but let us try how the thread of connexion runs,—

> "For this . . . . .
> The deeds of mercy, that embrace
> A distant sphere, an alien race,
> Shall virtue's lips record and claim
> The fairest honours of thy name."

I beg pardon if I misapprehend the matter, but this appears to me the only imperfect passage in the poem. The comparison of the sunbeam is fine.

The compliment to the Duke of Richmond is, I hope, as just as it is certainly elegant. The thought,

> "Virtue . . . . .
> Sends from her unsullied source,
> The gems of thought their purest force,"

is exceedingly beautiful. The idea, from verse 81st to the 85th, that the "blest decree" is like the beams of morning ushering in the glorious day of liberty, ought not to pass unnoticed or unapplauded. From verse 85th to verse 108th, is an animated contrast between the unfeeling selfishness of the oppressor on the one hand, and the misery of the captive on the other. Verse 88th might perhaps be amended thus: "Nor ever quit her narrow maze." We are said to pass a bound, but we quit a maze. Verse 100th is exquisitely beautiful:—

> "They, whom wasted blessings tire."

Verse 110th is I doubt a clashing of metaphors; "to lend a span" is, I am afraid, an unwarrantable expression. In verse 114th, "Cast the universe in shade," is a fine idea. From the 115th verse to the 142nd is a striking description of the wrongs of the poor African. Verse 120th, "The load of unremitted pain," is a remarkable, strong expression. The address to the advocates for abolishing the slave-trade, from verse 143rd to verse 208th is animated with the true life of genius. The picture of oppression,—

> "While she links her impious chain,
> And calculates the price of pain;
> Weighs agony in sordid scales,
> And marks if life or death prevails,"—

is nobly executed.

What a tender idea is in verse 180th! Indeed, that whole description of home may vie with Thomson's description of home, somewhere in the beginning of his Autumn. I do not remember to have seen a stronger expression of misery than is contained in these verses:—

> "Condemned, severe extreme, to live
> When all is fled that life can give."

The comparison of our distant joys to distant objects is equally original and striking.

The character and manners of the dealer in the infernal traffic is a well done though a horrid picture. I am not sure how far introducing the sailor was right; for though the sailor's common characteristic is generosity, yet, in this case, he is certainly not only an unconcerned witness, but, in some degree, an efficient agent in the business. Verse 224th is a nervous . . . . expressive—"The heart convulsive anguish breaks." The description of the captive wretch when he arrives in the West Indies is carried on with equal spirit. The thought that the oppressor's sorrows on seeing the slave pine, is like the butcher's regret when his destined lamb dies a natural death, is exceedingly fine.

I am got so much into the cant of criticism, that I begin to be afraid lest I have nothing except the cant of it; and instead of elucidating my author, am only benighting myself. For this reason, I will not pretend to go through the whole poem. Some few remaining beautiful lines, however, I cannot pass over. Verse 280th is the strongest description of selfishness I ever saw. The comparison in verses 285th and 286th is new and fine; and the line, "Your arms to penury you lend," is excellent. In verse 317th, "like" should certainly be "as" or "so;" for instance—

> "He sway the hardened bosom leads
> To cruelty's remorseless deeds;
> As (or, so) the blue lightning when it springs
> With fury on its livid wings,
> Darts on the goal with rapid force,
> Nor heeds that ruin marks its course."

If you insert the word "like" where I have placed "as," you must alter "darts" to "darting," and "heeds" to "heeding," in order to make it grammar. A tempest is a favourite subject with the poets, but I do not remember anything even in Thomson's Winter superior to your verses from the 347th to 351st. Indeed, the last simile, beginning with "Fancy may dress," &c., and ending with the 356th verse, is, in my opinion, the most beautiful passage in the poem; it would do honour to the greatest names that ever graced our profession.

I will not beg your pardon, Madam, for these strictures, as my conscience tells me, that for once in my life I have acted up to the duties of a Christian, in doing as I would be done by.

I had lately the honour of a letter from Dr. Moore, where he tells me that he has sent me some books: they are not yet come to hand, but I hear they are on the way.

Wishing you all success in your progress in the path of fame; and that you may equally escape the danger of stumbling through incautious speed, or losing ground through loitering neglect. I am, &c.,

R. B.

To Mrs. Rose, of Kilravock.

Edinburgh, February 17th, 1788.

MADAM,

You are much indebted to some indispensable business I have had on my hands, otherwise my gratitude threatened such a return for your obliging favour as would have tired your patience. It but poorly expresses my feelings to say, that I am sensible of your kindness; it may be said of hearts such as yours is, and such, I hope, mine is, much more justly than Addison applies it,—

> "Some souls by instinct to each other turn."

There was something in my reception at Kilravock so different from the cold, obsequious, dancing-school bow of politeness, that it almost got into my head that friendship had occupied her ground without the intermediate march of acquaintance. I wish I could transcribe, or rather transfuse into language, the glow of my heart when I read your letter. My ready fancy, with colours more mellow than life itself, painted the beautifully wild scenery of Kilravock—the venerable grandeur of the castle—the spreading woods—the winding river, gladly leaving his unsightly, heathy source, and lingering with apparent delight as he passes the fairy walk at the bottom of the garden;—your late distressful anxieties—your present enjoyments—your dear little angel, the pride of your hopes;—my aged friend, venerable in worth and years, whose loyalty and other virtues will strongly entitle her to the support of the Almighty Spirit here, and his peculiar favour in a happier state of existence. You cannot imagine, Madam, how much such feelings delight me: they are my dearest proofs of my own immortality. Should I never revisit the north, as probably I never will, nor again see your hospitable mansion, were I, some twenty years hence, to see your little fellow's name making a proper figure in a newspaper paragraph, my heart would bound with pleasure.

I am assisting a friend in a collection of Scottish songs, set to their proper tunes; every air worth preserving is to be included: among others I have given "Morag," and some few Highland airs which pleased me most, a dress which will be more generally known, though far, far inferior in real merit. As a small mark of my grateful esteem, I beg leave to present you with a copy of the work, so far as it is printed: the Man of Feeling, that first of men, has promised to transmit it by the first opportunity.

I beg to be remembered most respectfully to my venerable friend, and to your little Highland chieftain. When you see the "two fair spirits of the hill," at Kildrummie, tell them that I have done myself the honour of setting myself down as one of their admirers for at least twenty years to come, consequently they must look upon me as an acquaintance for the same period; but, as the Apostle Paul says, "this I ask of grace, not of debt."

I have the honour to be, Madam, &c.,   R. B.

[Mrs. Rose, a most accomplished amiable woman, was the representative of a very ancient Highland family; with which, by his mother's side, Henry Mackenzie, author of "The Man of Feeling," was connected. The "dear little angel" referred to was Hugh, who lived to be twentieth laird of Kilravock; "my venerable friend," Mrs. Rose's mother; and the "two fair spirits of the hill," Miss Rose and a Miss Brodie.—Partly from Chambers.]

(1.)   ## To Miss Davies.

[Date uncertain.]

MADAM,

I UNDERSTAND my very worthy neighbour, Mr. Riddel, has informed you that I have made you the subject of some verses. There is something so provoking in the idea of being the burthen of a ballad, that I do not think Job or Moses, though such patterns of patience and meekness, could have resisted the curiosity to know what that ballad was: so my worthy friend has done me a mischief, which I daresay he never intended; and reduced me to the unfortunate alternative of leaving your curiosity ungratified, or else disgusting you with foolish verses, the unfinished production of a random moment, and never meant to have met your ear. I have heard or read somewhere of a gentleman who had some genius, much eccentricity, and very considerable dexterity with his pencil. In the accidental group of life into which one is thrown, wherever this gentleman met with a character in a more than ordinary degree congenial to his heart, he used to steal a sketch of the face, merely, he said, as a *nota bene*, to point out the agreeable recollection to his memory. What this gentleman's pencil was to him, my muse is to me; and the verses I do myself the honour to send you are a *memento* exactly of the same kind that he indulged in.

It may be more owing to the fastidiousness of my caprice than the delicacy of my taste; but I am so often tired, disgusted, and hurt with the insipidity, affectation, and pride of mankind, that when I meet with a person "after my own heart," I positively feel what an orthodox Protestant would call a species of idolatry, which acts on my fancy like inspiration; and I can no more desist rhyming on the impulse, than an Æolian harp can refuse its tones to the streaming air. A distich or two would be the consequence, though the object which hit my fancy were gray-bearded age; but where my theme is youth and beauty, a young lady whose personal charms, wit, and sentiment are equally striking and unaffected—by Heavens! though I had lived three score years a married man, and three score years before I was a married man, my imagination would hallow the very idea: and I am truly sorry that the enclosed stanzas have done such poor justice to such a subject.

    R. B.

[Stanzas enclosed—"Lovely Davies."]

———

(2.)   ### TO MISS DAVIES.

[Date uncertain.]

IT is impossible, Madam, that the generous warmth and angelic purity of your youthful mind, can have any idea of that moral disease under which I unhappily must rank as the chief of sinners; I mean a torpitude of the moral powers, that may be called, a lethargy of conscience. In vain Remorse rears her horrent crest, and rouses all her snakes:

beneath the deadly fixed eye and leaden hand of Indolence, their wildest ire is charmed into the torpor of the bat, slumbering out the rigours of winter in the chink of a ruined wall. Nothing less, Madam, could have made me so long neglect your obliging commands. Indeed I had one apology—the bagatelle was not worth presenting. Besides, so strongly am I interested in Miss Davies's fate and welfare in the serious business of life, amid its chances and changes, that to make her the subject of a silly ballad is downright mockery of these ardent feelings; 'tis like an impertinent jest to a dying friend.

Gracious Heaven! why this disparity between our wishes and our powers? Why is the most generous wish to make others blest, impotent and ineffectual—as the idle breeze that crosses the pathless desert! In my walks of life, I have met with a few people to whom how gladly would I have said—"Go, be happy! I know that your hearts have been wounded by the scorn of the proud, whom accident has placed above you—or worse still, in whose hands are, perhaps, placed many of the comforts of your life. But there! ascend that rock, Independence, and look justly down on their littleness of soul. Make the worthless tremble under your indignation, and the foolish sink before your contempt; and largely impart that happiness to others, which, I am certain, will give yourselves so much pleasure to bestow."

Why, dear Madam, must I wake from this delightful reverie, and find it all a dream? Why, amid my generous enthusiasm, must I find myself poor and powerless, incapable of wiping one tear from the eye of Pity, or of adding one comfort to the friend I love!—Out upon the world, say I, that its affairs are administered so ill! They talk of reform;—good Heaven! what a reform would I make among the sons and even the daughters of men!—Down, immediately, should go fools from the high places, where misbegotten chance has perked them up, and through life should they skulk, over haunted by their native insignificance, as the body marches accompanied by its shadow.—As for a much more formidable class, the knaves, I am at a loss what to do with them: had I a world, there should not be a knave in it.

But the hand that could give, I would liberally fill: and I would pour delight on the heart that could kindly forgive, and generously love.

Still the inequalities of life are, among men, comparatively tolerable—but there is a delicacy, a tenderness, accompanying every view in which we can place lovely Woman, that are grated and shocked at the rude, capricious distinctions of fortune. Woman is the blood-royal of life: let there be slight degrees of precedency among them—but let them be ALL sacred.—Whether this last sentiment be right or wrong, I am not accountable; it is an original component feature of my mind.

    R. B.

———

To Mrs. M'Murdo,

DRUMLANRIG.

Ellisland, 2nd May, 1789.

MADAM,

I HAVE finished the piece which had the happy fortune to be honoured with your approbation; and never did little miss with more sparkling pleasure show her applauded sampler to partial mamma, than I now send my poem to you and Mr. M'Murdo, if he is returned to Drumlanrig. You cannot easily imagine what thin-skinned animals—what sensitive plants poor poets are. How do we shrink into the embittered corner of self-abasement, when neglected or condemned by those to whom we look up! and how do we, in erect importance, add another cubit to our stature on being noticed and applauded by those whom we honour and respect! My late visit to Drumlanrig, has I can tell you, Madam, given me a balloon waft up Parnassus, where on my fancied elevation I regard my poetic self with no small degree of complacency. Surely with all their sins, the rhyming tribe are not ungrateful creatures. I recollect your goodness to your humble guest—I see Mr. M'Murdo adding to the politeness of the gentleman the kindness of a friend, and my heart swells as it would burst, with warm emotions and ardent wishes! It may be it is not gratitude—it may be a mixed sensation. That strange, shifting, doubling animal MAN is so generally, at best, but a negative, often a worthless creature, that we cannot see real goodness and native worth without feeling the bosom glow with sympathetic approbation.

With every sentiment of grateful respect,

I have the honour to be

Madam,

Your obliged and grateful humble servant,

R. B.

To Lady W[inifred] M[axwell] Constable.

(1.) *Ellisland, 16th December,* 1789.

MY LADY,

IN vain have I from day to day expected to hear from Mrs. Young, as she promised me at Dalswinton that she would do me the honour to introduce me at Tinwald; and it was impossible, not from your ladyship's accessibility, but from my own feelings, that I could go alone. Lately, indeed, Mr. Maxwell of Carruchan, in his usual goodness, offered to accompany me, when an unlucky indisposition on my part hindered my embracing the opportunity. To court the notice or the tables of the great, except where I sometimes have had a little matter to ask of them, or more often the pleasanter task of witnessing my gratitude to them, is what I never have done, and I trust never shall do. But with your ladyship I have the honour to be connected by one of the strongest and most endearing ties in the whole moral world.

Common sufferers, in a cause where even to be unfortunate is glorious, the cause of heroic loyalty! Though my fathers had not illustrious honours and vast properties to hazard in the contest, though they left their humble cottages only to add so many units more to the unnoted crowd that followed their leaders, yet what they could they did, and what they had they lost: with unshaken firmness and unconcealed political attachments, they shook hands with ruin for what they esteemed the cause of their king and their country. The language and the enclosed verses are for your ladyship's eye alone. Poets are not very famous for their prudence; but as I can do nothing for a cause which is now nearly no more, I do not wish to hurt myself.

I have the honour to be,

My lady,

Your ladyship's obliged and obedient

Humble Servant,

R. B.

[Verses enclosed—those addressed to Mr. William Tytler.]

(2.) TO LADY W. M. CONSTABLE.

Ellisland, 11th April, 1791.

MY LADY,

NOTHING less than the unlucky accident of having lately broken my right arm, could have prevented me, the moment I received your ladyship's elegant present by Mrs. Miller, from returning you my warmest and most grateful acknowledgments. I assure your ladyship, I shall set it apart—the symbols of religion shall only be more sacred. In the moment of poetic composition, the box shall be my inspiring genius. When I would breathe the comprehensive wish of benevolence for the happiness of others, I shall recollect your ladyship; when I would interest my fancy in the distresses incident to humanity, I shall remember the unfortunate Mary.

R. B.

[The elegant present referred to was the valuable snuff-box, containing on lid the beautiful inlaid miniature of Queen Mary, which, however, when in possession of one of the Poet's sons, was unfortunately irreparably damaged in India.]

To Lady Glencairn.

[*Ellisland, December,* 1789.]

MY LADY,

THE honour you have done your poor poet, in writing him so very obliging a letter, and the pleasure the enclosed beautiful verses have given him, came very seasonably to his aid, amid the cheerless gloom and sinking despondency of diseased nerves and December weather. As to forgetting the family of Glencairn, Heaven is my witness with what sincerity

I could use those old verses which please me more in their rude simplicity than the most elegant lines I ever saw:—

> "If thee, Jerusalem, I forget,
>   Skill part from my right hand.
>
> My tongue to my mouth's roof let cleave,
>   If I do thee forget,
> Jerusalem, and thee above
>   My chief joy do not set."

When I am tempted to do anything improper, I dare not, because I look on myself as accountable to your ladyship and family. Now and then, when I have the honor to be called to the tables of the great, if I happen to meet with any mortification from the stately stupidity of self-sufficient squires, or the luxurious insolence of upstart nabobs, I get above the creatures by calling to remembrance that I am patronised by the noble house of Glencairn; and at gala-times, such as New-year's day, a christening, or the Kirn-night, when my punch-bowl is brought from its dusty corner and filled up in honor of the occasion, I begin with *The Countess of Glencairn!* My good woman, with the enthusiasm of a grateful heart, next cries, *My Lord!* and so the toast goes on until I end with *Lady Harriet's little angel!* whose epithalamium I have pledged myself to write.

When I received your ladyship's letter, I was just in the act of transcribing for you some verses I have lately composed; and meant to have sent them my first leisure hour, and acquainted you with my late change of life. I mentioned to my lord my fears concerning my farm. Those fears were indeed too true; it is a bargain would have ruined me but for the lucky circumstance of my having an excise commission.

People may talk as they please of the ignominy of the excise; 50l. a year will support my wife and children, and keep me independent of the world; and I would much rather have it said that my profession borrowed credit from me, than that I borrowed credit from my profession. Another advantage I have in this business is the knowledge it gives me of the various shades of human character, consequently assisting me vastly in my poetic pursuits. I had the most ardent enthusiasm for the muses when nobody knew me but myself, and that ardour is by no means cooled now that my lord Glencairn's goodness has introduced me to all the world. Not that I am in haste for the press. I have no idea of publishing, else I certainly had consulted my noble generous patron; but after acting the part of an honest man, and supporting my family, my whole wishes and views are directed to poetic pursuits. I am aware that though I were to give performances to the world superior to my former works, still if they were of the same kind with those, the comparative reception they would meet with would mortify me. I have turned my thoughts on the drama. I do not mean the stately buskin of the tragic muse.   *   *   *   *   *

Does not your ladyship think that an Edinburgh theatre would be more amused with affectation, folly, and whim of true Scottish growth, than manners which by far the greatest part of the audience can only know at second hand?

I have the honor to be

Your ladyship's ever devoted and grateful humble servant,

R. B.

(1.)

To Mrs. Graham,

OF FINTRA.

Ellisland [February], 1791.

MADAM,

WHETHER it is that the story of our Mary, Queen of Scots, has a peculiar effect on the feelings of a poet, or whether I have, in the inclosed ballad, succeeded beyond my usual poetic success, I know not; but it has pleased me beyond any effort of my muse for a good while past; on that account I inclose it particularly to you. It is true, the purity of my motives may be suspected. I am already deeply indebted to Mr. Graham's goodness; and what, *in the usual ways of men*, is of infinitely greater importance, Mr. G. can do me service of the utmost importance in time to come. I was born a poor dog; and however I may occasionally pick a better bone than I used to do, I know I must live and die poor: but I will indulge the flattering faith that my poetry will considerably outlive my poverty; and without any fustian affectation of spirit, I can promise and affirm, that it must be no ordinary craving of the latter shall ever make me do anything injurious to the honest fame of the former. Whatever may be my failings, for failings are a part of human nature, may they ever be those of a generous heart, and an independent mind! It is no fault of mine that I was born to dependence; nor is it Mr. Graham's chiefest praise that he can command influence; but it is his merit to bestow, not only with the kindness of a brother, but with the politeness of a gentleman; and I trust it shall be mine to receive with thankfulness, and remember with undiminished gratitude.

R. B.

(2.)

TO MRS. GRAHAM.
[WITH NEW EDITION OF HIS POEMS.]

IT is probable, Madam, that this page may be read, when the hand that now writes it shall be mouldering in the dust: may it then bear witness that I present you these volumes as a tribute of gratitude, on my part ardent and sincere, as your and Mr. Graham's goodness to me has been generous and noble! May every child of yours, in the hour of need, find such a friend as I shall teach every child of mine, that their father found in you.

R. B.

To Lady E. Cunningham.

MY LADY,

I WOULD, as usual, have availed myself of the privilege your goodness has allowed me, of sending you any thing I compose in my poetical way; but as I had resolved, so soon as the shock of my irreparable loss would allow me, to pay a tribute to my late benefactor, I determined to make that the first piece I should do myself the honor of sending you. Had the wing of my fancy been equal to the ardor of my heart, the inclosed had been much more worthy your perusal: as it is, I beg leave to lay it at your ladyship's feet.

* H

As all the world knows my obligations to the late Earl of Glencairn, I would wish to shew as openly that my heart glows, and shall ever glow, with the most grateful sense and remembrance of his lordship's goodness. The sables I did myself the honor to wear to his lordship's memory, were not the "mockery of woe." Nor shall my gratitude perish with me!—If, among my children, I shall have a son that has a heart, he shall hand it down to his child as a family honor and a family debt, that my dearest existence I owe to the noble house of Glencairn!

I was about to say, my lady, that if you think the poem* may venture to see the light, I would, in some way or other, give it to the world.

R. B.

* ["Lament for James, Earl of Glencairn."]

To Miss Benson.

Dumfries, 21st of March, 1793.

MADAM,

AMONG many things for which I envy those hale, long-lived old fellows before the flood, is this in particular, that when they met with anybody after their own heart, they had a charming long prospect of many, many happy meetings with them in after-life.

Now in this short, stormy, winter day of our fleeting existence, when you now and then, in the Chapter of Accidents, meet an individual whose acquaintance is a real acquisition, there are all the probabilities against you, that you shall never meet with that valued character more. On the other hand, brief as this miserable being is, it is none of the least of the miseries belonging to it, that if there is any miscreant whom you hate, or creature whom you despise, the ill-run of the chances shall be so against you, that in the overtakings, turnings, and jostlings of life, pop, at some unlucky corner, eternally comes the wretch upon you, and will not allow your indignation or contempt a moment's repose. As I am a sturdy believer in the powers of darkness, I take these to be the doings of that old author of mischief, the devil. It is well-known that he has some kind of short-hand way of taking down our thoughts, and I make no doubt that he is perfectly acquainted with my sentiments respecting Miss Benson: how much I admired her abilities and valued her worth, and how very fortunate I thought myself in her acquaintance. For this last reason, my dear Madam, I must entertain no hopes of the very great pleasure of meeting with you again.

Miss Hamilton tells me that she is sending a packet to you, and I beg leave to send you the inclosed sonnet, though, to tell you the real truth, the sonnet is a mere pretence, that I may have the opportunity of declaring with how much respectful esteem I have the honor to be, &c.

R. B.

To Miss Craik.

Dumfries, August, 1793.

MADAM,

SOME rather unlooked-for accidents have prevented my doing myself the honor of a second visit to Arbeigland, as I was so hospitably invited, and so positively meant to have done.—However, I still hope to have that pleasure before the busy months of harvest begin.

I inclose you two of my late pieces, as some kind of return for the pleasure I have received in perusing a certain MS. volume of poems in the possession of Captain Riddel. To repay one with an *old song*, is a proverb, whose force you, Madam, I know, will not allow. What is said of illustrious descent is, I believe, equally true of a talent for poetry: none ever despised it who had pretensions to it. The fates and characters of the rhyming tribe often employ my thoughts when I am disposed to be melancholy. There is not, among all the martyrologies that ever were penned, so rueful a narrative as the lives of the poets. In the comparative view of wretches, the criterion is not what they are doomed to suffer, but how they are formed to bear. Take a being of our kind, give him a stronger imagination and a more delicate sensibility, which between them will ever engender a more ungovernable set of passions than are the usual lot of man; implant in him an irresistible impulse to some idle vagary, such as arranging wild flowers in fantastical nose-guys, tracing the grasshopper to his haunt by his chirping song, watching the frisks of the little minnows in the sunny pool, or hunting after the intrigues of butterflies—in short, send him adrift after some pursuit which shall eternally mislead him from the paths of lucre, and yet curse him with a keener relish than any man living for the pleasures that lucre can purchase; lastly fill up the measure of his woes by bestowing on him a spurning sense of his own dignity, and you have created a wight nearly as miserable as a poet. To you, Madam, I need not recount the fairy pleasures the muse bestows to counterbalance this catalogue of evils. Bewitching poetry is like bewitching woman; she has in all ages been accused of mis-leading mankind from the counsels of wisdom and the paths of prudence, involving them in difficulties, baiting them with poverty, branding them with infamy, and plunging them in the whirling vortex of ruin; yet, where is the man but must own that all our happiness on earth is not worth the name—that even the holy hermit's solitary prospect of paradisiacal bliss is but the glitter of a northern sun rising over a frozen region, compared with the many pleasures, the nameless raptures that we owe to the lovely Queen of the heart of Man!

R. B.

To Miss Fontenelle.

MADAM,

IN such a bad world as ours, those who add to the scanty sum of our pleasures are positively our benefactors. To you, Madam, on our humble Dumfries boards, I have been more indebted for entertainment than ever I was in prouder theatres.

Your charms as a woman would insure applause to the most indifferent actress, and your theatrical talents would insure admiration to the plainest figure. This, Madam, is not the unmeaning or insidious compliment of the frivolous or interested; I pay it from the same honest impulse that the sublime of nature excites my admiration, or her beauties give me delight.

Will the foregoing lines be of any service to you on your approaching benefit night? If they will, I shall be prouder of my muse than ever. They are nearly extempore: I know they have no great merit; but though they should add but little to the entertainment of the evening, they give me the happiness of an opportunity to declare how much I have the honor to be, &c.,   R. B.

[With "Prologue."]

To a Lady.

MADAM,

You were so very good as to promise me to honor my friend with your presence on his benefit night. That night is fixed for Friday first: the play a most interesting one—"The Way to Keep Him." I have the pleasure to know Mr. G. well. His merit as an actor is generally acknowledged. He has genius and worth which would do honor to patronage: he is a poor and modest man; claims which, from their very *silence*, have the more forcible power on the generous heart. Alas, for pity! that from the indolence of those who have the good things of this life in their gift, too often does brazen-fronted importunity snatch that boon, the rightful due of retiring, humble want! Of all the qualities we assign to the Author and Director of Nature, by far the most enviable is, to be able "to wipe away all tears from all eyes." O what insignificant, sordid wretches are they, however chance may have loaded them with wealth, who go to their graves, to their magnificent mausoleums, with hardly the consciousness of having made one poor honest heart happy!

But I crave your pardon, Madam; I came to beg, not to preach.   R. B.

(1.)   To Mrs. Riddel.

[In January, 1792, Mrs. Riddel had a letter of introduction from our Author to Mr. William Smellie, Printer, Edinburgh, with a view to the publication of her voyage to Madeira and the Leeward Islands. The following letter, which we extract from Mr. Waller's Catalogue (Fleet Street, London), seems to refer to a presentation copy of that or some other work, and was probably the commencement of their correspondence.]

MADAM,   [1792.]

I RETURN you my most sincere thanks for the honor you have done me in presenting me a copy of your book. Be assured I shall ever keep it sacred.   *   *   *
                    R. B.

(2.)   TO MRS. RIDDEL.

I AM thinking to send my "Address" to some periodical publication, but it has not got your sanction, so pray look over it.

As to the Tuesday's play, let me beg of you, my dear Madam, to give us "The Wonder, a Woman keeps a Secret;" to which please add "The Spoilt Child"—you will highly oblige me by so doing.

Ah, what an enviable creature you are! There now, this cursed, gloomy, blue-devil day, you are going to a party of choice spirits—

> "To play the shapes
> Of frolic fancy, and incessant form
> Those rapid pictures, that assembled train
> Of fleet ideas, never join'd before,
> Where lively wit excites to gay surprise;
> Or folly-painting humour, grave himself,
> Calls laughter forth, deep-shaking every nerve."

But as you rejoice with them that do rejoice, do also remember to weep with them that weep, and pity your melancholy friend.   R. B.

(3.)   TO MRS. RIDDEL.

I WILL wait on you, my ever-valued friend, but whether in the morning I am not sure. Sunday closes a period of our curst revenue business, and may probably keep me employed with my pen until noon. Fine employment for a poet's pen! There is a species of the human genus that I call the *gin-horse class:* what enviable dogs they are! Round, and round, and round they go—Mundell's ox that drives his cotton-mill is their exact prototype—without an idea or wish beyond their circle; fat, sleek, stupid, patient, quiet, and contented; while here I sit, altogether Novemberish, a d—mn'd melange of fretfulness and melancholy; not enough of the one to rouse me to passion, nor of the other to repose me in torpor; my soul flouncing and fluttering round her tenement, like a wild finch, caught amid the horrors of winter, and newly thrust into a cage. Well, I am persuaded that it was of me the Hebrew sage prophesied, when he foretold—"And behold, on whatsoever this man doth set his heart, it shall not prosper!" If my resentment is awaked, it is sure to be where it dare not squeak; and if—   *   *   *   *   *

Pray that Wisdom and Bliss be more frequent visitors of
                    R. B.

(4.)   TO MRS. RIDDEL.

[*November, 1793.*]

DEAR MADAM,

I MEANT to have called on you yesternight, but as I edged up to your box-door, the first object which greeted my view, was one of those lobster-coated puppies, sitting like another dragon, guarding the Hesperian fruit. On the conditions and capitulations you so obligingly offer, I shall certainly make my weather-beaten rustic phiz a part of your box-furniture on Tuesday; when we may arrange the business of the visit.
    *   *   *   *   *   *

Among the profusion of idle compliments, which insidious craft, or unmeaning folly, incessantly offer at your shrine—a shrine, how far exalted above such adoration—permit me, were it but for rarity's sake, to pay you the honest tribute of a warm heart and an independent mind; and to assure you, that I am, thou most amiable and most accomplished of thy sex, with the most respectful esteem, and fervent regard, thine, &c.,   R. B.

(5.)   TO MRS. RIDDEL.

'The following exquisite fragment we extract, with explanatory clauses, from Waller's (Fleet Street, London) Catalogue; in hopes that a copy of the entire original may yet be procured.'

Friday, Noon, 1793.

[Two pages of this admirable and characteristic letter are devoted to strictures upon French gloves—the fair lady to whom it was written had stated to the Poet she could not exist without French gloves.] Had fate put it in my power any way to have added one comfort to your existence, it could not, perhaps, have done anything which would have gratified me more. * * * In order that you may have the higher idea of my merits in this momentous affair, I must tell you that all the haberdashers here are on the alarm as to the necessary article of French gloves. You must know that French gloves are contraband goods, and expressly forbidden by the laws of this wise-governed realm of ours. A satirist would say this is the reason why the ladies are so fond of them; but I, who have not one grain of *Gall* in my composition, shall alledge that it is the patriotism of the dear goddesses of man's idolatry that makes them so fond of dress from the land of Liberty and Equality. [He continues in this vein of humour to inform her how] on the very respectable character of a revenue officer, three of the principal merchants had been subpœnaed before the Court of Exchequer (a crabbed law expression for being ruined in a revenue court). * * * Still I have discovered one haberdasher who, at my particular request, will clothe your fair hands as they ought to be, to keep them from being profaned by the rude gaze of the gloating eye, or—horrid! from perhaps a—by the unhallowed lips of the Satyr Man. * * * [So much for this important matter. He had received a long letter from Mr. Thomson. who presides over the publication of Scotch music, &c.] Would you honour the publication with a song from you? I have just sent him a new song to "The last time I came o'er the moor," but I don't know if I have succeeded. I enclose it for your strictures. Mary was the name I intended my heroine to bear, but I altered it into your ladyship's, as being infinitely more musical. * * * * * *

                      R. B.

(6.)   TO MRS. RIDDEL.

MADAM,

I DARE say this is the first epistle you ever received from this nether world. I write you from the regions of Hell, amid the horrors of the damned. The time and manner of my leaving your earth I do not exactly know, as I took my departure in the heat of a fever of intoxication, contracted at your too hospitable mansion; but, on my arrival here, I was fairly tried, and sentenced to endure the purgatorial tortures of this infernal confine for the space of ninety-nine years, eleven months, and twenty-nine days, and all on account of the impropriety of my conduct yesternight under your roof. Here am I, laid on a bed of pitiless furze, with my aching head reclined on a pillow of ever-piercing thorn, while an infernal tormentor, wrinkled, and old, and cruel, his name I think is *Recollection*, with a whip of scorpions, forbids

peace or rest to approach me, and keeps anguish eternally awake. Still, Madam, if I could in any measure be reinstated in the good opinion of the fair circle whom my conduct last night so much injured, I think it would be an alleviation to my torments. For this reason, I trouble you with this letter. To the men of the company I will make no apology. —Your husband, who insisted on my drinking more than I chose, has no right to blame me; and the other gentlemen were partakers of my guilt. But to you, Madam, I have much to apologize. Your good opinion I valued as one of the greatest acquisitions I had made on earth, and I was truly a beast to forfeit it. There was a Miss I—— too, a woman of fine sense, gentle and unassuming manners—do make, on my part, a miserable d—mned wretch's best apology to her. A Mrs. G——, a charming woman, did me the honor to be prejudiced in my favor; this makes me hope that I have not outraged her beyond all forgiveness.—To all the other ladies please present my humblest contrition for my conduct, and my petition for their gracious pardon. O all ye powers of decency and decorum! whisper to them that my errors, though great, were involuntary—that an intoxicated man is the vilest of beasts—that it was not in my nature to be brutal to any one—that to be rude to a woman, when in my senses, was impossible with me—but—

Regret! Remorse! Shame! ye three hell-hounds that ever dog my steps and bay at my heels, spare me! spare me!

Forgive the offences, and pity the perdition of, Madam, your humble slave,

                      R. B.

[This letter, it is to be regretted, in which the writer's own conduct was perhaps a good deal exaggerated, had no effect. Coldness, alienation, and hostility at last succeeded; during which, whilst it continued, many painful and ungenerous things were said.]

(7.)   TO MRS. RIDDEL.

MADAM,

I RETURN your Common-place Book. I have perused it with much pleasure, and would have continued my criticisms, but as it seems the critic has forfeited your esteem, his strictures must lose their value.

If it is true that "offences come only from the heart," before you I am guiltless. To admire, esteem, and prize you as the most accomplished of women, and the first of friends—if these are crimes, I am the most offending thing alive.

In a face where I used to meet the kind complacency of friendly confidence, now to find cold neglect, and contemptuous scorn—is a wrench that my heart can ill bear. It is, however, some kind of miserable good luck, that while *de haut-en-bas* rigour may depress an unoffending wretch to the ground, it has a tendency to rouse a stubborn something in his bosom, which, though it cannot heal the wounds of his soul, is at least an opiate to blunt their poignancy.

With the profoundest respect for your abilities; the most sincere esteem and ardent regard for your gentle heart and amiable manners; and the most fervent wish and prayer for your welfare, peace, and bliss, I have the honor to be, Madam,

        Your most devoted humble servant,

                      R. B.

(8.)　　TO MRS. RIDDEL.

I HAVE this moment got the song from Syme, and I am sorry to see that he has spoilt it a good deal. It shall be a lesson to me how I lend him any thing again.

I have sent you "Werter," truly happy to have any the smallest opportunity of obliging you.

'Tis true, Madam, I saw you once since I was at Woodley; and that once froze the very life-blood of my heart. Your reception of me was such, that a wretch meeting the eye of his judge, about to pronounce sentence of death on him, could only have envied my feelings and situation. But I hate the theme, and never more shall write or speak on it.

One thing I shall proudly say, that I can pay Mrs. R. a higher tribute of esteem, and appreciate her amiable worth more truly, than any man whom I have seen approach her; *nor will I yield the pas to any man living*, subscribing myself, with the sincerest truth, her devoted humble servant,

　　　　　R. B.

(9.)　　TO MRS. RIDDEL.

Dumfries, 1793.

MR. BURNS's compliments to Mrs. Riddel—is much obliged to her for her polite attention in sending him the book. Owing to Mr. B.'s being at present acting as supervisor of excise, a department that occupies his every hour of the day, he has not that time to spare which is necessary for any belle-lettre pursuit; but, as he will, in a week or two, again return to his wonted leisure, he will then pay that attention to Mrs. R.'s beautiful song, "To thee, loved Nith"—which it so well deserves. When "Anacharsis' Travels" come to hand, which Mrs. Riddel mentioned as her gift to the public library, Mr. B. will thank her for a reading of it previous to her sending it to the library, as it is a book Mr. B. has never seen: he wishes to have a longer perusal of them than the regulations of the library allow.

　　　　　Friday Eve.

P.S.—Mr. Burns will be much obliged to Mrs. Riddel if she will favour him with a perusal of any of her poetical pieces which he may not have soon.

(10.)　　TO MRS. RIDDEL.

[From original in possession of Thos. Chas. S. Corry, Esq., M.D., Belfast. Letter seems to refer to miniature of the Poet's eldest son, which is confessedly an admirable likeness of the boy; but no likeness in such a case ever satisfied a parent. See "Kerry Miniatures"—Appendix.]

　　　　　Saturday, 6 p.m., 1793.

PER accident, meeting with Mrs. Scott in the street, and having the miniature in a book in my pocket, I send you it; as I understand that a servant of yours is in town. The painter, in my opinion, has spoilt the likeness. Return me the bagatelle per first opportunity. I am so ill as to be scarce able to hold this miserable pen to this miserable paper.

　　　　　R. B.

[Here should be inserted an affecting letter on the death of his infant daughter, of which, however, as yet, only the concluding words are known to us:—

(11.) That you may never experience such a loss as mine, sincerely prays　　　　　R. B.]

(12.)　　TO MRS. RIDDEL.

[Partly from original in Dr. T. C. S. Corry's possession, Belfast.]

　　　　　Dumfries, 20th January, 1796.

I CANNOT express my gratitude to you for allowing me a longer perusal of "Anacharsis." In fact, I never met with a book that bewitched me so much; and I, as a member of the library, must warmly feel the obligation you have laid us under. Indeed, to me the obligation is stronger than to any other individual of our society; as "Anacharsis" is an indispensable desideratum to a son of the Muses.

The health you wished me in your morning's card is, I think, flown from me for ever. I have not been able to leave my bed to-day till about an hour ago. These wickedly unlucky advertisements I lent (I did wrong) to a friend, and I am ill able to go in quest of him.

The Muses have not quite forsaken me. The following detached stanzas I intend to interweave in some disastrous tale of a shepherd, "Despairing beside a clear stream."

L'amour, toujours l'amour! Volte Subito.

　　The trout in yonder wimpling burn
　　That glides, a silver dart, &c.

Have you seen Clarke's Sonatas, the subjects from Scots airs? If not, send for my copy.

　　　　　R. B.

(13.)　　TO MRS. RIDDEL.

[From original in possession of George Masners, Esq., F.S.A., Croydon.]

　　　　　1796.

I THINK there is little doubt but that your interests, if judiciously directed, may procure, may procure' a tide-waiter's place for your protegé, Shaw; but, alas, that is doing little for him! Fifteen pounds per ann. is the salary; and the perquisites, in some lucky stations, such as Leith, Glasgow, Greenock, may be ten more; but in such a place as this, for instance, they will hardly amount to five. The appointment is not in the Excise, but in the Customs. The way of getting appointed, is just the application of great folks to the Commissioners of the Customs; the almanack will give you their names. The Excise is a superiour object, as the salary is fifty per annum. You mention that he has a family: if he has more than three children he cannot be admitted as an Excise officer. To apply there, is the same business as at the Customs. Garthland, if you can commit his sincere zeal in the cause, is, I think, able to do either the one or the other. Find out, among your acquaintances, who are the private friends of the Commissioners of the particular Board at which you wish to apply, and interest them—the more, the better. The Commissioners of both Boards are people quite in the fashionable circles, and must be known to many of your friends. I was going to mention some of your female acquaintance who might give you a lift, but, on recollection, your interest with the Women is, I believe, but a sorry business. So much the better! 'tis God's judgment upon you for making such a despotic use of your sway over the Men. You a Republican! You have an Empire over us; and you know it too; but the Lord's holy name be praised, you have something of the same propensity to get giddy (intoxicated is not a lady's word) with power; and a devilish deal of aptitude to the same blind undistinguishing Favoritism, which make other Despots less dangerous to the welfare and repose of mankind than they otherwise might be. So much for scolding you. I have perused your MSS. with a great deal of pleasure. I have taken the liberty to make a few marks with my pencil, which I trust you will pardon. Farewel!

R. B.

* [This repetition occurs in original, and seems to indicate either the abstraction or the earnestness of the writer's mind at the moment.]

(14.)   TO MRS. RIDDEL.

1796.

I HAVE perused with great pleasure your elegiac verses. In two or three instances I mark inequalities rather than faults. A line that in an ordinary mediocre production might pass, not only without censure, but with applause, in a brilliant composition glares in all its native halting inferiority. The last line of the second stanza I dislike most. If you cannot mend it (I cannot, after beating my brains to pap), I would almost leave out the whole stanza. *A Dieu je vous recommende.*

R. B.

(15.)   TO MRS. RIDDEL.

ON Monday, my dear Madam, I shall most certainly do myself the honour of waiting on you, whether the Muses will wait on me is, I fear, dubious. Please accept a new song which I have this moment received from Urbania. It is a trifling present, but—'Give all thou canst.'

R. B.

(16.)   TO MRS. RIDDEL.

Dumfries, 4th June, 1796.

I AM in such miserable health as to be utterly incapable of showing my loyalty in any way. Rackt as I am with rheumatisms, I meet every face with a greeting, like that of Balak to Balaam—" Come, curse me Jacob; and come, defy me Israel!" So say I—Come, curse me that east wind; and come, defy me the north! Would you have me in such circumstances copy you out a love-song?

*   *   *   *   *

I may perhaps see you on Saturday, but I will not be at the ball.*—Why should I? "man delights not me, nor woman either!" Can you supply me with the song, "Let us all be unhappy together?"—do if you can, and oblige, *le pauvre misérable*

R. B.

* [Birth-day Assembly.]

(17.)   TO MRS. RIDDEL.

I HAVE often told you, my dear friend, that you had a spice of caprice in your composition, and you have as often disavowed it; even perhaps while your opinions were, at the moment, irrefragably proving it. Could *any thing* estrange me from a friend such as you?—No! To-morrow I shall have the honor of waiting on you.

Farewell, thou first of friends, and most accomplished of women; even with all thy little caprices!

R. B.

[This seems to be acknowledging Mrs. Riddel's invitation to dine with her at Brow: the last time the Poet saw her—when he inquired if she had any commands for the other world.]

To Miss ———,

[*Dumfries, May or June,* 1794?]

MADAM,

NOTHING short of a kind of absolute necessity could have made me trouble you with this letter. Except my ardent and just esteem for your sense, taste, and worth, every sentiment arising in my breast, as I put pen to paper to you, is painful. The scenes I have past with the friend of my soul, and his amiable connexions! the wrench at my heart to think that he is gone, for ever gone from me, never more to meet in the wanderings of a weary world! and the cutting reflection of all, that I had most unfortunately, though most undeservedly, lost the confidence of that soul of worth, ere it took its flight! —these, Madam, are sensations of no ordinary anguish. However you also may be offended with some *imputed* improprieties of mine, sensibility you know I possess, and sincerity none will deny me.

To oppose those prejudices which have been raised against me, is not the business of this letter. Indeed, it is a warfare I know not how to wage. The powers of positive vice I can in some degree calculate, and against direct malevolence I can be on my guard; but who can estimate the fatuity of giddy caprice, or ward off the unthinking mischief of precipitate folly?

I have a favor to request of you, Madam; and of your sister, Mrs. [Riddel], through your means. You know that, at the wish of my late friend, I made a collection of all my trifles in verse which I had ever written. They are many of them local, some of them puerile and silly, and all of them unfit for the public eye. As I have some little fame at stake —a fame that I trust may live when the hate of those 'who watch for my halting,' and the contumelious sneer of those whom accident has made my superiors, will, with themselves, be gone to the regions of oblivion—I am uneasy now for the fate of those manuscripts. Will Mrs. [Riddel] have the goodness to destroy them, or return them to me? As a pledge of friendship they were bestowed; and that circumstance, indeed, was all their merit. Most unhappily for me, that merit they no longer possess; and I hope that Mrs. [Riddel]'s goodness, which I well know, and ever will revere, will not refuse this favor to a man whom she once held in some degree of estimation. With the sincerest esteem, I have the honor to be, Madam, &c.,

R. B.

[The Mrs. Riddel here referred to was the widow of Captain Riddel, of Friars-Carse.]

LITERARY CORRESPONDENCE.

BIOGRAPHICAL REMARKS.

BURNS AS PROFESSIONAL LETTER-WRITER.

Of Annibal Caro, incontestibly one of the most accomplished letter-writers in Europe, we shall have occasion hereafter to speak more fully: in the meantime, taking even him into account, we must observe that scarcely any letter-writer, whose unrevised indiscriminate correspondence pertains to us, has manifested such an extraordinary power of adapting himself in style and language simultaneously to such a variety of characters, and of attaining at the same time so perfectly the object of correspondence with all, as Robert Burns. To the plainest and the most fastidious; to men, to women, to children almost in capacity, he is precisely what he should be; and whether any of his innumerable epistles failed for the moment of producing the desired effect, they were all, or nearly all, that could be imagined or written most appropriate in the circumstances. That he had the heartiest ambition to excel in this difficult department of literary workmanship, is obvious; and would be obvious from a thousand marks in his epistles themselves, although we had no direct avowal of the fact under his own hand. It was his earliest study, and his most fascinating pursuit, in which he attained at last an ease and perfection rarely equalled by the most accomplished, and never excelled.

On his letter-writing to women we have already had an opportunity of commenting, and have also had an opportunity of judging of its variety, of its beauty, of its singular fitness for the correspon-dent's claims in rank, in taste, or disposition, in every individual case. Of his Literary, or what may be called his Professional Correspondence, we have now to speak, in which the same characteristics of artistic discrimination are apparent, but with greater latitude and license, as the case imports. His style in these literary communications is, distinctly, of two sorts. We have traces indeed of a third, instinctively adopted in certain peculiar cases, which does honour to his heart as well as to his head; although these specimens are too inconsiderable, perhaps, to merit a division by themselves. The two grand departments of his literary correspondence are those which include (1) the formal studied communications to men who were not only friends and patrons of his own, but acknowledged authorities themselves in the literary, or in the fashionable, world: and (2) the no less studied but much freer communications in which he himself was either the literary patron, or highest imaginable literary authority, for the time. The third sort, of which we have only a few examples (in connection at least with literary subjects), includes those special communications in which he addresses, with the respect and deference due to their position or character, the ministers of religion; or with the mingled authority and consideration suggested by circumstances, those who might apply to him for assistance or advice. To correspondents in each and all of these various classes, and to every man in his degree, are these literary communications of his adapted—with a freedom, a minuteness, and a propriety of diction that is truly astonishing.

The rudiments of his more formal style, as being that to which a young man almost invariably first addicts himself, and which is indeed most suitable always in certain cases, are to be found in those early studied fragments of which he has preserved us a selection from note books, &c., in his epistle to Captain Riddel. This style was suggested by his boyish admiration of Steele and Addison and other courtly letter-writers of that age, specimens of whose works were made slightly familiar to him at school; and it was cultivated with secret assiduous devotion, in ambitious rivalry of their finest models. Disraeli the elder, in his essay on the Literary Character, laments that the sketch of himself thus begun by Burns, in that epistle of his to Captain Riddel, was never completed; and satisfies himself by observing that " It was natural for such a creature of sensation and passion to project such a regular task, but quite impossible to get through it." Considerable additional portions of the documents from which that epistle was compiled, have been discovered and published, since Disraeli wrote; but they do not tend to throw much more light on the subject. The fact seems to be, that most of the entries are studiously sententious and reflective, after the fashion of a regular methodistical diary, and do not afford half so expressive an outline of the man's existence and character as his unpremeditated effusions to his fellow-men do. This studied style was not his happiest nor his truest; although he carried it to a point of perfection rarely attained even by its professed representatives. The style itself, which was formal at first, but by the infusion of higher elements became at last courtly in the highest sense, in tone and terms, continued with him throughout, but with an immense difference in ease or adaptation, as compared with his own original efforts, and even with the finest specimens of his admired original models. The letters in which this style is most conspicuous, although it gradually melts away towards the close, are those addressed to such noble patrons as Eglinton, or Glencairn, and partially to Buchan; or to literary magnates for the time, such as Dugald Stewart, Blair, and Moore. The letters to Moore,

indeed, of this type, are not only the most considerable, but the finest specimens of our Author in this kind extant. Of the celebrated autobiography addressed to that gentleman, after long consideration and much misgiving on the writer's part, as we learn from the Poet's own letter on the subject to Mrs. Dunlop, we cannot, after the most careful study, speak in the same very highest terms of critical eulogy in which Professor Wilson mentions it; for there are passages in it undoubtedly a little forced, and not a little stilted, in which style still contends with nature, and even with truth, to the disadvantage of both. But to be the first outline of his own life written by such a man in his then circumstances, and to such an authority at the moment, it is unquestionably both a wonderful and an admirable performance. On the other hand, his succeeding letters to Dr. Moore, all in the same style, are masterpieces of the sort; and the letter immediately succeeding, in which reference to Mr. Graham of Fintry occurs, is as near perfection in its way (and that a most difficult way) as any document written by a human pen. To criticise the various peculiar literary and artistic excellences of these letters, and to point out how the courtly and the familiar and the practical blend, and how the whole is uniquely fine, is unnecessary. The reader who cannot perceive and relish these points is beyond instruction: he does not know what a letter means, and never wrote one.

Of the same formal and deferential style, mixed with a tone of genuine respect and even reverence, is his correspondence with the clergy, or with persons in their position, where his faith in their own piety or respectability inspired such sentiments. With them, in such cases, he never jests, nor approaches them otherwise than as a gentlemanly correspondent should. His prejudices against the profession, too well founded in general at the time, neither blinded him to the highest claims of individuals, nor affected in the least degree the becoming and truly religious tenor of his correspondence with good or pious men.

That other style, however, which is by far the most frequent in his correspondence, and which is directly opposed to the formal or courtly, and may be described in a word as the natural or familiar, is characterised by the most apparently unstudied ease, the most unconditional freedom, the most extravagant abandon, and occasional license. It was in this sort of correspondence, confined entirely to persons of his own sex, that what may be called his natural want of reserve or reverence showed itself—more strongly even than in such extraordinary poetical productions as "Holy Willie's Prayer." Characteristic specimens of this style occur most frequently, perhaps, in his general correspondence; although in his literary correspondence also, more especially in his letters to Thomson and to Hill, strong enough illustrations of it, as the reader will soon discover, are to be found. His literary correspondence, however, even of this sort, is by no means to be mistaken for mere random or unlicensed letter-writing. It has indeed a character of its own, in freedom and in recklessness, appropriate enough to the various subjects as well as to the correspondents themselves, of which, or to whom he wrote; and might have been insipid or unnatural otherwise—which nothing from him could ever be. But the amazing readiness and extent of illustration, the variety of knowledge, the keen critical discernment, the inexhaustible humour, and inimitable charm of diction on the dullest theme, by which dross and ditch-water themselves seem to be illuminated, give a far higher tone to this very correspondence, than any mere literary abandon or the most sparkling profligacy of idea could ever communicate. What may be lost or hidden of this kind we know not, and will never inquire; but of what remains we can form no other honest judgment, than that it is the workmanship of one of the most gifted, accomplished, powerful, and versatile letter-writers that ever lived.

The date of this style in perfection was not till towards the concluding epoch of his life, when his powers were fully matured, and the fear of society or the restraints of competition had vanished. We have first the young man's solemn prose efforts, forced and formal enough, who was conscious of a great and glowing nature within him, but conscious of what seemed for the moment to be a greater, or at least a grander, model beyond him: we have then the courtly style to which these formal efforts naturally conducted, in which they are for a while visible, but in which they are ultimately lost or mellowed—as the green, hard, polished fruit is in the richness and roundness of maturity, and in which the heat and splendour of the inner man are

now dominant: and finally, we have the unrestrained, unmeasured effusions of that nature kindled and sometimes inflamed to the uttermost, on topics that might tempt to such freedom of display, or to correspondents alone who relished or provoked it; which was by no means always unblameable, but always brilliant and characteristic in a high degree. In the current of this correspondence, all ideas of restraint seem to have been abandoned, and all fear of competition out of the question. He had nobody's taste to consult but that of correspondents whom it would be difficult to displease; to whom in all literary respects he was absolutely superior, and on whose part any attempt at rivalry with him, even in license, would have been ridiculous. His correspondence in these latter years, therefore, might thus easily in many cases assume a questionable form; but it is to be remarked also, that wherever his own opinion in any mere critical discussion, or his own predilection on any favourite topic, or even his own feelings and interests as an author were concerned, in opposition to others—his modesty, his forbearance, and his self-denial together, are an example to mankind. So much, without fear of contradiction, we thus unreservedly affirm.

As a mere psychological study, this progressive change of style, and increase of license with increase of strength, is a most instructive theme. Topics, characters, opportunities, and years crowd in upon the man; faculties and freedom extend together; formulas of speech, once considered most elegant or appropriate, are gradually discarded or dropt, even in the presence of the great, as stilted, or shallow, or insincere; strength, fire, headlong eloquence, with the most difficult yet perfect involutions of speech, succeed; daring parallels, and yet more daring quotations, are often introduced with a levity that startles the most indifferent, and may possibly offend the devout: the man, in fact, seems to be revolutionised: yet, throughout the whole, the sense of beauty is never once obscured, nor the principles of benevolence, of tenderness, or of truth compromised in a hair's-breadth. Not even, when he visibly staggers on the very brink of mischief or distraction, does a single profane syllable escape his lips in the ear of woman; nay, so deeply does he venerate her nature, and so profoundly does he feel the loss of her respect or love, that when all offences are forgiven, he absolutely revels like an eagle in the restored sunshine of some fair correspondent's eyes. In many respects, these letters are more wonderful than his poems; and their study, after such philosophical fashion, an occupation as well as an amusement, to which the wisest reader may incline.

The subdivision or arrangement of our Author's literary correspondence, or rather to determine precisely where the line should be drawn between the literary and the general departments, has been a matter of some difficulty. By common arrangement, the literary correspondence is limited exclusively to his letters to Thomson, which are no doubt both literary and critical in the highest degree. But the letters to Johnson, although comparatively few, and in that sense unimportant, belong to the same category, and therefore ought not to be excluded; whilst the letters to Moore, and the earlier specimens of composition selected by our Author himself, at a later date, in his epistle addressed to Captain Riddel, are equally important in their own department. In a philosophical point of view, indeed, as we have already intimated, they are of the very highest importance; and in other respects have equal claims to a purely literary designation. These, therefore, without much hesitation, we have included in our selection; and as they are all of earlier dates, we have assigned them also precedence in place, as principal documents.

Of the strictly critical or literary correspondence itself there are two sorts, which we separate by distinctive titles accordingly—the one Principal, and the other Subsidiary or Subordinate. The Principal includes all the letters addressed directly to Johnson or to Thomson, about the proper position of which in the entire correspondence there can be no doubt: why they should ever have been separated we cannot understand. That there should be so few letters to Johnson now extant is indeed much to be regretted; but how their number should be so limited, except by accidental loss, we know not. The letters to Thomson, on the other hand, are so numerous, so well known, and so remarkable for their literary value in relation to Scottish song and music, that no commentary, beyond directing the reader's attention to them thus, is required; and having been carefully preserved and early submitted to editorial examina-

tion, they have been long before the world, as far as the world has a right to know them, in their own entirety.

Letters which we call Subsidiary or Subordinate, in a literary or sometimes in a critical point of view (for these terms are not always identical), are either such as were addressed on literary business to booksellers, publishers, editors, or collectors, with a view to obtain assistance and co-operation in literary work, or in some other way to promote the success of literary enterprise; such, for example, as the letters to Hill, Hoy, and Skinner; or such, on the other hand, as were addressed occasionally or accidentally to literary characters, although not expressly on his own literary concerns; or to others who had some sort of interest in literature, and, either as friends or admirers, found it expedient or agreeable to cultivate his acquaintance. Such we need hardly particularise, because they are comparatively few, and will be easily discriminated by their very style and titles.

The only sort of letters about the introduction of which in this division of our Author's correspondence, under any title whatever, we had some doubt, were those which are addressed directly to aristocratic patrons, or powerful political friends, with the avowed object of acknowledging their kindness or requesting the exercise of their influence in his favour. Such letters, although not strictly entitled to rank as purely literary productions, are just as far removed from what is commonly called general correspondence. They are at least elaborately, carefully, and, as a matter of course, elegantly written; and, as they refer to the prospects and interests of a man whose very existence was divided between the cultivation of literature and the painfullest anxieties of ordinary life, from which anxieties he was struggling in vain by these very applications to escape, they are admitted as subordinate within the limits of his literary correspondence, on these grounds.

Finally, there are one or two letters besides these, of a literary character to some extent, but so much mixed up with other letters on miscellaneous or indifferent topics, addressed to the same correspondent (Cunningham, for example), that we cannot prudently separate them from the rest, and reserve them therefore for a place with others in the next division of our work.

CORRESPONDENCE.

PRINCIPAL.

To Robert Riddel, Esq.
OF GLENRIDDEL.

MY DEAR SIR,

ON rummaging over some old papers I lighted on a MS. of my early years, in which I had determined to write myself out; as I was placed by fortune among a class of men to whom my ideas would have been nonsense. I had meant that the book should have lain by me, in the fond hope that some time or other, even after I was no more, my thoughts would fall into the hands of somebody capable of appreciating their value. It sets off thus:—

"OBSERVATIONS, HINTS, SONGS, SCRAPS OF POETRY, &c., by ROBERT BURNESS; a man who had little art in making money, and still less in keeping it; but was, however, a man of some sense, a great deal of honesty, and unbounded good-will to every creature, rational and irrational.—As he was but little indebted to scholastic education, and bred at a plough-tail, his performances must be strongly tinctured with his unpolished, rustic way of life; but as I believe they are really his own, it may be some entertainment to a curious observer of human nature to see how a ploughman thinks, and feels, under the pressure of love, ambition, anxiety, grief, with the like cares and passions, which, however diversified by the modes and manners of life, operate pretty much alike, I believe, on all the species."

"There are numbers in the world who do not want sense to make a figure, so much as an opinion of their own abilities to put them upon recording their observations, and allowing them the same importance which they do to those which appear in print."—SHENSTONE.

"Pleasing, when youth is long expired, to trace
The forms our pencil, or our pen design'd!
Such was our youthful air, and shape, and face,
Such the soft image of our youthful mind."—*Ibid.*

April, 1783.

Notwithstanding all that has been said against love, respecting the folly and weakness it leads a young inexperienced mind into; still I think it in a great measure deserves the highest encomiums that have been passed upon it. If any thing on earth deserves the name of rapture or transport, it is the feelings of green eighteen in the company of the mistress of his heart, when she repays him with an equal return of affection.

August.

There is certainly some connexion between love, and music, and poetry; and therefore, I have always thought it a fine touch of nature, that passage in a modern love composition:

"As towards her cot he jogg'd along,
Her name was frequent in his song."

For my own part I never had the least thought or inclination of turning poet till I got once heartily in love, and then rhyme and song were in a manner the spontaneous language of my heart. The following composition was the first of my performances, and done at an early period of my life, when my heart glowed with honest warm simplicity; unacquainted and uncorrupted with the ways of a wicked world. The performance is, indeed, very puerile and silly; but I am always pleased with it, as it recalls to my mind those happy days when my heart was yet honest, and my tongue was sincere. The subject of it was a young girl who really deserved all the praises I have bestowed on her. I not only had this opinion of her then—but I actually think so still, now that the spell is long since broken, and the enchantment at an end.

O once I lov'd a bonnie lass.

Lest my works should be thought below criticism; or meet with a critic, who, perhaps, will not look on them with so candid and favourable an eye, I am determined to criticise them myself.

The first distich of the first stanza is quite too much in the flimsy strain of our ordinary street ballads; and, on the other hand, the second distich is too much in the other extreme. The expression is a little awkward, and the sentiment too serious. Stanza the second I am well pleased with; and I think it conveys a fine idea of that amiable part of the sex —the agreeables; or what in our Scotch dialect we call a sweet sonsie lass. The third stanza has a little of the flimsy turn in it; and the third line has rather too serious a cast. The fourth stanza is a very indifferent one; the first line, is, indeed, all in the strain of the second stanza, but the rest is mere expletive. The thoughts in the fifth stanza come finely up to my favourite idea—a sweet sonsie lass: the last line, however, halts a little. The same sentiments are kept up with equal spirit and tenderness in the sixth stanza, but the second and fourth lines ending with short syllables hurt the whole. The seventh stanza has several minute faults; but I remember I composed it in a wild enthusiasm of passion, and to this hour I never recollect it but my heart melts, my blood sallies, at the remembrance.

*   *   *   *   *   *   *

[See song, " Handsome Nell," p. 186.]

September.

I entirely agree with that judicious philosopher, Mr. Smith, in his excellent Theory of Moral Sentiments, that remorse is the most painful sentiment that can embitter the human bosom. Any ordinary pitch of fortitude may bear up tolerably well under those calamities, in the procurement of which we ourselves have had no hand; but when our own follies, or crimes, have made us miserable and wretched, to bear up with manly firmness, and at the same time have a proper penitent sense of our misconduct, is a glorious effort of self-command.

> Of all the numerous ills that hurt our peace,
> That press the soul, or wring the mind with anguish,
> Beyond comparison the worst are those
> That to our folly or our guilt we owe.
> In every other circumstance, the mind
> Has this to say, ' It was no deed of mine;'
> But when to all the evil of misfortune
> This sting is added—' Blame thy foolish self:'
> Or worser far, the pangs of keen remorse;
> The torturing, gnawing consciousness of guilt—
> Of guilt, perhaps, where we've involved others;
> The young, the innocent, who fondly lov'd us,
> Nay, more, that very love their cause of ruin!
> O burning hell; in all thy store of torments
> There's not a keener lash!
> Lives there a man so firm, who, while his heart
> Feels all the bitter horrors of his crime,
> Can reason down its agonizing throbs;
> And, after proper purpose of amendment,
> Can firmly force his jarring thoughts to peace?
> O, happy! happy! enviable man!
> O glorious magnanimity of soul!

*   *   *   *   *   *   *

March, 1784.

I have often observed, in the course of my experience of human life, that every man, even the worst, has something good about him; though very often nothing else than a happy temperament of constitution inclining him to this or that virtue. For this reason, no man can say in what degree any person, besides himself, can be, with strict justice, called wicked. Let any of the strictest character for regularity of conduct among us examine impartially how many vices he has never been guilty of, not from any care or vigilance, but for want of opportunity, or some accidental circumstance intervening; how many of the weaknesses of mankind he has escaped, because he was out of the line of such temptation; and, what often, if not always, weighs more than all the rest, how much he is indebted to the world's good opinion, because the world does not know all: I say, any man who can thus think, will scan the failings, nay, the faults and crimes, of mankind around him, with a brother's eye.

I have often courted the acquaintance of that part of mankind, commonly known by the ordinary phrase of blackguards, sometimes farther than was consistent with the safety of my character; those who, by thoughtless prodigality or headstrong passions, have been driven to ruin. Though disgraced by follies, nay, sometimes, stained with guilt, I have yet found among them, in not a few instances, some of the noblest virtues, magnanimity, generosity, disinterested friendship, and even modesty.

April.

As I am what the men of the world, if they knew such a man, would call a whimsical mortal, I have various sources of pleasure and enjoyment, which are, in a manner, peculiar to myself, or some here and there such other out-of-the-way person. Such is the peculiar pleasure I take in the season of winter, more than the rest of the year. This, I believe, may be partly owing to my misfortunes giving my mind a melancholy cast: but there is something even in the

> " Mighty tempest, and the hoary waste
> Abrupt and deep, stretch'd o'er the buried earth,"

which raises the mind to a serious sublimity, favourable to every thing great and noble. There is scarcely any earthly object gives me more—I do not know if I should call it pleasure —but something which exalts me, something which enraptures me—than to walk in the sheltered side of a wood, or high plantation, in a cloudy winter-day, and hear the stormy wind howling among the trees, and raving over the plain. It is my best season for devotion; my mind is wrapt up in a kind of enthusiasm to Him, who, in the pompous language of the Hebrew bard, " walks on the wings of the winds." In one of these seasons, just after a train of misfortunes, I composed the following:—

The wintry West extends his blast.

[See Poetical Works, p. 54.]

Shenstone finely observes, that love-verses, writ without any real passion, are the most nauseous of all conceits: and I have often thought that no man can be a proper critic of love-composition, except he himself, in one or more instances, has been a warm votary of this passion. As I have been all along a miserable dupe to love, and have been led into a thousand weaknesses and follies by it, for that reason I put the more confidence in my critical skill, in distinguishing foppery and conceit from real passion and nature. Whether the following song will stand the test, I will not pretend to say, because it is my own; only I can say it was, at the time, genuine from the heart:—

> Behind yon hills where Stinchar flows,

[See Poetical Works, p. 25.]

—————

March, 1784.

There was a certain period of my life that my spirit was broke by repeated losses and disasters which threatened, and indeed effected, the utter ruin of my fortune. My body, too, was attacked by that most dreadful distemper, a hypochondria or confirmed melancholy. In this wretched state, the recollection of which makes me yet shudder, I hung my harp on the willow-trees, except in some lucid intervals, in one of which I composed the following:—

> O thou Great Being! what Thou art.

[See Poetical Works, p. 26.]

—————

April.

The following song is a wild rhapsody, miserably deficient in versification; but as the sentiments are the genuine feelings of my heart, for that reason I have a particular pleasure in conning it over.

> My father was a farmer
> Upon the Carrick border, O.

[See Posthumous Works.]

—————

April.

I think the whole species of young men may be naturally enough divided into two grand classes, which I shall call the *grave* and the *merry*; though, by the by, these terms do not with propriety enough express my ideas. The grave I shall cast into the usual division of those who are goaded on by the love of money, and those whose darling wish is to make a figure in the world. The merry are the men of pleasure of all denominations; the jovial lads, who have too much fire and spirit to have any settled rule of action; but, without much deliberation, follow the strong impulses of nature; the thoughtless, the careless, the indolent—in particular *he* who, with a happy sweetness of natural temper, and a cheerful vacancy of thought, steals through life—generally, indeed, in poverty and obscurity; but poverty and obscurity are only evils to him who can sit gravely down and make a repining comparison between his own situation and that of others; and lastly, to grace the quorum, such are, generally, those whose heads are capable of all the towerings of genius, and whose hearts are warmed with all the delicacy of feeling.

—————

August.

The foregoing was to have been an elaborate dissertation on the various species of men; but as I cannot please myself in the arrangement of my ideas, I must wait till farther experience and nicer observation throw more light on the subject. In the meantime I shall set down the following fragment, which, as it is the genuine language of my heart, will enable anybody to determine which of the classes I belong to:—

> There's nought but care on ev'ry han',
> In ev'ry hour that passes, O. *

As the grand end of human life is to cultivate an intercourse with that BEING to whom we owe life, with every enjoyment that renders life delightful; and to maintain an integritive conduct towards our fellow-creatures; that so, by forming piety and virtue into habit, we may be fit members for that society of the pious and the good, which reason and revelation teach us to expect beyond the grave, I do not see that the turn of mind, and pursuits of such an one as the above verses describe—one who spends the hours and thoughts which the vocations of the day can spare with Ossian, Shakspeare, Thomson, Shenstone, Sterne, &c.; or, as the maggot takes him, a gun, a fiddle, or a song to make or mend; and at all times some heart's-dear bonnie lass in view—I say I do not see that the turn of mind and pursuits of such an one are in the least more inimical to the sacred interests of piety and virtue, than the even lawful bustling and straining after the world's riches and honours: and I do not see but he may gain heaven as well—which, by the by, is no mean consideration—who steals through the vale of life, amusing himself with every little flower that fortune throws in his way, as he, who straining straight forward, and perhaps spattering all about him, gains some of life's little eminences, where, after all, he can only see and be seen a little more conspicuously than what, in the pride of his heart, he is apt to term the poor, indolent devil he has left behind him.

* [See Poetical Works, p. 26.]

—————

August.

A Prayer, when fainting fits, and other alarming symptoms of a pleurisy or some other dangerous disorder, which indeed still threatens me, first put nature on the alarm:—

> O thou unknown, Almighty Cause
> Of all my hope and fear!

[See Poetical Works, p. 54.]

—————

August,

Misgivings in the hour of *despondency* and prospect of death:—

> Why am I loth to leave this earthly scene?

[See Poetical Works, p. 55.]

—————

EGOTISMS FROM MY OWN SENSATIONS.

May [8].

I don't well know what is the reason of it, but somehow or other, though I am when I have a mind pretty generally beloved, yet I never could get the art of commanding respect. I imagine it is owing to my being deficient in what Sterne calls "that understrapping virtue of discretion." I am so apt to a *lapsus linguæ*, that I sometimes think the character of a certain great man I have read of somewhere is very much *apropos* to myself—that he was a compound of great talents and great folly. N.B.—To try if I can discover the causes of this wretched infirmity, and, if possible, to mend it.

———

August.

However I am pleased with the works of our Scotch poets, particularly the excellent Ramsay, and the still more excellent Fergusson, yet I am hurt to see other places of Scotland, their towns, rivers, woods, haughs, &c., immortalized in such celebrated performances, while my dear native country, the ancient bailieries of Carrick, Kyle, and Cunningham, famous both in ancient and modern times for a gallant and warlike race of inhabitants—a country where civil, and particularly religious liberty have ever found their first support, and their last asylum; a country, the birth-place of many famous philosophers, soldiers, statesmen, and the scene of many important events recorded in Scottish history, particularly a great many of the actions of the glorious WALLACE the SAVIOUR of his country—yet, we have never had one Scotch poet of any eminence, to make the fertile banks of Irvine, the romantic woodlands and sequestered scenes on Ayr, and the heathy mountainous source and winding sweep of Doon, emulate Tay, Forth, Ettrick, Tweed, &c. This is a complaint I would gladly remedy, but, alas! I am far unequal to the task, both in native genius and education. Obscure I am, and obscure I must be, though no young poet, nor young soldier's heart, ever bent more fondly for fame than mine—

> " And if there is no other scene of being
> Where my insatiate wish may have its fill,—
> This something at my heart that heaves for room,
> My best, my dearest part, was made in vain."

———

September.

There is a great irregularity in the old Scotch songs, a redundancy of syllables with respect to that exactness of accent and measure that the English poetry requires, but which glides in, most melodiously, with the respective tunes to which they are set. For instance, the fine old song of "The Mill, Mill, O," to give it a plain, prosaic reading, it halts prodigiously out of measure; on the other hand, the song set to the same tune in Bremner's collection of Scotch songs, which begins "To Fanny fair could I impart," &c., is most exact measure; and yet, let them both be sung before a real critic, one above the biases of prejudice but a thorough judge of nature, how flat and spiritless will the last appear, how trite, and lamely methodical, compared with the wild warbling cadence, the heart-moving melody of the first!—This is particularly the case with all those airs which end with a hypermetrical syllable. There is a degree of wild irregularity in many of the compositions and fragments which are daily sung to them by my compeers, the common people—a certain happy arrangement of old Scotch syllables, and yet, very frequently, nothing, not even like rhyme, or sameness of jingle, at the ends of the lines. This has made me sometimes imagine that perhaps it might be possible for a Scotch poet, with a nice judicious ear, to set compositions to many of our most favourite airs, particularly that class of them mentioned above, independent of rhyme altogether.

———

There is a noble sublimity, a heart-melting tenderness, in some of our ancient ballads, which show them to be the work of a masterly hand: and it has often given me many a heart-ache to reflect that such glorious old bards—bards who very probably owed all their talents to native genius, yet have described the exploits of heroes, the pangs of disappointment, and the meltings of love, with such fine strokes of nature—that their very names (O how mortifying to a bard's vanity!) are now " buried among the wreck of things which were."

O ye illustrious names unknown! who could feel so strongly and describe so well: the last, the meanest of the Muses' train—one who, though far inferior to your flights, yet eyes your path, and with trembling wing would sometimes soar after you—a poor rustic bard unknown, pays this sympathetic pang to your memory! Some of you tell us, with all the charms of verse, that you have been unfortunate in the world—unfortunate in love: he, too, has felt the loss of his little fortune, the loss of friends, and, worse than all, the loss of the woman he adored. Like you, all his consolation was his Muse: she taught him in rustic measures to complain. Happy could he have done it with your strength of imagination and flow of verse! May the turf lie lightly on your bones! and may you now enjoy that solace and rest which this world rarely gives to the heart tuned to all the feelings of poesy and love!

———

September [8].

The following fragment is done something in imitation of the manner of a noble old Scottish piece, called M'Millan's Peggy, and sings to the tune of Galla Water.—My Montgomery's Peggy was my deity for six or eight months. She had been bred (though, as the world says, without any just pretence for it) in a style of life rather elegant; but, as Vanburgh says in one of his comedies, my "d—d star found me out" there too; for though I began the affair merely in a *gaieté de cœur*, or, to tell the truth, which will scarcely be believed, a vanity of showing my parts in courtship, particularly my abilities at a *billet-doux*, which I always piqued myself upon, made me lay siege to her; and when, as I always do in my foolish gallantries, I had battered* myself into a very warm affection for her, she told me one day, in a flag of truce, that her fortress had been for some time before the rightful property of another; but, with the greatest friendship and politeness, she offered me every alliance except actual possession. I found out afterwards that what she told me of a pre-engagement was really true; but it cost me some heart-aches to get rid of the affair.

I have even tried to imitate in this extempore thing that irregularity in the rhymes, which, when judiciously done, has such a fine effect on the ear.

    "Altho' my bed were in yon muir."

* [This word seems to be very doubtful in original, for Cunningham prints it 'fettered,' whereas Chambers as above. If the original has it written 'battered,' then the word must be understood in the old Scotch sense of to *build up*, as in building a wall to the cope.]

September.

There is another fragment in imitation of an old Scotch song, well known among the country ingle sides.—I cannot tell the name, neither of the song nor the tune, but they are in fine unison with one another.—By the way, these old Scottish airs are so nobly sentimental, that when one would compose to them, to "sowth the tune," as our Scotch phrase is, over and over, is the readiest way to catch the inspiration, and raise the bard into that glorious enthusiasm so strongly characteristic of our old Scotch poetry. I shall here set down one verse of the piece mentioned above, both to mark the song and tune I mean, and likewise as a debt I owe to the author, as the repeating of that verse has lighted up my flame a thousand times:—

  When clouds in skies do come together
    To hide the brightness of the sun,
  There will surely be some pleasant weather
    When a' their storms are past and gone.'

  Though fickle fortune has deceived me,
    She promis'd fair and perform'd but ill;
  Of mistress, friends, and wealth bereav'd me,
    Yet I bear a heart shall support me still.

  I'll act with prudence as far as I'm able,
    But if success I must never find,
  Then come misfortune, I bid thee welcome,
    I'll meet thee with an undaunted mind.

* Alluding to the misfortunes he feelingly laments before this verse.—R. B.

The above was an extempore, under the pressure of a heavy train of misfortunes, which, indeed, threatened to undo me altogether. It was just at the close of that dreadful period mentioned already,* and though the weather has brightened up a little with me, yet there has always been since a tempest brewing round me in the grim sky of futurity, which I pretty plainly see will some time or other, perhaps ere long, overwhelm me, and drive me into some doleful dell, to pine in solitary, squalid wretchedness.—However, as I hope my poor country Muse, who, all rustic, awkward, and unpolished as she is, has more charms for me than any other of the pleasures of life beside—as I hope she will not then desert me. I may even then learn to be, if not happy, at least easy, and *sowth a song* to soothe my misery.

'Twas at the same time I set about composing an air in the old Scotch style.—I am not musical scholar enough to prick down my tune properly, so it can never see the light, and perhaps 'tis no great matter; but the following were the verses I composed to suit it:—

  O raging fortune's withering blast
    Has laid my leaf full low, O!

      [See Posthumous Works.]

The tune consisted of three parts, so that the above verses just went through the whole air.

* ['Commonplace-Book, date March, 1784.]

October, 1785.

If ever any young man, in the vestibule of the world, chance to throw his eye over these pages, let him pay a warm attention to the following observations, as I assure him they are the fruit of a poor devil's dear-bought experience. I have literally, like that great poet and great gallant, and by consequence, that great fool, Solomon, "turned my eyes to behold madness and folly." Nay, I have, with all the ardour of a lively, fanciful, and whimsical imagination, accompanied with a warm, feeling, poetic heart, shaken hands with their intoxicating friendship.

In the first place, let my pupil, as he tenders his own peace, keep up a regular, warm intercourse with the Deity. * * *

This is all worth quoting in my MSS. and more than all,

R. B.

[See Appendix.]

(1.)

To Dr. Moore.

Edinburgh [January], 1787.

Sir,

Mrs. Dunlop has been so kind as to send me extracts of letters she has had from you, where you do the rustic bard the honour of noticing him and his works. Those who have felt the anxieties and solicitudes of authorship, can only know what pleasure it gives to be noticed in such a manner by judges of the first character. Your criticisms, Sir, I receive with reverence; only I am sorry they mostly came too late; a peccant passage or two that I would certainly have altered, were gone to the press.

The hope to be admired for ages, is, in by far the greater part of those even who are authors of repute, an unsubstantial dream. For my part, my first ambition was, and still my strongest wish is, to please my compeers, the rustic inmates of the hamlet, while ever-changing language and manners shall allow me to be relished and understood. I am very willing to admit that I have some poetical abilities; and as few, if any, writers, either moral or poetical, are intimately acquainted with the classes of mankind among whom I have chiefly mingled, I may have seen men and manners in a different phasis from what is common, which may assist originality of thought. Still I know very well the novelty of my character has by far the greatest share in the learned and polite notice I have lately had; and in a language where Pope and Churchill have raised the laugh, and Shenstone and Gray have drawn the tear; where Thomson and Beattie have painted the landscape, and Lyttelton and Collins described the heart, I am not vain enough to hope for distinguished poetic fame.

R. B.

(2.)

TO DR. MOORE.

Edinburgh, 15th February, 1787.

Sir,

Pardon my seeming neglect in delaying so long to acknowledge the honour you have done me, in your kind notice of me, January 23rd. Not many months ago I knew no other employment than following the plough, nor could boast any thing higher than a distant acquaintance with a country clergyman. Mere greatness never embarrasses me; I have nothing to ask from the great, and I do not fear their judgment; but genius, polished by learning, and at its proper point of elevation in the eye of the world, this of late I frequently meet with, and tremble at its approach. I scorn the affectation of seeming modesty to cover self-conceit. That I have some merit I do not deny; but I see with frequent wringings of heart, that the novelty of my character, and the honest national prejudice of my countrymen have borne me to a height altogether untenable to my abilities.

For the honour Miss Williams has done me, please, Sir, return her in my name my most grateful thanks. I have more than once thought of paying her in kind, but have hitherto quitted the idea in hopeless despondency. I had never before heard of her; but the other day I got her poems, which for several reasons, some belonging to the head, and others the offspring of the heart, give me a great deal of pleasure. I have little pretensions to critic lore: there are, I think, two characteristic features in her poetry—the unfettered wild flight of native genius, and the querulous, sombre tenderness of "time-settled sorrow."

I only know what pleases me, often without being able to tell why.

R. B.

(3.)

TO DR. MOORE.

Edinburgh, 23rd April, 1787.

I received the books, and sent the one you mentioned to Mrs. Dunlop. I am ill skilled in beating the coverts of imagination for metaphors of gratitude. I thank you, Sir, for the honour you have done me; and to my latest hour will warmly remember it. To be highly pleased with your book is what I have in common with the world; but to regard these volumes as a mark of the author's friendly esteem, is a still more supreme gratification.

I leave Edinburgh in the course of ten days or a fortnight, and after a few pilgrimages over some of the classic ground of Caledonia, Cowden Knowes, Banks of Yarrow, Tweed, &c., I shall return to my rural shades, in all likelihood never more to quit them. I have formed many intimacies and friendships here, but I am afraid they are all of too tender a construction to bear carriage a hundred and fifty miles. To the rich, the great, the fashionable, the polite, I have no equivalent to offer; and I am afraid my meteor appearance will by no means entitle me to a settled correspondence with any of you, who are the permanent lights of genius and literature.

My most respectful compliments to Miss Williams. If once this tangent flight of mine were over, and I were returned to my wonted leisurely motion in my old circle, I may probably endeavour to return her poetic compliment in kind.

R. B.

(4.)

TO DR. MOORE.
[AUTHOR'S CELEBRATED AUTOBIOGRAPHY.]

Mauchline, 2nd August, 1787.

Sir,

For some months past I have been rambling over the country, but I am now confined with some lingering complaints, originating, as I take it, in the stomach. To divert my spirits a little in this miserable fog of *ennui*, I have taken a whim to give you a history of myself. My name has made some little noise in this country; you have done me the honour to interest yourself very warmly in my behalf; and I think a faithful account of what character of a man I am, and how I came by that character, may perhaps amuse you in an idle moment, I will give you an honest narrative, though I know it will be often at my own expense; for I assure you, Sir, I have, like Solomon, whose character, excepting in the trifling affair of *wisdom*, I sometimes think I resemble,—I have, I say, like him "turned my eyes to behold madness and folly," and like him, too, frequently shaken hands with their intoxicating friendship.—After you have perused these pages, should you think them trifling and impertinent, I only beg leave to tell you, that the poor author wrote them under some twitching qualms of conscience, arising from a suspicion that he was doing what he ought not to do; a predicament he has more than once been in before.

I have not the most distant pretensions to assume that character which the pye-coated guardians of escutcheons call a gentleman. When at Edinburgh last winter, I got acquainted in the herald's office; and, looking through that granary of honours, I there found almost every name in the kingdom: but for me

> "My ancient but ignoble blood
> Has crept thro' scoundrels ever since the flood."
>
> POPE.

Gules, Purpure, Argent, &c., quite disowned me.

My father was of the north of Scotland, the son of a farmer, and was thrown by early misfortunes on the world at large; where, after many years' wanderings and sojournings, he picked up a pretty large quantity of observation and experience, to which I am indebted for most of my little pretensions to wisdom. I have met with few who understood men, their manners, and their ways, equal to him; but stubborn, ungainly integrity, and headlong, ungovernable irascibility, are disqualifying circumstances; consequently, I was born a very poor man's son. For the first six or seven years of my life, my father was gardener to a worthy gentleman of small estate in the neighbourhood of Ayr. Had he continued in that station, I must have marched off to be one of the little underlings about a farm-house; but it was his dearest wish and prayer to have it in his power to keep his children under his own eye, till they could discern between good and evil; so, with the assistance of his generous master, my father ventured on a small farm on his estate. At those years, I was by no means a favourite with anybody. I was a good deal noted for a retentive memory, a stubborn sturdy something in my disposition, and an enthusiastic idiot piety. I say *idiot* piety, because I was then but a child. Though it cost the schoolmaster some thrashings, I made an excellent English scholar; and by the time I was ten or eleven years of age, I was a critic in substantives, verbs, and particles. In my infant and boyish days, too, I owed much to an old woman who resided in the family, remarkable for her ignorance, credulity, and superstition. She had, I suppose, the largest collection in the country of tales and songs concerning devils, ghosts, fairies, brownies, witches, warlocks, spunkies, kelpies, elf-candles, dead-lights, wraiths, apparitions, cantraips, giants, enchanted towers, dragons, and other trumpery. This cultivated the latent seeds of poetry; but had so strong an effect on my imagination, that to this hour, in my nocturnal rambles, I sometimes keep a sharp look out in suspicious places; and though nobody can be more sceptical than I am in such matters, yet it often takes an effort of philosophy to shake off those idle terrors. The earliest composition that I recollect taking pleasure in, was The Vision of Mirza, and a hymn of Addison's beginning, "How are thy servants blest, O Lord!" I particularly remember one half-stanza which was music to my boyish ear—

> "For though in dreadful whirls we hung
> High on the broken wave"—

I met with these pieces in Mason's English Collection, one of my school-books. The first two books I ever read in private,

and which gave me more pleasure than any two books I ever read since, were The Life of Hannibal, and The History of Sir William Wallace. Hannibal gave my young ideas such a turn, that I used to strut in raptures up and down after the recruiting drum and bag-pipe, and wish myself tall enough to be a soldier; while the story of Wallace poured a Scottish prejudice into my veins, which will boil along there till the flood-gates of life shut in eternal rest.

Polemical divinity about this time was putting the country half mad, and I, ambitious of shining in conversation parties on Sundays, between sermons, at funerals, &c., used a few years afterwards to puzzle Calvinism with so much heat and indiscretion, that I raised a hue and cry of heresy against me, which has not ceased to this hour.

My vicinity to Ayr was of some advantage to me. My social disposition, when not checked by some modifications of spirited pride, was like our catechism definition of infinitude, "without bounds or limits." I formed several connexions with other younkers, who possessed superior advantages; the youngling actors who were busy in the rehearsal of parts, in which they were shortly to appear on the stage of life, where, alas! I was destined to drudge behind the scenes. It is not commonly at this green age that our young gentry have a just sense of the immense distance that lies between them and their rugged playfellows. It takes a few dashes into the world, to give the young great man that proper, decent, unnoticing disregard for the poor, insignificant, stupid devils, the mechanics and peasantry around him, who were, perhaps, born in the same village. My young superiors never insulted the clouterly appearance of my plough-boy carcase, the two extremes of which were often exposed to all the inclemencies of all the seasons. They would give me stray volumes of books; among them, even then, I could pick up some observations, and one, whose heart, I am sure, not even the "Munny Begum" scenes have tainted, helped me to a little French. Parting with these my young friends and benefactors, as they occasionally went off for the East or West Indies, was often to me a sore affliction; but I was soon called to more serious evils. My father's generous master died! the farm proved a ruinous bargain; and to clench the misfortune, we fell into the hands of a factor, who sat for the picture I have drawn of one in my tale of "The Twa Dogs." My father was advanced in life when he married; I was the eldest of seven children, and he, worn out by early hardships, was unfit for labour. My father's spirit was soon irritated, but not easily broken. There was a freedom in his lease in two years more, and to weather these two years, we retrenched our expenses. We lived very poorly: I was a dexterous ploughman for my age; and the next eldest to me was a brother (Gilbert), who could drive the plough very well, and help me to thrash the corn. A novel-writer might, perhaps, have viewed these scenes with some satisfaction, but so did not I; my indignation yet boils at the recollection of the scoundrel factor's insolent threatening letters, which used to set us all in tears.

This kind of life—the cheerless gloom of a hermit, with the unceasing moil of a galley-slave, brought me to my sixteenth year; a little before which period I first committed the sin of

K

rhyme. You know our country custom of coupling a man and woman together as partners in the labours of harvest. In my fifteenth autumn, my partner was a bewitching creature, a year younger than myself. My scarcity of English denies me the power of doing her justice in that language, but you know the Scottish idiom: she was a "bonnie, sweet, sonsie lass." In short, she, altogether unwittingly to herself, initiated me in that delicious passion, which, in spite of acid disappointment, gin-horse prudence, and book-worm philosophy, I hold to be the first of human joys, our dearest blessing here below! How she caught the contagion I cannot tell; you medical people talk much of infection from breathing the same air, the touch, &c.; but I never expressly said I loved her.—Indeed, I did not know myself why I liked so much to loiter behind with her, when returning in the evening from our labours; why the tones of her voice made my heart-strings thrill like an Æolian harp; and particularly why my pulse beat such a furious rattan, when I looked and fingered over her little hand to pick out the cruel nettle-stings and thistles. Among her other love-inspiring qualities, she sung sweetly; and it was her favourite reel to which I attempted giving an embodied vehicle in rhyme. I was not so presumptuous as to imagine that I could make verses like printed ones, composed by men who had Greek and Latin; but my girl sung a song which was said to be composed by a small country laird's son, on one of his father's maids, with whom he was in love; and I saw no reason why I might not rhyme as well as he; for, excepting that he could smear sheep, and cast peats, his father living in the moorlands, he had no more scholar-craft than myself.

Thus with me began love and poetry; which at times have been my only, and till within the last twelve months, have been my highest enjoyment. My father struggled on till he reached the freedom in his lease, when he entered on a larger farm, about ten miles farther in the country. The nature of the bargain he made was such as to throw a little ready money into his hands at the commencement of his lease, otherwise the affair would have been impracticable. For four years we lived comfortably here, but a difference commencing between him and his landlord as to terms, after three years' tossing and whirling in the vortex of litigation, my father was just saved from the horrors of a jail, by a consumption, which, after two years' promises, kindly stepped in, and carried him away, to "where the wicked cease from troubling, and where the weary are at rest!"

It is during the time that we lived on this farm, that my little story is most eventful. I was, at the beginning of this period, perhaps, the most ungainly awkward boy in the parish —no *solitaire* was less acquainted with the ways of the world. What I knew of ancient story was gathered from Salmon's and Guthrie's Geographical Grammars; and the ideas I had formed of modern manners, of literature, and criticism, I got from the *Spectator*. These, with Pope's Works, some Plays of Shakespeare, Tull and Dickson on Agriculture, The Pantheon, Locke's Essay on the Human Understanding, Stackhouse's History of the Bible, Justice's British Gardener's Directory, Boyle's Lectures, Allan Ramsay's Works, Taylor's Scripture Doctrine of Original Sin, A Select Collection of English Songs,

and Hervey's Meditations, had formed the whole of my reading. The collection of Songs was my *vade mecum*. I pored over them, driving my cart, or walking to labour, song by song, verse by verse; carefully noting the true tender, or sublime, from affectation or fustian. I am convinced I owe to this practice much of my critic-craft, such as it is.*

In my seventeenth year, to give my manners a brush, I went to a country dancing-school. My father had an unaccountable antipathy against these meetings, and my going was, what to this moment I repent, in opposition to his wishes. My father, as I said before, was subject to strong passions; from that instance of disobedience in me, he took a sort of dislike to me, which, I believe, was one cause of the dissipation which marked my succeeding years.† I say dissipation, comparatively with the strictness, and sobriety, and regularity of Presbyterian country life; for though the will-o'-wisp meteors of thoughtless whim were almost the sole lights of my path, yet early ingrained piety and virtue kept me for several years afterwards within the line of innocence. The great misfortune of my life was to want an aim. I had felt early some stirrings of ambition, but they were the blind gropings of Homer's Cyclops round the walls of his cave. I saw my father's situation entailed on me perpetual labour. The only two openings by which I could enter the temple of fortune was the gate of niggardly economy, or the path of little chicaning bargain-making. The first is so contracted an aperture I never could squeeze myself into it—the last I always hated—there was contamination in the very entrance! Thus abandoned of aim or view in life, with a strong appetite for sociability, as well from native hilarity, as from a pride of observation and remark; a constitutional melancholy or hypochondriasm that made me fly solitude; add to these incentives to social life, my reputation for bookish knowledge, a certain wild logical talent, and a strength of thought, something like the rudiments of good sense; and it will not seem surprising that I was generally a welcome guest where I visited, or any great wonder that always, where two or three met together, there was I among them. But far beyond all other impulses of my heart, was *un penchant à l'adorable moitié du genre humain.* My heart was completely tinder, and was eternally lighted up by some goddess or other; and, as in every other warfare in this world, my fortune was various; sometimes I was received with favour, and sometimes I was mortified with a repulse. At the plough, scythe, or reap-hook, I feared no competitor, and thus I set absolute want at defiance; and as I never cared further for my labours than while I was in actual exercise, I spent the evenings in the way after my own heart. A country lad seldom carries on a love adventure without an assisting confidant. I possessed a curiosity, zeal, and intrepid

---

* [In the catalogue of books here transcribed, "Boyle's Lectures" has been misprinted by Currie "Bayle's Lectures." This inaccuracy was first pointed out by Chambers. The Select Collection of Songs here referred to was entitled "The Lark," a book published by Gordon of Edinburgh, in 1765. It contains 326 close printed pages, with some fine old songs and ballads, but a good deal also of inferior versification in its contents. From this little miscellany the Poet seems early to have picked up such names as Chloris and Chloe, which frequently occur on its pages.]

† [We have only again to state that the Author's remarks about his father's aversion to himself, and his own dissipation, are very much exaggerated; for what reason, it is not easy to conjecture.]

dexterity that recommended me as a proper second on these occasions; and I dare say, I felt as much pleasure in being in the secret of half the loves of the parish of Tarbolton, as ever did statesman in knowing the intrigues of half the courts of Europe. The very goose-feather in my hand seems to know instinctively the well-worn path of my imagination, the favourite theme of my song; and is with difficulty restrained from giving you a couple of paragraphs on the love-adventures of my compeers, the humble inmates of the farm-house and cottage; but the grave sons of science, ambition, or avarice baptize these things by the name of follies. To the sons and daughters of labour and poverty they are matters of the most serious nature: to them the ardent hope, the stolen interview, the tender farewell, are the greatest and most delicious parts of their enjoyments.

Another circumstance in my life which made some alteration in my mind and manners, was, that I spent my seventeenth summer on a smuggling coast, a good distance from home, at a noted school, to learn mensuration, surveying, dialling, &c., in which I made a pretty good progress.[*] But I made a greater progress in the knowledge of mankind. The contraband trade was at that time very successful, and it sometimes happened to me to fall in with those who carried it on. Scenes of swaggering riot and roaring dissipation were, till this time, new to me; but I was no enemy to social life. Here, though I learned to fill my glass, and to mix without fear in a drunken squabble, yet I went on with a high hand with my geometry, till the sun entered Virgo, a month which is always a carnival in my bosom, when a charming *fillette*, who lived next door to the school, overset my trigonometry, and set me off at a tangent from the sphere of my studies. I, however, struggled on with my sines and co-sines for a few days more; but stepping into the garden one charming noon to take the sun's altitude, there I met my angel,

> "Like Proserpine gathering flowers,
> Herself a fairer flower———"[+]

It was in vain to think of doing any more good at school. The remaining week I staid I did nothing but craze the faculties of my soul about her, or steal out to meet her; and the two last nights of my stay in the country, had sleep been a mortal sin, the image of this modest and innocent girl had kept me guiltless.

I returned home very considerably improved. My reading was enlarged with the very important addition of Thomson's and Shenstone's works; I had seen human nature in a new phasis; and I engaged several of my schoolfellows to keep up a literary correspondence with me. This improved me in composition. I had met with a collection of letters by the wits of Queen Anne's reign, and I pored over them most devoutly. I kept copies of any of my own letters that pleased me, and a comparison between them and the composition of most of my correspondents flattered my vanity. I carried this whim so far, that though I had not three-farthings' worth of business in the world, yet almost every post brought me as many letters as if I had been a broad plodding son of the day-book and ledger.

My life flowed on much in the same course till my twenty-third year. *Vive l'amour, et vive la bagatelle*, were my sole principles of action. The addition of two more authors to my library gave me great pleasure; Sterne and Mackenzie—Tristram Shandy and the Man of Feeling were my bosom favourites. Poesy was still a darling walk for my mind, but it was only indulged in according to the humour of the hour. I had usually half a dozen or more pieces on hand; I took up one or other, as it suited the momentary tone of the mind, and dismissed the work as it bordered on fatigue. My passions, when once lighted up, raged like so many devils, till they got vent in rhyme; and then the conning over my verses, like a spell, soothed all into quiet! None of the rhymes of those days are in print, except "Winter, a dirge," the oldest of my printed pieces; "The Death of poor Mailie," "John Barleycorn," and songs first, second, and third. Song second was the ebullition of that passion which ended the foregoing school-business.

My twenty-third year was to me an important one. Partly through whim, and partly that I wished to set about doing something in life, I joined a flax-dresser in a neighbouring town (Irvine), to learn his trade. This was an unlucky affair. My * * * and to finish the whole, as we were giving a welcome carousal to the new year, the shop took fire and burnt to ashes, and I was left, like a true poet, not worth a sixpence.

I was obliged to give up this scheme; the clouds of misfortune were gathering thick round my father's head; and, what was worst of all, he was visibly far gone in a consumption; and to crown my distresses, a *belle fille*, whom I adored, and who had pledged her soul to meet me in the field of matrimony, jilted me, with peculiar circumstances of mortification. The finishing evil that brought up the rear of this infernal file, was my constitutional melancholy being increased to such a degree, that for three months I was in a state of mind scarcely to be envied by the hopeless wretches who have got their mittimus—depart from me, ye cursed!

From this adventure I learned something of a town life: but the principal thing which gave my mind a turn, was a friendship I formed with a young fellow, a very noble character, but a hapless son of misfortune. He was the son of a simple mechanic; but a great man in the neighbourhood taking him under his patronage, gave him a genteel education, with a view of bettering his situation in life. The patron dying just as he was ready to launch out into the

---

[*] [The smuggling coast referred to, where the Author spent his seventeenth summer, was the Turnberry coast in Carrick; the village where his studies were then prosecuted, Kirkoswald; and the house where he resided with his maternal uncle Brown, a sweet picturesque locality by the roadside, in a glen about a mile to the west of that village—called Ballochneil. It was here, as the reader is aware, he became first acquainted with the original characters subsequently immortalised in 'Tam o' Shanter.' The date of his residence there has been long disputed,—the nineteenth and not the seventeenth summer having hitherto been universally printed; which undoubtedly implied miscalculation. We learn by a note in the *Inverness Courier* (June 11th, 1855) to whose accomplished editor we are indebted for the information, that this error was occasioned by Dr. Currie; who, not being satisfied about the date in question, deliberately struck out seventeenth and substituted nineteenth, which has ever since been adopted in all editions of the Poet's works. We are happy to be able to make this rectification in time.]

[+] [This quotation by our Author, from memory, doubtless, is slightly inaccurate in its form: the word "like" does not belong to Milton, and should not have been included in the quotation. The reader will find the passage in "Paradise Lost," B. iv., l. 268.]

world, the poor fellow in despair went to sea; where, after a variety of good and ill-fortune, a little before I was acquainted with him he had been set on shore by an American privateer, on the wild coast of Connaught, stripped of every thing. I cannot quit this poor fellow's story without adding, that he is at this time master of a large West-Indiaman belonging to the Thames.

His mind was fraught with independence, magnanimity, and every manly virtue. I loved and admired him to a degree of enthusiasm, and of course strove to imitate him. In some measure I succeeded; I had pride before, but he taught it to flow in proper channels. His knowledge of the world was vastly superior to mine, and I was all attention to learn. He was the only man I ever saw who was a greater fool than myself where woman was the presiding star; but he spoke of illicit love with the levity of a sailor, which hitherto I had regarded with horror. Here his friendship did me a mischief, and the consequence was, that soon after I resumed the plough, I wrote the "Poet's Welcome." My reading only increased while in this town by two stray volumes of Pamela, and one of Ferdinand Count Fathom, which gave me some idea of novels. Rhyme, except some religious pieces that are in print, I had given up; but meeting with Fergusson's Scottish Poems, I strung anew my wildly-sounding lyre with emulating vigour. When my father died, his all went among the hell-hounds that growl in the kennel of justice; but we made a shift to collect a little money in the family amongst us, with which, to keep us together, my brother and I took a neighbouring farm. My brother wanted my hair-brained imagination, as well as my social and amorous madness; but in good sense, and every sober qualification, he was far my superior.

I entered on this farm with a full resolution, "come, go to, I will be wise!" I read farming books, I calculated crops; I attended markets; and in short, in spite of the devil, and the world, and the flesh, I believe I should have been a wise man; but the first year, from unfortunately buying bad seed, the second from a late harvest, we lost half our crops. This overset all my wisdom, and I returned, "like the dog to his vomit, and the sow that was washed to her wallowing in the mire."

I now began to be known in the neighbourhood as a maker of rhymes. The first of my poetic offspring that saw the light was a burlesque lamentation on a quarrel between two reverend Calvinists both of them *dramatis personæ* in my "Holy Fair." I had a notion myself that the piece had some merit; but, to prevent the worst, I gave a copy of it to a friend, who was very fond of such things, and told him that I could not guess who was the author of it, but that I thought it pretty clever. With a certain description of the clergy, as well as laity, it met with a roar of applause. "Holy Willie's Prayer" next made its appearance, and alarmed the kirk-session so much, that they held several meetings to look over their spiritual artillery, if haply any of it might be pointed against profane rhymers. Unluckily for me, my wanderings led me on another side, within point-blank shot of their heaviest metal. This is the unfortunate story that gave rise to my printed poem, "The Lament." This was a most melancholy affair, which I cannot yet bear to reflect on, and had very nearly given me one or two of the principal qualifications for a place among those who have lost the chart, and mistaken the reckoning of rationality. I gave up my part of the farm to my brother; in truth it was only nominally mine; and made what little preparation was in my power for Jamaica. But, before leaving my native country for ever, I resolved to publish my poems. I weighed my productions as impartially as was in my power: I thought they had merit; and it was a delicious idea that I should be called a clever fellow, even though it should never reach my ears—a poor negro-driver—or perhaps a victim to that inhospitable clime, and gone to the world of spirits! I can truly say, that *pauvre inconnu* as I then was, I had pretty nearly as high an idea of myself and of my works as I have at this moment, when the public has decided in their favour. It ever was my opinion that the mistakes and blunders, both in a rational and religious point of view, of which we see thousands daily guilty, are owing to their ignorance of themselves.—To know myself had been all along my constant study. I weighed myself alone; I balanced myself with others; I watched every means of information, to see how much ground I occupied as a man and as a poet; I studied assiduously Nature's design in my formation—where the lights and shades in my character were intended. I was pretty confident my poems would meet with some applause; but, at the worst, the roar of the Atlantic would deafen the voice of censure, and the novelty of West Indian scenes make me forget neglect. I threw off six hundred copies, of which I had got subscriptions for about three hundred and fifty.—My vanity was highly gratified by the reception I met with from the public; and besides I pocketed, all expenses deducted, nearly twenty pounds. This sum came very seasonably, as I was thinking of indenting myself, for want of money to procure my passage. As soon as I was master of nine guineas, the price of wafting me to the torrid zone, I took a steerage passage in the first ship that was to sail from the Clyde, for

> "Hungry ruin had me in the wind."

I had been for some days skulking from covert to covert, under all the terrors of a jail; as some ill-advised people had uncoupled the merciless pack of the law at my heels. I had taken the last farewell of my few friends; my chest was on the road to Greenock; I had composed the last song I should ever measure in Caledonia—"The gloomy night is gathering fast," when a letter from Dr. Blacklock to a friend of mine, overthrew all my schemes, by opening new prospects to my poetic ambition. The doctor belonged to a set of critics for whose applause I had not dared to hope. His opinion, that I would meet with encouragement in Edinburgh for a second edition, fired me so much, that away I posted for that city, without a single acquaintance, or a single letter of introduction. The baneful star that had so long shed its blasting influence in my zenith, for once made a revolution to the nadir; and a kind Providence placed me under the patronage of one of the noblest of men, the Earl of Glencairn. *Oublie moi, grand Dieu, si jamais je l'oublie!*

I need relate no farther. At Edinburgh I was in a new world; I mingled among many classes of men, but all of them now to me, and I was all attention to "catch" the characters and the "manners living as they rise." Whether I have profited, time will show.

*   *   *   *   *   *

My most respectful compliments to Miss Williams. Her very elegant and friendly letter I cannot answer at present, as my presence is requisite in Edinburgh, and I set out to-morrow.

R. B.

(5.)   TO DR. MOORE.

Ellisland, near Dumfries, 4th Jan., 1789.

SIR,

As often as I think of writing to you, which has been three or four times every week these six months, it gives me something so like the idea of an ordinary-sized statue offering at a conversation with the Rhodian colossus, that my mind misgives me, and the affair always miscarries somewhere between purpose and resolve. I have, at last, got some business with you, and business letters are written by the style-book. I say my business is with you, Sir, for you never had any with me, except the business that benevolence has in the mansion of poverty.

The character and employment of a poet were formerly my pleasure, but are now my pride. I know that a very great deal of my late eclat was owing to the singularity of my situation, and the honest prejudice of Scotsmen; but still, as I said in the preface to my first edition, I do look upon myself as having some pretensions from Nature to the poetic character. I have not a doubt but the knack, the aptitude, to learn the muses' trade, is a gift bestowed by Him "who forms the secret bias of the soul;"—but I as firmly believe, that excellence in the profession is the fruit of industry, labour, attention, and pains. At least I am resolved to try my doctrine by the test of experience. Another appearance from the press I put off to a very distant day, a day that may never arrive—but poesy I am determined to prosecute with all my vigour. Nature has given very few, if any, of the profession the talents of shining in every species of composition. I shall try (for until trial it is impossible to know) whether she has qualified me to shine in any one. The worst of it is, by the time one has finished a piece, it has been so often viewed and reviewed before the mental eye, that one loses, in a good measure, the powers of critical discrimination. Here the best criterion I know is a friend—not only of abilities to judge, but with good-nature enough, like a prudent teacher with a young learner, to praise perhaps a little more than is exactly just, lest the thin-skinned animal fall into that most deplorable of all poetic diseases—heart-breaking despondency of himself. Dare I, Sir, already immensely indebted to your goodness, ask the additional obligation of your being that friend to me? I inclose you an essay of mine in a walk of poesy to me entirely new; I mean the Epistle addressed to R. G., Esq., or Robert Graham of Fintra, Esq., a gentleman of uncommon worth, to whom I lie under very great obligations.

The story of the poem, like most of my poems, is connected with my own story, and to give you the one, I must give you something of the other. I cannot boast of Mr. Creech's ingenuous fair dealing to me. He kept me hanging about Edinburgh from the 7th August, 1787, until the 13th April, 1788, before he would condescend to give me a statement of affairs; nor had I got it even then, but for an angry letter I wrote him, which irritated his pride. "I could" not a "tale" but a detail "unfold," but what am I that should speak against the Lord's anointed Bailie of Edinburgh.

I believe I shall, in whole, £100 copy-right included, clear about £400 some little odds; and even part of this depends upon what the gentleman has yet to settle with me. I give you this information, because you did me the honor to interest yourself much in my welfare. I give you this information, but I give it to yourself only, for I am still much in the gentleman's mercy. Perhaps I injure the man in the idea I am sometimes tempted to have of him—God forbid I should! A little time will try, for in a month I shall go to town to wind up the business if possible.

To give the rest of my story in brief, I have married "my Jean," and taken a farm: with the first step I have every day more and more reason to be satisfied: with the last, it is rather the reverse. I have a younger brother, who supports my aged mother; another still younger brother, and three sisters, in a farm. On my last return from Edinburgh, it cost me about £180 to save them from ruin. Not that I have lost so much—I only interposed between my brother and his impending fate by the loan of so much. I give myself no airs on this, for it was mere selfishness on my part: I was conscious that the wrong scale of the balance was pretty heavily charged, and I thought that throwing a little filial piety and fraternal affection into the scale in my favor, might help to smooth matters at the grand reckoning. There is still one thing would make my circumstances quite easy: I have an excise officer's commission, and I live in the midst of a country division. My request to Mr. Graham, who is one of the commissioners of excise, was, if in his power, to procure me that division. If I were very sanguine, I might hope that some of my great patrons might procure me a Treasury warrant for supervisor, surveyor-general, &c.

*   *   *   *   *

Thus, secure of a livelihood, "to thee, sweet Poetry, delightful maid," I would consecrate my future days.

R. B.

(6.)   TO DR. MOORE.

Ellisland, 23rd March, 1789.

SIR,

THE gentleman who will deliver you this is a Mr. Nielson, a worthy clergyman in my neighbourhood, and a very particular acquaintance of mine. As I have troubled him with this packet, I must turn him over to your goodness, to recompense him for it in a way in which he much needs your assistance, and where you can effectually serve him:—Mr. Nicbom is on his way for France, to wait on his Grace of Queensberry, on some little business of a good deal of importance to him, and he wishes for your instructions respecting the most eligible mode of travelling, &c., for him, when he has crossed the channel. I should not have dared to take this liberty with you, but that I am told, by those who have the honor of your personal acquaintance, that to be a poor honest Scotchman is a letter of recommendation to you, and that to have it in your power to serve such a character, gives you much pleasure.

The inclosed ode is a compliment to the memory of the late Mrs. Oswald, of Auchencruive. You, probably, knew her personally, an honor of which I cannot boast; but I spent my early years in her neighbourhood, and among her servants and tenants. I know that she was detested with the most heartfelt cordiality. However, in the particular part of her conduct which roused my poetic wrath, she was much less blameable. In January last, on my road to Ayrshire, I had put up at Bailie Wigham's, in Sanquhar, the only tolerable inn in the place. The frost was keen, and the grim evening and howling wind were ushering in a night of snow and drift. My horse and I were both much fatigued with the labors of the day, and just as my friend the Bailie and I were bidding defiance to the storm, over a smoking bowl, in wheels the funeral pageantry of the late great Mrs. Oswald; and poor I am forced to brave all the horrors of a tempestuous night, and jade my horse, my young favourite horse, whom I had just christened Pegasus, twelve miles farther on, through the wildest moors and hills of Ayrshire, to New Cumnock, the next inn. The powers of poesy and prose sink under me, when I would describe what I felt. Suffice it to say, that when a good fire at New Cumnock had so far recovered my frozen sinews, I sat down and wrote the inclosed ode.

I was at Edinburgh lately, and settled finally with Mr. Creech; and I must own, that, at last, he has been amicable and fair with me.

R. B.

(7.)   TO DR. MOORE.

Dumfries, Excise-Office, 14th July, 1790.

Sir,

Coming into town this morning to attend my duty in this office, it being collection-day, I met with a gentleman who tells me he is on his way to London; so I take the opportunity of writing to you, as franking is at present under a temporary death. I shall have some snatches of leisure through the day, amid our horrid business and bustle, and I shall improve them as well as I can; but let my letter be as stupid as * * * * * * * * *, as miscellaneous as a newspaper, as short as a hungry grace-before-meat, or as long as a law-paper in the Douglas cause; as ill-spelt as country John's billet-doux, or as unsightly a scrawl as Betty Byre-Mucker's answer to it; I hope, considering circumstances, you will forgive it; and as it will put you

to no expense of postage, I shall have the less reflection about it.

I am sadly ungrateful in not returning you my thanks for your most valuable present, "Zeluco." In fact, you are in some degree blameable for my neglect. You were pleased to express a wish for my opinion of the work, which so flattered me, that nothing less would serve my overweening fancy, than a formal criticism on the book. In fact, I have gravely planned a comparative view of you, Fielding, Richardson, and Smollet, in your different qualities and merits as novel-writers. This, I own, betrays my ridiculous vanity, and I may probably never bring the business to bear; but I am fond of the spirit young Elihu shows in the book of Job—"And I said, I will also declare my opinion." I have quite disfigured my copy of the book with my annotations. I never take it up without at the same time taking my pencil and marking with asterisms, parentheses, &c., wherever I meet with an original thought, a nervous remark on life and manners, a remarkably well-turned period, or a character sketched with uncommon precision.

Though I shall hardly think of fairly writing out my "Comparative View," I shall certainly trouble you with my remarks, such as they are.

I have just received from my gentleman that horrid summons in the book of Revelations—"That time shall be no more!"

The little collection of sonnets have some charming poetry in them. If indeed I am indebted to the fair author for the book, and not, as I rather suspect, to a celebrated author of the other sex, I should certainly have written to the lady, with my grateful acknowledgments, and my own ideas of the comparative excellence of her pieces. I would do this last, not from any vanity of thinking that my remarks could be of much consequence to Mrs. Smith, but merely from my own feelings as an author, doing as I would be done by.

R. B.

(8.)   TO DR. MOORE.

Ellisland, 28th February, 1791.

I do not know, Sir, whether you are a subscriber to "Grose's Antiquities of Scotland." If you are, the inclosed poem will not be altogether new to you. Captain Grose did me the favor to send me a dozen copies of the proof-sheet, of which this is one. Should you have read the piece before, still this will answer the principal end I have in view: it will give me another opportunity of thanking you for all your goodness to the rustic bard; and also of shewing you, that the abilities you have been pleased to commend and patronize are still employed in the way you wish.

The "Elegy on Captain Henderson," is a tribute to the memory of a man I loved much. Poets have in this the same advantage as Roman Catholics; they can be of service to their friends after they have passed that bourne where all other kindness ceases to be of avail. Whether, after all, either the one or the other be of any real service to the dead, is, I fear, very problematical; but I am sure they are highly gratifying to the living: and as a very orthodox text, I forget where in Scripture, says, "whatsoever is not of faith, is sin;" so say I, whatsoever is not detrimental to society, and is of positive enjoyment, is of God, the giver of all good things, and ought to be received and enjoyed by his creatures with thankful delight. As almost all my religious tenets originate from my heart, I am wonderfully pleased with the idea, that I can still keep up a tender intercourse with the dearly beloved friend, or still more dearly beloved mistress, who is gone to the world of spirits.

The ballad on Queen Mary was begun while I was busy with "Percy's Reliques of English Poetry." By the way, how much is every honest heart, which has a tincture of Caledonian prejudice, obliged to you for your glorious story of Buchanan and Targe. 'Twas an unequivocal proof of your loyal gallantry of soul, giving Targe the victory. I should have been mortified to the ground if you had not.

I have just read over, once more of many times, your "Zeluco." I marked with my pencil, as I went along, every passage that pleased me particularly above the rest; and one, or two I think, which, with humble deference, I am disposed to think unequal to the merits of the book. I have sometimes thought to transcribe these marked passages, or at least so much of them as to point where they are, and send them to you. Original strokes that strongly depict the human heart, is your and Fielding's province, beyond any other novelist I have ever perused. Richardson indeed might perhaps be excepted; but, unhappily, his *dramatis personæ* are beings of some other world; and however they may captivate the unexperienced, romantic fancy of a boy or a girl, they will ever, in proportion as we have made human nature our study, dissatisfy our riper years.

As to my private concerns, I am going on, a mighty tax-gatherer before the Lord, and have lately had the interest to get myself ranked on the list of excise as a supervisor. I am not yet employed as such, but in a few years I shall fall into the file of supervisorship by seniority. I have had an immense loss in the death of the Earl of Glencairn; the patron from whom all my fame and good fortune took its rise. Independent of my grateful attachment to him, which was indeed so strong that it pervaded my very soul, and was entwined with the thread of my existence; so soon as the prince's friends had got in (and every dog, you know, has his day), my getting forward in the excise would have been an easier business than otherwise it will be. Though this was a consummation devoutly to be wished, yet, thank Heaven, I can live and rhyme as I am; and as to my boys, poor little fellows! if I cannot place them on as high an elevation in life, as I could wish, I shall, if I am favored so much of the Disposer of events as to see that period, fix them on as broad and independent a basis as possible. Among the many wise adages which have been treasured up by our Scottish ancestors this is one of the best, *Better be the head o' the commonalty, as the tail o' the gentry.*

But I am got on a subject, which however interesting to me, is of no manner of consequence to you; so I shall give you a short poem on the other page, and close this with assuring you how sincerely I have the honor to be,

Yours, &c.   R. B.

Written on the blank leaf of a book, which I presented to a very young lady, whom I had formerly characterised under the denomination of *The Rose-Bud*.   * * * * *

(1.)   **To James Johnson.**

Lawn-market, Friday noon, 4th May, 1787.

DEAR SIR,

I HAVE sent you a song never before known, for your collection; the air by M'Gibbon, but I know not the author of the words, as I got it from Mr. Blacklock.

Farewell, my dear Sir! I wished to have seen you, but I have been dreadfully throng, as I march to-morrow. Had my acquaintance with you been a little older, I would have asked the favour of your correspondence, as I have met with few people whose company and conversation gives me so much pleasure, because I have met with few whose sentiments are so congenial to my own.

When Dunbar and you meet, tell him that I left Edinburgh with the idea of him hanging somewhere about my heart.

Keep the original of the song till we meet again, whenever that may be.   R. B.

(2.)   TO JAMES JOHNSON.

Mauchline, 25th [May] 17[88.]

MY DEAR SIR,

I AM really uneasy about that money which Mr. Creech owes me per note in your hand, and I want it much at present, as I am engaging in business pretty deeply both for myself and my brother. A hundred guineas can be but a trifling affair to him, and 'tis a matter of most serious importance to me. To-morrow I begin my operations as a farmer, and God speed the plough!

I am so enamoured with a certain girl's merit, that I have given her a legal title * * * * I found I had a long and much loved fellow-creature's happiness or misery among my hands; and though Pride and scorning Justice were murderous king's advocates on the one side, yet Humanity, Generosity, and Forgiveness, were such powerful, such irresistible counsel on the other side, that a jury of all endowments and attachments brought in an unanimous verdict— *Not Guilty!* And the panel, be it known unto all whom it may concern, is installed and instated into all the rights, privileges, immunities, and franchises, * * * * that at present do, or in any time coming may, belong to the name, title, designation, &c., of   R. B.

[This letter, we believe, was first printed by Mr. Chambers from original in possession of late Archibald Hastie, Esq., M.P.; and although not strictly literary in its contents, it is interesting for other reasons, and is here inserted to complete the correspondence with Johnson.]

(3.)   TO JAMES JOHNSON.

Mauchline, November 15th, 1788.

MY DEAR SIR,

I HAVE sent you two more songs. If you have got any tunes, or anything to correct, please send them by return of the carrier.

I can easily see, my dear friend, that you will very probably have four volumes. Perhaps you may not find your account lucratively in this business; but you are a patriot for the music of your country; and I am certain posterity will look on themselves as highly indebted to your public spirit. Be not in a hurry; let us go on correctly, and your name shall be immortal.

I am preparing a flaming preface for your third volume. I see every day new musical publications advertised; but what are they? Gaudy, hunted butterflies of a day, and then vanish for ever; but your work will outlive the momentary neglects of idle fashion, and defy the teeth of time.

Have you never a fair goddess that leads you a wild-goose chase of amorous devotion? Let me know a few of her qualities, such as whether she be rather black, or fair; plump, or thin; short, or tall, &c.; and choose your air, and I shall task my muse to celebrate her.

R. B.

[This letter was in all respects, both sorrowful and otherwise, a true prophecy.]

(4.)   TO JAMES JOHNSON.

Dumfries, 1794.

MY DEAR FRIEND,

YOU should have heard from me long ago; but over and above some vexatious share in the pecuniary losses of these accursed times, I have all this winter been plagued with low spirits and blue devils, so that *I have almost hung my harp on the willow-trees.*

I am just now busy correcting a new edition of my poems, and this, with my ordinary business, finds me in full employment.

I send you by my friend Mr. Wallace forty-one songs for your fifth volume; if we cannot finish it in any other way, what would you think of Scots words to some beautiful Irish airs? In the mean time, at your leisure, give a copy of the Museum to any worthy friend, Mr. Peter Hill, bookseller, to bind for me, interleaved with blank leaves, exactly as he did the Laird of Glenriddel's, that I may insert every anecdote I can learn, together with my own criticisms and remarks on the songs. A copy of this kind I shall leave with you, the editor, to publish at some after period, by way of making the Museum a book famous to the end of time, and you renowned for ever.

I have got an Highland Dirk, for which I have great veneration; as it once was the dirk of *Lord Balmerino.* It fell into bad hands, who stripped it of the silver mounting, as well as the knife and fork. I have some thoughts of sending it to your care, to get it mounted anew.

Thank you for the copies of my Volunteer Ballad.—Our friend Clarke has done *indeed* well! 'tis chaste and beautiful. I have not met with any thing that has pleased me so much. You know I am no connoisseur: but that I am an amateur—will be allowed me.

R. B.

(5.)   TO JAMES JOHNSON.

How are you, my dear Friend? and how comes on your fifth volume? You may probably think that for some time past I have neglected you and your work; but, alas! the hand of pain, and sorrow, and care has these many months lain heavy on me! Personal and domestic affliction have almost entirely banished that alacrity and life with which I used to woo the rural Muse of Scotia. In the meantime let us finish what we have so well begun.

The gentleman, Mr. Lewars, a particular friend of mine, will bring out any proofs (if they are ready) or any message you may have. Farewell!

R. BURNS.

Turn over.

You should have had this when Mr. Lewars called on you, but his saddle-bags miscarried. I am extremely anxious for your work, as indeed I am for everything concerning you and your welfare.

You are a good, worthy, honest fellow, and have a good right to live in this world—because you deserve it. Many a merry meeting this Publication has given us, and possibly it may give us more, though, alas! I fear it. This protracting, slow, consuming illness which hangs over me, will, I doubt much, my ever dear friend, arrest my sun before he has well reached his middle career, and will turn over the Poet to far other and more important concerns than studying the brilliancy of wit, or the pathos of sentiment! However, Hope is the cordial of the human heart, and I endeavour to cherish it as well as I can.

Let me hear from you as soon as convenient.—Your work is a great one; and though, now that it is near finished, I see, if we were to begin again, two or three things that might be mended; yet I will venture to prophesy, that to future ages your Publication will be the text-book and standard of Scottish song and music.

I am ashamed to ask another favor of you, because you have been so very good already; but my wife has a very particular friend of hers, a young lady who sings well, to whom she wishes to present the "Scots Musical Museum." If you have a spare copy, will you be [so] obliging as to send it by the very first Fly, as I am anxious to have it soon.

Yours ever,   R. BURNS.

[This letter is now, for the first time, we believe, accurately printed from fac-simile of the original in "Stenhouse's Illustrations." The hand-writing, although still strong and good, is marked with signs of irritation—slips, and slight errors in orthography. The letter, as the reader will perceive, has two distinct signatures, having been written at two separate times; but has no date of any kind whatever. The presumed date is July, 1796. It is addressed to "Mr. James Johnson, Engraver, Lawn Market, Edinr.," and sealed with the Author's coat of arms. It bore originally on the outside to be delivered by Mr. Lewars; but this, as explained by the letter itself, was impossible. The letter had then been opened, and finished, and despatched by post or carrier. These particulars are the more interesting, because it is presumably among the last letters written by the Author, either to Johnson, or to any one else. This is one, we have no doubt, among many instances in which the letters of Burns, from careless editorial reproduction, lose one half of their character and their interest. Let the reader compare the above letter as it now stands, with the common edition as it appears in Cunningham, and he will perceive the difference. On Cunningham's authority, we learn that the copy of the "Museum" here applied for was never sent. This is to be much regretted for Johnson's own sake, *if true*, **although he was then in** very straitened circumstances. For Chambers's **edition of letter (4.) see end of** Principal Literary Correspondence.]

(1.) To Mr. Thomson.

[Here begins the celebrated Thomson Correspondence, so valuable and interesting in relation to Scottish song and music. Only the titles of songs, or the first lines of quotations will be here given; except where the quotation is important, or not elsewhere to be found in the text. As between Dr. Currie and Mr. Chambers, there is a considerable difference in this correspondence, Mr. Chambers having added many important passages which Dr. Currie at the moment thought proper to omit. The passages thus added by Mr. Chambers from the originals we preserve in brackets. Mr. Thomson's letters to Burns we do not include.]

Dumfries, 16th Sept., 1792.

Sir,

I HAVE just this moment got your letter. As the request you make to me will positively add to my enjoyments in complying with it, I shall enter into your undertaking with all the small portion of abilities I have, strained to their utmost exertion by the impulse of enthusiasm. Only, don't hurry me: "Deil tak the hindmost" is by no means the *cri de guerre* of my muse. Will you, as I am inferior to none of you in enthusiastic attachment to the poetry and music of old Caledonia, and, since you request it, have chearfully promised my mite of assistance—will you let me have a list of your airs, with the first line of the printed verses you intend for them, that I may have an opportunity of suggesting any alteration that may occur to me? You know 'tis in the way of my trade; still leaving you, gentlemen, the undoubted right of publishers to approve or reject, at your pleasure, for your own Publication. Apropos, if you are for *English* verses, there is, on my part, an end of the matter. Whether in the simplicity of the ballad, or the pathos of the song, I can only hope to please myself in being allowed at least a sprinkling of our native tongue. English verses, particularly the works of Scotsmen, that have merit, are certainly very eligible. "Tweedside;" "Ah! the poor Shepherd's mournful fate;" "Ah! Chloris, could I now but sit," &c., you cannot mend: but such insipid stuff as "To Fanny fair could I impart," &c., usually set to "The Mill mill, O," is a disgrace to the collections in which it has already appeared, and would doubly disgrace a collection that will have the very superior merit of yours. But more of this in the farther prosecution of the business, if I am called on for my strictures and amendments —I say amendments, for I will not alter except where I myself at least think that I amend.

As to any remuneration, you may think my songs either above or below price; for they shall absolutely be the one or the other. In the honest enthusiasm with which I embark in your undertaking, to talk of money, wages, fee, hire, &c.,

would be downright *prostitution of soul!* A proof of each of the songs that I compose or amend, I shall receive as a favor. In the rustic phrase of the season, "Gude speed the wark!"

I am, Sir, Your very humble servant,

R. BURNS.

P.S.—I have some particular reasons for wishing my interference to be known as little as possible.

(2.) TO MR. THOMSON.

My DEAR SIR,

LET me tell you, that you are too fastidious in your ideas of songs and ballads. I own that your criticisms are just; the songs you specify in your list have, *all but one*, the faults you remark in them; but who shall mend the matter? Who shall rise up and say—"Go to, I will make a better?" For instance, on reading over "The Lea-rig," I immediately set about trying my hand on it, and, after all, I could make nothing more of it than the following, which, Heaven knows, is poor enough.

> When o'er the hill the eastern star, &c.

Your observation as to the aptitude of Dr. Percy's ballad to the air, "Nanie O," is just. It is besides, perhaps, the most beautiful ballad in the English language. But let me remark to you, that in the sentiment and style of our Scottish airs, there is a pastoral simplicity, a something that one may call the Doric style and dialect of vocal music, to which a dash of our native tongue and manners is particularly, nay peculiarly, apposite. For this reason, and, upon my honor, for this reason alone, I am of opinion (but, as I told you before, my opinion is yours, freely yours, to approve or reject, as you please) that my ballad of "Nanie O" might perhaps do for one set of verses to the tune. Now don't let it enter into your head that you are under any necessity of taking my verses. I have long ago made up my mind as to my own reputation in the business of authorship, and have nothing to be pleased or offended at, in your adoption or rejection of my verses. Though you should reject one half of what I give you, I shall be pleased with your adopting the other half, and shall continue to serve you with the same assiduity.

In the printed copy of my "Nanie O," the name of the river is horridly prosaic. I will alter it,

> Behind yon hills where *Lugar* flows.

Girran is the name of the river that suits the idea of the stanza best, but Lugar is the most agreeable modulation of syllables.

I will soon give you a great many more remarks on this business; but I have just now an opportunity of conveying you this scrawl, free of postage, an expense that it is ill able to pay: so, with my best compliments to honest Allan, Good be wi' ye, &c.

Friday Night.

Saturday Morning.

As I find I have still an hour to spare this morning before my conveyance goes away, I will give you "Nanie O" at length. [Here follows the song.]

Your remarks on "Ewe-bughts, Marion," are just; still it has obtained a place among our more classical Scottish songs; and what with many beauties in its composition, and more prejudices in its favor, you will not find it easy to supplant it.

In my very early years, when I was thinking of going to the West Indies, I took the following farewell of a dear girl. It is quite trifling, and has nothing of the merits of "Ewe-bughts;" but it will fill up this page. You must know that all my earlier love-songs were the breathings of ardent passion, and though it might have been easy in after-times to have given them a polish, yet that polish, to me, whose they were, and who perhaps alone cared for them, would have defaced the legend of my heart, which was so faithfully inscribed on them. Their uncouth simplicity was, as they say of wines, their *race*.

Will ye go to the Indies, my Mary? &c.

"Galla Water" and "Auld Rob Morris," I think, will most probably be the next subject of my musings. However, even on my *verses*, speak out your criticisms with equal frankness. My wish is, not to stand aloof, the uncomplying bigot of *opiniâtreté*, but cordially to join issue with you in the furtherance of the work.

R. B.

(3.)   TO MR. THOMSON.

November 8th, 1792.

If you mean, my dear Sir, that all the songs in your collection shall be poetry of the first merit, I am afraid you will find more difficulty in the undertaking than you are aware of. There is a peculiar rhythmus in many of our airs, and a necessity of adapting syllables to the emphasis, or what I would call the feature-notes of the tune, that cramp the poet, and lay him under almost insuperable difficulties. For instance, in the air, "My wife's a wanton wee thing," if a few lines smooth and pretty can be adapted to it, it is all you can expect. The following were made extempore to it; and though, on further study, I might give you something more profound, yet it might not suit the light-horse gallop of the air so well as this random clink:—

MY WIFE'S A WINSOME WEE THING.

I have just been looking over the "Collier's bonny Dochter;" and, if the following rhapsody, which I composed the other day, on a charming Ayrshire girl, Miss Lesley Baillie, as she passed through this place to England, will suit your taste better than the "Collier Lassie," fall on and welcome.

O, saw ye bonie Lesley, &c.

I have hitherto deferred the sublimer, more pathetic airs, until more leisure, as they will take, and deserve, a greater effort. However, they are all put into your hands, as clay into the hands of the potter, to make one vessel to honour, and another to dishonour. Farewell, &c.,

R. B.

(4.)   TO MR. THOMSON.

[SONG.]

Ye banks, and braes, and streams around
The castle o' Montgomery, &c.

14th November, 1792.

MY DEAR SIR,

I AGREE with you that the song "Katharine Ogie," is very poor stuff, and unworthy, altogether unworthy of so beautiful an air. I tried to mend it; but the awkward sound, *Ogie*, recurring so often in the rhyme, spoils every attempt at introducing sentiment into the piece. The foregoing song pleases myself; I think it is in my happiest manner; you will see at first glance that it suits the air. The subject of the song is one of the most interesting passages of my youthful days, and I own that I should be much flattered to see the verses set to an air which would insure celebrity. Perhaps, after all, 'tis the still glowing prejudice of my heart that throws a borrowed lustre over the merits of the composition.

I have partly taken your idea of "Auld Rob Morris." I have adopted the two first verses, and am going on with the song on a new plan, which promises pretty well. I take up one or another, just as the bee of the moment buzzes in my bonnet-lug; and do you, *sans cérémonie*, make what use you chuse of the productions.

Adieu, &c.

R. B.

(5.)   TO MR. THOMSON.

Dumfries, 1st Dec., 1792.

YOUR alterations of my "Nanie O" are perfectly right. So are those of "My wife's a winsome wee thing." Your alteration of the second stanza is a positive improvement. Now, my dear Sir, with the freedom which characterises our correspondence, I must not, cannot alter "Bonie Leslie." You are right; the word "Alexander" makes the line a little uncouth, but I think the thought is pretty. Of Alexander, beyond all other heroes, it may be said, in the sublime language of Scripture, that "he went forth conquering and to conquer."

"For nature made her *what she is*,
    And never made anither."   (such a person as she is.)

This is, in my opinion, more poetical than "Ne'er made sic anither." However, it is immaterial: make it either way. "Caledonie," I agree with you, is not so good a word as could be wished, though it is sanctioned in three or four instances by Allan Ramsay; but I cannot help it. In short, that species of stanza is the most difficult that I have ever tried.

The "Lea-rig" is as follows:

[The song is here given at full length.]

I am interrupted.

Yours, &c.,

R. B.

* The second stanza as Thomson proposed to write it would have been

O leeze me on my wee thing,
My bonny blithesome wee thing;
Sae lang's I hae my wee thing,
I'll think my lot divine, &c.

See Posthumous Poetical Works, p. 327, with Note on Song.]

(6.) TO MR. THOMSON.

[SONGS.]

There's auld Rob Morris, &c.

Duncan Gray cam here to woo, &c.

4th December, 1792.

THE foregoing I submit, my dear Sir, to your better judgment. Acquit them, or condemn them, as seemeth good in your sight. "Duncan Gray" is that kind of light-horse gallop of an air, which precludes sentiment. The ludicrous is its ruling feature.

R. B.

(7.) TO MR. THOMSON.

[SONGS.]

O Poortith cauld, and restless love, &c.

There's braw, braw lads on Yarrow braes, &c.

Jan. 1793.

MANY returns of the season to you, my dear Sir. How comes on your Publication?—will these two foregoing be of any service to you? I should like to know what songs you print to each tune, besides the verses to which it is set. In short, I would wish to give you my opinion on all the poetry you publish. You know it is my trade; and a man in the way of his trade may suggest useful hints, that escape men of much superior parts and endowments in other things.

If you meet with my dear, and much-valued Cunningham, greet him, in my name, with the compliments of the season.

Yours, &c.

R. B.

(8.) TO MR. THOMSON.

20th January, 1793.

I APPROVE greatly, my dear Sir, of your plans. Dr. Beattie's essay will, of itself, be a treasure. On my part, I mean to draw up an appendix to the Doctor's essay, containing my stock of anecdotes, &c., of our Scots songs. All the late Mr. Tytler's anecdotes I have by me, taken down in the course of my acquaintance with him, from his own mouth. I am such an enthusiast, that in the course of my several peregrinations through Scotland, I made a pilgrimage to the individual spot from which every song took its rise, "Lochaber" and the "Braes of Ballenden" excepted. So far as the locality, either from the title of the air, or the tenor of the song, could be ascertained, I have paid my devotions at the particular shrine of every Scots muse.

I do not doubt but you might make a very valuable collection of Jacobite songs; but would it give no offence? In the meantime, do not you think that some of them, particularly "The Sow's tail to Geordie," as an air, with other words, might be well worth a place in your collection of lively songs?

If it were possible to procure songs of merit, it would be proper to have one set of Scots words to every air, and that the set of words to which the notes ought to be set. There is a *naïveté*, a pastoral simplicity, in a slight intermixture of Scots words and phraseology, which is more in unison (at least to my taste, and, I will add, to every genuine Caledonian taste) with the simple pathos, or rustic sprightliness of our native music, than any English verses whatever.

The very name of Peter Pindar is an acquisition to your work. His "Gregory" is beautiful. I have tried to give you a set of stanzas in Scots, on the same subject, which are at your service. Not that I intend to enter the lists with Peter: that would be presumption indeed. My song, though much inferior in poetic merit, has, I think, more of the ballad simplicity in it.

O mirk, mirk is this midnight hour, &c.

My most respectful compliments to the honourable gentleman* who favoured me with a postscript in your last. He shall hear from me and receive his MSS. soon.

R. B.

* (Hon. A. Erskine.)

(9.) TO MR. THOMSON.

[SONG.]

O Mary, at thy window be, &c.

20th March, 1793.

MY DEAR SIR,

THE song prefixed is one of my juvenile works. I leave it in your hands. I do not think it very remarkable, either for its merits or demerits. It is impossible (at least I feel it so in my stinted powers) to be always original, entertaining, and witty.

What is become of the list, &c., of your songs? I shall
be out of all temper with you by and by. I have always
looked on myself as the prince of indolent correspondents,
and valued myself accordingly; and I will not, cannot, bear
rivalship from you, nor any body else.

R. B.

(10.)   TO MR. THOMSON.

March, 1793.

[SONG.]

Here awa, there awa, wandering Willie, &c.

I LEAVE it to you, my dear Sir, to determine whether the
above, or the old "Thro' the lang muir" be the best.

R. B.

(11.)   TO MR. THOMSON.

OPEN THE DOOR TO ME, OH!
With Alterations.

Oh open the door, some pity to show,
   Oh, open the door to me, Oh,* &c.

I DO not know whether this song be really mended.

R. B.

* ' The second line was originally

If lore it may na be, Oh.]

(12.)   TO MR. THOMSON.

JESSIE.
Tune.—" Bonie Dundee."

TRUE-HEARTED was he, the sad swain o' the Yarrow,
   And fair are the maids on the banks o' the Ayr, &c.

(13.)   TO MR. THOMSON.

WHEN WILD WAR'S DEADLY BLAST WAS BLAWN.
Air.—" The Mill mill, O."

When wild war's deadly blast was blawn,
   And gentle peace returning, &c.

MEG O' THE MILL.
Air.—" O Bonie Lass will you lie in a Barrack?"

O ken ye what Meg o' the Mill has gotten? &c.

(14.)   TO MR. THOMSON.

7th April, 1793.

THANK you, my dear Sir, for your packet. You cannot
imagine how much this business of composing for your Publication has added to my enjoyments. What with my early
attachment to ballads, your book, &c., ballad-making is now
as completely my hobby-horse as ever fortification was Uncle
Toby's; so I'll e'en canter it away till I come to the limit of
my race—God grant that I may take the right side of the
winning post!—and then cheerfully looking back on the
honest folks with whom I have been happy, I shall say or
sing, "Sae merry as we a' hae been," and, raising my last
looks to the whole human race, the last words of the voice of
"Coila" shall be "Good night, and joy be wi' you a'!" So
much for my last words: now for a few present remarks, as
they have occurred at random, on looking over your list.

The first lines of "The last time I came o'er the moor,"
and several other lines in it, are beautiful; but, in my opinion
—pardon me! revered shade of Ramsay!—the song is unworthy of the divine air. I shall try to *mend* or *mend*.

"For ever Fortune wilt thou prove" is a charming song;
but "Logan burn and Logan braes" are sweetly susceptible of
rural imagery: I'll try that likewise, and if I succeed, the
other song may class among the English ones. I remember
the two last lines of a verse in some of the old songs of
"Logan Water" (for I know a good many different ones)
which I think pretty:

     "Now my dear lad maun face his faes,
     Far, far frae me and Logan Braes."

"My Patie is a lover gay," is unequal. "His mind is
never muddy," is a muddy expression indeed.

     "Then I'll resign and marry Patie,
     And syne my cockernony.—"

This is surely far unworthy of Ramsay or your book. My
song "Rigs of barley," to the same tune, does not altogether
please me; but if I can mend it, and thresh a few loose sentiments out of it, I will submit it to your consideration. "The
lass o' Patie's mill" is one of Ramsay's best songs; but there
is one loose sentiment in it, which my much-valued friend
Mr. Erskine will take into his critical consideration. In Sir
J. Sinclair's Statistical volumes, are two claims—one, I
think from Aberdeenshire, and the other from Ayrshire—for
the honour of this song. The following anecdote, which I had
from the present Sir William Cunningham of Robertland, who
had it of the late John, Earl of Loudon, I can, on such
authorities, believe:—

Allan Ramsay was residing at Loudon Castle with the then
Earl, father to Earl John; and one forenoon, riding, or walking out together, his lordship and Allan passed a sweet
romantic spot on Irwine water, still called "Patie's Mill,"
where a bonie lass was "todding hay, barehended on the
green." My lord observed to Allan, that it would be a fine
theme for a song. Ramsay took the hint, and, lingering
behind, he composed the first sketch of it, which he produced
at dinner.

"One day I heard Mary say," is a fine song; but, for con-
sistency's sake alter the name "Adonis." Were there ever

such burns published, as a purpose of marriage between Adonis and Mary? I agree with you that my song, "There's nought but care on every hand," is much superior to "Poortith cauld." The original song, "The Mill mill, O!" though excellent, is, on account of delicacy, inadmissible; still I like the title, and think a Scottish song would suit the notes best; and let your chosen song, which is very pretty, follow as an English set. "The Banks of the Dee" is, you know, literally "Langolee," to slow time. The song is well enough, but has some false imagery in it: for instance,

"And sweetly the nightingale sang from the tree."

In the first place, the nightingale sings in a low bush, but never from a tree; and in the second place, there never was a nightingale seen or heard on the banks of Dee, or on the banks of any other river in Scotland. Exotic rural imagery is always comparatively flat. If I could hit on another stanza equal to "The small birds rejoice," &c., I do myself honestly avow, that I think it a superior song. "John Anderson, my jo"— the song to this tune in Johnson's Museum is my composition, and I think it not my worst: if it suit you, take it, and welcome. Your collection of sentimental and pathetic songs is, in my opinion, very compleat; but not so your comic ones. Where are "Tullochgorum," "Lumps o' puddin," "Tibbie Fowler," and several others, which, in my humble judgment, are well worthy of preservation? There is also one sentimental song of mine in the Museum, which never was known out of the immediate neighbourhood, until I got it taken down from a country girl's singing. It is called "Craigieburn Wood," and, in the opinion of Mr. Clarke, is one of our sweetest Scottish songs. He is quite an enthusiast about it; and I would take his taste in Scottish music against the taste of most connoisseurs.

You are quite right in inserting the last five in your list, though they are certainly Irish. "Shepherds, I have lost my love;" is to me a heavenly air—what would you think of a set of Scottish verses to it? I have made one to it, a good while ago, which I think * * *, but in its original state is not quite a lady's song. I inclose an altered, not amended copy for you, if you chuse to set the tune to it, and let the Irish verses follow.*

Mr. Erskine's songs are all pretty, but his "Lone Vale" is divine.

Yours, &c.
R. B.

Let me know just how you like these random hints.

*[Song above referred to is probably "Yestreen I got a pint o' wine." &c.]

(15.)
TO MR. THOMSON.

April, 1793.

I HAVE yours, my dear Sir, this moment. I shall answer it and your former letter, in my desultory way of saying whatever comes uppermost.

The business of many of our tunes wanting, at the beginning, what fiddlers call a starting-note, is often a rub to us poor rhymers.

"There's braw, braw lads on Yarrow braes,
That wander through the blooming heather,"

you may alter to

Braw, braw lads on Yarrow braes,
Ye wander, &c.

My song, "Here awa, there awa," as amended by Mr. Erskine, I entirely approve of, and return you.*

Give me leave to criticise your taste in the only thing in which it is, in my opinion, reprehensible. You know I ought to know something of my own trade. Of pathos, sentiment, and point, you are a complete judge; but there is a quality more necessary than either in a song, and which is the very essence of a ballad—I mean simplicity: now, if I mistake not, this last feature you are a little apt to sacrifice to the foregoing.

Ramsay, as every other poet, has not been always equally happy in his pieces; still I cannot approve of taking such liberties with an author as Mr. W[alker] proposes doing with "The last time I came o'er the moor." Let a poet, if he chuses, take up the idea of another, and work it into a piece of his own; but to mangle the works of the poor bard whose tuneful tongue is now mute for ever in the dark and narrow house—by Heaven, 'twould be sacrilege! I grant that Mr. W.'s version is an improvement: but I know Mr. W. well, and esteem him much; let him mend the song, as the Highlander mended his gun—he gave it a new stock, a new lock, and a new barrel.

I do not, by this, object to leaving out improper stanzas, where that can be done without spoiling the whole. One stanza in "The lass o' Patie's mill" must be left out: the song will be nothing worse for it. I am not sure if we can take the same liberty with "Corn rigs are bonnie." Perhaps it might want the last stanza, and be the better for it. "Cauld kail in Aberdeen," you must leave with me yet awhile. I have vowed to have a song to that air, on the lady whom I attempted to celebrate in the verses, "Poortith cauld and restless love." At any rate, my other song, "Green grow the rashes," will never suit. That song is current in Scotland under the old title, and to the merry old tune of that name, which, of course would mar the progress of your song to celebrity. Your book will be the standard of Scots songs for the future; let this idea ever keep your judgment on the alarm.

I send a song on a celebrated toast in this country, to suit "Bonie Dundee." I send you also a ballad to the "Mill mill, O!"

"The last time I came o'er the moor," I would fain attempt to make a Scots song for, and let Ramsay's be the English set. You shall hear from me soon. When you go to London on this business, can you come by Dumfries? I have still several MS. Scots airs by me, which I have pickt up, mostly from the singing of country lasses. They please me vastly; but your learned lugs would perhaps be displeased with the very feature for which I like them. I call them simple; you would pronounce them silly. Do you know a fine air called "Jackie Hume's Lament?" I have a song of considerable merit to that air. I'll inclose you both the song and the tune, as I had them ready to send to Johnson's Museum.* I send you likewise, to me, a beautiful little air, which I have taken down from viva voce.‡

Adieu.
R. B.

* [This is more complaisant than correct. Our Author did indeed adopt one or two of the changes suggested—but was very far from accepting them all. It is astonishing, indeed, considering the value and importance of his contributions, how he should have endured so much interference so patiently. But there was a limit to that patience. Compare note to letter (17).]

† ["O ken ye what Meg o' the Mill has gotten?" &c.]

‡ ["There was a lass, and she was fair," &c.]

(16.)

TO MR. THOMSON.

April, 1793.

[SONG.]

Farewell thou stream that winding flows, &c.

MY DEAR SIR,

I HAD scarcely put my last letter into the post-office, when I took up the subject of "The last time I came o'er the moor," and ere I slept drew the outlines of the foregoing. How far I have succeeded, I leave on this, as on every other occasion, to you to decide. I own my vanity is flattered, when you give my songs a place in your elegant and superb work; but to be of service to the work is my first wish. As I have often told you, I do not in a single instance wish you, out of compliment to me, to insert anything of mine. One hint let me give you—whatever Mr. Pleyel does, let him not alter one iota of the original Scottish airs; I mean in the song department; but let our national music preserve its native features. They are, I own, frequently wild and irreducible to the more modern rules; but on that very eccentricity, perhaps, depends a great part of their effect.

R. B.

(17.)

TO MR. THOMSON.

June, 1793.

WHEN I tell you, my dear Sir, that a friend of mine, in whom I am much interested, has fallen a sacrifice to these accursed times, you will easily allow that it might unhinge me for doing any good among ballads. My own loss as to pecuniary matters is trifling; but the total ruin of a much-loved friend is a loss indeed. Pardon my seeming inattention to your last commands.

I cannot alter the disputed lines in the "Mill mill, O!" What you think a defect, I esteem as a positive beauty; so you see how doctors differ.* I shall now, with as much alacrity as I can muster, go on with your commands.

You know Frazer, the haut-boy player in Edinburgh—he is here, instructing a band of music for a fencible corps quartered in this country. Among many of his airs that please me, there is one, well known as a reel, by the name of "The Quaker's wife;" and which, I remember, a grand-aunt of mine used to sing, by the name of "Liggeram Cosh, my bonnie wee lass." Mr. Frazer plays it slow, and with an expression that quite charms me. I became such an enthusiast about it, that I made a song for it, which I here subjoin, and inclose Frazer's set of the tune. If they hit your fancy, they are at your service; if not, return me the tune, and I will put it in Johnson's Museum. I think the song is not in my worst manner.

Blythe hae I been on yon hill, &c.

I should wish to hear how this pleases you.

R. B.

* [It is manifest that our Author was at last offended by the editorial liberties so often taken with his contributions. Notwithstanding the hint thus plainly conveyed, Messrs. Thomson and Erskine had the confidence to make the forbidden alteration—a liberty which the Poet, as we are informed by his widow, silently resented. See Note on the Song.]

(18.)

TO MR. THOMSON.

June 25th, 1793.

HAVE you ever, my dear Sir, felt your bosom ready to burst with indignation, on reading of those mighty villains who divide kingdoms, desolate provinces, and lay nations waste, out of the wantonness of ambition, or often from still more ignoble passions? In a mood of this kind to-day I recollected the air of "Logan Water," and it occurred to me that its querulous melody probably had its origin from the plaintive indignation of some swelling, suffering heart, fired at the tyrannic strides of some public destroyer, and overwhelmed with private distress, the consequence of a country's ruin. If I have done anything at all like justice to my feelings, the following song, composed in three-quarters of an hour's meditation in my elbow-chair, ought to have some merit.

O Logan, sweetly didst thou glide, &c.

Do you know the following beautiful little fragment, in Witherspoon's collection of Scots songs?

Air—"Hughie Graham."

"Oh gin my love were yon red rose,
That grows upon the castle wa';
And I mysel' a drap o' dew,
Into her bonie breast to fa'!
"Oh there, beyond expression blest,
I'd feast on beauty a' the night,
Seal'd on her silk-saft faulds to rest,
Till fley'd awa by Phœbus' light."

This thought is inexpressibly beautiful; and quite, so far as I know, original. It is too short for a song, else I would forswear you altogether, unless you gave it a place. I have often tried to eke a stanza to it, but in vain. After balancing myself for a musing five minutes, on the hind-legs of my elbow-chair, I produced the following.

The verses are far inferior to the foregoing, I frankly confess: but if worthy of insertion at all, they might be first in place; as every poet who knows anything of his trade, will husband his best thoughts for a concluding stroke.

> Oh were my love yon lilac fair,
>   Wi' purple blossoms to the spring;
> And I a bird to shelter there,
>   When wearied on my little wing:
> How I wad mourn, when it was torn
>   By autumn wild and winter rude!
> But I wad sing on wanton wing,
>   When youthfu' May its bloom renew'd.

R. B.

(19.)   TO MR. THOMSON.

July 2nd, 1793.

MY DEAR SIR,

I HAVE just finished the following ballad, and, as I do think it in my best style, I send it you. Mr. Clarke, who wrote down the air from Mrs. Burns's wood-note wild, is very fond of it, and has given it a celebrity by teaching it to some young ladies of the first fashion here. If you do not like the air enough to give it a place in your collection, please return it. The song you may keep, as I remember it.

> There was a lass, and she was fair, &c.

I have some thoughts of inserting in your index, or in my notes, the names of the fair ones, the themes of my songs. I do not mean the name at full; but dashes or asterisms, so as ingenuity may find them out.

[The heroine of the foregoing is Miss M'Murdo, daughter to Mr. M'Murdo, of Drumlanrig, one of your subscribers. I have not painted her in the rank which she holds in life, but in the dress and character of a cottager.]

R. B.

[This sentence does not appear in the original letter.—*Chambers*.]

(20.)   TO MR. THOMSON.

July, 1793.

I ASSURE you, my dear Sir, that you truly hurt me with your pecuniary parcel. It degrades me in my own eyes. However, to return it would savour of affectation; but, as to any more traffic of that debtor and creditor kind, I swear by that HONOUR which crowns the upright statue of ROBERT BURNS's INTEGRITY—on the least motion of it, I will indignantly spurn the bypast transaction, and from that moment commence entire stranger to you! BURNS's character for generosity of sentiment and independence of mind, will, I trust, long outlive any of his wants which the cold unfeeling ore can supply; at least, I will take care that such a character he shall deserve.

Thank you for my copy of your Publication. Never did my eyes behold in any musical work such elegance and correctness. Your preface, too, is admirably written, only your partiality to me has made you say too much: however, it will bind me down to double every effort in the future progress of the work. The following are a few remarks on the songs in the list you sent me. I never copy what I write to you, so I may often be tautological, or perhaps contradictory.

"The Flowers of the Forest" is charming as a poem, and should be, and must be, set to the notes; but, though out of your rule, the three stanzas beginning

> "I've seen the smiling o' fortune beguiling,"

are worthy of a place, were it but to immortalise the author of them, who is an old lady of my acquaintance, and at this moment living in Edinburgh. She is a Mrs. Cockburn, I forget of what place; but from Roxburghshire. What a charming apostrophe is

> "Oh fickle fortune, why this cruel sporting,
> Why thus perplex us—poor sons of a day!"

The old ballad, "I wish I were where Helen lies," is silly to contemptibility. My alteration of it, in Johnson's, is not much better. Mr. Pinkerton, in his, what he calls, ancient ballads (many of them notorious, though beautiful enough, forgeries), has the best set. It is full of his own interpolations—but no matter.

In my next I will suggest to your consideration a few songs which may have escaped your hurried notice. In the meantime, allow me to congratulate you now, as a brother of the quill. You have committed your character and fame, which will now be tried, for ages to come, by the illustrious jury of the SONS AND DAUGHTERS OF TASTE—all whom poesy can please, or music charm.

Being a bard of nature, I have some pretensions to second sight; and I am warranted by the spirit to foretell and affirm, that your great-grand-child will hold up your volumes, and say, with honest pride, "This so much admired selection was the work of my ancestor."*

R. B.

* [The family of the illustrious novelist Charles Dickens occupy this relationship.]

(21.)   TO MR. THOMSON.

August, 1793.

MY DEAR THOMSON,

I HOLD the pen for our friend Clarke, who at present is studying the music of the spheres at my elbow. The *Georgium Sidus* he thinks is rather out of tune; so, until he rectify that matter, he cannot stoop to terrestrial affairs.

He sends you six of the *Rondeau* subjects, and if more are wanted, he says you shall have them.

*   *   *   *   *

Confound* your long stairs!

S. CLARKE.

* [No in Currie: in manuscript a stronger word. The signature 'S. Clarke' is in Clarke's hand.—*Chambers*.]

(22.) TO MR. THOMSON.

August, 1793.

Your objection, my dear Sir, to the passages in my song of "Logan Water," is right in one instance; but it is difficult to mend it; if I can, I will. The other passage you object to does not appear in the same light to me.

I have tried my hand on "Robin Adair," and, you will probably think, with little success; but it is such a cursed, cramp, out-of-the-way measure, that I despair of doing any thing better to it.

While larks with little wing, &c.

So much for namby-pamby. I may, after all, try my hand on it in Scots verse. There I always find myself most at home.

I have just put the last hand to the song I meant for "Cauld Kail in Aberdeen." If it suits you to insert it, I shall be pleased, as the heroine is a favorite of mine; if not, I shall also be pleased: because I wish, and will be glad, to see you act decidedly on the business.* 'Tis a tribute as a man of taste, and as an editor, which you owe yourself.

R. B.

*[The song herewith sent is that in p. 29 of this (iv.) volume.—Currie. The song on that page is "O Poortith cauld."]

(23.) TO MR. THOMSON.

August, 1793.

That crinkum-crankum tune, "Robin Adair," has run so in my head, and I succeeded so ill in my last attempt, that I have ventured, in this morning's walk, one essay more. You, my dear Sir, will remember an unfortunate part of our worthy friend C[unningham]'s story, which happened about three years ago. That struck my fancy, and I endeavoured to do the idea justice as follows:

Had I a cave on some wild distant shore, &c.

By the way, I have met with a musical Highlander in Breadalbane's Fencibles, which are quartered here, who assures me that he well remembers his mother's singing Gaelic songs to both "Robin Adair" and "Gramachree." They certainly have more of the Scotch than Irish taste in them.

This man comes from the vicinity of Inverness; so it could not be any intercourse with Ireland that could bring them; except, what I shrewdly suspect to be the case, the wandering minstrels, harpers, and pipers, used to go frequently errant through the wilds both of Scotland and Ireland, and so some favourite airs might be common to both. A case in point— They have lately, in Ireland, published an Irish air, as they say, called "Caun du delish." The fact is, in a publication of Corri's, a great while ago, you will find the same air, called a Highland one, with a Gaelic song set to it. Its name there, I think, is "Oran Gaoil," and a fine air it is. Do ask honest Allan, or the Rev. Gaelic Parson, about these matters.

R. B.

(24.) TO MR. THOMSON.

August, 1793.

My dear Sir,

"Let me in this ae night" I will reconsider. I am glad that you are pleased with my song, "Had I a cave," &c., as I liked it myself.

I walked out yesterday evening with a volume of the Museum in my hand, when, turning up "Allan Water," "What numbers shall the muse repeat," &c., as the words appeared to me rather unworthy of so fine an air, and recollecting that it is on your list, I sat and raved under the shade of an old thorn, till I wrote one to suit the measure. I may be wrong; but I think it not in my worst style. You must know, that in Ramsay's Tea-table, where the modern song first appeared, the ancient name of the tune, Allan says, is "Allan Water," or "My love Annie's very bonie." This last has certainly been a line of the original song; so I took up the idea, and, as you will see, have introduced the line in its place, which I presume it formerly occupied; though I likewise give you a chusing line, if it should not hit the cut of your fancy.

By Allan stream I chanced to rove, &c.

Bravo! say I; it is a good song. Should you think so too (not else) you can set the music to it, and let the other follow as English verses.

Autumn is my propitious season. I make more verses in it than all the year else. God bless you!

R. B.

(25.) TO MR. THOMSON.

August, 1793.

You may readily trust, my dear Sir, that any exertion in my power is heartily at your service. But one thing I must hint to you; the very name of Peter Pindar is of great service to your Publication, so get a verse from him now and then; though I have no objection, as well as I can, to bear the burden of the business.'

Is "Whistle, and I'll come to you, my lad," one of your airs? I admire it much; and yesterday I set the following verses to it. Urbani, whom I have met with here, begged them of me, as he admires the air much; but as I understand that he looks with rather an evil eye on your work, I did not chuse to comply. However, if the song does not suit your taste I may possibly send it him. [He is, *entre nous*, a narrow, contracted creature; but he sings so delightfully, that whatever he introduces at your concert must have immediate celebrity.] The set of the air which I had in my eye is in Johnson's Museum.

O whistle, and I'll come to you, my lad, &c.

Another favorite air of mine is, "The muckin o' Geordie's byre." When sung slow with expression, I have wished that it had had better poetry; that I have endeavoured to supply as follows:

Adown winding Nith I did wander, &c.

Mr. Clarke begs you to give Miss Phillis a corner in your book, as she is a particular flame of his, and out of compliment to him I have made the song. She is a Miss P[hillis] M'[Murdo], sister to "Bonie Jean." They are both pupils of his. You shall hear from me, the very first grist I get from my rhyming-mill.

R. B.

* [Dr. Currie has transferred this paragraph from the present, its proper place, to the head of a subsequent Letter.—Chambers.]

(26.)   TO MR. THOMSON.

[28th] August, 1793.

THAT tune, "Cauld kail," is such a favorite of yours, that I once more roved out yesterday, for a gloamin-shot at the muses; when the muse that presides o'er the shores of Nith, or rather my old inspiring dearest nymph, Coila, whispered me the following. I have two reasons for thinking that it was my early, sweet, simple inspirer that was by my elbow, "smooth gliding without step," and pouring the song on my glowing fancy. In the first place, since I left Coila's native haunts, not a fragment of a poet has arisen to cheer her solitary musings, by catching inspiration from her, so I more than suspect that she has followed me hither, or, at least, makes me occasional visits; secondly, the last stanza of this song I send you is the very words that Coila taught me many years ago, and which I set to an old Scots reel in Johnson's Museum.

Come, let me take thee to my breast, &c.

If you think the above will suit your idea of your favorite air, I shall be highly pleased. "The last time I came o'er the moor" I cannot meddle with, as to mending it; and the musical world have been so long accustomed to Ramsay's words, that a different song, though positively superior, would not be so well received. I am not fond of choruses to songs, so I have not made one for the foregoing.

R. B.

(27.)   TO MR. THOMSON.

[28th] August, 1793.

[MY dear Sir, I have written you already by to-day's post, where I hinted at a song of mine which might suit "Dainty Davie." I have been looking over another and a better song of mine in the Museum, which I have altered as follows, and which I am persuaded will please you. The words 'Dainty Davie' glide so sweetly in the air, that, to a Scots ear, any song to it, without Davie being the hero, would have a lame effect.]

[SONG.]

Now rosy May comes in wi' flowers, &c.

So much for Davie. The chorus, you know, is to the low part of the tune. See Clarke's set of it in the Museum.

N. B. In the Museum they have drawled out the tune to twelve lines of poetry, which is —— nonsense. Four lines of song, and four of chorus, is the way.

(28.)   TO MR. THOMSON.

Sept., 1793.

You know that my pretensions to musical taste are merely a few of nature's instincts, untaught and untutored by art. For this reason, many musical compositions, particularly where much of the merit lies in counterpoint, however they may transport and ravish the ears of you connoisseurs, affect my simple lug no otherwise than merely as melodious din. On the other hand, by way of amends, I am delighted with many little melodies, which the learned musician despises as silly and insipid. I do not know whether the old air "Hey tuttie, taitie," may rank among this number; but well I know that, with Frazer's hautboy, it has often filled my eyes with tears. There is a tradition, which I have met with in many places of Scotland, that it was Robert Bruce's march at the battle of Bannockburn. This thought, in yesternight's evening walk* warmed me to a pitch of enthusiasm on the theme of liberty and independence, which I threw into a kind of Scottish ode, fitted to the air, that one might suppose to be the gallant Royal Scot's address to his heroic followers on that eventful morning.

Bruce to his Troops on the Eve of the Battle of
BANNOCKBURN.

TO ITS AIN TUNE.

Scots, wha hae wi' Wallace bled, &c.†

So may God ever defend the cause of truth and liberty, as he did that day! Amen.

P.S. I showed the air to Urbani, who was highly pleased with it, and begged me to make soft verses for it; but I had no idea of giving myself any trouble on the subject, till the accidental recollection of that glorious struggle for freedom, associated with the glowing ideas of some other struggles of the same nature, not quite so ancient, roused my rhyming mania. Clarke's set of the tune, with his bass, you will find in the Museum, though I am afraid that the air is not what will entitle it to a place in your elegant selection.

R. B.

* [Currie prints this passage "This thought in my solitary wanderings warmed me," &c., in which Mr. Chambers convicts his distinguished predecessor of an improper liberty with the text. See Notes on Song: Poetical Works, p. 201, &c.]
† [See Author's own version, Poetical Works, p. 213.]

---

* M

(29.)

TO MR. THOMSON.

[*Sept.*, 1793.]

I DARE say, my dear Sir, that you will begin to think my correspondence is persecution. No matter, I can't help it; a ballad is my hobby-horse, which, though otherwise a simple sort of harmless idiotical beast enough, has yet this blessed headstrong property, that when it has once fairly made off with a hapless wight, it gets so enamoured with the tinkle-gingle, tinkle-gingle of its own bells, that it is sure to run poor pilgarlick, the bedlam jockey, quite beyond any useful point or post in the common race of man.

The following song I have composed for "Oran-gaoil," the Highland air that, you tell me in your last, you have resolved to give a place to in your book. I have this moment finished the song, so you have it glowing from the mint. If it suit you, well!—if not, 'tis also well!

Behold the hour, the boat arrive, &c.

R. B.

(30.)

TO MR. THOMSON.

Sept., 1793.

I HAVE received your list, my dear Sir, and here go my observations on it.

"Down the burn, Davie." I have this moment tried an alteration, leaving out the last half of the third stanza, and the first half of the last stanza, thus:

As down the burn they took their way,
  And thro' the flowery dale;
His cheek to hers he aft did lay,
  And love was ay the tale.
With "Mary, when shall we return,
  Sic pleasure to renew?"
Quoth Mary, "Love, I like the burn,
  And ay shall follow you."

"Thro' the wood, Laddie"—I am decidedly of opinion that both in this, and "There'll never be peace till Jamie comes hame," the second or high part of the tune being a repetition of the first part an octave higher, is only for instrumental music, and would be much better omitted in singing.

["Banks of the Dee"—Leave it out entirely—'tis rank Irish—every other Irish air you have adopted is in the Scotch taste; but "Langolee"—why, 'tis no more like a Scots air than Lunardi's balloon is like Diogenes's tub. But why don't you take also the "Humours of Glen," "Captain O'Kean," "Coolin," and many other Irish airs, much more beautiful than it? In place of this blackguard Irish jig, let me recommend to you our beautiful Scots air "Saw ye my Peggy"—a tune worth ten thousand of it; or "Fy! let us a' to the Bridal," worth twenty thousand of it.

"White Cockade"—I have forgot the Cantata you allude to, as I kept no copy, and indeed did not know that it was in existence; however, I remember that none of the songs pleased myself, except the last—something about

Courts for cowards were erected,
  Churches built to please the priest.

But there is another song of mine, a composition of early life, in the Museum, beginning—

Nae gentle dames, though e'er sae fair,

which suits the measure, and has tolerable merit.]

"Cowden-knowes"—Remember in your index that the song in pure English to this tune, beginning

"When summer comes, the swains on Tweed,"

is the production of Crawford. Robert was his christian name.

["Bonnie Dundee"—Your objection of the stiff line is just; but mending my colouring would spoil my likeness; so the picture must stand as it is.*

"Flowers of the Forest"—The verses, "I've seen the smiling," &c., with a few trifling alterations, putting "no more" for "nae mair," and the word "turbid" in a note at the bottom of your page, to shew the meaning of "drumlie," the song will serve you for an English set. A small sprinkling of Scotticisms is no objection to an English reader.]

"Laddie, lie near me," must lie by me for some time. I do not know the air; and until I am complete master of a tune, in my own singing (such as it is) I can never compose for it. My way is: I consider the poetic sentiment correspondent to my idea of the musical expression; then chuse my theme; begin one stanza: when that is composed, which is generally the most difficult part of the business, I walk out, sit down now and then, look out for objects in nature around me that are in unison or harmony with the cogitations of my fancy, and workings of my bosom; humming every now and then the air with the verses I have framed. When I feel my muse beginning to jade, I retire to the solitary fire-side of my study, and there commit my effusions to paper; swinging at intervals on the hind-legs of my elbow-chair, by way of calling forth my own critical strictures, as my pen goes on. Seriously, this, at home, is almost invariably my way.

What cursed egotism!

"Gill Morice" I am for leaving out. It is a plaguy length; the air itself is never sung; and its place can well be supplied by one or two songs for fine airs that are not in your list—for instance "Craigieburn-wood" and "Roy's wife." The first, beside its intrinsic merit, has novelty, and the last has high merit as well as great celebrity. I have the original words of a song for the last air, in the handwriting of the lady who composed it; and they are superior to any edition of the song which the public has yet seen.

"Highland-laddie." The old set will please a mere Scotch ear best; and the new an Italianised one. There is a third, and what Oswald calls the old "Highland-laddie," which pleases me more than either of them. It is sometimes called "Ginglin Johnnie;" it being the air of an old humorous tawdry song of that name. You will find it in the Museum. "I hae been at Crookieden," &c. I would advise you, in this musical quandary, to offer up your prayers to the muses for inspiring direction; and in the meantime, waiting for this direction, bestow a libation to Bacchus; and there is not a doubt but you will hit on a judicious choice. *Probatum est.*

"Auld Sir Simon" I must beg you to leave out, and put in its place "The Quaker's wife."

"Blythe hae I been o'er the hill" is one of the finest songs ever I made in my life, and, besides, is composed on a young lady, positively the most beautiful, lovely woman in the world. As I purpose giving you the names and designations of all my heroines, to appear in some future edition of your work, perhaps half a century hence, you must certainly include "The boniest lass in a' the warld," in your collection.

"Dainty Davie" I have heard sung nineteen thousand nine hundred and ninety-nine times, and always with the chorus to the low part of the tune; and nothing has surprised me so much as your opinion on this subject. If it will not suit as I proposed, we will lay two of the stanzas together, and then make the chorus follow [exactly as "Lucky Nancy" in the Museum].

"Fee him, father"—I enclose you Frazer's set of this tune when he plays it slow: in fact he makes it the language of despair. I shall here give you two stanzas, in that style, merely to try if it will be any improvement. Were it possible, in singing, to give it half the pathos which Frazer gives it in playing, it would make an admirably pathetic song. I do not give these verses for any merit they have. I composed them at the time in which "Patie Allan's mither died—that was about the back o' midnight," and by the lee-side of a bowl of punch, which had overset every mortal in company except the hautbois and the muse.

Thou hast left me ever, Jamie, &c.

"Jockie and Jenny" I would discard, and in its place would put "There's nae luck about the House," which has a very pleasant air, and which is positively the finest love-ballad in that style in the Scottish or perhaps in any other language. "When she cam ben she bobbit," as an air, is more beautiful than either, and in the *andante* way would unite with a charming sentimental ballad.

"Saw ye my father?" is one of my greatest favorites. The evening before last, I wandered out, and began a tender song, in what I think is its native style. I must premise that the old way, and the way to give most effect, is to have no starting note, as the fiddlers call it, but to burst at once into the pathos. Every country girl sings "*Saw* ye my father?" &c.

My song is but just begun; and I should like, before I proceed, to know your opinion of it. I have sprinkled it with the Scottish dialect, but it may be easily turned into correct English.†

"Todlin hame." Urbani mentioned an idea of his, which has long been mine, that this air is highly susceptible of pathos; accordingly, you will soon hear him at your concert try it to a song of mine in the Museum, "Ye banks and braes o' bonnie Doon." [Clarke has told me what a creature he is; but if he will bring any more of our tunes from darkness into light, I would be pleased.] One song more and I have done; "Auld lang syne." The air is but mediocre; but the following song, the old song of the olden times, and which has never been in print, nor even in manuscript, until I took it down from an old man's singing, is enough to recommend any air.

Should auld acquaintance be forgot? &c.

Now, I suppose, I have tired your patience fairly. You must, after all is over, have a number of ballads, properly so called. "Gill Morice," "Tranent Muir," "Macpherson's Farewell," "Battle of Sheriff-muir," or "We ran, and they ran" (I know the author of this charming ballad, and his history), "Hardiknute," "Barbara Allan" (I can furnish a finer set of this tune than any that has yet appeared); and besides, do you know that I really have the old tune to which "The Cherry and the Slae" was sung, and which is mentioned as a well-known air in "Scotland's Complaint," a book published before poor Mary's days? It was then called "The banks o' Helicon;" an old poem which Pinkerton has brought to light. You will see all this in Tytler's History of Scottish music. The tune, to a learned ear, may have no great merit; but it is a great curiosity. I have a good many original things of this kind.

R. B.

* [See Letter (12), Jessie.]
† [Where are the joys I hae met in the morning! &c.]

(31.) TO MR. THOMSON.

[8th] *September*, 1793.

I AM happy, my dear Sir, that my ode pleases you so much. Your idea, "honor's bed," is, though a beautiful, a hackneyed idea; so, if you please, we will let the line stand as it is. I have altered the song as follows:—

BANNOCKBURN.

ROBERT BRUCE'S ADDRESS TO HIS ARMY.

Scots, wha hae wi' Wallace bled, &c.*

N.B.—I have borrowed the last stanza from the common stall edition of Wallace—

"A false usurper sinks in every foe,
And liberty returns with every blow."

A couplet worthy of Homer. Yesterday you had enough of my correspondence. The post goes, and my head aches miserably. One comfort! I suffer so much, just now, in this world, for last night's joviality, that I shall escape scot-free for it in the world to come. Amen!

R. B.

* [See Second Version, Poetical Works, p. 213.]

(32.) TO MR. THOMSON.

[15th] *September*, 1793.

"WHO shall decide when doctors disagree?" My ode pleases me so much that I cannot alter it. Your proposed alterations would, in my opinion, make it tame. I am exceedingly obliged to you for putting me on reconsidering it, as I think I have much improved it. Instead of "sodger! hero!" I will have it "Caledonian, on wi' me."

I have scrutinized it over and over; and to the world, some way or other, it shall go as it is. At the same time, it will not in the least hurt me, should you leave it out altogether, and adhere to your first intention of adopting Logan's verses.

I have finished my song to "Saw ye my father?" and in English as you will see. That there is a syllable too much for the expression of the air, is true; but, allow me to say, that the mere dividing of a dotted crotchet into a crotchet and a quaver, is not a great matter: however, in that I have no pretensions to cope in judgment with you. Of the poetry I speak with confidence; but the music is a business where I hint my ideas with the utmost diffidence.

The old verses have merit, though unequal, and are popular: my advice is to set the air to the old words, and let mine follow as English verses. Here they are:

Where are the joys I have met in the morning? &c.

Adieu, my dear Sir! the post goes, so I shall defer some other remarks until more leisure.

R. B.

———

(33.)   TO MR. THOMSON.

September, 1793.

I HAVE been turning over some volumes of songs, to find verses whose measures would suit the airs for which you have allotted me English songs.

For "Muirland Willie," you have, in Ramsay's Tea-Table, an excellent song beginning, "Ah, why those tears in Nelly's eyes?" As for "The Collier's Dochter," take the following old bacchanal:—

Deluded swain, the pleasure, &c.

The faulty line in Logan-Water, I mend thus:

How can your flinty hearts enjoy
The widow's tears, the orphan's cry?

The song otherwise will pass. As to "M'Gregoir-a-Rura," you will see a song of mine to it, with a set of the air superior to yours, in the Museum, vol. ii. p. 181. The song begins,

Raving winds around her blowing.

Your Irish airs are pretty, but they are downright Irish. If they were like the "Banks of Banna," for instance, though really Irish, yet in the Scottish taste, you might adopt them. Since you are so fond of Irish music, what say you to twenty-five of them in an additional number? We could easily find this quantity of charming airs, I will take care that you shall not want songs; and I assure you that you will find it the most saleable of the whole. If you do not approve of "Roy's wife," for the music's sake, we shall not insert it. "Deil tak the wars" is a charming song: so is "Saw ye my Peggy?" "There's nae luck about the House" well deserves a place. I cannot say that "O'er the hills and far awa" strikes me as equal to your selection. "This is no my ain House" is a great favorite of mine; and if you will send me your set of

it, I will task my muse to her highest effort. What is your opinion of "I hae laid a herrin' in saut?" I like it much. Your jacobite airs are pretty, and there are many others of the same kind pretty; but you have not room for them. You cannot, I think, insert "Fy! let us a' to the bridal," to any other words than its own.

What pleases me, as simple and *naïve*, disgusts you as ludicrous and low. For this reason, "Fy! gie me my coggie, Sirs," "Fy! let us a' to the bridal," with several others of that cast, are to me highly pleasing; while "Saw ye my father, or saw ye my mother?" delights me with its descriptive simple pathos. Thus my song, "Ken ye what Meg o' the mill has gotten?" pleases myself so much, that I cannot try my hand at another song to the air, so I shall not attempt it. I know you will laugh at all this; but "ilka man wears his belt his ain gait."

R. B.

———

(34.)   TO MR. THOMSON.

October, 1793.

YOUR last letter, my dear Thomson, was indeed laden with heavy news. Alas, poor Erskine! The recollection that he was a condjutor in your Publication has till now scared me from writing to you, or turning my thoughts on composing for you.

I am pleased that you are reconciled to the air of the "Quaker's wife;" though, by the bye, an old Highland gentleman, and a deep antiquarian, tells me it is a Gaelic air, and known by the name of "Leiger m' chose." The following verses, I hope, will please you, as an English song to the air.

Thine am I, my faithful fair, &c.

Your objection to the English song I proposed for "John Anderson my jo," is certainly just. The following is by an old acquaintance of mine, and I think has merit. The song was never in print, which I think is so much in your favor. The more original good poetry your collection contains, it certainly has so much the more merit.

SONG.—BY GAVIN TURNBULL.

O condescend, dear charming maid,
    My wretched state to view;
A tender swain to love betray'd,
    And sad despair, by you.

While here, all melancholy,
    My passion I deplore,
Yet, urg'd by stern, resistless fate,
    I love thee more and more.

I heard of love, and with disdain
    The urchin's power denied;
I laugh'd at every lover's pain,
    And mock'd them when they sigh'd.

But how my state is alter'd!
    Those happy days are o'er;
For all thy unrelenting hate,
    I love thee more and more.

O yield, illustrious beauty, yield!
  No longer let me mourn;
And tho' victorious in the field,
  Thy captive do not scorn.

Let generous pity warm thee,
  My wonted peace restore;
And grateful I shall bless thee still,
  And love thee more and more.

The following address of Turnbull's to the Nightingale will suit as an English song to the air "There was a lass, and she was fair." By the bye, Turnbull has a great many songs in MS., which I can command, if you like his manner. Possibly, as he is an old friend of mine, I may be prejudiced in his favor; but I like some of his pieces very much.

THE NIGHTINGALE.
By G. Turnbull.

Thou sweetest minstrel of the grove,
  That ever tried the plaintive strain,
Awake thy tender tale of love,
  And soothe a poor forsaken swain.

For tho' the muses deign to aid,
  And teach him smoothly to complain;
Yet Delia, charming, cruel maid,
  Is deaf to her forsaken swain.

All day, with fashion's gaudy sons,
  In sport, she wanders o'er the plain:
Their tales approves, and still she shuns
  The notes of her forsaken swain.

When evening shades obscure the sky,
  And bring the solemn hours again,
Begin, sweet bird, thy melody,
  And soothe a poor forsaken swain.

I shall just transcribe another of Turnbull's, which would go charmingly to "Lewie Gordon."

LAURA.
By G. Turnbull.

Let me wander where I will,
By shady wood, or winding rill;
Where the sweetest May-born flowers
Paint the meadows, deck the bowers;
Where the linnet's early song
Echoes sweet the woods among:
Let me wander where I will,
Laura haunts my fancy still.

If at rosy dawn I chase
To indulge the smiling muse;
If I count some cool retreat,
To avoid the noontide heat;
If beneath the moon's pale ray,
Thro' unfrequented wilds I stray:
Let me wander where I will,
Laura haunts my fancy still.

When at night the drowsy god
Waves his sleep-compelling rod,
And to fancy's wakeful eyes
Bids celestial visions rise;
While with boundless joy I rove
Thro' the fairy land of love:
Let me wander where I will,
Laura haunts my fancy still.

The rest of your letter I shall answer at some other opportunity.   R. B.

* [The Honourable A. Erskine, brother to Lord Kelly, whose melancholy death Mr. Thomson had communicated in an excellent letter, which he has suppressed.—Currie. Mr. Erskine was found drowned in the Firth of Forth, with his pockets full of stones. The distressing event was believed to have been the consequence of a habit of gambling.—Chambers.]

(35.)   TO MR. THOMSON.

December, 1793.

TELL me how you like the following verses to the tune of "Jo Janet."

Husband, husband cease your strife, &c.

[Then follows]

Air—"The Sutor's Dochter."
Wilt thou be my dearie, &c.

(36.)   TO MR. THOMSON.

May, 1794.

MY DEAR SIR,

I RETURN you the plates, with which I am highly pleased; I would humbly propose, instead of the younker knitting stockings, to put a stock and horn into his hands. A friend of mine, who is positively the ablest judge on the subject I have ever met with, and though an unknown, is yet a superior artist with the burin, is quite charmed with Allan's manner. I got him a peep of the "Gentle Shepherd;" and he pronounces Allan a most original artist of great excellence.

For my part, I look on Mr. Allan's chusing my favorite poem for his subject, to be one of the highest compliments I have ever received.

I am quite vexed at Pleyel's being cooped up in France, as it will put an entire stop to our work. Now, and for six or seven months, *I shall be quite in song,* as you shall see by and by. I got an air, pretty enough, composed by Lady Elizabeth Heron of Heron, which she calls "The Banks of Cree." Cree is a beautiful romantic stream, and as her ladyship is a particular friend of mine, I have written the following song to it.

Here is the glen, and here the bower, &c.

[The air, I fear, is not worth your while; else I would send it you. I am hurried, so farewell until next post. My seal is all well, except that my holly must be a *bush,* not a *tree,* as in the present shield. I also inclose it, and will send the pebble by the first opportunity.]

          R. B.

(37.)   TO MR. THOMSON.

July, 1794.

Is there no news yet of Pleyel? Or is your work to be at a dead stop until the allies set our modern Orpheus at liberty from the savage thraldom of democratic discords? Alas the day! And woe is me! That auspicious period, pregnant with the happiness of millions * * * seems by no means near.

I have presented a copy of your songs to the daughter of a much-valued and much-honored friend of mine, Mr. Graham of Fintray. I wrote on the blank side of the title-page the following address to the young lady.

Here, where the Scottish muse immortal lives, &c.

R. B.

[This letter contains an ironical tirade on the mishaps of Prussia in her war against France, which Dr. Currie had deemed unfit for publication.—*Chambers*.]

———

(38.)

TO MR. THOMSON.

30th August, 1794.

The last evening, as I was straying out, and thinking of "O'er the hills and far away," I spun the following stanza for it; but whether my spinning will deserve to be laid up in store, like the precious thread of the silk-worm, or brushed to the devil, like the vile manufacture of the spider, I leave, my dear Sir, to your usual candid criticism. I was pleased with several lines in it at first, but I own that now it appears rather a flimsy business.

This is just a hasty sketch, until I see whether it be worth a critique. We have many sailor songs, but as far as I at present recollect, they are mostly the effusions of the jovial sailor, not the wailings of his love-lorn mistress. I must here make one sweet exception—"Sweet Annie frae the sea-beach came." Now for the song:—

ON THE SEAS AND FAR AWAY.

How can my poor heart be glad, &c.

I give you leave to abuse this song, but do it in the spirit of Christian meekness.

R. B.

———

(39.)

TO MR. THOMSON.

Sept., 1794.

[Little do the Trustees for our Manufactures, when they frank my letters to you, little do they consider what kind of manufacture they are encouraging. The Manufacture of Nonsense was certainly not in idea when the act of Parliament was framed, and yet, under my hands and your cover, it thrives amazingly. Well, there are more pernicious manufactures, that is certain.]

I shall withdraw my "On the seas and far away" altogether: it is unequal and unworthy the work. Making a poem is like begetting a son: you cannot know whether you have a wise man or a fool, until you produce him to the world and try him.

For that reason I send you the offspring of my brain, abortions and all; and, as such, pray look over them, and forgive them, and burn them. I am flattered at your adopting

"Ca' the yowes to the knowes," as it was owing to me that ever it saw the light. About seven years ago I was well acquainted with a worthy little fellow of a clergyman, a Mr. Clunzie, who sung it charmingly; and, at my request, Mr. Clarke took it down from his singing. When I gave it to Johnson, I added some stanzas to the song, and mended others, but still it will not do for you. In a solitary stroll which I took to-day, I tried my hand on a few pastoral lines, following up the idea of the chorus, which I would preserve. Here it is, with all its crudities and imperfections on its head.

Ca' the yowes to the knowes, &c.

I shall give you my opinion of your other newly adopted songs my first scribbling fit.

R. B.

———

(40.)

TO MR. THOMSON.

Sept., 1794.

Do you know a blackguard Irish song called "Onagh's Waterfall?" The air is charming, and I have often regretted the want of decent verses to it. It is too much, at least for my humble rustic Muse, to expect that every effort of hers shall have merit; still I think that it is better to have mediocre verses to a favorite air, than none at all. On this principle I have all along proceeded in the Scots Musical Museum; and as that publication is at its last volume, I intend the following song, to the air above mentioned, for that work.

If it does not suit you as an editor, you may be pleased to have verses to it that you can sing in the company of ladies.

Sae flaxen were her ringlets, &c.

Not to compare small things with great, my taste in music is like the mighty Frederick of Prussia's taste in painting: we are told that he frequently admired what the connoisseurs derided, and always, without any hypocrisy, confessed his admiration. I am sensible that my taste in music must be inelegant and vulgar, because people of undisputed and cultivated taste can find no merit in my favorite tunes. Still, because I am cheaply pleased, is that any reason why I should deny myself that pleasure? Many of our strathspeys, ancient and modern, give me most exquisite enjoyment, where you and other judges would probably be showing disgust. For instance, I am just now making verses for "Rothe-murche's rant," an air which puts me in raptures; and, in fact, unless I can be pleased with the tune, I never can make verses to it. Here I have Clarke on my side; who is a judge that I will pit against any of you. "Rothemurche," he says, "is an air both original and beautiful;" and, on his recommendation, I have taken the first part of the tune for a chorus, and the fourth or last part for the song. I am but two stanzas deep in the work, and possibly you may think, and justly, that the poetry is as little worth your attention as the music. [Here follow two stanzas of "Lassie wi' the lint-white locks."]

I have begun anew, "Let me in this ae night." Do you think that we ought to retain the old chorus? I think we must retain both the old chorus and the first stanza of the old song. I do not altogether like the third line of the first stanza, but cannot alter it to please myself. I am just three stanzas deep in it. Would you have the *denouément* to be successful or otherwise?—should she "let him in" or not?

Did you not once propose "The Sow's tail to Geordie" as an air for your work? I am quite delighted with it; but I acknowledge that is no mark of its real excellence. I once set about verses for it, which I meant to be in the alternate way of a lover and his mistress chanting together. I have not the pleasure of knowing Mrs. Thomson's christian name, and yours, I am afraid, is rather burlesque for sentiment, else I had meant to have made you [two] the hero and heroine of the little piece.

How do you like the following epigram which I wrote the other day on a lovely young girl's recovery from a fever? Doctor Maxwell was the physician who seemingly saved her from the grave; and to him I address the following:—

TO DR. MAXWELL,

ON MISS JESSIE STAIG'S RECOVERY.

Maxwell, if merit here you crave,
 That merit I deny;
You save fair Jessie from the grave:—
 An angel could not die.

God grant you patience with this stupid epistle!

R. B.

(41.) TO MR. THOMSON.

19th October, 1794.

MY DEAR FRIEND,

By this morning's post I have your list, and, in general, I highly approve of it. I shall, at more leisure, give you a critique on the whole. [In the meantime, let me offer at a new improvement, or rather restoring old simplicity, in one of your newly adopted songs:—

When she cam ben she bobbit—*a crotchet stop*
When she cam ben she bobbit—*a crotchet stop*
And when she cam ben she kiss'd Cockpen,
And syne she denied that she did it—*a crotchet stop.*

This is the old rhythm, and by far the most original and beautiful. Let the harmony of the bass, at the stops, be full; and thin and dropping through the rest of the air, and you will give the tune a noble and striking effect. Perhaps I am betraying my ignorance; but Mr. Clarke is decidedly of my opinion. He) goes to your town by to-day's fly, and I wish you would call on him and take his opinion in general: you know his taste is a standard. He will return here again in a week or two, so please do not miss asking for him. One

thing I hope he will do [which would give me high satisfaction], persuade you to adopt my favorite "Craigieburn-wood" in your selection: it is as great a favorite of his as of mine. The lady on whom it was made is one of the finest women in Scotland; and in fact (*entre nous*) is in a manner to me what Sterne's Eliza was to him—a mistress, or friend, or what you will, in the guileless simplicity of Platonic love. (Now, don't put any of your squinting constructions on this, or have any clishmaclaiver about it among our acquaintances.) I assure you that to my lovely friend you are indebted for many of your best songs of mine. Do you think that the sober, gin-horse routine of existence could inspire a man with life, and love, and joy—could fire him with enthusiasm, or melt him with pathos, equal to the genius of your book? No! no! Whenever I want to be more than ordinary *in song* —to be in some degree equal to your diviner airs—do you imagine I fast and pray for the celestial emanation? *Tout au contraire!* I have a glorious recipe; the very one that for his own use was invented by the divinity of healing and poetry, when erst he piped to the flocks of Admetus. I put myself in a regimen of admiring a fine woman; and in proportion to the adorability of her charms, in proportion you are delighted with my verses. The lightning of her eye is the godhead of Parnassus, and the witchery of her smile the divinity of Helicon!

To descend to business; if you like my idea of " When she cam ben she bobbit," the following stanzas of mine, altered a little from what they were formerly, when set to another air, may perhaps do instead of worse stanzas:—

O saw ye my dear, my Phely, &c.

Now for a few miscellaneous remarks. "The Posie" (in the Museum) is my composition; the air was taken down from Mrs. Burns's voice. It is well known in the West Country, but the old words are trash. By the bye, take a look at the tune again, and tell me if you do not think it is the original from which "Roslin Castle" is composed. The second part in particular, for the first two or three bars, is exactly the old air. "Strathallan's Lament" is mine; the music is by our right trusty and deservedly well-beloved Allan Masterton. "Donocht-Head" is not mine; I would give ten pounds it were. It appeared first in the *Edinburgh Herald,* and came to the editor of that paper with the Newcastle post-mark on it." "Whistle o'er the lave o't" is mine; the music said to be by a John Bruce, a celebrated violin player in Dumfries, about the beginning of this century. This I know, Bruce, who was an honest man, though a red-wud Highlandman, constantly claimed it; and by all the old musical people here is believed to be the author of it.

"O how can I be blythe and glad" is mine; but as it is already appropriated to an air by itself, both in the Museum and from thence into Ritson—I have got that book—I think it would be as well to leave it out.

"M'Pherson's Farewell" is mine, excepting the chorus and one stanza.

"Andrew and his cutty gun."—The song to which this is set in the Museum is mine, and was composed on Miss

Euphemia Murray, of Lintrose, commonly and deservedly called the Flower of Strathmore.

["The Quaker's wife."—Do not give the tune that name, but the old Highland one, "Leiger m' chose." The only fragment remaining of the old words is the chorus, still a favorite lullaby of my old mother, from whom I learned it:

> Leiger m' chose, my bonny wee lass,
> An' leiger m' chose, my dearie:
> A' the lee-lang winter night,
> Leiger m' chose, my dearie.

The current name for the reel to this day at country weddings is "Laggeram Cosh," a Lowland corruption of the original Gaelic. I have altered the first stanza, which I would have to stand thus:

> Thine am I, my faithful fair,
> Well thou may'st discover;
> Every pulse along my veins
> Tells the ardent lover.

"Saw ye my father."—I am still decidedly of opinion that you should set the tune to the old song, and let mine follow for English verses; but as you please. "In summer when the hay was mawn," "An' O for ane-and-twenty, Tam," are both mine. The set of the last in the Museum does not please me; but if you will get any of our ancienter Scots fiddlers to play you in our strathspey time "The Moudiewort"—that is the name of the air—I think it will delight you.]

"How long and dreary is the night!" I met with some such words in a collection of songs somewhere, which I altered and enlarged; and to please you, and to suit your favorite air, I have taken a stride or two across my room and have arranged it anew, as you will find on the other page.

> How long and dreary is the night, &c.

Tell me how you like this. I differ from your idea of the expression of the tune. There is, to me, a great deal of tenderness in it. You cannot, in my opinion, dispense with a bass to your addenda airs. A lady of my acquaintance, a noted performer, plays ["Nae Luck about the House"] and sings [it] at the same time so charmingly, that I shall never bear to see any of her songs sent into the world, as naked as Mr. What-d'ye-call-um has done in his London Collection.†

These English songs gravel me to death. I have not that command of the language that I have of my native tongue. [In fact, I think my ideas are more barren in English than in Scotch.] I have been at "Duncan Gray," to dress it in English, but all I can do is deplorably stupid. For instance:—

> Let not woman e'er complain, &c.

[If you insert both Peter's song and mine, to the "Bonny Brucket Lassie," it will cost you engraving the first verse of both songs, as the rhythm of the two is considerably different. As "Fair Eliza" is already published, I am totally indifferent whether you give it a place or not; but to my taste, the rhythm of my song to that air would have a much more original effect.

"Love never more shall give me Pain" has long been appropriated to a popular air of the same title, for which reason, in my opinion, it would be improper to set it to "My Lodging is on the cold Ground." There is a song in the Museum by a ci-devant goddess of mine, which I think not unworthy of the air, and suits the rhythm equally with "Love never more," &c. It begins—

> "Talk not of love, it gives me pain."]

Since the above, I have been out in the country, taking a dinner with a friend, where I met with the lady whom I mentioned in the second page in this odds-and-ends of a letter. As usual, I got into song; and returning home I composed the following:

> Sleep'st thou, or wak'st thou, fairest creature, &c.

[I allow the first four lines of each stanza to be repeated; but if you inspect the air, in the first part, you will find that it also, without a quaver of difference, is the same passage repeated; which will exactly put it on the footing of our other slow Scottish airs, as they, you know, are twice sung over.]

If you honor my verses by setting the air to them, I will vamp up the old song, and make it English enough to be understood.

[I have sent you my song noted down to the air, in the way I think it should go: I believe you will find my set of the air to be one of the best.]

I inclose you a musical curiosity, an East Indian air, which you would swear was a Scottish one. I know the authenticity of it, as the gentleman who brought it over is a particular acquaintance of mine. Do preserve me the copy I send you, as it is the only one I have. Clarke has set a bass to it, and I intend putting it into the Musical Museum. Here follow the verses I intend for it.

> But lately seen in gladsome green, &c.

I would be obliged to you if you would procure me a sight of Ritson's collection of English songs, which you mention in your letter. I will thank you for another information, and that as speedily as you please: whether this miserable drawling hotchpotch epistle has not completely tired you of my correspondence?

R. B.

---

* "The reader will be curious to see this poem, so highly praised by Burns. Here it is.

> Keen blaws the wind o'er Donocht-Head,
>   The snaw drives snelly thro' the dale,
> The Gaber-lunzie tirls my sneck,
>   And shivering tells his waefu' tale.
> "Cauld is the night, O let me in,
>   "And dinna let your minstrel fa',
> "And dinna let his winding sheet
>   "Be naething but a wreath o' snaw,
>
> "Full ninety winters hae I seen,
>   "And pip'd where gor-cocks whirring flew,
> "And mony a day I've danc'd, I ween,
>   "To lilts which from my drone I blew."
> My Eppie wak'd, and soon she cry'd,
>   "Get up gudeman, and let him in;
> "For weel ye ken the winter night
>   "Was short when he began his din."

> My Eppie's voice, O wow it's sweet,
>   Even tho' she bann and scaulds a wee;
> But when it's tun'd to sorrow's tale,
>   O, haith, it's doubly dear to me!
> Come in, auld carl, I'll steer my fire,
>   I'll make it bleeze a bonnie flame;
> Your bluid is thin, ye've tint the gate,
>   Ye should na stray sae far frae hame.
>
>   "Nae hame hae I," the minstrel said,
>   "Sad party-strife o'erturned my ha';
>   "And, weeping at the eve of life,
>   "I wander thro' a wreath o' snaw."
>   *   *   *   *   *   *   *

This affecting poem is apparently incomplete. **The author need not be ashamed to own himself. It is worthy of Burns, or of Macneill.—Currie. It was written by a gentleman of Newcastle, named Pickering.—Chambers.]** Dunnecht Head is a mountain promontory in extreme north of Scotland.

+ [Mr. Ritson.—Currie.]

(42.)   TO MR. THOMSON.

November, 1794.

MANY thanks to you, my dear Sir, for your present; it is a book of the utmost importance to me. I have yesterday begun my anecdotes, &c., for your work. I intend drawing them up in the form of a letter to you, which will save me from the tedious dull business of systematic arrangement. Indeed, as all I have to say consists of unconnected remarks, anecdotes, scraps of old songs, &c., it would be impossible to give the work a beginning, a middle, and an end, which the critics insist to be absolutely necessary in a work. [As soon as I have a few pages in order, I will send you them as a specimen. I only fear that the matter will grow so large among my hands as to be more expense than you can allot for it. Now for my desultory way of writing to you.

I am happy that I have at last pleased you with verses to your right-hand tune "Cauld Kail." I see a little unpliancy in the line you object to, but cannot alter it for a better. It is one thing to know one's error, and another and much more difficult affair to amend that error.] In my last, I told you my objections to the song you had selected for " My lodging is on the cold ground." On my visit the other day to my fair Chloris (that is the poetic name of the lovely goddess of my inspiration) she suggested an idea, which I, on my return from the visit, wrought into the following song. [It is exactly in the measure of " My dearie an thou die," which you say is the precise rhythm of the air:]

> My Chloris, mark how green the groves, &c.

How do you like the simplicity and tenderness of this pastoral? I think it pretty well.

I like you for entering so candidly and so kindly into the story of " Ma chere Amie." I assure you I was never more in earnest in my life, than in the account of that affair which I sent you in my last. Conjugal love is a passion which I deeply feel, and highly venerate; but, somehow, it does not make such a figure in poesy as that other species of the passion,

> " Where Love is liberty, and Nature law."

Musically speaking, the first is an instrument of which the gamut is scanty and confined, but the tones inexpressibly sweet, while the last has powers equal to all the intellectual modulations of the human soul. Still, I am a very poet in my enthusiasm of the passion. The welfare and happiness of the beloved object is the first and inviolate sentiment that pervades my soul; and whatever pleasures I might wish for, or whatever might be the raptures they would give me, yet, if they interfere [and clash] with that first principle, it is having these pleasures at a dishonest price; and justice forbids, and generosity disdains the purchase.   *   *   * [Where the parties are capable of, and the Passion is, the true Divinity of Love—the man who can act otherwise is a VILLAIN!]

[The Poet, as Mr. Chambers informs us, here leaves a small space at the bottom of a page, and at the top of the next goes on: ' It was impossible, you know, to take up the subject of your songs in the last sheet: that would have been a falling off indeed!]

Despairing of my own powers to give you variety enough in English songs, I have been turning over old collections, to pick out songs, of which the measure is something similar to what I want: and, with a little alteration, so as to suit the rhythm of the air exactly, to give you them for your work. Where the songs have hitherto been but little noticed, nor have ever been set to music, I think the shift a fair one. A song, which, under the same first verse, you will find in Ramsay's Tea-Table Miscellany, I have cut down for an English dress to your " Dainty Davie," as follows:—

> It was the charming month of May, &c.

You may think meanly of this, but take a look at the bombast original, and you will be surprised that I have made so much of it. I have finished my song to " Rothemurche's rant," and you have Clarke to consult as to the set of the air for singing.

> Lassie wi' the lint-white locks, &c.

This piece has at least the merit of being a regular pastoral; the vernal morn, the summer noon, the autumnal evening, and the winter night, are regularly rounded. If you like it, well; if not, I will insert it in the Museum.

I am out of temper that you should set so sweet, so tender an air, as " Deil tak the wars," to the foolish old verses. You talk of the silliness of " Saw ye my father?"—By heavens! the odds is gold to brass! Besides, the old song, though now pretty well modernized into the Scottish language, is originally, and in the early editions, a bungling low imitation of the Scottish manner, by that genius Tom D'Urfey, so has no pretensions to be a Scottish production. There is a pretty English song by Sheridan, in the " Duenna," to this air, which is out of sight superior to D'Urfey's. It begins,

> " When sable night each drooping plant restoring."

The air, if I understand the expression of it properly, is the very native language of simplicity, tenderness, and love. I have again gone over my song to the tune, as follows,

> Sleep'st thou, or wak'st thou, fairest creature? * &c.

* N

[I could easily throw this into an English mould; but to my taste, in the simple and tender of the pastoral song, a sprinkling of the old Scottish has an inimitable effect. You know I never encroach on your privilege as an Editor. You may reject my song altogether, and keep by the old one; or you may give mine as a second Scottish one; or lastly, you may set the air to my verses, still giving the old song, as a second one, and as being well known; in which last case, I would find you in English verses of my own, a song, the exact rhythm of my Scottish one. If you keep by the old words, Sheridan's song will do for an English one. I once more conjure you to have no manner of false delicacy in accepting or refusing my compositions, either in this or any other of your songs.]

Now for my English song to "Nancy's to the greenwood," &c.

Farewell thou stream that winding flows, &c.

["Young Jockey was the blithest lad."—My English song, "Here is the Glen, and here the Bower," cannot go to this air. However, the measure is so common that you may have your choice of five hundred English songs. Do you know the air "Lumps of Pudding?" It is a favorite of mine, and I think would be worth a place among your additional songs, as soon as several on your list. It is in a measure in which you will find songs enow to chuse from; but if you were to adopt it, I would take it in my own hand.

There is an air, "The Caledonian Hunt's delight," to which I wrote a song that you will find in Johnson, "Ye banks and braes o' bonie Doon:" this air I think might find a place among your hundred, as Lear says of his knights. [To make room for it, you may take out—to my taste—either "Young Jockey was the blithest lad," or "There's nae Luck about the House," or "The Collier's Bonny Lassie," or "The tither morn," or "The Sow's Tail;" and put into your additional list. Not but that these songs have great merit; but still they have not the pathos of "The Banks of Doon."] Do you know the history of the air? It is curious enough. A good many years ago, Mr. James Miller, writer in your good town, a gentleman whom possibly you know, was in company with our friend Clarke; and talking of Scottish music, Miller expressed an ardent ambition to be able to compose a Scots air. Mr. Clarke, partly by way of joke, told him to keep to the black keys of the harpsichord, and preserve some kind of rhythm, and he would infallibly compose a Scots air. Certain it is that, in a few days, Mr. Miller produced the rudiments of an air, which Mr. Clarke, with some touches and corrections, fashioned into the tune in question. Ritson, you know, has the same story of the *Black keys:* but this account which I have just given you, Mr. Clarke informed me of several years ago. Now, to show you how difficult it is to trace the origin of our airs, I have heard it repeatedly asserted that this was an Irish air: nay, I met with an Irish gentleman who affirmed he had heard it in Ireland among the old women: while, on the other hand, a lady of fashion, no less than a countess, informed me, that the first person who introduced the air into this country, was a baronet's lady of her acquaintance, who took down the notes from an itinerant piper in the Isle of Man. How difficult, then, to ascertain the truth respecting our poesy and music! I myself have lately seen a couple of ballads sung through the streets of Dumfries, with my name at the head of them as the author, though it was the first time I had ever seen them.

I thank you for admitting "Craigieburn-wood;" and I shall take care to furnish you with a new chorus. In fact, the chorus was not my work, but a part of some old verses to the air. If I can catch myself in a more than ordinarily propitious moment, I shall write a new "Craigieburn-wood" altogether. My heart is much in the theme.

I am ashamed, my dear fellow, to make the request; 'tis dunning your generosity; but in a moment when I had forgotten whether I was rich or poor, I promised Chloris a copy of your songs. It wrings my honest pride to write you this; but an ungracious request is doubly so by a tedious apology. To make you some amends, as soon as I have extracted the necessary information out of them, I will return you Ritson's volumes.†

The lady is not a little proud that she is to make so distinguished a figure in your collection, and I am not a little proud that I have it in my power to please her so much. Lucky it is for your patience that my paper is done, for when I am in a scribbling humour, I know not when to give over.

R. B.

* [Second version: see both versions, Poetical Works (Thomson's Collection), p. 224.]

† [We think it right here to quote Mr. Thomson's reply to this request. "Let me beseech you not to use ceremony in telling me when you wish to present any of your friends with the songs. The next carrier will bring you three copies, and you are as welcome to twenty as to a pinch of snuff."]

(43.)
TO MR. THOMSON.

19th November, 1794.

You see, my dear Sir, what a punctual correspondent I am; though, indeed, you may thank yourself for the *tedium* of my letters, as you have so flattered me on my horsemanship with my favorite hobby, and have praised the grace of his ambling so much, that I am scarcely ever off his back. For instance, this morning, though a keen blowing frost, in my walk before breakfast, I finished my duet, which you were pleased to praise so much. Whether I have uniformly succeeded, I will not say; but here it is for you, though it is not an hour old.

O Philly, happy be the day, &c.

Tell me honestly how you like it, and point out whatever you think faulty.

I am much pleased with your idea of singing our songs in alternate stanzas, and regret that you did not hint it to me sooner. In those that remain I shall have it in my eye. I remember your objections to the name Philly; but it is the common abbreviation of Phillis. Sally, the only other name that suits, has, to my ear, a vulgarity about it, which unfits it for any thing except burlesque. The legion of Scottish poetasters of the day, whom your brother editor, Mr. Ritson, ranks with me as my coevals, have always mistaken vulgarity for simplicity; whereas, simplicity is as much *éloignée* from vulgarity on the one hand, as from affected point and puerile conceit on the other.

I agree with you as to the air, "Craigieburn-wood," that a chorus would, in some degree, spoil the effect, and shall certainly have none in my projected song to it. It is not, however, a case in point with "Rothemurche;" there, as in "Roy's Wife of Aldivalloch," a chorus goes, to my taste, well enough. As to the chorus going first, that is the case with "Roy's Wife" as well as "Rothemurche." In fact, in the first part of both tunes, the rhythm is so peculiar and irregular, and on that irregularity depends so much of their beauty, that we must e'en take them with all their wildness, and humour the verse accordingly. Leaving out the starting note in both tunes, has, I think, an effect that no regularity could counterbalance the want of.

Try,   { Oh Roy's Wife of Aldivalloch.
        { O lassie wi' the lint-white locks.

and

Compare with   { *Roy's* Wife of Aldivalloch.
                { *Lassie* wi' the lint-white locks.

Does not the tameness of the prefixed syllable strike you? In the last case, with the true furor of genius, you strike at once into the wild originality of the air; whereas, in the first insipid method, it is like the grating screw of the pins before the fiddle is brought into tune. This is my taste; if I am wrong, I beg pardon of the *cognoscenti*.

[I am also of your mind as to the "Caledonian Hunt;" but to fit it with verses to suit these dotted crotchets will be a task indeed. I differ from you as to the expression of the air. It] is so charming, that it would make any subject in a song go down; but pathos is certainly its native tongue. Scottish bacchanalians we certainly want, though the few we have are excellent. For instance, "Todlin hame" is, for wit and humour, an unparalleled composition; and "Andrew and his cutty gun" is the work of a master. By the way, are you not quite vexed to think that those men of genius, for such they certainly were, who composed our fine Scottish lyrics should be unknown? It has given me many a heart-ache. Apropos to bacchanalian songs in Scottish; I composed one yesterday, for an air I like much—"Lumps o' pudding."

Contented wi' little and cantie wi' mair, &c.

If you do not relish this air, I will send it to Johnson.

[The two songs you saw in Clarke's are neither of them worthy of your attention. The words of "Auld Lang Syne" are good, but the music is an old air, the rudiments of the modern tune of that name. The other tune you may hear as a common country-dance.]

Since yesterday's penmanship, I have framed a couple of English stanzas, by way of an English song to "Roy's wife." You will allow me, that in this instance my English corresponds in sentiment with the Scottish.

Canst thou leave me thus, my Katy? &c.

Well! I think this to be done in two or three turns across my room, and with two or three pinches of Irish blackguard, is not so far amiss. You see I am determined to have my quantum of applause from somebody.

[Now for "When she cam ben she bobbit."

[Burns here repeats the song "Oh, saw ye my dear, my Phely?" but with the names Mary and Harry instead of Phely and Willy.]

I think these names will answer better than the former; and the rhythm of the song is as you desired.

I dislike your proposed alterations in two instances. "Logie o' Buchan," and "There's my Thumb, I'll ne'er beguile thee," are certainly fittest for your additional songs; and in their place, as two of the hundred, I would put the most beautiful of airs—"Whistle and I'll come to ye, my Lad," at all rates, as one. It is surely capable of feeling and sentiment, and the song is one of my best. For the other, keep your favorite "Muirland Willy," and with it close your hundred. As to the first being Irish, all that you can say is, that it has a twang of the Irish manner; but to infer from that, that of course it must be an Irish production, is unfair. In the neighbourhood and intercourse of the Scots and Irish, and both musical nations too, it is highly probable that composers of one nation would sometimes imitate or emulate the manner of the other. I never met with an Irishman who claimed this air; a pretty strong proof that it is Scottish. Just the same is the case with "Gramachree;" if it be really Irish, it is decidedly in the Scottish taste. That other air in your collection, "Oran-Gaoil," which you think is Irish, that nation claim as theirs by the name of "Caun du delish;" but look into Gow's publication of Scottish Songs, and you will find it as a Gaelic song, with the words in that language, a wretched translation of which original words is set to the tune in the Museum. Your worthy Gaelic priest gave me that translation, and at his table I heard both the original and the translation sung by a pretty large party of Highland gentlemen, all of whom had no other idea of the air than that it was a native of their country.

I am obliged to you for your goodness in your three copies, but will certainly return you two of them. Why should I take money out of your pocket?]

Tell my friend Allan (for I am sure that we only want the trifling circumstance of being known to one another, to be the best friends on earth) that I much suspect he has, in his plates, mistaken the figure of the stock and horn. I have, at last, gotten one, but it is a very rude instrument. It is composed of three parts; the stock, which is the hinder thigh-bone of a sheep, such as you see in a mutton ham; the horn, which is a common Highland cow's horn, cut off at the smaller end, until the aperture be large enough to admit the stock to be pushed up through the horn until it be held by the thicker end of the thigh-bone; and lastly, an oaten reed exactly cut and notched like that which you see every shepherd boy have, when the corn stems are green and full-grown. The reed is not made fast in the bone, but is held by the lips, and plays loose in the smaller end of the stock; while the stock, with the horn hanging on its larger end is held by the hands in playing. The stock has six or seven ventiges on the upper side, and one back ventige, like the common flute,

This of mine was made by a man from the braes of Athole, and is exactly what the shepherds wont to use in that country.

However, either it is not quite properly bored in the holes, or else we have not the art of blowing it rightly; for we can make little of it. If Mr. Allan chuses, I will send him a sight of mine, as I look on myself to be a kind of brother-brush with him. "Pride in poets is nae sin;" and I will say it, that I look on Mr. Allan and Mr. Burns to be the only genuine and real painters of Scottish costume in the world.

R. B.

* (In reply, Mr. Thomson says, "Do not, I beseech you, return my books." Allan had seen a stock and horn: Thomson says, on the authority of a friend, that "the sound was abominable.")

(44.)　　　TO MR. THOMSON.

[Postmark, December 9th,] 1794.

It is, I assure you, the pride of my heart to do any thing to forward or add to the value of your book; and as I agree with you that the Jacobite song in the Museum to "There'll never be peace till Jamie comes hame," would not so well consort with Peter Pindar's excellent love-song to that air, I have just framed for you the following:—

Now in her green mantle, &c.

How does this please you? As to the point of time for the expression, in your proposed print from my "Sodger's Return," it must certainly be at—"She gaz'd." The interesting dubiety and suspense taking possession of her countenance, and the gushing fondness, with a mixture of roguish playfulness in his, strike me as things of which a master will make a great deal. In great haste, but in great truth, yours,

R. B.

(45.)　　　TO MR. THOMSON.

January, 1795.

I FEAR for my songs; however a few may please, yet originality is a coy feature in composition, and in a multiplicity of efforts in the same style, disappears altogether. For these three thousand years, we poetic folks have been describing the spring for instance; and as the spring continues the same, there must soon be a sameness in the imagery, &c., of these said rhyming folks * * * * * * *

A great critic (Aikin) on songs, says that love and wine are the exclusive themes for song-writing. The following is on neither subject, and consequently is no song; but will be allowed, I think, to be two or three pretty good prose thoughts inverted into rhyme:—

Is there for honest poverty, &c.

Jan. 15th.

The foregoing has lain by me this fortnight, for want of a spare moment. The Supervisor of Excise here being ill, I have been acting for him, and I assure you I have hardly

five minutes to myself to thank you for your elegant present of Pindar. The typography is admirable, and worthy of the truly original bard.

I do not give you the foregoing song for your book, but merely by way of vive la bagatelle; for the piece is not really poetry. How will the following do for "Craigie-burn Wood?"—

Sweet fa's the eve on Craigie-burn, &c.

Farewell! God bless you!

R. B.

(46.)　　　TO MR. THOMSON.

Ecclefechan, 7th February, 1795.

MY DEAR THOMSON,

You cannot have any idea of the predicament in which I write to you. In the course of my duty as Supervisor (in which capacity I have acted of late), I came yesternight to this unfortunate, wicked little village.* I have gone forward, but snows of ten feet deep have impeded my progress; I have tried to "gae back the gate I cam again," but the same obstacle has shut me up within insuperable bars. To add to my misfortune, since dinner, a scraper has been torturing catgut, in sounds that would have insulted the dying agonies of a sow under the hands of a butcher, and thinks himself, on that very account, exceeding good company. In fact, I have been in a dilemma, either to get drunk, to forget these miseries; or to hang myself to get rid of them: like a prudent man (a character congenial to my every thought, word, and deed) I, of two evils, have chosen the least, and am very drunk, at your service!

I wrote you yesterday from Dumfries. I had not time then to tell you all I wanted to say; and, Heaven knows, at present I have not capacity.

Do you know an air—I am sure you must know it—"We'll gang nae mair to yon town?" I think, in slowish time, it would make an excellent song. I am highly delighted with it; and if you should think it worthy of your attention, I have a fair dame in my eye to whom I would consecrate it. [Try it with this doggrel—until I give you a better:

O wat ye wha's in yon town, &c.]

As I am just going to bed, I wish you a good night.

R. B.

[P.S.—As I am likely to be storm-staid here to-morrow, if I am in the humour, you shall have a long letter from me.]

* (Dr. Currie, who was a native of the district, thus protests against our Author's verdict—"The Bard must have been tipsy indeed, to abuse sweet Ecclefechan at this rate." It is worth remarking, that before the end of this very year (4th December, 1795), no less distinguished a personage than Thomas Carlyle was born in the immediate neighbourhood.)

(47.) **TO MR. THOMSON.**

[Post-mark, February 9,] 1795.

[I AM afraid, my dear Sir, that printing your songs in the manner of Ritson's would counteract the sale of your greater work; but, secluded as I am from the world, its humours and caprices, I cannot pretend to judge in the matter. If you are ultimately frustrated of Pleyel's assistance, what think you of applying to Clarke? This, you will say, would be breaking faith with your subscribers; but, bating that circumstance, I am confident that Clarke is equal, in *Scottish song*, to take up the pen even after Pleyel.

I shall at a future period write you my sentiments as to sending my bagatelles to a newspaper.]

Here is another trial at your favorite air:

[SONG.]

Tune.—"Let me in this ae night."

O lassie, art thou sleeping yet? &c.

[HER ANSWER.]

O tell na me o' wind and rain, &c.

I do not know whether it will do.

R. B.

———

(48.) **TO MR. THOMSON.**

[May,] 1795.

[SONG.]

O wat ye wha's in yon town, &c.

[YOUR objection to the last two stanzas of my song, "Let me in this ae night," does not strike me as just. You will take notice that my heroine is replying quite at her ease, and when she talks of "faithless man," she gives not the least reason to believe that she speaks from her own experience, but merely from observation of what she has seen around her. But of all boring matters in this boring world, criticising my own works is the greatest bore.]

[SONG.]

O stay, sweet warbling woodlark, stay, &c.

Let me know, your very first leisure, how you like this song.

[SONG.]

Long, long the night, &c.

How do you like the foregoing? The Irish air, "Humors of Glen," is a great favorite of mine, and as, except the silly stuff in the "Poor Soldier," there are not any decent verses for it, I have written for it as follows:—

Their groves o' sweet myrtle let foreign lands reckon, &c.

Yours, R. B.

P.S.—Stop! Turn over. [Here follows song,]

'Twas na her bonnie blue e'e was my ruin, &c.

Let me hear from you.

(49.) **TO MR. THOMSON.**

[Post-mark, May 9,] 1795.

[SONG.]

How cruel are the parents, &c.

Mark yonder pomp of costly fashion, &c.

WELL, this is not amiss. You see how I answer your orders—your tailor could not be more punctual. I am just now in a high fit for poetising, provided the strait-jacket of criticism don't cure me. If you can, in a post or two, administer a little of the intoxicating potion of your applause, it will raise your humble servant's phrenzy to any height you want. I am at this moment "holding high converse" with the muses, and have not a word to throw away on such a prosaic dog as you.

R. B.

———

(50.) **TO MR. THOMSON.**

May, 1795.

TEN thousand thanks for your elegant present—though I am ashamed of the value of it being bestowed on a man who has not, by any means, merited such an instance of kindness. I have shown it to two or three judges of the first abilities here, and they all agree with me in classing it as a first-rate production. My phiz is sae kenspeckle, that the very joiner's apprentice, whom Mrs. Burns employed to break up the parcel (I was out of town that day), knew it at once. My most grateful compliments to Allan, who has honoured my rustic muse so much with his masterly pencil. One strange coincidence is, that the little one who is making the felonious attempt on the cat's tail, is the most striking likeness of an ill-deedie, d—n'd, wee ramble-gairie urchin of mine, whom from that propensity to witty wickedness, and manfu' mischief, which, even at twa days' auld, I foresaw would form the striking features of his disposition, I named Willie Nicol, after a certain friend of mine, who is one of the masters of a grammar-school in a city which shall be nameless. [Several people think that Allan's likeness of me is more striking than Nasmyth's, for which I sat to him half-a-dozen times. However, there is an artist of considerable merit just now in this town, who has hit the most remarkable likeness of what I am at this moment, that I think ever was taken of anybody. It is a small miniature, and as it will be in your town getting itself be-crystallised, &c., I have some thoughts of suggesting to you to prefix a vignette taken from it to my song, "Contented wi' Little, and Cantie wi' Mair," in order the portrait of my face and the picture of my mind may go down the stream of Time together.'

Now to business. I enclose you a song of merit, to a well-known air, which is to be one of yours. It was written by a lady, and has never yet seen the press. If you like it better than the ordinary "Woo'd and Married," or if you chuse to insert this also, you are welcome; only, return me this copy. "The Lothian Lassie" I also enclose; the song is well-known, but was never in notes before. The first part is the old tune. It is a great favorite of mine, and here I have the honor of being of the same opinion with STANDARD CLARKE. I think it would make a fine andante ballad.]

Give the enclosed epigram to my much-valued friend Cunningham, and tell him, that on Wednesday I go to visit a friend of his, to whom his friendly partiality in speaking of me in a manner introduced me—I mean, a well-known military and literary character, Colonel Dirom.

You do not tell me how you liked my two last songs. Are they condemned?

R. B.

* [See History of Kerry Miniatures—Appendix.]

(51.)   TO MR. THOMSON.

[ENGLISH SONG.]

Forlorn, my love, no comfort near, &c.

How do you like the foregoing? I have written it within this hour: so much for the speed of my Pegasus; but what say you to his bottom?

R. B.

(52.)   TO MR. THOMSON.

[SCOTTISH BALLAD.]

Last May a braw wooer, &c.

[FRAGMENT.]

Why, why tell thy lover? &c.

Such is the peculiarity of the rhythm of this air, that I find it impossible to make another stanza to suit it.

I am at present quite occupied with the charming sensations of the toothache, so have not a word to spare.

R. B.

(53.)   TO MR. THOMSON.

[Post-mark, August 3,] 1795.

[DID I mention to you that I wish to alter the first line of the English song to "Luiger m' chuse," or the "Quaker's Wife," from

Thine am I, my faithful fair,

to

Thine am I, my Chloris fair.

If you neglect the alteration, I call on all the NINE, conjunctly and severally, to anathematise you!]

In "Whistle, and I'll come to ye, my lad," the iteration of that line is tiresome to my ear. Here goes what I think is an improvement:—

O whistle, and I'll come to ye, my lad;
O whistle, and I'll come to ye, my lad;
Tho' father and mother and a' should gae mad,
Thy Jeanie will venture wi' ye, my lad.

In fact, a fair dame, at whose shrine I, the Priest of the Nine, offer up the incense of Parnassus—a dame whom the Graces have attired in witchcraft, and whom the Loves have armed with lightning—a fair one, herself the heroine of the song, insists on the amendment, and dispute her commands if you dare!

Gateslack, the word you object to, is the name of a particular place, a kind of passage up among the Lawther Hills, on the confines of this county. Dalgarnock is also the name of a romantic spot near the Nith, where are still a ruined church and a burial-ground. However, let the first run—

He up the lang loan, &c.

[SONG.]

O this is no my ain lassie, &c.

Do you know that you have roused the torpidity of Clarke at last? He has requested me to write three or four songs for him, which he is to set to music himself. The enclosed sheet contains two songs for him, which please to present to my valued friend Cunningham.

I enclose the sheet open, both for your inspection, and that you may copy the song "O bonnie was yon rosy brier." I do not know whether I am right, but that song pleases me; and as it is extremely probable that Clarke's newly-roused celestial spark will soon be smothered in the fogs of indolence, if you like the song, it may go as Scottish verses to the air of " I wish my love was in a mire;" and poor Erskine's English lines may follow.

I enclose you a " For a' that and a' that," which was never in print; it is a much superior song to mine. I have been told that it was composed by a lady. [At this point comes "enclosed sheet" containing songs—

Now Spring has clad the groves in green, &c.,

and   O bonnie was yon rosy brier, &c.

Then follow lines] written on the blank leaf of a copy of the last edition of my poems, presented to the lady whom, in so many fictitious reveries of passion, but with the most ardent sentiments of real friendship, I have so often sung under the name of Chloris:—

'Tis friendship's pledge, my young, fair friend, &c.

Une bagatelle de l'amitié.   COILA.

(54.)   TO MR. THOMSON.

February, 1796.

MANY thanks, my dear Sir, for your handsome, elegant present to Mrs. Burns, and for my remaining volume of P. Pindar. Peter is a delightful fellow, and a first favorite of mine. I am much pleased with your idea of publishing a collection of our songs in octavo, with etchings. I am extremely willing to lend every assistance in my power. The Irish airs I shall cheerfully undertake the task of finding verses for.

I have already, you know, equipt three with words, and the other day I strung up a kind of rhapsody to another Hibernian melody, which I admire much.

Awa wi' your witchcraft o' beauty's alarms, &c.

If this will do, you have now four of my Irish engagement. In my by-past songs I dislike one thing, the name Chloris— I meant it as the fictitious name of a certain lady; but, on second thoughts, it is a high incongruity to have a Greek appellation to a Scottish pastoral ballad. Of this, and some things else, in my next; I have more amendments to propose. What you once mentioned of "flaxen locks" is just: they cannot enter into an elegant description of beauty. Of this also again—God bless you!

R. B.

(55.)   TO MR. THOMSON.

April, 1796.

ALAS! my dear Thomson, I fear it will be some time ere I tune my lyre again! "By Babel streams I have sat and wept" almost ever since I wrote you last; I have only known existence by the pressure of the heavy hand of sickness, and have counted time by the repercussions of pain! Rheumatism, cold, and fever have formed to me a terrible combination. I close my eyes in misery, and open them without hope. I look on the vernal day, and say with poor Fergusson,

> "Say wherefore has an all-indulgent heaven
> Light to the comfortless and wretched given?"

This will be delivered to you by Mrs. Hyslop, landlady of the Globe Tavern here, which for these many years has been my howff, and where our friend Clarke and I have had many a merry squeeze. I am highly delighted with Mr. Allan's etchings. "Woo'd an' married an' a'," is admirable! The grouping is beyond all praise. The expression of the figures, conformable to the story in the ballad, is absolutely faultless perfection. I next admire "Turnimspike." What I like least is "Jenny said to Jockey." Besides the female being in her appearance [quite a virago], if you take her stooping into the account, she is at least two inches taller than her lover. Poor Cleghorn! I sincerely sympathise with him. Happy I am to think that he has yet a well-grounded hope of health and enjoyment in this world. As for me—but that is a damning subject!

R. B.

(56.)   TO MR. THOMSON.

[About May 17, 1796.]

MY DEAR SIR,

I once mentioned to you an air which I have long admired —"Here's a health to them that's awa, Hiney," but I forget if you took any notice of it. I have just been trying to suit it with verses, and I beg leave to recommend the air to your attention once more. I have only begun it.

Here's a health to ane I lo'e dear, &c.

This will be delivered by a Mr. Lewars, a young fellow of uncommon merit, [indeed by far the cleverest fellow I have met with in this part of the world. His only fault is D-m-cratic heresy]. As he will be a day or two in town, you will have leisure, if you chuse, to write me by him; and if you have a spare half-hour to spend with him, I shall place your kindness to my account. I have no copies of the songs I have sent you, and I have taken a fancy to review them all, and possibly may mend some of them; so when you have complete leisure, I will thank you for either the originals or copies. I had rather be the author of five well-written songs than of ten otherwise. [My verses to "Cauld Kail" I will suppress; as also those to "Laddie lie near me." They are neither worthy of my name nor of your book.] I have great hopes that the genial influence of the approaching summer will set me to rights, but as yet I cannot boast of returning health. I have now reason to believe that my complaint is a flying gout—a sad business.

Do let me know how Cleghorn is, and remember me to him.

This should have been delivered to you a month ago, [but my friend's trunk miscarried, and was not recovered till he came here again].* I am still very poorly, but should like much to hear from you.

R. B.

* [Our readers will remember that the last letter to Johnson was in the same predicament. Mr. Lewars's trunk is there called saddle-bags. See Letter (5) to Johnson.]

[The letter appears to have been dispatched by post on the 17th June. Currie unaccountably divides the letter into two.—Chambers. This so far determines the date of last letter to Johnson. Compare Note to Chambers's Edition of Letter (4) to Johnson, infra.]

(57.)   TO MR. THOMSON.

Brow, on the Solway-firth, 12th July, 1796.

AFTER all my boasted independence, curst necessity compels me to implore you for five pounds. A cruel wretch of a haberdasher, to whom I owe an account, taking it into his head that I am dying, has commenced a process, and will infallibly put me into jail. Do, for God's sake, send me that sum, and that by return of post. Forgive me this earnestness, but the horrors of a jail have made me half distracted. I do not ask all this gratuitously; for, upon returning health, I hereby promise and engage to furnish you with five pounds' worth of the neatest song-genius you have seen. I tried my hand on "Rothemurche" this morning. The measure is so difficult that it is impossible to infuse much genius into the lines; they are on the other side. Forgive, forgive me!"

Fairest maid on Devon's banks, &c.

R. B.

* [To this application Mr. Thomson replied as follows—

11th July, 1796.

MY DEAR SIR,

Ever since I received your melancholy letter, by Mrs. Hyslop, I have been ruminating in what manner I could endeavour to alleviate your sufferings. Again and again I thought of a pecuniary offer, but the recollection of one of your letters on this subject, and the fear of offending your independent spirit, checked my resolution. I thank you heartily therefore for the frankness of your letter of the 12th, and with great pleasure inclose a draft for the very sum I proposed sending. Would I were Chancellor of the Exchequer but for one day, for your sake!

Pray, my good Sir, is it not possible for you to muster a volume of poetry? If too much trouble to you in the present state of your health, some literary friend might be found here, who would select and arrange from your manuscripts, and take upon him the task of Editor. In the meantime, it could be advertised to be published by subscription. Do not shun this mode of obtaining the value of your labour: remember Pope published the Iliad by subscription. Think of this, my dear Burns, and do not reckon me intrusive with my advice. You are too well convinced of the respect and friendship I bear you, to impute any thing I say to an unworthy motive. Yours faithfully,

The verses to *Rothiemurche* will answer finely. I am happy to see you can still tune your lyre.]

[In Mr. Chambers's edition the following version of Letter (4) to James Johnson appears; which, as it differs considerably from the one given in our own text, we think proper to present entire.]

[To Mr. James Johnson.]

Dumfries [*February*], 1794.

MY DEAR SIR,

I SEND you by my friend, Mr. Wallace, forty-one songs for your fifth volume. Mr. Clarke has also a good many, if he have not, with his usual indolence, *cast them at the cocks.* I have still a good parcel amongst my hands in scraps and fragments; so that I hope we will make shift with our last volume.

You should have heard from me long ago; but over and above some vexatious share in the pecuniary losses of these accursed times, I have all this winter been plagued with low spirits and blue devils; so that *I have almost hung my harp on the willow trees.*

In the meantime, at your leisure, give a copy of the *Museum* to my worthy friend, Mr. Peter Hill, bookseller, to bind for me, interleaved with blank leaves, exactly as he did the Laird of Glenriddel's, that I may insert every anecdote I can learn, together with my own criticisms and remarks on the songs. A copy of this kind I shall leave with you, the editor, to publish at some after-period, by way of making the *Museum* a book famous to the end of time, and you renowned for ever.

I have got a Highland dirk, for which I have great veneration, as it once was the dirk of Lord Balmerino. It fell into bad hands, who stripped it of the silver mounting, as well as the knife and fork. I have some thoughts of sending it to your care, to get it mounted anew. Our friend Clarke owes me an account, somewhere about one pound, which would go a good way in paying the expense. I remember you once settled an account in this way before, and as you still have money-matters to settle with him, you might accommodate us both * * * * My best compliments to your worthy old father and your better half.

Yours,

R. B.

[It is obvious at a glance, that this edition by Mr. Chambers has been from a rough draft, which the writer on consideration, and with great delicacy and good taste, had thrown aside. The reference to Clarke's debt in the circumstances was not like Robert Burns, neither were "best compliments" to his correspondent's "worthy old father"—and so the original idea of the letter was abandoned. Besides, in the mean time, "copies of my Volunteer Ballad" had come to hand (see Letter (4), *p.* 80), in which "Our friend Clarke has done *indeed* well! 'tis chaste and beautiful!" &c. So it appears, after all, that Clarke had *not* been casting his musical pearls "*at the cocks.*" The receipt of the Volunteer Ballad, in short, had occasioned the re-writing of the whole letter, in which all reference to debt and indolence disappears: a very beautiful illustration of the Poet's moral nature, and the writer's private life.

A similar confusion occurs with respect to the last letter (5) of the same series; where, however, Mr. Chambers appears simply to have quoted from Cromek, who seems to have had nothing more than a copy *ex parte* by the Author before him. He states expressly, indeed, that "This letter was written on the 4th of July—the Poet died on the 21st." We have already explained that the letter actually sent to Johnson had no date whatever; and we see from letter to Thomson (5), posted 17th June, that it must have been written, or rather opened and finished, about the same time. The edition by Cromek and Chambers contains no reference at all to Lewars or the lost saddle-bags, but only the substance of the document itself; from which it appears undoubtedly to have been a mere copy.]

SUBORDINATE.

<table><tr><td>(1.)</td><td>

To Mr. John Murdoch,

SCHOOLMASTER,

STAPLES-INN BUILDINGS, LONDON.

</td></tr></table>

Lochlea, 15th January, 1783.

DEAR SIR,

As I have an opportunity of sending you a letter without putting you to that expense, which any production of mine would but ill repay, I embrace it with pleasure, to tell you that I have not forgotten, nor ever will forget, the many obligations I lie under to your kindness and friendship.

I do not doubt, Sir, but you will wish to know what has been the result of all the pains of an indulgent father, and a masterly teacher; and I wish I could gratify your curiosity with such a recital as you would be pleased with; but that is what I am afraid will not be the case. I have, indeed, kept pretty clear of vicious habits; and in this respect, I hope, my conduct will not disgrace the education I have gotten; but, as a man of the world, I am most miserably deficient. One would have thought that, bred as I have been, under a father who has figured pretty well as *un homme des affaires,* I might have been what the world calls a pushing, active fellow; but to tell you the truth, Sir, there is hardly anything more my reverse. I seem to be one sent into the world to see and observe; and I very easily compound with the knave who tricks me of my money, if there be anything original about him, which shows me human nature in a different light from anything I have seen before. In short, the joy of my heart is to "study men, their manners, and their ways;" and for this darling subject, I cheerfully sacrifice every other consideration. I am quite indolent about those great concerns that set the bustling, busy sons of care a-gog; and if I have to answer for the present hour, I am very easy with regard to anything further. Even the last, worst shift of the unfortunate and the wretched does not much terrify me: I know that my talent for what country folks call "a sensible crack," when once it is sanctified by a hoary head, would procure me so much esteem, that even then—I would learn to be happy.* However, I am under no apprehensions about that; for though indolent, yet so far as an extremely delicate constitution permits, I am not lazy; and in many things, especially in tavern matters, I am a strict economist—not, indeed, for the sake of the money; but one of the principal parts in my composition is a kind of pride of stomach; and I scorn to fear the face of any man living: above everything, I abhor as hell the idea of sneaking. in a corner to avoid a dun—possibly some pitiful, sordid wretch, whom in my heart I despise and detest. 'Tis this, and this alone, that endears economy to me. In the matter of books, indeed, I am very profuse. My favorite authors are of the sentimental kind, such as Shenstone, particularly his "Elegies;" Thomson; "Man of Feeling"—a book I prize next to the Bible; "Man of the World;" Sterne, especially his "Sentimental Journey;" Macpherson's "Ossian," &c.; these are the glorious models after which I endeavour to form my conduct, and 'tis incongruous, 'tis absurd to suppose that the man whose mind glows with sentiments lighted up at their sacred flame—the man whose heart distends with benevolence to all the human race—he "who can soar above this little scene of things"—can he descend to mind the paltry concerns about which the terrestrial race fret, and fume, and vex themselves! O how the glorious triumph swells my heart! I forgot that I am a poor, insignificant devil, unnoticed and unknown, stalking up and down fairs and markets, when I happen to be in them, reading a page or two of mankind, and "catching the manners living as they rise," whilst the men of business jostle me on every side, as an idle incumbrance in their way. But I daresay I have by this time tired your patience; so I shall conclude with begging you to give Mrs. Murdoch—not my compliments, for that is a mere commonplace story—but my warmest, kindest wishes for her welfare; and accept of the same for yourself, from,

Dear Sir, yours,

R. B.

* [This last shift here alluded to, must be the condition of an itinerant beggar.—Currie.]

[Thus also, exactly two years afterwards, in "Epistle to Davie"—
The last o't, the warst o't,
Is only but to beg.]

(2.) TO MR. MURDOCH,
TEACHER OF FRENCH, LONDON.

Ellisland, 16th July, 1790.

MY DEAR SIR,

I RECEIVED a letter from you a long time ago, but unfortunately, as it was in the time of my peregrinations and journeyings through Scotland, I mislaid or lost it, and by consequence your direction along with it. Luckily my good star brought me acquainted with Mr. Kennedy, who, I understand, is an acquaintance of yours: and by his means and mediation I hope to replace that link which my unfortunate negligence had so unluckily broke in the chain of our correspondence. I was the more vexed at the vile accident, as my brother William, a journeyman saddler, has been for some time in London; and wished above all things for your direction, that he might have paid his respects to his father's friend.

His last address he sent to me was, "Wm. Burns, at Mr. Barber's, saddler, No. 181 Strand." I writ him by Mr. Kennedy, but neglected to ask him for your address; so, if you find a spare half-minute, please let my brother know by a card where and when he will find you, and the poor fellow will joyfully wait on you, as one of the few surviving friends of the man whose name, and christian name too, he has the honor to bear.*

The next letter I write you shall be a long one. I have much to tell you of "hair-breadth 'scapes in th' imminent deadly breach," with all the eventful history of a life, the early years of which owed so much to your kind tutorage; but this at an hour of leisure. My kindest compliments to Mrs. Murdoch, and family. I am ever, my dear Sir,

Your obliged friend,

R. B.

* [In less than a month, this worthy man was called on to officiate as chief mourner at William's funeral; see Domestic Correspondence.]

To Mr. Walker,
BLAIR OF ATHOLE.

Inverness, 5th September, 1787.

MY DEAR SIR,

I HAVE just time to write the foregoing, and to tell you that it was (at least most part of it) the effusion of an half-hour I spent at Bruar.* I do not mean it was extempore, for I have endeavoured to brush it up as well as Mr. Nicol's chat and the jogging of the chaise would allow. It eases my heart a good deal, as rhyme is the coin with which a poet pays his debts of honor or gratitude. What I owe to the noble family of Athole, of the first kind, I shall ever proudly boast; what I owe of the last, so help me God in my hour of need! I shall never forget.

The "little angel-band!" I declare I prayed for them very sincerely to-day at the Fall of Fyers. I shall never forget the fine family-piece I saw at Blair; the amiable, the truly noble duchess, with her smiling little seraph in her lap, at the

* O

head of the table; the lovely "olive plants," as the Hebrew bard finely says, round the happy mother; the beautiful Mrs. Graham; the lovely sweet Miss Cathcart, &c. I wish I had the powers of Guido to do them justice! My Lord Duke's kind hospitality—markedly kind indeed. Mr. Graham of Fintry's charms of conversation—Sir W. Murray's friendship. In short, the recollection of all that polite, agreeable company raises an honest glow in my bosom.

R. B.

* [The poem here referred to was "The humble Petition of Bruar Water." Mr. Josiah Walker, then tutor to His Grace's family at Athole, was afterwards, as our readers are already aware, Professor of Humanity in Glasgow College, and a biographer of Burns. His somewhat pedantic manner in the chair did great injustice to his own worth and literary attainments. He was in reality both a kind-hearted obliging man, and one of the most accomplished scholars, both in Latinity and in English Classic Literature, of his day. We think it only right to make this addition to our former note. Poet. Works, p. 249.]

(1.)   To James Hoy, Esq.,

GORDON CASTLE.

[At Gordon Castle, Burns had formed an acquaintance with a Mr. James Hoy, ostensibly librarian to the Duke, but rather a kind of humble companion; a sensible, learned person, who is described as having lived in that princely mansion for forty-six years (previous to his death in 1828) without ever losing the Dominie-Sampson-like purity of heart and simplicity of manners by which he was distinguished.—Chambers.]

Edinburgh, 20th October, 1787.

Sir,

I will defend my conduct in giving you this trouble, on the best of Christian principles,—"Whatsoever ye would that men should do unto you, do ye even so unto them." I shall certainly, among my legacies, leave my latest curse to that unlucky predicament which hurried—tore me away from Castle Gordon. May that obstinate son of Latin prose [Nicol] be curst to Scotch-mile periods, and damned to seven-league paragraphs; while Declension and Conjugation, Gender, Number, and Tense, under the ragged banners of Dissonance and Disarrangement, eternally rank against him in hostile array.

Allow me, Sir, to strengthen the small claim I have to your acquaintance, by the following request. An engraver, James Johnson, in Edinburgh, has, not from mercenary views, but from an honest Scotch enthusiasm, set about collecting all our native songs and setting them to music; particularly those that have never been set before. Clarke, the well-known musician, presides over the musical arrangement, and Drs. Beattie and Blacklock, Mr. Tytler of Woodhouselee, and your humble servant to the utmost of his small power, assist in collecting the old poetry, or sometimes for a fine air make a stanza, when it has no words. The bruts, too tedious to mention, claim a parental pang from my bardship. I suppose it will appear in Johnson's second number —the first was published before my acquaintance with him. My request is—"Cauld Kail in Aberdeen" is one intended for this number, and I beg a copy of his Grace of Gordon's words to it, which you were so kind as to repeat to me. You

may be sure we won't prefix the author's name, except you like, though I look on it as no small merit to this work that the names of so many of the authors of our old Scotch songs, names almost forgotten, will be inserted. I do not well know where to write to you—I rather write at you: but if you will be so obliging, immediately on receipt of this, as to write me a few lines, I shall perhaps pay you in kind, though not in quality. Johnson's terms are:—each number a handsome pocket volume, to consist at least of a hundred Scotch songs, with basses for the harpsichord, &c. The price to subscribers, 5s.; to non-subscribers, 6s. He will have three numbers, I conjecture.

My direction for two or three weeks will be at Mr. William Cruikshank's, St. James's Square, New-town, Edinburgh.

I am, Sir, yours to command,

R. B.

(2.)   TO JAMES HOY, Esq.,

AT GORDON CASTLE, FOCHABERS.

Edinburgh, 6th November, 1787.

Dear Sir,

I would have wrote you immediately on receipt of your kind letter, but a mixed impulse of gratitude and esteem whispered to me that I ought to send you something by way of return. When a poet owes anything, particularly when he is indebted for good offices, the payment that usually recurs to him—the only coin indeed in which he probably is conversant—is rhyme. Johnson sends the books by the fly, as directed, and begs me to enclose his most grateful thanks: my return I intended should have been one or two poetic bagatelles which the world have not seen, or, perhaps, for obvious reasons, cannot see. These I shall send you before I leave Edinburgh. They may make you laugh a little, which, on the whole, is no bad way of spending one's precious hours and still more precious breath: at any rate, they will be, though a small, yet a very sincere mark of my respectful esteem for a gentleman whose further acquaintance I should look upon as a peculiar obligation.

The Duke's song, independent totally of his dukeship, charms me. There is I know not what of wild happiness of thought and expression peculiarly beautiful in the old Scottish song style, of which his Grace, old venerable Skinner, the author of "Tullochgorum," &c., and the late Ross, at Lochlee, of true Scottish poetic memory, are the only modern instances that I recollect, since Ramsay with his contemporaries, and poor Bob Fergusson went to the world of deathless existence and truly immortal song. The mob of mankind, that many-headed beast, would laugh at so serious a speech about an old song; but, as Job says, "O that mine adversary had written a book!" Those who think that composing a Scotch song is a trifling business—let them try it.

I wish my Lord Duke would pay a proper attention to

the Christian admonition—"Hide not your candle under a bushel," but "let your light shine before men." I could name half a dozen dukes that I guess are a devilish deal worse employed: nay, I question if there are half a dozen better: perhaps there are not half that scanty number whom Heaven has favored with the tuneful, happy, and, I will say, glorious gift.

 I am, dear Sir,
  Your obliged humble servant,
        R. B.

(1.)   **To Rev. John Skinner.**

Edinburgh, October 25, 1787.

REVEREND AND VENERABLE SIR,

ACCEPT, in plain dull prose, my most sincere thanks for the best poetical compliment I ever received.* I assure you, Sir, as a poet, you have conjured up an airy demon of vanity in my fancy, which the best abilities in your other capacity would be ill able to lay. I regret, and while I live I shall regret, that when I was in the north, I had not the pleasure of paying a younger brother's dutiful respects to the author of the best Scotch song ever Scotland saw—"Tullochgorum's my delight!" The world may think slightingly of the craft of song-making if they please, but, as Job says—"O! that mine adversary had written a book!"—let them try. There is a certain something in the old Scotch songs, a wild happiness of thought and expression, which peculiarly marks them not only from English songs, but also from the modern efforts of song-wrights, in our native manner and language. The only remains of this enchantment, these spells of the imagination, rest with you. Our true brother, Ross of Lochlee, was likewise "owre cannie"—"a wild warlock"—but now he sings among the "sons of the morning."

I have often wished, and will certainly endeavour to form a kind of common acquaintance among all the genuine sons of Caledonian song. The world, busy in low prosaic pursuits, may overlook most of us; but "reverence thyself." The world is not our peers, so we challenge the jury. We can lash that world, and find ourselves a very great source of amusement and happiness independent of that world.

There is a work going on in Edinburgh just now which claims your best assistance. An engraver in this town has set about collecting and publishing all the Scotch songs, with the music, that can be found. Songs in the English language, if by Scotchmen, are admitted, but the music must all be Scotch. Drs. Beattie and Blacklock are lending a hand, and the first musician in town presides over that department. I have been absolutely crazed about it, collecting old stanzas, and every information remaining respecting their origin, authors, &c., &c. This last is but a very fragment business; but at the end of his second number—the first is already published—a small account will be given of the authors, particularly to preserve those of latter times. Your three

songs, "Tullochgorum," "John of Badenyon," and "Ewie wi' the Crookit Horn," go in this second number. I was determined, before I got your letter, to write you, begging that you would let me know where the editions of these pieces may be found, as you would wish them to continue in future times; and if you would be so kind to this undertaking as send any songs, of your own or others, that you would think proper to publish, your name will be inserted among the other authors,—"Nill ye, will ye." One half of Scotland already give your songs to other authors. Paper is done. I beg to hear from you; the sooner the better, as I leave Edinburgh in a fortnight or three weeks.

 I am, with the warmest sincerity, Sir,
  Your obliged humble servant,
        R. B.

* [See conclusion of Literary Correspondence.]

(2.)   TO REV. JOHN SKINNER.

Edinburgh, February 14th, 1788.

REVEREND AND DEAR SIR,

I HAVE been a cripple now near three months, though I am getting vastly better, and have been very much hurried besides, or else I would have wrote you sooner. I must beg your pardon for the epistle you sent me appearing in the Magazine. I had given a copy or two to some of my intimate friends, but did not know of the printing of it till the publication of the Magazine. However, as it does great honor to us both, you will forgive it.

The second volume of the songs I mentioned to you in my last is published to-day. I send you a copy, which I beg you will accept as a mark of the veneration I have long had, and shall ever have, for your character, and of the claim I make to your continued acquaintance. Your songs appear in the third volume, with your name in the index; as, I assure you, Sir, I have heard your "Tullochgorum," particularly among our west-country folks, given to many different names, and most commonly to the immortal author of "The Minstrel," who, indeed, never wrote anything superior to "Gie's a sang, Montgomery cried." Your brother has promised me your verses to the Marquis of Huntly's reel, which certainly deserve a place in the collection. My kind host, Mr. Cruikshank, of the High School here, and said to be one of the best Latins in this age, begs me to make you his grateful acknowledgments for the entertainment he has got in a Latin publication of yours, that I borrowed for him from your acquaintance and much respected friend in this place, the Reverend Dr. Webster. Mr. Cruikshank maintains that you write the best Latin since Buchanan. I leave Edinburgh to-morrow, but shall return in three weeks. Your song you mentioned in your last, to the tune of "Dumbarton Drums," and the other, which you say was done by a brother in trade of mine, a ploughman, I shall thank you for a copy of each. I am ever, Reverend Sir, with the most respectful esteem and sincere veneration, yours,

        R. B.

(1.) To Professor Dugald Stewart.

Mauchline, 3d May, 1788.

Sir,

I enclose you one or two more of my bagatelles. If the fervent wishes of honest gratitude have any influence with that great unknown Being who frames the chain of causes and events, prosperity and happiness will attend your visit to the continent, and return you safe to your native shore.

Wherever I am, allow me, Sir, to claim it as my privilege to acquaint you with my progress in my trade of rhymes; as I am sure I could say it with truth, that next to my little fame, and the having it in my power to make life more comfortable to those whom nature has made dear to me, I shall ever regard your countenance, your patronage, your friendly good offices, as the most valued consequence of my late success in life.

R. B.

(2.) TO PROFESSOR DUGALD STEWART.

Ellisland, 20th Jan., 1789.

Sir,

The inclosed sealed packet I sent to Edinburgh a few days after I had the happiness of meeting you in Ayrshire, but you were gone for the Continent. I have now added a few more of my productions, those for which I am indebted to the Nithsdale muses. The piece inscribed to R. G., Esq., is a copy of verses I sent Mr. Graham, of Fintray, accompanying a request for his assistance in a matter to me of very great moment. To that gentleman I am already doubly indebted for deeds of kindness of serious import to my dearest interests, done in a manner grateful to the delicate feelings of sensibility. This poem is a species of composition new to me, but I do not intend it shall be my last essay of the kind, as you will see by the " Poet's Progress." These fragments, if my design succeed, are but a small part of the intended whole. I propose it shall be the work of my utmost exertions, ripened by years; of course I do not wish it much known. The fragment beginning "A little, upright, pert, tart, &c.," I have not shown to man living, till I now send it you. It forms the postulata, the axioms, the definition of a character, which, if it appear at all, shall be placed in a variety of lights. This particular part I send you merely as a sample of my hand at portrait-sketching; but, lest idle conjecture should pretend to point out the original, please to let it be for your single, sole inspection.

Need I make any apology for this trouble to a gentleman who has treated me with such marked benevolence and peculiar kindness—who has entered into my interests with so much zeal, and on whose critical decisions I can so fully depend? A poet as I am by trade, these decisions are to me of the last consequence. My late transient acquaintance among some of the mere rank and file of greatness, I resign with ease; but to the distinguished champions of genius and learning, I shall be ever ambitious of being known. The native genius and accurate discernment in Mr. Stewart's critical strictures; the justness (iron justice, for he has no bowels of compassion for a poor poetic sinner) of Dr. Gregory's remarks, and the delicacy of Professor Dalziel's taste, I shall ever revere.

I shall be in Edinburgh some time next month.

I have the honor to be, Sir,

Your highly obliged, and very humble Servant,

R. B.

[Dugald Stewart, born 1753, died 1828, was one of the most eloquent and influential teachers of his day in Europe. He occupied the chair of Moral Philosophy in Edinburgh for the space of twenty-five years.]

(1.) To Mr. Peter Hill.

[In this series of letters the order of Mr. Chambers's edition is followed. Mr. Hill, who had lately been chief assistant to Mr. Creech in Edinburgh, had now commenced business for himself in that city; and, as we learn from Mr. Chambers, had " the afterwards famous Archibald Constable as his apprentice.]

Mauchline, 18th July, 1788.

You injured me, my dear Sir, in your construction of the cause of my silence. From Ellisland in Nithsdale to Mauchline in Kyle is forty-and-five miles. *There*, a house a-building, and farm enclosures and improvements to tend; *here*, a new—not, indeed, so much a *new* as a *young* wife: Good God, Sir, could my dearest brother expect a regular correspondence from me! * * * I am certain that my liberal-minded and much-respected friend would have acquitted me, though I had obeyed to the very letter that famous statute among the irrevocable decrees of the Medes and Persians, not to ask petition, for forty days, of either God or man, save thee, O Queen, only!

I am highly obliged to you, my dearest Sir, for your kind, your elegant compliments on my becoming one of that most respectable, that most truly venerable corps, they who are, without a metaphor, the fathers of posterity * * * * *

Your book came safe, and I am going to trouble you with further commissions. I call it troubling you—because I want only books; the cheapest way, the best; so you may have to hunt for them in the evening auctions. I want Smollett's works, for the sake of his incomparable humour. I have already Roderick Random and Humphrey Clinker. Peregrine Pickle, Launcelot Greaves, and Ferdinand Count Fathom, I still want; but as I said, the veriest ordinary copies will serve me. I am nice only in the appearance of my poets. I forget the price of Cowper's poems, but, I believe, I must have them. I saw the other day proposals for a publication entitled " Banks's new and complete Christian's Family Bible," printed by C. Cooke, Paternoster-row, London. He promises at least to give in the work, I think it is three hundred and odd engravings, to which he has put the names of the first artists in London. You will know the character of the performance, as some numbers of it are published; and if it is really what it pretends to be, set me down as a subscriber, and send me the published numbers.

Let me hear from you your first leisure minute, and trust me you shall in future have no reason to complain of my silence. The dazzling perplexity of novelty will dissipate, and leave me to pursue my course in the quiet path of methodical routine.

R. B.

(2.)　　　TO MR. PETER HILL.

Mauchline, 1st October, 1788.

I HAVE been here in this country about three days, and all that time my chief reading has been the "Address to Lochlomond" you were so obliging as to send to me. Were I impannelled one of the author's jury, to determine his criminality respecting the sin of poesy, my verdict should be "Guilty! A poet of nature's making!" It is an excellent method for improvement, and what I believe every poet does, to place some favorite classic author in his own walks of study and composition before him as a model. Though your author had not mentioned the name, I could have, at half a glance, guessed his model to be Thomson. Will my brother-poet forgive me, if I venture to hint that his imitation of that immortal bard is in two or three places rather more servile than such a genius as his required:—*e. g.*

"To soothe the maddening passions all to peace."
Address.

"To soothe the throbbing passions into peace."
Thomson.

I think the "Address" is in simplicity, harmony, and elegance of versification, fully equal to the "Seasons." Like Thomson, too, he has looked into nature for himself; you meet with no copied description. One particular criticism I made at first reading; in no one instance has he said too much. He never flags in his progress, but, like a true poet of nature's making, kindles in his course. His beginning is simple and modest, as if distrustful of the strength of his pinion; only, I do not altogether like—

————————————————"Truth,
The soul of every song that's nobly great."

Fiction is the soul of many a song that is nobly great. Perhaps I am wrong; this may be but a prose criticism. Is not the phrase, in line 7, page 6, "Great lake," too much vulgarized by every-day language for so sublime a poem?

"Great mass of waters, theme for nobler song,"

is perhaps no emendation. His enumeration of a comparison with other lakes is at once harmonious and poetic. Every reader's ideas must sweep the

"Winding margin of an hundred miles."

The perspective that follows, mountains blue—the imprisoned billows beating in vain—the wooded isles—the digression on the yew-tree—"Ben-Lomond's lofty, cloud-envelop'd head," &c., are beautiful. A thunder-storm is a subject which has been often tried, yet our poet in his grand picture has interjected a circumstance, so far as I know, entirely original:—

————————————————"the gloom
Deepened'd with frequent streaks of moving fire."

In his preface to the storm, "the glens how dark between," is noble Highland landscape! The "rain ploughing the red mould," too, is beautifully fancied. "Ben-Lomond's lofty, pathless top," is a good expression; and the surrounding view from it is truly great: the

————"silver mist,
Beneath the beaming sun,"

is well described; and here he has contrived to enliven his poem with a little of that passion which bids fair, I think, to usurp the modern Muses altogether. I know not how far this episode is a beauty upon the whole, but the swain's wish to carry "some faint idea of the vision bright," to entertain her "partial listening ear," is a pretty thought. But in my opinion the most beautiful passages in the whole poem are the fowls crowding, in wintry frosts, to Lochlomond's "hospitable flood;" their wheeling round, their lighting, mixing, diving, &c.; and the glorious description of the sportsman. This last is equal to any thing in the "Seasons." The idea of "the floating tribes distant seen, far glistering to the moon," provoking his eye as he is obliged to leave them, is a noble ray of poetic genius. "The howling winds," the "hideous roar" of the "white cascades," are all in the same style.

I forgot that while I am thus holding forth with the heedless warmth of an enthusiast, I am perhaps tiring you with nonsense. I must, however, mention that the last verse of the sixteenth page is one of the most elegant compliments I have ever seen. I must likewise notice that beautiful paragraph beginning, "The gleaming lake," &c. I dare not go into the particular beauties of the last two paragraphs, but they are admirably fine, and truly Ossianic.

I must beg your pardon for this lengthened scrawl. I had no idea of it when I began—I should like to know who the author is; but, whoever he be, please present him with my grateful thanks for the entertainment he has afforded me.*

A friend of mine desired me to commission for him two books, "Letters on the Religion essential to Man," a book you sent me before; and "The World Unmasked, or the Philosopher the Greatest Cheat." Send me them by the first opportunity. The Bible you sent me is truly elegant; I only wish it had been in two volumes.

R. B.

* [The poem, entitled *An Address to Loch-Lomond*, is said to be written by a gentleman, now one of the Masters of the High-School at Edinburgh, and the same who translated the beautiful story of the *Paria*, as published in the *Bee* of Dr. Anderson.—*Currie.* The author was Rev. Dr. Cririe, afterwards minister of Dalton, in Dumfriesshire.—*Chambers.*]

(3.)　　　TO MR. PETER HILL.

[*Ellisland, March, 1789?*]

MY DEAR HILL,

I SHALL say nothing to your mad present*—you have so long and often been of important service to me, and I suppose you mean to go on conferring obligations until I shall not be able to lift up my face before you. In the mean time, as

Sir Roger de Coverley, because it happened to be a cold day in which he made his will, ordered his servants great coats for mourning, so, because I have been this week plagued with an indigestion, I have sent you by the carrier a fine old ewe-milk cheese.

Indigestion is the devil; nay, 'tis the devil and all. It besets a man in every one of his senses. I lose my appetite at the sight of successful knavery, and sicken to loathing at the noise and nonsense of self-important folly. When the hollow-hearted wretch takes me by the hand, the feeling spoils my dinner: the proud man's wine so offends my palate that it chokes me in the gullet; and the pulvilised, feathered, pert coxcomb is so disgustful in my nostril that my stomach turns.

If ever you have any of those disagreeable sensations, let me prescribe for you patience and a bit of my cheese. I know that you are no niggard of your good things among your friends, and some of them are in much need of a slice. There, in my eye is our friend Smellie; a man positively of the first abilities and greatest strength of mind, as well as one of the best hearts and keenest wits that I have ever met with; when you see him, as, alas! he too is smarting at the pinch of distressful circumstances, aggravated by the sneer of contumelious greatness—a bit of my cheese alone will not cure him, but if you add a tankard of brown stout, and super-add a magnum of right Oporto, you will see his sorrow vanish like the morning mist before the summer sun.

Candlish, the earliest friend, except my only brother, that I have on earth, and one of the worthiest fellows that ever any man called by the name of friend, if a luncheon of my best cheese would help to rid him of some of his superabundant modesty, you would do well to give it him.

David, with his *Courant*,[†] comes, too, across my recollection, and I beg you will help him largely from the said ewe-milk cheese, to enable him to digest those damned bedaubing para-graphs with which he is eternally larding the lean characters of certain great men in a certain great town. I grant you the periods are very well turned; so, a fresh egg is a very good thing, but, when thrown at a man in a pillory, it does not at all improve his figure, not to mention the irreparable loss of the egg.

My facetious friend Dunbar I would wish also to be a par-taker; not to digest his spleen, for that he laughs off, but to digest his last night's wine at the last field-day of the Croch-allan corps.

Among our common friends I must not forget one of the dearest of them—Cunningham. The brutality, insolence, and selfishness of a world unworthy of having such a fellow as he is in it, I know sticks in his stomach, and if you can help him to anything that will make him a little easier on that score, it will be very obliging.

As to honest J[ohn] S[omervill]e, he is such a contented, happy man, that I know not what can annoy him, except, perhaps, he may not have got the better of a parcel of modest anecdotes which a certain poet gave him one night at supper, the last time the said poet was in town.

Though I have mentioned so many men of law, I shall have nothing to do with them professionally—the faculty are be-yond my prescription. As to their clients, that is another thing; God knows they have much to digest.

The clergy I pass by; their profundity of erudition, and their liberality of sentiment; their total want of pride, and their detestation of hypocrisy, are so proverbially notorious as to place them far, far above either my praise or censure.

I was going to mention a man of worth whom I have the honor to call friend, the Laird of Craigdarroch; but I have spoken to the landlord of the King's Arms Inn here, to have at the next county meeting a large ewe-milk cheese on the table, for the benefit of the Dumfries-shire Whigs, to enable them to digest the Duke of Queensberry's late political conduct.

I have just this moment an opportunity of a private hand to Edinburgh, as perhaps you would not digest double postage.

So God bless you!

R. B.

* ['Mr. Hill had sent the Poet a present of Books.—*Chambers.*]
† [Mr. David Ramsay, of *Edinburgh Evening Courant*: see also Letter [4].]

(4.)

TO MR. PETER HILL.

Ellisland, 2nd April, 1789.

I WILL make no excuses, my dear Bibliopolus, (GOD forgive me for murdering language!) that I have sat down to write you on this vile paper, stained with the sanguinary scores of " thae curs'd horse-leeches o' the Excise."

It is economy, Sir; it is that cardinal virtue, prudence: so I beg you will sit down, and either compose or borrow a panegyric. If you are going to borrow, apply to our friend Ramsay for the assistance of the author of the pretty little buttering paragraphs of eulogium on your thrice-honored, and never-enough-to-be-praised, MAGISTRACY—how they hunt down a housebreaker with the sanguinary persever-ance of a bloodhound—how they out-do a terrier in a badger-hole in unearthing a resetter of stolen goods—how they steal on a thoughtless troop of night-nymphs as a spaniel winds the unsuspecting covey—or how they riot over a ravaged ' ' as a cat does o'er a plundered mouse-nest—how they new-vamp old churches, aiming at appear-ances of piety; plan squares and colleges, to pass for men of taste and learning, &c., &c., &c.; while Old Edinburgh, like the doting mother of a parcel of rakehelly prodigals, may sing *Hooly and fairly,* or cry *War's me that e'er I saw ye!* but still must put her hand in her pocket, and pay whatever scores the young dogs think proper to contract.

I was going to say—but this parenthesis has put me out of breath—that you should get that manufacturer of the tinselled crockery of magistratial reputations, who makes so distinguished and distinguishing a figure in the *Evening Courant*, to compose, or rather to compound, something very clever on my remarkable frugality; that I write to one of my most esteemed friends on this wretched paper, which was originally intended for the venal fist of some drunken exciseman, to take dirty notes in a miserable vault of an ale-cellar.

O Frugality! thou mother of ten thousand blessings—thou cook of fat beef and dainty greens!—thou manufacturer of warm Shetland hose, and comfortable surtouts!—thou old housewife, darning thy decayed stockings with thy ancient spectacles on thy aged nose!—lend me, hand me in thy clutching palsied fist, up those heights, and through those thickets, hitherto inaccessible and impervious to my anxious, weary feet:—not those Parnassian crags, bleak and barren, where the hungry worshippers of fame are breathless clambering, hanging between heaven and hell; but those glittering cliffs of Potosi, where the all-sufficient, all powerful deity, Wealth, holds his immediate court of joys and pleasures; where the sunny exposure of Plenty, and the hot-walls of Profusion, produce those blissful fruits of Luxury, exotics in this world, and natives of Paradise!—Thou withered sybil, my sage conductress, usher me into thy refulgent, adored presence!—The power, splendid and potent as he now is, was once the puling nursling of thy faithful care and tender arms! Call me thy son, thy cousin, thy kinsman, or favourite, and adjure the god by the scenes of his infant years, no longer to repulse me as a stranger or an alien, but to favour me with his peculiar countenance and protection?—He daily bestows his greatest kindness on the undeserving and the worthless—assure him, that I bring ample documents of meritorious demerits! Pledge yourself for me, that, for the glorious cause of LUCRE, I will do any thing, be any thing—but the horse-leech of private oppression, or the vulture of public robbery!

But to descend from heroics—what, in the name of all * * at once, have you done with my trunk? Please let me have it by the first carrier.

I want a Shakspeare: let me know what plays your used copy of Bell's Shakspeare wants. I want likewise an English dictionary—Johnson's, I suppose, is best. In these and all my prose commissions, the cheapest is always the best for me. There is a small debt of honour that I owe Mr. Robert Cleghorn, in Saughton Mills, my worthy friend, and your well-wisher. Please give him, and urge him to take it, the first time you see him, ten shillings' worth of any thing you have to sell, and place it to my account.

The library scheme that I mentioned to you is already begun, under the direction of Captain Riddel and me. There is another in emulation of it going on at Closeburn, under the auspices of Mr. Monteith of Closeburn, which will be on a greater scale than ours. I have, likewise, secured it for you. Captain Riddel gave his infant society a great many of his old books, else I had written you on that subject; but, one of these days, I shall trouble you with a commission for The Monkland Friendly Society. A copy of The Spectator, Mirror, and Lounger, Man of Feeling, Man of the World, Guthrie's Geographical Grammar, with some religious pieces will likely be our first order.*

When I grow richer, I will write to you on gilt-post, to make amends for this sheet. At present, every guinea has a five-guinea errand with, my dear Sir,

Your faithful, poor, but honest friend,

R. B.

* Compare letter to Sir J. Sinclair.]

(5.)   TO MR. PETER HILL.

Ellisland, 2nd Feb., 1790.

No! I will not say one word about apologies or excuses for not writing.—I am a poor, rascally gauger, condemned to gallop at least 200 miles every week to inspect dirty ponds and yeasty barrels, and where can I find time to write to, or importance to interest anybody? The upbraidings of my conscience, nay, the upbraidings of my wife, have persecuted me on your account these two or three months past.—I wish to God I was a great man, that my correspondence might throw light upon you, to let the world see what you really are; and then I would make your fortune without putting my hand in my pocket for you, which, like all other great men, I suppose I would avoid as much as possible. What are you doing, and how are you doing? Have you lately seen any of my few friends? What is become of the honovari REFORM, or how is the fate of my poor namesake, Mademoiselle Burns, decided? Which of their grave lordships can lay his hand on his heart, and say that he has not taken advantage of such frailty? * * * O man! but for thee and thy selfish appetites and dishonest artifices, that beauteous form, and that once innocent and still ingenuous mind, might have shone conspicuous and lovely in the faithful wife and the affectionate mother; and shall the unfortunate sacrifice to thy pleasures have no claim on thy humanity! * * *

I saw lately in a Review some extracts from a new poem, called the Village Curate; send it me. I want likewise a cheap copy of The World. Mr. Armstrong, the young poet, who does me the honor to mention me so kindly in his works, please give him my best thanks for the copy of his book. I shall write him my first leisure hour. I like his poetry much, but I think his style in prose quite astonishing.

What is become of that veteran in genius, wit, and ——, Smellie, and his book? Give him my compliments. Does Mr. Graham of Gartmore ever enter your shop now? He is the noblest instance of great talents, great fortune, and great worth that ever I saw in conjunction. Remember me to Mrs. Hill; and believe me to be, my dear Sir, ever yours,

R. B.

————

(6.)   TO MR. PETER HILL.

Ellisland, 2nd March, 1790.

AT a late meeting of the Monkland Friendly Society, it was resolved to augment their library by the following books, which you are to send us as soon as possible:—The Mirror, The Lounger, Man of Feeling, Man of the World (these, for my own sake, I wish to have by the first carrier); Knox's History of the Reformation; Rae's History of the Rebellion in 1715; any good History of the Rebellion in 1745; A Display of the Secession Act and Testimony, by Mr. Gibb; Hervey's Meditations; Beveridge's Thoughts; and another copy of Watson's Body of Divinity. This last heavy performance is so much admired by many of our members, that they will not be content with one copy.

I wrote to Mr. A. Masterton three or four months ago, to pay some money he owed me into your hands, and lately I wrote to you to the same purpose, but I have heard from neither one nor other of you.

In addition to the books I commissioned in my last, I want very much, An Index to the Excise Laws, or an Abridgment of all the Statutes now in force, relative to the Excise: by Jellinger Symons. I want three copies of this book; if it is now to be had, cheap or dear, get it for me. An honest country neighbour of mine wants too a Family Bible, the larger the better; but second-handed, for he does not chuse to give above ten shillings for the book. I want likewise for myself, as you can pick them up, second-handed or cheap copies of Otway's Dramatic Works, Ben Jonson's, Dryden's, Congreve's, Wycherley's, Vanbrugh's, Cibber's, or any dramatic works of the more modern Macklin, Garrick, Foote, Colman, or Sheridan. A good copy, too, of Molière in French I much want. Any other good dramatic authors in that language I want also; but comic authors chiefly, though I should wish to have Racine, Corneille, and Voltaire too. I am in no hurry for all, or any of these, but if you accidentally meet with them very cheap, get them for me.

And now, to quit the dry walk of business, how do you do, my dear friend? and how is Mrs. Hill? I trust, if now and then not so *elegantly* handsome, at least as amiable, and sings as divinely as ever. My good wife too has a charming " wood-note wild;" now could we four get anyway snugly together in a corner of the New Jerusalem (remember, I bespeak your company there), you and I, though Heaven knows we are no singers, &c. ————.

I am out of all patience with this vile world for one thing. Mankind are by nature benevolent creatures, except in a few scoundrelly instances. I do not think that avarice of the good things we chance to have is born with us; but we are placed here amid so much nakedness and hunger and poverty and want, that we are under a cursed necessity of studying selfishness, in order that we may EXIST! Still there are, in every age, a few souls that all the wants and woes of life cannot debase to selfishness, or even to the necessary alloy of caution and prudence. If ever I am in danger of vanity, it is when I contemplate myself on this side of my disposition and character. God knows I am no saint; I have a whole host of follies and sins to answer for; but if I could, and I believe I do it as far as I can, I would wipe away all tears from all eyes. Even the knaves who have injured me, I would oblige them; though, to tell the truth, it would be more out of vengeance, to show them that I was independent of and above them, than out of the over-flowings of my benevolence. Adieu!

R. B.

————

(7.)   TO MR. PETER HILL.

Ellisland, 17th January, 1791.

TAKE these two guineas,* and place them over against that damned account of yours, which has gagged my mouth these five or six months! I can as little write good things as apologies to the man I owe money to. O the supreme curse of making three guineas do the business of five! Not all the labours of Hercules; not all the Hebrews' three centuries of Egyptian bondage, were such an insuperable business, such an infernal task!! Poverty! thou half-sister of death, thou cousin-german of hell! where shall I find force of execration equal to the amplitude of thy demerits? Oppressed by thee, the venerable ancient, grown hoary in the practice of every virtue, laden with years and wretchedness, implores a little—little aid to support his existence, from a stony-hearted son of Mammon, whose sun of prosperity never knew a cloud; and is by him denied and insulted. Oppressed by thee, the man of sentiment, whose heart glows with independence, and melts with sensibility, inly pines under the neglect, or writhes, in bitterness of soul, under the contumely of arrogant, unfeeling wealth. Oppressed by thee, the son of Genius, whose ill-starred ambition plants him at the tables of the fashionable and polite, must see, in suffering silence, his remark neglected, and his person despised, while shallow greatness, in his idiot attempts at wit, shall meet with countenance and applause. Nor is it only the family of Worth that have reason to complain of thee: the children of Folly and Vice, though in common with thee the offspring of Evil, smart equally under thy rod. Owing to thee, the man of unfortunate disposition and neglected education is condemned as a fool for his dissipation; despised and shunned as a needy wretch when his follies, as usual, bring him to want; and when his unprincipled necessities drive him to dishonest practices, he is abhorred as a miscreant, and perishes by the justice of his country. But far otherwise is the lot of the man of family and fortune. *His* early follies and extravagances are spirit and fire; *his* consequent wants are the embarrassments of an honest fellow; and when, to remedy the matter, he has gained a legal commission to plunder distant provinces, or massacre peaceful nations, he returns, perhaps, laden with the spoils of rapine and murder; lives wicked and respected, and dies a scoundrel and a lord. Nay, worst of all, alas for helpless woman! the needy prostitute, who has shivered at the corner of the street, waiting to earn the wages of casual prostitution, is left neglected and insulted, ridden down by the chariot wheels of the coroneted Rip, hurrying on to the guilty assignation—she who, without the same necessities to plead, riots nightly in the same guilty trade.

Well! divines may say of it what they please; but execration is to the mind what phlebotomy is to the body; the vital sluices of both are wonderfully relieved by their respective evacuations.

R. B.

* [Mr. Chambers mentions that the sum of three guineas is placed to Burns's credit in Mr. Hill's books of this date, and suggests that *two* had been written in our Author's letter by mistake. This is very likely to be the case; compare next sentence, in which he laments that three guineas cannot do the work of five.]

(8.)　　　　TO MR. PETER HILL.

[*Spring?* 1791.]

MY DEAR FRIEND,

I was never more unfit for writing. A poor devil, nailed to an elbow-chair, writhing in anguish with a bruised leg laid on a stool before him, is in a fine situation truly for saying bright things.

I may perhaps see you about Martinmas. I have sold to my landlord the lease of my farm, and as I roup off everything then, I have a mind to take a week's excursion to see old acquaintance. At all events, you may reckon on [payment of] your account about that time. So much for business. I do not know if I ever informed you that I am now ranked on the list as a supervisor, and I have pretty good reason to believe that I shall soon be called out to employment. The appointment is worth from one to two hundred a year, according to the place of the country in which one is settled. I have not been so lucky in my farming. Mr. Miller's kindness has been just such another as Creech's was:

> "His meddling vanity, a busy fiend,
> Still making work his selfish craft must mend."

By the way, I have taken vengeance on Creech. He wrote me a fine, fair letter, telling me that he was going to print a third edition; and as he had a brother's care of my fame, he wished to add every new thing I have written since, and I should be amply rewarded with—a copy or two to present to my friends. He has sent me a copy of the last edition to correct, &c. But I have as yet taken no notice of it; and I hear he has published without me.* You know, and all my friends know, that I do not value money; but I owed the gentleman a debt, which I am happy to have it in my power to repay.

Farewell, and prosperity attend all your undertakings! I shall try, if my unlucky limb would give me a little ease, to write you a letter a little better worth reading.

R. B.

* [The reader's attention is directed to this statement, as one among many proofs how editions of our Author, with or without editorial revision, were sometimes printed. There seems to be some little confusion here about dates, which it is not easy to rectify. The form was not actually given up till much later—November 18th—but there may have been a private agreement to that effect at this date. What may be called Creech's *third* edition was published in July, 1790; and the next edition, that containing the new pieces, in April, 1793. One of the previous editions, therefore, the one in which the London publishers had an interest, may have been omitted by our Author in this calculation. In any case, there had been manifestly a long interval of silence between him and Creech.]

(9.)　　　　TO [MR. PETER HILL.]

[*Dumfries*, 13th *July*, 1791.]

MY DEAR FRIEND,

I TAKE Glenriddel's kind offer of a corner for a postscript to you, though I have nothing particular to tell you. It is with the greatest pleasure I learn from all hands, and particularly from your warm friend and patron, the Laird here, that you are going on, spreading and thriving like the palm-tree that shades the fragrant vale in the Holy Land of the Prophet. May the richest juices from beneath, and the dews of heaven from above, foster your root and refresh your branches, until you be as conspicuous among your fellows as the stately Goliah towering over the little pigmy Philistines around him! Amen, so be it!!!

R. B.

(10.)　　　　TO MR. PETER HILL.

Dumfries, 5th *Feb.*, 1792.

MY DEAR FRIEND,

I SEND you by the bearer, Mr. Clarke, a particular friend of mine, six pounds and a shilling, which you will dispose of as follows:—five pounds ten shillings per account I owe Mr. R. Burn, architect, for erecting the stone over the grave of poor Fergusson. He was two years in erecting it after I had commissioned him for it, and I have been two years in paying him, after he sent me his account; so he and I are quits. He had the *hardiesse* to ask me interest on the sum; but, considering that the money was due by one poet for putting a tombstone over another, he may, with grateful surprise, thank Heaven that he ever saw a farthing of it.

With the remainder of the money, pay yourself for the "Office of a Messenger" that I bought of you; and send me by Mr. Clarke a note of its price. Send me, likewise, the fifth volume of the *Observer* by Mr. Clarke; and if any money remain, let it stand to account.

My best compliments to Mrs. Hill.

I sent you a maukin by last week's Fly, which I hope you received. Yours, most sincerely,

R. B.

(11.)　　　　TO MR. PETER HILL.

(*Dumfries, May*, 1793?)

*　　　.　　　.　　　.*

I HOPE and trust that this unlucky blast which has overturned so many, and many worthy characters, who, four months ago, little dreaded any such thing—will spare my friend.

O may the wrath and curse of all mankind haunt and harass these turbulent, unprincipled miscreants who have involved a People in this ruinous business!

I have not a moment more. Blessed be he that blesseth

* P

thee, and cursed be he that curseth thee, and the wretch whose envious malice would injure thee, may the Giver of every good and perfect gift say unto him, "Thou shalt not prosper."

R. B.

[Compare this and following letter with letter (1) to Captain John Hamilton, in General Correspondence.]

(12.)   TO MR. PETER HILL.

[Dumfries, July, 1793?]

My dear Sir,

* * * * Now that business is over, how are you, and how do you weather this accursed time? God only knows what will be the consequence; but in the meantime the country, at least in our part of it, is still progressive to the devil. For my part, "I jouk, and let the jaw flee o'er." As my hopes in this world are but slender, I am turning rapidly devotee, in the prospect of sharing largely in the world to come.

How is old sinful Smellie coming on? Is there any talk of his second volume? If you meet with my much-valued old friend, Colonel Dunbar, of the Crochallan Fencibles, remember me most affectionately to him. Alas! not unfrequently, when my heart is in a wandering humour, I live past scenes over again. To my mind's eye, you, Dunbar, Cleghorn, Cunningham, &c., present their friendly phiz[es], and my bosom aches with tender recollections. Adieu!

R. B.

(13.)   TO MR. PETER HILL.

[Dumfries, end of October, 1794?]

My dear Hill,

By a carrier of yesterday, Henry Osborn by name, I sent you a kippered salmon, which I trust you will duly receive, and which I also trust will give you many a toothful of satisfaction. If you have the confidence to say that there is anything of the kind in all your great city superior to this in true kipper relish and flavour, I will be revenged by—not sending you another next season. In return, the first party of friends that dine with you —provided that your fellow-travellers and my trusty and well-beloved veterans in intimacy, Messrs Ramsay and Cameron be of the party—about that time in the afternoon when a relish or devil becomes grateful, give them two or three slices of the kipper, and drink a bumper to your friends in Dumfries. Moreover, by last Saturday's fly, I sent you a hare, which I hope came, and carriage-free, safe to your hospitable mansion and social table. So much for business.

How do you like the following pastoral, which I wrote the other day for a tune that I daresay you well know?

[Here follows song—"Ca' the Yowes to the Knowes."]

And how do you like the following?—

ON SEEING MRS. KEMBLE IN YARICO.

Kemble, thou cur'st my unbelief
   Of Moses and his rod;
At Yarico's sweet notes of grief
   The rock with tears had flowed.

Or this?—

ON W——— R———, ESQ.

So vile was poor Wat, such a miscreant slave,
That the worms even damned him when laid in his grave;
' In his skull there is famine!' a starved reptile cries;
' And his heart it is poison!' another replies.

My best good wishes to Mrs. Hill; and believe me to be ever yours,

R. Burns.*

* [This letter appeared in the Knickerbocker (New York magazine) for September, 1848.—Chambers.]

To the Rev. G. Laurie,

NEWMILLS, NEAR KILMARNOCK.

Edinburgh, Feb. 5, 1787.

Reverend and dear Sir,

When I look at the date of your kind letter, my heart reproaches me severely with ingratitude in neglecting so long to answer it. I will not trouble you with any account, by way of apology, of my hurried life and distracted attention; do me the justice to believe that my delay by no means proceeded from want of respect. I feel, and ever shall feel for you the mingled sentiments of esteem for a friend, and reverence for a father.

I thank you, Sir, with all my soul for your friendly hints, though I do not need them so much as my friends are apt to imagine. You are dazzled with newspaper accounts and distant reports; but, in reality, I have no great temptation to be intoxicated with the cup of prosperity. Novelty may attract the attention of mankind awhile; to it I owe my present éclat; but I see the time not far distant when the popular tide which has borne me to a height of which I am, perhaps, unworthy, shall recede with silent celerity, and leave me a barren waste of sand, to descend at my leisure to my former station. I do not say this in the affectation of modesty; I see the consequence is unavoidable, and am prepared for it. I had been at a good deal of pains to form a just, impartial estimate of my intellectual powers before I came here; I have not added, since I came to Edinburgh, anything to the account; and I trust I shall take every atom of it back to my shades, the coverts of my unnoticed, early years.

In Dr. Blacklock, whom I see very often, I have found what I would have expected in our friend, a clear head and an excellent heart.

By far the most agreeable hours I spend in Edinburgh must be placed to the account of Miss Laurie and her pianoforte. I cannot help repeating to you and Mrs. Laurie a compliment that Mr. Mackenzie, the celebrated "Man of Feeling," paid to Miss Laurie the other night, at the concert. I had come in at the interlude, and sat down by him till I saw Miss Laurie in a seat not very far distant, and went up to pay my respects to her. On my return to Mr. Mackenzie, he asked me who she was; I told him 'twas the daughter of a reverend friend of mine in the west country. He returned, there was something very striking, to his idea, in her appearance. On my desiring to know what it was, he was pleased to say, "She has a great deal of the elegance of a well-bred lady about her, with all the sweet simplicity of a country girl.

My compliments to all the happy inmates of St. Margaret's.

I am, my dear Sir,

Yours most gratefully,

R. B.

[Our readers need hardly be reminded that this estimable gentleman was the friend who first introduced our Author's name and works to the notice of Dr. Blacklock—with what strange consequences of success the world knows.]

To the Rev. Dr. Hugh Blair.

Lawn-Market, Edinburgh, 3rd May, 1787.

REVEREND AND MUCH-RESPECTED SIR,

I LEAVE Edinburgh to-morrow morning, but could not go without troubling you with half a line, sincerely to thank you for the kindness, patronage, and friendship you have shown me. I often felt the embarrassment of my singular situation; drawn forth from the veriest shades of life to the glare of remark; and honored by the notice of those illustrious names of my country whose works, while they are applauded to the end of time, will ever instruct and mend the heart. However the meteor-like novelty of my appearance in the world might attract notice, and honor me with the acquaintance of the permanent lights of genius and literature, those who are truly benefactors of the immortal nature of man, I knew very well that my utmost merit was far unequal to the task of preserving that character when once the novelty was over: I have made up my mind that abuse, or almost even neglect, will not surprise me in my quarters.

I have sent you a proof impression of Beugo's work for me, done on Indian paper, as a trifling but sincere testimony with what heart-warm gratitude I am, &c.,

R. B.

[Hugh Blair, born at Edinburgh, 1718, died 1790, minister of Lady Yester's Church and professor of rhetoric in the University of that city, was long esteemed the most eloquent and accomplished lecturer and preacher of his day in Great Britain. His sermons were translated, as models of their kind, into almost every language in Europe.]

To Bishop Geddes.

Ellisland, 3rd Feb., 1789.

VENERABLE FATHER,

AS I am conscious that wherever I am, you do me the honor to interest yourself in my welfare, it gives me pleasure to inform you that I am here at last, stationary in the serious business of life, and have now not only the retired leisure, but the hearty inclination, to attend to those great and important questions—what I am? where I am? and for what I am destined?

In that first concern, the conduct of the man, there was ever but one side on which I was habitually blameable, and there I have secured myself in the way pointed out by Nature and Nature's God. I was sensible that to so helpless a creature as a poor poet, a wife and family were incumbrances, which a species of prudence would bid him shun; but when the alternative was, being at eternal warfare with myself, on account of habitual follies, to give them no worse name, which no general example, no licentious wit, no sophistical infidelity would, to me, ever justify, I must have been a fool to have hesitated, and a madman to have made another choice. Besides, I had in "my Jean" a long and much loved fellow-creature's happiness or misery among my hands, and who could trifle with such a deposit?

In the affair of a livelihood, I think myself tolerably secure; I have good hopes of my farm, but should they fail, I have an Excise commission, which, on my simple petition, will at any time procure me bread. There is a certain stigma affixed to the character of an Excise officer, but I do not pretend to borrow honor from my profession; and though the salary be comparatively small, it is luxury to anything that the first twenty-five years of my life taught me to expect.

Thus, with a rational aim and method in life, you may easily guess, my reverend and much-honoured friend, that my characteristical trade is not forgotten. I am, if possible, more than ever an enthusiast to the Muses. I am determined to study man and nature, and in that view incessantly; and to try if the ripening and corrections of years can enable me to produce something worth preserving.

You will see in your book, which I beg your pardon for detaining so long, that I have been tuning my lyre on the banks of Nith. Some large poetic plans that are floating in my imagination, or partly put in execution, I shall impart to you when I have the pleasure of meeting with you; which, if you are then in Edinburgh, I shall have about the beginning of March.

That acquaintance, worthy Sir, with which you were pleased to honor me, you must still allow me to challenge; for with whatever unconcern I give up my transient connexion with the merely great, those self-important beings whose intrinsic * * * [con]cealed under the accidental advantages of their * * * I cannot lose the patronizing notice of the learned and good, without the bitterest regret.

R. B.

[Bishop Alexander Geddes, of the Roman Catholic Church, a man of singular character and original genius, was born in Banffshire, of humble parentage, in 1737, and died in London, 1802. The 'book' here referred to was a copy of our Author's own poems, into which he had transcribed some additional verses. Bishop Geddes had a high admiration of, and fatherly regard for, Robert Burns.]

To the Rev. Peter Carfrae.

[Ellisland, March, 1789?]

Rev. Sir,

I do not recollect that I have ever felt a severer pang of shame, than on looking at the date of your obliging letter which accompanied Mr. Mylne's poem.

I am much to blame; the honor Mr. Mylne has done me, greatly enhanced in its value by the endearing, though melancholy circumstance, of its being the last production of his muse, deserved a better return.

I have, as you hint, thought of sending a copy of the poem to some periodical publication; but, on second thoughts, I am afraid, that in the present case, it would be an improper step. My success, perhaps as much accidental as merited, has brought an inundation of nonsense under the name of Scottish poetry. Subscription-bills for Scottish poems have so dunned, and daily do dun the public, that the very name is in danger of contempt. For these reasons, if publishing any of Mr. Mylne's poems in a magazine, &c., be at all prudent, in my opinion it certainly should not be a Scottish poem. The profits of the labours of a man of genius are, I hope, as honourable as any profits whatever; and Mr. Mylne's relations are most justly entitled to that honest harvest which fate has denied himself to reap. But let the friends of Mr. Mylne's fame (among whom I crave the honor of ranking myself) always keep in eye his respectability as a man and as a poet, and take no measure that, before the world knows anything about him, would risk his name and character being classed with the fools of the times.

I have, Sir, some experience of publishing; and the way in which I would proceed with Mr. Mylne's poems is this:—I will publish, in two or three English and Scottish public papers, any one of his English poems which should, by private judges, be thought the most excellent, and mention it at the same time as one of the productions of a Lothian farmer of respectable character, lately deceased, whose poems his friends had it in idea to publish soon by subscription, for the sake of his numerous family:—not in pity to that family, but in justice to what his friends think the poetic merits of the deceased; and to secure in the most effectual manner, to those tender connexions, whose right it is, the pecuniary reward of those merits. *

R. B.

* [A volume of these poems, including two tragedies, was published by Creech in 1790. Rev. Mr. Carfrae seems to have been a friend of Mrs. Dunlop's—compare letter (20) to her.]

To Sir John Sinclair.

[1791.]

Sir,

The following circumstance has, I believe, been omitted in the statistical account transmitted to you of the parish of Dunscore, in Nithsdale. I beg leave to send it to you, because it is new, and may be useful. How far it is deserving of a place in your patriotic publication, you are the best judge.

To store the minds of the lower classes with useful knowledge is certainly of very great importance, both to them as individuals and to society at large. Giving them a turn for reading and reflection is giving them a source of innocent and laudable amusement; and besides, raises them to a more dignified degree in the scale of rationality. Impressed with this idea, a gentleman in this parish, Robert Riddel, Esq., of Glenriddel, set on foot a species of circulating library, on a plan so simple as to be practicable in any corner of the country; and so useful, as to deserve the notice of every country gentleman, who thinks the improvement of that part of his own species, whom chance has thrown into the humble walks of the peasant and the artizan, a matter worthy of his attention.

Mr. Riddel got a number of his own tenants and farming neighbours to form themselves into a society, for the purpose of having a library among themselves. They entered into a legal engagement to abide by it for three years; with a saving clause or two, in case of removal to a distance, or of death. Each member at his entry paid five shillings; and at each of their meetings, which were held every fourth Saturday, sixpence more. With their entry-money, and the credit which they took on the faith of their future funds, they laid in a tolerable stock of books at the commencement. What authors they were to purchase, was always decided by the majority. At every meeting, all the books, under certain fines and forfeitures, by way of penalty, were to be produced; and the members had their choice of the volumes in rotation. He whose name stood for that night first on the list had his choice of what volume he pleased, in the whole collection; the second had his choice after the first; the third, after the second; and so on, to the last. At next meeting, he who had been first on the list at the preceding meeting was last at this; he who had been second was first; and so on, through the whole three years. At the expiration of the engagement the books were sold by auction, but only among the members themselves; and each man had his share of the common stock, in money or in books, as he chose to be a purchaser or not.

At the breaking up of this little society, which was formed under Mr. Riddel's patronage, what with benefactions of books from him, and what with their own purchases, they had collected together upwards of one hundred and fifty volumes. It will easily be guessed that a good deal of trash would be bought. Among the books, however, of this little library were Blair's Sermons, Robertson's History of Scotland, Hume's History of the Stewarts, The Spectator, Idler,

Adventurer, Mirror, Lounger, Observer, Man of Feeling, Man of the World, Chrysal, Don Quixote, Joseph Andrews, &c. A peasant who can read and enjoy such books is certainly a much superior being to his neighbour who perhaps stalks beside his team, very little removed, except in shape, from the brutes he drives.

Wishing your patriotic exertions their so much merited success,

I am, Sir,

Your humble servant,

A PEASANT.

[This letter (which seems to have been intended as a rebuke to the minister of the parish for neglect of the library) was forwarded with a brief accompanying note by Captain Riddel to Sir John Sinclair, explaining our Author's valuable services "as treasurer, librarian, and censor to this little society"—and both letters appear in third volume of Sir John's celebrated *Statistical Account of Scotland.* Compare letters to P. Hill, with reference to books ordered.]

To Charles Sharpe, Esq.,

OF HODDAM.

[ENCLOSING A BALLAD.]

[1790 or 1791.]

IT is true, Sir, you are a gentleman of rank and fortune, and I am a poor devil; you are a feather in the cap of society, and I am a very hobnail in his shoes; yet I have the honor to belong to the same family with you, and on that score I now address you. You will perhaps suspect that I am going to claim affinity with the ancient and honourable house of Kirkpatrick. No, no, Sir; I cannot indeed be properly said to belong to any house, or even any province or kingdom; as my mother, who for many years was spouse to a marching regiment, gave me into this bad world, aboard the packet-boat, somewhere between Donaghadee and Portpatrick. By our common family, I mean, Sir, the family of the Muses. I am a fiddler, and a poet; and you, I am told, play an exquisite violin, and have a standard taste in the *Belles Lettres.* The other day, a brother-catgut gave me a charming Scots air of your composition. If I was pleased with the tune, I was in raptures with the title you have given it; and taking up the idea I have spun it into the three stanzas enclosed. Will you allow me, Sir, to present you them, as the dearest offering that a misbegotten son of Poverty and Rhyme has to give? I have a longing to take you by the hand and unburthen my heart by saying, "Sir, I honor you as a man who supports the dignity of human nature, amid an age when frivolity and avarice have, between them, debased us below the brutes that perish!" But, alas! Sir, to me you are unapproachable. It is true, the Muses baptized me in Castalian streams, but the thoughtless gipsies forgot to give me a name. As the sex have served many a good fellow, the Nine have given me a great deal of pleasure, but, bewitching jades! they have beggared me. Would they but spare me a little of their cast-linen! were it only to put it in my power to say that

I have a shirt on my back! But the idle wenches, like Solomon's lilies, "they toil not, neither do they spin;" so I must e'en continue to tie my remnant of a cravat, like the hangman's rope, round my naked throat, and coax my galligaskins to keep together their many-coloured fragments. As to the affair of shoes, I have given that up. My pilgrimages in my ballad-trade, from town to town, and on your stony-hearted turnpikes too, are what not even the hide of Job's Behemoth could bear. The coat on my back is no more: I shall not speak evil of the dead. It would be equally unhandsome and ungrateful to find fault with my old surtout, which so kindly supplies and conceals the want of that coat. My hat indeed is a great favourite; and though I got it literally for an old song, I would not exchange it for the best beaver in Britain. I was, during several years, a kind of fac-totum servant to a country clergyman, where I pickt up a good many scraps of learning, particularly in some branches of the mathematics. Whenever I feel inclined to rest myself on my way, I take my seat under a hedge, laying my poetic wallet on the one side, and my fiddle-case on the other, and placing my hat between my legs, I can, by means of its brim, or rather brims, go through the whole doctrine of the conic sections.

However, Sir, don't let me mislead you, as if I would interest your pity. Fortune has so much forsaken me, that she has taught me to live without her; and amid all my rags and poverty, I am as independent, and much more happy, than a monarch of the world. According to the hackneyed metaphor, I value the several actors in the great drama of life, simply as they act their parts. I can look on a worthless fellow of a duke with unqualified contempt, and can regard an honest scavenger with sincere respect. As you, Sir, go through your rôle with such distinguished merit, permit me to make one in the chorus of universal applause, and assure you that with the honor to be, &c.,

I have the honor to be, &c.

JOHNNY FAA.

[All further trace of literary correspondence between our Author and this accomplished but somewhat eccentric gentleman, to whom he thus introduced himself in quaint enough character, seems to be lost. There is indeed in Mr. Chambers's edition (vol. III. p. 105) some account of a masonic apron, on the authority of Mr. John Ramsay (author of the *Woodnotes of a Wanderer*), understood by him to have been a gift from Sharpe to Burns, and which bore an inscription under the over-lap to that effect—thus quoted by Mr. Chambers:—

—

CHARLES SHARPE, of Hoddam,

TO

RABBIE BURNS.

DUMFRIES, *Dec.* 12, 1791.

This alleged memorial of their friendship, however, has been subjected to examination by Thomas Thorburn, Esq., Ryedale, Dumfries,—who estimates its value at a shilling or eighteenpence, exclusive of the lettering, which is good; and disproves its authenticity in a communication of considerable length, evidencing minute acquaintance with the whole subject, in *Dumfries Courier,* May 17, 1855. Among other arguments, he states that "the handwriting is not that of the Laird of Hoddam, nor of the illustrious 'Rabbie,' and it is abundantly obvious that neither of them would have been guilty of so gross a solecism as to spell Mr. Sharpe's name without an 'e' any more than to call his patrimonial property Hotham instead of Hoddam, by which it is universally known and recognised. The ink is not that of 1791, though of course it might have been refreshed or renewed." From this it appears that Mr. Ramsay or Mr. Chambers had not examined with sufficient care the actual inscription when transcribing it for the press. According to Mr. Thorburn, the writing reads as follows:—

CHARLES SHARP of Hotham,

To

ROBERT BURNS.

Dumfries, December 12, 1791.

which, beside the style of the handwriting, goes far to prove that it was not a genuine inscription at all. He further demonstrates, from entries in the Lodge Book, that Sharpe and Burns could hardly ever have met as masons; so that all ground for imagining an intercourse of that kind, however natural it might seem, is removed. We are much indebted to Mr. Thorburn for his kindness in directing our attention to this and to some other points of interest, to which hereafter we shall have occasion to refer.]

To Dr. Anderson.

[FRAGMENT.]

[1790.]

SIR,

I AM much indebted to my worthy friend, Dr. Blacklock, for introducing me to a gentleman of Dr. Anderson's celebrity; but when you do me the honor to ask my assistance in your proposed publication, alas! Sir, you might as well think to cheapen a little honesty at the sign of an advocate's wig, or humility under the Geneva band. I am a miserable hurried devil, worn to the marrow in the friction of holding the noses of the poor publicans to the grindstone of the excise! and, like Milton's Satan, for private reasons, am forced

    "To do what yet though damn'd I would abhor,"

—and, except a couplet or two of honest execration   *   *   *

[We adopt Mr. Chambers's order in this letter, who seems correctly to have settled its date, and some other particulars respecting it, which had been misstated by Currie and Cromek. Dr. James Anderson was a celebrated writer on agriculture, also on miscellaneous subjects. The *Bee* began in December, 1790. Blacklock addressed a playful poetical epistle to Burns in September of that year, entreating his assistance as a contributor. The above letter manifestly refers to this subject.]

To William Tytler, Esq.,

OF WOODHOUSELEE.*

Lawn-Market, August, 1790.

SIR,

ENCLOSED I have sent you a sample of the old pieces that are still to be found among our peasantry in the west. I had once a great many of these fragments, and some of these here entire; but as I had no idea then that any body cared for them, I have forgotten them. I invariably hold it sacrilege to add anything of my own to help out with the shattered wrecks of these venerable old compositions; but they have many, various readings. If you have not seen these before, I know they will flatter your true old-style Caledonian feelings; at any rate I am truly happy to have an opportunity of assuring you how sincerely I am, revered Sir,

    Your gratefully indebted humble Servant,

R. B.

* [Author of *An Inquiry, Historical and Critical, into the Evidence against Mary Queen of Scots*, 1790; addressed elsewhere by Burns as "Revered defender of beauteous Stuart."]

(1.)   To A. F. Tytler, Esq.

Ellisland, [April,] 1791.

SIR,

NOTHING less than the unfortunate accident I have met with could have prevented my grateful acknowledgments for your letter. His own favourite poem, and that an essay in the walk of the Muses entirely new to him, where consequently his hopes and fears were on the most anxious alarm for his success in the attempt—to have that poem so much applauded by one of the first judges, was the most delicious vibration that ever thrilled along the heart-strings of a poor poet. However, Providence, to keep up the proper proportion of evil with the good, which it seems is necessary in this sublunary state, thought proper to check my exultation by a very serious misfortune. A day or two after I received your letter, my horse came down with me and broke my right arm. As this is the first service my arm has done me since its disaster, I find myself unable to do more than just, in general terms, thank you for this additional instance of your patronage and friendship. As to the faults you detected in the piece, they are truly there; one of them, the hit at the lawyer and priest, I shall cut out; as to the falling off in the catastrophe, for the reason you justly adduce, it cannot easily be remedied. Your approbation, Sir, has given me such additional spirits to persevere in this species of poetic composition, that I am already revolving two or three stories in my fancy. If I can bring these floating ideas to bear any kind of embodied form, it will give me an additional opportunity of assuring you how much I have the honor to be, &c.

R. B.

[Alexander Fraser Tytler, Esq., eldest son of the above William Tytler of Woodhouselee, was at this time highly distinguished in Edinburgh both as a littérateur and as a professorial lecturer in the University. The letter acknowledged by Burns contained a criticism on "Tam o' Shanter," which was highly complimentary, but which we need not here reproduce. Mr. Fraser Tytler was appointed Judge-Advocate of Scotland in 1790, and was afterwards raised to the bench in 1802, with the title of Lord Woodhouselee, by which he is most commonly distinguished. See note to next letter.]

(2.)   TO A. F. TYTLER, ESQ.

SIR,

A POOR caitiff, driving as I am at this moment with an Excise quill, at the rate of "Devil take the hindmost," is ill qualified to round the period of gratitude, or swell the pathos of sensibility. Gratitude, like some other amiable qualities of the mind, is now-a-days so abused by imposters, that I have sometimes wished that the project of that sly dog Momus, I think it is, had gone into effect—planting a window in the breast of man. In that case, when a poor fellow comes, as I do at this moment, before his benefactor, tongue-tied with the sense of these very obligations, he would have nothing to do but place himself in front of his friend, and lay bare the workings of his bosom.

I again trouble you with another, and my last, parcel of manuscript. I am not interested in any of these; blot them at your pleasure. I am much indebted to you for taking the trouble of correcting the press work. One instance, indeed, may be rather unlucky; if the lines to Sir John Whiteford are printed, they ought to end—

"And tread the shadowy path to that dark world unknown."

"Shadowy," instead of "dreary," as I believe it stands at present. I wish this could be noticed in the Errata. This comes of writing, as I generally do, from the memory.

I have the honour to be, Sir, your deeply indebted humble servant,

ROBT. BURNS.

6th Decr., 1795.

[This letter, now in possession of Lord Woodhouselee's grandson, Colonel Fraser Tytler of Aldourie, was printed for the first time in *Inverness Courier*, October 11, 1855. We have already had occasion to observe that the request of the Poet does not seem to have been attended to, in the necessary revision of the Press, in as much as the error referred to remains to this day. It is proper to mention, however, that Mr. Fraser Tytler, in 1795, was suffering from a very severe indisposition. By the same complaint, which returned in 1812, he was finally prostrated, and died on the 5th January, 1813, in the sixty-sixth year of his age.]

To the Rev. Arch. Alison.

Ellisland, near Dumfries, 14th Feb., 1791.

SIR,

YOU must by this time have set me down as one of the most ungrateful of men. You did me the honour to present me with a book, which does honour to science and the intellectual powers of man, and I have not even so much as acknowledged the receipt of it. The fact is, you yourself are to blame for it. Flattered as I was by your telling me that you wished to have my opinion of the work, the old spiritual enemy of mankind, who knows well that vanity is one of the sins that most easily beset me, put it into my head to ponder over the performance with the look-out of a critic, and to draw up forsooth a deep-learned digest of strictures on a composition, of which, in fact, until I read the book, I did not even know the first principles. I own, Sir, that at first glance, several of your propositions startled me as paradoxical. That the martial clangor of a trumpet had something in it vastly more grand, heroic, and sublime, than the twingle-twangle of a Jew's harp; that the delicate flexure of a rose-twig, when the half-blown flower is heavy with the tears of the dawn, was infinitely more beautiful and elegant than the upright stub of a burdock; and that from something innate and independent of all associations of ideas —these I had set down as irrefragable, orthodox truths, until perusing your book shook my faith. In short, Sir, except Euclid's Elements of Geometry, which I made a shift to unravel by my father's fire-side, in the winter evenings of the first season I held the plough, I never read a book which gave me such a quantum of information, and added so much

to my stock of ideas, as your "Essays on the Principles of Taste." One thing, Sir, you must forgive my mentioning as an uncommon merit in the work, I mean the language. To clothe abstract philosophy in elegance of style, sounds something like a contradiction in terms; but you have convinced me that they are quite compatible.

I enclose you some poetic bagatelles of my late composition. The one in print is my first essay in the way of telling a tale.

I am, Sir, &c.,

R. B.

[On reading this letter, Dugald Stewart expressed his surprise, in a letter printed by Currie, that an Ayrshire peasant should have formed, independently, "a distinct conception of the general principles of the doctrine of association"—a favorite theme at that time, and since, with Scottish metaphysicians. The learned professor did not seem to see that the Poet was quietly heaping ridicule on the whole system. On the other hand, we do not know whether Mr. Ruskin, who has so eloquently illustrated the principles of architectural design and painting, may have studied this letter, but he certainly does seem to have adopted its principles—although the doctrine of association, subordinately, by him, is very beautifully blended with them. Our readers need hardly be reminded, perhaps, that the reverend gentleman here addressed, who was an Episcopalian clergyman in Edinburgh, was father of the late Sir Archibald Alison, Bart., author of the *History of Europe*.]

To the Rev. G. Baird.°

Ellisland, [February,] 1791.

REVEREND SIR,

WHY did you, my dear Sir, write to me in such a hesitating style on the business of poor Bruce? Don't I know, and have I not felt, the many ills, the peculiar ills that poetic flesh is heir to? You shall have your choice of all the unpublished poems I have; and had your letter had my direction so as to have reached me sooner (it only came to my hand this moment), I should have directly put you out of suspense on the subject. I only ask that some prefatory advertisement in the book, as well as the subscription bills, may bear that the publication is solely for the benefit of Bruce's mother. I would not put it in the power of ignorance to surmise, or malice to insinuate, that I clubbed a share in the work from mercenary motives. Nor need you give me credit for any remarkable generosity in my part of the business. I have such a host of peccadilloes, failings, follies, and backslidings (any body but myself might perhaps give some of them a worse appellation), that by way of some balance, however trifling, in the account, I am fain to do any good that occurs in my very limited power to a fellow-creature, just for the selfish purpose of clearing a little the vista of retrospection.†

R. B.

* [Rev. George Husband Baird—afterwards Principal of Edinburgh University.]
† [It does not appear that the contributions here promised by Burns were ultimately availed of.]

TO PRINTERS, PUBLISHERS, &c.

To Mr. Sibbald,

BOOKSELLER IN EDINBURGH.

Lawn-Market, [1787.]

SIR,

So little am I acquainted with the words and manners of the more public and polished walks of life, that I often feel myself much embarrassed how to express the feelings of my heart, particularly gratitude:—

> "Rude am I in speech,
> And little therefore shall I grace my cause
> In speaking for myself—"

The warmth with which you have befriended an obscure man and a young author, in the last three magazines—I can only say, Sir, I feel the weight of the obligation: I wish I could express my sense of it. In the meantime, accept of the conscious acknowledgment from,

Sir,
Your obliged servant,
R. B.

[This letter first appeared in Nichols's Illustrations of Literature. Mr. James Sibbald was himself distinguished in more than one walk of literary enterprise, but is best known by his 'Chronicle of Scottish Poetry,' an admirable and valuable, though now comparatively rare, work.]

To William Creech, Esq.,

EDINBURGH.

Selkirk, 13th May, 1787.

MY HONOURED FRIEND,

THE enclosed I have just wrote, nearly extempore, in a solitary inn in Selkirk, after a miserably wet day's riding. I have been over most of East Lothian, Berwick, Roxburgh, and Selkirk-shires: and next week I begin a tour through the north of England. Yesterday I dined with Lady Harriet,[*] sister to my noble patron—*Quem Deus conservet!* I would write till I would tire you as much with dull prose, as I dare say by this time you are with wretched verse, but I am jaded to death; so, with a grateful farewell,

I have the honor to be,
Good Sir, yours sincerely,
R. B.

[Verses enclosed were]

WILLIE'S AWA.

Auld chuckie Reekie's sair distrest, &c.

[*] [Lady Harriet Don, sister to the Earl of Glencairn. See 'Journal'—Appendix.]

(2.)   TO WILLIAM CREECH, ESQ.

Ellisland, 30th May, 1789.

SIR,

I HAD intended to have troubled you with a long letter, but at present the delightful sensations of an omnipotent Toothache so engross all my inner man, as to put it out of my power even to write nonsense. However, as in duty bound, I approach my Bookseller with an offering in my hand—a few poetic clinches and a song:—To expect any other kind of offering from the RHYMING TRIBE, would be to know them much less than you do. I do not pretend that there is much merit in these *morceaux,* but I have two reasons for sending them; *primo,* they are mostly ill-natured, so are in unison with my present feelings, while fifty troops of infernal spirits are driving post from ear to ear along my jawbones; and *secondly,* they are so short, that you cannot leave off in the middle, and so hurt my pride in the idea that you found any work of mine too heavy to get through.

I have a request to beg of you, and I not only beg of you, but conjure you—by all your wishes and by all your hopes, that the Muse will spare the satiric wink in the moment of your foibles; that she will warble the song of rapture round your hymeneal couch; and that she will shed on your turf the honest tear of elegiac gratitude! grant my request as speedily as possible:—Send me by the very first fly or coach for this place, three copies of the last edition of my poems; which place to my account.

Now, may the good things of prose, and the good things of verse, come among thy hands until they be filled with the *good things of this life!* prayeth

ROBT. BURNS.

[Our **Author's** generosity in thus forwarding to Mr. Creech, after previous experience, so many new poetical effusions to enrich a new edition of his works, very much for that gentleman's advantage (see letter (8) to Hill), needs no commentary here, any more than the style in which that edition seems to have been conducted. After all attempts at adjustment or reconciliation, no permanent friendship seems to have been established between them. Dr. Currie indeed informs us on Mr. C.'s authority, "that whatever little differences subsisted between Burns and him had been made up long before the bard's death, and that he would do everything in his power to serve the family"—which, if not a questionable statement, looks very like a piece of special pleading. The two letters above printed are all we can now find extant of our Author's to Creech. His business letters to that gentleman, which were full of unpleasant recriminations—perhaps exaggerated complaints, were by Mrs. Hay's (Margaret Chalmers) advice, to whom they were submitted, finally destroyed.]

To Mr. Beugo,

ENGRAVER, EDINBURGH.

Ellisland, 9th Sept., 1788.

MY DEAR SIR,

THERE is not in Edinburgh above the number of the Graces whose letters would have given me so much pleasure as yours of the 3rd instant, which only reached me yesternight.

I am here on my farm, busy with my harvest; but for all

that most pleasurable part of life called SOCIAL COMMUNICA-
TION, I am here at the very elbow of existence. The only
things that are to be found in this country, in any degree
of perfection, are stupidity and canting. Prose they only
know in graces, prayers, &c., and the value of these they
estimate as they do their plaiding webs—by the ell! As
for the Muses, they have as much an idea of a rhinoceros
as of a poet. For my old capricious but good-natured huzzy
of a Muse—

> "By banks of Nith I sat and wept
> When Coila I thought on,
> In midst thereof I hung my harp
> The willow-trees upon."

I am generally about half my time in Ayrshire with my
"darling Jean," and then I, at lucid intervals, throw my
horny fist across my be-cobwebbed lyre, much in the same
manner as an old wife throws her hand across the spokes
of her spinning-wheel.

I will send you the "Fortunate Shepherdess" as soon
as I return to Ayrshire, for there I keep it with other
precious treasure. I shall send it by a careful hand, as I
would not for any thing it should be mislaid or lost. I
do not wish to serve you from any benevolence, or other
grave Christian virtue; 'tis purely a selfish gratification
of my own feelings whenever I think of you.

You do not tell me if you are going to be married. Depend
upon it, if you do not make some foolish choice, it will be a
very great improvement on the dish of life. I can speak
from experience, though, God knows, my choice was as
random as blind man's buff.   *   *   *

If your better functions would give you leisure to write
me, I should be extremely happy; that is to say, if you
neither keep nor look for a regular correspondence. I hate
the idea of being obliged to write a letter. I sometimes
write a friend twice a week, at other times once a quarter.

I am exceedingly pleased with your fancy in making the
author you mention place a map of Iceland instead of his
portrait before his works: 'twas a glorious idea.*

Could you conveniently do me one thing?—whenever you
finish any head I should like to have a proof copy of it.
I might tell you a long story about your fine genius; but
as what every body knows cannot have escaped you, I
shall not say one syllable about it.

If you see Mr. Nasmyth, remember me to him most
respectfully, as he both loves and deserves respect: though,
if he would pay less respect to the mere carcass of greatness, I should think him much nearer perfection.

R. B.

* [This is undoubtedly an allusion to Creech, who had been publishing some
frozen stuff of his own from the newspapers.]

[Mr. Beugo was an engraver of great skill, and of the highest reputation then
in Edinburgh. He was employed to transfer Nasmyth's celebrated picture of
our Author to copper, as a frontispiece for the new edition of his works. Into
this engraving he introduced finishing touches of his own from the life, having
had the Poet himself frequently as a sitter before him. His work has, therefore,
been considered by many superior to the original. Having a photograph of
Nasmyth's portrait before us, we are by no means of this opinion; and having
carefully studied the expression of both, in comparison with the miniature of
1795, we cease to regard either the one or the other as a reliable representation
of Robert Burns.]

To Mr. William Smellie,

PRINTER.

Dumfries, 22nd January, 1792.

I SIT down, my dear Sir, to introduce a young lady to you,
and a lady in the first ranks of fashion too. What a task! to
you who care no more for the herd of animals called young
ladies, than you do for the herd of animals called young
gentlemen. To you—who despise and detest the groupings
and combinations of fashion, as an idiot painter that seems
industrious to place staring fools and unprincipled knaves
in the foreground of his picture, while men of sense and
honesty are too often thrown in the dimmest shades. Mrs.
Riddel, who will take this letter to town with her, and send
it to you, is a character that, even in your own way, as a
naturalist and a philosopher, would be an acquisition to
your acquaintance. The lady, too, is a votary to the Muses;
and as I think myself somewhat of a judge in my own
trade, I assure you that her verses, always correct, and
often elegant, are much beyond the common run of the
lady-poetesses of the day. She is a great admirer of your
book; and hearing me say that I was acquainted with
you, she begged to be known to you, as she is just going
to pay her first visit to our Caledonian capital. I told her
that her best way was, to desire her near relation, and
your intimate friend, Craigdarroch, to have you at his
house while she was there; and lest you might think of
a lively West Indian girl of eighteen, as girls of eighteen
too often deserve to be thought of, I should take care to
remove that prejudice. To be impartial, however, in appreciating the lady's merits, she has one unlucky failing—
a failing which you will easily discover, as she seems
rather pleased with indulging in it; and a failing that you
will easily pardon, as it is a sin which very much besets
yourself—where she dislikes or despises, she is apt to make
no more a secret of it than where she esteems and respects.

I will not present you with the unmeaning *compliments of
the season,* but I will send you my warmest wishes and most
ardent prayers, that FORTUNE may never throw your SUB-
SISTENCE to the mercy of a KNAVE, or set your CHARACTER on
the judgment of a FOOL; but, that upright and erect, you
may walk to an honest grave, where men of letters shall
say, "Here lies a man who did honor to science;" and men
of worth shall say, "Here lies a man who did honor to
human nature."

R. B.

[This admirable letter was to introduce Mrs. W. Riddel (Maria Woodley),
who was anxious to obtain Mr. Smellie's assistance in the publication of her
voyage to Madeira and the Leeward Isles. On this work the old gentleman
pronounced the highest eulogium, and subsequently paid a visit to the authoress.
See Heroines of Burns—Appendix. "Your book" referred to ("Sinful old
Smellie and his second volume") was a work published by him entitled *The
Philosophy of Natural History*—in which there was much shrewd speculation;
of which the first volume had already been published, and the second was
anxiously expected by his friends.]

To Francis Grose, Esq., F.S.A.

(1.)   *Dumfries,* 1792.

Sir,

I believe among all our Scots literati you have not met with Professor Dugald Stewart, who fills the moral philosophy chair in the University of Edinburgh. To say that he is a man of the first parts, and, what is more, a man of the first worth, to a gentleman of your general acquaintance, and who so much enjoys the luxury of unencumbered freedom and undisturbed privacy, is not perhaps recommendation enough; but when I inform you that Mr. Stewart's principal characteristic is your favorite feature—*that* sterling independence of mind which, though every man's right, so few men have the courage to claim, and fewer still the magnanimity to support; when I tell you that, unseduced by splendour, and undisgusted by wretchedness, he appreciates the merits of the various actors in the great drama of life merely as they perform their parts—in short, he is a man after your own heart, and I comply with his earnest request in letting you know that he wishes above all things to meet with you. His house, Catrine, is within less than a mile of Sorn Castle, which you proposed visiting; or if you could transmit him the enclosed, he would, with the greatest pleasure, meet you anywhere in the neighbourhood. I write to Ayrshire to inform Mr. Stewart that I have acquitted myself of my promise. Should your time and spirits permit your meeting with Mr. Stewart, 'tis well; if not, I hope you will forgive this liberty, and I have at least an opportunity of assuring you with what truth and respect

I am, Sir,

Your great admirer,

and very humble servant,

R. B.

(2.)   TO FRANCIS GROSE, ESQ., F.S.A.

Dumfries, 1792.

Among the many witch-stories I have heard relating to Alloway Kirk, I distinctly remember only two or three.

Upon a stormy night, amid whistling squalls of wind, and bitter blasts of hail—in short, on such a night as the devil would choose to take the air in—a farmer, or farmer's servant, was plodding and plashing homeward with his plough-irons on his shoulder, having been getting some repairs on them at a neighbouring smithy. His way lay by the Kirk of Alloway; and being rather on the anxious look-out in approaching a place so well known to be a favourite haunt of the devil, and the devil's friends and emissaries, he was struck aghast by discovering, through the horrors of the storm and stormy night, a light, which on his nearer approach plainly showed itself to proceed from the haunted edifice. Whether he had been fortified from above, on his devout supplication, as is customary with people when they suspect the immediate presence of Satan; or whether, according to another custom, he had got courageously drunk at the smithy, I will not pretend to determine; but so it was that he ventured to go up to, nay, into the very kirk. As luck would have it, his temerity came off unpunished.

The members of the infernal junto were all out on some midnight business or other, and he saw nothing but a kind of kettle, or cauldron, depending from the roof, over the fire, simmering some heads of unchristened children, limbs of executed malefactors, &c., for the business of the night. It was in for a penny in for a pound, with the honest ploughman: so without ceremony he unhooked the cauldron from off the fire, and pouring out the damnable ingredients, inverted it on his head, and carried it fairly home, where it remained long in the family, a living evidence of the truth of the story.

Another story, which I can prove to be equally authentic, was as follows:—

On a market-day in the town of Ayr, a farmer from Carrick, and consequently whose way lay by the very gate of Alloway Kirkyard, in order to cross the river Doon at the old bridge, which is about two or three hundred yards farther on than the said gate, had been detained by his business, till by the time he reached Alloway it was the wizard-hour—between night and morning.

Though he was terrified with a blaze streaming from the kirk, yet as it is a well-known fact that to turn back on these occasions is running by far the greatest risk of mischief, he prudently advanced on his road. When he had reached the gate of the kirkyard, he was surprised and entertained, through the ribs and arches of an old Gothic window, which still faces the highway,* to see a dance of witches merrily footing it round their old sooty blackguard master, who was keeping them all alive with the power of his bagpipe. The farmer, stopping his horse to observe them a little, could plainly descry the faces of many old women of his acquaintance and neighbourhood. How the gentleman was dressed tradition does not say; but that the ladies were all in their smocks: and one of them happening unluckily to have a smock which was considerably too short to answer all the purposes of that piece of dress, our farmer was so tickled that he involuntarily burst out, with a loud laugh, "Weel luppen, Maggy wi' the short sark!" and recollecting himself, instantly spurred his horse to the top of his speed. I need not mention the universally known fact, that no diabolical power can pursue you beyond the middle of a running stream. Lucky it was for the poor farmer that the river Doon was so near, for notwithstanding the speed of his horse, which was a good one, against he reached the middle of the arch of the bridge, and consequently the middle of the stream, the pursuing, vengeful hags were so close at his heels, that one of them actually sprung to seize him: but it was too late; nothing was on her side of the stream but the horse's tail, which immediately gave way at her infernal grip, as if blasted by a stroke of lightning; but the farmer was beyond her reach. However, the unsightly, tail-less condition of the vigorous steed was,

to the last hour of the noble creature's life, an awful warning to the Carrick farmers not to stay too late in Ayr markets.

The last relation I shall give, though equally true, is not so well identified as the two former, with regard to the scene; but as the best authorities give it for Alloway, I shall relate it.

On a summer's evening, about the time nature puts on her sables to mourn the expiry of the cheerful day, a shepherd-boy, belonging to a farmer in the immediate neighbourhood of Alloway Kirk, had just folded his charge, and was returning home. As he passed the kirk, in the adjoining field he fell in with a crew of men and women, who were busy pulling stems of the plant ragwort. He observed that as each person pulled a ragwort, he or she got astride of it, and called out, " Up, horsie!" on which the ragwort flew off, like Pegasus, through the air with its rider. The foolish boy likewise pulled his ragwort, and cried with the rest. "Up, horsie!" and, strange to tell, away he flew with the company. The first stage at which the cavalcade stopt was a merchant's wine-cellar in Bordeaux, where, without saying by your leave, they quaffed away at the best the cellar could afford, until the morning, foe to the imps and works of darkness, threatened to throw light on the matter, and frightened them from their carousals.

The poor shepherd-lad, being equally a stranger to the scene and the liquor, heedlessly got himself drunk; and when the rest took horse, he fell asleep, and was found so next day by some of the people belonging to the merchant. Somebody that understood Scotch, asking him what he was, he said such-a-one's herd in Alloway, and by some means or other getting home again, he lived long to tell the world the wondrous tale.

I am, &c.

R. B.

" [That is the old highway, which passed on the south-west side of the kirk.]

[This letter was communicated by Mr. Gilchrist, of Stamford, to Sir Egerton Brydges, by whom it was published in the *Censura Literaria*, 1796. The reader may compare note on "Tam o' Shanter," *Poetical Works*, p. 247. There is a most singular correspondence between the whole of the third story and several scenes in *Faust*—especially the Witches' ride, and the revel in the Wine-shop: *Faust*, we may remind our readers, was not published till 1808.]

(1.)　　　**To Mr. [Peter Stuart.]**

Edinburgh, March, 1787.

MY DEAR SIR,

You may think, and too justly, that I am a selfish, ungrateful fellow, having received so many repeated instances of kindness from you, and yet never putting pen to paper to say thank you; but if you knew what a devil of a life my conscience has led me on that account, your good heart would think yourself too much avenged. By the bye, there is nothing in the whole frame of man which seems to me so unaccountable as that thing called conscience. Had the

troublesome yelping cur powers officient to prevent a mischief, he might be of use; but at the beginning of the business, his feeble efforts are to the workings of passion as the infant frosts of an autumnal morning to the unclouded fervour of the rising sun; and no sooner are the tumultuous doings of the wicked deed over, than, amidst the bitter native consequences of folly, in the very vortex of our horrors, up starts conscience, and harrows us with the feelings of the damned.

I have inclosed you, by way of expiation, some verse and prose, that, if they merit a place in your truly entertaining miscellany, you are welcome to. The prose extract is literally as Mr. Sprott sent it me.

The inscription on the stone is as follows:

HERE LIES ROBERT FERGUSSON, POET.

Born, September 5th, 1751—Died, 16th October, 1774.

No sculptur'd marble here, nor pompous lay,
"No storied urn, nor animated bust;"
This simple stone directs pale Scotia's way
To pour her sorrows o'er her poet's dust.

On the other side of the stone is as follows:

" By special grant of the managers to Robert Burns, who erected this stone, this burial-place is to remain for ever sacred to the memory of Robert Fergusson."

Session-house, within the Kirk of Canongate, the twenty-second day of February, one thousand seven hundred eighty-seven years.

Soderunt of the Managers of the Kirk and Kirk-Yard funds of Canongate.

Which day, the treasurer to the said funds produced a letter from Mr. Robert Burns, of date the 6th current, which was read and appointed to be engrossed in their soderunt book, and of which letter the tenor follows:—

"To the honourable baillies of Canongate, Edinburgh.— Gentlemen, I am sorry to be told that the remains of Robert Fergusson, the so justly celebrated poet, a man whose talents for ages to come will do honor to our Caledonian name, lie in your church-yard among the ignoble dead, unnoticed and unknown.

"Some memorial to direct the steps of the lovers of Scottish song, when they wish to shed a tear over the 'narrow house' of the bard who is no more, is surely a tribute due to Fergusson's memory: a tribute I wish to have the honor of paying.

"I petition you then, gentlemen, to permit me to lay a simple stone over his revered ashes, to remain an unalienable property to his deathless fame. I have the honor to be, gentlemen, your very humble servant (*sic subscribitur*),

ROBERT BURNS."

Thereafter the said managers, in consideration of the laudable and disinterested motion of Mr. Burns, and the propriety of his request, did, and hereby do, unanimously, grant power and liberty to the said Robert Burns to erect a headstone at the grave of the said Robert Fergusson, and to keep up and preserve the same to his memory in all time coming. Extracted forth of the records of the managers, by

WILLIAM SPROTT, Clerk.

(2.)*   TO MR. [PETER STUART.]

[Autumn,] 1789.

MY DEAR SIR,

THE hurry of a farmer in this particular season, and the indolence of a poet at all times and seasons, will, I hope, plead my excuse for neglecting so long to answer your obliging letter of the 5th of August.

That you have done well in quitting your laborious concern in * * * * I do not doubt; the weighty reasons you mention were, I hope, very, and deservedly indeed, weighty ones, and your health is a matter of the last importance; but whether the remaining proprietors of the paper have also done well, is what I much doubt. The [Star,] so far as I was a reader, exhibited such a brilliancy of point, such an elegance of paragraph, and such a variety of intelligence, that I can hardly conceive it possible to continue a daily paper in the same degree of excellence: but if there was a man who had abilities equal to the task, that man's assistance the proprietors have lost.   *   *   *

When I received your letter I was transcribing for [the Star] my letter to the magistrates of the Canongate, Edinburgh, begging their permission to place a tomb-stone over poor Fergusson, and their edict in consequence of my petition; but now I shall send them to * * * * * *. Poor Fergusson! If there be a life beyond the grave, which I trust there is; and if there be a good God presiding over all nature, which I am sure there is—thou art now enjoying existence in a glorious world, where worth of the heart alone is distinction in the man; where riches, deprived of all their pleasure-purchasing powers, return to their native sordid matter; where titles and honors are the disregarded reveries of an idle dream; and where that heavy virtue, which is the negative consequence of steady dulness, and those thoughtless, though often destructive follies, which are the unavoidable aberrations of frail human nature, will be thrown into equal oblivion as if they had never been!

Adieu, my dear Sir! So soon as your present views and schemes are concentered in an aim, I shall be glad to hear from you; as your welfare and happiness is by no means a subject indifferent to,

Yours,   R. B.

* [Dr. Currie having concealed the name of the correspondent to whom these two letters were addressed, they have long been printed without any address at all. We are indebted to Mr. Chambers for having determined to whom they belong. Mr. Stuart was one of three brothers—Charles, Peter, and Daniel—all men of literary celebrity at the time. To the same gentleman, in his professional character as editor of the Star, the following letter had been addressed about a twelvemonth before the above; but in the meantime, as we may conclude from the above, he had resigned his editorship. His admiration of Fergusson (who was eight years older than himself, and the intimate friend of his elder brother Charles) seems to have been unbounded. See Appendix—Scottish Language. For Burns's opinion of the Star, see Poetical Works, p. 342, v. 1.]

To the Editor of "The Star."

November 8th, 1788.

SIR,

NOTWITHSTANDING the opprobrious epithets with which some of our philosophers and gloomy sectarians have branded our nature—the principle of universal selfishness, the proneness to all evil, they have given us; still, the detestation in which inhumanity to the distressed, and insolence to the fallen, are held by all mankind, shows that they are not natives of the human heart. Even the unhappy partner of our kind who is undone—the bitter consequence of his follies or his crimes—who but sympathizes with the miseries of this ruined profligate brother? We forget the injuries, and feel for the man.

I went, last Wednesday, to my parish church, most cordially to join in grateful acknowledgment to the AUTHOR OF ALL GOOD, for the consequent blessings of the glorious Revolution. To that auspicious event we owe no less than our liberties, civil and religious; to it we are likewise indebted for the present Royal Family, the ruling features of whose administration have ever been mildness to the subject, and tenderness of his rights.

Bred and educated in revolution principles, the principles of reason and common sense, it could not be any silly political prejudice which made my heart revolt at the harsh abusive manner in which the reverend gentleman mentioned the House of Stuart, and which, I am afraid, was too much the language of the day. We may rejoice sufficiently in our deliverance from past evils, without cruelly raking up the ashes of those whose misfortune it was, perhaps as much as their crime, to be the authors of those evils; and we may bless GOD for all his goodness to us as a nation, without at the same time cursing a few ruined, powerless exiles, who only harboured ideas, and made attempts, that most of us would have done, had we been in their situation.

"The bloody and tyrannical House of Stuart" may be said with propriety and justice, when compared with the present royal family, and the sentiments of our days; but is there no allowance to be made for the manners of the times? Were the royal contemporaries of the Stuarts more attentive to their subjects' rights? Might not the epithets of "bloody and tyrannical" be, with at least equal justice, applied to the House of Tudor, of York, or any other of their predecessors?

The simple state of the case, Sir, seems to be this:—At that period, the science of government, the knowledge of the true relation between king and subject, was like other sciences and other knowledge, just in its infancy, emerging from dark ages of ignorance and barbarity.

The Stuarts only contended for prerogatives which they knew their predecessors enjoyed, and which they saw their contemporaries enjoying; but these prerogatives were inimical to the happiness of a nation and the rights of subjects.

In this contest between prince and people, the consequence of that light of science which had lately dawned over Europe, the monarch of France, for example, was victorious over the struggling liberties of his people; with us, luckily the monarch failed, and his unwarrantable pretensions fell a sacrifice to our rights and happiness. Whether it was owing to the wisdom of leading individuals, or to the justling of parties, I cannot pretend to determine; but, likewise happily for us, the kingly power was shifted into another branch of the family, who, as they owed the throne solely to the call of a free people, could claim nothing inconsistent with the covenanted terms which placed them there.

The Stuarts have been condemned and laughed at for the folly and impracticability of their attempts in 1715 and 1745. That they failed, I bless God: but cannot join in the ridicule against them. Who does not know that the abilities or defects of leaders and commanders are often hidden until put to the touchstone of exigency; and that there is a caprice of fortune, an omnipotence in particular accidents and conjunctures of circumstances, which exalt us as heroes, or brand us as madmen, just as they are for or against us?

Man, Mr. Publisher, is a strange, weak, inconsistent being: who would believe, Sir, that in this our Augustan age of liberality and refinement, while we seem so justly sensible and jealous of our rights and liberties, and animated with such indignation against the very memory of those who would have subverted them—that a certain people under our national protection should complain, not against our monarch and a few favorite advisers, but against our WHOLE LEGISLATIVE BODY, for similar oppression, and almost in the very same terms, as our forefathers did of the House of Stuart! I will not, I cannot, enter into the merits of the cause; but I dare say the American Congress, in 1776, will be allowed to be as able and as enlightened as the English Convention was in 1688; and that their posterity will celebrate the centenary of their deliverance from us, as duly and sincerely as we do ours from the oppressive measures of the wrong-headed House of Stuart.

To conclude, Sir; let every man who has a tear for the many miseries incident to humanity, feel for a family illustrious as any in Europe, and unfortunate beyond historic precedent; and let every Briton (and particularly every Scotsman), who ever looked with reverential pity on the dotage of a parent, cast a veil over the fatal mistakes of the kings of his forefathers.   R. B.

[This letter, which contains such an admirable statement of the whole case, and which is so decidedly prophetic not only in its tone but in its very terms, demonstrates the writer to have been, both in politics and philosophy, a hundred years at least before his day. It was provoked by the illiberality of Rev. Mr. Kirkpatrick's sermon on occasion of the Assembly's Thanksgiving-day, Nov. 5th, 1788, to celebrate the centenary of King William's arrival at Torbay, to assume the government of these Islands and maintain Protestant ascendency.]

<hr>

TO THE

Editor of the "Morning Chronicle."

[*Dumfries*, 1795.]

SIR,

You will see, by your subscribers' list, that I have been about nine months of that number.

I am sorry to inform you, that in that time seven or eight of your papers either have never been sent me, or else have never reached me. To be deprived of any one number of the first newspaper in Great Britain for information, ability, and independence, is what I can ill brook and bear; but to be deprived of that most admirable oration of the Marquis of Lansdowne, when he made the great, though ineffectual attempt (in the language of the poet, I fear too true) "to save a SINKING STATE"—this was a loss that I neither can nor will forgive you.—That paper, Sir, never reached me; but I demand it of you. I am a BRITON; and must be interested in the cause of LIBERTY: I am a MAN; and the RIGHTS OF HUMAN NATURE cannot be indifferent to me. However, do not let me mislead you: I am not a man in that situation of life which, as your subscriber, can be of any consequence to you, in the eyes of those to whom SITUATION OF LIFE ALONE is the criterion of MAN.—I am but a plain tradesman, in this distant, obscure country town; but that humble domicile in which I shelter my wife and children is the CASTELLUM of a BRITON; and that scanty, hard-earned income which supports them, is as truly my property, as the most magnificent fortune of the most PUISSANT MEMBER of your HOUSE OF NOBLES.

These, Sir, are my sentiments; and to them I subscribe my name: and were I a man of ability and consequence enough to address the PUBLIC, with that name should they appear.

I am, &c.

[This letter owes its origin to the following circumstance. A neighbour of the Poet's at Dumfries called on him, and complained that he was greatly disappointed in the irregular delivery of the Paper of *The Morning Chronicle*. Burns asked, "Why do not you write to the Editors of the Paper?" "Good God, Sir, can *I* presume to write to the learned Editors of a Newspaper?"—"Well, if you are afraid of writing to the Editors of a Newspaper, *I* am not; and if you think proper, I'll draw up a sketch of a letter, which you may copy."

Burns tore a leaf from his copie book and instantly produced the sketch which I have transcribed, and which is here printed. The poor man thanked him, and took the letter home. However, that caution which the watchfulness of his enemies had taught him to exercise, prompted him to the prudence of begging a friend to wait on the person for whom it was written, and request the favor to have it returned. This request was complied with, and the paper never appeared in print.—*Crossek.*]

<hr>

TO PATRONS.

<hr>

To the Earl of Eglintoun.

[*Edinburgh, January* 11, 1787.]

MY LORD,

As I have but slender pretensions to philosophy, I cannot rise to the exalted ideas of a citizen of the world, but have all those national prejudices which I believe glow peculiarly strong in the breast of a Scotchman. There is scarcely any thing to which I am so feelingly alive as the honor and welfare of my country: and, as a poet, I have no higher enjoyment than singing her sons and daughters. Fate had cast my station in the veriest shades of life, but never did a heart pant more ardently than mine to be distinguished; though, till very lately, I looked in vain on every side for a ray of light. It is easy then to guess how much I was gratified with the countenance and approbation of one of my country's most illustrious sons, when Mr. Wauchope called on me yesterday on the part of your lordship. Your munificence, my lord, certainly deserves my very grateful acknowledgments; but your patronage is a bounty peculiarly suited to my feelings.* I am not master enough of the etiquette of life to know whether there be not some impropriety in troubling your lordship with my thanks, but my heart whispered me to do it. From the emotions of my inmost soul I do it. Selfish ingratitude I hope I am incapable of; and mercenary servility, I trust, I shall ever have so much honest pride as to detest.

R. B.

* [His lordship had become a subscriber for the new edition of our Author's poems, and had also presented him with a donation of ten guineas, by the gentleman's hand above mentioned.]

(1.)   To the Earl of Glencairn.

[Edinburgh, February, 1787.]

My Lord,

I WANTED to purchase a profile of your lordship, which I was told was to be got in town; but I am truly sorry to see that a blundering painter has spoiled a "human face divine." The enclosed stanzas I intended to have written below a picture or profile of your lordship, could I have been so happy as to procure one with anything of a likeness.

As I will soon return to my shades, I wanted to have something like a material object for my gratitude; I wanted to have it in my power to say to a friend, there is my noble patron, my generous benefactor. Allow me, my lord, to publish these verses. I conjure your lordship, by the honest throe of gratitude, by the generous wish of benevolence, by all the powers and feelings which compose the magnanimous mind, do not deny me this petition. I owe much to your lordship; and, what has not in some other instances always been the case with me, the weight of the obligation is a pleasing load. I trust I have a heart as independent as your lordship's, than which I can say nothing more; and I would not be beholden to favours that would crucify my feelings. Your dignified character in life, and manner of supporting that character, are flattering to my pride; and I would be jealous of the purity of my grateful attachment, where I was under the patronage of one of the much-favored sons of fortune.

Almost every poet has celebrated his patrons, particularly when they were names dear to fame, and illustrious in their country; allow me, then, my lord, if you think the verses have intrinsic merit, to tell the world how much I have the honor to be,

Your lordship's highly indebted,
and ever grateful humble servant,

R. B.

[The permission here requested was not granted. The verses will be found among Posthumous Works.]

(2.)   TO THE EARL OF GLENCAIRN.

[Edinburgh, May 4, 1787.]

My Lord,

I go away to-morrow morning early, and allow me to vent the fulness of my heart, in thanking your lordship for all that patronage, that benevolence, and that friendship with which you have honored me. With brimful eyes, I pray that you may find in that great Being, whose image you so nobly bear, that friend which I have found in you. My gratitude is not selfish design—that I disdain; it is not dodging after the heels of greatness—that is an offering you disdain. It is a feeling of the same kind with my devotion.

R. B.

[Written on the eve of our Author's leaving Edinburgh on his border tour, in company with his young friend Ainslie. If the reader will compare this letter with that addressed to Rev. Dr. Blair (p. 115), he will perceive by the difference of one day in the date, that there had been a little delay on the occasion of their starting. They did actually leave town on Saturday, the 5th day of May. Mr. Chambers has discovered that Burns was at Covington Mains, Lanarkshire, between 30th April and 3rd May—an entry in Mr. Prentice's journal there, May 1, 1787, bearing "Mr. Burns here." Mr. Chambers concludes that this secret short excursion had reference to some temporary love affair. Not improbably: compare our own note on the song—" Yon Wild Mossy Mountains!" Poetical Works, p. 203.]

(3.)   TO THE EARL OF GLENCAIRN.

[Edinburgh, 1787.]

My Lord,

I KNOW your lordship will disapprove of my ideas in a request I am going to make to you; but I have weighed, long and seriously weighed, my situation, my hopes, and turn of mind, and am fully fixed to my scheme if I can possibly effectuate it. I wish to get into the Excise; I am told that your lordship's interest will easily procure me the grant from the commissioners; and your lordship's patronage and goodness, which have already rescued me from obscurity, wretchedness, and exile, embolden me to ask that interest. You have likewise put it in my power to save the little tie of home that sheltered an aged mother, two brothers, and three sisters from destruction. There, my lord, you have bound me over to the highest gratitude.

My brother's farm is but a wretched lease, but I think he will probably weather out the remaining seven years of it; and after the assistance which I have given and will give him, to keep the family together, I think, by my guess, I shall have rather better than two hundred pounds; and instead of seeking, what is almost impossible at present to find, a farm that I can certainly live by, with so small a stock, I shall lodge this sum in a banking-house, a sacred deposit, excepting only the calls of uncommon distress or necessitous old age.

These, my lord, are my views: I have resolved from the maturest deliberation; and now I am fixed, I shall leave no stone unturned to carry my resolve into execution. Your lordship's patronage is the strength of my hopes; nor have I yet applied to any body else. Indeed, my heart sinks within me at the idea of applying to any other of the great who have honoured me with their countenance. I am ill qualified to dog the heels of greatness with the impertinence of solicitation, and tremble nearly as much at the thought of the cold promise as the cold denial; but to your lordship I have not only the honor, the comfort, but the pleasure of being

   Your lordship's much obliged
    and deeply indebted humble servant,
         R. B.

[The above letters are all addressed to James, Fourteenth Earl of Glencairn, the Poet's well-known, generous, and much-loved patron—on occasion of whose death the celebrated "Lament" was written. His lordship was pre-eminently remarkable for manly beauty.]

To the Earl of Glencairn.

          May, 1794.

MY LORD,

WHEN you cast your eye on the name at the bottom of this letter, and on the title-page of the book I do myself the honor to send your lordship, a more pleasurable feeling than my vanity tells me that it must be a name not entirely unknown to you. The generous patronage of your late illustrious brother found me in the lowest obscurity: he introduced my rustic Muse to the partiality of my country; and to him I owe all. My sense of his goodness, and the anguish of my soul at losing my truly noble protector and friend, I have endeavoured to express in a poem to his memory, which I have now published. This edition is just from the press; and in my gratitude to the dead, and my respect for the living (fame belies you, my lord, if you possess not the same dignity of man, which was your noble brother's characteristic feature), I had destined a copy for the Earl of Glencairn. I learnt just now that you are in town: allow me to present it you.

I know, my lord, such is the vile, venal contagion which pervades the world of letters, that professions of respect from an author, particularly from a poet to a lord, are more than suspicious. I claim my by-past conduct, and my feelings at this moment, as exceptions to the too just conclusion. Exalted as are the honors of your lordship's name, and unnoted as is the obscurity of mine; with the uprightness of an honest man, I come before your lordship with an offering—however humble, 'tis all I have to give—of my grateful respect; and to beg of you, my lord—'tis all I have to ask of you—that you will do me the honor to accept of it.

    I have the honor to be, &c.,
         R. B.

[John, Fifteenth Earl of Glencairn, succeeded his brother James in 1791, and died in 1796. He was the last male representative of the ancient and influential House of Cunningham, and with him the title of Glencairn became extinct.]

To the Earl of Buchan.

MY LORD,

THE honor your lordship has done me, by your notice and advice in yours of the 1st instant, I shall ever gratefully remember:—

> "Praise from thy lips 'tis mine with joy to boast,
> They best can give it who deserve it most."

Your lordship touches the darling chord of my heart, when you advise me to fire my muse at Scottish story and Scottish scenes. I wish for nothing more than to make a leisurely pilgrimage through my native country; to sit and muse on those once hard-contended fields, where Caledonia, rejoicing, saw her bloody lion borne through broken ranks to victory and fame: and, catching the inspiration, to pour the deathless names in song. But, my lord, in the midst of these enthusiastic reveries, a long-visaged, dry, moral-looking phantom strides across my imagination, and pronounces these emphatic words:—

"I, Wisdom, dwell with Prudence. Friend, I do not come to open the ill-closed wounds of your follies and misfortunes, merely to give you pain: I wish through these wounds to imprint a lasting lesson on your heart. I will not mention how many of my salutary advices you have despised: I have given you line upon line and precept upon precept; and while I was chalking out to you the straight way to wealth and character, with audacious effrontery you have zigzagged across the path, contemning me to my face: you know the consequences. It is not yet three months since home was so hot for you, that you were on the wing for the western shore of the Atlantic, not to make a fortune, but to hide your misfortune.

"Now that your dear-loved Scotia puts it in your power to return to the situation of your forefathers, will you follow those will-o'-wisp meteors of fancy and whim, till they bring you once more to the brink of ruin? I grant that the utmost ground you can occupy is but half a step from the veriest poverty; but still it *is* half a step from it. If all that I can urge be ineffectual, let her who seldom calls to you in vain, let the call of pride prevail with you. You know how you feel at the iron gripe of ruthless oppression: you know how you bear the galling sneer of contumelious greatness. I hold you out the conveniences, the comforts of life, independence and character, on the one hand; I tender you servility, dependence, and wretchedness, on the other. I will not insult your understanding by bidding you make a choice."

This, my lord, is unanswerable. I must return to my humble station, and woo my rustic muse in my wonted way at the plough-tail. Still, my lord, while the drops of life warm my heart, gratitude to that dear-loved country in which I boast my birth, and gratitude to those her distinguished sons, who have honored me so much with their patronage and approbation, shall, while stealing through my humble shades, over distend my bosom, and at times, as now, draw forth the swelling tear.

R. B.

(2.)   TO THE EARL OF BUCHAN.

Ellisland, August 29th, 1791.

MY LORD,

LANGUAGE sinks under the ardour of my feelings when I would thank your lordship for the honor you have done me in inviting me to make one at the coronation of the bust of Thomson. In my first enthusiasm in reading the card you did me the honor to write me, I overlooked every obstacle, and determined to go; but I fear it will not be in my power. A week or two's absence, in the very middle of my harvest, is what I much doubt I dare not venture on. I once already made a pilgrimage *up* the whole course of the Tweed, and fondly would I take the same delightful journey *down* the windings of that delightful stream.

Your lordship hints at an ode for the occasion: but who would write after Collins? I read over his verses to the memory of Thomson, and despaired. I got, indeed, to the length of three or four stanzas, in the way of address to the shade of the bard on crowning his bust. I shall trouble your lordship with the subjoined copy of them, which, I am afraid, will be but too convincing a proof how unequal I am to the task. However, it affords me an opportunity of approaching your lordship, and declaring how sincerely and gratefully I have the honor to be, &c.   R. B.

[Here follows ADDRESS TO THE SHADE OF THOMSON.]

(3.)   TO THE EARL OF BUCHAN,

WITH A COPY OF "BRUCE'S ADDRESS TO HIS TROOPS
AT BANNOCKBURN."

Dumfries, 12th Jan., 1794.

MY LORD,

WILL your lordship allow me to present you with the enclosed little composition of mine, as a small tribute of gratitude for that acquaintance with which you have been

pleased to honor me. Independent of my enthusiasm as a Scotsman, I have rarely met with any thing in history which interests my feelings as a man, equal with the story of Bannockburn. On the one hand, a cruel, but able usurper, leading on the finest army in Europe to extinguish the last spark of freedom among a greatly-daring and greatly-injured people: on the other hand, the desperate relics of a gallant nation, devoting themselves to rescue their bleeding country, or perish with her.

Liberty! thou art a prize truly, and indeed invaluable!— for never canst thou be too dearly bought!

If my little ode has the honor of your lordship's approbation, it will gratify my highest ambition.

I have the honor to be, &c.,

R. B.

[David Stewart Erskine, the Earl of Buchan to whom these letters are addressed, seems to have been a weak-minded, vain, intrusive personage, who believed himself to be a man of genius and affected literature. He undertook at the same time to advise the living, and to patronise the memory of the dead, in a style which made himself at last ridiculous. We do not think it at all necessary to rehearse his sayings and doings in the present case: Burns sufficiently understood his character, and wrote to him accordingly, as to a grown child. Henry Erskine, and Thomas, Lord (Chancellor) Erskine, so celebrated for their eloquence and wit, were younger brothers of the Earl.]

To Sir John Whitefoord.

Edinburgh, December, 1787.

SIR,

MR. MACKENZIE, in Mauchline, my very warm and worthy friend, has informed me how much you are pleased to interest yourself in my fate as a man, and (what to me is incomparably dearer) my fame as a poet. I have, Sir, in one or two instances, been patronized by those of your character in life, when I was introduced to their notice by * * * * , friends to them, and honored acquaintances to me! but you are the first gentleman in the country whose benevolence and goodness of heart has interested himself for me, unsolicited and unknown. I am not master enough of the etiquette of these matters to know, nor did I stay to inquire, whether formal duty bade, or cold propriety disallowed, my thanking you in this manner, as I am convinced, from the light in which you kindly view me, that you will do me the justice to believe this letter is not the manœuvre of the needy, sharping author, fastening on those in upper life, who honor him with a little notice of him or his works. Indeed, the situation of poets is generally such, to a proverb, as may, in some measure, palliate that prostitution of heart and talents they have at times been guilty of. I do not think prodigality is, by any means, a necessary concomitant of a poetic turn, but I believe a careless indolent attention to economy, is almost inseparable from it; then there must be in the heart of every bard of Nature's making a certain modest sensibility, mixed with a kind of pride, that will ever keep him out of the way of those windfalls of fortune which frequently light on hardy impudence

and foot-licking servility. It is not easy to imagine a more helpless state than his whose poetic fancy unfits him for the world, and whose character as a scholar gives him some pretensions to the *politesse* of life—yet is as poor as I am.

For my part, I thank Heaven my star has been kinder; learning never elevated my ideas above the peasant's shed, and I have an independent fortune at the plough-tail.

I was surprised to hear that any one who pretended in the least to the manners of the gentleman should be so foolish, or worse, as to stoop to traduce the morals of such a one as I am, and so inhumanly cruel, too, as to meddle with that late most unfortunate, unhappy part of my story. With a tear of gratitude, I thank you, Sir, for the warmth with which you interposed in behalf of my conduct. I am, I acknowledge, too frequently the sport of whim, caprice, and passion; but reverence to God, and integrity to my fellow-creatures, I hope I shall ever preserve. I have no return, Sir, to make you for your goodness but one—a return which, I am persuaded, will not be unacceptable—the honest warm wishes of a grateful heart for your happiness, and every one of that lovely flock, who stand to you in a filial relation. If ever calumny aim the poisoned shaft at them, may friendship be by to ward the blow!

R. B.

To Dr. Blacklock.

Mauchline, November 15th, 1788.

REVEREND AND DEAR SIR,

As I hear nothing of your motions, but that you are, or were, out of town, I do not know where this may find you, or whether it will find you at all. I wrote you a long letter, dated from the land of Matrimony, in June; but either it had not found you, or, what I dread more, it found you or Mrs. Blacklock in too precarious a state of health and spirits to take notice of an idle packet.

I have done many little things for Johnson since I had the pleasure of seeing you; and I have finished one piece in the way of Pope's "Moral Epistles;" but, from your silence, I have every thing to fear, so I have only sent you two melancholy things, which I tremble lest they should too well suit the tone of your present feelings.

In a fortnight I move, bag and baggage, to Nithsdale; till then, my direction is at this place; after that period, it will be at Ellisland, near Dumfries. It would extremely oblige me were it but half a line, to let me know how you are, and where you are. Can I be indifferent to the fate of a man to whom I owe so much? A man whom I not only esteem, but venerate.

My warmest good wishes and most respectful compliments to Mrs. Blacklock, and Miss Johnson, if she is with you.

I cannot conclude without telling you that I am more and more pleased with the step I took respecting "my Jean." Two things, from my happy experience, I set down

as apophthegms in life—A wife's head is immaterial, compared with her heart; and—"Virtue's (for wisdom, what poet pretends to it?) ways are ways of pleasantness, and all her paths are peace." Adieu!

R. B.

[DR. BLACKLOCK]
TO
MR. GEORGE LAWRIE, V.D.M.,*
ST. MARGARET'S HILL, KILMARNOCK.

Edin., Sept. 4, 1786.

REVEREND AND DEAR SIR,

I OUGHT to have acknowledged your favor long ago, not only as a testimony of your kind remembrance, but as it gave me an opportunity of sharing one of the finest, and, perhaps, one of the most genuine entertainments of which the human mind is susceptible. A number of avocations retarded my progress in reading the poems; at last, however, I have finished that pleasing perusal. Many instances have I seen of Nature's force and beneficence exerted under numerous and formidable disadvantages; but none equal to that with which you have been kind enough to present me. There is a pathos and delicacy in his serious poems, a vein of wit and humour in those of a more festive turn, which cannot be too much admired, nor too warmly approved; and I think I shall never open the book without feeling my astonishment renewed and increased. It was my wish to have expressed my approbation in verse; but whether from declining life, or a temporary depression of spirits, it is at present out of my power to accomplish that agreeable intention.

Mr. Stewart, Professor of Morals in this University, had formerly read me three of the poems, and I had desired him to get my name inserted among the subscribers: but whether this was done, or not, I never could learn. I have little intercourse with Dr. Blair, but will take care to have the poems communicated to him by the intervention of some mutual friend. It has been told me by a gentleman, to whom I showed the performances, and who sought a copy with diligence and ardour, that the whole impression is already exhausted. It were, therefore, much to be wished, for the sake of the young man, that a second edition, more numerous than the former, could immediately be printed; as it appears certain that its intrinsic merit, and the exertion of the author's friends, might give it a more universal circulation than any thing of the kind which has been published within my memory. * * * * *

T. BLACKLOCK.

[* V.D.M.—*i.e.* Verbi Dei Minister; Minister of the Word of God—a formal style equivalent to Reverend, and assigned to gentlemen in the church long ago who had not yet attained the dignity of Doctorship in Divinity. Notices of Dr. Blacklock himself, so amiable, so gentle, and so unfortunate in his blindness, occur elsewhere in this edition.]

[This letter, certainly one of the most interesting documents connected with Scottish literary history, is now in the possession (1856) of the Rev. Balfour

* K

Graham, minister of North Berwick, son-in-law of the late Rev. Archibald Lawrie, the son of Blacklock's correspondent.—*Chambers.* We entirely agree with Mr. Chambers as to the interest attaching to this modest, affectionate, and manly document, as the first formal critical recognition of Robert Burns, and first practical introduction of his name to the notice of the world; and assign it thus prominently, in equal type, a place in the correspondence of our Author himself with his Patrons. A copy of the letter was first forwarded by Mr. Lawrie to Gavin Hamilton, and by him communicated to Burns; among whose papers **that copy** was found.]

To ———

Ellisland, 22nd January, 1789.

Sir,

There are two things which, I believe, the blow that terminates my existence alone can destroy—my attachment and propensity to poesy, and my sense of what I owe to your goodness. There is nothing in the different situations of a Great and a Little man that vexes me more than the ease with which the one practises some virtues that to the other are extremely difficult, or perhaps wholly impracticable. A man of consequence and fashion shall richly repay a deed of kindness with a nod and a smile, or a hearty shake of the hand; while a poor fellow labours under a sense of gratitude, which, like copper coin, though it loads the bearer, is yet of small account in the currency and commerce of the world. As I have the honor, Sir, to stand in the poor fellow's predicament with respect to you, will you accept of a device I have thought on to acknowledge these obligations I can never cancel? Mankind, in general, agree in testifying their devotion, their gratitude, their friendship, or their love, by presenting whatever they hold dearest. Everybody who is in the least acquainted with the character of a poet, knows that there is nothing in the world on which he sets so much * * * * * * * * * * * to time, as she may bestow her favors, to present you with the productions of my humble Muse. The enclosed are the principal of her works on the banks of the Nith. The poem inscribed to R. G., Esq., is some verses, accompanying a request, which I sent to Mr. Graham of Fintry—a gentleman who has given double value to some important favors he has bestowed on me by his manner of doing them, and on whose future patronage, likewise, I must depend for matters to me of the last consequence.

I have no great faith in the boastful pretensions to intuitive propriety and unlaboured elegance. The rough material of Fine Writing is certainly the gift of Genius; but I as firmly believe that the workmanship is the united effort of Pains, Attention, and Repeated-trial. The piece addressed to Mr. Graham is my first essay in that didactic, epistolary way; which circumstance, I hope, will bespeak your indulgence. To your friend Captain Erskine's strictures I lay claim as a relation; not, indeed, that I have the honor to be akin to the peerage, but because he is a son of Parnassus.

I intend being in Edinburgh in four or five weeks, when I shall certainly do myself the honor of waiting on you, to testify with what respect and gratitude, &c.

R. B.

[This letter is conjectured by Mr. Chambers, with probability, to have been addressed to Henry Erskine : whether ever sent is uncertain. It contains many good and true thoughts, in a somewhat formal style, and another among the many references which occur in our Author's correspondence to the Epistle addressed to Mr. Graham of Fintry.]

Supplementary.

[The following letters or notes to James Johnson, transcribed from originals, formerly in possession of Archibald Hastie, Esq., M.P. for Paisley, now in the British Museum, but hitherto inedited, have been politely placed at our disposal by Robert Carruthers, Esq., of the *Inverness Courier.* They came unfortunately a little too late to appear in their appropriate place, but we introduce them without hesitation here, that the series to which they belong (still imperfect, we have no doubt), may be supplemented as far as possible. Other memoranda for which we are indebted to Mr. Carruthers will be found elsewhere.]

[Supplement.]

To James Johnson.

(1.)

Ellisland, 24th April, 1789.

I have sent you a list that I approve of; but I beg and insist that you will never allow my opinion to override yours.

[Supplement.]

TO JAMES JOHNSON.

(2.)

[No Date.]

I was much obliged to you, my dear friend, for making me acquainted with Gow. He is a modest, intelligent worthy, besides his being a man of great genius in his way. I have spent many happy hours with him in the short while he has been here.

Why did you not send me those tunes and verses that Clarke and you cannot make out? Let me have them as soon as possible, that while he is at hand I may settle the matter with him. He and I have been very busy providing and laying out materials for your fifth volume; I want no more. As soon as the bound copy of all the volumes is ready, take the trouble of forwarding it. In haste,

Yours ever,   R. B.

[A very pleasant blink this is into the ganger's parlour at Dumfries, with the immortal composer of Scotch strathspeys at his elbow; labouring both, gratuitously and lovingly, for the honour of Scottish melody. It appears from our Author's Journal (see Appendix) that he had seen Neil Gow and heard him perform at Dunkeld, in August, 1787, and that he had also called at his house. It does not appear, however, that Neil Gow himself was at home—only 'Margot Gow;' and the probability is that Neil, to compensate for this disappointment, as well as for other reasons, had afterwards obtained an introduction to our Author from Johnson, with whom they were both intimately acquainted. Neil's visit to Dumfries might be in the October of 1792, when the Caledonian Hunt met there; or it might be later, perhaps in 1793—we have no satisfactory evidence in the meantime; but that such an interview as this took place is certain.]

[Supplement.]

TO JAMES JOHNSON.

(3.)

June 29th, [1794.]

I THANK you for your kind present of poor Riddel's book.
Depend upon it that your fifth volume shall not be forgotten.
* * * * I have just been getting three or four songs for
your book. Pray will you let me know how many and what
are the songs Urbani has borrowed from your Museum.

Yours,

R. B.

[It is enough to remark that these letters show the very reverse of negligence
or niggardliness on Johnson's part, so far as copies of the Museum are concerned.
Compare note to letter (3), p. 86.]

Poetical Epistles

ADDRESSED TO ROBERT BURNS,

And referred to in foregoing Correspondence.

FROM JANET LITTLE:

DAIRY-MAID TO MRS. DUNLOP.

[Referred to in Letter (23) to Mrs. Dunlop, p. 20.]

Loudoun House, 12th July, 1789.

Fair fa' the honest rustic swain,
The pride o' a' our Scottish plain:
Thou gi'es us joy to hear thy stra'n,
    And notes sae sweet:
Old Ramsay's shade revived again
    In thee we greet.

Loved Thalia, that delightful muse,
Seem'd lang shut up as a recluse;
To all she did her aid refuse
    Since Allan's day,
Till Burns arose, then did she choose
    To grace his lay.

To hear thy sang all ranks desire,
Sae weel you strike the dormant lyre;
Apollo with poetic fire
    Thy breast does warm,
And critics silently admire
    Thy art to charm.

Camac and Louth weel can speak,
'Tis pity e'er their gabs should steek,
Poet into human nature keek,
    And knots unravel:
To hear their lectures once a-week,
    Nine miles I'd travel.

Thy dedication to G. H.,
An' unco bonnie homespun speech,
Wi' whatsome glee the heart can teach
    A better lesson,
Than servile bards who fan and fleech
    Like beggar's messan.

When slighted love becomes your theme,
And woman's faithless vows you blame,
With so much pathos you exclaim,
    In your Lament;
But glanced by the most rigid dame,
    She would relent.

The daisy, too, ye sing wi' skill,
And weel ye praise the whisky gill:
In vain I blunt my reckless quill
    Your fame to raise;
While Echo sounds from ilka hill
    To Burns's praise.

Did Addison or Pope but hear,
Or Sam, that critic most severe,
A ploughboy sing with throat sae clear,
    They in a rage
Their works would a' in pieces tear,
    And curse your page.

Sure Milton's eloquence were faint
The beauties of your verse to paint:
My rude unpolish'd strokes but taint
    Their brilliancy;
Th' attempt would doubtless vex a saint,
    And weel may thee.

The task I'll drop—with heart sincere
To Heaven present my humble pray'r,
That all the blessings mortals share
    May be by turns
Dispensed by an indulgent care,
    To Robert Burns!

[Janet Little, born near Ecclefechan, 1759: died at Loudoun Castle, 1813. She
published a small volume of poems in 1792, dedicated to the then Countess of
Loudoun.]

FROM DR. BLACKLOCK.

[Referred to in Letter to Dr. Anderson, p. 118.]

Edinburgh, 1st September, 1790.

How does my dear friend, much I languish to hear,
His fortune, relations, and all that are dear?
With love of the Muses so strongly still smitten,
I meant this epistle in verse to have written;
But from age and infirmity indolence flows,
And this, much I fear, will restore me to prose.
Anon to my business I wish to proceed,
Dr. Anderson guides and provokes me to speed,
A man of integrity, genius, and worth,
Who soon a performance intends to set forth;
A work miscellaneous, extensive, and free,
Which will weekly appear by the name of the *Bee.*
Of this from himself I enclose you a plan,
And hope you will give what assistance you can.
Entangled with business, and haunted with care,
In which more or less human nature must share,
Some moments of leisure the Muses will claim,
A sacrifice due to amusement and fame.
The Bee, which sucks honey from ev'ry gay bloom,
With some rays of your genius her work may illume,
Whilst the flow'r whence her honey spontaneously flows,
As fragrantly smells, and as vig'rously grows.

Now with kind gratulations 'tis time to conclude,
And add, your promotion is here understood;
Thus free from the servile employ of excise, Sir,
We hope soon to hear you commence Supervisor;
You then more at leisure, and free from control,
May indulge the strong passion that reigns in your soul.
But I, feeble I, must to nature give way;
Devoted cold death's, and longevity's prey.
From verses tho' languid my thoughts must unbend,
Tho' still I remain your affectionate friend,

THO. BLACKLOCK.

POETICAL EPISTLE TO BURNS,

BY THE

REV. JOHN SKINNER.

O! happy hour for ever mair,
That led my Chiel up Cha'mers' stair,
And gae him, what he values sair,
                Sae braw a skance
Of Ayrshire's dainty Poet there,
                By lucky chance.

Whan my auld heart I was na wi' you,
Tho' worth your while I cou'd na gie you,
But sin' I had na hap to see you
                Whan ye was North,
I'm bauld to send my service to you
                Hyne o'er the Forth.

Sae proud 's I am that ye hae heard
O' my attempts to be a Bard,
And thinks my muse mae that ill far'd
                Sell o' your face!
I wad na wiss for mair reward
                Than your good grace.

Your bonnie bookie, line by line
I've read, and think it freely fine:
Indeed, I darena ca't divine,
                As others might;
For that, ye ken, frae pen like mine,
                Wad no be right.

But, by my sang, I dinna wonner,
That your admirers, mony hunner,
Let gowkit fleeps pretend to scunner
                And tak' offence;
Ye've naething said that looks like blunner
                To fowks o' sense.

Your pawky "Dream" has humour in't,
I never saw the like in print;
The birth-day Laurit durst na mint
                As ye hae dane;
And yet there's nae a single hint
                Can be mista'en.

Your "Maillie," and your guid "Auld Mare,"
And "Hallow-even's" funny cheer;
There's nane that's read them, far or near,
                But reeses Robie,
And thinks them as diverting gear
                As Yorick's Tobie.

But, O! the weel tauld "Cotter's Night"
Is what gies me the maist delight;
A piece sae finished, and sae tight,
                There's nane o's a'
Cou'd preachment-timmer cleaner dight
                In kirk nor ha'.

But what need this or that to name!
It's own'd by a' there's no a theme
Ye tak' in hand, but's a' the same,
                And nae ane o' them
But weel may challenge a' the fame
                That we can gi' them.

For me, I heartily allow you
The waid o' praise ane justly due you:
And but a Plowman! Sall I true you!
                Gin it be sae,
A miracle I will avow you,
                Deny't wha may.

What recks a hash o' classic lair,
Thro' seven years, and some guide mair;
When plow-man-clad, wi' nature bare,
                Sae far surpasses
A' we can do wi' study sair
                To climb Parnassus.

But, thanks to praise, ye're i' your prime,
And may chaunt on this lang, lang time;
For, let me tell you, 'twere a crime
                To haud your tongue,
Wi' sic a knack's ye hae at rhyme,
                And you sae young.

Ye ken it's nae for ane like me
To be sae droll as ye can be;
But ony help that I can gie,
                Tho't be but sma',
Your least command, I'se let you see,
                Sall gar me draw.

An hour or twa, by hook or crook,
And may be three, some orrow owk
That I can spare frae haly buik,
                (For that's my hobby,)
I'll steal awa' to some by-neuk,
                And crack wi' Robie.

Wad ye but only crack again,
Just what ye like, in ony strain,
I'll tak it kind; for, to be plain,
                I do expect it;
And, mair than that, I'll no be fain
                Gin ye neglect it.

To Linshart, gin my name ye spier,
Whare I hae been near fifty year,
'Twill come in course, ye need na fear;
                The pairt's weel kent;
And postage, be it cheap or dear
                I'll pay content.

Now, after a', hae me excused
For wishing nae to be refeus'd;
I dinna covet to be reus'd
                For this fiel lilt;
But fiel or wise, gin ye be pleas'd,
                Ye're welcome till't.

Sae, canty Plowman, fare ye weel;
Lord bless ye lang wi' hae and heft,
And keep you aye the honest chiel
                That ye hae been;
Syne lift you to a better biel
                Whane this is dane!

POSTSCRIPT.

This auld Scots muse I've courted lang,
      And spar'd nae pains to win her;
Dowff tho' I be in rustic sang,
      I'm no a late beginner,
But now auld age taks dowie turns,
      Yet troth, as I'm a sinner,
I'll aye be fond of Robbie Burns,
      While I can sign.

                          JOHN SKINNER.

Linshart, Sept. 25th, 1787.

GENERAL CORRESPONDENCE.

BIOGRAPHICAL REMARKS.

BURNS COMPARED WITH OTHER LETTER-WRITERS.

HAVING now arrived at the general mass of our Author's Letters, which are devoted to no special subject nor limited to any particular class of correspondents, and in which a number of his best and most characteristic effusions are to be found, we have less of more criticism to advance than the extent of the subject might seem to call for. It remains, indeed, only farther to say, critically—that in this general department there is more variety and freedom, more abandon and sometimes even more license of style than in most of what (if we except certain letters to Hill) we have yet had before us; as much luxuriance of humour, of eloquence, of illustration, and more diversity of topic than in almost anything, perhaps, of the same sort to be met with in the same number of pages. At this point, however, to illustrate the principles on which our remarks have hitherto been founded, and to justify in some degree the high opinion we have expressed of our Author's epistolary work in comparison with that of others, we think it almost indispensable to present a parallel or two from the same department of literature.

In judging a Letter critically, two distinct considerations must be taken into account: *first*, the style of its composition—its ease, its elegance, its force; its clearness, its conciseness, its fluency; its adaptation to circumstances or to persons; its general excellence and perfection, as a piece of artistic workmanship—according to which, its rank as a literary composition must be determined: and *second*, its moral characteristics as an exponent of the writer's mind—such as its frankness, its suggestiveness, its reserve; its sprightliness, its tenderness, its humour; its moral dignity or delicacy, its solemnity, its pathos, as the subject or the case may imply: two considerations in criticism which are entirely distinct, but which in judging of letters can hardly ever be separated. The best intentioned letter in the world might be a comparative failure in composition, and the most perfect piece of epistolary workmanship might be contemptible in moral aspect; so that excellence in one way should by no means be accepted as necessarily implying excellence in the other. But because letters, more than any other sort of composition, are understood to be the transcript of the writer's heart, or the reflection of his mind, or the revelation of himself in various ways,—without which they would be of no value at all—both the moral and the artistic qualities of such compositions are almost invariably taken into account together; indeed, the moral are not improperly preferred; although the highest excellence and variety in both are indispensable to give a letter the highest rank in its own department of literature. The goodness and the honesty which blunder, are not precisely for epistles: but the elegance or perfection which lies, or fawns, or grossly flatters, or outrages, or insults, damns the writer: prolixity and monotony fatigue, and too much brevity disappoints the reader. In short, it requires heart, intellect, and pen—the heart predominating chiefly—to produce a letter; and nothing short of the finest native instinct, or greatest acquired skill, can regulate their union to perfection.

Letter-writing, as a distinct branch of literature, has been cultivated by some of the most distinguished authors in ancient and modern times; but the letter-writing of the moderns has the advantage, perhaps, of being more varied and natural; and foremost, as well as first, among the letter-writers of modern Europe, the Italians demand our critical attention and homage. As for the ancients, we cannot now afford space for criticism on them, nor would it be of much service in our present work. Cicero, for example, as being purely classic and altogether unimaginative; whose letters, although ornate and beautiful, are more elaborate, didactic, or prosaic works than sympathetic or spontaneous effusions—we need not here quote; nor Pliny. They stand by themselves there, as models of their sort; but have little or nothing in common with the passionate or poetic Scotsman. Before all other letter-writers of the highest reputation, we select at once, for comparison with Burns, the name of Annibal Caro, already referred to, as justly entitled to the very foremost rank in that department. Montaigne, who informs us in his vehement entertaining way, that he had (so early as 1580) not fewer than "an hundred several volumes" of Italian letters in his own library, prefers, without hesitation, to them all, those of Annibal Caro, then recently published; and no one who has glanced at the admirable specimens of epistolary writing long known to the world as the "Lettere Famigliari" of that author, can have any doubt at all about his pre-eminence.

Annibal Caro—who, besides being a poet and poetical translator of note, and a dignitary in the church, whose shrewdness and accomplishments together secured his own promotion from the humblest sphere, was a recognised letter-writer of well-known faculty among his own contemporaries; to whom application for a letter to instruct or to enliven them was their favourite order of the day—had an incomparable style of his own, with a certain interwoven charm of familiar elegance in diction, almost indefinable. We speak from some reasonable acquaintance with his text. The style itself is easy, equable, and varied—equable and varied; respectful, deferential, insinuating; entertaining in narrative, gossiping in detail; persistent and effective; jocular, and solemnly absurd at carnival seasons, or on carnival topics—such as masks and noses; clear, concise, methodical on business affairs, and affectionately earnest on all matters of moment; with a vein of friendliest humour, like quicksilver in solution, pervading all. The diction is always elegant:—no slips in that, no inequalities, no blunders, no mistakes. It may not rise to eloquence, for the writer affects nothing; but it never sinks to commonplace, for he knows his capabilities and his rank. Any topic—social, political, religious, artistic or absurd; or no topic at all, but the simple demand of some friend *for* a letter, is enough for him. He adopts, or creates, or constitutes a topic, from the instant he puts pen to paper till he kisses hands and retires from view. A perfect, masterly, and accomplished letter-writer is this man. In addition to which, certain moral qualities are conspicuous in his epistles, which ought particularly in the present case to be specified. There is much good nature, much inclination to oblige, much real kindness of disposition; amazing discrimination of character, and an almost incomparable tact, when addressing a correspondent with some object of his own in view. It would be difficult, indeed, to imagine anything more perfect than his manner on such occasions. Yet withal, and in the most delicate or even dangerous cases of that kind, a composure resulting from consciousness of superior capacity is perceptible throughout; so that no result, whatever it might be, should seem to take him by surprise. Some expressions of his, indeed (that might be quoted), in such difficult circumstances, with every possible condition of success or failure implied, addressed to those who might have life or death in their hands, are absolute perfection. In these various qualities as an epistolary writer, and in their combination, he is perhaps unrivalled.

As between him and Burns, there are many points of resemblance in this view of their qualifications—in the ease, the fluency, and the adaptation of language to the character and theme in hand; but there are also points of difference most remarkable, which must now be more minutely specified. The most prominent of these are (1) the passionate abandon and luxury of speech in Burns on any, and conspicuously on certain topics, which is scarcely, if ever, manifest in the ecclesiastic. (2) The occasional restlessness, and inequality of tone corresponding to the constitution of the Poet and the Scotchman, which is totally imperceptible in the Italian and the Priest. With him, all thoughts seem to be regulated, all passions subdued, all personal interests kept in decorous abeyance, and all opinions or expressions on all themes however varied (except where display or prominence would be becoming or imperative), dovetailed and adjusted with absolute nicety, and yet with the utmost ease: Burns also *could do* this, but he did not stoop to do it—did often, in fact, to his own disadvantage, the very reverse. (3) Finally, which makes the characteristic distinction between the men as men, and also as letter-writers—and which those who read them for comparison will do well to note, as indicating a most singular moral power, of opposite description and yet of similar effect, in each—that the one with a sort of passionate eloquence assimilates his correspondent to himself, where the other, with elegant adaptation of thought and language, assimilates himself to his correspondent. Burns sympathetically, sometimes forcibly, appropriates his correspondent—takes for granted that there can be no answer, no reply, no effectual resistance at least, when he speaks: Caro sympathetically allows himself to *be* appropriated; is all things, by anticipation, to all men: but in both cases, the process is effected with the hand of a master, and the effect is substantially the same—the correspondent is attracted, or propitiated, or subdued—stormed or taken—and the writer for the moment is triumphant. In writing to 'Clarinda' sometimes, for obvious reasons; and occasionally to Thomson on controverted topics, and in one or two other solitary instances, our Author does indeed adopt the self-assimilating style; but never consistently or long. That style

was, in fact, impossible for him; and he inevitably breaks through it, awkwardly or with violence. To Annibal Caro, on the contrary, it was a second nature. There may be solitary instances in him too, in which a little assumption of conscious superiority, or the slightest strain of vehemence occurs; but it is so qualified with easy badinage, or so interwoven with dexterous compliment, that it is scarcely felt or seen. It is impossible, in fact, in such cases, to tell whether it be there or no. To have been anything else to his correspondent than an accomplished, persuasive, entertaining, and irresistible *alter ego*, would with him have been at once an outrage on etiquette and on humanity. No distinction between two writers of the same sort, and writing undeniably for the most part with the same object—the enlightenment or delectation of their correspondents—in view, could be more obvious or complete. The adroitest of the two was Annibal Caro; the manliest of the two was Robert Burns.

Having attempted such a comparison of our Author with so distinguished a model of epistolary excellence, we can hardly avoid referring for a moment to his English counterpart in style, the amiable and illustrious author of 'The Task,' who stands confessedly pre-eminent among the letter-writers of his age and country. Cowper in his easy, fluent, elegant self-adaptation, and in his quiet artistic handling of the slightest, of the very slightest themes—imperceptible almost from their mere tenuity till he developes them, and evanescent until he fixes them in ink—investing them with the interest of new discoveries or dreamy narration in the hush of an afternoon, whilst the clock clicks in the neighbourhood or pictures eye him from the wall, reminds a reader at once of Annibal Caro; is Annibal Caro's second self, in fact, so far as style is concerned, although Annibal Caro's life and habits were by no means of the secluded sort. He has not, however, the same versatility of power for all subjects as the old Italian; would labour more conspicuously, for example, in handling certain solemn or painful themes; nor has he the same sort of light-heartedness—unqualified, unscrupulous gaiety of soul. In these, the Italian surpasses him. But he has a light-heartedness of his own, most engaging, most beautiful; and a gentle humour that plays upon the paper like a beam—that could disport itself without excess among butterflies and tea cups, or indulge its utmost vagaries within the limits of a garden walk; but that would certainly never ensconce itself for observation on a ladder, or sun itself, even in the company of nobles, with arms akimbo at a public-house. As to their treatment of trifles, they differ thus from Burns —that they both systematically make much of their difficulty before beginning, and forewarn you they have nothing to say: he says nothing of difficulties at all, yet leaves an admirable letter out of nothing, in your hands.

Cowper's mere diction is, if possible, more like Caro's than his style—a most perfect arrangement of words and unexceptionable choice of phrases. Some expressions, some entire sentences, indeed, both introductory and valedictory (in which he much excels), seem to be actually copied from Caro; and it is difficult to believe that he was not intimately acquainted with him, although anything like mere appropriation of terms from him is not to be conjectured. His pretty frequent elaboration on the other hand, and careful attention to periods and periodic rhythm, to give point and emphasis and periphrasis their proper place, remind us not only of Caro throughout, but also of Burns's earlier and more studied efforts: there is, however, a perceptible difference in the latter case. In Burns one can perceive that the most studied effort of his is far unequal to express, or oftener to repress, himself. There is more below than any formal utterance of his own is adequate either to conceal or divulge. In Cowper it is just the reverse: nothing remains to be written, after what you see. Burns's early formality was the decorous epistolary performance of a youth eager for applause or conscious of superiority; and was never so perfect as Cowper's: Cowper's, on the other hand, was the finished work of a weaker and a smaller man, thankful to have escaped from madness, and conscious of no other passion; who had no other aspirations of the sort beyond those of the moment—which were to amuse himself or gratify a friend, or illustrate his own piety and narrate his own occupations; and who longed again, good-naturedly, to endite another epistle in another "frank," with the same innocent object in view.

In variety of topics and corresponding variety of style, there is no comparison to be made between them. There was, indeed, a difference in the circumstances of their lives, and in the respective circles of their acquaintance, sufficient to account for this. The seclusion of Huntingdon and Olney, enlivened by an occasional newspaper, was not very likely to suggest much deep or diversified acquaintance with the world; nor the correspondence of two amiable lady cousins, or a couple of orthodox clergymen of the most exemplary sect, endowed equally with all the graces of the Christian life and all the advantages of comfortable livings, to stimulate to much variety of style or elicit untried gifts of epistolary eloquence. The wonder rather is, how with such correspondents only or chiefly, and subjects alone that could be acceptable to them; with hares and pigeons only for playfellows or dependents, and above all wanting that absorbing passion which blazed in Burns like a fiery fountain of inspiration, his correspondence should be so varied as it is. His uniformity, nevertheless, it must be admitted, borders on monotony, and we long in vain for the appearance of some ruder element to endanger its tranquillity and divert its course. But then, it would no longer have been Cowper's. Upon the whole, it seems evident that, with any number of correspondents and with any choice of topics, Cowper could not have written in a lifetime the same number of first-class letters on the same variety of topics, and to the same multitude of correspondents, that Burns did simultaneously in the course of a few months or years.

In one other respect, on which we desire now to touch most briefly, they also differed widely. Cowper's religion as manifested in his letters— however genuine and consolatory it might be to himself—would have been utterly abhorrent to Robert Burns, and could nowhere have found any place in his correspondence. They were both constitutionally subject to the profoundest religious melancholy, and had both, in their youth at least, a strong tendency to doctrinal speculations in theology; but the relief obtained in their respective cases, even by theoretical apprehension of the truth, was diametrically opposite. In his earlier letters, which are full of it; and wherever else he touches on the theme, it is self, religious self, self-humiliation—that is, unconscious self-complacency; gratitude for gifts of grace, which gifts imply of course his own gracious experience; and most affectionate prayerful concern for the spiritual safety of other men, which means that he and all his are spiritually safe: but apparently, an utter inability to extend religious sympathy beyond the smallest section of the world, or to see anything, or at least much, in the wisdom or providence of God beyond what may contribute to the temporal and eternal advantage of the chosen few. These are traits and topics which, if they pervaded the whole of his correspondence, as happily they do not, would fatigue any general reader; and mark the very narrowest phase of complacent pharisaical childhood. But such was the model religion of the age, in the midst of abounding social and political corruption, and such the sort of piety in which this gifted yet be-clouded soul took refuge. A rebel fancy or two, and some natural longings after social endearments unincumbered with religious bigotries and drawbacks are no doubt to be met with, even among these very epistles, which cannot be concluded *always* in the appropriate solemn style. But in this respect alone, so great a difference appears between him and Burns, that no sort of comparison can be attempted. It is serious contrast, all. Yet the geniality, the humility, and godlike charity of Burns are worth a thousand such scriptural epistolary disquisitions as we frequently find in Cowper, and are a thousand times better atonement for the very rudeness and licence which here and there appear, than the most elaborate declarations of repentance.

It was our intention at this point to have quoted at some length one other illustrious name, more nearly resembling our Author's own than perhaps any other—the name of a poet who, like him, was an extensive and spontaneous letter-writer also; but as our limits now preclude any lengthened notice, we shall content ourselves with but a brief reference to Lord Byron. An elaborate notice of Lord Byron's correspondence, indeed, is perhaps less necessary, inasmuch as a very considerable number of the numerous letters his lordship wrote were more descriptive journals of travel—always admirable, with remarks on society in which he mingled—gossipy and shrewd, or diplomatic communications with respect to Greece, than letters properly so called, or such at least as could be

critically compared with the remains of other letter-writers differently situated. A very considerable number also do not rank much higher than mere hurried scrawls about the typographical emendations, or editorial accuracy of his works, and are hardly therefore to be dignified with the name of letters, although they are included as such among the rest. Of the comparatively small number which remain, from a collection amounting to more than five hundred and fifty, and which as letters, in our acceptation of the term, are to be compared with other letters, two things with respect to their style are first to be considered, before any comparisons can be made at all. In the first place, the sort of language, being at the commencement of the modern era, is perceptibly different from that of Burns or Cowper, who were the last representatives of an older era: and secondly, the tone being essentially aristocratic, with the careless dash of nonchalant indifference about it, insensibly assumed in familiar intercourse with social inferiors and sometimes dependents, with the generous enough purpose of breaking down all conventional barriers between himself and them, gives an air of ease and readiness to the diction which, in other circumstances, it might not have retained. With all these deductions and conditions, however, Lord Byron's correspondence is the correspondence of a great letter-writer, and exhibits some of the finest specimens of epistolary composition in the language.

To speak farther of its literary characteristics, however, the monotony of selfish complaint without cause, and of petulant aspersion of his fellow-creatures without end or object, both of which pervade the whole; and the inexcusable accumulation of oaths, and occasional use of slang, which disfigure so much of it, are faults which must offend the most partial reader. They seem utterly inconsistent with his own indisputable greatness, and drag the writer down to the level of the mere misanthrope or flash-man on town. A murmur of dissatisfaction with himself or the world now and then, as we sometimes find in the best writers, would have been natural or excusable in him; and a passionate ejaculation such as frequently occurs in Burns, or even a downright oath upon occasion, interjected to relieve his spleen or to give piquancy to a dull theme, might be explained and relished in such a man; but page after page of sneering, of wilful swearing, or of petty scandal, with scarcely the relief of a single tear or the sunshine of a genuine smile—is overwhelming at once to taste and patience. In two hundred and fifty letters we remember only one that afforded ourselves a hearty burst of laughter, and not more than a score that rose to the highest level of dignity or beauty—not one of them with pathos. In his journal, indeed, one pathetic touch about the unlucky shooting of an eaglet, which reminds us much of Burns, appears.

On the moral secrets these letters unfold we have nothing here to advance. Many a noble deed of charity and forbearance they record; many an incomprehensible folly, to say the least of it, they suggest. It is of their literary characteristics alone we now speak. All that we see and blame, or at least lament, might be affectation; if so, it was in sorrowful taste. But the perceptible want of geniality and tenderness, to all but a few literary cronies and admiring worshipping friends, defaces the beauty of the whole scroll; and we sigh with dissatisfaction and regret ourselves in the very reading of it, that he who wrote so easily and well, and might have written so delightfully if he would, should have understood so little, after all, the penman's art of human sympathy. In variety of topic, there is nothing in him at all like Burns; and in appropriate diversity of style—on this or that theme, as it occurs—there is but little approach to him. The student who reads carefully five letters of Lord Byron's (except for biographical purposes) has read fifty in fact. The topics are his own works and travels, his extravagancies, his difficulties, and his contemporaries, with a dash of politics; and the style, the highest—sometimes the lowest—style of the clubs, with postscripts out of number. In this view of the matter, few collections of letters perhaps could be imagined more characteristic or reliable; but beyond that, as in relation to other letter-writers—Burns in particular—the comparison ends. In Burns we have sometimes an oath, and sometimes an indecorum—but sympathy and sincerity always, and slang never.

In concluding these remarks, it is perhaps necessary to observe that they refer to our Author's entire correspondence at large, and not exclusively to the miscellaneous or any other particular portion of it; and farther, that in making such comparison between him and the highest models of epistolary-writing, we are much disposed to limit our review to letters written by him from after the commencement of his authorship. There are comparatively few indeed before that date, but they are not to be compared in general excellence with those which were then and subsequently indited. It seemed to require the encouragement of decided success to liberate his hand, and induce the flow of humours and of eloquence by which his correspondence was invariably after distinguished.

Of the miscellaneous correspondence now immediately before us—setting the letters to Mr. Graham of Fintry, which, from their special character, have an importance of their own, aside—and looking to the combination of various elements in the several series, we are inclined to select those addressed to Mr. Ainslie (which, after all, is a series very likely incomplete) as the most characteristic of our Author. The letters of that series still preserved to us are all humorous, natural, and varied—humorous and natural, beyond the ordinary sense of these terms. The letters to Cunningham, which have more of the literary cast about them, without being absolutely literary, are characteristic also, but they are not always so natural; whilst those to Nicol have a good deal of exaggerated banter in them—not rising to perfect humour as those to Ainslie generally do, and sometimes overstepping the fair limitations of banter itself. The letters to Smith, in which mirth and humour verge occasionally on uproar, are excellent specimens of their kind; whilst those to Richmond, Brown, Brice, and Candlish are pretty much what one brother might indite in affectionate confidence to another on affairs of the heart, or on prospects in life in which brothers only had an interest: those to Richmond, however, appear to us extremely beautiful in their way, as specimens of such correspondence. The letters to Ballantyne, Gavin Hamilton, Dalrymple, and others of their standing in society, are necessarily somewhat in the style of letters to a patron; but with such an admixture of freedom and jocularity, nevertheless, as to indicate the independence of the writer. One at least, of those addressed to Gavin Hamilton, is inimitable in its solemn sarcastic tone;

and several other individual specimens are conspicuous in their place. The letters to Muir, which are various, ranging from mere notes of exuberant jocularity to something like religious confessions or consolatory thoughts for a dying man, constitute what seems, unfortunately for the world, to be a hopelessly imperfect series. One fragment only we have been able, through the kindness of an esteemed friend and school-fellow, Mr. John Reid of this city, to add to the previous list; the rest, whatever were, we have reason to believe, are irretrievably lost. Their history, which is somewhat singular, may be briefly stated. One of our Author's earliest friends was the late William Reid, Esq., of Messrs. Brash & Reid, booksellers, Glasgow —himself a poet. Of their friendship we shall hereafter have some interesting details to record: but as regards the present correspondence, the following statement, on his son's authority, must suffice. Muir himself, or members of his family, seem to have had some intimate business or other relations with Mr. William Reid; in consequence of which, not only portions of the correspondence now in question, but a considerable amount of other literary property, the remains of our Author, in Muir's possession, came ultimately into Mr. Reid's hands. Some of these pieces found their way to the world by various uncertain channels—most probably in Stewart's Glasgow edition of 1801. But the correspondence and other miscellaneous documents were, shortly before Mr. Reid's death, accidentally so damaged by water, through an inundation of the Clyde,* as to be not only illegible, but beyond all hope of restoration. Single fragments recovered from the mass were carefully preserved, and have since from time to time obtained circulation. The remaining documents, still in Mr. John Reid's possession, include two of the letters to Muir; one of

which has already been published almost entire, and both of which we have been kindly permitted to transcribe for the present edition.

But of all the series here represented, that addressed to Mr. Aiken was originally the most beautiful and perfect. Only *three* letters, however, out of twenty or thirty, to that early friend and patron of our Author's, are now extant; and of these, one now appears for the first time. This valuable collection, treasured always with the utmost care, was surreptitiously removed from Mr. Aiken's repositories the very year of the Poet's death, and has never since been heard of. The particulars of this loss we learn from Mr. Aiken's grandson, P. F. Aiken, Esq., Wallcroft House, Bristol, who has politely forwarded us a copy of his aunt Miss Aiken's letter to Allan Cunningham on this, and on some other matters affecting the correspondence. Certain erroneous conclusions by Allan Cunningham, with respect to the continuance of our Author's friendly relation to Mr. Aiken, founded apparently on the want of this correspondence, and other circumstances hereafter to be referred to—occasioned some just regret, if not annoyance, to Miss Aiken; who accordingly addressed the letter in question to Mr. Cunningham, July, 1835, to anticipate the second edition of his Life and Works of Burns—which letter, we are sorry to learn, Mr. Cunningham never condescended to answer. So far as the loss of the correspondence is concerned, the following quotation from the document now before us will be interesting:

Having heard in the spring of 1796 that our poor friend was in very bad health, we felt how doubly valuable his letters would be in the event of his death, and I collected them all, and tied them up according to their dates, laying them away safely, as I then thought, before setting out for Dumfries and Liverpool where my brother Andrew was settled as a merchant, and recently married. At the former place I staid some days with my uncle Dr. Copeland, and one of them my emaciated, but still animated friend, Burns, spent delightfully with me there—our last meeting! He, alas, sank rapidly after; and before winter I had much communication with Dr. Currie at Liverpool, our friend and medical man, as to his proposed work: and finding a want of letters, and knowing there were few so favourable to the Poet's memory as those to my father, I wrote to him to send them by the mail. On going to the place where the parcel had been deposited, *it was gone!* and although every exertion was made *then* and often since to

---

* In spring of 1831, by the breaking up of the ice on the Clyde above Glasgow, that river came down in such flood as to carry all the vessels then in harbour from their moorings, together with much of the strong breast-work to which they were made fast. All the houses in Clyde Buildings, where Mr. Reid's family then resided, were inundated several feet above the street level, and the inhabitants had to employ ladders from the second storey windows to obtain egress. A pillar, since removed in course of improvements, was erected by the Clyde Trustees at Yoker, opposite Renfrew, to mark the height of the inundation there. Date of flood, Tuesday, February 8, 1831.

discover and recover the Letters, we could never trace them; and we were forced to conclude that a gay youth of some genius, then a clerk of my Father's, had secretly taken them to peruse, and my demand coming unexpectedly he could not *restore* and so had *destroyed* them, as he soon after left his situation and the country, and died some years after without making any discovery. I merely, Sir, state these circumstances to you, to prove that there was no interruption in the correspondence between Burns and my father. * * *

The correspondence, thus lost, extended over a period of ten years, and never ceased till Burns had been long in Dumfriesshire. It is described by Miss Aiken elsewhere in the same letter, as "beautiful, pure and interesting." How an attestation of this kind so honourable to all honestly concerned, and so important to the credit of Burns's memory, should have been contemptuously ignored by Mr. Cunningham, we are much at a loss to imagine—unless he had some theory of his own to maintain, which evidence so unimpeachable would have overthrown. This, indeed, seems to have been the case, as we shall hereafter see. In the meantime, it may be observed that the very letter to Mr. Aiken published by Cunningham himself—(2) in our edition of this series—and misplaced by him, demonstrates the inaccuracy of his own conclusion; and if farther evidence were required, letter (3), now for the first time presented to the public, corroborates Miss Aiken's testimony and finishes the argument.

Of the letters to Graham of Fintry, already alluded to as being of special peculiar interest, we have now farther to add that they are in many respects, both literary and biographical, among the most important in the whole of our Author's correspondence. Mr. Graham was not only a true literary friend—to whom therefore many epistolary poetical effusions, as well as prose letters, were addressed; but he was also a generous professional patron, whose influence at the board of Excise, to procure promotion where possible, or to represent the true facts of the case when defence against injurious accusations was required, was of the utmost value; and to this much honoured influential friend, in both these relations, our Author had frequent occasion to address himself. The letters are all of the very highest rank as epistolary compositions; one of them, indeed—letter (5)

—considering the delicacy of the writer's position in asking or acknowledging so many favours, we hold to be one of the most perfect compositions of its kind (his own included) in any language. Of those which refer to, and contain refutations of, the calumnious charges so frequently made against the writer, about the time of the French Revolution, one—letter (9)—we have already had occasion to lament as unworthy of his own dignity, and could wish almost it had never been indited; but the other which follows on the same subject, and written manifestly with more composure, is a clear, manly, and unexceptionable document, which those who have been accustomed to traduce his conduct or his reputation, in this matter, would do well dispassionately to consider. For this valuable series, originally most incomplete, the world is indebted to the editorial care of Mr. Chambers, through whose instrumentality it was first made known, in its present form, to the public.

Among the remaining documents in this department, with special biographical interest attached, we cannot conclude these general remarks without directing our readers' attention to one now for the first time published, which throws much and long desiderated light on the social and financial difficulties of our Author's later years. The true source of these pecuniary troubles, and of the humiliating embarrassments connected with them, so often obscurely referred to, or misapprehended and misrepresented to his disadvantage, the letter (1) to Captain John Hamilton—most beautiful and affecting in its manly avowal of inability and distress, originating in the purest generosity, in a great measure adequately explains. What the full amount of the disastrous obligation referred to might be, we are not informed, and who the very person was to whom it had been incurred we can only conjecture; but that it was enough to originate a debt which was never discharged, we know, and enough to bring a cloud of despondency on the writer's mind for the brief remaining portion of his life, we see. For such opportune elucidation of this painful subject as the letter in question affords, and for the light which it reflects at last on the whole of that period long so dark, we, and all true friends of the Poet's memory, are indebted to Mr. Manners of Croydon.

BURNS'S MONUMENT, AYR.

CORRESPONDENCE.

(1.) ## To Mr. John Richmond.

EDINBURGH.

Mossgiel, Feb. 17, 1786.

MY DEAR SIR,

I HAVE not time at present to upbraid you for your silence and neglect; I shall only say I received yours with great pleasure. I have enclosed you a piece of rhyming ware for your perusal. I have been very busy with the Muses since I saw you, and have composed, among several others, "The Ordination," a poem on Mr. M'Kinlay's being called to Kilmarnock; "Scotch Drink," a poem; "The Cotter's Saturday Night;" "An Address to the Devil," &c. I have likewise completed my poem on the "Dogs," but have not shown it to the world. My chief patron now is Mr. Aiken, in Ayr, who is pleased to express great approbation of my works. Be so good as send me Fergusson, by Connel, and I will remit you the money. I have no news to acquaint you with about Mauchline, they are just going on in the old way. I have some very important news with respect to myself, not the most agreeable—news that I am sure you cannot guess, but I shall give you the particulars another time. I am extremely happy with Smith; he is the only friend I have now in Mauchline. I can scarcely forgive your long neglect of me, and I beg you will let me hear from you regularly by Connel. If you would act your part as a friend, I am sure neither good nor bad fortune should estrange or alter me. Excuse haste, as I got yours but yesterday.

I am, my dear Sir, yours,

R. B.

(2.) ## TO MR. JOHN RICHMOND.

EDINBURGH.

Mossgiel, 9th July, 1786.

MY DEAR FRIEND,

WITH the sincerest grief I read your letter. You are truly a son of misfortune. I shall be extremely anxious to hear from you how your health goes on; if it is in any way re-establishing, or if Leith promises well; in short, how you feel in the inner man.

No news worth any thing: only godly Bryan was in the inquisition yesterday, and half the country-side as witnesses against him. He still stands out steady and denying; but proof was led yesternight of circumstances highly suspicious: almost *de facto*, one of the servant girls made faith that she upon a time rashly entered the house—to speak in your cant, "in the hour of cause."

I have waited on Armour since her return home; not from any the least view of reconciliation, but merely to ask for her health and—to you I will confess it—from a foolish hankering fondness—very ill placed indeed. The mother forbade me the house, nor did Jean show the penitence that might have been expected. However, the priest, I am informed, will give me a certificate as a single man, if I comply with the rules of the church, which for that very reason I intend to do.

I am going to put on sack-cloth and ashes this day. I am indulged so far as to appear in my own seat. *Peccavi, pater; miserere mei.* My book will be ready in a fortnight. If you have any subscribers, return them by Connel. The Lord stand with the righteous: Amen, amen!

R. B.

(3.) ## TO MR. JOHN RICHMOND.

Old Rome Forest,[*] *30th July,* 1786.

MY DEAR RICHMOND,

MY hour is now come—you and I will never meet in Britain more. I have orders, within three weeks at farthest, to repair aboard the Nancy, Captain Smith, from Clyde to Jamaica, and to call at Antigua. This, except to our friend Smith, whom God long preserve, is a secret about Mauchline. Would you believe it? Armour has got a warrant to throw me in jail till I find security for an enormous sum. This they keep an entire secret, but I got it by a channel they little dream of; and I am wandering from one friend's house to another, and, like a true son of the gospel, "have no where to lay my head." I know you will pour an execration on her head, but spare the poor, ill-advised girl, for my sake; though may all the furies that rend the injured, enraged lover's bosom, await her mother until her latest hour! I write in a moment of rage, reflecting on my miserable situation—exiled, abandoned, forlorn. I can write no more—let me hear from you by the return of coach. I will write you ere I go.

I am, dear Sir,

Yours here and hereafter,

R. B.

[*] [Near Kilmarnock.]

(4.)   TO MR. JOHN RICHMOND.

Mossgiel, 7th July, 1787.

MY DEAR RICHMOND,

I AM all impatience to hear of your fate since the old confounder of right and wrong has turned you out of place, by his journey to answer his indictment at the bar of the other world. He will find the practice of the court so different from the practice in which he has for so many years been thoroughly hackneyed, that his friends, if he had any connections truly of that kind, which I rather doubt, may well tremble for his sake. His chicane, his left-handed wisdom, which stood so firmly by him, to such good purpose, here, like other accomplices in robbery and plunder, will, now the piratical business is blown, in all probability turn king's evidence, and then the devil's bagpiper will touch him off "Bundle and go!"

If he has left you any legacy, I beg your pardon for all this; if not, I know you will swear to every word I said about him.

I have lately been rambling over by Dumbarton and Inveraray, and running a drunken race on the side of Loch Lomond with a wild Highlandman; his horse, which had never known the ornaments of iron or leather, zigzagged across before my old spavin'd hunter, whose name is Jenny Geddes, and down came the Highlandman, horse and all, and down came Jenny and my bardship; so I have got such a skinful of bruises and wounds, that I shall be at least four weeks before I dare venture on my journey to Edinburgh.

Not one new thing under the sun has happened in Mauchline since you left it. I hope this will find you as comfortably situated as formerly, or, if heaven pleases, more so; but, at all events, I trust you will let me know of course how matters stand with you, well or ill. 'Tis but poor consolation to tell the world when matters go wrong; but you know very well your connection and mine stands on a different footing.

I am ever, my dear friend, yours,

R. B.

[The young friend to whom these letters are addressed was originally a clerk in Mr. Hamilton's office at Mauchline. He removed afterwards to pursue his legal studies in Edinburgh; where he received Burns on his first visit to the capital, in his own humble apartment, Baxter's Close, Lawnmarket. Burns shared both room and bed, and seems to have been on terms of brotherly friendship with his correspondent.]

(1.)   To Mr. John Kennedy,
DUMFRIES HOUSE.

Mossgiel, 3rd March, 1786.

SIR,

I HAVE done myself the pleasure of complying with your request in sending you my Cottager. If you have a leisure minute, I should be glad you would copy it, and return me either the original or the transcript, as I have not a copy of it by me, and I have a friend who wishes to see it.

"Now, Kennedy, if foot or horse, &c."

ROBT. BURNESS.

[Mr. Kennedy, afterwards factor to the Earl of Breadalbane, occupied at this time some office in a similar department at Dumfries House, residence of Patrick, last Earl of Dumfries; from whom, by his only daughter and heiress, it accrued, together with extensive estates, to the family of Bute. The house itself was built by Jean Armour's grandfather, and is situated about half-way between Auchinleck and Ochiltree. The generosity on our Author's part of risking the safety of such a treasure as the "Cotter's Saturday Night," without the security of a duplicate, for the gratification of a comparative stranger, may well excite astonishment, and certainly requires no commentary.]

(2.)   TO MR. JOHN KENNEDY.

Mossgiel, 20th April, 1786.

SIR,

By some neglect in Mr. Hamilton, I did not hear of your kind request for a subscription paper 'till this day. I will not attempt any acknowledgment for this, nor the manner in which I see your name in Mr. Hamilton's subscription list. Allow me only to say, Sir, I feel the weight of the debt.

I have here likewise enclosed a small piece, the very latest of my productions.* I am a good deal pleased with some sentiments myself, as they are just the native querulous feelings of a heart, which, as the elegantly melting Gray says, "melancholy has marked for her own."

Our race comes on a-pace; that much-expected scene of revelry and mirth; but to me it brings no joy equal to that meeting with which your last flattered the expectation of,

Sir, your indebted humble Servant,

R. B.

*[Lines "To a Mountain Daisy."]

(3.)   TO MR. JOHN KENNEDY.

Mossgiel, 16th May, 1786.

DEAR SIR,

I HAVE sent you the above hasty copy as I promised. In about three or four weeks I shall probably set the press a-going. I am much hurried at present, otherwise your diligence, so very friendly in my subscription, should have a more lengthened acknowledgment from,

Dear Sir, your obliged Servant,

R. B.

(4.)   TO MR. JOHN KENNEDY.

Kilmarnock, [August,] 1786.

MY DEAR SIR,

YOUR truly facetious epistle of the 3rd inst. gave me much entertainment. I was only sorry I had not the pleasure of seeing you as I passed your way, but we shall bring up all our leeway on Wednesday, the 16th current, when I hope to have it in my power to call on you and take a kind, very probably a last adieu, before I go for Jamaica: and I expect orders to repair to Greenock every day. I have at last made my public appearance, and am solemnly inaugurated into the numerous class. Could I have got a carrier, you should have had a score of vouchers for my authorship; but now you have them, let them speak for themselves.—

> Farewell, dear friend! may guid luck hit you,
> And 'mang her favorites admit you!
> If e'er Detraction shore to smit you,
>   May nane believe him!
> And ony de'il that thinks to get you,
>   Good Lord deceive him.
>
>   R. B.

(1.) To Mr. Robert Muir,
KILMARNOCK.

Mossgiel, 20th March, 1789.

DEAR SIR,

I am heartily sorry I had not the pleasure of seeing you as you returned through Mauchline; but as I was engaged, I could not be in town before the evening.

I here enclose you my "Scotch Drink," and "may the —— follow with a blessing for your edification." I hope, some time before we hear the gowk,* to have the pleasure of seeing you at Kilmarnock, when I intend we shall have a gill between us, in a mutchkin-stoup; which will be a great comfort and consolation to,

Dear Sir, your humble Servant,

ROBERT BURNESS.

* [The cuckoo is heard in this country, for the first time in the season, in the month of April.]

(2.) TO MR. ROBERT MUIR,
KILMARNOCK.

Mossgiel, Friday Morning, [Sept.? 1786.]

MY FRIEND, MY BROTHER,

WARM recollection of an absent friend presses so hard upon my heart, that I send him the prefixed bagatelle,* pleased with the thought that it will greet the man of my bosom, and be a kind of distant language of friendship.

You will have heard that poor Armour has repaid me double. A very fine boy and a girl have awakened a thought and feelings that thrill, some with tender pleasure and some with foreboding anguish, through my soul.

The poem was nearly an extemporaneous production, on a wager with Mr. Hamilton, that I would not produce a poem on the subject in a given time.

If you think it worth while, read it to Charles and Mr. W. Parker, and if they choose a copy of it, it is at their service, as they are men whose friendship I shall be proud to claim, both in this world and that which is to come.

I believe all hopes of staying at home will be abortive; but more of this when, in the latter part of next week, you shall be troubled with a visit from, my dear Sir,

Your most devoted,

R. B.

* [Copy of "The Calf."]

(3.) TO MR. ROBERT MUIR.

Mossgiel, 18th Nov., 1786.

MY DEAR SIR,

INCLOSED you have "Tam Samson," as I intend to print him. I am thinking for my Edinburgh expedition on Monday or Tuesday come se'ennight, for pos. I will see you on Tuesday first.—I am ever, your much indebted,

R. B.

(4.) [TO MR. ROBERT MUIR.]

MY DEAR SIR,

I DELAYED writing you till I [was] able to give you some rational account of [myself] and my affairs. I am got under the p[atronage] of the Duchess of Gordon, Countess Dowager of Glencairn, Sir John Whitefoord, the Dean of Faculty, Professors Blair, Stewart, Gre[gory] and several others of the noblesse and literati. I believe I shall begin at Mr. Creech's as [publisher]. I am still undetermined as to the future; and, as usual, [ne]ver think of it. I have now neither house nor home that I can call my own, but live on the world at large. I am just a poor wayfaring Pilgrim on the road to Parnassus; thoughtless wanderer and sojourner in a strange land. [I] received a very kind letter from Mr. A. Dalziel, for which please return him my thanks; and [tell] him I will write him in a day or two. Mr. Parker, Charles, Dr. Corsan, and honest John [Wilson?] quondam printer, I remember in my prayers when I pray in rhyme. To all of [whom], till I have an opportunity * * * *

Edinr., 15th Dec., 1786.

I forgot to tell you how honest-hearted [Andrew?] and [his wife?] Matty * * * * She is [no]blest of the Creator's * * * *

[The above fragment, which has no address, but which manifestly, from the names and references which occur in it, belongs to this series, we carefully print from original in possession of our friend John Reid, Esq., Kingston Place, Glasgow; to whom, for this and other similar favours we have again to record our acknowledgements. In consequence of this letter, Mr. Muir seems to have interested himself on behalf of the Edinburgh edition, which is acknowledged in the next letter, in our Author's affectionate but independent manner. In filling up the blanks (recommended, as we have already explained how, p. 129,) the only two about which we have any doubt are those in the concluding sentence; but we are much disposed to believe that the parties alluded to are Andrew Bruce and his wife, or some other female relative, mentioned in letter (6), who seem to have been well known to the Kilmarnock folk, and to whose care, it appears, the letters for Burns from Kilmarnock were addressed. So much, however, is but conjecture.]

(5.)

TO MR. ROBERT MUIR.

Edinburgh, Dec. 20th, 1786.

MY DEAR FRIEND,

I HAVE just time for the carrier, to tell you that I received your letter; of which I shall say no more but what a lass of my acquaintance said of her bastard wean; she said she "did na ken wha was the father exactly, but she suspected it was some o' the bonny blackguard smugglers, for it was like them." So I only say your obliging epistle was like you. I enclose you a parcel of subscription bills. Your affair of sixty copies is also like you: but it would not be like me to comply.

Your friend's notion of my life has put a crotchet in my head of sketching it in some future epistle to you. My compliments to Charles and Mr. Parker.

R. B.

———

(6.)

TO MR. ROBERT MUIR.

Stirling, 26th August, 1787.

MY DEAR SIR,

I INTENDED to have written you from Edinburgh, and now write you from Stirling to make an excuse. Here am I, on my way to Inverness, with a truly original, but very worthy man, a Mr. Nicol, one of the masters of the High School in Edinburgh. I left Auld Reekie yesterday morning, and have passed, besides by-excursions, Linlithgow, Borrowstounness, Falkirk, and here am I undoubtedly. This morning I knelt at the tomb of Sir John the Graham, the gallant friend of the immortal Wallace; and two hours ago I said a fervent prayer for Old Caledonia, over the hole in a blue whinstone, where Robert de Bruce fixed his royal standard on the banks of Bannockburn; and just now, from Stirling Castle, I have seen by the setting sun the glorious prospect of the windings of Forth through the rich carse of Stirling, and skirting the equally rich carse of Falkirk. The crops are very strong, but so very late, that there is no harvest, except a ridge or two perhaps in ten miles, all the way I have travelled from Edinburgh.

I left Andrew Bruce and family all well. I will be at least three weeks in making my tour, as I shall return by the coast, and have many people to call for.

My best compliments to Charles, our dear kinsman and fellow-saint; and Messrs. W. and H. Parkers. I hope Hughoc is going on and prospering with God and Miss M'Causlin.

If I could think on any thing sprightly, I should let you hear every other post; but a dull, matter-of-fact business, like this scrawl, the less and seldomer one writes the better.

Among other matters-of-fact I shall add this, that I am and ever shall be, my dear Sir,

Your obliged,

R. B.

(7.)

TO MR. ROBERT MUIR.

Mauyiel, 7th March, 1788.

I HAVE partly changed my ideas, my dear friend, since I saw you. I took old Glenconner with me to Mr. Miller's farm, and he was so pleased with it, that I have wrote an offer to Mr. Miller, which, if he accepts, I shall sit down a plain farmer—the happiest of lives when a man can live by it. In this case I shall not stay in Edinburgh above a week. I set out on Monday, and would have come by Kilmarnock, but there are several small sums owing me for my first edition about Galston and Newmills, and I shall set off so early as to dispatch my business and reach Glasgow by night. When I return, I shall devote a forenoon or two to make some kind of acknowledgment for all the kindness I owe your friendship. Now that I hope to settle with some credit and comfort at home, there was not any friendship or friendly correspondence that promised me more pleasure than yours; I hope I will not be disappointed. I trust the spring will renew your shattered frame, and make your friends happy. You and I have often agreed that life is no great blessing on the whole. The close of life, indeed, to a reasoning eye, is

> "Dark as was chaos, ere the infant sun
> Was roll'd together, or had try'd his beams
> Athwart the gloom profound."

But an honest man has nothing to fear. If we lie down in the grave, the whole man a piece of broke machinery, to moulder with the clods of the valley, be it so; at least there is an end of pain, care, woes, and wants: if that part of us called Mind does survive the apparent destruction of the man—away with old-wife prejudices and tales! Every age and every nation has had a different set of stories; and as the many are always weak, of consequence, they have often, perhaps always, been deceived: a man conscious of having acted an honest part among his fellow-creatures—even granting that he may have been the sport at times of passions and instincts—he goes to a great unknown Being, who could have no other end in giving him existence but to make him happy; who gave him those passions and instincts, and well knows their force.

These, my worthy friend, are my ideas; and I know they are not far different from yours. It becomes a man of sense to think for himself; particularly in a case where all men are equally interested, and where indeed all men are equally in the dark.

These copies of mine you have on hand: please send ten of them to Mr. John Ballantine, of the Bank in Ayr; for the remainder, I'll write you about them from Glasgow.

Adieu, my dear Sir! God send us a cheerful meeting—

ROBT. BURNS.

[This letter, important in many ways, is printed by us from original copy now in possession of Mr. John Reid, Kingston Place, Glasgow. The external address is to Mr. Robert Muir, wine merchant, Kilmarnock, and it is probably the last letter now extant (as already explained) of those addressed by our Author to that correspondent. How long Mr. Muir survived after this date, we are not at present able to determine. That his death, however, had taken place sometime, perhaps shortly, before the month of December, 1788, appears from letter (24) to Mrs. Dunlop (p. 21); so that several letters, now supposed to be lost, may have been addressed to him during this interval.]

(1.) 𝕿𝖔 𝕸𝖗. [𝕽𝖔𝖇𝖊𝖗𝖙] 𝕬𝖎𝖐𝖊𝖓.

[VERBATIM.]

DEAR SIR,

I RECEIVED your kind letter with double pleasure, in* account of this second flattering instance of Mrs. C.'s notice and approbation. I assure you I

"Turn out the truant side o' my shin,"

as the famous Ramsay of jingling memory says, at such a Patroness. Present her my most grateful acknowledgements, in your very best manner of telling Truth. I have inscribed the following stanza on the blank leaf of Miss More's works:—

Thou flatt'ring mark of friendship kind, &c. †

My proposals for publishing I am just going to send to the press. I expect to hear from you first opportunity.

I am ever, dear Sir, yours,

ROBT. BURNESS.

Mossgiel, 3rd April, 1786.

* [So, in original, distinctly—possibly by mistake for on.]
† [See Posthumous Poetical Works.]

[We need hardly remind our readers that Mr. Aiken was the esteemed friend and patron to whom "The Cotter's Saturday Night" was inscribed. He seems to have been a man of most amiable disposition, of fine taste, and of the highest honour. To his review many of our Author's earliest productions were submitted, and he ensured a sort of publicity for these by the admirable manner in which he read or recited them to his own friends in private. He was in this respect peculiarly entitled to be called the Patron of the Poet's "Virgin Muse"—for according to our Author's own account, "Mr. Aiken read me into fame." Mr. Aiken died at Ayr, March 24, 1807.

The above letter, by kind permission, we print from the original, which is now in possession of Mr. Edward Broadfield of this city, who received it from a Mr. James M'Creadie, Ayr, about 14 years ago—that is, about 1854. Its history beyond this, we regret to say, is not now known; but the letter has been folded and docketed in the usual business style—

Mossgiel :
3d April, 1786.
R. Burns to
Mr. Aiken.

We are thus particular for reasons which the reader can now understand, in hopes that some intelligence may possibly be obtained of letters still awanting in this important series.]

(2.) TO MR. ROBERT AIKEN.

[*A little after Oct. 6* † 1786.]

SIR,

I WAS with Wilson, my printer, t'other day, and settled all our by-gone matters between us. After I had paid him all demands, I made him the offer of the second edition, on the hazard of being paid out of the first and readiest, which he declines. By his account, the paper of a thousand copies would cost about twenty-seven pounds, and the printing about fifteen or sixteen: he offers to agree to this for the printing, if I will advance for the paper, but this, you know, is out of my power; so farewell hopes of a second edition till I grow richer! an epocha which I think will arrive at the payment of the British national debt.

There is scarcely any thing hurts me so much in being disappointed of my second edition, as not having it in my power to show my gratitude to Mr. Ballantine, by publishing my poem of "The Brigs of Ayr." I would detest myself as a wretch, if I thought I were capable in a very long life of forgetting the honest, warm, and tender delicacy with which he enters into my interests. I am sometimes pleased with myself in my grateful sensations; but I believe, on the whole, I have very little merit in it, as my gratitude is not a virtue, the consequence of reflection, but merely the instinctive emotion of my heart, too inattentive to allow worldly maxims and views to settle into selfish habits.

I have been feeling all the various rotations and movements within, respecting the Excise. There are many things plead strongly against it; the uncertainty of getting soon into business; the consequence of my follies, which may perhaps make it impracticable for me to stay at home; and besides, I have for some time been pining under secret wretchedness, from causes which you pretty well know—the pang of disappointment, the sting of pride, with some wandering stabs of remorse, which never fail to settle on my vitals like vultures, when attention is not called away by the calls of society or the vagaries of the Muse. Even in the hour of social mirth, my gaiety is the madness of an intoxicated criminal under the hands of the executioner. All these reasons urge me to go abroad, and to all these reasons I have only one answer—the feelings of a father. This, in the present mood I am in, overbalances every thing that can be laid in the scale against it. * * * *

You may perhaps think it an extravagant fancy, but it is a sentiment which strikes home to my very soul: though sceptical in some points of our current belief, yet, I think I have every evidence for the reality of a life beyond the stinted bourne of our present existence; if so, then how should I, in the presence of that tremendous Being, the Author of existence, how should I meet the reproaches of those who stand to me in the dear relation of children, whom I deserted in the smiling innocency of helpless infancy? Oh thou great unknown Power!—thou Almighty God! who hast lighted up reason in my breast, and blessed me with immortality!—I have frequently wandered from that order and regularity necessary for the perfection of thy works, yet thou hast never left me nor forsaken me! * * * *

Since I wrote the foregoing sheet, I have seen something of the storm of mischief thickening over my folly-devoted head. Should you, my friends, my benefactors, be successful in your applications for me, perhaps it may not be in my power, in that way, to reap the fruit of your friendly efforts. What I have written in the preceding pages, is the settled tenor of my present resolution; but should inimical circumstances forbid me closing with your kind offer, or enjoying it only threaten to entail farther misery—* * * *

To tell the truth, I have little reason for complaint; as the world, in general, has been kind to me fully up to my deserts. I was, for some time past, fast getting into the pining, distrustful snarl of the misanthrope. I saw myself alone, unfit for the struggle of life, shrinking at every rising cloud in the chance-directed atmosphere of fortune, while all defenceless I looked about in vain for a cover. It never

* T

occurred to me, at least never with the force it deserved, that this world is a busy scene, and man a creature destined for a progressive struggle; and that, however I might possess a warm heart and inoffensive manners (which last, by the bye, was rather more than I could well boast), still, more than these passive qualities, there was something to be done. When all my school-fellows and youthful compeers (those misguided few excepted who joined, to use a Gentoo phrase, the "hallachores" of the human race) were striking off with eager hope and earnest intent in some one or other of the many paths of busy life, I was "standing idle in the market-place," or only left the chase of the butterfly from flower to flower, to hunt fancy from whim to whim. *   *   *   *

You see, Sir, that if to know one's errors were a probability of mending them, I stand a fair chance; but according to the reverend Westminster divines, though conviction must precede conversion, it is very far from always implying it. *   *   *   *   *   *

[In the conjectural date of this imperfect letter we adopt Mr. Chambers's suggestion. It was manifestly written at least after the settlement of accounts with Wilson and the proposal for a new edition made to him, to which it refers. In Cunningham's edition, although no date except the year is assigned to this letter, the letter itself is placed in order between June 12 and July 9, which is obviously incorrect, because the first edition of the Poems had not then been published; and on the contents of a letter assumed by him to have been written by Burns to Mr. Ballantine (1), also without date, but in order before July 17, and certainly before publication of the Poems, he formed the supposition that some "coldness" had occurred between Burns and Mr. Aiken. The above letter to that gentleman, so full of gratitude and confidence, absolutely disproves the truth of any such supposition. If "coldness" ever did exist, it must have been short, and easily removed—which, in Burns's mind at least, would have been a kind of moral impossibility. (Compare note on above letter to Ballantine.)

(3.)   TO MR. ROBERT AIKEN.

DEAR PATRON OF MY VIRGIN MUSE,

I WROTE Mr. Ballantine at large all my operations and "eventful story," since I came to town.—I have found in Mr. Creech, who is my agent forsooth, and Mr. Smellie who is to be my printer, that honor and goodness of heart which I always expect in Mr. Aiken's friends. Mr. Dalrymple of Orangefield I shall ever remember: my Lord Glencairn I shall ever pray for. The Maker of man has great honor in the workmanship of his lordship's heart. May he find that patronage and protection in his guardian angel that I have found in him! His lordship has sent a parcel of subscription bills to the Marquiss of Graham, with downright orders to get them filled up with all the first Scottish names about Court.—He has likewise wrote to the Duke of Montague and is about to write to the Duke of Portland for their Graces' interest in behalf of the Scotch Bard's subscription.

You will very probably think, my honored friend, that a hint about the mischievous nature of intoxicated vanity may not be unseasonable; but, alas! you are wide of the mark.—Various concurring circumstances have raised my

fame as a Poet to a height which I am absolutely certain I have not merits to support; and I look down on the future as I would into the bottomless pit.—

You shall have one or two more bills when I have an opportunity of a Carrier.

I am ever,
      with the sincerest gratitude,
        Honored Sir,
      Your most devoted humble servt.,
          ROBERT BURNS.
Edinr., 16th Dec., 1786.

[Addressed Mr. Robert Aiken, Writer, Ayr.—This letter, which came to light in Glasgow at the centenary celebration of the Poet's birth, was acquired for the late James Crum, Esq., of Busby, a devout admirer of his genius. It appears in this collection by the courteous permission of Mr. Crum's widow; and, with the exception of the following—(4)—is presumably the only remaining extant letter of the series addressed to Mr. Aiken. There is certainly no appearance of any diminution of respect or gratitude towards Mr. Aiken on the writer's part in either.]

(4.)   TO ROBERT AIKEN, ESQ.,
               AYR.

[*Mauchline, July*, 1787.]

MY HONORED FRIEND,

THE melancholy occasion of the foregoing poem affects not only individuals but a country. That I have lost a friend is but repeating after Caledonia. This copy, rather an incorrect one, I beg you will accept, till I have an opportunity in person, which I expect to have on Tuesday first, of assuring you how sincerely I ever am,

      Honored and dear Sir,
        Your oft oblidged,
          ROBT. BURNS.

MR. H——'s *Office,*
    Saturday Evening.

[This letter which we print, with thanks, from original in Mr. P. F. Aiken's possession (Bristol), was written most probably in the beginning of July, from Mr. Hamilton's office, Mauchline. The poem it enclosed was the Elegy on Sir J. H. Blair, Bart., who died on the 1st of July, 1787. Burns, wherever else he might be in the interval, spent the month of July at Mauchline, from which he returned again to Edinburgh in the beginning of August. The Elegy, therefore, must have been written in the meantime. (Compare note on Elegy—Posthumous Poetical Works.) Along with the above document we receive from Mr. Aiken the following interesting statement in reference to the lost correspondence between our Author and Robert Aiken, Esq.:—

"It was pre-eminently valuable, not only as being addressed to his early, and, I believe, his constant friend and patron, but because, as his best poems were successively written, they were sent to my grandfather—in whose friendship and literary taste Burns had confidence; and each letter was, in some degree, the Poet's commentary on his own composition, descriptive of the circumstances by which it was suggested, and the feelings which prompted or influenced it. One cannot but deplore the loss of such an accompaniment to The Cotter's Saturday Night, Tam o' Shanter, The Mouse, &c." The Lost Correspondence, restored only to the extent of a single letter, we now commit to the affectionate solicitude and research of our readers everywhere, in Great Britain and America. If it anywhere yet exists, let it be forthcoming. The above letter, we may add, comes to hand after our editorial remarks, p. 130, are in type.]

To Mr. M'Whinnie,

WRITER, AYR.

Mossgiel, 17th April, 1786.

It is injuring some hearts, those hearts that elegantly bear the impression of the good Creator, to say to them you give them the trouble of obliging a friend; for this reason, I only tell you that I gratify my own feelings in requesting your friendly offices with respect to the enclosed, because I know it will gratify yours to assist me in it to the utmost of your power.

I have sent you four copies, as I have no less than eight dozen, which is a great deal more than I shall ever need.

Be sure to remember a poor poet militant in your prayers. He looks forward with fear and trembling to that, to him, important moment which stamps the die with—with—with, perhaps the eternal disgrace of, my dear Sir,

Your humbled, afflicted, tormented,

ROBT. BURNS.

(1.) To Mons. James Smith,

MAUCHLINE.

Monday Morning, Mossgiel [1786].

MY DEAR SIR,

I WENT to Dr. Douglas yesterday, fully resolved to take the opportunity of Captain Smith; but I found the Doctor with a Mr. and Mrs. White, both Jamaicans, and they have deranged my plans altogether. They assure him that to send me from Savannah la Mar to Port Antonio will cost my master, Charles Douglas, upwards of fifty pounds; besides running the risk of throwing myself into a pleuritic fever, in consequence of hard travelling in the sun. On these accounts, he refuses sending me with Smith, but a vessel sails from Greenock the first of September, right for the place of my destination. The Captain of her is an intimate friend of Mr. Gavin Hamilton's, and as good a fellow as heart could wish; with him I am destined to go. Where I shall shelter, I know not, but I hope to weather the storm. Perish the drop of blood of mine that fears them; I know their worst, and am prepared to meet it:—

> "I'll laugh, an' sing, an' shake my leg,
> As lang's I dow."

On Thursday morning, if you can muster as much self-denial as to be out of bed about seven o'clock, I shall see you as I ride through to Cumnock. After all, Heaven bless the sex! I feel there is still happiness for me among them:—

> "O woman, lovely woman! Heaven designed you
> To temper man!—we had been brutes without you."

R. B.

[James Smith, our readers are doubtless aware, was the friend to whom the celebrated Epistle by our Author is addressed: Compare note on which, Poetical Works, p. 96.]

(2.) TO MR. JAMES SMITH,

AT MILLER AND SMITH'S OFFICE, LINLITHGOW.

Mauchline, 11th June, 1787.

MY EVER DEAR SIR,

I DATE this from Mauchline, where I arrived on Friday even last. I slept at John Dow's, and called for my daughter; Mr. Hamilton and family; your mother, sister, and brother; my quondam Eliza, &c., all, all well. If any thing had been wanting to disgust me completely at Armour's family, their mean, servile compliance would have done it.

Give me a spirit like my favorite hero, Milton's Satan:

> Hail, horrors! hail,
> Infernal world! and thou profoundest hell
> Receive thy new possessor! one who brings
> A mind not to be changed by place or time!

I cannot settle to my mind.—Farming, the only thing of which I know any thing, and heaven above knows, but little do I understand of that, I cannot, dare not risk on farms as they are. If I do not fix, I will go for Jamaica. Should I stay in an unsettled state at home, I would only dissipate my little fortune, and ruin what I intend shall compensate my little ones, for the stigma I have brought on their names.

I shall write you more at length soon; as this letter costs you no postage, if it be worth reading you cannot complain of your penny-worth.

I am ever, my dear Sir, yours,

R. B.

P.S.—The cloot has unfortunately broke, but I have provided a fine buffalo-horn, on which I am going to affix the same cypher which you will remember was on the lid of the cloot.*

* [A calf's cloot, polished and ornamented, was a favourite snuff-box in those days.]

[Mr. Chambers's edition of this letter differs considerably from above, which is nearly Cunningham's.]

(3.) TO MR. JAMES SMITH,

LINLITHGOW.

June 30, 1787.

[MY DEAR FRIEND,]

ON our return, at a Highland gentleman's hospitable mansion, we fell in with a merry party, and danced till the ladies left us, at three in the morning. Our dancing was none of the French or English insipid formal movements; the ladies sung Scotch songs like angels, at intervals: then we flew at Bab at the Bowster, Tullochgorum, Loch Erroch Side, &c., like midges sporting in the mottie sun, or craws prognosticating a storm in a hairst day.—When the dear lasses left us, we ranged round the bowl till the good-fellow hour of six; except a few minutes that we went out to pay our devotions to the glorious lamp of day peering over the towering top of Benlomond. We all kneeled; our worthy landlord's son held the bowl; each man a full glass in his hand; and I, as priest, repeated some rhyming nonsense, like Thomas-a-Rhymer's prophecies I suppose.—After a small refreshment of the gifts of Somnus, we proceeded to spend the day on Lochlomond, and reach Dumbarton in the evening. We dined at another good fellow's house, and consequently pushed the bottle; when we went out to mount our horses, we found ourselves "No vera fou but gaylie yet." My two friends and I rode soberly down the Loch side, till by came a Highlandman at the gallop, on a tolerably good horse, but which had never known the ornaments of iron or leather. We scorned to be out-galloped by a Highlandman, so off we started, whip and spur. My companions, though seemingly gaily mounted, fell sadly astern; but my old mare, Jenny Geddes, one of the Rosinante family, she strained past the Highlandman in spite of all his efforts with the hair halter. Just as I was passing him, Donald wheeled his horse, as if to cross before me to mar my progress, when down came his horse, and threw his rider's breekless a—o in a clipt hedge; and down came Jenny Geddes over all, and my hardship between her and the Highlandman's horse. Jenny Geddes trode over me with such cautious reverence, that matters were not so bad as might well have been expected; so I came off with a few cuts and bruises, and a thorough resolution to be a pattern of sobriety for the future.

I have yet fixed on nothing with respect to the serious business of life. I am, just as usual, a rhyming, mason-making, raking, aimless, idle fellow. However, I shall some-where have a farm soon. I was going to say, a wife too; but that must never be my blessed lot. I am but a younger son of the house of Parnassus, and like other younger sons of great families, I may intrigue, if I choose to run all risks, but must not marry.

I am afraid I have almost ruined one source, the principal one, indeed, of my former happiness—that eternal propensity I always had to fall in love. My heart no more glows with feverish rapture. I have no paradisaical evening interviews, stolen from the restless cares and prying inhabitants of this weary world. I have only ' * * '. This last is one of your distant acquaintances, has a fine figure, and elegant manners; and, in the train of some great folks whom you know, has seen the politest quarters in Europe. I do like her a good deal; but what piques me is her conduct at the commence-ment of our acquaintance. I frequently visited her when I was in ——, and after passing regularly the intermediate degrees between the distant formal bow and the familiar grasp round the waist, I ventured, in my careless way, to talk of friendship in rather ambiguous terms; and after her return to ——, I wrote to her in the same style. Miss, construing my words farther than even I intended, flow off in a tangent of female dignity and reserve, like a mounting lark in an April morning; and wrote me an answer which measured me out very completely what an immense way I had to travel before I could reach the climate of her favour. But I am an old hawk at the sport, and wrote her such a cool, deliberate, prudent reply, as brought my bird from her aerial towerings, pop, down at my foot, like Corporal Trim's hat.

As for the rest of my acts, and my wars, and all my wise

sayings, and why my mare was called Jenny Geddes, they shall be recorded in a few weeks hence at Linlithgow, in the chronicles of your memory, by

R. B.

(4.)

TO MR. JAMES SMITH,
AVON PRINTFIELD, LINLITHGOW.

Mauchline, April 28, 1788.

BEWARE of your Strasburgh, my good Sir! Look on this as the opening of a correspondence, like the opening of a twenty-four gun battery!

There is no understanding a man properly, without know-ing something of his previous ideas (that is to say, if the man has any ideas; for I know many, who in the animal-muster pass for men, that are the scanty masters of only one idea on any given subject, and by far the greatest part of your acquaintances and mine can barely boast of ideas, 1·25—1·5—1·75 or some such fractional matter); so to let you a little into the secrets of my pericranium, there is, you must know, a certain clean-limbed, handsome, bewitching young hussy of your acquaintance, to whom I have lately and privately given a matrimonial title to my corpus.

" Bode a robe and wear it,"*

says the wise old Scots adage! I hate to presage ill-luck; and as my girl has been *doubly* kinder to me than even the best of women usually are to their partners of our sex, in similar circumstances, I reckon on twelve times a brace of children against I celebrate my twelfth wedding-day: these twenty-four will give me twenty-four gossipings, twenty-four christenings (I mean one equal to two), and I hope, by the blessing of the God of my fathers, to make them twenty-four dutiful children to their parents, twenty-four useful members of society, and twenty-four approven servants of their God!

    *   *   *   *   *

"Light's heartsome," quo' the wife when she was stealing sheep. You see what a lamp I have hung up to lighten your paths, when you are idle enough to explore the combinations and relations of my ideas. 'Tis now as plain as a pike-staff, why a twenty-four gun battery was a metaphor I could readily employ.

Now for business.—I intend to present Mrs. Burns with a printed shawl, an article of which I dare say you have variety: 'tis my first present to her since I have *irrevocably* called her mine, and I have a kind of whimsical wish to get her the said first present from an old and much-valued friend of hers and mine, a trusty Trojan, on whose friendship I count myself possessed of a life-rent lease. * * * *

Look on this letter as a "beginning of sorrows;" I'll write you till your eyes ache with reading nonsense.

Mrs. Burns ('tis only her private designation) begs her best compliments to you.

R. B.

* [The entire proverbial couplet runs—

"Bade a robe and wear it,
Bade a poke and bear it;"

but as the writer did not wish "to presage ill-luck," he quotes only the pleasant first half of it—at least so, according to Cromek, whose edition we take to be correct.]

(1.)

To Mr. David Brice.

Mossgiel, June 12, 1786.

DEAR BRICE,

I RECEIVED your message by G. Paterson, and as I am not very throng at present, I just write to let you know that there is such a worthless, rhyming reprobate, as your humble servant, still in the land of the living, though I can scarcely say, in the place of hope. I have no news to tell you that will give me any pleasure to mention, or you to hear.

Poor ill-advised ungrateful Armour came home on Friday last. You have heard all the particulars of that affair, and a black affair it is. What she thinks of her conduct now, I don't know; one thing I do know—she has made me completely miserable. Never man loved, or rather adored, a woman more than I did her; and, to confess a truth between you and me, I do still love her to distraction after all, though I won't tell her so if I were to see her, which I don't want to do. My poor dear unfortunate Jean! how happy have I been in thy arms! It is not the losing her that makes me so unhappy, but for her sake I feel most severely: I foresee she is in the road to, I am afraid, eternal ruin. * * * *

May Almighty God forgive her ingratitude and perjury to me, as I from my very soul forgive her: and may his grace be with her and bless her in all her future life! I can have no nearer idea of the place of eternal punishment than what I have felt in my own breast on her account. I have tried often to forget her: I have run into all kinds of dissipation and riots, mason-meetings, drinking-matches, and other mischief, to drive her out of my head, but all in vain. And now for a grand cure: the ship is on her way home that is to take me out to Jamaica; and then, farewell dear old Scotland! and farewell dear ungrateful Jean! for never, never will I see you more.

You will have heard that I am going to commence Poet in print; and to-morrow my works go to the press. I expect it will be a volume of about two hundred pages—it is just the last foolish action I intend to do; and then turn a wise man as *fast as possible.*

Believe me to be, dear Brice,
Your friend and well-wisher,

R. B.

(2.)

TO MR. DAVID BRICE,
SHOEMAKER, GLASGOW.

Mossgiel, 17th July, 1786.

I HAVE been so throng printing my Poems, that I could scarcely find as much time as to write to you. Poor Armour is come back again to Mauchline, and I went to call for her, and her mother forbade me the house, nor did she herself express much sorrow for what she has done. I have already appeared publicly in church, and was indulged in the liberty of standing in my own seat. I do this to get a certificate as a bachelor, which Mr. Auld has promised me. I am now fixed to go for the West Indies in October. Jean and her friends insisted much that she should stand along with me in the kirk, but the minister would not allow it, which bred a great trouble I assure you, and I am blamed as the cause of it, though I am sure I am innocent; but I am very much pleased, for all that, not to have had her company. I have no news to tell you that I remember. I am really happy to hear of your welfare, and that you are so well in Glasgow. I must certainly see you before I leave the country. I shall expect to hear from you soon, and am,

Dear Brice, yours,

R. B.

[FROM CUNNINGHAM'S EDITION.]

(1.)

To John Ballantyne,
OF AYR.

HONOURED SIR,

MY proposals came to hand last night, and knowing that you would wish to have it in your power to do me a service as early as any body, I enclose you half a sheet of them. I must consult you, first opportunity, on the propriety of sending my quondam friend, Mr. Aiken, a copy. If he is now reconciled to my character as an honest man, I would do it with all my soul; but I would not be beholden to the noblest being ever God created, if he imagined me to be a rascal. Apropos, old Mr. Armour prevailed with him to mutilate that unlucky paper yesterday. Would you believe it? though I had not a hope, nor even a wish, to make her mine after her conduct; yet, when he told me the names were all out of the paper, my heart died within me, and he cut my veins with the news. Perdition seize her falsehood!

R. B.

We invite the reader's special attention to the following note.

[This letter, which has neither date nor address, and is most probably a mere scroll, seems to have been discovered by Allan Cunningham, who, without hesitation, allocates it to Mr. Ballantine, and prefixes the following note: "There is a plain account in this letter of the destruction of the lines of marriage which united, as far as civil contract in a matter civil can, the Poet and Jean Armour. Aiken was consulted, and in consequence of his advice the certificate of marriage was destroyed." With reference to which allegation, Miss Aiken, in the letter already quoted (p. 139) addressed to Mr. Cunningham, says—

"I was much distressed by the impression left on the public mind by the 18th letter in the 6th volume, without date and believed to have been addressed to my relative Mr. Ballantine; and would immediately have written to you on the subject, had not the last volume of your work been published before I saw it. It was only yesterday that I learnt from my cousins, the Misses Stewart of Afton, that a second edition is now in the press, and I hope to anticipate the re-publication of your 6th volume by stating, that I am sure no such letter as the above was received by Mr. Ballantine, and unless I saw the autograph I cannot believe that it was ever written by the Poet. Because, however grieved my father was on his account for all his irregularities, Mr. Aiken had no knowledge of or interest in the Armours, even if his principles could have allowed him to be a party in any such transaction, which was impossible. Besides, as there never was any interruption in their friendship or correspondence, Burns could not have applied the phrase quondam *friend* to my father, and your idea in the note* that they were no longer correspondents is quite a mistake. * * The sacred motive which prompts this communication, will, with a man of your feeling, be I hope sufficient apology for, Sir,

Yours, &c.

Ayr, 6th July, 1835. GRACE AIKEN."

Allan Cunningham, we regret to say, neither acknowledged this communication, nor made any correction of his text in consequence. The only explanation of this neglect we can imagine is, that believing the document in question to be genuine, and having founded some theory of his own upon its contents, he did not feel disposed to withdraw it. But the document might be genuine and yet written in error; and, having been so written in error, was therefore never sent, nor even addressed, to the party for whom it was intended; in which case, it ceased to be a document at all in the cause to which it referred, and should never have been founded on for any *conclusion whatever*. Mr. Cunningham ought at least to have added a mark of interrogation to the address of the letter, or to have placed the address in brackets, to intimate its absence or uncertainty in the original. Compare concluding note to this series.

We are thus particular, because Mr. Chambers, influenced apparently by the boldness of Allan Cunningham's assumption, not only adopts his view but speaks of Mr. Aiken as having "presided on the occasion" (vol. ii. 209); and because, until present evidence came before us, we were ourselves (Biography p. xxv.) of the same opinion. The whole affair seems now to be an apocryphal myth, originating in the Poet's own misapprehension, or in some angry threat of Mr. Armour's—in which Mr. Aiken's name might be incautiously used—to perplex and punish him. This we believe to be the simple truth regarding Burns's marriage, which never was, and never could be dissolved by any such irregular proceeding, even if it had been adopted—which it was not, although the Poet in his passionate frenzy believed it had; and the conviction, thus originated, has been confirmed and circulated by mere reiteration to the present day. It should now cease, unless supported by other and much clearer evidence.]

* [See note on letter (2) to Mr. Aiken.]

[FROM CROMEK'S EDITION.]

(2.)

TO JOHN BALLANTINE, ESQ.,
BANKER, AYR.

Edinburgh, 13th Dec., 1786.

MY HONORED FRIEND,

I WOULD not write you till I could have it in my power to give you some account of myself and my matters, which, by the bye, is often no easy task. I arrived here on Tuesday was se'nnight, and have suffered ever since I came to town with a miserable head-ache and stomach complaint, but am now a good deal better. I have found a worthy warm friend in Mr. Dalrymple, of Orangefield, who introduced me to Lord Glencairn, a man whose worth and brotherly kindness to me I shall remember, when time shall be no more. By his interest it is passed in the "Caledonian Hunt," and entered in their books, that they are to take each a copy of the second edition, for which they are to pay one guinea. I have been introduced to a good many of the *Noblesse*, but my avowed

patrons and patronesses are the Duchess of Gordon—the Countess of Glencairn, with my Lord, and Lady Betty—the Dean of Faculty—Sir John Whitefoord. I have likewise warm friends among the literati; Professors Stewart, Blair, and Mr. Mackenzie—the Man of Feeling. An unknown hand left ten guineas for the Ayrshire bard with Mr. Sibbald, which I got. I since have discovered my generous unknown friend to be Patrick Miller, Esq., brother to the Justice Clerk; and drank a glass of claret with him, by invitation, at his own house yesternight. I am nearly agreed with Creech to print my book, and I suppose I will begin on Monday. I will send a subscription bill or two, next post; when I intend writing my first kind patron, Mr. Aiken. I saw his son to-day, and he is very well.

Dugald Stewart, and some of my learned friends, put me in the periodical paper called The Lounger, a copy of which I here enclose you. I was, Sir, when I was first honored with your notice, too obscure; now I tremble lest I should be ruined by being dragged too suddenly into the glare of polite and learned observation.

I shall certainly, my ever honored patron, write you an account of my every step; and better health and more spirits may enable me to make it something better than this stupid matter-of-fact epistle.

I have the honor to be, good Sir,

Your ever grateful humble servant,

R. B.

If any of my friends write me, my direction is, care of Mr. Creech, bookseller.

[The reader may compare this letter with letter (4) to Mr. Robert Muir, and also with letter (3) to Mr. Aiken. They contain many similar expressions, and have been written all in immediate succession.—The Lady Betty here alluded to was Lady Betty Cunningham; and the paper alluded to was the review of our Author's poems by Mackenzie the celebrated author of the 'Man of Feeling.']

(3.)

TO JOHN BALLANTINE, ESQ.

Edinburgh, Jan. 14, 1787.

MY HONORED FRIEND,

IT gives me a secret comfort to observe in myself that I am not yet so far gone as Willie Gaw's Skate, "post redemption;" for I have still this favorable symptom of grace, that when my conscience, as in the case of this letter, tells me I am leaving something undone that I ought to do, it teazes me eternally till I do it.

I am still "dark as was Chaos" in respect to futurity. My generous friend, Mr. Patrick Miller, has been talking with me about a lease of some farm or other in an estate called Dalswinton, which he has lately bought, near Dumfries. Some life-rented embittering recollections whisper me that I will be happier any where than in my old neighbourhood, but Mr. Miller is no judge of land; and though I dare say he means to favor me, yet he may give me, in his opinion, an advantageous bargain that may ruin me. I am to take a tour by Dumfries as I return, and have promised to meet Mr. Miller on his lands some time in May.

I went to a Mason-lodge yesternight, where the most Worshipful Grand Master Charters, and all the Grand Lodge of Scotland visited. The meeting was numerous and elegant; all the different Lodges about town were present, in all their pomp. The Grand Master, who presided with great solemnity and honor to himself as a gentleman and mason, among other general toasts, gave "Caledonia, and Caledonia's Bard, Brother B——," which rung through the whole assembly with multiplied honors and repeated acclamations. As I had no idea such a thing would happen, I was downright thunderstruck, and, trembling in every nerve made the best return in my power. Just as I had finished, some of the grand officers said, so loud that I could hear, with a most comforting accent, "Very well indeed!" which set me something to rights again.

I have to-day corrected my 152d page. My best good wishes to Mr. Aiken. I am over, Dear Sir,

Your much indebted humble Servant,

R. B.

———

(4.)　　TO JOHN BALLANTINE, ESQ.

[*January* —, 1787.]

WHILE here I sit, sad and solitary by the side of a fire in a little country inn, and drying my wet clothes, in pops a poor fellow of a sodger, and tells me he is going to Ayr. By heavens! say I to myself, with a tide of good spirits which the magic of that sound, Auld Toon o' Ayr, conjured up, I will send my last song to Mr. Ballantine. Here it is—

Ye flowery banks o' bonnie Doon, &c. *

* [See Posthumous Poetical Works.]

———

(5.)　　TO JOHN BALLANTINE, ESQ.

Edinburgh, Feb. 24, 1787.

MY HONORED FRIEND,

I 'WILL soon be with you now, *in guid black prent ;*—in a week or ten days at farthest. I am obliged, against my own wish, to print subscribers' names; so if any of my Ayr friends have subscription bills, they must be sent in to Creech directly. I am getting my phix done by an eminent engraver; and if it can be ready in time, I will appear in my book, looking like other *fools* to my title-page.

R. B.

[John Ballantine, Esq., to whom "The Brigs of Ayr" was dedicated, was a banker and for sometime provost in that town—a gentleman held in the highest estimation for his many excellent qualities, both as a citizen and as a magistrate.

His name is spelt in most modern editions with a *y* in the last syllable; but in the older editions, and by our Author himself, as well as by Miss Aiken his own relative, the name is spelt otherwise, and we have retained it accordingly. In these letters as it was written—Ballantine. This circumstance, although trivial, is strong enough proof that letter (1) as published by Cunningham—where the name is printed with a *y*, had either no address at all, or was not addressed by our Author. Compare Gilbert Burns's account of Mr. Ballantine, in Appendix. Mr. Ballantine, who lived a bachelor, died at Ayr, July 15, 1812.]

———

(1.)　　**To Dr. Mackenzie,**

MAUCHLINE.

ENCLOSING THE VERSES ON DINING WITH LORD DAER.

Wednesday Morning, [*End of October ?* 1786.]

DEAR SIR,

I NEVER spent an afternoon among great folks with half that pleasure as when, in company with you, I had the honor of paying my devoirs to that plain, honest, worthy man, the Professor.* I would be delighted to see him perform acts of kindness and friendship, though I were not the object; he does it with such a grace.

I think his character, divided into ten parts, stands thus —four parts Socrates—four parts Nathaniel—and two parts Shakspeare's Brutus.

The foregoing verses were really extempore, but a little corrected since. They may entertain you a little with the help of that partiality with which you are so good as to favor the performances of,

Dear Sir, your very humble Servant,

R. B.

* [Dugald Stewart, Esq., who resided then at his own villa of Catrine, in the neighbourhood of Mauchline. Burns and Mr. M'Kenzie, surgeon in Mauchline—a man universally respected there, dined together at the Professor's on the 23rd of October, 1786. "Lord Daer," the Professor informs us, "happened to arrive at Catrine the same day, and by the kindness and frankness of his manner, left an impression on the mind of the Poet which was never effaced." This was the first occasion of our Author's meeting either with his Lordship or the Professor. Compare note on the Verses.]

———

(2.)　　TO DR. MACKENZIE,

MAUCHLINE.

Edinburgh, 11th January, 1787.

MY DEAR SIR,

YOURS gave me something like the pleasure of an old friend's face. I saw your friend and *my* honored patron, Sir John Whitefoord, just after I received your letter, and gave him your compliments. He was pleased to say many handsome things of you, which I heard with the more satisfaction as I know them to be just.

His son John, who calls very frequently on me, is in a fuss to-day like a coronation. This is the great day—the assembly and ball of the Caledonian Hunt; and John has had the good luck to pre-engage the hand of the beauty-famed, and wealth-celebrated Miss M'Adam, our country-woman. Between friends, John is desperately in for it there, and I am afraid will be desperate indeed.

I am sorry to send you the last speech and dying words of "The Lounger."

A gentleman waited on me yesterday, and gave me, by Lord Eglinton's orders, ten guineas by way of subscription for a brace of copies of my second edition.

I met with Lord Maitland* and a brother of his to-day at breakfast. They are exceedingly easy, accessible, agreeable fellows, and seemingly pretty clever.

I am ever, my dear Sir,
Yours,
ROBERT BURNS.

* [Afterwards eighth Earl of Lauderdale, at this time a conspicuous member of the House of Commons, on the side of Opposition.]

(1.) To Gavin Hamilton, Esq.,
MAUCHLINE.

Edinburgh, Dec. 7th, 1786.

HONORED SIR,

I HAVE paid every attention to your commands, but can only say what perhaps you will have heard before this reach you, that Muirkirklands were bought by a John Gordon, W.S., but for whom I know not; Mauchlands, Haugh-Miln, &c.,* by a Frederick Fotheringham, supposed to be for Ballochmyle Laird, and Adamhill and Shawood were bought for Oswald's folks.—This is so imperfect an account, and will be so late ere it reach you, that were it not to discharge my conscience I would not trouble you with it; but after all my diligence I could make it no sooner nor better.

For my own affairs, I am in a fair way of becoming as eminent as Thomas à Kempis or John Bunyan; and you may expect henceforth to see my birth-day inserted among the wonderful events, in the Poor Robin's and Aberdeen Almanacks, along with the black Monday, and the battle of Bothwell bridge.—My Lord Glencairn and the Dean of Faculty, Mr. H. Erskine, have taken me under their wing; and by all probability I shall soon be the tenth worthy, and the eighth wise man of the world. Through my lord's influence it is inserted in the records of the Caledonian Hunt, that they universally, one and all, subscribe for the second edition.—My subscription bills come out to-morrow, and you shall have some of them next post.—I have met, in Mr. Dalrymple, of Orangefield, what Solomon emphatically calls "A friend that sticketh closer than a brother."—The warmth with which he interests himself in my affairs is of the same enthusiastic kind which you, Mr. Aiken, and the few patrons that took notice of my earlier poetic days showed for the poor unlucky devil of a poet.

I always remember Mrs. Hamilton and Miss Kennedy in my poetic prayers, but you both in prose and verse.

> May cauld ne'er catch you but a hap,
> Nor hunger but in plenty's lap!
> Amen!

* [These lands, the property of the Loudoun family, were disposed of by public roup in Edinburgh, Dec. 5th, of this year. The Earl, as our readers are aware, had perished some months before by an act of despair, in consequence of embarrassment. Compare note on some "Raving Winds," &c., Poetical Works, p. 260.]
[We need hardly direct our readers' attention to the strange truthful prophecy of fame which occurs in this letter.]

(2.) TO GAVIN HAMILTON, ESQ.

Edinburgh, Jan. 7, 1787.

To tell the truth among friends, I feel a miserable blank in my heart, with the want of her, and I don't think I shall ever meet with so delicious an armful again. She has her faults; and so have you and I; and so has every body:

> Their tricks and craft hae put me daft;
> They've ta'en me in and a' that;
> But clear your decks, and here's the sex,
> I like the jads for a' that:
> For a' that and a' that,
> And twice as muckle's a' that.

I have met with a very pretty girl, a Lothian farmer's daughter, whom I have almost persuaded to accompany me to the west country, should I ever return to settle there. By the bye, a Lothian farmer is about an Ayrshire squire of the lower kind; and I had a most delicious ride from Leith to her house yesternight, in a hackney-coach, with her brother and two sisters, and brother's wife. We had dined all together at a common friend's house in Leith, and danced, drank, and sang till late enough. The night was dark, the claret had been good, and I thirsty. * * * * *
R. B.

(3.) TO GAVIN HAMILTON, ESQ.

Edinburgh, March 8, 1787.

DEAR SIR,

YOURS came safe, and I am, as usual, much indebted to your goodness. Poor Captain Montgomery is cast. Yesterday it was tried whether the husband could proceed against the unfortunate lover without first divorcing his wife; and their gravities on the bench were unanimously of opinion that M—— may prosecute for damages directly, and need not divorce his wife at all if he pleases. * * * * O all ye Powers of love unfortunate, and friendless wo, pour the balm of sympathising pity on the grief-torn, tender heart of the hapless fair one!

My two songs on Miss W. Alexander and Miss P[eggy] K[ennedy] were likewise tried yesterday by a jury of literati, and found defamatory libels against the fastidious powers of Poesy and Taste; and the author forbidden to print them under pain of forfeiture of character. I cannot help almost shedding a tear to the memory of two songs that had cost me some pains, and that I valued a good deal; but I must submit.

My most respectful compliments to Mrs. Hamilton and Miss Kennedy.

My poor unfortunate songs come again across my memory. D[amn] the pedant, frigid soul of criticism for ever and ever !

R. B.

[The case of divorce, or no-divorce with penalties, above referred to, was one that seems to have occasioned a good deal of scandal at the time, not without sympathy for the lady. A handsome estate would have been lost if divorce had been sued for; that plea, therefore, was abandoned, and penalties alone enforced. The songs mentioned as being considered unsuitable for publication, were 'The Female Loss of Ballochmyle,' and 'Banks o' Doon.' Compare notes on Songs, Poetical Works, p. 294, and p. 270.]

(4.) TO GAVIN HAMILTON, ESQ.

Stirling, 28th August, 1787.

MY DEAR SIR,

HERE am I on my way to Inverness. I have rambled over the rich, fertile carses of Falkirk and Stirling, and am delighted with their appearance: richly waving crops of wheat, barley, &c., but no harvest at all yet, except, in one or two places, an old wife's ridge. Yesterday morning I rode from this town up the meandering Devon's banks, to pay my respects to some Ayrshire folks at Harvieston. After breakfast, we made a party to go and see the famous Caudron-linn, a remarkable cascade in the Devon, about five miles above Harvieston; and after spending one of the most pleasant days I ever had in my life, I returned to Stirling in the evening. They are a family, Sir, though I had not had any prior tie—though they had not been the brothers and sisters of a certain generous friend of mine—I would never forget them. I am told you have not seen them these several years, so you can have very little idea of what these young folks are now. Your brother is as tall as you are, but slender rather than otherwise; and I have the satisfaction to inform you that he is getting the better of those consumptive symptoms which I suppose you know were threatening him. His make, and particularly his manner, resemble you, but he will have a still finer face. (I put in the word *still,* to please Mrs. Hamilton.) Good sense, modesty, and at the same time a just idea of that respect that man owes to man, and has a right in his turn to exact, are striking features in his character; and, what with me is the Alpha and Omega, he has a heart that might adorn the breast of a poet ! Grace has a good figure, and the look of health and cheerfulness, but nothing else remarkable in her person. I scarcely ever saw so striking a likeness as is between her and your little Beenie; the mouth and chin

particularly. She is reserved at first; but as we grew better acquainted, I was delighted with the native frankness of her manner, and the sterling sense of her observation. Of Charlotte I cannot speak in common terms of admiration; she is not only beautiful but lovely. Her form is elegant; her features not regular, but they have the smile of sweetness and the settled complacency of good nature in the highest degree; and her complexion, now that she has happily recovered her wonted health, is equal to Miss Burnet's. After the exercise of our riding to the Falls, Charlotte was exactly Dr. Donne's mistress :—

> " Her pure and eloquent blood
> Spoke in her cheeks, and so distinctly wrought,
> That one would almost say her body thought."

Her eyes are fascinating; at once expressive of good sense, tenderness, and a noble mind.

I do not give you all this account, my good Sir, to flatter you. I mean it to reproach you. Such relations the first peer in the realm might own with pride; then why do you not keep up more correspondence with these so amiable young folks? I had a thousand questions to answer about you. I had to describe the little ones with the minuteness of anatomy. They were highly delighted when I told them that John was so good a boy, and so fine a scholar, and that Willie was going on still very pretty; but I have it in commission to tell her from them that beauty is a poor silly bauble, without she be good. Miss Chalmers I had left in Edinburgh, but I had the pleasure of meeting with Mrs. Chalmers, only Lady Mackenzie being rather a little alarmingly ill of a sore throat somewhat marred our enjoyment.

I shall not be in Ayrshire for four weeks. My most respectful compliments to Mrs. Hamilton, Miss Kennedy, and Doctor Mackenzie. I shall probably write him from some stage or other. I am ever, Sir,

Yours most gratefully,

R. B.

[Mrs. Hamilton, the stepmother of Gavin—Mrs. Chalmers—and the deceased Mrs. Tait of Harvieston, were sisters—the children of Murdoch of Cumlodden in Galloway, the representative of a gallant peasant who had got lands for the help he gave to Bruce on a perilous occasion. Mr. Tait, being left a widower, invited his sister-in-law, Mrs. Hamilton, with her children, to reside at Harvieston; Mrs. Chalmers also occasionally lived there in summer with her daughters—one of whom was Margaret, and the other the wife of Sir Hector Mackenzie. The Charlotte alluded to in the letter was Mrs. Hamilton's daughter. We summarise the above information from *Chambers.*]

(5.) TO GAVIN HAMILTON, ESQ.

[*Edinburgh, Dec.,* 1787.]

MY DEAR SIR,

IT is indeed with the highest pleasure that I congratulate you on the return of days of ease, and nights of pleasure, after the horrid hours of misery in which I saw you suffering existence when last in Ayrshire: I seldom pray for any body, " I'm baith dead-sweer and wretched ill o't;" but most fervently do I beseech the Power that directs the world, that you may live long and be happy, but live no longer than you are happy. It is needless for me to advise you to have a reverend care of your health. I know you will make it a point never at one time to drink more than a pint of wine (I mean an English pint), and that you will never be witness to more than one bowl of punch at a time, and that cold drams you will never more taste; and, above all things, I am convinced, that after drinking perhaps boiling punch, you will never mount your horse and gallop home in a chill late hour. Above all things, as I understand you are in the habits of intimacy with that Boanerges of gospel powers, Father Auld, be earnest with him that he will wrestle in prayer for you, that you may see the vanity of vanities in trusting to, or even practising the carnal moral works of charity, humanity, generosity, and forgiveness of things, which you practised so flagrantly that it was evident you delighted in them, neglecting, or perhaps profanely despising, the wholesome doctrine of faith without works, the only [means] of salvation. A hymn of thanksgiving would, in my opinion, be highly becoming from you at present, and in my zeal for your well-being, I earnestly press on you to be diligent in chaunting over the two enclosed pieces of sacred poesy. My best compliments to Mrs. Hamilton and Miss Kennedy. Yours in the L—d,

R. B.

(G.)   TO [MR. GAVIN HAMILTON.]

Mossgiel, Friday Morning.

THE language of refusal is to me the most difficult language on earth, and you are the man in the world, excepting one of Right Honorable designation,* to whom it gives me the greatest pain to hold such language. My brother has already got money, and shall want nothing in my power to enable him to fulfil his engagement with you; but to be security on so large a scale, even for a brother, is what I dare not do, except I were in such circumstances of life as that the worst that might happen could not greatly injure me.

I never wrote a letter which gave me so much pain in my life, as I know the unhappy consequences: I shall incur the displeasure of a gentleman for whom I have the highest respect, and to whom I am deeply obliged. I am ever, Sir,

Your obliged and very humble Servant,

ROBERT BURNS.

* [The Earl of Glencairn is no doubt here referred to.]

[Some time after the date of this letter, and before he settled in Dumfriesshire, our Author advanced from the proceeds of his poems the sum of £180 to Gilbert, to maintain him in the farm, and as some acknowledgment of the filial obligation which devolved on himself as a member of the family. The money was understood to be a loan without interest. See Domestic Correspondence.]

[*The following series to Logan and Campbell should have been earlier placed, had the necessary documents been to hand.*]

(1.)   To John Logan, Esq.,

OF KNOCKSHINNOCH:

[OTHERWISE OF AFTON.]

SIR,

I GRATEFULLY thank you for your kind offices in promoting my sub[s]cription, and still more for your very friendly letter.—The first was doing me a Favour, but the last was doing me an Honour.—I am in such a bustle at present, preparing for my West-India voyage, as I expect a letter every day from the Master of the vessel, to repair directly to Greenock; that I am under a necessity to return you the subscription bills, and trouble you with the quantum of Copies till called for, or otherwise transmitted to the Gentlemen who have subscribed. Mr. Bruce Campbell is already supplied with two copies, and I here send you 20 copies more.—If any of the Gentlemen are supplied from any other quarter, 'tis no matter; the copies can be returned.

If orders from Greenock do not hinder, I intend doing myself the honour of waiting on you, Wednesday the 16th Inst.

I am much hurt, Sir, that I must trouble you with the Copies; but circumstanced as I am, I know no other way your friends can be supplied.

I have the honour to be,

SIR,

Your much indebted humble Servt.,

ROBERT BURNS.

KILMARNOCK, *10th Aug:*
    1786.

[By the above letter, which we print from original in possession of Miss Logan (Mr. John Logan's eldest daughter, residing at Bishopsleugh, Lockerbie), obtained for us by the obliging assistance of her cousin, G. Gemmell, Esq., banker, Ayr, it appears that our Author had been much earlier acquainted with Mr. Logan than is commonly supposed. The letter itself is written in a very close, plain, formal hand, smaller than usual, and has all the appearance of being a 'clean copy.' It has a few orthographical slips, as is very often the case in 'clean copies,' and it has had spaces originally left blank for a day or two, till days, dates and numbers could be settled. In the interval, we may imagine the young Author counting over and allotting the 'copies,' or bundling them up for despatch, before leaving his native land. The blanks, filled up with different ink on the 10th of August, are as follows, 20—in large figures; Wednesday—crowded a little and so spelt in haste; 16th—straight up and down; 10th—without intervening comma and close to Kilmarnock. Subscription—as our readers observe in one case, wants an s, and necessity, in original, has an s too many; honour—contrary to his usual custom, is formally spelt with a u in last syllable throughout. We delight to trace these curious proofs of over-care and over-sight, and dwell on them as records of the past with reverence and love. The Bruce Campbell here referred to was of Sornbeg near Galston, but no relative of the Thomas Campbell whose name occurs immediately below; from the letter to whom it should seem that the above engagement, in which also Mr. Kennedy, at Dumfries House—compare letter (4) to him—was concerned, was never fulfilled.]

(2.)   TO JOHN LOGAN, ESQ.

OF AFTON.

Ellisland, near Dumfries, 7th Aug., 1789.

DEAR SIR,

I INTENDED to have written you long ere now, and as I told you, I had gotten three stanzas and a half on my way in a poetic epistle to you; but that old enemy of all *good works*, the Devil, threw me into a prosaic mire, and for the soul of me I cannot get out of it. I dare not write you a long letter, as I am going to intrude on your time with a long Ballad. I have, as you will shortly see, finished "The Kirk's Alarm;" but now that it is done, and that I have laughed once or twice at the conceits in some of the stanzas, I am determined not to let it get into the Public; so I send you this copy, the first I have sent to Ayrshire, except some few of the stanzas, which I wrote off in embryo for Gavin Hamilton, under the express provision and request—that you will only read it to a few *of us*, and do not on any account give, or permit to be taken, any copy of the Ballad. If I could be of any service to Dr. M'Gill, I would do it, though it should be at a much greater expence than irritating a few bigotted Priests; but as I am afraid, serving him in his present embarras is a task too hard for me. I have enemies enow, God knows, tho' I do not wantonly add to the number. Still, as I think that there is some merit in two or three of the thoughts, I send it you as a small but sincere testimony how much, and with what respectful esteem, I am, dear Sir,

Your obliidged humble servant,
Robt. Burns.

[This letter, as the preceding, we print from original in Miss Logan's possession.]

To Monsr. Thomas Campbell,
PENCLOE.

[12th August ? 1786.]

My dear Sir,

I HAVE met with few men in my life whom I more wished to see again than you, and Chance seems industrious to disappoint me of that pleasure. I came here yesterday fully resolved to see you and Mr. Logan, at New Cumnock; but a conjuncture of circumstances conspired against me. Having an opportunity of sending you a line, I joyfully embraced it. It is perhaps the last mark of our friendship you can receive from me on this side of the Atlantic.

Farewell! May you be happy up to the wishes of parting Friendship!

Robt. Burns.

Mr. J. MERRY'S, *Saturday Morn.*

[This letter we print from original in possession of George Pagon, Esq., New Cumnock, obtained for us by the same obliging hand as the above. It has been manifestly written in haste; is on a small square scrap of paper, but duly folded, and sealed with an old-fashioned cipher-seal on red wax, too much broken to be now perfectly legible. It bears on the address to be forwarded per Mr. Good; and seems to refer very plainly to the agreement to meet Mr. Logan at New Cumnock, on Wednesday, 16th August. It was therefore probably written on the Saturday before that day, and at New Cumnock itself; for Mr. Merry's public-house (Annie Rankine's husband, heroine of the 'Rigs o' Barley') was in that town. The Poet was most likely called away before the engagement could be fulfilled. A blot in the original proves all this—the sentence stood at first: "but at New Cumnock, a conjuncture, &c."

Mr. Pagon, we may mention, in whose possession this letter now is, was a nephew of Mr. Logan's of Afton, and a near kinsman to Mr. Campbell of Pencloe.]

To Mr. William Chalmers,
WRITER, AYR.

Edinburgh, Dec. 27, 1786.

My dear Friend,

I CONFESS I have sinned the sin for which there is hardly any forgiveness—ingratitude to friendship—in not writing you sooner; but of all men living, I had intended to have sent you an entertaining letter; and by all the plodding, stupid powers, that in nodding, conceited majesty, preside over the dull routine of business—a heavily solemn oath this!—I am, and have been, ever since I came to Edinburgh, as unfit to write a letter of humor, as to write a commentary on the Revelation of St. John the Divine, who was banished to the Isle of Patmos, by the cruel and bloody Domitian, son to Vespasian, and brother to Titus, both emperors of Rome, and who was himself an emperor, and raised the second or third persecution, I forget which, against the Christians, and after throwing the said Apostle John, brother to the Apostle James, commonly called James the Greater, to distinguish him from another James, who was, on some account or other, known by the name of James the Less—after throwing him into a cauldron of boiling oil, from which he was miraculously preserved, he banished the poor son of Zebedee to a desert island in the Archipelago, where he was gifted with the second sight, and saw as many wild beasts as I have seen since I came to Edinburgh; which, a circumstance not very uncommon in story-telling, brings me back to where I set out.

To make you some amends for what, before you reach this paragraph, you will have suffered, I enclose you two poems I have carded and spun since I past Glenbuck.

One blank in the address to Edinburgh—"Fair B——," is heavenly Miss Burnet, daughter to Lord Monboddo, at whose house I have had the honor to be more than once. There has not been anything nearly like her in all the combinations of beauty, grace, and goodness the great Creator has formed since Milton's Eve on the first day of her existence.

My direction is—Care of Andrew Bruce, Merchant, Bridge Street.

R. B.

(1.) To Mr. James Candlish,
STUDENT IN PHYSIC, COLLEGE, GLASGOW.

Edinburgh, March 21, 1787.

My ever dear old Acquaintance,

I WAS equally surprised and pleased at your letter; though I dare say you will think by my delaying so long to write to you, that I am so drowned in the intoxication of good fortune as to be indifferent to old, and once dear connections. The truth is, I was determined to write a good letter, full of argument, amplification, erudition, and, as Bayes says, *all that*, I thought of it, and thought of it, but for my soul, I can not; and, lest you should mistake the cause of my silence, I just sit down to tell you so. Don't give yourself credit, though, that the strength of your logic scares me: the truth is, I never mean to meet you on that ground at all. You have shown me one thing which was to be demonstrated; that strong pride of reasoning, with a little affectation of singularity, may mislead the best of hearts. I, likewise, since you and I were first acquainted, in the pride of despising old women's stories, ventured in "the daring path Spinosa trod;" but experience of the weakness, not the strength, of human powers, made me glad to grasp at revealed religion.

I must stop, but don't impute my brevity to a wrong cause. I am still, in the Apostle Paul's phrase, "The old man with his deeds," as when we were sporting about the "Lady Thorn." I shall be four weeks here yet at least; and so I shall expect to hear from you—welcome sense, welcome nonsense.

I am, with the warmest sincerity,
R. B.

[Mr. Candlish married Miss Smith, celebrated for her wit as one of the Belles of Mauchline. A son of this marriage is the Rev. Robert Smith Candlish, D.D., Principal of the Free Church College, Edinburgh. Mr. Candlish died in 1806.]

(2.)   ## TO MR. JAMES CANDLISH.

[Edinburgh, 1787.]

MY DEAR FRIEND,

IF once I were gone from this scene of hurry and dissipation, I promise myself the pleasure of that correspondence being renewed which has been so long broken. At present I have time for nothing. Dissipation and business engross every moment. I am engaged in assisting an honest Scotch enthusiast,* a friend of mine, who is an engraver, and has taken it into his head to publish a collection of all our songs set to music, of which the words and music are done by Scotsmen. This, you will easily guess, is an undertaking exactly to my taste. I have collected, begged, borrowed, and stolen all the songs I could meet with. Pompey's Ghost, words and music, I beg from you immediately, to go into his second number: the first is already published. I shall show you the first number when I see you in Glasgow, which will be in a fortnight or less. Do be so kind as to send me the song in a day or two; you cannot imagine how much it will oblige me.

Direct to me at Mr. W. Cruikshank's, St. James's Square, New Town, Edinburgh.

R. B.

* [Johnson, the publisher of the 'Scots Musical Museum.']

To Mr. William Dunbar, W.S.,
(1.)   EDINBURGH.

Lawnmarket, Monday Morning.

DEAR SIR,

IN justice to Spenser, I must acknowledge that there is scarcely a poet in the language could have been a more agreeable present to me; and in justice to you, allow me to say, Sir, that I have not met with a man in Edinburgh to whom I would so willingly have been indebted for the gift. The tattered rhymes I herewith present you, and the handsome volumes of Spenser for which I am so much indebted to your goodness, may perhaps be not in proportion to one another; but be that as it may, my gift, though far less valuable, is as sincere a mark of esteem as yours.

The time is approaching when I shall return to my shades; and I am afraid my numerous Edinburgh friendships are of so tender a construction, that they will not bear carriage with me. Yours is one of the few that I could wish of a more robust constitution. It is indeed very probable that when I leave this city, we part never more to meet in this sublunary sphere; but I have a strong fancy that in some future eccentric planet, the comet of happier systems than any with which astronomy is yet acquainted, you and I, among the harum-scarum sons of imagination and whim, with a hearty shake of a hand, a metaphor, and a laugh, shall recognise old acquaintance:

Where Wit may sparkle all its rays,
Uncurst with Caution's fears;
And Pleasure, basking in the blaze,
Rejoice for endless years.

I have the honor to be, with the warmest sincerity,
Dear Sir, &c.,
R. B.

[William Dunbar, Esq., to whom this admirable series of letters is addressed, was, professionally, a Writer to the Signet in Edinburgh; convivially, Colonel of the "Crochallan Corps;" and poetically, the "Rattling Roaring Willie" of our Author's well-known song. He seems to have been a man of a very genial, mirthful disposition. He was ultimately promoted to the office of Inspector-General of Stamp-duties for Scotland.]

(2.)   ## TO MR. WILLIAM DUNBAR, W.S.

Mauchline, 7th April, 1788.

I HAVE not delayed so long to write you, my much respected friend, because I thought no farther of my promise. I have long since given up that kind of formal correspondence, where one sits down irksomely to write a letter, because we think we are in duty bound so to do.

I have been roving over the country, as the farm I have taken is forty miles from this place, hiring servants and preparing matters; but most of all, I am earnestly busy to bring about a revolution in my own mind. As, till within these eighteen months, I never was the wealthy master of ten guineas, my knowledge of business is to learn; add to this, my late scenes of idleness and dissipation have enervated my mind to an alarming degree. Skill in the sober science of life is my most serious and hourly study. I have dropt all conversation and all reading (prose reading) but what tends in some way or other to my serious aim. Except one worthy young fellow, I have not one single correspondent in Edinburgh. You have indeed kindly made me an offer of that kind. The world of wits, and *gens comme il faut* which I lately left, and with whom I never again will intimately mix—from that port, Sir, I expect your Gazette: what *les beaux esprits* are saying, what they are doing, and what they are singing. Any sober intelligence from my sequestered walks of life; any droll original; any passing remark, important forsooth, because it is mine; any little poetic effort, however embryoth; these, my dear Sir, are all you have to expect from me. When I talk of poetic efforts, I must have it always understood, that I appeal from your wit and taste to your friendship and good nature. The first would be my favorite tribunal, where I defied censure; but the last, where I declined justice.

I have scarcely made a single distich since I saw you. When I meet with an old Scots air that has any facetious idea in its name, I have a peculiar pleasure in following out that idea for a verse or two.

I trust that this will find you in better health than I did last time I called for you. A few lines from you, directed to me at Mauchline, were it but to let me know how you are, will set my mind a good deal [at rest.] Now, never shun the idea of writing me because perhaps you may be out of humour or spirits. I could give you a hundred good consequences attending a dull letter; one, for example, and the remaining ninety-nine some other time—it will always serve to keep in countenance, my much respected Sir, your obliged friend and humble servant,

R. B.

(3.)　　TO MR. WILLIAM DUNBAR, W.S.

Ellisland, 14*th January*, 1790.

SINCE we are here creatures of a day, since "a few summer days, and a few winter nights, and the life of man is at an end," why, my dear much-esteemed Sir, should you and I let negligent indolence, for I know it is nothing worse, step in between us and bar the enjoyment of a mutual correspondence? We are not shapen out of the common, heavy, methodical clod, the elemental stuff of the plodding selfish race, the sons of Arithmetic and Prudence; our feelings and hearts are not benumbed and poisoned by the cursed influence of riches, which, whatever blessing they may be in other respects, are no friends to the nobler qualities of the heart: in the name of random Sensibility, then, let never the moon change on our silence any more. I have had a tract of bad health most part of this winter, else you had heard from me long ere now. Thank Heaven, I am now got so much better as to be able to partake a little in the enjoyments of life.

Our friend Cunningham will perhaps have told you of my going into the Excise. The truth is, I found it a very convenient business to have £50 per annum, nor have I yet felt any of those mortifying circumstances in it that I was led to fear.

Feb. 2.

I have not, for sheer hurry of business, been able to spare five minutes to finish my letter. Besides my farm-business, I ride on my Excise matters at least two hundred miles every week. I have not by any means given up the Muses. You will see in the 3d vol. of Johnson's Scots Songs that I have contributed my mite there.

But, my dear Sir, little ones that look up to you for paternal protection are an important charge. I have already two fine, healthy, stout little fellows, and I wish to throw some light upon them. I have a thousand reveries and schemes about them, and their future destiny—Not that I am a Utopian projector in these things. I am resolved never to breed up a son of mine to any of the learned professions. I know the value of independence; and since I cannot give my sons an independent fortune, I shall give them an independent line of life. What a chaos of hurry, chance, and changes is this world, when one sits soberly down to reflect on it! To a father, who himself knows the world, the thought that he shall have sons to usher into it must fill him with dread; but if he have daughters, the prospect in a thoughtful moment is apt to shock him.

I hope Mrs. Fordyce and the two young ladies are well. Do let me forget that they are nieces of yours, and let me say that I never saw a more interesting, sweeter pair of sisters in my life. I am the fool of my feelings and attachments. I often take up a volume of my Spenser to realise you to my imagination, and think over the social scenes we have had together. God grant that there may be another world more congenial to honest fellows beyond this: a world where those rubs and plagues of absence, distance, misfortunes, ill-health, &c., shall no more damp hilarity and divide friendship. This I know is your throng season, but half a page will much oblige, my dear Sir, yours sincerely,

R. B.

(4.)　　TO COL. W. DUNBAR.

Ellisland, 17*th January*, 1791.

I AM not gone to Elysium, most noble Colonel, but am still here in this sublunary world, serving my God by propagating his image, and honoring my king by begetting him loyal subjects. Many happy returns of the season await my friend! May the thorns of Care never beset his path! May Peace be an inmate of his bosom, and Rapture a frequent visitor of his soul! May the blood-hounds of Misfortune never trace his steps, nor the screech-owl of Sorrow alarm his dwelling! May Enjoyment tell thy hours, and Pleasure number thy days, thou friend of the Bard! Blessed be he that blesseth thee, and cursed be he that curseth thee!!!

As a further proof that I am still in the land of existence, I send you a poem, the latest I have composed. I have a particular reason for wishing you only to show it to select friends, should you think it worthy a friend's perusal; but if, at your first leisure hour, you will favour me with your opinion of, and strictures on, the performance, it will be an additional obligation on, dear Sir, your deeply indebted humble servant,

R. B.

To Mr. Pattison,

BOOKSELLER, PAISLEY.

Berry-well, near Dunse, May 17, 1787.

Dear Sir,

I am sorry I was out of Edinburgh, making a slight pilgrimage to the classic scenes of this country, when I was favoured with yours of the 11th instant, enclosing an order of the Paisley Banking Company on the Royal Bank for twenty-two pounds seven shillings sterling, payment in full, after carriage deducted, for ninety copies of my book I sent you. According to your motions, I see you will have left Scotland before this reaches you, otherwise I would send you "Holy Willie" with all my heart. I was so hurried that I absolutely forgot several things I ought to have minded, among the rest, sending books to Mr. Cowan; but any order of yours will be answered at Creech's shop. You will please remember that non-subscribers pay six shillings—this is Creech's profit; but those who have subscribed, though their names have been neglected in the printed list, which is very incorrect, are supplied at the subscription price. I was not at Glasgow, nor do I intend for London; and I think Mrs. Fame is very idle to tell so many lies on a poor poet. When you or Mr. Cowan write for copies, if you should want any, direct to Mr. Hill, at Mr. Creech's shop, and I write to Mr. Hill by this post, to answer either of your orders. Hill is Mr. Creech's first clerk, and Creech himself is presently in London. I suppose I shall have the pleasure, against your return to Paisley, of assuring you how much I am, dear Sir, your obliged humble servant,

R. B.

(1.)　To Mr. William Nicol,

MASTER OF THE HIGH SCHOOL, EDINBURGH.

Carlisle, June 1, 1787,
(or, I believe, the 30th o' May rather.)

Kind, honest-hearted Willie,

I'm sitten down here after seven and forty miles' ridin, e'en as forjesket and forniaw'd as a forfoughten cock, to gie you some notion o' my land-lowper-like stravaguin sin' the sorrowfu' hour that I shook hands and parted wi' auld Reekie.

My auld, ga'd gleyde o' a meere has huchyall'd up hill and down brae, in Scotland and England, as tough and birnie as a very deevil wi' me. It's true, she's as poor's a sang-maker and as hard's a kirk, and tipper-taipers when she taks the gate, just like a lady's gentlewoman in a minuwae, or a hen on a het girdle; but she's a yauld, poutherie Girran for a' that, and has a stomack like Willie Stalker's meere, that wad hae disgeested tumbler-wheels, for she'll whip me aff her five stimparts o' the best aits at a down-sittin and ne'er fash her thumb. When ance her ringbanes and spavies, her crucks and cramps, are fairly soupl'd, she beets to, beets to, and ay the hindmost hour the tightest. I could wager her price to a thretty pennies, that for twa or three wooks' ridin at fifty miles a day, the deil-sticket [o'] five gallopers acqueesh Clyde and Whithorn could cast saut on her tail.

I hae dander'd owre a' the kintra frae Dumbar to Selcraig, and hae forgather'd wi' monie a guid fallow, and monie a weelfar'd huzzie. I met wi' twa dink quines in particlar, ane o' them a sonsie, fine, fodgel lass, baith braw and bonnie; the tither was a clean-shankit, straught, tight, weelfar'd winch, as blythe's a lintwhite on a flowerie thorn, and as sweet and modest's a new-blawn plumrose in a hazle shaw. They were baith bred to mainers by the beuk, and onie ane o' them had as muckle smeddum and rumblegumtion as the half o' some presbytries that you and I baith ken. They play'd me sik a deevil o' a shavie that I daur say if my harigals were turn'd out, ye wad see twa nicks i' the heart o' me like the mark o' a kail-whittle in a castock.

I was gaun to write you a lang pystle, but, Gude forgie me, I gat mysel sae notouriously bitchify'd the day after kail-time, that I can hardly stoiter but and ben.

My best respecks to the guidwife and a' our common friens, especiall Mr. and Mrs. Cruikshank, and the honest guidman o' Jock's Lodge.

I'll be in Dumfries the morn gif the beast be to the fore, and the branks bide hale. Gude be wi' you, Willie! Amen!

R. B.

(2.)　TO MR. WILLIAM NICOL.

Mauchline, June 18, 1787.

My dear Friend,

I am now arrived safe in my native country, after a very agreeable jaunt, and have the pleasure to find all my friends well. I breakfasted with your gray-headed, reverend friend, Mr. Smith; and was highly pleased both with the cordial welcome he gave me, and his most excellent appearance and sterling good sense.

I have been with Mr. Miller at Dalswinton, and am to meet him again in August. From my view of the lands, and his reception of my bardship, my hopes in that business are rather mended; but still they are but slender.

I am quite charmed with Dumfries folks—Mr. Burnside, the clergyman, in particular, is a man whom I shall ever gratefully remember; and his wife, Gude forgie me! I had almost broke the tenth commandment on her account! Simplicity, elegance, good sense, sweetness of disposition, good-humour, kind hospitality, are the constituents of her manner and heart; in short—but if I say one word more about her, I shall be directly in love with her.

I never, my friend, thought mankind very capable of anything generous; but the stateliness of the patricians in Edinburgh, and the servility of my plebeian brethren (who perhaps formerly eyed me askance) since I returned home, have nearly put me out of conceit altogether with my species. I have bought a pocket Milton, which I carry perpetually about with me, in order to study the sentiments—the dauntless magnanimity, the intrepid, unyielding independence, the desperate daring, and noble defiance of hardship, in that great personage, SATAN. 'Tis true, I have just now a little cash; but I am afraid the star that hitherto has shed its malignant, purpose-blasting rays full in my zenith; that noxious planet so baneful in its influences to the rhyming tribe, I much dread it is not yet beneath my horizon. Misfortune dodges the path of human life; the poetic mind finds itself miserably deranged in, and unfit for, the walks of business; add to all, that thoughtless follies and harebrained whims, like so many *ignes fatui*, eternally diverging from the right line of sober discretion, sparkle with stepbewitching blaze in the idly-gazing eyes of the poor heedless bard, till pop, "he falls like Lucifer, never to hope again." God grant this may be an unreal picture with respect to me! but should it not, I have very little dependence on mankind. I will close my letter with this tribute my heart bids me pay you—the many ties of acquaintance and friendship which I have, or think I have, in life, I have felt along the lines, and, damn them, they are almost all of them of such frail contexture, that I am sure they would not stand the breath of the least adverse breeze of fortune; but from you, my ever dear Sir, I look with confidence for the apostolic love that shall wait on me "through good report and bad report"— the love which Solomon emphatically says "is strong as death." My compliments to Mrs. Nicol, and all the circle of our common friends.   R. B.

P.S.—I shall be in Edinburgh about the latter end of July.

(3.)   TO MR. WILLIAM NICOL.

Auchtertyre, Monday, [*Oct.* 15, 1787.]

MY DEAR SIR,

I FIND myself very comfortable here, neither oppressed by ceremony nor mortified by neglect. Lady Augusta is a most engaging woman, and very happy in her family, which makes one's outgoings and incomings very agreeable. I called at Mr. Ramsay's of Auchtertyre as I came up the country, and am so delighted with him that I shall certainly accept of his invitation to spend a day or two with him as I return. I leave this place on Wednesday or Thursday.

Make my kind compliments to Mr. and Mrs. Cruikshank, and Mrs. Nicol, if she is returned. I am ever, dear Sir,

Your deeply indebted,

R. B.

(4.)   TO MR. WILLIAM NICOL.

Ellisland, Feb. 9, 1790.

MY DEAR SIR,

THAT d—mned mare of yours is dead. I would freely have given her price to have saved her; she has vexed me beyond description. Indebted as I was to your goodness beyond what I can ever repay, I eagerly grasped at your offer to have the mare with me. That I might at least show my readiness in wishing to be grateful, I took every care of her in my power. She was never crossed for riding above half a score of times by me or in my keeping. I drew her in the plough, one of three, for one poor week. I refused fifty-five shillings for her, which was the highest bode I could squeeze for her. I fed her up and had her in fine order for Dumfries fair; when four or five days before the fair, she was seized with an unaccountable disorder in the sinews, or somewhere in the bones of the neck; with a weakness or total want of power in her fillets; and in short the whole vertebræ of her spine seemed to be diseased and unhinged, and in eight-and-forty hours, in spite of the two best farriers in the country, she died, and be d—mned to her! The farriers said that she had been quite strained in the fillets beyond cure before you had bought her; and that the poor devil, though she might keep a little flesh, had been jaded and quite worn out with fatigue and oppression. While she was with me, she was under my own eye, and I assure you, my much-valued friend, every thing was done for her that could be done; and the accident has vexed me to the heart. In fact I could not pluck up spirits to write to you, on account of the unfortunate business.

There is little new in this country. Our theatrical company, of which you must have heard, leave us this week. Their merit and character are indeed very great, both on the stage and in private life: not a worthless creature among them; and their encouragement has been accordingly. Their usual run is from eighteen to twenty-five pounds a night; seldom less than the one, and the house will hold no more than the other. There have been repeated instances of sending away six, eight, and ten pounds a night for want of room. A new theatre is to be built by subscription; the first stone is to be laid on Friday first to come. Three hundred guineas have been raised by thirty subscribers, and thirty more might have been got if wanted. The manager, Mr. Sutherland, was introduced to me by a friend from Ayr; and a worthier or cleverer fellow I have rarely met with. Some of our clergy have slipt in by stealth now and then; but they have got up a farce of their own. You must have heard how the Rev. Mr. Lawson of Kirkmahoe, seconded by the Rev. Mr. Kirkpatrick of Dunscore, and the rest of that faction, have accused, in formal process, the unfortunate and Rev. Mr. Heron of Kirkgunzeon, that in ordaining Mr. Nielson to the cure of souls in Kirkbean, he, the said Heron, feloniously and treasonably bound the said Nielson to the Confession of Faith, *so far as it was agreeable to Reason and the Word of God!*

Mrs. B. begs to be remembered most gratefully to you.

Little Bobby and Frank are charmingly well and healthy. I am jaded to death with fatigue. For these two or three months, on an average, I have not ridden less than two hundred miles per week. I have done little in the poetic way. I have given Mr. Sutherland two Prologues; one of which was delivered last week. I have likewise strung four or five barbarous stanzas, to the tune of Chevy Chase, by way of Elegy on your poor unfortunate mare, beginning (the name she got here was Peg Nicholson)—

> Peg Nicholson was a good bay mare, &c.[*]

My best compliments to Mrs. Nicol, and little Neddy, and all the family; I hope Ned is a good scholar, and will come out to gather nuts and apples with me next harvest.

R. B.

[*] [See Posthumous Poetical Works.]

(5.)   TO MR. WILLIAM NICOL.

20th *February*, 1792.

O THOU, wisest among the Wise, meridian blaze of Prudence, full-moon of Discretion, and chief of many Counsellors! How infinitely is thy puddle-headed, rattle-headed, wrong-headed, round-headed slave indebted to thy super-eminent goodness, that from the luminous path of thy own right-lined rectitude, thou lookest benignly down on an erring wretch, of whom the zig-zag wanderings defy all the powers of calculation, from the simple copulation of units, up to the hidden mysteries of fluxions! May one feeble ray of that light of wisdom which darts from thy sensorium, straight as the arrow of heaven, and bright as the meteor of inspiration, may it be my portion, so that I may be less unworthy of the face and favour of that father of Proverbs and master of Maxims, that anti-pode of Folly, and magnet among the Sages, the wise and witty Willie Nicol! Amen! Amen! Yea, so be it!

For me! I am a beast, a reptile, and know nothing! From the cave of my ignorance, amid the fogs of my dulness, and pestilential fumes of my political heresies, I look up to thee, as doth a toad through the iron-barred lucerne of a pestiferous dungeon, to the cloudless glory of a summer sun! Sorely sighing in bitterness of soul, I say, When shall my name be the quotation of the wise, and my countenance be the delight of the godly, like the illustrious lord of Laggan's many hills? As for him, his works are perfect: never did the pen of Calumny blur the fair page of his reputation, nor the bolt of Hatred fly at his dwelling.

Thou mirror of Purity, when shall the elfin-lamp of my glimmerous understanding, purged from sensual appetites and gross desires, shine like the constellation of thy intellectual powers!—As for thee, thy thoughts are pure, and thy lips are holy. Never did the unhallowed breath of the powers of darkness, and the pleasures of darkness, pollute the sacred flame of thy sky-descended and heaven-bound desires: never did the vapours of impurity stain the unclouded serene of thy cerulean imagination. O that like thine were the tenor of my life, like thine the tenor of my conversation!—then should no friend fear for my strength, no enemy rejoice in my weakness! Then should I lie down and rise up, and none to make me afraid. May thy pity and thy prayer be exercised for, O thou lamp of Wisdom and mirror of Morality! thy devoted slave,

R. B.

[In connection with the above series of Letters, the reader may compare note on ' Willie Brew'd a Peck o' Maut :' also 'Highland Tour,' Appendix.]

(1.)   To Mr. Robert Ainslie.

Arrochar, by Loch Long, June 28,[*] 1787.

MY DEAR SIR,

I WRITE you this on my tour through a country where savage streams tumble over savage mountains, thinly over-spread with savage flocks, which starvingly support as savage inhabitants. My last stage was Inverary—to-morrow night's stage, Dumbarton. I ought sooner to have answered your kind letter, but you know I am a man of many sins.

R. B.

[*] [Mr. Chambers corrects this date, by interrogation, to 27.]

[The tour here referred to is the West Highland Tour, of the return from which we have an account in letter (3) to Mr. J. Smith at Linlithgow. On his way to Ayrshire, Burns seems to have passed through Paisley.]

(2.)   TO MR. ROBERT AINSLIE.

Mauchline, 23rd July, 1787.

MY DEAR AINSLIE,

THERE is one thing for which I set great store by you as a friend, and it is this—that I have not a friend upon earth, besides yourself, to whom I can talk nonsense without forfeiting some degree of his esteem. Now, to one like me, who never cares for speaking any thing else but nonsense, such a friend as you is an invaluable treasure. I was never a rogue, but have been a fool all my life; and, in spite of all my endeavours, I see now plainly that I shall never be wise. Now it rejoices my heart to have met with such a fellow as you, who, though you are not just such a hopeless fool as I, yet I trust you will never listen so much to the temptations of the devil, as to grow so very wise that you will in the least disrespect an honest fellow because he is a fool. In short, I have set you down as the staff of my old age, when the whole list of my friends will, after a decent share of pity, have forgot me.

> ' Though in the morn comes sturt and strife,
>   Yet joy may come at noon;
> And I hope to live a merry, merry life
>   When a' thir days are done.'

Write me soon, were it but a few lines just to tell me how that good sagacious man your father is—that kind dainty body your mother—that strapping chiel your brother Douglas—and my friend Rachel, who is as far before Rachel of old, as she was before her blear-eyed sister Leah.

R. B.

(3.)   TO MR. ROBERT AINSLIE, JUNIOR,
BERRYWELL, DUNSE.

Edinburgh, 23rd August, 1787.

> "As I gaed up to Dunse
> To warp a pickle yarn,
> Robin, silly body,
> He gat me wi' bairn."

FROM henceforth, my dear Sir, I am determined to set off with my letters like the periodical writers; namely, prefix a kind of text, quoted from some classic of undoubted authority, such as the author of the immortal piece, of which my text is a part. What I have to say on my text is exhausted in the chatter which I wrote you the other day, before I had the pleasure of receiving yours from Inverleithing; and sure never was anything more lucky, as I have but the time to write this, that Mr. Nicol, on the opposite side of the table, takes to correct a proof-sheet of a thesis. They are gabbling Latin so loud that I cannot hear what my own soul is saying in my own skull, so must just give you a matter-of-fact sentence or two, and end, if time permit, with a verse *de rei generatione*.

To-morrow I leave Edinburgh in a chaise; Nicol thinks it more comfortable than horse-back, to which I say, Amen; so Jenny Geddes goes home to Ayrshire, to use a phrase of my mother's, "wi' her finger in her mouth."

Now for a modest verse of classical authority:—

> The cats like kitchen ;
> The dogs like broo ;
> The lasses like the lads weel,
> And th' auld wives too.
> And we're a' noddin,
> Nid, nid, noddin,
> We're a' noddin fou at e'en.

If this does not please you, let me hear from you: if you write any time before the 1st of September, direct to Inverness, to be left at the post-office till called for; the next week at Aberdeen, the next at Edinburgh.

The sheet is done, and I shall just conclude with assuring you that I am, and ever with pride shall be,

My dear Sir, yours, &c.,

R. B.

Call your boy what you think proper, only interject Burns. What do you say to a Scripture name? Zimri Burns Ainslie, or Architophel, &c. Look your Bible for these two heroes; if you do this, I will repay the compliment.

(4.)   TO MR. ROBERT AINSLIE,
EDINBURGH.

Edinburgh, Sunday Morning,
Nov. 23, [25?] 1787.

I WISH, my dear Sir, you would not make any appointment to take us to Mr. Ainslie's to-night. On looking over my engagements, constitution, present state of my health, some little vexatious soul concerns, &c., I find I can't sup abroad to-night. I shall be in to-day till one o'clock, if you have a leisure hour.

You will think it romantic when I tell you, that I find the idea of your friendship almost necessary to my existence.—You assume a proper length of face in my bitter hours of blue-devilism, and you laugh fully up to my highest wishes at my good things. I don't know, upon the whole, if you are one of the first fellows in God's world, but you are so to me. I tell you this just now, in the conviction that some inequalities in my temper and manner may perhaps sometimes make you suspect that I am not so warmly as I ought to be your friend,

R. B.

(5.)   TO MR. ROBERT AINSLIE.

[Mauchline, 3rd March, 1788.] [*]

MY DEAR FRIEND,

I AM just returned from Mr. Miller's farm. My old friend whom I took with me was highly pleased with the bargain, and advised me to accept of it. He is the most intelligent sensible farmer in the county, and his advice has staggered me a good deal.[†] I have the two plans before me: I shall endeavour to balance them to the best of my judgment, and fix on the most eligible. On the whole, if I find Mr. Miller in the same favourable disposition as when I saw him last, I shall in all probability turn farmer.

I have been through sore tribulation and under much buffetting of the Wicked One since I came to this country. Jean I found banished like a martyr—forlorn, destitute, and friendless: I have reconciled her to her fate, and I have reconciled her to her mother. * * * *

I shall be in Edinburgh the middle of next week. My farming ideas I shall keep private till I see. I got a letter from Clarinda yesterday, and she tells me she has got no letter of mine but one. Tell her that I wrote to her from Glasgow, from Kilmarnock, from Mauchline, and yesterday from Cumnock as I returned from Dumfries. Indeed, she is the only person in Edinburgh I have written to till this day. How are your soul and body putting up?—a little like man and wife, I suppose.

Your faithful friend,

R. B.

* [This date is given by Mr. Ainslie. Compare letter to Mr. ——, immediately following this series.]
† [Mr. James Tennant of Glenconner is the person here referred to.]

(6.)   TO MR. ROBERT AINSLIE.

Mauchline, May 26, 1788.

MY DEAR FRIEND,

I AM two kind letters in your debt, but I have been from home, and horridly busy, buying and preparing for my farming business, over and above the plague of my Excise instructions, which this week will finish.

As I flatter my wishes that I foresee many future years' correspondence between us, 'tis foolish to talk of excusing dull epistles; a dull letter may be a very kind one. I have the pleasure to tell you that I have been extremely fortunate in all my buyings and bargainings hitherto—Mrs. Burns not excepted; which title I now avow to the world. I am truly pleased with this last affair: it has indeed added to my anxieties for futurity, but it has given a stability to my mind, and resolutions unknown before; and the poor girl has the most sacred enthusiasm of attachment to me, and has not a wish but to gratify my every idea of her deportment. I am interrupted.—Farewell! my dear Sir.

R. B.

(7.)   TO MR. ROBERT AINSLIE.

Ellisland, June 14, 1788.

THIS is now the third day, my dearest Sir, that I have sojourned in these regions; and during these three days you have occupied more of my thoughts than in three weeks preceding: in Ayrshire I have several variations of friendship's compass, here it points invariably to the pole. My farm gives me a good many uncouth cares and anxieties, but I hate the language of complaint. Job, or some one of his friends, says well—"Why should a living man complain?"

I have lately been much mortified with contemplating an unlucky imperfection in the very framing and construction of my soul: namely, a blundering inaccuracy of her olfactory organs in hitting the scent of craft or design in my fellow-creatures. I do not mean any compliment to my ingenuousness, or to hint that the defect is in consequence of the unsuspicious simplicity of conscious truth and honor; I take it to be, in some way or other, an imperfection in the mental sight; or, metaphor apart, some modification of dullness. In two or three small instances lately, I have been most shamefully out.

I have all along hitherto, in the warfare of life, been bred to arms among the light-horse—the piquet-guards of fancy; a kind of Hussars and Highlanders of the *Brain*; but I am firmly resolved to *sell out* of these giddy battalions, who have no ideas of a battle but fighting the foe, or of a siege but storming the town. Cost what it will, I am determined to *buy in* among the grave squadrons of heavy-armed Thought, or the artillery corps of plodding Contrivance.

What books are you reading, or what is the subject of your thoughts, besides the great studies of your profession? You said something about religion in your last. I don't exactly remember what it was, as the letter is in Ayrshire; but I thought it not only prettily said, but nobly thought. You will make a noble fellow if once you were married. I make no reservation of your being well-married; you have so much sense, and knowledge of human nature, that though you may not realize perhaps the ideas of romance, yet you will never be ill-married.

Were it not for the terrors of my ticklish situation respecting provision for a family of children, I am decidedly of opinion that the step I have taken is vastly for my happiness. As it is, I look to the Excise scheme as a certainty of maintenance. A maintenance!—luxury to what either Mrs. Burns or I were born to. Adieu!

R. B.

(8.)   TO MR. ROBERT AINSLIE.

Mauchline, 23rd June, 1788.

THIS letter, my dear Sir, is only a business scrap. Mr. Miers, profile painter in your town, has executed a profile of Dr. Blacklock for me: do me the favour to call for it, and sit to him yourself for me, which put in the same size as the Doctor's. The account of both profiles will be fifteen shillings, which I have given to James Connell, our Mauchline carrier, to pay you when you give him the parcel. You must not, my friend, refuse to sit. The time is short: when I sat to Mr. Miers, I am sure he did not exceed two minutes. I propose hanging Lord Glencairn, the Doctor, and you in trio, over my new chimney-piece that is to be. Adieu!

R. B.

(9.)   TO MR. ROBERT AINSLIE.

Ellisland, 30th June, 1788.

MY DEAR SIR,

I JUST now received your brief epistle; and, to take vengeance on your laziness, I have, you see, taken a long sheet of writing-paper, and have begun at the top of the page, intending to scribble on to the very last corner.

I am vexed at that affair of the   *   *   *, but dare not enlarge on the subject until you send me your direction, as I suppose that will be altered on your late master and friend's death. I am concerned for the old fellow's exit, only as I fear it may be to your disadvantage in any respect —for an old man's dying, except he have been a very benevolent character, or in some particular situation of life that the welfare of the poor or the helpless depended on him, I think it an event of the most trifling moment to the world. Man is naturally a kind, benevolent animal, but he is dropped into such a needy situation here in this vexatious world, and has such a whoreson hungry, growling, multiplying pack of necessities, appetites, passions, and desires about him, ready to devour him for want of other food;

that in fact he must lay aside his cares for others that he may look properly to himself. You have been imposed upon in paying Mr. Miers for the profile of a Mr. H. I did not mention it in my letter to you, nor did I ever give Mr. Miers any such order. I have no objection to lose the money, but I will not have any such profile in my possession.

I desired the carrier to pay you, but as I mentioned only fifteen shillings to him, I will rather enclose you a guinea note. I have it not, indeed, to spare here, as I am only a sojourner in a strange land in this place; but in a day or two I return to Mauchline, and there I have the bank-notes through the house like salt permits.

There is a great degree of folly in talking unnecessarily of one's private affairs. I have just now been interrupted by one of my new neighbours, who has made himself absolutely contemptible in my eyes, by his silly, garrulous pruriency. I know it has been a fault of my own, too; but from this moment I abjure it as I would the service of hell! Your poets, spendthrifts, and other fools of that kidney, pretend forsooth to crack their jokes on prudence; but 'tis a squalid vagabond glorying in his rags. Still, imprudence respecting money matters is much more pardonable than imprudence respecting character. I have no objection to prefer prodigality to avarice, in some few instances; but I appeal to your observation, if you have not met, and often met, with the same disingenuousness, the same hollow-hearted insincerity, and disintegritive depravity of principle, in the hackneyed victims of profusion, as in the unfeeling children of parsimony. I have every possible reverence for the much-talked-of world beyond the grave, and I wish that which piety believes, and virtue deserves, may be all matter of fact. But in things belonging to, and terminating in this present scene of existence, man has serious and interesting business on hand. Whether a man shall shake hands with welcome in the distinguished elevation of respect, or shrink from contempt in the abject corner of insignificance; whether he shall wanton under the tropic of plenty, at least enjoy himself in the comfortable latitudes of easy convenience, or starve in the arctic circle of dreary poverty; whether he shall rise in the manly consciousness of a self-approving mind, or sink beneath a galling load of regret and remorse —these are alternatives of the last moment.

You see how I preach. You used occasionally to sermonize too; I wish you would, in charity, favor me with a sheet full in your own way. I admire the close of a letter Lord Bolingbroke writes to Dean Swift: "Adieu, dear Swift! with all thy faults I love thee entirely; make an effort to love me with all mine!" Humble servant, and all that trumpery, is now such a prostituted business, that honest Friendship, in her sincere way, must have recourse to her primitive, simple,—farewell!

R. B.

*[Mr. Samuel Mitchelson, W.S., had been Mr. Ainslie's master. He died June 21, 1788.—Chambers.]

<hr>

(10.)   TO MR. ROBERT AINSLIE.

Ellisland, January 6, 1789.

MANY happy returns of the season to you, my dear Sir! May you be comparatively happy up to your comparative worth among the sons of men; which wish would, I am sure, make you one of the most blest of the human race.

I do not know if passing a "Writer to the Signet" be a trial of scientific merit, or a mere business of friends and interest. However it be, let me quote you my two favourite passages, which, though I have repeated them ten thousand times, still they rouse my manhood and steel my resolution like inspiration:—

> ————————On reason build resolve,
> That column of true majesty in man.—*Young.*

> "Hear, Alfred, hero of the state,
> Thy genius Heaven's high will declare;
> The triumph of the truly great,
> Is never, never to despair!
> Is never to despair!"—*Masque of Alfred.*

I grant you enter the lists of life, to struggle for bread, business, notice, and distinction, in common with hundreds. —But who are they? Men like yourself: and of that aggregate body your compeers, seven-tenths of them come short of your advantages natural and accidental; while two of those that remain either neglect their parts, as flowers blooming in a desert, or mis-spend their strength, like a bull goring a bramble-bush.

But to change the theme: I am still catering for Johnson's publication; and among others, I have brushed up the following favourite song a little, with a view to your worship. I have only altered a word here and there; but if you like the humour of it, we shall think of a stanza or two to add to it.

R. B.

<hr>

(11.)   TO MR. ROBERT AINSLIE.

Ellisland, 8th June, 1789.

MY DEAR FRIEND,

I AM perfectly ashamed of myself when I look at the date of your last. It is not that I forget the friend of my heart and the companion of my peregrinations; but I have been condemned to drudgery beyond sufferance, though not, thank God, beyond redemption. I have had a collection of poems by a lady put into my hands to prepare them for the press; which horrid task, with sowing corn with my own hand, a parcel of masons, wrights, plasterers, &c., to attend to, roaming on business through Ayrshire—all this was against me, and the very first dreadful article was of itself too much for me.

13th. I have not had a moment to spare from incessant toil since the 8th. Life, my dear Sir, is a serious matter. You know by experience that a man's individual self is a good deal; but believe me, a wife and family of children, whenever you have the honour to be a husband and a father, will show you that your present and most anxious hours of solitude are spent on trifles. The welfare of those who are very dear to us, whose only support, hope, and stay we are—this, to a generous mind, is another sort of more important object of care than any concerns whatever which centre merely in the individual. On the other hand, let no young, unmarried, rakehelly dog among you, make a song of his pretended liberty and freedom from care. If the relations we stand in to king, country, kindred, and friends, be any thing but the visionary fancies of dreaming metaphysicians; if religion, virtue, magnanimity, generosity, humanity, and justice, be aught but empty sounds; then the man who may be said to live only for others, for the beloved, honourable female, whose tender faithful embrace endears life, and for the helpless little innocents who are to be the men and women, the worshippers of his God, the subjects of his king, and the support, nay the very vital existence of his COUNTRY, in the ensuing age;—compare such a man with any fellow whatever, who, whether he bustle and push in business among labourers, clerks, statesmen; or whether he roar and rant, and drink and sing in taverns—a fellow over whose grave no one will breathe a single heigh-ho, except from the cobweb-tie of what is called good-fellowship—who has no view nor aim but what terminates in himself—if there be any grovelling earthborn wretch of our species, a renegade to common sense, who would fain believe that the noble creature Man is no better than a sort of fungus, generated out of nothing, nobody knows how, and soon dissipated in nothing, nobody knows where; such a stupid beast, such a crawling reptile, might balance the forgoing unexaggerated comparison, but no one else would have the patience.

Forgive me, my dear Sir, for this long silence. *To make you amends*, I shall send you soon, and more encouraging still, without any postage, one or two rhymes of my later manufacture.

R. B.

I know not how the word exciseman, or still more opprobrious, gauger, will sound in your ears. I too have seen the day when my auditory nerves would have felt very delicately on this subject; but a wife and children are things which have a wonderful power in blunting those kind of sensations. Fifty pounds a year for life, and a provision for widows and orphans, you will allow, is no bad settlement for a *poet*. For the ignominy of the profession, I have the encouragement which I once heard a recruiting sergeant give to a numerous, if not a respectable audience, in the streets of Kilmarnock.—" Gentlemen, for your further and better encouragement, I can assure you that our regiment is the most blackguard corps under the crown, and consequently with us an honest fellow has the surest chance for preferment."

You need not doubt that I find several very unpleasant and disagreeable circumstances in my business; but I am tired with and disgusted at the language of complaint against the evils of life. Human existence in the most favourable situations does not abound with pleasures, and has its inconveniences and ills; capricious, foolish man mistakes these inconveniences and ills, as if they were the peculiar property of his particular situation; and hence that eternal fickleness, that love of change, which has ruined, and daily does ruin, many a fine fellow, as well as many a blockhead, and is almost without exception a constant source of disappointment and misery.

I long to hear from you how you go on—not so much in business as in life. Are you pretty well satisfied with your own exertions, and tolerably at ease in your internal reflections? 'Tis much to be a great character as a lawyer, but beyond comparison more to be a great character as a man. That you may be both the one and the other is the earnest wish, and that you *will* be both is the firm persuasion of,

My dear Sir, &c.,

R. B.

     TO MR. ROBERT AINSLIE.

Ellisland, 1st Nov., 1789.

MY DEAR FRIEND,

I HAD written you long ere now, could I have guessed where to find you, for I am sure you have more good sense than to waste the precious days of vacation-time in the dirt of business and Edinburgh.—Wherever you are, God bless you, and lead you not into temptation, but deliver you from evil!

I do not know if I have informed you that I am now appointed to an Excise division, in the middle of which my house and farm lie. In this I was extremely lucky. Without ever having been an expectant, as they call their journeymen excisemen, I was directly planted down to all intents and purposes an officer of Excise; there to flourish and bring forth fruits—worthy of repentance.

     TO MR. ROBERT AINSLIE.

[Dumfries, 1791.]

MY DEAR AINSLIE,

CAN you minister to a mind diseased? can you, amid the horrors of penitence, regret, remorse, head-ache, nausea, and all the rest of the d——d hounds of hell, that beset a poor wretch who has been guilty of the sin of drunkenness—can you speak peace to a troubled soul?

Misérable perdu that I am! I have tried every thing that used to amuse me, but in vain; here must I sit, a monument of the vengeance laid up in store for the wicked, slowly counting every click of the clock as it slowly, slowly numbers over these lazy scoundrels of hours, who, d——n them, are ranked up before me, every one at his neighbour's backside, and every one with a burthen of anguish on his back, to pour on my devoted head—and there is none to pity me.

My wife scolds me! my business torments me, and my sins come staring me in the face, every one telling a more bitter tale than his fellow. * * * I began *Eldbanks and Elibraes*, but the stanzas fell unenjoyed and unfinished from my listless tongue: at last I luckily thought of reading over an old letter of yours, that lay by me in my book-case, and I felt something for the first time since I opened my eyes, of pleasurable existence.——Well—I begin to breathe a little since I began to write to you. How are you, and what are you doing? How goes Law? Apropos, for connexion's sake, do not address to me supervisor, for that is an honor I cannot pretend to.—I am on the list, as we call it, for a supervisor, and will be called out by and by to act as one; but at present, I am a simple gauger, tho' t'other day I got an appointment to an excise division of £25 per annum better than the rest. My present income, down money, is £70 per annum.

I have one or two good fellows here whom you would be glad to know.

R. B.

(14.)   TO MR. ROBERT AINSLIE,
ST. JAMES'S STREET, EDINBURGH.

[*April 26, 1793.*]

I AM d—mnably out of humour, my dear Ainslie, and that is the reason why I take up the pen to you; 'tis the nearest way (*probatum est*) to recover my spirits again.

I received your last, and was much entertained with it; but I will not at this time, nor at any other time, answer it. —Answer a letter! I never could answer a letter in my life! —I have written many a letter in return for letters I have received; but then—they were original matter—spurt-away! zig here, zag there; as if the devil that, my Grannie (an old woman *indeed*) often told me, rode on Will-o'-wisp, or in her more classic phrase, SPUNKIE, were looking over my elbow. A happy thought that idea has engendered in my head! SPUNKIE—thou shalt henceforth be my Symbol, Signature, and Tutelary Genius! Like thee, hap-step-and-lowp, here-awa-there-awa, higglety-pigglety, pell-mell, hither-and-yont, ram-stam, happy-go-lucky, up-tails-a'-by-the-light-o'-the-moon—has been, is, and shall be, my progress through the mosses and moors of this vile, bleak, barren, wilderness of a life of ours.

Come then, my guardian spirit! like thee may I skip away, amusing myself by and at my own light: and if any opaque-souled lubber of mankind complain that my elfine, lambent, glimmerous wanderings have misled his stupid steps over precipices, or into bogs, let the thick-headed blunderbuss recollect that he is not SPUNKIE:—that

"SPUNKIE'S wanderings could not copied be;
Amid these perils none durst walk but he."—

I feel vastly better. I give you joy * * * * * * *
I have no doubt but scholarcraft may be caught, as a Scotchman catches the itch,—by friction. How else can you account for it, that born blockheads, by mere dint of *handling* books, grow so wise that even they themselves are equally convinced of and surprised at their own parts? I once carried this philosophy to that degree that in a knot of country folks who had a library amongst them, and who, to the honor of their good sense, made me factotum in the business;* one of our members, a little, wise-looking, squat, upright, jabbering body of a tailor, I advised him, instead of turning over the leaves, *to bind the book on his back,*— Johnnie took the hint; and as our meetings were every fourth Saturday, and Prickhouse having a good Scots mile to walk in coming, and of course another in returning, Bodkin was sure to lay his hand on some heavy quarto or ponderous folio, with, and under which, wrapt up in his grey plaid, he grew wise as he grew weary, all the way home. He carried this so far, that an old musty Hebrew concordance, which we had in a present from a neighbouring priest, by mere dint of applying it as doctors do a blistering plaster, between his shoulders, Stitch, in a dozen pilgrimages, acquired as much rational theology as the said priest had done by forty years' perusal of the pages.†

Tell me, and tell me truly, what you think of this theory.

Yours,

SPUNKIE.

* [Compare letter to Sir John Sinclair—p. 116.]
† [The reader will observe in this, and in several other sentences in immediately preceding letters—(11) and (12) particularly—of this series, a sort of unconnected desultory style—which seems to indicate the occasional irritability and haste the writer was exposed to at this period of his life; which, although they were not allowed to appear before all correspondents, could hardly be concealed from a friend.]

To Mr. [———]*

[*Mauchline, March 3d—8th,*] 1788.

MY DEAR SIR,

My life, since I saw you last, has been one continued hurry; that savage hospitality which knocks a man down with strong liquors, is the devil. I have a sore warfare in this world; the devil, the world, and the flesh are three formidable foes. The first I generally try to fly from; the second, alas! generally flies from me; but the third is my plague, worse than the ten plagues of Egypt.

I have been looking over several farms in this country; one in particular, in Nithsdale, pleased me so well, that if my offer to the proprietor is accepted, I shall commence farmer at Whitsunday. If farming do not appear eligible, I shall have recourse to my other shift: but this to a friend.

I set out for Edinburgh on Monday morning; how long I stay there is uncertain, but you will know so soon as I can inform you myself. However I determine, poesy must be laid aside for some time; my mind has been vitiated with idleness, and it will take a good deal of effort to habituate it to the routine of business.

I am, my dear Sir,

Yours sincerely,

R. B.

* [This letter is published by Cunningham as addressed to Ainslie; but the letter, it appears, has no address of its own, and is most reasonably supposed by Chambers to have been addressed to some other correspondent, name unknown. Two letters at the same time, on the same subject, and almost in the same words, were not likely to be addressed by our Author to the same person. Compare letter (5) to Ainslie, also (7) to Cruikshank.]

To Mr. William Cruikshank,

(1.)   ST. JAMES'S SQUARE, EDINBURGH.

Auchtertyre, Monday, [*Oct.* 15, 1787.]

I HAVE nothing, my dear Sir, to write to you, but that I feel myself exceedingly comfortably situated in this good family; just notice enough to make me easy but not to embarrass me. I was storm-staid two days at the foot of the Ochil-hills, with Mr. Tait of Herveyston and Mr. Johnston of Alva; but was so well pleased, that I shall certainly spend a day on the banks of the Devon, as I return. I leave this place I suppose on Wednesday, and shall devote a day to Mr. Ramsay at Auchtertyre, near Stirling—a man to whose worth I cannot do justice. My respectful kind compliments to Mrs. Cruikshank, and my dear little Jeanie; and if you see Mr. Masterton, please remember me to him.

I am ever, my dear Sir, &c.,

R. B.

[Mr. Cruikshank, our readers are aware, is the friend by whom our Author was so kindly entertained after his accident in Edinburgh. This letter was first published in the *Gentleman's Magazine*, 1832, without an address, but manifestly belongs to Mr. Cruikshank. The reader may compare letter (3) to Nicol, of the same date, p. 159.]

(2.)   TO MR. WILLIAM CRUIKSHANK.

Mauchline, 3rd March, 1788.

MY DEAR SIR,

APOLOGIES for not writing are frequently like apologies for not singing—the apology better than the song. I have fought my way severely through the savage hospitality of this country, [the object of all hosts being] to send every guest drunk to bed if they can.

I executed your commission in Glasgow, and I hope the cocoa came safe. 'Twas the same price and the very same kind as your former parcel, for the gentleman recollected your buying there perfectly well.

I should return my thanks for your hospitality (I leave a blank for the epithet, as I know none can do it justice) to a poor, wayfaring bard, who was spent and almost overpowered fighting with prosaic wickednesses in high places; but I am afraid lest you should burn the letter whenever you come to the passage, so I pass over it in silence. I am just returned from visiting Mr. Miller's farm. The friend whom I told you I would take with me was highly pleased with the farm; and as he is, without exception, the

most intelligent farmer in the country, he has staggered me a good deal. I have the two plans of life before me; I shall balance them to the best of my judgment, and fix on the most eligible. I have written Mr. Miller, and shall wait on him when I come to town, which shall be the beginning or middle of next week; I would be in sooner, but my unlucky knee is rather worse, and I fear for some time will scarcely stand the fatigue of my Excise instructions. I only mention these ideas to you; and, indeed, except Mr. Ainslie, whom I intend writing to to-morrow, I will not write at all to Edinburgh till I return to it. I would send my compliments to Mr. Nicol, but he would be hurt if he knew I wrote to anybody and not to him: so I shall only beg my best, kindest, kindest compliments to my worthy hostess and the sweet little Rose-bud.*

So soon as I am settled in the routine of life, either as an Excise-officer, or as a farmer, I propose myself great pleasure from a regular correspondence with the only man almost I ever saw who joined the most attentive prudence with the warmest generosity.

I am much interested for that best of men, Mr. Wood; I hope he is in better health and spirits than when I saw him last. I am ever, my dearest friend,

Your obliged, humble servant,

R. B.

* [Mr. Cruikshank's daughter. Compare note on Lines to Miss C., Poetical Works, p. 268.]

(3.)   TO MR. WILLIAM CRUIKSHANK.

Ellisland, [*December,*] 1788.

I HAVE not room, my dear friend, to answer all the particulars of your last kind letter. I shall be in Edinburgh on some business very soon; and as I shall be two days, or perhaps three, in town, we shall discuss matters *vivâ voce*. My knee, I believe, will never be entirely well; and an unlucky fall this winter has made it still worse. I well remember the circumstance you allude to respecting Creech's opinion of Mr. Nicol; but, as the first gentleman owes me still about fifty pounds, I dare not meddle in the affair.

It gave me a very heavy heart to read such accounts of the consequences of your quarrel with that puritanic, rotten-hearted, hell-commissioned scoundrel, A——. If, notwithstanding your unprecedented industry in public, and your irreproachable conduct in private life, he still has you so much in his power, what ruin may he not bring on some others I could name?

Many and happy returns of seasons to you, with your dearest and worthiest friend, and the lovely little pledge of your happy union. May the great Author of life, and of every enjoyment that can render life delightful, make her that comfortable blessing to you both, which you so ardently wish for, and which, allow me to say, you so well deserve! Glance over the foregoing verses, and let me have your blots.

R. B.

To James Dalrymple, Esq.,
ORANGEFIELD.

Edinburgh, [December 10, 1786?]

DEAR SIR,

I SUPPOSE the Devil is so elated with his success with you, that he is determined by a *coup de main* to complete his purposes on you all at once, in making you a poet. I broke open the letter you sent me; hummed over the rhymes; and, as I saw they were extempore, said to myself, they were very well; but when I saw at the bottom a name that I shall ever value with grateful respect, "I gapit wide, but naething spak." I was nearly as much struck as the friends of Job, of affliction-bearing memory, when they sat down with him seven days and seven nights, and spake not a word.

I am naturally of a superstitious cast, and as soon as my wonder-scared imagination regained its consciousness, and resumed its functions, I cast about what this mania of yours might portend. My foreboding ideas had the wide stretch of possibility; and several events, great in their magnitude, and important in their consequences, occurred to my fancy. The downfal of the conclave, or the crushing of the Cork rumps; a ducal coronet to Lord George Gordon and the Protestant interest; or St. Peter's keys to * * * *

You want to know how I come on. I am just *in statu quo,* or, not to insult a gentleman with my Latin, in "auld use and wont." The noble Earl of Glencairn took me by the hand to-day, and interested himself in my concerns, with a goodness like that benevolent Being whose image he so richly bears. He is a stronger proof of the immortality of the soul, than any that philosophy ever produced. A mind like his can never die. Let the worshipful squire H. L., the reverend Mass J. M., go into their primitive nothing. At best, they are but ill-digested lumps of chaos—only, one of them strongly tinged with bituminous particles and sulphureous effluvia. But my noble patron, eternal as the heroic swell of magnanimity, and the generous throb of benevolence, shall look on with princely eye at "the war of elements, the wreck of matter, and the crush of worlds."

R. B.

[Mr. Dalrymple of Orangefield, near Ayr, was, by the mother's side, cousin-german to the Earl of Glencairn.]

To St. James's Lodge,
TARBOLTON.

Edinburgh, 23rd August, 1787.

MEN AND BRETHREN,

I AM truly sorry it is not in my power to be at your quarterly meeting. If I must be absent in body, believe me, I shall be present in spirit. I suppose those who owe us monies, by bill or otherwise, will appear.—I mean those we summoned. If you please, I wish you would delay prosecuting defaulters till I come home. The court is up, and I will be home before it sits down. In the meantime, to take a note of who appear and who do not, of our faulty debtors, will be right in my humble opinion; and those who confess debt and crave days, I think we should spare them. Farewell!

> Within your dear mansion may wayward Contention,
>   And withered Envy ne'er enter;
> May Secrecy round be the mystical bound,
>   And Brotherly Love be the centre.

ROBT. BURNS.

To the Free Masons of
  ST. JAMES'S LODGE,
    Care of H. Manson,
      TARBOLTON.

[The insignia used by the Poet are still preserved with religious care in this Lodge.]

To Charles Hay, Esq.,
ADVOCATE.

[ENCLOSING VERSES ON THE DEATH OF THE LORD PRESIDENT.]

SIR,

THE enclosed poem was written in consequence of your suggestion, last time I had the pleasure of seeing you. It cost me an hour or two of next morning's sleep, but did not please me; so it lay by, an ill-digested effort, till the other day that I gave it a critic brush. These kind of subjects are much hackneyed; and, besides, the wailings of the rhyming tribe over the ashes of the great are cursedly suspicious, and out of all character for sincerity. These ideas damped my Muse's fire; however, I have done the best I could, and, at all events, it gives me an opportunity of declaring that I have the honor to be, Sir, your obliged humble servant,

R. B.

To Mr. Francis Howden.
JEWELLER, PARLIAMENT SQUARE.

THE bearer of this will deliver you a small shade to set; which, my dear sir, if you would highly oblige a poor cripple devil as I am at present, you will finish at furthest against to-morrow evening. It goes a hundred miles into the country; and if it is at me by five o'clock to-morrow evening, I have an opportunity of a private hand to convey it; if not, I don't know how to get it sent. Set it just as you did the others you did for me—"in the neatest and cheapest manner;" both to answer as a breast-pin, and with a ring to answer as a locket. Do despatch it; as it

is, I believe, the pledge of love, and perhaps the prelude
to ma-tri-mo-ny. Everybody knows the auld wife's observation when she saw a poor dog going to be hanged—
"God help us! it's the gate we ha'e a' to gang!"

The parties, one of them at least, is a very particular
acquaintance of mine—the honest lover. He only needs a
little of an advice which my grandmother, rest her soul,
often gave me, and I as often neglected—

> "Look twice ere ye loup ance."   [see]

Let me conjure you, my friend, by the bended bow of
Cupid—by the unloosed cestus of Vestus—by the lighted
torch of Hymen—that you will have the locket finished by
the time mentioned? And if your worship would have as
much Christian charity as call with it yourself, and comfort
a poor wretch, not wounded indeed by Cupid's arrow, but
bruised by a good, serious, agonising, damned, hard knock
on the knee, you will gain the earnest prayers, when he
does pray, of, dear sir, your humble servant,

ROBT. BURNS.

ST. JAMES'S SQUARE, No. 2, Attic Story.

(1.)   To Mr. Richard Brown,
IRVINE.

Edinburgh, 30th Dec., 1787.

MY DEAR SIR,

I HAVE met with few things in life which have given me
more pleasure than Fortune's kindness to you since those
days in which we met in the vale of misery; as I can
honestly say, that I never knew a man who more truly
deserved it, or to whom my heart more truly wished it. I
have been much indebted since that time to your story and
sentiments for steeling my mind against evils, of which I
have had a pretty decent share. My will-o'-wisp fate you
know: do you recollect a Sunday we spent together in Eglintoun woods? You told me, on my repeating some verses
to you, that you wondered I could resist the temptation of
sending verses of such merit to a magazine. It was from
this remark I derived that idea of my own pieces, which
encouraged me to endeavour at the character of a poet. I
am happy to hear that you will be two or three months at
home. As soon as a bruised limb will permit me, I shall
return to Ayrshire, and we shall meet; "and faith, I hope
we'll not sit dumb, nor yet cast out!"

I have much to tell you "of men, their manners, and
their ways," perhaps a little of the other sex. Apropos, I
beg to be remembered to Mrs. Brown. There I doubt not,
my dear friend, but you have found substantial happiness.
I expect to find you something of an altered but not a
different man; the wild, bold, generous young fellow composed into the steady affectionate husband, and the fond
careful parent. For me, I am just the same will-o'-wisp
being I used to be. About the first and fourth quarters

of the moon, I generally set in for the trade-wind of wisdom;
but about the full and change, I am the luckless victim of
mad tornadoes, which blow me into chaos. Almighty love
still reigns and revels in my bosom; and I am at this moment
ready to hang myself for a young Edinburgh widow, who has
wit and wisdom more murderously fatal than the assassin-
ating stiletto of the Sicilian bandit, or the poisoned arrow
of the savage African. My Highland dirk, that used to hang
beside my crutches, I have gravely removed into a neighbouring closet, the key of which I cannot command in case of
spring-tide paroxysms. You may guess of her wit by the
following verses, which she sent me the other day.*

My best compliments to our friend Allan. Adieu!

R. B.

* ["Talk not of love, it gives me pain," &c.—Letter (3) to Clarinda, p. 37.]

(2.)   TO MR. RICHARD BROWN.

Edinburgh, February 15, 1788.

MY DEAR FRIEND,

I RECEIVED yours with the greatest pleasure, I shall arrive
at Glasgow on Monday evening, and beg, if possible, you will
meet me on Tuesday. I shall wait you Tuesday all day. I
shall be found at Davie's Black Bull Inn. I am hurried, as
if hunted by fifty devils, else I should go to Greenock; but
if you cannot possibly come, write me, if possible, to Glasgow,
on Monday; or direct to me at Mossgiel by Mauchline; and
name a day and place in Ayrshire, within a fortnight from
this date, where I may meet you. I only stay a fortnight
in Ayrshire, and return to Edinburgh.

I am ever, my dearest friend, yours,

R. B.

(3.)   TO MR. RICHARD BROWN.

Mossgiel, 24th February, 1788.

MY DEAR SIR,

I CANNOT get the proper direction for my friend in Jamaica,
but the following will do:—To Mr. Jo. Hutchinson, at Jo.
Brownrigg's, Esq., care of Mr. Benjamin Henriquez, merchant, Orange Street, Kingston. I arrived here, at my
brother's, only yesterday, after fighting my way through
Paisley and Kilmarnock, against those old powerful foes of
mine, the devil, the world, and the flesh—so terrible in the
fields of dissipation. I have met with few incidents in my
life which gave me so much pleasure as meeting you in
Glasgow. There is a time of life beyond which we cannot
form a tie worth the name of friendship. "O youth! enchanting stage, profusely blest." Life is a fairy scene;
almost all that deserves the name of enjoyment or pleasure
is only a charming delusion; and in comes repining age in

all the gravity of hoary wisdom, and wretchedly chases away the bewitching phantom. When I think of life, I resolve to keep a strict look-out in the course of economy, for the sake of worldly convenience and independence of mind: to cultivate intimacy with a few of the companions of youth, that they may be the friends of age; never to refuse my liquorish humour a handful of the sweetmeats of life, when they come not too dear; and, for futurity—

> "The present moment is our ain,
> The niest we never saw!"

How like you my philosophy? Give my best compliments to Mrs. B., and believe me to be,

My dear Sir, yours most truly,

R. B.

(4.)   TO MR. RICHARD BROWN.

Mauchline, 7th March, 1788.

I HAVE been out of the country, my dear friend, and have not had an opportunity of writing till now, when I am afraid you will be gone out of the country too. I have been looking at farms, and, after all, perhaps I may settle in the character of a farmer. I have got so vicious a bent to idleness, and have ever been so little a man of business, that it will take no ordinary effort to bring my mind properly into the routine: but you will say a "great effort is worthy of you." I say so myself; and butter up my vanity with all the stimulating compliments I can think of. Men of grave, geometrical minds, the sons of "which was to be demonstrated," may cry up reason as much as they please: but I have always found an honest passion, or native instinct, the truest auxiliary in the warfare of this world. Reason almost always comes to me like an unlucky wife to a poor devil of a husband—just in sufficient time to add her reproaches to his other grievances.

[He speaks afterwards of Jean and her then unpleasant circumstances, and adds]

I am gratified with your kind enquiries after her [Jean]: as, after all, I may say with Othello:—

> ———— "Excellent wretch!
> Perdition catch my soul, but I do love thee."

I go for Edinburgh on Monday. Yours,

R. B.

(5.)   TO MR. RICHARD BROWN.

Glasgow, 26th March, 1788.

I AM monstrously to blame, my dear Sir, in not writing to you, and sending you the Directory. I have been getting my tack extended, as I have taken a farm; and I have been racking shop accounts with Mr. Creech; both of which, to-

gether with watching, fatigue, and a load of care almost too heavy for my shoulders, have in some degree actually fevered me.* I really forgot the Directory yesterday, which vexed me; but I was convulsed with rage a great part of the day. I have to thank you for the ingenious, friendly, and elegant epistle from your friend Mr. Crawford.† I shall certainly write to him, but not now. This is merely a card to you, as I am posting to Dumfries-shire, where many perplexing arrangements await me. I am vexed about the Directory; but, my dear Sir, forgive me: these eight days I have been positively crazed. My compliments to Mrs. B. I shall write to you at Grenada.

I am ever, my dearest friend, yours,

R. B.

* [Mr. Chambers computes that at this time, all accidental and other expenses taken into account as deductions from his capital, our Author could not have more than £380 in pocket. Mr. Creech's business relations to the Poet will be found more fully stated in note to "Willie's Awa"—Posthumous Works.]

† [Mr. Thomas Crawford of Cartsburn, Greenock, from whom the Poet a few days before had a friendly, jocular invitation to visit him—much too highly spoken of in above terms.]

(6.)   TO MR. RICHARD BROWN.

Mauchline, 21st May, 1789.

MY DEAR FRIEND,

I WAS in the country by accident, and hearing of your safe arrival, I could not resist the temptation of wishing you joy on your return—wishing you would write to me before you sail again—wishing you would always set me down as your bosom-friend—wishing you long life and prosperity, and that every good thing may attend you—wishing Mrs. Brown and your little ones as free of the evils of this world, as is consistent with humanity—wishing you and she were to make two at the ensuing lying-in, with which Mrs. B. threatens very soon to favour me—wishing I had longer time to write to you at present; and, finally, wishing that, if there is to be another state of existence, Mr. B., Mrs. B., our little ones, and both families, and you and I, in some snug retreat, may make a jovial party to all eternity!

My direction is at Ellisland, near Dumfries. Yours,

R. B.

(7.)   TO MR. RICHARD BROWN.

Ellisland, 4th November, 1789.

I HAVE been so hurried, my ever-dear friend, that though I got both your letters, I have not been able to command an hour to answer them as I wished; and, even now, you are to look on this as merely confessing debt, and craving days. Few things could have given me so much pleasure as the news that you were once more safe and sound on

* Y

terra firma, and happy in that place where happiness is alone to be found—in the fireside circle. May the benevolent Director of all things peculiarly bless you in all those endearing connexions consequent on the tender and venerable names of husband and father! I have indeed been extremely lucky in getting an additional income of £50 a year, while, at the same time, the appointment will not cost me above £10 or £12 per annum of expenses more than I must have inevitably incurred. The worst circumstance is, that the Excise division which I have got is so extensive—no less than ten parishes to ride over; and it abounds besides with so much business, that I can scarcely steal a spare moment. However, labour endears rest, and both together are absolutely necessary for the proper enjoyment of human existence. I cannot meet you any where. No less than an order from the Board of Excise, at Edinburgh, is necessary before I can have so much time as to meet you in Ayrshire. But do you come, and see me. We must have a social day, and perhaps lengthen it out half the night, before you go again to sea. You are the earliest friend I now have on earth, my brothers excepted: and is not that an endearing circumstance? When you and I first met, we were at the green period of human life. The twig would easily take a bent, but would as easily return to its former state. You and I not only took a mutual bent, but, by the melancholy, though strong influence of being both of the family of the unfortunate, we were entwined with one another in our growth towards advanced age; and blasted be the sacrilegious hand that shall attempt to undo the union! You and I must have one bumper to my favorite toast, "May the companions of our youth be the friends of our old age!" Come and see me one year; I shall see you at Port-Glasgow the next; and if we can contrive to have a gossiping between our two bed-fellows, it will be so much additional pleasure. Mrs. Burns joins me in kind compliments to you and Mrs. Brown. Adieu! I am ever, my dear Sir, yours,

R. B.

[On the above correspondence Professor Walker remarks—"The letters to Richard Brown, written at a period when the Poet was in the full blaze of reputation, showed that he was at no time so dazzled with success as to forget the friends who had anticipated the public by discovering his merit."

Brown himself, we are informed by Cunningham, "retrieved his fortunes, and lived much respected in Greenock to a good old age. He said Burns had little to learn in matters of levity, when he became acquainted with him." To judge by all the letters now before us, our own conviction certainly is, that our Author, in his celebrated letter to Dr. Moore, has exaggerated both his own failings in this respect and those of his young friend Brown. He could never have written such letters as the above to any man who had done him so grievous a moral injury as there implied. Compare Autobiographical Letter to Dr. Moore—p. 72.]

(1.)

To Mr. Robert Cleghorn,
[SAUGHTON MILLS, EDINBURGH.]

Mauchline, 31st March, 1788.

YESTERDAY, my dear Sir, as I was riding thro' a track of melancholy, joyless muirs, between Galloway and Ayrshire; it being Sunday, I turned my thoughts to psalms, and

hymns, and spiritual songs; and your favorite air, "Captain O'Kean," coming at length into my head, I tried those words to it. You will see that the first part of the tune must be repeated.

> The small birds rejoice in the green leaves returning,
> 　The murmuring streamlet winds clear through the vale;
> The hawthorn-trees blow in the dew of the morning,
> 　And wild scatter'd cowslips bedeck the green dale;
> But what can give pleasure, or what can seem fair,
> While the lingering moments are number'd by care?
> 　No flowers gaily springing, nor birds sweetly singing,
> Can soothe the sad bosom of joyless despair.

I am tolerably pleased with those verses, but as I have only a sketch of the tune, I leave it with you to try if they suit the measure of the music.

I am so harassed with care and anxiety about this farming project of mine, that my Muse has degenerated into the veriest prose-wench that ever picked cinders, or followed a tinker. When I am fairly got into the routine of business, I shall trouble you with a longer epistle; perhaps with some queries respecting farming; at present, the world sits such a load on my mind, that it has effaced almost every trace of the [poet]' in me.

My very best compliments and good wishes to Mrs. Cleghorn.

R. B.

' (This word was left purposely by our Author, in the original, a ——. So at least it stands in Currie's edition, significantly and well.)

(Mr. Cleghorn, who, in reply to the above, addresses our Author as "My dear Brother Farmer," was a jovial man and also a musician. At his special request, the above lines were modified, and by the addition of as many more were converted into the beautiful Jacobite song entitled "The Chevalier's Lament." The air, as we learn from other sources, from the testimony of his widow in particular, was a great favourite of our Author's. The reader may compare note on the "Chevalier's Lament," Poetical Works, p. 201. Mr. Cleghorn promised some practical advice on farming, which, however, was of slight avail.)

(2.)

TO MR. ROBERT CLEGHORN,
SAUGHTON.

[Dumfries, 21st August, 1795.]

MY DEAR CLEGHORN,

INCLOSED you have Clarke's Gaffer Gray.—I have not time [to take a] copy of it, so, when you have taken a copy for yourself, please return me the original. I need not caution you against giving copies to any other person. Peggy Ramsay I shall expect to find in Gaffer Gray's company, when he returns to Dumfries.

I intended to have taken the advantage of the frank, and given you a long letter; but cross accident has detained me untill the Post is just going.—Pray, has Mr. Wight got the better of his fright, and how is Mr. Allan? I hope you got all safe home. Dr. Maxwell and honest John Syme beg leave to be remembered to you all. They both speak in high terms of the acquisition they have made to their acquaintance. I in

No. 263. & 4 Rounds Dumfries Roll
D. 1st Dev.
Permit Thos. Harkness, Mitchelslack, Dumfries Cy
to receive one Casks of foreign Rum proof
Quantity ten Gallons No.
as under. Part of the Stock of John Hutton, Dumfries —
Witness my hand this thirtieth day of Nov. — 1792
& This Permit to be in force two off — for the Goods
being sent out of Mr. Hutton's Stock and
five hours more for the same being delivered and
received into Mr. Harkness's Stock, Granted 30 1792

Nov. — 10 g. F. R. M. Robt. Burns

The above Goods sent by a Cart —

Thomson meet you on Sunday? If so, you would have a world of conversation. Mrs. Burns joins in thanks for your obliging, *very obliging* visit.

Yours ever,

R. BURNS.

P.S.—Did you ever meet with the following "Todlin Hame," by the late Mr. M'Culloch of Airdwell, Galloway?

[A good deal of conjectural interest is connected with this short epistle; for if the Mr. Allan referred to was David Allan the painter, commonly known as the "Scottish Hogarth"—which seems possible, from the occurrence of his name and Cleghorn's again in a letter (16) to Thomson, p. 163—then he must have been on a visit to the Poet at Dumfries along with Cleghorn in 1795, which would be the first and only time in their lives these two men of genius met. Before that date our Author had not the pleasure of Allan's acquaintance, although Allan had been illustrating his works, and had even hit an imaginary likeness of him in his picture of the "Cotter's Saturday Night"—compare letters (45) and (50) to Thomson;—and after that date there was no opportunity. This interview, therefore, between "Mr. Allan and Mr. Burns," "the only genuine and real painters of Scottish costume in the world," as our Poet honours Allan by saying, would be interesting to see—like the interview with Neil Gow; and it would be a source of great gratification to themselves, more especially as they were both indebted for early patronage and friendship to the same liberal hand. David Allan, although born at Alloa, was educated as an artist first in Glasgow and then at Rome, chiefly by the interest or at the personal expense of Gavin Hamilton. On the other hand—we find a Mr. John Allan associated with Robert Cleghorn and Robert Wight as a subscriber on behalf of the Poet's family; which looks like presumptive evidence equally strong against the above pleasant theory. Having nothing more to guide us to a conclusion in the matter, we must leave it thus undetermined with our readers.

This final interview with Cleghorn himself seems to have been social and friendly in the truest sense, and one in which not only Maxwell and Syme, but Mrs. Burns herself could join, and which doubtless she enlivened with her voice, agreeably. The letter itself, which we print from original in possession of George Manners, Esq., F.S.A., Croydon, has no date of its own inside, but is dated at full outside, and franked by P. Miller—that is, younger of Dalswinton, who was then Member for the Dumfries Burghs. Compare letter (6) to Robert Graham, Esq., of Fintry.]

To Mr. George Lockhart,

MERCHANT, GLASGOW.

Mauchline, 18th July, 1788.

MY DEAR SIR,

I am just going for Nithsdale, else I would certainly have transcribed some of my rhyming things for you. The Miss Baillies I have seen in Edinburgh. "Fair and lovely are thy works, Lord God Almighty! Who would not praise Thee for those Thy gifts in Thy goodness to the sons of men!" It needed not your fine taste to admire them. I declare, one day I had the honor of dining at Mr. Baillie's, I was almost in the predicament of the children of Israel, when they could not look on Moses' face for the glory that shone in it when he descended from Mount Sinai.

I did once write a poetic address from the Falls of Bruar to his Grace of Athole, when I was in the Highlands. When you return to Scotland, let me know, and I will send such of my pieces as please myself best. I return to Mauchline in about ten days.

My compliments to Mr. Purden. I am in truth, but at present in haste, yours sincerely,

R. B.

[Burns had never felt the full measure of the beauty of his poems till he heard Mr. Aiken read them. Mr. Lockhart of Glasgow did him a similar service regarding his songs. On hearing him for the first time sing some of those pieces, he exclaimed with great naïveté—"I'll be hanged if I ever knew half their merit till now!"—Chambers.]

(1.)   To Robert Graham, Esq.,

OF FINTRY.*

SIR,

When I had the honour of being introduced to you at Athole-house, I did not think so soon of asking a favour of you. When Lear, in Shakspeare, asked Old Kent why he wished to be in his service, he answers, "Because you have that in your face which I would fain call master." For some such reason, Sir, do I now solicit your patronage. You know, I dare say, of an application I lately made to your Board to be admitted an officer of Excise. I have, according to form, been examined by a supervisor, and to-day I gave in his certificate, with a request for an order for instructions. In this affair, if I succeed, I am afraid I shall but too much need a patronizing friend. Propriety of conduct as a man, and fidelity and attention as an officer, I dare engage for; but with any thing like business, except manual labour, I am totally unacquainted.

I had intended to have closed my late appearance on the stage of life, in the character of a country farmer; but after discharging some filial and fraternal claims, I find I could only fight for existence in that miserable manner, which I have lived to see threw a venerable parent into the jaws of a jail; whence death, the poor man's last and often best friend, rescued him.

I know, Sir, that to need your goodness, is to have a claim on it; may I, therefore, beg your patronage to forward me in this affair, till I be appointed to a division; where, by the help of rigid economy, I will try to support that independence so dear to my soul, but which has been too often so distant from my situation.

R. B.

* [Mr. Graham, of Fintry, Fintra, or Fintray (for his designation is thus variously spelt), was cousin to Sir William Murray of Auchtertyre; and seems to have been introduced to our Author at supper, in the house of Athole's at Blair—compare Highland Tour, Appendix; also letter to Mr. Walker. The important series of letters addressed to him appeared for the first time complete in Appendix to Mr. Chambers's edition, from which we now quote them, with some explanatory notes of our own. Mr. Graham, as our readers are aware, was a Commissioner at the Board of Excise, and one of our Author's warmest friends there in his professional capacity.]

(2.) TO ROBERT GRAHAM, ESQ.

Ellisland, 10th Sept., 1788.

Sir,

The scrapes and premunires into which our indiscretions and follies, in the ordinary constitution of things, often bring us, are bad enough; but it is peculiarly hard that a man's virtues should involve him in disquiet, and the very goodness of his heart cause the persecution of his peace. You, Sir, have patronized and befriended me—not by barren compliments, which merely fed my vanity, or little marks of notice, which perhaps only encumbered me more in the awkwardness of my native rusticity, but by being my persevering friend in real life; and now, as if your continued benevolence had given me a prescriptive right, I am going again to trouble you with my importunities.

Your Honourable Board sometime ago gave me my Excise commission, which I regard as my sheet-anchor in life. My farm, now that I have tried it a little, though I think it will in time be a saving bargain, yet does by no means promise to be such a pennyworth as I was taught to expect. It is in the last stage of worn-out poverty, and it will take some time before it pay the rent. I might have had cash to supply the deficiencies of these hungry years; but I have a younger brother and three sisters on a farm in Ayrshire, and it took all my surplus over what I thought necessary for my farming capital, to save not only the comfort, but the very existence of that fireside family circle from impending destruction. This was done before I took the farm; and rather than abstract my money from my brother—a circumstance which would ruin him—I will resign the farm, and enter immediately into the service of your Honours. But I am embarked now in the farm; I have commenced married man; and I am determined to stand by my lease till resistless necessity compel me to quit my ground.

There is one way by which I might be enabled to extricate myself from this embarrassment—a scheme which I hope and am certain is in your power to effectuate. I live here, Sir, in the very centre of a country Excise division; the present officer lately lived on a farm which he rented, in my nearest neighbourhood; and as the gentleman, owing to some legacies, is quite opulent, a removal could do him no manner of injury; and on a month's warning to give me a little time to look again over my instructions, I would not be afraid to enter on business. I do not know the name of his division, as I have not yet got acquainted with any of the Dumfries Excise people; but his own name is Leonard Smith. It would suit me to enter on it beginning of next summer; but I shall be in Edinburgh to wait upon you about the affair, sometime in the ensuing winter.

When I think how and on what I have written to you, Sir, I shudder at my own *hardiesse*. Forgive me, Sir, I have told you my situation. If asking anything less could possibly have done, I would not have asked so much.

If I were in the service, it would likewise favour my poetical schemes. I am thinking of something in the rural way, of the drama kind. Originality of character is, I think, the most striking beauty in that species of composition, and my wanderings in the way of my business would be vastly favourable to my picking up original traits of human nature.

I again, Sir, earnestly beg your forgiveness for this letter. I have done violence to my own feelings in writing it.

——' If I in aught have done amiss,
    Impute it not!'——

My thoughts on this business, as usual with me when my mind is burdened, vented themselves in the enclosed verses, which I have taken the liberty to inscribe to you.

You, Sir, have the power to bless; but the only claim I have to your friendly offices is my having already been the object of your goodness, which (indeed looks like) producing my debt instead of my discharge.

I am sure I go on Scripture grounds in this affair, for I "ask in faith, nothing doubting;" and for the true Scripture reason too, because I have the fullest conviction that "my benefactor is good."

I have the honour to be, Sir, your deeply indebted humble servant,

ROBT. BURNS.

(3.) TO ROBERT GRAHAM, ESQ.

Ellisland, 23rd Sept. 1788.

Sir,

Though I am scarce able to hold up my head with this fashionable influenza, which is just now the rage hereabouts, yet, with half a spark of life, I would thank you for your most generous favour of the 14th, which, owing to my infrequent calls at the post-office in the hurry of harvest, came only to hand yesternight. I assure you, my ever-honoured Sir, I read it with eyes brimful of other drops than those of anguish. Oh, what means of happiness the Author of goodness has put in their hands to whom he has given the power to bless!—and what real happiness has he given to those on whom he has likewise bestowed kind, generous, benevolent dispositions! Did you know, Sir, from how many fears and forebodings the friendly assurance of your patronage and protection has freed me, it would be some reward for your goodness.

I am cursed with a melancholy prescience, which makes me the veriest coward in life. There is not any exertion which I would not attempt, rather than be in that horrid situation—to be ready to call on the mountains to fall on me, and the hills to cover me from the presence of a haughty landlord, or his still more haughty underling, to whom I owed—what I could not pay. My muse, too, the circumstance that, after my domestic comfort, is by far the dearest to my soul, to have it in my power to cultivate her acquaintance to advantage—in short, Sir, you have, like the great Being whose image you so richly bear, made a creature happy, who had no other claim to your goodness than his necessity, and who can make you no other return than his grateful acknowledgment.

My farm, I think I am certain, will in the long-run be an object for me; and as I rent it the first three years something under [its value], I will be able to weather by a twelvemonth, or perhaps more; though it would make me set fortune more at defiance, if it can be in your power to grant my request, as I mentioned, in the beginning of next summer. I was thinking that, as I am only a little more than five miles from Dumfries, I might perhaps officiate there, if any of these officers could be removed with more propriety than Mr. Smith; but besides the monstrous inconvenience of it to me, I could not bear to injure a poor fellow by outing him to make way for myself; to a wealthy son of good-fortune like Smith, the injury is imaginary where the propriety of your rules admits.

Had I been well, I intended to have troubled you further with a description of my soil and plan of farming; but business will call me to town about February next. I hope then to have the honour of assuring you in *proprid persond*, how much and how truly I am, Sir, your deeply indebted and ever-grateful, humble servant,

ROBT. BURNS.

(4.)

TO ROBERT GRAHAM, ESQ.

Ellisland, 13th May, 1789.

SIR,

THOUGH I intend making a little manuscript-book of my unpublished poems for Mrs. Graham, yet I cannot forbear in the meantime sending her the enclosed, which was the production of the other day. In the plea of humanity, the ladies, to their honour be it spoken, are ever warmly interested. That is one reason of my troubling you with this; another motive I have is a hackneyed subject in my letters to you—God help a poor devil who carries about with him a load of gratitude, of which he can never hope to ease his shoulders but at the expense of his heart! I waited on Collector Mitchell with your letter. It happened to be collection-day, so he was very busy; but he received me with the utmost politeness, and made me promise to call on him soon. As I don't wish to degrade myself to a hungry rook, gaping for a morsel, I shall just give him a hint of my wishes. I am going on with a bold hand in my farm, and am certain of holding it with safety for three or four years; and I think, if some cursed malevolent star have not taken irremovable possession of my zenith, that your patronage and my own priority then as an expectant, should run a fair chance for the division I want. By the bye, the Excise instructions you mentioned were not in the bundle; but 'tis no matter; Marshall in his *Yorkshire*, and particularly that extraordinary man, Smith, in his *Wealth of Nations*, find my leisure employment enough. I could not have given any more new credit for half the intelligence Mr. Smith discovers in his book. I would covet much to have his ideas respecting the present state of some quarters of the world that are, or have been, the

scenes of considerable revolutions since his book was written. Though I take the advantage of your goodness, and presume to send you any new poetic thing of mine, I must not tax you with answers to each of my idle letters. I remember you talked of being this way with my honoured friend, Sir William Murray, in the course of this summer. You cannot imagine, Sir, how happy it would make me, should you, too, illuminate my humble domicile. You will certainly do me the honour to partake of a farmer's dinner with me. I shall promise you a piece of good old beef, a chicken, or perhaps a Nith salmon, fresh from the wear, and a glass of good punch, on the shortest notice; and allow me to say that Cincinnatus or Fabricius, who presided in the august Roman senate, and led their invincible armies, would have jumped at such a dinner. I expect your honours with a kind of enthusiasm. I shall mark the year, and mark the day, and hand it down to my children's children, as one of the most distinguished honours of their ancestor.

I have the honour to be, with sincerest gratitude, your obliged and very humble servant,

ROBT. BURNS.

(5.)

TO ROBERT GRAHAM, ESQ.

Ellisland, 31st July, 1789.

SIR,

THE language of gratitude has been so prostituted by servile adulation and designing flattery, that I know not how to express myself when I would acknowledge the receipt of your last letter. I beg and hope, ever-honoured

"*Friend of my life! true patron of my rhymes,*"

that you will always give me credit for the sincerest, chastest gratitude! The callous hypocrite may be louder than I in his grateful professions—professions which he never felt; or the selfish heart of the covetous may pocket the bounties of beneficence with more rejoicing exultation; but for the brimful eye, springing from the ardent throbbings of an honest bosom, at the goodness of a kindly active benefactor and politely generous friend, I dare call the Searcher of hearts and Author of all goodness to witness how truly these are mine to you.

Mr. Mitchell did not wait my calling on him, but sent me a kind letter, giving me a hint of the business, and on my waiting on him yesterday, he entered with the most friendly ardour into my views and interests. He seems to think, and from my own private knowledge I am certain he is right, that removing the officer who now does, and for these many years has done, duty in the division in the middle of which I live, will be productive of at least no disadvantage to the revenue, and may likewise be done without any detriment to him. Should the Honourable Board think so, and should they deem it eligible to appoint me to officiate in his present place, I am then at the top of my wishes. The emoluments of my office will enable me to carry on and enjoy those improvements in my farm, which, but for this additional assistance, I might in a year or two have abandoned. Should it be judged improper to place me in this division, I am deliberating whether I had not better give up my farming altogether, and go into the Excise wherever I can find employment. Now that the salary is £50 per annum, the Excise is surely a much superior object to a farm, which, without some foreign assistance, must for half a lease be a losing bargain. The worst of it is, I know there are some respectable characters who do me the honour to interest themselves in my welfare and behaviour, and as leaving the farm so soon may have an unsteady, giddy-headed appearance, I had perhaps better lose a little money than hazard such people's esteem.

You see, Sir, with what freedom I lay before you all my little matters—little indeed to the world, but of the most important magnitude to me. You are so good, that I trust I am not troublesome. I have heard and read a good deal of philanthropy, generosity, and greatness of soul, and when rounded with the flourish of declamatory periods, or poured in the mellifluence of Parnassian measure, they have a tolerable effect on a musical ear; but when these high-sounding professions are compared with the very act and deed as they are usually performed, I do not think there is anything in or belonging to human nature so baldly disproportionate. In fact, were it not for a very few of our kind, among whom an honoured friend of mine, that to you, Sir, I will not name, is a distinguished individual, the very existence of magnanimity, generosity, and all their kindred virtues, would be as much a question among metaphysicians, as the existence of witchcraft. Perhaps the nature of man is not so much to blame for all this, as the situation in which, by some miscarriage or other, he is placed in this world. The poor, naked, helpless wretch, with such voracious appetites and such a famine of provision for them, is under a kind of cursed necessity of turning selfish in his own defence. Except here and there a scelerat, who seems to be a scoundrel from the womb by original sin, thorough-paced selfishness is always a work of time. Indeed, in a little time, we generally grow so attentive to ourselves, and so regardless of others, that I have often in poetic frenzy looked on this world as one vast ocean, occupied and commoved by innumerable vortices, each whirling round its centre, which vortices are the children of men; and that the great design and merit, if I may say so, of every particular vortex consists, in how wide it can extend the influence of its circle, and how much floating trash it can suck in and absorb.

I know not why I have got into this preaching vein, except it be to shew you, Sir, that it is not my ignorance but my knowledge of mankind which makes me so much admire your goodness to your humble servant.

I hope this will find my amiable young acquaintance, John, recovered from his indisposition, and all the members of your charming fireside circle well and happy. I am sure I am anxiously interested in all their welfares; I wish it

with all my soul; nay, I believe I sometimes catch myself praying for it. I am not impatient of my own impotence under that immense debt which I owe to your goodness, but I wish and beseech that BEING who has all good things in His hands, to bless and reward you with all those comforts and pleasures which He knows I would bestow on you, were they mine to give.

I shall return your books very soon. I only wish to give Dr. Smith one other perusal, which I will do in two or three days. I do not think that I must trouble you for another cargo, at least for some time, as I am going to apply to Leadbetter and Symons on Gauging, and to study my Sliding Rule, Brannan's Rule, &c., with all possible attention.

An apology for the impertinent length of this epistle would only add to the evil.

I have the honour to be, Sir,
> Your deeply indebted humble Servt.,
> > ROBT. BURNS.

(G.)   TO ROBERT GRAHAM, ESQ.

9th December, 1789.

SIR,

I HAVE a good while had a wish to trouble you with a letter, and had certainly done it long ere now—but for a humiliating something that throws cold water on the resolution, as if one should say, "You have found Mr. Graham a very powerful and kind friend indeed, and that interest he is so kindly taking in your concerns, you ought by every thing in your power to keep alive and cherish." Now, though, since God has thought proper to make one powerful and another helpless, the connection of obliger and obliged is all fair; and though my being under your patronage is to me highly honourable, yet, Sir, allow me to flatter myself, that, as a poet, and an honest man you first interested yourself in my welfare, and principally as such still you permit me to approach you.

I have found the Excise business go on a great deal smoother with me than I expected; owing a good deal to the generous friendship of Mr. Mitchell, my collector, and the kind assistance of Mr. Findlater, my supervisor. I dare to be honest, and I fear no labour. Nor do I find my hurried life greatly inimical to my correspondence with the Muses. Their visits to me, indeed, and I believe, to most of their acquaintance, like the visits of good angels, are "short and far between;" * but I meet them now and then as I jog through the hills of Nithsdale, just as I used to do on the banks of Ayr. I take the liberty to enclose you a few bagatelles, all of them the productions of my leisure thoughts in my Excise rides.

If you know or have ever seen Captain Grose, the antiquary, you will enter into any humour that is in the verses on him. Perhaps you have seen them before, as I sent them to a London newspaper. Though I dare say you have none of the Solemn-League-and-Covenant fire, which shone so conspicuous in Lord George Gordon, and the Kilmarnock weavers, yet I think you must have heard of Dr. M'Gill, one of the Clergymen of Ayr, and his heretical book. God help him, poor man! Though he is one of the worthiest, as well as one of the ablest of the whole priesthood of the Kirk of Scotland, in every sense of that ambiguous term, yet the poor Doctor and his numerous family are in imminent danger of being thrown out to the mercy of the winter-winds. The enclosed ballad on that business is, I confess, too local, but I laughed myself at some conceits in it, though I am convinced in my conscience that there are a good many heavy stanzas in it too.†

The Election Ballad, as you will see, alludes to the present canvass in our string of burghs. I do not believe there will be a harder-run match in the whole general election. The great man here, like all renegadoes, is a flaming zealot kicked out before the astonished indignation of his deserted master, and despised, I suppose, by the party who took him in to be a mustering faggot at the mysterious orgies of their midnight iniquities, and a useful drudge in the dirty work of their country elections; he would fain persuade this part of the world that he is turned patriot, and, where he knows his men, has the impudence to aim away at the unmistrusting manner of a man of conscience and principle. Nay, to such an intemperate height has his zeal carried him that in convulsive violence to every feeling in his bosom, he has made some desperate attempts at the hopeless business of getting himself a character for benevolence; and, in one or two late terrible strides in pursuit of party-interest, has actually stumbled on something like meaning the welfare of his fellow-creatures.

I beg your pardon, Sir, if I differ from you in my idea of this great man; but were you to know his sins, as well as omission as commission, to this outraged land, you would club your curse with the execrating voice of the country. I am too little a man to have any political attachments; I am deeply indebted to, and have the warmest veneration for, individuals of both parties; but a man who has it in his power to be the father of a country, and who is only known to that country by the mischiefs he does in it, is a character of which one cannot speak with patience.

Sir James Johnston does "what man can do," but yet I doubt his fate. Of the burgh of Annan he is secure; Kirkcudbright is dubious. He has the provost; but Lord Daer, who does the honours of great man to the place, makes every effort in his power for the opposite interest. Luckily for Sir James, his lordship, though a very good lord, is a very poor politician. Dumfries and Sanquhar are decidedly the duke's "to let or sell;" so Lochmaben, a city containing upwards of fourscore living souls that cannot discern between their right hand and their left—for drunkenness—has at present the balance of power in her hands. The honourable council of that ancient burgh are fifteen in number; but alas! their fifteen names indorsing a bill of fifteen pounds, would not discount the said bill in any banking-office. My lord provost, who is one of the soundest-headed, best-hearted, whisky-drinking fellows in the south of Scotland, is devoted to Sir James;

but his Grace thinks he has a majority of the council, though I, who have the honour to be a burgess of the town, and know somewhat behind the curtain, could tell him a different story.

The worst of it for the buff and blue folks is, that their candidate, Captain M[iller], my landlord's son, is, entre nous, a youth by no means above mediocrity in his abilities, and is said to have a huckster-lust for shillings, pence, and farthings. This is the more remarkable, as his father's abilities and benevolence are so justly celebrated.‡

The song beginning "Thou lingering star," &c., is the last, and, in my own opinion, by much the best of the enclosed compositions. I beg leave to present it with my most respectful compliments to Mrs. Graham.

I return you by the carrier, the bearer of this, Smith's *Wealth of Nations*, Marshall's *Yorkshire*, and *Angola*. *Les Contes de Fontaine* is in the way of my trade, and I must give it another reading or two. *Chansons Joyeuses*, and another little French book, I keep for the same reason. I think you will not be reading them, and I will not keep them long.

Forgive me, Sir, for the stupid length of this epistle. I pray Heaven it may find you in a humour to read *The Belfast New Almanac*, or *The Bachelor's Garland*, containing five excellent new songs, or the Paisley poet's version of the Psalms of David, and then my importunence may disgust the less.

I have the honour to be, Sir, your ever-grateful, humble servant,

ROBT. BURNS.

* [Marsh, of America, in his Lectures on the English Language, thus traces the origin of this celebrated idea:—John Norris, about close of the seventeenth century, has—

"Like angels' visits, short and bright:"

Dr. Blair, fifty years later, improves into—

"Visits, like those of angels, short and far between:"

Thomas Campbell perfects, by help of more alliteration, in the well-known line—

"Like angels' visits, few and far between."

Our Author, whom Marsh seems not to have observed, manifestly quotes from Blair, but with an alteration most characteristic of himself, and which renders the idea not only more significant in every way, but entirely new: Not all angels (he seems to say) seldom visit this world; but only "good angels"—alas!]

† [Kirk's Alarm is here no doubt referred to. Compare letter (5) to Logan of Afton, to whom a few months before, with the very same expressions regarding it, the original copy was sent.]

‡ [This gentleman was the successful candidate, notwithstanding. His supporter, "the great man" referred to above, was the Duke of Queensberry.—Compare Election Ballads.]

————

(7.)   TO ROBERT GRAHAM, ESQ.

Dumfries, Globe Inn, 4th Sept., 1790.

SIR,

THE very kind letter you did me the honour to write me reached me just as I was setting in to the whirlpool of an Excise fraud-court, from the vortex of which I am just emerged,—Heaven knows in a very unfit situation to do justice to the workings of my bosom when I sit down to write to the

"Friend of my life—true patron of my rhymes."

As my division consists of ten large parishes, and, I am sorry to say, hitherto very carelessly surveyed, I had a good deal of business for the justices; and I believe my decreet will amount to between fifty and sixty pounds. I took, I fancy, rather a new way with my frauds. I recorded every defaulter; but at the court I myself begged off every poor body that was unable to pay, which seeming candour gave me so much implicit credit with the honourable bench, that, with high compliments, they gave me such ample vengeance on the rest, that my *decreet* is double the amount of any division in the district.*

I am going either to give up or subset my farm directly. I have not liberty to subset; but if my master will grant it me, I propose giving it, just as I have it to myself, to an industrious fellow of a near relation of mine. Farming this place in which I live would just be a livelihood to a man who would be the greatest drudge in his own family; so is no object; and living here hinders me from that knowledge in the business of Excise which it is absolutely necessary for me to attain.

I did not like to be an incessant beggar from you. A port-division I wish, if possible, to get; my kind, funny friend, Captain Grose, offered to interest Mr. Brown, and perhaps Mr. Wharton, for me: a very handsome opportunity offered of getting Mr. Corbet, supervisor-general, to pledge every service in his power; and then I was just going to acquaint you with what I had done, or rather what was done for me, that as everybody have their particular friends to serve, you might find the less obstacle in what, I assure you, Sir, I constantly count on—your wishes and endeavours to be of service to me. As I had an eye to getting on the examiner's list, if attainable by me, I was going to ask you if it would be of any service to try the interest of some great, and some *very* great folks, to whom I have the honour to be known—I mean in the way of a Treasury warrant. But much as early impressions have given me of the horrors of spectres, &c., still I would face the arch-fiend, in Miltonic pomp, at the head of all his legions, and hear that infernal shout which blind John says "tore hell's concave," rather than crawl in, a dust-licking petitioner, before the lofty presence of a mighty man, and bear, amid all the mortifying pangs of self-annihilation, the swelling consequence of his d —— state, and the cold monosyllables of his hollow heart!

It was in the view of trying for a port, that I asked Collector Mitchell to get me appointed, which he has done, to a vacant foot-walk in Dumfries. If ever I am so fortunate as to be called out to do business as a supervisor, I would then choose the north of Scotland; but until that Utopian period, I own I have some wayward feelings of appearing as a simple gauger in a country where I am only known by fame. Port-Glasgow, Greenock, or Dumfries ports would, in the meantime, be my ultimatum.

I enclose you a tribute I have just been paying to the memory of my friend, Matthew Henderson, whom I daresay you must have known. I had acknowledged your goodness sooner, but for want of time to transcribe the poem. Poor Matthew! I can forgive poverty for hiding virtue and piety. They are not only plants that flourish best in the shade, but

they also produce their sacred fruits, more especially for another world; but when the haggard beldam throws her invidious veil over wit, spirit, &c.,—but I trust another world will cast light on the subject.

I have the honour to be, Sir, your deeply obliged and very humble servant,   ROBT. BURNS.

* [Compare letter to Collector Mitchell, and Answers to Petition of T. J. immediately following. These decreets were, of course, additions to salary.]

(8.)   TO ROBERT GRAHAM, ESQ.

[Post-mark, Oct. 6.]

I OUGHT to have written you long ago; but a mere letter of thanks must be to you an insipid business. I wish to send you something that will give you at least as much amusement as *The Aberdeen New Prognostication*, or *Six Excellent New Songs*. Along with two other pieces, I enclose you a sheetful of groans, wrung from me in my elbow-chair, with one unlucky leg on a stool before me. I will make no apology for addressing it to you: I have no longer a *choice* of patrons: the truly noble Glencairn is no more! I intend soon to do myself the honour of writing Mrs. Graham, and sending her some other lesser pieces of late date. My Muse will sooner be in mischief than be idle; so I keep her at work.

I thought to have mentioned some Excise ideas that your late goodness has put in my head; but it is so like the sorning impudence of a sturdy beggar, that I cannot do it. It was something in the way of an officiating job. With the most ardent wish that you may be rewarded by *Him* who can do it, for your generous patronage to a man who, though feeling sensible of it, is quite unable to repay it, I have the honour, &c.

[Here follows Note to Mrs. Graham, with Prologue, "Rights of Woman."—See note on.]

(9.)   TO ROBERT GRAHAM, ESQ.

December, 1792.

SIR,

I HAVE been surprised, confounded, and distracted by Mr. Mitchell, the collector, telling me that he has received an order from your Board to enquire into my political conduct, and blaming me as a person disaffected to government.

Sir, you are a husband—and a father. You know what you would feel, to see the much-loved wife of your bosom, and your helpless, prattling little ones, turned adrift into the world, degraded and disgraced from a situation in which they had been respectable and respected, and left almost without the necessary support of a miserable existence. Alas, Sir! must I think that such, soon, will be my lot! and from the d-mned, dark insinuations of hellish, groundless envy too! I believe, Sir, I may aver it, and in the sight of Omniscience, that I would not tell a deliberate falsehood, no, not though even worse horrors, if worse can be, than those I have mentioned, hung over my head; and I say, that the allegation, whatever villain has made it, is a lie! To the British constitution on Revolution principles, next after my God, I am most devoutly attached. You, Sir, have been much and generously my friend. Heaven knows how warmly I have felt the obligation, and how gratefully I have thanked you. Fortune, Sir, has made you powerful, and me impotent; has given you patronage, and me dependence. I would not, for my single self, call on your humanity; were such my insular, unconnected situation, I would despise the tear that now swells in my eye—I could brave misfortune, I could face ruin; for at the worst, "Death's thousand doors stand open;" but, Good God! the tender concerns that I have mentioned, the claims and ties that I see at this moment, and feel around me, how they unnerve courage and wither resolution! To your patronage, as a man of some genius, you have allowed me a claim; and your esteem, as an honest man, I know is my due. To those, Sir, permit me to appeal; by these may I adjure you to save me from that misery which threatens to overwhelm me, and which, with my latest breath I will say it, I have not deserved.

R. B.

(10.)   TO ROBERT GRAHAM, ESQ.

Dumfries, 5th Jan., 1793.

Sir,

I am this moment honoured with your letter; with what feelings I received this other instance of your goodness, I shall not pretend to describe.

Now to the charges which malice and misrepresentation have brought against me. It has been said, it seems, that I not only belong to, but head a disaffected party in this place. I know of no party in this place, either republican or reform, except an old party of borough-reform, with which I never had anything to do. Individuals, both republican and reform, we have, though not many of either; but if they have associated, it is more than I have the least knowledge of, and if there exists such an association, it must consist of such obscure nameless beings, as precludes any possibility of my being known to them, or they to me. I was in the playhouse one night when *Ça ira* was called for. I was in the middle of the pit, and from the pit the clamour arose. One or two individuals with whom I occasionally associate were of the party, but I neither knew of the plot nor joined in the plot, nor ever opened my lips either to hiss or huzza that or any other political tune whatever. I looked on myself as far too obscure a man to have any weight in quelling a riot; at the same time, as a character of higher respectability than to yell in the howlings of a rabble. This was the conduct of all the first characters in the place; and these characters know, and will avow, that such was my conduct.

I never uttered any invectives against the king. His

private worth it is altogether impossible that such a man as I can appreciate; and in his public capacity I always revered, and always will, with the soundest loyalty, revere the monarch of Great Britain, as, to speak in masonic, the sacred Keystone of Our Royal Arch Constitution.

As to Reform Principles, I look upon the British constitution, as settled at the Revolution, to be the most glorious constitution on earth, or that perhaps the wit of man can frame; at the same time, I think, and you know what high and distinguished characters have for some time thought so, that we have a good deal deviated from the original principles of that constitution; particularly, that an alarming system of corruption has pervaded the connection between the executive power and the House of Commons. This is the truth, and the whole truth, of my reform opinions, which, before I was aware of the complexion of these innovating times, I too unguardedly (now I see it) sported with; but henceforth I seal up my lips. However, I never dictated to, corresponded with, or had the least connection with, any political association whatever—except, that when the magistrates and principal inhabitants of this town met to declare their attachment to the constitution, and their abhorrence of riot, which declaration you would see in the papers, I, as I thought my duty as a subject at large, and a citizen in particular, called upon me, subscribed the same declaratory creed. Of Johnston, the publisher of the *Edinburgh Gazetteer*, I know nothing. One evening, in company with four or five friends, we met with his prospectus, which we thought manly and independent; and I wrote to him, ordering his paper for us. If you think that I act improperly in allowing his paper to come addressed to me, I shall immediately countermand it. I never, so judge me God! wrote a line of prose for the *Gazetteer* in my life. An occasional address, spoken by Miss Fontenelle on her benefit-night here, which I called the *Rights of Women*, I sent to the *Gazetteer*, as also some extempore stanzas on the commemoration of Thomson; both these I will subjoin for your perusal. You will see that they have nothing whatever to do with politics. At the time when I sent Johnston one of those poems, but which one I do not remember, I enclosed, at the request of my warm and worthy friend, Robert Riddel, Esq., of Glenriddel, a prose essay, signed Cato, written by him, and addressed to the delegates for the County Reform, of which he was one for this country. With the merits or demerits of that essay I have nothing to do, further than transmitting it in the same frank, which frank he had procured me.

As to France, I was her enthusiastic votary in the beginning of the business. When she came to show her old avidity for conquest, in annexing Savoy, &c., to her dominions, and invading the rights of Holland, I altered my sentiments. A tippling ballad, which I made on the Prince of Brunswick's breaking up his camp, and sung one convivial evening, I shall likewise send you, sealed up, as it is not everybody's reading. This last is not worth your perusal; but lest Mrs. Fame should, as she has already done, use, and even abuse her old privilege of lying, you shall be master of everything, *le pour et le contre,* of my political writings and conduct.

This, my honoured patron, is all. To this statement I

* z

challenge disquisition. Mistaken prejudice, or unguarded passion, may mislead, and have often misled me; but when called on to answer for my mistakes, though—I will say it—no man can feel keener compunction for his errors, yet, I trust, no man can be more superior to evasion or disguise.

I shall do myself the honour to thank Mrs. Graham for her goodness in a separate letter.

If, Sir, I have been so fortunate as to do away these misapprehensions of my conduct and character, I shall, with the confidence which you were wont to allow me, apply to your goodness on every opening in the way of business where I think I, with propriety, may offer myself. An instance that occurs just now: Mr. M'Farlane, supervisor of the Galloway district, is and has been for some time very ill. I spoke to Mr. Mitchell as to his wishes to forward my application for the job; but though he expressed, and ever does express, every kindness for me, he hesitates, in hopes that the disease may be of short continuance. However, as it seems to be a paralytic affection, I fear that it may be some time ere he can take charge of so extended a district. There is a great deal of fatigue and very little business in the district—two things suitable enough to my hardy constitution, and inexperience in that line of life.

I have the honour to be, Sir, your over-grateful, as highly obliged, humble servant,

ROBERT BURNS.

   * [We have somewhere seen a letter giving a different and very disadvantageous account of Burns's conduct on this occasion. The writer, according to our recollection, seemed to speak with political prejudice; but the above, from its very minuteness as well as from its earnestness, is manifestly a truthful statement of what occurred—if the occasion referred to be the same.]

(11.)   TO ROBERT GRAHAM, ESQ.

[Jan., 1794.]

SIR,

I AM going to venture on a subject which, I am afraid, may appear, *from me*, improper; but as I do it from the best of motives, if you should not approve of my ideas, you will forgive them.

Economy of the public monies is, I know, highly the wish of your honourable board; and any hint conducive thereto which may occur to any, though the meanest, individual in your service, it is surely his duty to communicate it.

I have been myself accustomed to labour, and have no notion that a servant of the public should eat the bread of idleness; so, what I have long digested, and am going to propose, is the reduction of one of our Dumfries divisions. Not only in those unlucky times, but even in the highest flush of business, my division, though by far the heaviest, was mere trifling—the others, still less. I would plan the reduction as thus: Let the second division be annihilated, and be divided among the others. The duties in it are, two chandlers, a common brewer, and some victuallers: these, with some tea and spirit stocks, are the whole division. The

two chandlers I would give to the third or tobacco division; it is the idlest of us all. That I may seem impartial, I shall willingly take under my charge the common brewer and the victuallers. The tea and spirit stocks divide between the Bridgend and Dumfries second divisions. They have at present but very little, *comparatively*, to do, and are quite adequate to the task,

I assure you, Sir, that by my plan the duties will be equally well charged, and thus an officer's appointment saved to the public. You must remark one thing—that our common brewers are, every man of them in Dumfries, completely and unexceptionally, fair traders. One or two rascally creatures are in the Bridgend division; but besides being nearly ruined, as all smugglers deserve, by fine and forfeiture, their business is on the most trifling scale you can fancy.

I must beg of you, Sir, should my plan please you, that you will conceal my hand in it, and give it as your own thought. My warm and worthy friend, Mr. Corbet, may think me an impertinent intermeddler in his department; and Mr. Findlater, my supervisor, who is not only one of the first, if not the very first, excisemen in your service, but is also one of the worthiest fellows in the universe—he, I know, would feel hurt at it; and as he is one of my most intimate friends, you can easily figure how it would place me to have my plan known to be mine.*

For further information on the subject, permit me to refer you to a young beginner whom you lately sent among us—Mr. Andrew Pearson, a gentleman that, I am happy to say, from manner, abilities, and attention, promises, indeed, to be a great acquisition to the service of your honourable board.

This is a letter of business; in a future opportunity I may, and most certainly will, trouble you with one in my own way *à la Parnasse*.

I have the honour to be, Sir, your much indebted, and over-grateful servant,

ROBT. BURNS.

P.S.—I forgot to mention that, if my plan takes, let me recommend to your humanity and justice the present officer of the second division. He is a very good officer, and is burdened with a family of small children, which, with some debts of early days, crush him much to the ground.

R. B.

   * [The reader will find the whole of this and a kindred subject more fully treated in letter to Provost Staig—*infra*.]

To Mr. Morison,
MAUCHLINE.

Ellisland, September 22, 1788.

MY DEAR SIR,

NECESSITY obliges me to go into my new house even before it be plaistered. I will inhabit the one end until the other is finished. About three weeks more, I think, will at farthest be my time, beyond which I cannot stay in this present house.

If ever you wished to deserve the blessing of him that was ready to perish; if ever you were in a situation that a little kindness would have rescued you from many evils; if ever you hope to find rest in future states of untried being—get these matters of mine ready.* My servant will be out in the beginning of next week for the clock. My compliments to Mrs. Morison. I am, after all my tribulation,

Dear Sir, yours,

R. B.

* [The "matters" here referred to were chiefly articles of household furniture, chairs and tables of hardwood. These are the same, if we mistake not, which were given by Mrs. Burns as a marriage plenishing to a faithful domestic—Mary M'Lachlan, for fourteen years housekeeper to Mrs. Burns—and are now in possession of her husband, Andrew Nicolson, who survives her—a humble artisan in Dumfries, but a devout worshipper of the Poet's, and who would not part with these reliques of his study for a ransom. The eight-day clock, we are told by Cunningham, was sold at Mrs. Burns's death "for thirty-eight pounds, to one who would have paid one hundred sooner than wanted it."]

To Mr. John Tennant.

December 22, 1788.

I YESTERDAY tried my cask of whiskey for the first time, and I assure you it does you great credit. It will bear five waters, strong; or six, ordinary toddy. The whiskey of this country is a most rascally liquor; and, by consequence, only drunk by the most rascally part of the inhabitants. I am persuaded, if you once get a footing here, you might do a great deal of business, in the way of consumpt; and should you commence distiller again, this is the native barley country. I am ignorant if, in your present way of dealing, you would think it worth your while to extend your business so far as this country side. I write you this on the account of an accident, which I must take the merit of having partly designed to. A neighbour of mine, a John Currie, miller in Carse-mill—a man who is, in a word, a "very" good man, even for a £500 bargain,—he and his wife were in my house the time I broke open the cask. They keep a country public-house and sell a great deal of foreign spirits, but all along thought that whiskey would have degraded their house. They were perfectly astonished at my whiskey, both for its taste and strength; and, by their desire, I write you to know if you could supply them with liquor of an equal quality, and what price. Please write me by first post, and direct to me at Ellisland, near Dumfries. If you could take a jaunt this way yourself, I have a spare spoon, knife, and fork very much at your service. My compliments to Mrs. Tennant, and all the good folks in Glenconner and Barquharrie.

R. B.

[In Mr. Chambers's edition we find the following note attached to this letter: "If this is rightly addressed, it might refer to a different person from the Tennant of Glenconner, to whom Burns wrote a rhymed epistle, as the latter is called 'Jamie.' Perhaps John was a brother, engaged in business as a distiller." James had several brothers, or half-brothers; and the person most probably addressed in this letter was Mr. Tennant of Auchenbay, who is described by a correspondent in *Notes and Queries* as a "sagacious, decisive business man; he minded No. 1." —For further information, compare note on the Epistle to James Tennant.]

To Mr. Cunningham.

Ellisland, 4th May, 1789.

MY DEAR SIR,

YOUR *duty-free* favour of the 26th April I received two days ago: I will not say I perused it with pleasure—that is the cold compliment of ceremony—I perused it, Sir, with delicious satisfaction;—in short, it is such a letter, that not you, nor your friend, but the legislature, by express proviso in their postage laws, should frank. A letter informed with the soul of friendship is such an honour to human nature, that they should order it free ingress and egress to and from their bags and mails, as an encouragement and mark of distinction to supereminent virtue.

I have just put the last hand to a little poem, which I think will be something to your taste. One morning lately, as I was out pretty early in the fields, sowing some grass seeds,* I heard the burst of a shot from a neighbouring plantation, and presently a poor little wounded hare came crippling by me. You will guess my indignation at the inhuman fellow who could shoot a hare at this season, when all of them have young ones. Indeed, there is something in that business of destroying for our sport individuals in the animal creation that do not injure us materially, which I could never reconcile to my ideas of virtue.

. . . .

ON SEEING A FELLOW WOUND A HARE WITH A SHOT,
April, 1789.

Inhuman man! curse on thy barb'rous art,
  And blasted be thy murder-aiming eye!
May never pity soothe thee with a sigh,
Nor never pleasure glad thy cruel heart!

Go live, poor wanderer of the wood and field!
  The bitter little that of life remains:
No more the thickening brakes or verdant plains
To thee a home, or food, or pastime yield.

Seek, mangled innocent, some wonted form;
  That wonted form, alas! thy dying bed!
The sheltering rushes whistling o'er thy head,
The cold earth with thy blood-stained bosom warm.

Perhaps a mother's anguish adds its wo;
  The playful pair crowd fondly by thy side:
Ah! helpless nurslings, who will now provide
That life a mother only can bestow?

Oft as by winding Nith, I, musing, wait
  The sober eve, or hail the cheerful dawn;
I'll miss thee sporting o'er the dewy lawn,
And curse the ruthless wretch and mourn thy hapless fate?

Let me know how you like my poem. I am doubtful whether it would not be an improvement to keep out the last stanza but one altogether.

Cruikshank is a glorious production of the Author of man. You, he, and the noble Colonel of the Crochallan Fencibles are to me

> "Dear as the ruddy drops which warm my heart."

I have got a good mind to make verses on you all, to the tune of *Three gude fellows ayont the glen.*

R. B.

* [On this subject, compare Memoranda by Mrs. Burns, of the Poet's life as a farmer—Appendix.]

† [The version here quoted is the original draft of the poem, which the Author submitted to Dr. Gregory for revision. Compare the poem as published after revision—Poetical Works, p. 122. The person referred to in the poem was a young man of the name of Thomson, who rehearsed the incident to Allan Cunningham, and stated that Burns not only cursed him for his thoughtlessness, but threatened to throw him into the Nith. Thomson, when he told Cunningham this, had not seen the poem.]

(2.)   TO MR. CUNNINGHAM.

Ellisland, 13th February, 1790.

I BEG your pardon, my dear and much valued friend, for writing to you on this very unfashionable, unsightly sheet—

> "My poverty but not my will consents."

But to make amends, since of modish post I have none, except one poor widowed half-sheet of gilt, which lies in my drawer among my plebeian fool's-cap pages, like the widow of a man of fashion, whom that unpolite scoundrel, Necessity, has driven from Burgundy and Pine-apple, to a dish of Bohea with the scandal-bearing help-mate of a village-priest; or a glass of whisky-toddy with a ruby-nosed yoke-fellow of a foot-padding exciseman—I make a vow to enclose this sheet-ful of epistolary fragments in that my only scrap of gilt paper.

I am indeed your unworthy debtor for three friendly letters. I ought to have written to you long ere now, but it is a literal fact, I have scarcely a spare moment. It is not that I *will not* write to you; Miss Burnet is not more dear to her guardian angel, nor his grace the Duke of Queensberry to the powers of darkness, than my friend Cunningham to me. It is not that I *cannot* write to you; should you doubt it, take the following fragment, which was intended for you some time ago, and be convinced that I can *antithesize* sentiment, and *circumvolute* periods, as well as any coiner of phrase in the regions of philology.

December, 1789.

MY DEAR CUNNINGHAM,

WHERE are you? And what are you doing? Can you be that son of levity who takes up a friendship as he takes up a fashion; or are you, like some other of the worthiest fellows in the world, the victim of indolence, laden with fetters of ever-increasing weight?

What strange beings we are! Since we have a portion of conscious existence, equally capable of enjoying pleasure, happiness, and rapture, or of suffering pain, wretchedness, and misery, it is surely worthy of an inquiry, whether there be not such a thing as a science of life; whether method,

economy, and fertility of expedients be not applicable to enjoyment, and whether there be not a want of dexterity in pleasure, which renders our little scantling of happiness still less; and a profuseness, an intoxication in bliss, which leads to satiety, disgust, and self-abhorrence. There is not a doubt but that health, talents, character, decent competency, respectable friends, are real substantial blessings; and yet do we not daily see those who enjoy many or all of those good things, contrive notwithstanding to be as unhappy as others to whose lot few of them have fallen? I believe one great source of this mistake or misconduct is owing to a certain stimulus, with us called ambition, which goads us up the hill of life—not as we ascend other eminences, for the laudable curiosity of viewing an extended landscape, but rather for the dishonest pride of looking down on others of our fellow-creatures, seemingly diminutive in humbler stations, &c., &c.

Sunday, 14th February, 1790.

GOD help me! I am now obliged to

> "Join night to day, and Sunday to the week."

If there be any truth in the orthodox faith of those churches, I am d—mned past redemption, and what is worse, d—mned to all eternity. I am deeply read in Boston's Four-fold State, Marshall on Sanctification, Guthrie's Trial of a Saving Interest, &c.; but "there is no balm in Gilead, there is no physician there," for me; so I shall e'en turn Arminian, and trust to "sincere though imperfect obedience."

Tuesday, 16th.

Luckily for me, I was prevented from the discussion of the knotty point at which I had just made a full stop. All my fears and cares are of this world: if there is another, an honest man has nothing to fear from it. I hate a man that wishes to be a Deist; but I fear, every fair, unprejudiced enquirer must in some degree be a sceptic. It is not that there are any very staggering arguments against the immortality of man; but like electricity, phlogiston, &c., the subject is so involved in darkness, that we want data to go upon. One thing frightens me much: that we are to live for ever, seems *too good news to be true.* That we are to enter into a new scene of existence, where, exempt from want and pain, we shall enjoy ourselves and our friends without satiety or separation—how much should I be indebted to any one who could fully assure me that this was certain!

My time is once more expired. I will write to Mr. Cleghorn soon. God bless him and all his concerns! And may all the powers that preside over conviviality and friendship be present with all their kindest influence, when the bearer of this, Mr. Syme, and you meet! I wish I could also make one. I think we should be ＊ ＊ ＊

Finally, brethren, farewell! Whatsoever things are lovely, whatsoever things are gentle, whatsoever things are charitable, whatsoever things are kind, think on these things, and think on

ROBERT BURNS.

(3.)

TO MR. CUNNINGHAM.

Ellisland, 8th August, 1790.

FORGIVE me, my once dear, and ever dear friend, my seeming negligence. You cannot sit down and fancy the busy life I lead.

I laid down my goose-feather to beat my brains for an apt simile, and had some thoughts of a country grannum at a family christening; a bride on the market-day before her marriage; an orthodox clergyman at a Paisley sacrament * * * or a tavern-keeper at an election-dinner; &c., &c.: but the resemblance that hits my fancy best is that blackguard miscreant, Satan, who roams about like a roaring lion, seeking, *searching* whom he may devour. However, tossed about as I am, if I chuse (and who would not chuse?) to bind down with the crampets of attention the brazen foundation of integrity, I may rear up the superstructure of Independence, and from its daring turrets, bid defiance to the storms of fate. And is not this a "consummation devoutly to be wished?"

> "Thy spirit, Independence, let me share;
> Lord of the lion-heart, and eagle-eye!
> Thy steps I follow with my bosom bare,
> Nor heed the storm that howls along the sky!"

Are not these noble verses? They are the introduction of Smollet's "Ode to Independence:" if you have not seen the poem, I will send it to you.—How wretched is the man that hangs on by the favours of the great! To shrink from every dignity of man, at the approach of a lordly piece of self-consequence, who amid all his tinsel glitter, and stately hauteur, is but a creature formed as thou art—and perhaps not so well formed as thou art—came into the world a paling infant as thou didst, and must go out of it, as all men must, a naked corse. * * *

[Compare letter (27) to Mrs. Dunlop—p. 23. With respect to which Dr. Currie observes—"The preceding letter explains the feelings under which this was written. The strain of indignant invective goes on some time longer in the style which our bard was too apt to indulge, and of which the reader has already seen so much."—Mr. Chambers explains the circumstance of these two letters (the one to Mrs. Dunlop, and the other to Cunningham) having been written on the same day, when the writer's time was so much occupied, by stating "that the 8th of August, 1790, was a Sunday."—Certainly not a day of rest to him, as the letter to Mrs. Dunlop painfully shows.]

(4.)

TO MR. CUNNINGHAM.

Ellisland, 23rd January, 1791.

MANY happy returns of the season to you, my dear friend! As many of the good things of this life, as is consistent with the usual mixture of good and evil in the cup of Being!

I have just finished a poem—Tam o' Shanter—which you will receive enclosed. It is my first essay in the way of tales.

I have these several months been hammering at an elegy on the amiable and accomplished Miss Burnet. I have got, and can get, no farther than the following fragment, on which please give me your strictures. In all kinds of poetic composition, I set great store by your opinion; but in sentimental verses, in the poetry of the heart, no Roman Catholic ever set more value on the infallibility of the Holy Father than I do on yours.

I mean the introductory couplets as text verses.

ELEGY ON THE LATE MISS BURNET OF MONBODDO.

> Life ne'er exulted in so rich a prize,
> As Burnet lovely from her native skies;
> Nor envious death so triumph'd in a blow,
> As that which laid th' accomplish'd Burnet low.
> &c.   &c.

Let me hear from you soon. Adieu!

R. B.

(5.)

TO MR. CUNNINGHAM.

Ellisland, 12th March, 1791.

IF the foregoing piece be worth your strictures, let me have them. For my own part, a thing that I have just composed always appears through a double portion of that partial medium in which an author will ever view his own works. I believe in general, novelty has something in it that inebriates the fancy, and not unfrequently dissipates and fumes away like other intoxication, and leaves the poor patient, as usual, with an aching heart. A striking instance of this might be adduced, in the revolution of many a hymeneal honeymoon. But lest I sink into stupid prose, and so sacrilegiously intrude on the office of my parish-priest, I shall fill up the page in my own way, and give you another song of my late composition, which will appear perhaps in Johnson's work, as well as the former.

You must know a beautiful Jacobite air, "There'll never be peace till Jamie comes hame." When political combustion ceases to be the object of princes and patriots, it then, you know, becomes the lawful prey of historians and poets.

> By yon castle wa' at the close of the day,
> I heard a man sing, tho' his head it was grey;
> And as he was singing, the tears fast down came—
> There'll never be peace till Jamie comes hame.*

If you like the air, and if the stanzas hit your fancy, you cannot imagine, my dear friend, how much you would oblige me, if, by the charms of your delightful voice, you would give my honest effusion to "the memory of joys that are past," to the few friends whom you indulge in that pleasure. But I have scribbled on till I hear the clock has intimated the near approach of

That hour, o' night's black arch the key-stane.—

So good night to you! Sound be your sleep and delectable your dreams! Apropos, how do you like this thought in a ballad, I have just now on the tapis?

> I look to the west when I gae to rest,
> That happy my dreams and my slumbers may be;
> † Far, far in the west is he I lo'e best,
> The lad that is dear to my babie and me!

Good night, once more, and God bless you!

R. B.

* [Compare perfect edition—" There'll never be peace "—Poetical Works, p. 175.]
† [Compare correct edition—" Out over the Forth "—Poetical Works, p. 181.]

(6.)   ## TO MR. CUNNINGHAM.

11th June, 1791.

LET me interest you, my dear Cunningham, in behalf of the gentleman who waits on you with this. He is a Mr. Clarke, of Moffat, principal schoolmaster there, and is at present suffering severely under the persecution of one or two powerful individuals of his employers. He is accused of harshness to boys that were placed under his care. God help the teacher, if a man of sensibility and genius—and such is my friend Clarke—when a booby father presents him with his booby son, and insists on lighting up the rays of science in a fellow's head whose skull is impervious and inaccessible by any other way than a positive fracture with a cudgel: a fellow whom in fact it savours of impiety to attempt making a scholar of, as he has been marked a blockhead in the book of fate, at the almighty fiat of his Creator.

The patrons of Moffat-school are, the ministers, magistrates, and town-council of Edinburgh, and as the business comes now before them, let me beg my dearest friend to do every thing in his power to serve the interests of a man of genius and worth, and a man whom I particularly respect and esteem. You know some good fellows among the magistracy and council, but particularly you have much to say with a reverend gentleman to whom you have the honour of being very nearly related, and whom this country and age have had the honour to produce. I need not name the historian of Charles V.* I tell him through the medium of his nephew's influence, that Mr. Clarke is a gentleman who will not disgrace even his patronage. I know the merits of the cause thoroughly, and say it, that my friend is falling a sacrifice to prejudiced ignorance, and   *   *   *

God help the children of dependence! Hated and persecuted by their enemies, and too often, alas! almost unexceptionally, received by their friends with disrespect and reproach, under the thin disguise of cold civility and humiliating advice. O! to be a sturdy savage, stalking in the pride of his independence, amid the solitary wilds of his deserts; rather than in civilized life, helplessly to tremble for a subsistence, precarious as the caprice of a fellow-creature! Every man has his virtues, and no man is without his failings; and curse on that privileged plain-dealing of friendship, which, in the hour of my calamity, cannot reach forth the helping hand without at the same time pointing out those failings, and apportioning them their share in procuring my present distress. My friends, for such the world calls ye, and such ye think yourselves to be, pass by my virtues if you please, but do also spare my follies: the first will witness in my breast for themselves, and the last will give pain enough to the ingenuous mind without you. And since deviating more or less from the paths of propriety and rectitude must be incident to human nature, do thou, Fortune, put it in my power, always from myself, and of myself, to bear the consequence of those errors! I do not want to be independent that I may sin, but I want to be independent in my sinning.

To return in this rambling letter to the subject I set out with, let me recommend my friend, Mr. Clarke, to your acquaintance and good offices; his worth entitles him to the one, and his gratitude will merit the other. I long much to hear from you. Adieu!

R. B.

* [Mr. Cunningham was nephew to Dr. Robertson, the historian.]

(7.)   ## TO MR. CUNNINGHAM.

Dumfries, 10th September, 1792.

No! I will not attempt an apology.—Amid all my hurry of business, grinding the faces of the publican and the sinner on the merciless wheels of the Excise; making ballads, and then drinking, and singing them; and, over and above all, the correcting the press-work of two different publications; still, still I might have stolen five minutes to dedicate to one of the first of my friends and fellow-creatures. I might have done, as I do at present, snatched an hour near " witching time of night," and scrawled a page or two. I might have congratulated my friend on his marriage; or I might have thanked the Caledonian archers for the honour they have done me (though to do myself justice, I intended to have done both in rhyme, else I had done both long ere now). Well then, here is to your good health! for you must know, I have set a nipperkin of toddy by me, just by way of spell, to keep away the meikle horned deil, or any of his subaltern imps who may be on their nightly rounds.

But what shall I write to you?—" The voice said cry," and I said, " what shall I cry?"—O, thou spirit! whatever thou art, or wherever thou makest thyself visible! be thou a bogle by the eerie side of an auld thorn, in the dreary glen through which the herd-callan maun bicker in his gloamin route frae the fauldie!—Be thou a brownie, set, at dead of night, to thy task by the blazing ingle, or in the solitary barn, where the repercussions of thy iron flail half affright thyself, as thou performest the work of twenty of the sons of men, ere the cock-crowing summon thee to thy ample cog of substantial brose—Be thou a kelpie, haunting the ford or ferry in the starless night, mixing thy laughing yell with the howling of the storm and the roaring of the flood, as thou viewest the perils and miseries of man on the foundering horse, or in the tumbling boat!—Or, lastly, be thou a ghost, paying thy nocturnal visits to the hoary ruins of decayed grandeur; or performing thy mystic rites in the shadow of the time-worn church, while the moon looks, without a cloud, on the silent, ghastly dwellings of the dead around thee: or taking thy stand by the bedside of the villain, or the murderer, pourtraying on his dreaming fancy, pictures, dreadful as the horrors of unveiled hell, and terrible as the wrath of incensed Deity! —Come, thou spirit, but not in these horrid forms; come with the milder, gentle, easy inspirations, which thou breathest round the wig of a prating advocate, or the *tête-à-tête* of a tea-sipping gossip, while their tongues run at the light-horse gallop of clish-maclaver for ever and ever—come and assist a poor devil who is quite jaded in the attempt to share half an idea among half a hundred words; to fill up four quarto pages, while he has not got one single sentence of recollection, information, or remark worth putting pen to paper for.

I feel, I feel the presence of supernatural assistance! circled in the embrace of my elbow-chair, my breast labours, like the bloated Sybil on her three-footed stool, and like her, too, labours with Nonsense.—Nonsense, auspicious name! Tutor, Friend, and Finger-post in the mystic mazes of law; the cadaverous paths of physic; and particularly in the sightless soarings of SCHOOL DIVINITY, who, leaving Common Sense, confounded at his strength of pinion; Reason, delirious with eyeing his giddy flight; and Truth creeping back into the bottom of her well, cursing the hour that ever she offered her scorned alliance to the wizard power of Theologic Vision—raves abroad on all the winds. "On earth Discord! a gloomy Heaven above, opening her jealous gates to the nineteen-thousandth part of the tithe of mankind! and below, an inescapable and inexorable hell, expanding its leviathan jaws for the vast residue of mortals!!!"—O doctrine! comfortable and healing to the weary, wounded soul of man! Ye sons and daughters of affliction, ye *pauvres misérables*, to whom day brings no pleasure, and night yields no rest, be comforted! "'Tis but one to nineteen hundred thousand that your situation will mend in this world;" so, alas, the experience of the poor and the needy too often affirms; and 'tis nineteen hundred thousand to one, by the dogmas of * * * * * * * * that you will be damned eternally in the world to come! *

But of all Nonsense, Religious Nonsense is the most nonsensical; so enough, and more than enough of it. Only, by the bye, will you, or can you tell me, my dear Cunningham, why a sectarian turn of mind has always a tendency to narrow and illiberalize the heart? They are orderly; they may be just; nay, I have known them merciful; but still your children of sanctity move among their fellow-creatures with a nostril—snuffing putrescence, and a foot—spurning filth; in short, with a conceited dignity that your titled * * * * * , or any other of your Scottish lordlings of seven centuries standing display, when they accidentally mix among the many apron'd sons of mechanical life. I remember, in my plough-boy days, I could not conceive it possible that a noble lord could be a fool, or a godly man could be a knave. How ignorant are plough-boys!—Nay, I have since discovered that a *godly woman* may be a * * * * *!—But hold—Here's t'ye again— this rum is generous Antigua, so a very unfit menstruum for scandal.

Apropos, how do you like—I mean *really* like—the married life? Ah, my friend! matrimony is quite a different thing from what 'your love-sick youths and sighing girls take it to be! But marriage, we are told, is appointed by God, and I shall never quarrel with any of his institutions. I am a husband of older standing than you, and shall give you my ideas of the conjugal state (*en passant*—you know I am no Latinist—is not *conjugal* derived from *jugum*, a yoke?). Well then, the scale of good wifeship I divide into ten parts:—Good-nature, four; Good Sense, two; Wit, one; Personal Charms, viz.—a sweet face, eloquent eyes, fine limbs, graceful carriage (I would add a fine waist too, but that is so soon spoilt, you know), all these, one; as for the other qualities belonging to, or attending on, a wife, such as Fortune, Connexions, Education (I mean education extraordinary), Family Blood, &c., divide the two remaining degrees among them as you please; only, remember that all these minor properties must be expressed by *fractions*, for there is not any one of them, in the aforesaid scale, entitled to the dignity of an *integer*.

As for the rest of my fancies and reveries—how I lately met with Miss Lesley Baillie, the most beautiful, elegant woman in the world—how I accompanied her and her father's family fifteen miles on their journey, out of pure devotion, to admire the loveliness of the works of God, in such an unequalled display of them—how, in galloping home at night, I made a ballad on her, of which these two stanzas make a part—

> Thou, bonie Lesley, art a queen,
> 　Thy subjects we before thee;
> Thou, bonie Lesley, art divine,
> 　The hearts o' men adore thee.
>
> The very deil he could na scaith
> 　Whatever wad belang thee!
> He'd look into thy bonie face
> 　And say, "I canna wrang thee."†

—behold all these things are written in the chronicles of my imaginations, and shall be read by thee, my dear friend, and by thy beloved spouse, my other dear friend, at a more convenient season.

Now, to thee, and to thy before-designed bosom-companion, be given the precious things brought forth by the sun, and the precious things brought forth by the moon, and the benignest influences of the stars, and the living streams which flow from the fountains of life, and by the tree of life, for ever and ever! Amen!

R. B.

* [Compare "Holy Willie's Prayer," "Address to the Deil," and similar poetico-religious effusions. Compare also letter (9) of this series, on genuine religion.]

† [Rough draft apparently: compare song as finished for Thomson's Collection —Poetical Works, p. 205.]

(8.)   TO MR. CUNNINGHAM.

3rd March, 1793.

SINCE I wrote to you the last lugubrious sheet, I have not had time to write you further. When I say that I had not time, that, as usual, means that the three demons, indolence, business, and ennui, have so completely shared my hours among them, as not to leave me a five minutes' fragment to take up a pen in.

Thank heaven, I feel my spirits buoying upwards with the renovating year. Now I shall in good earnest take up Thomson's songs. I dare say he thinks I have used him unkindly, and I must own with too much appearance of truth. Apropos, do you know the much admired old Highland air called "The Sutor's Dochter?" It is a first-rate favourite of mine, and I have written what I reckon one of my best songs to it. I will send it to you as it was sung with great applause in some fashionable circles by Major Robertson, of Ludo, who was here with his corps.

    *   *   *   *   *   *   *

There is one commission that I must trouble you with. I lately lost a valuable seal, a present from a departed friend, which vexes me much.

I have gotten one of your Highland pebbles which I fancy would make a very decent one; and I went to cut my armorial bearing on it; will you be so obliging as enquire what will be the expense of such a business? I do not know that my name is matriculated, as the heralds call it, at all; but I have invented arms for myself, so you know I shall be chief of the name; and, by courtesy of Scotland, will likewise be entitled to supporters. These, however, I do not intend having on my seal. I am a bit of a herald, and shall give you, *secundum artem,* my arms. On a field, azure, a holly-bush, seeded, proper, in base; a shepherd's pipe and crook, saltier-wise, also proper, in chief. On a wreath of the colours, a wood-lark perching on a sprig of bay-tree, proper, for crest. Two mottoes; round the top of the crest, *Wood Notes Wild;* at the bottom of the shield, in the usual place, *Better a wee bush than nae bield.* By the shepherd's pipe and crook I do not mean the nonsense of painters of Arcadia, but a *Stock and Horn* and a *Club,* such as you see at the head of Allan Ramsay, in Allan's quarto edition of the *Gentle Shepherd.* By the bye, do you know Allan? He must be a man of very great genius—Why is he not more known?—Has he no patrons? or do "Poverty's cold wind and crushing rain beat keen and heavy" on him? I once, and but once, got a glance of that noble edition of the noblest pastoral in the world; and dear as it was, I mean, dear as to my pocket, I would have bought it; but I was told that it was printed and engraved for subscribers only. He is the *only* artist who has hit *genuine* pastoral *costume.* What, my dear Cunningham, is there in riches, that they narrow and harden the heart so? I think, that were I as rich as the sun, I should be as generous as the day; but as I have no reason to imagine my soul a nobler one than any other man's, I must conclude that wealth imparts a bird-lime quality to the possessor, at which the man, in his native poverty, would have revolted. What has led me to this, is the idea of such merit as Mr. Allan possesses, and such riches as a nabob or government contractor possesses, and why they do not form a mutual league. Let wealth shelter and cherish unprotected merit, and the gratitude and celebrity of that merit will richly repay it.

    *   *   *   *   *   *   *

                                R. B.

(9.)   TO MR. CUNNINGHAM.

25th February, 1794.

CANST thou minister to a mind diseased? Canst thou speak peace and rest to a soul tost on a sea of troubles, without one friendly star to guide her course, and dreading that the next surge may overwhelm her? Canst thou give to a frame, tremblingly alive as the tortures of suspense, the stability and hardihood of the rock that braves the blast? If thou canst not do the least of these, why wouldst thou disturb me in my miseries, with thy inquiries after me?

    *   *   *   *   *   *   *

For these two months I have not been able to lift a pen. My constitution and frame were, *ab origine,* blasted with a deep incurable taint of hypochondria, which poisons my existence. Of late a number of domestic vexations, and some pecuniary share in the ruin of these cursed times; losses which, though trifling, were yet what I could ill bear, have so irritated me, that my feelings at times could only be envied by a reprobate spirit listening to the sentence that dooms it to perdition.

Are you deep in the language of consolation? I have exhausted in reflection every topic of comfort. *A heart at ease* would have been charmed with my sentiments and reasonings; but as to myself, I was like Judas Iscariot preaching the gospel; he might melt and mould the hearts of those around him, but his own kept its native incorrigibility.

Still there are two great pillars that bear us up amid the wreck of misfortune and misery. The ONE is composed of the different modifications of a certain noble stubborn something in man, known by the names of courage, fortitude, magnanimity. The OTHER is made up of those feelings and sentiments, which, however the sceptic may deny them, or the enthusiast disfigure them, are yet, I am convinced, original and component parts of the human soul; those *senses of the mind,* if I may be allowed the expression, which connect us with, and link us to, those awful obscure realities—an all-powerful, and equally beneficent God; and a world to come, beyond death and the grave. The first gives the nerve of combat, while a ray of hope beams on the field: the last pours the balm of comfort into the wounds which time can never cure.

I do not remember, my dear Cunningham, that you and I ever talked on the subject of religion at all. I know some who laugh at it, as the trick of the crafty FEW, to lead the undiscerning MANY; or at most as an uncertain obscurity, which mankind can never know any thing of, and with which they are fools if they give themselves much to do.* Nor would

I quarrel with a man for his irreligion, any more than I would for his want of a musical ear. I would regret that he was shut out from what, to me and to others, were such superlative sources of enjoyment. It is in this point of view, and for this reason, that I will deeply imbue the mind of every child of mine with religion. If my son should happen to be a man of feeling, sentiment, and taste, I shall thus add largely to his enjoyments. Let me flatter myself that this sweet little fellow, who is just now running about my desk, will be a man of a melting, ardent, glowing heart; and an imagination, delighted with the painter, and rapt with the poet. Let me figure him wandering out in a sweet evening, to inhale the balmy gales, and enjoy the growing luxuriance of the spring; himself the while in the blooming youth of life.† He looks abroad on all nature, and through nature up to nature's God. His soul, by swift delighting degrees, is rapt above this sublunary sphere, until he can be silent no longer, and bursts out into the glorious enthusiasm of Thomson—

> "These, as they change, Almighty Father, these
> Are but the varied God.—The rolling year
> Is full of thee."

And so on in all the spirit and ardour of that charming hymn.

These are no ideal pleasures, they are real delights; and I ask what of the delights among the sons of men are superior, not to say equal, to them? And they have this precious, vast addition, that conscious virtue stamps them for her own; and lays hold on them to bring herself into the presence of a witnessing, judging, and approving God.‡

R. B.

* [Compare Memoranda by Mrs. Burns—Burns's Habit of Reading the Bible—Appendix.]

† [Compare Miniature of Poet's son—Boy with flowers in his hand—in which this idea seems to have been carried out.]

‡ [The reader may advantageously compare the whole of this letter with letter (7), in which so strong a contrast of religious dogmatism is made. It is worthy of notice, however, that there is a slight inconsistency between the theory here admitted of religion being like a musical ear—which is certainly most true, and the practice inculcated of "imbuing the mind of every child with it"—unless by that only is meant the affectionate and prayerful cultivation of the religious sense—which is indeed all that can possibly be done in that way—and which, on multiplied evidence, we know the Poet as a father tried to do. Compare Memoranda by Mrs. Burns—Poet's Bearing to his Children—Appendix.]

(10.)

TO MR. CUNNINGHAM.

Brow, Sea-bathing quarters, 7th July, 1796.

MY DEAR CUNNINGHAM,

I RECEIVED yours here this moment, and am indeed highly flattered with the approbation of the literary circle you mention; a literary circle inferior to none in the two kingdoms. Alas! my friend, I fear the voice of the bard will soon be heard among you no more! For these eight or ten months I have been ailing, sometimes bedfast and sometimes not; but these last three months I have been tortured with an excruciating rheumatism, which has reduced me to nearly the last stage. You actually would not know me if you saw me.—Pale, emaciated, and so feeble, as occasionally to need help

from my chair—my spirits fled! fled! but I can no more on the subject—only the medical folks tell me that my last and only chance is bathing and country-quarters, and riding.—The deuce of the matter is this: when an exciseman is off duty, his salary is reduced to £35 instead of £50.—What way, in the name of thrift, shall I maintain myself, and keep a horse in country-quarters—with a wife and five children at home, on £35? I mention this, because I had intended to beg your utmost interest, and that of all the friends you can muster, to move our Commissioners of Excise to grant me the full salary; I dare say you know them all personally. If they do not grant it me, I must lay my account with an exit truly *en poëte*—if I die not of disease, I must perish with hunger.

I have sent you one of the songs; the other my memory does not serve me with, and I have no copy here; but I shall be at home soon, when I will send it you.—Apropos to being at home: Mrs. Burns threatens, in a week or two, to add one more to my paternal charge, which, if of the right gender, I intend shall be introduced to the world by the respectable designation of *Alexander Cunningham Burns.* My last was *James Glencairn,* so you can have no objection to the company of nobility. Farewell!

R. B.

[Alexander Cunningham, Esq., to whom this beautiful and important series of letters is addressed, was a Writer to the Signet in Edinburgh, of most respectable position, and connection. He was also one of a convivial set with whom Burns associated much when in that city; members of the Crochallan corps, and similar spirits, among whom a certain freedom of social intercourse was the bond of union. Whatever their failings or excesses, in this respect, may have been, they seem all to have been most affectionate friends of the Poet, and by their kindness to him to have merited the honour of his gratitude and the distinction of his correspondence. Dunbar was one of these; and Cunningham in particular, after the Poet's death, manifested the sincerity of his attachment by the most generous efforts on behalf of his widow and family.]

(1.)

To John M'Murdo, Esq.,
[DRUMLANRIG.]

Ellisland, 9th Jan., 1789.

SIR,

A POET and a beggar are, in so many points of view, alike, that one might take them for the same individual character under different designations; were it not that, though with a trifling poetic license most poets may be styled beggars, yet the converse of the proposition does not hold, that every beggar is a poet. In one particular, however, they remarkably agree: if you help either the one or the other to a mug of ale, or the picking of a bone, they will very willingly repay you with a song. This occurs to me at present, as I have just dispatched a well-lined rib of John Kirkpatrick's Highlander;" a bargain for which I am indebted to you, in the style of our ballad printers, "Five excellent new songs." The enclosed is nearly my newest song, and one that has cost me some pains, though that is but an equivocal mark of its excellence. Two or three others, which I have by me, shall

* 2 A

do themselves the honour to wait on your after leisure: petitioners for admittance into favour must not harass the condescension of their benefactors.

You see, Sir, what it is to patronise a poet. 'Tis like being a magistrate in Petty-borough: you do them the favour to preside in their council for one year, and your name bears the prefatory stigma of Bailie for life.

With, not the compliments, but the best wishes, the sincerest prayers of the season for you, that you may see many happy years with Mrs. M'Murdo and your family—two blessings by the bye, to which your rank does not, by any means, entitle you; a loving wife and fine family being almost the only good things of this life to which the farmhouse and cottage have an exclusive right.

    I have the honor to be, Sir,
   Your much indebted and very humble servant,
            R. B.

* [Mr. Chambers explains this allusion with reference to some present of a piece of Highland mutton, conveyed to the Author at Mr. M'Murdo's instance, by Kirkpatrick; whose name in Chambers's edition is given as Kilpatrick—a neighbouring blacksmith.]

(2.)   TO JOHN M'MURDO, ESQ.

         Ellisland, 2nd August, 1790.
 Sir,

Now that you are over with the sirens of Flattery, the harpies of Corruption, and the furies of Ambition—those infernal deities, that on all sides, and in all parties, preside over the villainous business of politics—permit a rustic Muse of your acquaintance to do her best to soothe you with a song.—

  You know Henderson*—I have not flattered his memory.
    I have the honor to be, Sir,
     Your obliged humble servant,
            R. B.

* [Matthew Henderson, subject of the well-known Elegy. Mr. Chambers, it appears, had searched the obituaries in vain for some notice of his death; and the fact itself was not known to us except from its commemoration in the Elegy. We have been favoured, however, by Mr. Carruthers of the *Inverness Courier* with the following extract from the *Scots Magazine.*

1788, "November 21, at Edinburgh, Matthew Henderson, Esq."—Which determines the matter. Compare note on *Elegy*—Poetical Works, p. 212.]

(3.)   TO JOHN M'MURDO, ESQ.

           Dumfries, 1793.

WILL Mr. M'Murdo do me the favour to accept of these volumes? a trifling but sincere mark of the very high respect I bear for his worth as a man, his manners as a gentleman, and his kindness as a friend. However inferior now, or afterwards, I may rank as a poet, one honest virtue to which few poets can pretend I trust I shall ever claim as mine—to no man, whatever his station in life, or his power to serve me, have I ever paid a compliment at the expense of TRUTH.

         THE AUTHOR.

[These words appear as Prefatory Note on blank leaf of his Poems—Two vols. octavo, 1793.]

(4.)   TO JOHN M'MURDO, ESQ.,
      WITH A PARCEL.

       [*Dumfries,*] *December,* 1793.
 Sir,

IT is said that we take the greatest liberties with our greatest friends, and I pay myself a very high compliment in the manner in which I am going to apply the remark. I have owed you money longer than ever I owed it to any man. Here is Ker's account, and here are six guineas; and now I don't owe a shilling to man—or woman either. But for these damned dirty dog's-ear'd little pages, I had done myself the honour to have waited on you long ago. Independent of the obligations your hospitality has laid me under; the consciousness of your superiority in the rank of man and gentleman, of itself was fully as much as I could ever make head against; but to owe you money too, was more than I could face.

I think I once mentioned something of a collection of Scots songs I have for some years been making: I send you a perusal of what I have got together. I could not conveniently spare them above five or six days, and five or six glances of them will probably more than suffice you. A very few of them are my own. When you are tired of them, please leave them with Mr. Clint, of the King's Arms. There is not another copy of the collection in the world; and I should be sorry that any unfortunate negligence should deprive me of what has cost me a good deal of pains.

            R. B.

[Mr. M'Murdo, as our readers are aware, was chamberlain to the Duke of Queensberry, and resided at his Grace's mansion of Drumlanrig in the neighbourhood of Thornhill. He was one of our Author's most hospitable friends and distinguished patrons in that district. His family circle afforded most attractive society, and his daughter, Miss Philadelphia, was one of the most celebrated and beautiful of the Poet's heroines.

We think it right to state that in this series of letters to Mr. M'Murdo, there are a few slight variations as between the editions of Cunningham and Chambers. The explanation in such cases generally is, that there have been rough drafts as well as finished copies of the several letters; and that they have been printed accordingly by the respective editors, as the rough draft or finished copy was before them. In the present instance, we incline rather to Mr. Chambers's reading, without invalidating Cunningham's at all, except in the date of letter (1), where he is manifestly wrong in reading *June* for *Jan.*]

To Mr. James Hamilton,
GROCER, GLASGOW.

        Ellisland, May 26, 1789.
 DEAR SIR,

I SEND you by John Glover, carrier, the above account for Mr. Turnbull, as I suppose you know his address.

I would fain offer, my dear Sir, a word of sympathy with your misfortunes; but it is a tender string, and I know not how to touch it. It is easy to flourish a set of high-flown sentiments on the subject that would give great satisfaction to—a breast quite at ease; but as ONE observes, who was very seldom mistaken in the theory of life, "The heart knoweth its own sorrows, and a stranger intermeddleth not therewith."

Among some distressful emergencies that I have experienced in life, I ever laid this down as my foundation of comfort—*That he who has lived the life of an honest man has by no means lived in vain!*

With every wish for your welfare and future success,

I am, my dear Sir, sincerely yours,

R. B.

[This letter—which we print from Cromek, in Chambers's edition wants the introductory sentence. In this, as in other cases, one editor may have printed from a rough draft, and the other from a finished copy. The Mr. Hamilton addressed, we are told by Cunningham, was a friend in Glasgow, "who had interested himself early in the fortunes of the Poet."]

To Mr. [John] M'Auley,

[DUMBARTON.]

Ellisland, 4th June, 1789.

DEAR SIR,

THOUGH I am not without my fears respecting my fate at that grand, universal inquest of right and wrong, commonly called *The Last Day*, yet I trust there is one sin which that arch-vagabond, Satan, who I understand is to be king's evidence, cannot throw in my teeth—I mean ingratitude. There is a certain pretty large quantum of kindness for which I remain, and from inability, I fear, must still remain, your debtor; but though unable to repay the debt, I assure you, Sir, I shall ever warmly remember the obligation. It gives me the sincerest pleasure to hear by my old acquaintance, Mr. Kennedy, that you are, in immortal Allan's language, "Hale, and weel, and living;" and that your charming family are well, and promising to be an amiable and respectable addition to the company of performers, whom the Great Manager of the Drama of Man is bringing into action for the succeeding age.

With respect to my welfare, a subject in which you once warmly and effectively interested yourself, I am here in my old way, holding my plough, marking the growth of my corn, or the health of my dairy; and at times sauntering by the delightful windings of the Nith, on the margin of which I have built my humble domicile, praying for seasonable weather, or holding an intrigue with the Muses; the only gypseys with whom I have now any intercourse. As I am entered into the holy state of matrimony, I trust my face is turned completely Zion-ward; and as it is a rule with all honest fellows to repeat no grievances, I hope that the little poetic licences of former days will, of course, fall under the oblivious influence of some good-natured statute of celestial prescription. In my family devotion, which, like a good Presbyterian, I occasionally give to my household folks, I am extremely fond of the psalm, "Let not the errors of my youth," &c., and that other, "Lo children are

God's heritage," &c., in which last Mrs. Burns, who by the bye has a glorious "wood-note wild" at either old song or psalmody, joins me with the pathos of Handel's Messiah.

*   *   *   *   *   *   *   *

R. B.

[Mr. M'Auley, who was a legal practitioner of respectability in Dumbarton, seems to have been remarkable also for handsome personal exterior. The following anecdote corroborative, and highly characteristic so far as Lord Affleck is concerned, which Mr. Chambers quotes from *Glasgow Reformers' Gazette, Dec. 4, 1852,* we here transcribe. "He was at one time examined as a witness before Lord Affleck, at the Circuit Court here, who asked M'Auley "where he came frae?" "From Dumbarton, my Lord." "The deevil, ye do! I did not think there had been sae weel-faured a fellow in a' Dumbarton."—This must have been some time before Burns's day as a poet, for Lord Affleck died in 1782. M'Auley must therefore have been either a mere youth at the time, or was considerably older than Burns at the date of their acquaintance. From the mention made of Mr. Kennedy in this letter, it seems very probable, as Mr. Chambers conjectures, that it was through the medium of that gentleman our Author was introduced to the hospitable gentry of Dumbartonshire and Lochlomondside. Compare letter (3) to Smith—*Prose Works, p. 147.*]

To Captain Riddel,

(1.)   CARSE.

Ellisland, 16th Oct., 1789.

SIR,

BIG with the idea of this important day at Friars-Carse, I have watched the elements and skies in the full persuasion that they would announce it to the astonished world by some phenomena of terrific portent. Yesternight until a very late hour did I wait with anxious horror, for the appearance of some Comet firing half the sky; or aerial armies of sanguinary Scandinavians, darting athwart the startled heavens, rapid as the ragged lightning, and horrid as those convulsions of nature that bury nations.

The elements, however, seem to take the matter very quietly: they did not even usher in this morning with triple suns and a shower of blood, symbolical of the three potent heroes, and the mighty claret-shed of the day. For me, as Thomson in his Winter says of the storm—I shall "Hear astonished, and astonished sing"

> The whistle and the man I sing;
> The man that won the whistle, &c.

> " Here are we met, three merry boys,
> Three merry boys I trow are we;
> And mony a night we've merry been,
> And mony mae we hope to be.

> " Wha first shall rise to gang awa,
> A cuckold coward loon is he;
> Wha last beside his chair shall fa'
> He is the king amang us three."†

To leave the heights of Parnassus and come to the humble vale of prose. I have some misgivings that I take too much upon me, when I request you to get your guest, Sir Robert Lowrie, to frank the two enclosed covers for me, the one of them to Sir William Cunningham, of Robertland, Bart., at Auchenskeith, Kilmarnock—the other to Mr. Allan Masterton, Writing-Master, Edinburgh. The first has a kindred claim on Sir Robert, as being a brother Baronet, and likewise a keen Foxite; the other is one of the worthiest men in the world, and a man of real genius; so, allow me to say, he has a fraternal claim on you. I want them franked for to-morrow, as I cannot get them to the post to-night. I shall send a servant again for them in the evening. Wishing that your head may be crowned with laurels to-night,* and free from aches to-morrow, I have the honor to be, Sir,

Your deeply indebted humble servant,

R. B.

* [The day on which "the Whistle" was to be contended for. The Poet's own date of this contest, as in 1790, was an error of the pen undoubtedly.]
+ [Compare note on "Willie Brew'd a Peck o' Maut"—Poetical Works, p. 267.]

(2.)   TO CAPTAIN RIDDEL.

[*Ellisland*, 1789.]

SIR,

I WISH from my inmost soul it were in my power to give you a more substantial gratification and return for all your goodness to the poet, than transcribing a few of his idle rhymes.—However, "an old song," though to a proverb an instance of insignificance, is generally the only coin a poet has to pay with.

If my poems which I have transcribed, and mean still to transcribe, into your book, were equal to the grateful respect and high esteem I bear for the gentleman to whom I present them, they would be the finest poems in the language.— As they are, they will at least be a testimony with what sincerity I have the honor to be, Sir,

Your devoted humble servant,

R. B.

[The reader may compare with this the letter to Captain Riddel at commencement of Literary Correspondence, containing a collection of fragments from our Author's earliest writings.]

MEMORANDUM

FOR

Provost E[dward] W[higham.]

To get from John French his sets of the following old Scots airs——

1st. The auld yowe jumpt o'er the tether—

2d. Nine nights awa, welcome hame my dearie—

3d. A' the nights o' the year, the chapman drinks nae water.

If Mr. Whigham will either of himself, or through the medium of that [hardy?] hearty Veteran of original wit, and social iniquity—Clackleith—procure these airs, it will be extremely obliging to

R. B.

[Edward Whigham, Esq., was at that time Provost of Sanquhar. The original document is now in possession of Miss Johnston, Sanquhar, a daughter of Mr. Johnston's, Clackleith. We are under obligation to G. Gemmell, Esq., Ayr, for the privilege of introducing this as well as several other documents in the present edition. The MS. being slightly decayed at the place, we have some difficulty in deciding whether the word in brackets should be hardy or hearty; we incline to the latter reading.]

To Provost Maxwell,

OF LOCHMABEN.

Ellisland, 20th December, 1789.

DEAR PROVOST,

As my friend Mr. Graham goes for your good town to-morrow, I cannot resist the temptation to send you a few lines, and as I have nothing to say I have chosen this sheet of foolscap, and begun as you see at the top of the first page, because I have ever observed, that when once people have fairly set out they know not where to stop. Now that my first sentence is concluded, I have nothing to do but to pray heaven to help me on to another. Shall I write you on Politics or Religion, two master subjects for your sayers of nothing. Of the first I dare say by this time you are nearly surfeited: and for the last, whatever they may talk of it, who make it a kind of company concern, I never could endure it beyond a soliloquy. I might write you on farming, on building, on marketing, but my poor distracted mind is so torn, so jaded, so racked and bedevilled with the task of the superlatively damned to make *one guinea do the business of three*, that I detest, abhor, and swoon at the very word business, though no less than four letters of my very short surname are in it.

Well, to make the matter short, I shall betake myself to a subject ever fruitful of themes; a subject the turtle-feast of the sons of Satan, and the delicious secret sugar-plum of the babes of grace—a subject sparkling with all the jewels that wit can find in the mines of genius; and pregnant with all the stores of learning from Moses and Confucius to Franklin and Priestley—in short, may it please your Lordship, I intend to write · · · ·

If at any time you expect a field-day in your town, a day when Dukes, Earls, and Knights pay their court to weavers, tailors, and cobblers, I should like to know of it two or three days beforehand. It is not that I care three skips of a cur dog for the politics, but I should like to see such an exhibition of human nature. If you meet with that worthy old veteran in religion and good-fellowship, Mr. Jaffrey, or any of his amiable family, I beg you will give them my best compliments.

R. B.

To Mr. Sutherland,

PLAYER,

ENCLOSING A PROLOGUE.

Monday Morning.

I WAS much disappointed, my dear Sir, in wanting your most agreeable company yesterday. However, I heartily pray for good weather next Sunday; and whatever aërial Being has the guidance of the elements, may take any other half-dozen of Sundays he pleases, and clothe them with

> "Vapours, and clouds, and storms,
> Until he terrify himself
> At combustion of his own raising."

I shall see you on Wednesday forenoon. In the greatest hurry,

R. B.

To Collector Mitchell.

Ellisland, [Oct. 13. 1790.]

SIR,

I SHALL not fail to wait on Captain Riddel to-night—I wish and pray that the goddess of Justice herself would appear to-morrow among our hon. gentlemen, merely to give them a word in their ear that mercy to the thief is injustice to the honest man. For my part, I have galloped over my ten parishes these four days, until this moment that I am just alighted, or rather, that my poor jackass-skeleton of a horse has let me down; for the miserable devil has been on his knees half a score of times within the last twenty miles, telling me in his own way, "Behold, am not I thy faithful jade of a horse, on which thou hast ridden these many years!"

In short, Sir, I have broke my horse's wind, and almost broke my own neck, besides some injuries in a part that shall be nameless, owing to a hard-hearted stone of a saddle. I find that every offender has so many great men to espouse his cause, that I shall not be surprised if I am not* committed to the strong hold of the law to-morrow for insolence to the dear friends of the gentlemen of the country.

I have the honor to be, Sir,

Your obliged and obedient humble

R. B.

* [Negative too many, in haste.]

Answer to the Petition of T. J.

1. Whether the Petitioner has been in use formerly to malt all his grain at one operation, is foreign to the purpose: this last season he certainly malted his crop at four or five operations; but be that as it may, Mr. J. ought to have known that by express act of parliament no malt, however small the quantity, can be legally manufactured until previous entry be made in writing of all the ponds, burns, floors, &c., so as to be used before the grain can be put to steep. In the Excise entry-books for the division, there is not a syllable of T. J.'s name for a number of years bygone.

2. True it is that Mr. Burns, on his first ride, in answer to Mr. J.'s question anent the conveying of the notices, among other ways pointed out the sending it by post as the most eligible method, but at the same time added this express clause, and to which Mr. Burns is willing to make faith: "At the same time, remember, Mr. J., that the notice is at your risk until it reach me!" Further, when Mr. Burns came to the Petitioner's kiln, there was a servant belonging to Mr. J. ploughing at a very considerable distance from the kiln, who left his plough and three horses without a driver, and came into the kiln, which Mr. B. thought was rather a suspicious circumstance, as there was nothing extraordinary in an Excise-officer going into a legal malt-floor so as to [induce a man to] leave three horses yoked to a plough in the distant middle of a moor. This servant, on being repeatedly questioned by Mr. Burns, could not tell when the malt was put to steep, when it was taken out, &c.—in short, was determined to be entirely ignorant of the affair. By and by, Mr. J.'s son came in; and on being questioned as to the steeping, taking out of the grain, &c., Mr. J., junior, referred me to this said servant, this ploughman, who, he said, must remember it best, as having been the principal actor in the business. The lad then, having gotten his cue, circumstantially recollected all about it.

All this time, though I was telling the son and servant the nature of the premunire they had incurred, though they pleaded for mercy keenly, the affair of the notice having been sent never once occurred to them, not even the son, who is said to have been the bearer. This was a stroke reserved for, and worthy of the gentleman himself. As to Mrs. Kelloch's oath, it proves nothing. She did, indeed, depone to a line being left for me at her house, which said line miscarried. It was a sealed letter; she could not tell whether it was a malt-notice or not; she could not even condescend on the month, nor so much as the season of the year. The truth is, T. J. and his family being Seceders, and consequently coming every Sunday to Thornhill Meeting-house, they were a good conveyance for the several maltsters and traders in their neighbourhood to transmit to post their notices, permits, &c.

But why all this tergiversation? It was put to the Petitioner in open court, after a full investigation of the cause: "Was he willing to swear that he meant no fraud in the matter?" And the Justices told him, that if he swore he would be assoilzied [absolved], otherwise he should be fined; still the Petitioner, after ten minutes' consideration, found his conscience unequal to the task, and declined the oath.

Now, indeed, he says he is willing to swear; he has been exercising his conscience in private, and will perhaps stretch a point. But the fact to which he is to swear was equally and in all parts known to him on that day when he refused to swear as to-day: nothing can give him further light as to the intention of his mind, respecting his meaning or not meaning *a fraud in the affair. No time can cast further light on the present resolves of the mind; but time will reconcile, and has reconciled many a man to that iniquity which he at first abhorred.*

[The above document forms Burns's official share of the business to which the previous letter to Collector Mitchell refers; and is an illustration of the system adopted by him, and explained in letter (7) to Robert Graham, Esq., in prosecuting the defaulters of his district. The document appeared for the first time in Chambers's Edition, 1856. It is worthy of notice how the Poet's peculiar style of observation characterises the document—"the distant middle of a name" being an expression, descriptive and truthful, that nobody almost but himself, in such a case, would have used. The rest of the document, in moral and other respects, is equally characteristic. The Petitioner, it appears, was a farmer at Mirecleugh, and had been fined £5 for contravension; against which he had reclaimed.]

To A. Fergusson, Esq.,

[OF CRAIGDARROCH.]

Globe Inn, Noon, Wednesday.
[Oct. ? 1789.]

"Blessed be he that kindly doth
The poor man's case consider."

I HAVE sought you all over the town, good Sir, to learn what you have done, or what can be done, for poor Robie Gordon. The hour is at hand when I must assume the execrable office of whipper-in to the blood-hounds of Justice, and must let loose the carrion sons * * * on poor Robie. I think you can do something to save the unfortunate man, and am sure, if you can, you will. I know that Benevolence is supreme in your bosom, and has the first voice in, and last check on, all you do; but that insidious * *, Politics, may [word wanting] the honest cully Attention, until the practicable moment of doing good is no more. I have the honor to be, Sir, your obliged humble servant,

ROBT. BURNS.

[This letter to Alexander Ferguson of Craigdarroch, Esq., in juxta-position with the above document, shows how anxiously solicitous the writer was to save from guilt, or even from suffering, the unfortunate victim of law, however stern he might be in bringing regular transgressors to punishment. This note, Mr. Chambers informs us, was found in Craigdarroch House, along with another very brief metrical note from our Author, in reply to the invitation to Carse.—See Miscellaneous Poetical Pieces.]

To Crauford Tait, Esq.,

EDINBURGH.

Ellisland, Oct. 15, 1790.

DEAR SIR,

ALLOW me to introduce to your acquaintance the bearer, Mr. Wm. Duncan, a friend of mine, whom I have long known and long loved. His father, whose only son he is, has a decent little property in Ayrshire, and has bred the young man to the law, in which department he comes up an adventurer to your good town. I shall give you my friend's character in two words: as to his head, he has talents enough, and more than enough, for common life; as to his heart, when Nature had kneaded the kindly clay that composes it, she said —" I can no more."

You, my good Sir, were born under kinder stars; but your fraternal sympathy, I well know, can enter into the feelings of the young man, who goes into life with the laudable ambition to *do* something, and to *be* something among his fellow-creatures; but whom the consciousness of friendless obscurity presses to the earth, and wounds to the soul!

Even the fairest of his virtues are against him. That independent spirit, and that ingenuous modesty, qualities inseparable from a noble mind, are, with the million, circumstances not a little disqualifying. What pleasure is in the power of the fortunate and the happy, by their notice and patronage, to brighten the countenance and glad the heart of such depressed youth! I am not so angry with mankind for their deaf economy of the purse:—the goods of this world cannot be divided without being lessened—but why be a niggard of that which bestows bliss on a fellow-creature, yet takes nothing from our own means of enjoyment! We wrap ourselves up in the cloak of our own better fortune, and turn away our eyes, lest the wants and woes of our brother-mortals should disturb the selfish apathy of our souls!

I am the worst hand in the world at asking a favor. That indirect address, that insinuating implication, which, without any positive request, plainly expresses your wish, is a talent not to be acquired at a plough-tail. Tell me then, for you can, in what periphrasis of language, in what circumvolution of phrase, I shall envelope, yet not conceal this plain story.— " My dear Mr. Tait, my friend Mr. Duncan, whom I have the pleasure of introducing to you, is a young lad of your own profession, and a gentleman of much modesty, and great worth. Perhaps it may be in your power to assist him in the, to him, important consideration of getting a place; but at all events, your notice and acquaintance will be a very great acquisition to him; and I dare pledge myself that he will never disgrace your favor."

You may possibly be surprised, Sir, at such a letter from me; 'tis, I own, in the usual way of calculating these matters, more than our acquaintance entitles me to; but my answer is short:—Of all the men at your time of life, whom I knew in Edinburgh, you are the most accessible on the side on which I have assailed you. You are very much altered indeed from what you were when I knew you, if generosity point the path you will not tread, or humanity call to you in vain.

As to myself, a being to whose interest I believe you are still a well-wisher; I am here, breathing at all times, thinking sometimes, and rhyming now and then. Every situation has its share of the cares and pains of life, and my situation, I am persuaded, has a full ordinary allowance of its pleasures and enjoyments.

My best compliments to your father and Miss Tait. If you have an opportunity, please remember me in the solemn league and covenant of friendship to Mrs. Lewis Hay. I am a wretch for not writing her; but I am so hackneyed with self-accusation in that way, that my conscience lies in my bosom with scarce the sensibility of an oyster in its shell. Where is Lady M‘Kenzie?—wherever she is, God bless her! I likewise beg leave to trouble you with compliments to Mr. Wm. Hamilton; Mrs. Hamilton and family; and Mrs. Chalmers, when you are in that country. Should you meet with Miss Nimmo, please remember me kindly to her.

R. B.

* [This gentleman was, we believe, the only son of Mr. Tait of Harveyston, Clackmannanshire, to whose hospitable mansion our Author paid two visits, whilst his correspondent was a youth. Mr. Crawford Tait, who settled as a Writer to the Signet in Edinburgh, married there a daughter of the late Sir Ilay Campbell, Bart., of Succoth; the fifth and youngest son of which marriage is the Right Rev. Archibald Campbell Tait, D.D., Archbishop of Canterbury.]

To ————.

[Ellisland, 1790.]

DEAR SIR,

WHETHER in the way of my trade I can be of any service to the Rev. Doctor is, I fear, very doubtful. Ajax's shield consisted, I think, of seven bull-hides and a plate of brass, which altogether set Hector's utmost force at defiance. Alas! I am not a Hector, and the worthy Doctor's foes are as securely armed as Ajax was. Ignorance, superstition, bigotry, stupidity, malevolence, self-conceit, envy—all strongly bound in a massy frame of brazen impudence. Good God, Sir! to such a shield, humour is the peck of a sparrow, and satire the pop-gun of a school-boy. Creation-disgracing *Scélérats* such as they, God only can mend, and the devil only can punish. In the comprehending way of Caligula, I wish they all had but one neck. I feel impotent as a child to the ardour of my wishes! O for a withering curse to blast the germins of their wicked machinations. O for a poisonous Tornado, winged from the Torrid Zone of Tartarus, to sweep the spreading crop of their villainous contrivances to the lowest hell:

R. B.

To Mr. Alexander Dalziel,
FACTOR, FINDLAYSTON.*

Ellisland, 19th March, 1791.

MY DEAR SIR,

I HAVE taken the liberty to frank this letter to you, as it encloses an idle poem of mine, which I send you; and God knows you may perhaps pay dear enough for it if you read it through. Not that this is my own opinion; but the author by the time he has composed and corrected his work, has quite pored away all his powers of critical discrimination.

I can easily guess from my own heart, what you have felt

on a late most melancholy event. God knows what I have suffered, at the loss of my best friend, my first, my dearest patron and benefactor; the man to whom I owe all that I am and have! I am going into mourning for him, and with more sincerity of grief than I fear some will, who by nature's ties ought to feel on the occasion.

I will be exceedingly obliged to you, indeed, to let me know the news of the noble family, how the poor mother and the two sisters support their loss. I had a packet of poetic bagatelles ready to send to Lady Betty, when I saw the fatal tidings in the newspaper. I see by the same channel, that the honored REMAINS of my noble patron are designed to be brought to the family burial-place. Dare I trouble you to let me know privately before the day of interment, that I may cross the country, and steal among the crowd to pay a tear to the last sight of my over revered benefactor? It will oblige me beyond expression.

R. B.

* [This gentleman, the factor, or steward, of Burns's noble friend, Lord Glencairn, with a view to encourage a second edition of the poems, laid the volume before his lordship, with such an account of the rustic bard's situation and prospects as from his slender acquaintance with him he could furnish. The result, as communicated to Burns by Mr. Dalziel, is highly creditable to the character of Lord Glencairn. After reading the book, his lordship declared that its merits greatly exceeded his expectation, and he took it with him as a literary curiosity to Edinburgh. He repeated his wishes to be of service to Burns, and desired Mr. Dalziel to inform him, that in patronising the book, ushering it with effect into the world, or treating with the booksellers, he would most willingly give every aid in his power; adding his request that Burns would take the earliest opportunity of letting him know in what way he could best further his interests. He also expressed a wish to see some of the unpublished manuscripts, with a view to establishing his character with the world.—Cromek.]

To Mr. Thomas Sloan.

Ellisland, 1st Sept., 1791.

MY DEAR SLOAN,

SUSPENSE is worse than disappointment; for that reason I hurry to tell you, that I just now learn that Mr Ballantine does not choose to interfere more in the business. I am truly sorry for it, but cannot help it.

You blame me for not writing you sooner; but you will please to recollect that you omitted one little necessary piece of information—your address.

However, you know equally well my hurried life, indolent temper, and strength of attachment. It must be a longer period than the longest life "in the world's hale and undegenerate days," that will make me forget so dear a friend as Mr. Sloan. I am prodigal enough at times, but I will not part with such a treasure as that.

I can easily enter into the *embarras* of your present situation. You know my favourite quotation from Young—

———————————"On Reason build RESOLVE!
That column of true majesty in man;"

And that other favourite one from Thomson's *Alfred*—

"What proves the hero truly GREAT
Is never, never, to despair."

Or, shall I quote you an author of your acquaintance?

> "——Whether morn, sleep- rising, or press arise,
> You may do miracles by—perseverance."

I have nothing new to tell you. The few friends we have are going on in the old way. I sold my crop on this day se'ennight, and sold it very well. A guinea an acre, on an average, above value. But such a scene of drunkenness was hardly ever seen in this country. After the roup was over, about thirty people engaged in a battle, every man for his own hand, and fought it out for three hours. Nor was the scene much better in the house. No fighting, indeed, but folks lying drunk on the floor, and decanting, until both my dogs got so drunk by attending them, that they could not stand. You will easily guess how I enjoyed the scene; as I was no farther over than you used to see me.

Mrs. B. and family have been in Ayrshire these many weeks.

Farewell! and God bless you, my dear Friend!

R. B.

[Readers may perhaps be shocked at such an account of rural debauchery at a sale, but the present was no exception to the usual routine at that time in such cases—and at funerals, it is lamentable to think, as well as at "Roups" and "Holy Fairs," the abuse of refreshments provided for visitors was the same. The reader will find an interesting anecdote of Burns and Mr. Sloan at Wanlockhead, in Chambers's edition, vol. iii. p. 9.—See also verses to John Taylor—Posthumous Works.]

To Col. Fullarton,

OF FULLARTON.

Ellisland, October 3, 1791.

SIR,

I HAVE just this minute got the frank, and next minute must send it to post, else I purposed to have sent you two or three other bagatelles, that might have amused a vacant hour about as well as "Six excellent new songs," or, the Aberdeen "Prognostications for the Year to come." I shall probably trouble you soon with another packet. About the gloomy month of November, when " the people of England hang and drown themselves," any thing generally is better than one's own thought.

Fond as I may be of my own productions, it is not for their sake that I am so anxious to send you them. I am ambitious, covetously ambitious of being known to a gentleman whom I am proud to call my countryman; a gentleman who was a foreign ambassador as soon as he was a man, and a leader of armies as soon as he was a soldier, and that with an *éclat* unknown to the usual minions of a court—men who, with all the adventitious advantages of princely connexions and princely fortune, must yet, like the caterpillar, labour a whole lifetime before they reach the wished for height, there to roost a stupid chrysalis, and doze out the remaining glimmering existence of old age.

If the gentleman that accompanied you when you did me the honor of calling on me, is with you, I beg to be respect-

fully remembered to him. I have the honor to be, Sir, your highly obliged, and most devoted humble servant,

R. B.

[Compare Note on " Vision "—Poetical Works, p. 99—" Brydon's brave Ward I well could spy.")

To ————,

Ellisland, 1791.

DEAR SIR,

I AM exceedingly to blame in not writing you long ago; but the truth is, that I am the most indolent of all human beings; and when I matriculate in the herald's office, I intend that my supporters shall be two sloths, my crest a slow-worm, and the motto, " Deil tak the foremost." So much by way of apology for not thanking you sooner for your kind execution of my commission.

I would have sent you the poem; but somehow or other it found its way into the public papers, where you must have seen it.   *   *   *

I am ever, dear Sir, yours sincerely.

R. B.

(1.)   To James Gracie, Esq.

Globe Inn, 8 o'clock p.m. [1791.]

SIR,

I have your letter anent Crombie's bill. Your forbearance has been very great. I did it to accommodate the thoughtless fellow. He asks till Wednesday week. If he fail, I pay it myself. In the meantime, if horning and caption be absolutely necessary, *grip him by the neck, and welcome.*   Yours,

ROBERT BURNS.

[Mr. Chambers, from whose edition we quote this letter, informs us that the defaulter alluded to was a mason about Dalswinton, Alexander Crombie by name, who had been employed at the building of the farm-steading at Ellisland, and whom Burns had accommodated with his name, as a worthy man struggling with difficulties in the world. Mr. Gracie was an official in the Bank at Dumfries.]

(2.)   TO JAMES GRACIE, ESQ.

Brow, Wednesday Morning, [13th *July,* 1796.]

MY DEAR SIR,

It would [be] doing high injustice to this place not to acknowledge that my rheumatisms have derived great benefits from it already; but, alas! my loss of appetite still continues. I shall not need your kind offer *this week*, and I return to town the beginning of next week, it not being a tide-week. I am detaining a man in a burning hurry. So, God bless you!

R. B.

[Mr. Gracie had been a kind friend to our Author; and the offer here referred to, was that of his carriage, to bring the Poet home from some salutary quarters to Dumfries.—Chambers.]

To Mr. James C[larke],

(1.)　　　　MOFFAT.

Dumfries, 10th January, 1792.

I RECEIVED yours this moment, my dear Sir. I sup with Captain Riddel in town to-night, else I had gone to Carse directly. Courage, *mon ami!* The day may, after all, be yours; but at any rate, there is other air to breathe than that of Moffat, pestiferously tainted as it is with the breath of that arch-scoundrel, J——. There are two quotations from two poets which, in situations such as yours, were congenial to my soul. Thomson says:

> "What proves the hero truly great,
> Is never, never to despair."

And Dr. Young:

> ——"On Reason build Resolve,
> That column of true majesty in man."

To-morrow, you shall know the result of my consultation with Captain Riddel.—Yours,

R. B.

(2.)　　　TO MR. JAMES C[LARKE],
　　　　　MOFFAT.

Dumfries, 17th Feb., 1792.

MY DEAR SIR,

IF this finds you at Moffat, or as soon as it finds you at Moffat, you must without delay wait on Mr. Riddel, as he has been very kindly thinking of you in an affair that has occurred of a clerk's place in Manchester; which, if your hopes are desperate in your present business, he proposes procuring for you. I know your gratitude for past, as well as hopes of future favors, will induce you to pay every attention to Glenriddel's wishes; as he is almost the only, and undoubtedly the best friend that your unlucky fate has left you.

Apropos, I just now hear that you have beat your foes *every tail hollow*. Huzza! *Io triumphe!* Mr. Riddel, who is at my elbow, says that if it is so, he begs that you will wait on him directly, and I know you are too good a man not to pay your respects to your saviour. Yours,

R. B.

[These two letters, for the discovery of which the public is indebted to Mr. Chambers, read in connection with letter (6) to Cunningham, indicate very plainly the affectionate interest the Poet had taken in the welfare of his friend the then schoolmaster of Moffat. What triumph is here celebrated over his "foes," we do not learn;—but whatever it might be, it is certain that he required and received still further assistance from our Author, and finally relinquished his situation at Moffat for another of the same kind at Forfar, as the following letter, given by Mr. Chambers, shows:—

CLARKE TO BURNS.

MY DEAR FRIEND,　　　　*　　　(Forfar, 18th Feb., 1796.)

Your letter makes me very unhappy; the more so, as I had heard very flattering accounts of your situation some months ago. A note [20s.] is enclosed; and if such partial payment will be acceptable, this shall soon be followed by more. My appointment here has more than answered my expectations; but furnishing a large house, &c., has kept me still very poor; and the persecution I suffered from that rascal, Lord H——, brought me into expenses which, with all my economy, I have not yet rubbed off. Be so kind as write me. Your disinterested friendship has made an impression which time cannot efface. Believe me, my dear Burns, yours in sincerity,　　　JAMES CLARKE.]

(3.)　　　TO MR. CLARKE,
　　　　　SCHOOLMASTER, FORFAR.

Dumfries, 26th June, 1796.

MY DEAR CLARKE,

STILL, still the victim of affliction! Were you to see the emaciated figure who now holds the pen to you, you would not know your old friend. Whether I shall ever get about again is only known to Him, the Great Unknown, whose creature I am. Alas, Clarke! I begin to fear the worst. As to my individual self, I am tranquil, and would despise myself if I were not; but Burns's poor widow, and half-a-dozen of his dear little ones—*helpless orphans!—there* I am weak as a woman's tear.* Enough of this! 'Tis half of my disease.

I duly received your last, enclosing the note. It came extremely in time, and I am much obliged by your punctuality. Again I must request you to do me the same kindness. Be so very good as, by return of post, to enclose me *another note*. I trust you can do it without inconvenience, and it will seriously oblige me.† If I must go, I shall leave a few friends behind me, whom I shall regret while consciousness remains. I know I shall live in their remembrance. Adieu, dear Clarke. That I shall ever see you again, is, I am afraid, highly improbable.

R. B.

* [This adaptation from Shakspeare—
"But I am weaker than a woman's tear,"
Troilus and Cressida: Act I., Scene I.—

is far from being merely rhetorical. It is manifestly employed to save the use of terms by himself that would have been too painful and enervating for him to utter, in prospect of the desolation to which he could not help looking forward.]
† [Compare note on letter (1) to Captain John Hamilton. The forbearance and gentleness of this application to a debtor, in the circumstances of the case, are beyond mere commentary: sermons might be written on them.]

To Mr. Stephen Clarke,

EDINBURGH.

July 16, 1792.

MR. BURNS begs leave to present his most respectful compliments to Mr. Clarke.—Mr. B. some time ago did himself the honor of writing Mr. C. respecting coming out to the country, to give a little musical instruction in a highly respectable family, where Mr. C. may have his own terms, and may be as happy as indolence, the Devil, and the gout will permit him. Mr. B. knows well how Mr. C. is engaged with another family; but cannot Mr. C. find two or three weeks to spare to each of them? Mr. B. is deeply impressed with, and awefully conscious of, the high importance of Mr. C.'s time, whether in the winged moments of symphonious exhibition, at the keys of harmony, while listening Seraphs cease their own less delightful strains; or in the drowsy hours of slumb'rous Repose, in the arms of his dearly

* 2 B

beloved elbow-chair, where the frowsy, but potent power of Indolence circumfuses her vapours round, and sheds her dews on the head of her darling son. But half a line conveying half a meaning from Mr. C. would make Mr. B. the happiest of mortals.

[The gentleman here addressed is the celebrated musician so frequently alluded to in the correspondence with Thomson; and Mr. M'Murdo's, at Drumlanrig, is understood to be the "highly respectable family" where Mr. C.'s services were in requisition; and where, it is said, a tender impression was afterwards made on Mr. C.'s heart by one of his elegant and accomplished pupils. In Cromek's *Reliques* the letter is addressed, by misprint, to "Mr. T. Clarke."]

To Captain Johnstone.

Dumfries, Nov. 13, 1792.

Sir,

I HAVE just read your prospectus of the *Edinburgh Gazetteer*. If you go on in your paper with the same spirit, it will, beyond all comparison, be the first composition of the kind in Europe. I beg leave to insert my name as a subscriber, and if you have already published any papers, please send me them from the beginning. Point out your own way of settling payments in this place, or I shall settle with you through the medium of my friend, Peter Hill, bookseller in Edinburgh.

Go on Sir! Lay bare with undaunted heart and steady hand that horrid mass of corruption called politics and state-craft. Dare to draw in their native colours those

"Calm thinking villains whom no faith can fix,"

whatever be the shibboleth of their pretended party.

The address to me at Dumfries will find, Sir, your very humble servant,

ROBERT BURNS.

[Compare letter (10) to Robert Graham, Esq., on this subject.]

To Captain [John] Hamilton,

(1.)   DUMFRIES.

[After Martinmas, 1793.]

Sir,

IT is even so. —You are the only person in Dumfries or in the world, to whom I have *run in debt*; and I took the freedom with you, because I believed, and do still believe, that I may do it with more impunity as to my feelings than any other person almost that I ever met with.—I will settle with you soon; and I assure you, Sir, it is with infinite pain that I have transgressed on your goodness. The unlucky fact for me is, that about the beginning of these disastrous times, in a moment of imprudence I lent my name to a friend who has since been unfortunate; and of course, I had a sum to pay which my very

limited income and large family could ill afford.—God forbid, Sir, that anything should ever distress you as much as writing this card has done me.

With the sincerest gratitude and most respectful esteem,
    I have the honor to be,
        Sir,
            Your very humble sert.,
                ROBERT BURNS.

[We have no conclusive evidence either as to the exact date of this painfully interesting letter, or the unfortunate monetary transaction to which it refers. We have more than one reference to "these disastrous times" in the correspondence with Hill, which enable us to fix the date as being at least posterior to summer of 1793; and one obscure reference to money matters—letters (11) and (12) to Hill—which seems to imply that Hill himself had knowledge of, perhaps disagreeable interest in, some such transaction. But Gilbert Burns's distinct statement about Mr. Clark's bill (schoolmaster at Forfar—see letter (3) to him), and the well-known fact that the Poet had in some way, by pecuniary advance or otherwise, befriended him, and was still a creditor of his at the time of his own death, seem to leave very little doubt on the subject. "The Poet would appear to have never quite succeeded in squaring accounts with his landlord, Captain Hamilton," says Mr. Chambers. The above letter, which appears now for the first time in print, explains satisfactorily the origin of those painful obligations, which so darkened and distressed his last hours, and which were undoubtedly the cause of his self-alienation from Captain Hamilton, and perhaps other esteemed friends, in pride and sorrow. The above document, as our readers are already aware, has been opportunely supplied to us by George Manners, Esq., F.S.A., Croydon, and completes the *elucidation* of a subject on which Mr. Chambers has bestowed much care.]

---

(2)   TO CAPTAIN HAMILTON.

Saturday Morning, [January 31, 1795.]

Sir,

I WAS from home, and had not the opportunity of seeing your more than polite, your most friendly card. It is not possible, most worthy Sir, that you could do anything to offend anybody. My backwardness proceeds alone from the abashing consciousness of my obscure station in the ranks of life. Many an evening have I sighed to call in and spend it at your social fireside; but a shyness of appearing obtrusive amid the fashionable visitants occasionally there, kept me at a distance. It shall do so no more. On Monday, I must be in the country, and most part of the week; but the first leisure evening I shall avail myself of your hospitable goodness. With the most ardent sentiments of gratitude and respect, I have the honor to be, Sir,

    Your highly-obliged humble servant,
        ROBT. BURNS.

[The friendly communication to which the above letter is a reply we find in Mr. Chambers's Edition, vol. iv., p. 131,—as follows:—

DUMFRIES, 30th Jan., 1795.

DEAR SIR,

AT same time that I acknowledge the receipt of three guineas to account of house-rent, will you permit me to enter a complaint of a different nature? When you first came here, I courted your acquaintance; I wished to see you; I asked you to call in and take a family-dinner now and then, when it suited your convenience. For more than twelve months you have never entered my door, but seemed rather shy when we met. This kept me from sending any further particular invitation. If I have in any shape offended, or from inadvertency hurt the delicacy of your feelings, tell me so, and I will endeavour to set it to rights.

If you are disposed to renew our acquaintance (I) will be glad to see you to a family-dinner at three o'clock on Sunday; and, at any rate, hope you will believe me, dear Sir, your sincere friend,

JOHN HAMILTON.]

[On our Author's reply—(2)—to the above, Mr. Chambers remarks:—"One can scarcely doubt that there were other considerations pressing upon him—the unpleasant sense of debt towards his landlord, and the consciousness that he was under the ban of a large part of respectable society on account of politics, the Riddel quarrel, and his own many imprudences." So far as a painful sense of indebtedness to his landlord was a cause of this unwillingness on the Poet's part to intrude on Captain Hamilton, the reader has now the clearest evidence; and if it was probably the chief, if not the only cause—although, as we perceive, he was honestly endeavouring to repay it. Captain Hamilton, proprietor of Allershaw, was landlord of both the houses our Author tenanted in succession at Dumfries, and was a man of the highest respectability and most amiable disposition.]

To Captain ——————[*]

Dumfries, 6th December, 1793.

Sir,

Heated as I was with wine yesternight, I was perhaps rather seemingly impertinent in my anxious wish to be honoured with your acquaintance. You will forgive it—it was the impulse of heart-felt respect. "He is the father of Scottish county reform, and is a man who does honour to the business, at the same time that the business does honour to him," said my worthy friend Glenriddel to somebody by me, who was talking of your coming to this country with your corps. "Then," I said "I have a woman's longing to take him by the hand, and say to him, 'Sir, I honour you as a man to whom the interests of humanity are dear, and as a patriot to whom the rights of your country are sacred.'"

In times like these, Sir, when our commoners are barely able by the glimmering of their own twilight understandings to scrawl a frank, and when lords are what gentlemen would be ashamed to be, to whom shall a sinking country call for help? To the independent country gentleman. To him who has too deep a stake in his country not to be in earnest for her welfare; and who, in the honest pride of man, can view with equal contempt the insolence of office and the allurements of corruption.

I mentioned to you a Scots ode or song I had lately composed, and which, I think, has some merit. Allow me to enclose it. When I fall in with you at the theatre, I shall be glad to have your opinion of it. Accept of it, Sir, as a very humble but most sincere tribute of respect from a man who, dear as he prizes poetic fame, yet holds dearer an independent mind.

I have the honour to be, &c.,

R. B.

[*] [Supposed by Mr. Chambers to be Captain or Major Robertson, of Lude; Compare letter (3) to Cunningham. The poem enclosed was "Bruce's Address"—of which our Author distributed, among literary and political friends, several copies about this time.]

To John Syme, Esq.

You know that among other high dignities, you have the honor to be my supreme court of critical judicature, from which there is no appeal. I enclose you a song which I composed since I saw you, and I am going to give you the history of it. Do you know that among much that I admire in the characters and manners of those great folks whom I have now the honor to call my acquaintance, the Oswald family, there is nothing charms me more than Mr. Oswald's unconcealable attachment to that incomparable woman? Did you ever, my dear Syme, meet with a man who owed more to the Divine Giver of all good things than Mr. O.? A fine fortune; a pleasing exterior; self-evident amiable dispositions, and an ingenuous upright mind, and that informed too, much beyond the usual run of young fellows of his rank and fortune: and to all this, such a woman!—but of her I shall say nothing at all, in despair of saying anything adequate: in my song I have endeavoured to do justice to what would be his feelings on seeing, in the scene I have drawn, the habitation of his Lucy. As I am a good deal pleased with my performance, I, in my first fervour, thought of sending it to Mrs. Oswald, but on second thoughts, perhaps what I offer as the honest incense of genuine respect might, from the well-known character of poverty and poetry, be construed into some modification or other of that servility which my soul abhors. Do let me know some convenient moment, ere the worthy family leave town, that I, *with propriety*, may wait on them. In the circle of the fashionable herd, those who come either to show their own consequence, or to borrow consequence from the visit—in such a mob I will not appear; mine is a different errand.—Yours,

ROBERT BURNS.

[John Syme, Esq., of Ryedale, was distributor of stamps for the district, and had his office on the ground floor of the house in which Burns took up his residence on coming to Dumfries. Here they got acquainted. Mr. Syme was perhaps a true enough friend of Burns—he was at least a constant associate; and, being a man of taste and literary accomplishments, was often consulted by the Poet on such subjects, and was, indeed, selected by Dr. Currie himself as the person to whom the writing of the Poet's life should be entrusted. At the same time, it appears to us that Mr. Syme's egotism and propensity to exaggerate, in his own favour and for his own glory, any incident or detail of the Poet's life connected with himself, render him a very doubtful authority in such matters. The well-known story, for example, of Burns drawing his sword-cane to avenge an imaginary insult at Syme's table, and trembling at Syme's affectionate remonstrance, is manifestly an absurd exaggeration of some convivial joke. The reader is referred for a variety of incidents in his teens, to Chambers's edition, 1836, vol. iv. p. 151, &c. It need hardly be mentioned that the lady referred to in the letter was Mrs. Richard Oswald of Auchencruive, and that the song enclosed for Mr. Syme's critical examination is the beautiful lyric, "O, Wat ye wha's in yon town!"—see Poetical Works, p. 308.]

To David M'Culloch, Esq.

Dumfries, 21st June, 1794.

My Dear Sir,

My long projected journey through your country is at last fixed: and on Wednesday next, if you have nothing of more importance than to take a saunter down to Gatehouse about

two or three o'clock, I shall be happy to take a draught of M'Kune's best with you. Collector Syme will be at Glen's about that time, and will meet us about dish-of-tea hour. Syme goes also to Kerroughtree, and let me remind you of your kind promise to accompany me there : I will need all the friends I can muster, for I am indeed ill at ease whenever I approach your honourables and right honourables.

Yours sincerely,

R. B.

* [So, elliptically, in original.]

[Mr. David M'Culloch, younger of Ardwell, is the gentleman to whom we are indebted, through Mr. Lockhart, for the sentimental account of an interview with Burns at Dumfries, as he, Burns, was " walking alone on the shady side of the street, while the opposite side was gay with successive groups of ladies and gentlemen, all drawn together for the festivities of the night [King's Birth-day assembly night, 1794], not one of whom appeared willing to recognise him," &c. ; a story about which, like some of Syme's stories, we must be allowed to express a little qualifying scepticism.—Compare Memoranda by Mrs. Burns—Appendix. The visit here alluded to was to Mr. Heron of Heron.—see Ballads on his election.]

To Mr. Samuel Clarke, Jun.,
DUMFRIES.

(1.)

Sunday Morning [1794.]

DEAR SIR,

I was, I know, drunk last night, but I am sober this morning. From the expressions Capt. [Dods] made use of to me, had I had nobody's welfare to care for but my own, we should certainly have come, according to the manners of the world, to the necessity of murdering one another about the business. The words were such as generally, I believe, end in a brace of pistols; but I am still pleased to think that I did not ruin the peace and welfare of a wife and a family of children in a drunken squabble. Further, you know that the report of certain political opinions being mine, has already once before brought me to the brink of destruction. I dread lest last night's business may be misrepresented in the same way,— You, I beg, will take care to prevent it. I tax your wish for Mrs. Burns's welfare with the task of waiting, as soon as possible, on every gentleman who was present, and state this to him, and, as you please, show him this letter. What, after all, was the obnoxious toast?—" May our success in the present war be equal to the justice of our cause "—a toast that the most outrageous frenzy of loyalty cannot object to. I request and beg that this morning you will wait on the parties present at the foolish dispute. I shall only add, that I am truly sorry that a man who stood so high in my estimation as Mr. ——, should use me in the manner in which I conceive he has done.

R. B.

[The above letter refers to one of those painful, and sometimes dangerous, political discussions into which the Poet was precipitated at this crisis by the violence of his own zeal, and his contempt for the "holster-coated epauletted puppies" of the service, who took every occasion to assert offensively their own professional loyalty in his presence. Neither have nor respect, it may be imagined, was lost on either side. Compare letter (1) to Mrs. Riddel, p. 59. Wine may have had something to do with such ebullitions, but not so much as sheer political animosity.]

By some unexplained oversight, Mr. Chambers allocates this letter to " Mr. Stephen Clarke, jun."—being ignorant, perhaps, of Mr. Samuel Clarke, jun.'s acquaintance with the Poet. There were three Clarkes, correspondents of our Author's, who may be here briefly distinguished : 1—James Clarke, schoolmaster at Moffat, afterwards at Forfar : 2—Stephen Clarke, teacher of music, and organist of the Episcopal Chapel, Cowgate, Edinburgh—a man of great musical genius, frequently referred to in our Author's correspondence with Thomson—died August, 1797 : 3—Samuel Clarke, jun., a resident in Dumfries, and who occupied an important legal position there, as Assessor, if we mistake not, to the Burgh. To him this letter is undoubtedly addressed, as well as that, on a similar topic, which immediately follows.]

(2.)

TO MR. SAMUEL CLARKE, JUN.

MY DEAR SIR,

I RECOLLECT something of a drunken promise yesternight to breakfast with you this morning.—I am very sorry that it is impossible. I remember too, you very obligingly mentioning something of your intimacy with Mr. Corbet, our Supervisor-General. Some of our folks about the Excise Office, Edinr., had and perhaps still have conceived a prejudice against me as being a drunken dissipated character.—I might be all this, you know, and yet be an honest fellow ; but you know that I am an honest fellow, and am nothing of this. You may in your own way let him know that I am not unworthy of subscribing myself, my dear Clarke, your friend,

R. BURNS.

[This letter, already quoted and commented on by us in Biography (p. xlv.), is thus in original " Docketted : R. Burns's—S. Clarke, jun., witness, Dumfries." No trace of any date visible. The original is in possession of his daughter, Mrs. Stewart Gladstone of Capenoch, Dumfriesshire.]

To Mr. Alexander Findlater,
SUPERVISOR OF EXCISE, DUMFRIES.

[1795 ?]

SIR,

INCLOSED are the two schemes. I would not have troubled you with the Collector's one, but for suspicion lest it be not right. Mr. Erskine promised me to make it right, if you will have the goodness to shew him how. As I have no copy of the scheme for myself, and the alterations being very considerable from what it was formerly, I hope that I shall have access to this scheme I send you, when I come to face up my new books. *So much for schemes*—And that no scheme to betray a FRIEND, or mislead a STRANGER ; to seduce a YOUNG GIRL, or rob a HENROOST ; to subvert LIBERTY, or bribe an EXCISEMAN ; to disturb the GENERAL ASSEMBLY, or annoy a GOSSIPPING ; to overthrow the credit of ORTHODOXY, or the authority of OLD SONGS ; to oppose *your wishes*, or frustrate *my hopes*—MAY PROSPER—is the sincere wish and prayer of

ROBT. BURNS.

[In Mr. Findlater's opinion, who was a true friend of our Author's in life, and to whose affectionate vindication in some respects his reputation since death has been indebted, the rebuke administered to Burns, by authority of the Board, was not so severe as commonly supposed at the time ; and in this opinion of his on that subject, the Poet's widow herself concurs. Compare Memoranda by Mrs. Burns, also Reminiscences, *—Appendix.]

To Mr. Heron,

OF HERON.

[*Dumfries*, 1794 or 1795.]

SIR,

I INCLOSE you some copies of a couple of political ballads; one of which, I believe, you have never seen. Would to Heaven I could make you master of as many votes in the Stewartry! But—

"Who does the utmost that he can,
Does well, acts nobly—angels could no more."

In order to bring my humble efforts to bear with more effect on the foe, I have privately printed a good many copies of both ballads, and have sent them among friends all about the country.

To pillory upon Parnassus the rank reprobation of character, the utter dereliction of all principle, in a profligate junto which has not only outraged virtue, but violated common decency, spurning even hypocrisy as paltry iniquity below their daring—to unmask their flagitiousness to the broadest day—to deliver such over to their merited fate, is surely not merely innocent, but laudable; is not only propriety, but virtue. You have already, as your auxiliary, the sober detestation of mankind on the heads of your opponents; and I swear by the lyre of Thalia, to muster on your side all the votaries of honest Laughter, and fair, candid Ridicule!

I am extremely obliged to you for your kind mention of my interests in a letter which Mr. Syme showed me. At present, my situation in life must be in a great measure stationary, at least for two or three years. The statement is this—I am on the supervisors' list, and as we come on there by precedency, in two or three years I shall be at the head of that list, and be appointed, *of course*. *Then*, a FRIEND might be of service to me in getting me into a place of the kingdom which I would like. A supervisor's income varies from about a hundred and twenty to two hundred a year; but the business is an incessant drudgery, and would be nearly a compleat bar to every species of literary pursuit. The moment I am appointed supervisor, in the common routine, I may be nominated on the collectors' list; and this is always a business purely of political patronage. A collectorship varies much, from better than two hundred a year to near a thousand. They also come forward by precedency on the list; and have, besides a handsome income, a life of compleat leisure. A life of literary leisure with a decent competence, is the summit of my wishes. It would be the prudish affectation of silly pride in me to say that I do not need, or would not be indebted to a political friend; at the same time, Sir, I by no means lay my affairs before you thus, to hook my dependent situation on your benevolence. If, in my progress of life, an opening should occur where the good offices of a gentleman of your public character and political consequence might bring me forward, I shall petition your goodness with the same frankness as I now do myself the honor to subscribe myself,

R. B.

[Compare Ballads on Mr. Heron's election, &c.]

To [Richard A. Oswald, Esq.]

Dumfries, 23d April, 1795.

SIR,

You see the danger of patronizing the rhyming tribe: you flatter the Poet's vanity—a most potent ingredient in the composition of a son of rhyme—by a little notice; and he, in return, persecutes your good-nature with his acquaintance. In these days of volunteering, I have come forward with my services, as Poet Laureate to a highly respectable political party, of which you are a distinguished member. The enclosed are, I hope, only a beginning to the songs of triumph which you will earn in that contest.—I have the honor to be,
Sir,
Your obliged and devoted humble servant,
R. BURNS.

[This letter, Mr. Chambers informs us, was found among the papers of the Auchencruive family, and is supposed to have enveloped our Author's Election Ballads of the crisis.]

To Mr. John Edgar,

EXCISE-OFFICE, EDINBURGH.

25th April, 1795.

SIR,

I UNDERSTAND that I am to incur censure by the wine-account of this district not being sent in. Allow me to state the following circumstances to you, which, if they do not apologise for, will at least extenuate my part of the offence.

The general letter was put into my hands sometime about the beginning of this month, as I was then in charge of the district, Mr. Findlater being indisposed. I immediately, as far as in my power, made a survey of the wine-stocks; and where I could not personally survey, I wrote the officer of the division. In a few days more, and previous to collection-week, Mr. Findlater resumed charge; and as, in the course of collection, he would have both the officers by him, and the old books among his hands, it very naturally occurred to me the wine-account business would rest with him. At the close of that week, I got a note from the collector that the account-making-up was thrown on my hands. I immediately set about it; but one officer's books, James Graham of Sanquhar, not being at hand, I wrote him to send me them by first post. Mr. Graham has not thought proper to pay the least attention to my request, and to day I have sent an express for his stock-book.

This, Sir, is a plain state of facts; and if I must still be thought censurable, I hope it will be considered that this officiating job being my first, I cannot be supposed to be completely master of all the etiquette of the business.

If my supposed neglect is to be laid before the Honourable Board, I beg you will have the goodness to accompany the complaint with this letter.

I am, Sir, your very humble servant,
ROBT. BURNS.

ADDRESS OF THE SCOTTISH DISTILLERS

To the Right Hon. William Pit.

Sir,

While pursy burgesses crowd your gate, sweating under the weight of heavy addresses, permit us, the quondam distillers in that part of Great Britain called Scotland, to approach you, not with venal approbation, but with fraternal condolence; not as what you are just now, or for some time have been; but as what, in all probability, you will shortly be.—We shall have the merit of not deserting our friends in the day of their calamity, and you will have the satisfaction of perusing at least one honest address. You are well acquainted with the dissection of human nature; nor do you need the assistance of a fellow-creature's bosom to inform you that man is always a selfish, often a perfidious being.—This assertion, however the hasty conclusions of superficial observation may doubt of it, or the raw inexperience of youth may deny it, those who make the fatal experiment we have done will feel.—You are a statesman, and consequently are not ignorant of the traffic of these corporation compliments.—The little great man who drives the borough to market, and the very great man who buys the borough in that market, they two do the whole business; and you well know they, likewise, have their price. With that sullen disdain which you can so well assume, rise, illustrious Sir, and spurn these hireling efforts of venal stupidity. At best they are the compliments of a man's friends on the morning of his execution; they take a decent farewell, resign you to your fate, and hurry away from your approaching hour.

If fame say true, and omens be not very much mistaken, you are about to make your exit from that world where the sun of gladness gilds the paths of prosperous men: permit us, great Sir, with the sympathy of fellow-feeling to hail your passage to the realms of ruin.

Whether this sentiment proceed from the selfishness or cowardice of mankind is immaterial; but to point out to a child of misfortune those who are still more unhappy, is to give him some degree of positive enjoyment. In this light, Sir, our downfall may be again useful to you:—though not exactly in the same way, it is not perhaps the first time it has gratified your feelings. It is true, the triumph of your evil star is exceedingly despiteful.—At an age when others are the votaries of pleasure, or underlings in business, you had attained the highest wish of a British statesman; and with the ordinary date of human life, what a prospect was before you! Deeply rooted in *Royal Favour*, you overshadowed the land. The birds of passage, which follow ministerial sunshine through every clime of political faith and manners, flocked to your branches; and the beasts of the field (the lordly possessors of hills and valleys) crowded under your shade. "But behold a watcher, a holy one, came down from heaven, and cried aloud, and said thus: Hew down the tree, and cut off his branches; shake off his leaves, and scatter his fruit; let the beasts get away from under it, and the fowls from his branches!" A blow from an unthought-of quarter, one of those terrible accidents which peculiarly mark the hand of Omnipotence, overset your career, and laid all your fancied honours in the dust. But turn your eyes, Sir, to the tragic scenes of our fate:—an ancient nation, that for many ages had gallantly maintained the unequal struggle for independence with her much more powerful neighbour, at last agrees to a union which should ever after make them one people. In consideration of certain circumstances, it was covenanted that the former should enjoy a stipulated alleviation in her share of the public burdens, particularly in that branch of the revenue called the Excise. This just privilege has of late given great umbrage to some interested, powerful individuals of the more potent part of the empire, and they have spared no wicked pains, under insidious pretexts, to subvert what they dared not openly to attack, from the dread which they yet entertained of the spirit of their ancient enemies.

In this conspiracy we fell; nor did we alone suffer, our country was deeply wounded. A number of (we will say) respectable individuals, largely engaged in trade, where we were not only useful, but absolutely necessary to our country in her dearest interests; we, with all that was near and dear to us, were sacrificed, without remorse, to the infernal deity of political Expediency!* We fell to gratify the wishes of dark Envy, and the views of unprincipled Ambition! Your foes, Sir, were avowed; were too brave to take an ungenerous advantage; you fell in the face of day.—On the contrary, our enemies, to complete our overthrow, contrived to make their guilt appear the villainy of a nation.—Your downfall only drags with you your private friends and partizans: in our misery are more or less involved the most numerous and most valuable part of the community—all those who immediately depend on the cultivation of the soil, from the landlord of a province down to his lowest hind.

Allow us, Sir, yet further, just to hint at another rich vein of comfort in the dreary regions of adversity;—the gratulations of an approving conscience. In a certain great assembly, of which you are a distinguished member, panegyrics on your private virtues have so often wounded your delicacy, that we shall not distress you with anything on the subject. There is, however, one part of your public conduct which our feelings will not permit us to pass in silence: our gratitude must trespass on your modesty; we mean, worthy Sir, your whole behaviour to the Scots Distillers.—In evil hours, when obtrusive recollection presses bitterly on the sense, let that, Sir, come like a healing angel, and speak the peace to your soul which the world can neither give nor take away.

We have the honor to be, Sir,

Your sympathizing fellow-sufferers,

And grateful humble Servants,

JOHN BARLEYCORN—*Præses.*

* [Compare "Author's Earnest Cry and Prayer"—*Poetical Works*, p. 19.]

[" This ironical letter," we are informed by Cunningham, " was found among the papers of Burns." It first appeared, however, in Cromek's Reliques. We are afraid so admirable a piece of satire never found its way to the Right Honourable Gentleman's eye for whom it was intended. It is in the very best style of Junius, with a genial vein of merriment and solemnity combined running through it, which he was not capable of; and it is pleasant to see by such evidence, that Burns could rightly appreciate both the character and position of the great legislator by whom he, in his obscurity, and for his too great honesty, had been neglected, if not condemned.]

To the Hon. Provost, Bailies, and Town Council of Dumfries.

GENTLEMEN,　　　　　　　　　　　　　　　　[1793?]

THE literary taste and liberal spirit of your good town has so ably filled the various departments of your schools, as to make it a very great object for a parent to have his children educated in them. Still, to me, a stranger, with my large family, and very stinted income, to give my young ones that education I wish, at the high school-fees which a stranger pays, will bear hard upon me.

Some years ago your good town did me the honor of making me an honorary burgess.—Will you allow me to request that this mark of distinction may extend so far, as to put me on the footing of a real freeman of the town, in the schools?

[That I may not appear altogether unworthy of this favor, allow me to state to you some little services I have lately done a branch of your revenue. The two-pennies exigible on foreign ale vended within your limits: in this rather neglected article of your income I am ready to shew that within these few weeks my exertions have secured for you of those duties nearly the sum of Ten Pounds; and in this too, I was the only one of the gentlemen of the Excise (except Mr. Mitchell, whom *you pay* for his trouble) who took the least concern in the business.*]

If you are so very kind as to grant my request, it will certainly be a constant incentive to me to strain every nerve where I can officially serve you; and will, if possible, increase that grateful respect with which I have the honor to be,

Gentlemen,

Your devoted humble Servant,

R. B.

* [For supplying this important paragraph we are indebted to Mr. Carruthers of the *Inverness Courier.*

[The request contained in this letter, one is glad to know, was immediately complied with. Burns had been made an honorary burgess on occasion of his first visit to Dumfries in 1787, as he was returning from England, and the above application was certainly not made till 1793; so there had been no haste on his part, to convert this honour to advantage: and by the letter which follows, it appears he was still going on, doing all in his power to augment the revenues of the Burgh, and more than compensate for the privilege conferred of free education for his children. His boys, under the special care of his esteemed friend, Rev. James Gray, then master of the grammar-school, Dumfries, were in the full enjoyment of its advantages at the time of their father's death.]

To Provost Staig.

Friday, Noon, [1795.]

I KNOW, Sir, that anything which relates to the Burgh of Dumfries's interests will engage your readiest attention, so shall make no apology for this letter. I have been for some time turning my attention to a branch of your good town's revenue, where, I think, there is much to amend: I mean the "Twa-Pennies" on ale. The Brewers and Victuallers within the jurisdiction pay accurately: but three common brewers in the Bridgend, whose consumpt is almost entirely in Dumfries, pay nothing: Annan Brewer, who daily sends in great quantities of ale, pays nothing: because in both cases Ale certificates are never asked for; and of all the English ale, porter, &c., scarcely any of it pays. For my part, I never recorded an ale certificate in Dumfries, and I know most of the other officers are in the same predicament. It makes no part of our official duty, and besides, until it is universally assessed on all dealers, it strikes me as injustice to assess one. I know that our collector has a per-centage on the collection: but as it is no great object to him he gives himself no concern as to what is brought into the town. The supervisor would suit you better. He is an abler and a keener man, and what is all important in the business, such is his official influence over, and power among his offrs.,* that were he to signify that such was his wish, not a "pennie" would be left unaccounted. It is by no means the case with the collector. The offrs. are not so immediately among his hands, and they would not pay the same attention to his mandates. Your brewers here, the Richardsons, one of whom, Gabriel, I survey, pay annually in "twa-pennies" about thirty pounds, and they complain, with great justice, of the unfair balance against them in their competition with the Bridgend, Annan, and English traders. As they are respectable characters, both as citizens and men of business, I am sure they will meet with every encouragement from the Magistracy of Dumfries. For their sakes partly I have interested myself in this business, but still much more on account of many obligations which I feel myself to lie under to Mr. Staig's civility and goodness. Could I be of the smallest service in anything which he has at heart, it would give me great pleasure. I have been at some pains to ascertain what your annual loss on this business may be, and I have reason to think it may amount fully to one-third of what you at present receive. These crude hints, Sir, are entirely for your private use. I have by no means any wish to take a sixpence from Mr. Mitchell's income: nor do I wish to serve Mr. Findlater; I wish to show any attempt, I can, to do anything to declare with what sincerity I have the honour to be, Sir, your obliged humble Servant,

ROBERT BURNS.

* [Contraction for "officers".]

[The above interesting document first appeared, as a note, in a local pamphlet, published by Mr. M'Diarmid, on the Established Churches of Dumfries. Our attention having been directed to it by Mr. W. R. M'Diarmid, we extract it with much satisfaction, as one among the many proofs now accumulating of the care with which Burns discharged all the duties, directly or indirectly, devolving on him; and that he could not have been so much the slave of dissipation, as he has frequently been represented to be, at this period.

Provost Staig, we are further informed, took the opinion of counsel on the question, which confirmed the views set forth in this letter that the Burgh had the power to tax all imported malt liquor. Our readers will remember that a similar subject, the reduction of Excise Divisions in Dumfries with a view to economise the public, as well as the local revenues, was fully represented by our Author to Mr. Graham of Fintry, in his capacity of Commissioner—letter (11) to him. How Robert Burns, on any rational ground, could be accused of neglecting his duties, as a citizen or as a public official, is to us incomprehensible. Let our readers compare the above and similar preceding documents with our own remarks on the subject, in Reminiscences, &, Excise Rebuke—Appendix—and judge for themselves in the matter.]

[FOR special reasons assigned, our Author's correspondence with Mr. Miller and his family at Dalswinton; and his letter of thanks, now for the first time published, for the gift of a Pair of Pistols, since much spoken of, occupy here a separate and more conspicuous place at the end of this department.]

CORRESPONDENCE
WITH THE
DALSWINTON FAMILY.

As our Author's connection with Mr. Miller—patron, friend, and landlord—was peculiar, and upon the whole unsatisfactory; and as the reader may naturally desire to see all now extant of the correspondence on his part with that gentleman and his family, we think it advisable to arrange these letters in a separate group, with a few introductory remarks, that all necessary information may be presented at once.

Patrick Miller, Esq., then of Dalswinton, and brother to the Lord Justice-Clerk of that day, was by profession a banker, by taste an amateur in practical science, by position a country gentleman of influence and character; also, a sort of self-constituted patron of struggling genius in poetry and the fine arts; but with a sufficiently high estimate of his own importance, crotchety and capricious—the last person in the world, perhaps, to be really serviceable to a man like Burns. Burns accordingly was never on very cordial terms with him, and we have no doubt was glad enough to get rid of Ellisland without an open rupture. Mr. Miller, however, showed all the sort of interest in, and attention to the Poet a man of his kind could be expected to show; and it is a pleasant memento of their friendship to learn that, besides being an occasional guest at the mansion, Burns was present by invitation at the first trial trip of the first steamboat in the world, on Dalswinton Loch. The incident has been thus commemorated:

"An engine was built under Symington (James Symington) the engineer's direction and superintendence, sent to Dalswinton and put together in October, 1788. This engine and the little vessel in which it was placed formed the first steamer that was ever built. The little boat was launched on Dalswinton Loch, and steamed across the Loch at the rate of five miles an hour. The company on board on that memorable occasion were Mr. Miller; Mr. Taylor, tutor to Mr. Miller's boys; and Alexander Nasmyth, the well-known painter. Besides these, there was a brisk stripling with strongly marked features, by name Harry Brougham, afterwards to be Lord-Chancellor of England; and last, but not least of the group, was one of Mr. Miller's tenants, the farmer of Ellisland—Robert Burns, the great bard of Scotland. 'Many a time,' says Mr. James Nasmyth, son of the distinguished painter, 'I have heard my father describe the delights of the party in question at this first and successful essay of steam navigation. I only wish Burns had immortalised it in verse; for it was worthy of his highest muse.'"

Mr. Miller, as our readers may remember, first introduced himself to the Poet with a handsome enough donation of ten guineas—letter (2) to John Ballantine, Esq.; and afterwards proposed the taking of a farm by him on his own estate of Dalswinton—letter (3) to the same. This estate, which Mr. Miller had recently purchased (1785 or 1786), was, on his own public avowal, in a wretched condition—"It was in the most miserable state of exhaustion, and all the tenants in poverty."[*] Burns, it should seem, was expected to invest both labour and capital in a portion of this exhausted soil, at far too high a rental for its value, and with whatever prospects of remuneration he could hope for.

Before concluding this disadvantageous bargain, however, Burns twice or thrice visited the locality; first in June, 1787, on returning from his Border Tour by Dumfries; again, in

[*] [*General View of the Agriculture, &c., of Dumfriesshire*, 8vo. Edinburgh: 1812. Account by Mr. Miller—as quoted by Chambers.]

September of the same year; and again, it would appear, at some later date—before deciding: Compare letters to Miss Chalmers (1) and (2); also (7), March 14th, 1788, when the lease was agreed on. According to Cunningham, whose father was steward on the estate, Burns had the choice of three farms, including Ellisland; two of which, Foregirth and Bankhead, were infinitely superior in an agricultural point of view, but not so romantically situated as Ellisland; and therefore had made a "poet's choice rather than a farmer's." Mrs. Burns, indeed, admits that "this may be true." [Memoranda by her—Appendix.] Gilbert Burns, on the contrary, maintained that no such choice was ever offered; that Mr. Miller not only specified the farm, but fixed the rent, with all conditions: so that the Poet had no option but either to take or not; which his own first letter seems to imply.

However this may be, Mr. Miller ultimately "granted a lease of seventy-six years at the annual rent of £50 for the three first years, and £70 for the remainder; agreeing farther to give his tenant £300 to build a new farm-steading and enclose the fields." Mr. Chambers, whose words we here quote, is of opinion, all things considered, that "there is no reason to suppose that Mr. Miller drove a hard bargain with Burns." Cunningham, however, distinctly assures us that, in the opinion of his neighbours, it would require the utmost economy and hard labour for the tenant to save £20 a year from Ellisland—no fortune assuredly! and Burns himself we know, by repeated intimations in his letters, was of the same opinion—also had he never thought seriously of the Excise, as a provision against poverty.

Thus, then, stood the bargain in March, 1788, when the Poet entered on the farm; and in November, 1791, with curses on its yet hopeless sterility, he quitted the scene for ever—leaving nothing behind him, as Cunningham tells us, "but a putting-stone with which he loved to exercise his strength, a memory of his musings which can never die; and £300 of his money sunk beyond redemption" in its furrows!

Ellisland, including the Isle—an old tower-like residence on some level land, at one time surrounded by water from the river—lies on the south side of the Nith, opposite the mansion house and policies of Dalswinton. The Poet lived in this old fabric till the new steading on the farm was built—the Ellisland that now is—of his own designing; where he spent the two remaining years of his brief sojourn here, and which is still an object of universal interest to readers of his works. The name of this now celebrated farm was originally Aillies-land, then Ellesland, finally Ellisland. It was purchased from Mr. Miller, as a reasonable investment, by a Mr. Morine, for £2000, when Burns was prepared to give it up. This gentleman, therefore, must either have had some special fancy for the spot, or believed in the possibility of realising a much handsomer percentage from it than the Poet ever dreamed of; and, with capital for improvements, he might not be wrong.

Dalswinton, now a magnificent estate, although no longer in possession of Mr. Miller's family, was originally the patrimony of the noble House of Cummin; whose representative—cousin and rival of the Bruce—was by him slain at the altar of the Grey-Friars in Dumfries.

(1.)   ## To Patrick Miller, Esq.,
DALSWINTON.

Edinburgh, 28th September, 1787.

Sir,

I HAVE been on a tour through the Highlands, and arrived in town but the other day, so could not wait on you at Dalswinton about the latter end of August, as I had promised and intended.

Independent of any views of future connections, what I owe you for the past, as a friend and benefactor, when friends I had few, and benefactors I had none, strongly in my bosom prohibits the most distant instance of ungrateful disrespect. I am informed you do not come to town for a month still, and within that time I shall certainly wait on you, as by this time I suppose you will have settled your scheme with respect to your farms.

My journey through the Highlands was perfectly inspiring, and I hope I have laid in a good stock of new poetical ideas from it. I shall make no apology for sending you the enclosed: it is a small but grateful tribute to the memory of our common countryman.[*] I have the honour to be, with the most grateful sincerity, Sir, your obliged humble servant,

ROBT. BURNS.

P.S.—I have added another poem, partly as it alludes to some folks nearly and dearly connected with Ayrshire, and partly as rhymes are the only coin in which the poor poet can pay his debts of gratitude. The lady alluded to is Miss Isabella M'Leod, aunt to the young Countess of Loudon.

As I am determined not to leave Edinburgh till I wind up my matters with Mr. Creech, which I am afraid will be a tedious business, should I unfortunately miss you at Dalswinton, perhaps your factor will be able to inform me of your intentions with respect to the Elesland farm [*so in MS.*], which will save me a jaunt to Edinburgh again.

There is something so suspicious in the professions of attachment from a little man to a great man, that I know not how to do justice to the grateful warmth of my heart, when I would say how truly I am interested in the welfare of your little troop of angels, and how much I have the honour to be again, Sir, your obliged humble servant,

ROBT. BURNS.

* [Most probably the elegy on Sir James Hunter Blair: Mr. Miller's family, of Barskimming and Glenlee, belonged also to Ayrshire. He was therefore a fellow-countryman both of the deceased baronet's and of our Author's.]

(2.)   ## TO PATRICK MILLER, ESQ.,
DALSWINTON.

Edinburgh, 20th October, 1787.

Sir,

I WAS spending a few days at Sir William Murray's, Ochtertyre, and did not get your obliging letter till to-day I came to town. I was still more unlucky in catching a miserable cold, for which the medical gentlemen have ordered me into close confinement, "under pain of death"—the soverest of penalties. In two or three days, if I get better, and if I hear at your lodgings that you are still at Dalswinton, I will take a ride to Dumfries directly. From something in your last, I would wish to explain my idea of being your tenant. I want to be a farmer in a small farm, about a plough-gang, in a pleasant country, under the auspices of a good landlord. I have no foolish notion of being a tenant on easier terms than another. To find a farm where one can live at all is not easy —I only mean living soberly, like an old-style farmer, and joining personal industry. The banks of the Nith are as sweet poetic ground as any I ever saw; and besides, Sir, 'tis but justice to the feelings of my own heart, and the opinion of my best friends, to say that I would wish to call you landlord sooner than any landed gentleman I know. These are my views and wishes; and in whatever way you think best to lay out your farms, I shall be happy to rent one of them. I shall certainly be able to ride to Dalswinton about the middle of next week, if I hear you are not gone.

I have the honour to be, Sir,

Your obliged, humble servant.

ROBT. BURNS.

[On this letter Mr. Chambers, chiefly, and justly relies to prove that our Author's second Tour by Stirling to Clackmannanshire was in the month of October, and not in August, as Dr. Adair by an error of memory imagined. Compare Second Tour—Appendix.

Both the above letters, which we quote from Mr. Chambers's edition, were first printed by him from copies of the originals in possession of Mr. W. C. Aitken, Broad Street, Birmingham.]

(3.)   ## TO PATRICK MILLER, ESQ.,
OF DALSWINTON.

Dumfries, April, 1793.

Sir,

MY poems having just come out in another edition, will you do me the honor to accept of a copy? A mark of my gratitude to you, as a gentleman to whose goodness I have been much indebted; of my respect for you, as a patriot who, in a venal, sliding age, stands forth the champion of the liberties of my country; and of my veneration for you, as a man, whose benevolence of heart does honor to human nature.

There was a time, Sir, when I was your dependant: this language *then* would have been like the vile incense of flattery —I could not have used it. Now that that connection is at an end, do me the honor to accept of this *honest* tribute of respect from, Sir,

Your much indebted humble servant,

R. B.

To Captain Miller,

DALSWINTON.

[ENCLOSING COPY OF "SCOTS WHA HAE."]

[1793, *or* 1794.]

DEAR SIR,

THE following ode is on a subject which I know you by no means regard with indifference.

> "O Liberty, ——
> Thou mak'st the gloomy face of nature gay,
> Giv'st beauty to the sun, and pleasure to the day." *

It does me so much good to meet with a man whose honest bosom glows with the generous enthusiasm, the heroic daring, of liberty, that I could not forbear sending you a composition of my own on the subject, which I really think is in my best manner.　I have the honour to be,

Dear Sir, &c.,

ROBERT BURNS.

* [*Address*.]

[At a sale of old manuscripts and books in London lately, the following lot was included:—Robert Burns's ode, "Bruce's Address to his troops at Bannockburn"—*Tune*, "Lewie Gordon." The autograph manuscript of this poem is written on two sides of a letter addressed to Captain Miller, Dalswinton. This precious relic of the great Scottish Poet is framed and glazed, and enclosed in a handsome mahogany case; it went for £17, and was purchased by Mr. Robert Thallon, who immediately drew a cheque for the amount, and was congratulated by the auctioneer on his obtaining so great a bargain.—*Newspaper Notice*, 1865.]

To Patrick Miller, Jun., Esq.,

OF DALSWINTON.

Dumfries, Nov. 1794.

DEAR SIR,

YOUR offer is indeed truly generous, and most sincerely do I thank you for it; but in my present situation, I find that I dare not accept it. You well know my political sentiments; and were I an insular individual, unconnected with a wife and a family of children, with the most fervid enthusiasm I would have volunteered my services; I then could and would have despised all consequences that might have ensued.

My prospect in the Excise is something; at least it is, encumbered as I am with the welfare, the very existence, of near half-a-score of helpless individuals, what I dare not sport with.

In the mean time, they are most welcome to my Ode; only, let them insert it as a thing they have met with by accident, and unknown to me. Nay, if Mr. Perry—whose honor, after your character of him, I cannot doubt—if he will give me an address and channel by which any thing will come safe from those spies with which he may be certain that his correspondence is beset, I will now and then send him any bagatelle that I may write. In the present hurry of Europe, nothing but news and politics will be regarded; but against the days of peace, which Heaven send soon, my little assistance may perhaps fill up an idle column of a newspaper. I have long had it in my head to try my hand in the way of little prose essays, which I propose sending into the world through the medium of some newspaper; and should these be worth his while, to these Mr. Perry shall be welcome; and all my reward shall be, his treating me with his paper, which, by the bye, to any body who has the least relish for wit, is a high treat indeed. With the most grateful esteem, I am ever,

Dear Sir, &c.,

R. B.

The gentleman addressed in the above two letters is presumably one and the same person—Captain Patrick Miller, younger of Dalswinton, and M.P. for the Dumfries district of Boroughs. He is described in the 'Five Carlins' as a "sodger youth, wi' modest grace;" but our Author certainly did not entertain the highest opinion of his capabilities in any way—compare letter (6) to Robert Graham, Esq. His recommending Burns to the editor of the *Morning Chronicle*, however, was friendly, and, as a friendly act, acknowledged; but the engagement proposed would have been manifestly dangerous to Burns—besides being, in our humble opinion, morally unsuitable for him. It was wise in him to decline it. The "Ode" referred to in both letters is, no doubt, also one and the same—viz. "Bruce's Address"—for which the Author seems to have been anxious to secure publicity, knowing its value; but which, through the delay or pottering stupidity of editors, he was doomed never to see.

The above distinction of the individual addressed was rendered necessary by the fact, that Captain Patrick Miller had a younger brother William, also Captain, afterwards Major Miller, who married Miss Jessy Staig, second daughter of Provost Staig, Dumfries, celebrated by our Author in his song of "True-hearted was he," &c.—*Poetical Works*, p. 205.]

To D. Newal,

[DUMFRIES.]

DR. SIR,

ENCLOSED is a state of the account between you and me and James Halliday respecting the drain. I have stated it at 20d. per rood, as, in fact, even at that they have not the wages they ought to have had, and I cannot for the soul of me see a poor devil a loser at my hand.

Humanity, I hope, as well as Charity, will cover a multitude of sins; a mantle of which—between you and me—I have some little need.—I am, Sir, yours,

R. B.

[The above letter, which first appeared in Chambers's edition, was addressed to Mr. David Newal, writer in Dumfries, and factor on the Dalswinton estate. It refers to some agricultural improvement, in which the tenant and the landlord seem to have been equally concerned; but in which humanity on the tenant's part is foremost. Besides this, Mr. Chambers, at the same place, gives the substance of another account with one D. Halliday, some relative of James's, doubtless, which infers a debit on Burns's side of £30, 17s. 5d., as wages to D. H. for building a yard-dike; and a credit of £11, 1s. 6d., "composed of so much in cash, so much in meal and shoes, and certain other sums paid for Halliday." It is not the same account as that referred to in above letter, but a memorandum only of D. Halliday's wages at the Martinmas Term. "It contains, however, equally characteristic matter," says Mr. Chambers; "for the Poet makes an error of summation to the extent of 3s. in Halliday's favour, and overpays him 3s. 3d. besides. As to this 'poor devil' too, he took special care that 'he should not be a loser at his hand;'"—A very rare and beneficent illustration of the 'truck system,' surely !

Mr. Newal had been tenant of the Isle before Burns went to reside there, but left it in consequence of strange "nocturnal sounds in the old tower," which his family would no doubt imagine to be haunted.* He seems to have been afterwards an intimate friend of our Author's at Dumfries, who, according to Mr. Chambers, would occasionally step in to hear a Scotch air on the piano from his daughters.

* The notorious persecutor, Grierson of Lagg, whose ghost might well disturb any ordinary household, lies buried in the neighbourhood.]

BURNS'S PISTOLS:

LETTER OF THANKS TO THE MAKER.

FROM ORIGINAL IN POSSESSION OF MISS MARY S. GLADSTONE,
FASQUE, LAWRENCEKIRK.

———

To Mr. David Blair,

GUN-MAKER, ST. PAUL'S SQUARE, BIRMINGHAM.

Ellisland, 23d Jany., 1789.

My dear Sir,

My honor has lien bleeding these two months almost, as
'tis near that time since I received your kind tho' short
epistle of the 29th Oct. The defensive tools do more than
half mankind do, they do honor to their maker; but I trust
that with me they shall have the fate of a miser's gold—to
be often admired, but never used.

Long before your letter came to hand, I sent you, by way
of Mr. Nicol, a copy of the book, and a proof-copy of the
print, loose, among the leaves of the book. These, I hope,
are safe in your possession some time ago. If I could think
of any other channel of communication with you than the
villainous expensive one of the Post, I could send you a
parcel of my Rhymes; partly as a small return for your
kind, handsome compliment, but much more as a mark of my
sincere esteem and respect for Mr. Blair. A piece I did
lately I shall try to cram into this letter, as I think the
turn of thought may perhaps please you.

WRITTEN IN FRIARS-CARSE HERMITAGE, ON THE
BANKS OF THE NITH.

OCT. 1788.

[Here follows version alluded to, Poetical Works—Various Readings—p. 23b.]

I remember with pleasure, my dear Sir, a visit you talked
of paying to Dumfries, in Spring or Summer.—I shall only
say, I have never parted with a man, after so little acquaintance, whom I more ardently wished to see again. At your
first convenience, a line to inform me of an affair in which I
am much interested—just an answer to the question, How
you do, will highly oblidge, my dear Sir,

Yours very sincerely,

ROBT. BURNS.

[The above letter, which, by Miss Gladstone's courteous permission, we have
the privilege of first presenting to the public, seems to have been originally
among the documents entrusted to Dr. Currie, but why not employed by him
does not appear. It is connected with, and indeed forms, in part, the subject of
a most interesting discussion, in which Dr. Maxwell, Bishop Gillis, and other
parties claiming to be possessors of the celebrated pistols, are involved.

The reader, whose attention is thus invited to the subject, will find the whole
circumstances detailed in the Appendix—Reminiscences Original, Part I, 10.—Dr.
Maxwell, &c.]

———

FRAGMENTS, NOTES, &c.

———

To ——,

Ellisland, 1792.

Thou Eunuch of language: thou Englishman, who never
was south of the Tweed: thou servile echo of fashionable bar-
barisms: thou quack, vending the nostrums of empirical
elocution: thou marriage-maker between vowels and consonants, on the Gretna-green of caprice: thou cobbler, botch-
ing the flimsy socks of bombast oratory: thou blacksmith,
hammering the rivets of absurdity: thou butcher, embruing
thy hands in the bowels of orthography: thou arch-heretic in
pronunciation: thou pitch-pipe of affected emphasis: thou
carpenter, mortising the awkward joints of jarring sentences:
thou squeaking dissonance of cadence: thou pimp of gender:
thou Lyon Herald to silly etymology: thou antipode of
grammar: thou executioner of construction: thou brood of
the speech-distracting builders of the Tower of Babel: thou
lingual confusion worse confounded: thou scape-gallows from
the land of syntax: thou scavenger of mood and tense: thou
murderous accoucheur of infant learning: thou *ignis fatuus*,
misleading the steps of benighted ignorance: thou pickle-
herring in the puppet-show of nonsense: thou faithful re-
corder of barbarous idiom: thou persecutor of syllabication:
thou baleful meteor, foretelling and facilitating the rapid approach of Nox and Erebus.

[The above extraordinary invective, which it would require some solidity of
moral constitution to withstand, and which reminds one very much of the
"flytings" of Polwart, Kennedy, Dunbar, &c., is supposed by some to have
been intended for the same hypercritical reviewer referred to by our Author
in his Epistle to Graham of Fintra—Poetical Works, p. 117. "It first appeared
in the *Gentleman's Magazine* for August, 1832. The original MS. was in possession of Mr. Andrew Henderson, surgeon, Berwick-upon-Tweed—one of the sons
of the Bard."—Chambers.]

———

(1.) Draught of Love Letter.
[FOR A FARMER.]

Madam,

What excuse to make for the liberty I am going to assume
in this letter, I am utterly at a loss. If the most unfeigned
respect for your accomplished worth—if the most ardent
attachment—if sincerity and truth—if these, on my part, will
in any degree weigh with you, my apology is these, and these
alone. Little as I have had the pleasure of your acquaintance,
it has been enough to convince me what enviable happiness
must be his whom you shall honour with your particular
regard, and more than enough to convince me how unworthy
I am to offer myself a candidate for that partiality. In this
kind of trembling hope, Madam, I intend very soon doing
myself the honour of waiting on you, persuaded that, how-

ever little Miss G—— may be disposed to attend to the suit of a lover as unworthy of her as I am, who is still too good to despise an honest man, whose only fault is loving her too much for his own peace. I have the honour to be, Madam, your most devoted humble servant.

(2.)   DRAUGHT OF LOVE LETTER.
[FOR THE SAME.]

DEAR MADAM,

THE passion of love had need to be productive of much delight; as where it takes thorough possession of the man, it almost unfits him for anything else. The lover who is certain of an equal return of affection, is surely the happiest of men; but he who is a prey to the horrors of anxiety and dreaded disappointment, is a being whose situation is by no means enviable. Of this, my present experience gives me sufficient proof. To me, amusement seems impertinent, and business intrusion, while you alone engross every faculty of my mind. May I request you to drop me a line, to inform me when I may wait on you? For pity's sake, do: and let me have it soon. In the meantime, allow me, in all the artless sincerity of truth, to assure you, that I truly am, my dearest Madam, your ardent lover, and devoted humble servant.

[Love is perhaps the only passion pathetic in reality that is ridiculous by proxy, and it is certainly ridiculous here. The worthy swain whose ardour thus found vent, we learn from Mr. Carruthers of the *Inverness Courier*, through Mr. Chambers, was a farmer on the estate of Rockhall in the neighbourhood of Dumfries, and the lady a Miss G——, of respectable connections, in the same locality. Which of the two 'draughts,' or whether both were employed to propitiate her favour, we do not know, but the suit was successful. The worthy man was blessed with an excellent wife, in consequence of this vicarious intercession; and both the couple themselves, and the Poet for a while, lived to enjoy the marriage-making joke. The originals are, or lately were, in possession of Mr. W. Smith, perfumer, Dumfries.]

Inscriptions on Books.

(1.)   [CICERO'S SELECT ORATIONS TRANSLATED.*]

Edin., 23d April, 1787.

THIS book, a present from the truly worthy and learned DR. GREGORY, I shall preserve to my latest hour, as a mark of the gratitude, esteem, and veneration I bear the Donor. So help me God!   ROBERT BURNS.

* [London, 1736.]

(2.)   [DELOLME ON THE BRITISH CONSTITUTION.]

Mr. Burns presents this book to the Library, and begs they will take it as a creed of British liberty—until they find a better.   R. B.

[Early in March, 1793, our Author was admitted by vote of committee, a free member of the Public Library, Dumfries, "out of respect and esteem for his abilities as a literary man." On the 30th of the same month, he presented to the library the following books;— *Humphry Clinker*, *Julia de Roubigné*, *Knox's History of the Reformation*, and *Delolme on the British Constitution*; the last of which had the above characteristic inscription. The tradition is, that "early in the morning after Delolme had been presented, Burns came to Provost Thomson's bedside before he was up, anxiously desiring to see the volume, as he feared he had written something upon it, 'which might bring him into trouble.' On the volume being shown to him, he looked at the inscription which he had written upon it the previous night, and having procured some paste, he pasted over it the fly-leaf in such a way as completely to conceal it. I have seen the volume," says Mr. Chambers's informant, "which is the edition of 1790, neatly bound, with a portrait of the Author at the beginning. Some stains of ink shine through the paper, indicating that there is something written on the back of the engraving; but the fly-leaf being pasted down upon it, there is nothing legible. On holding the leaf up to the light, however, I distinctly read, in the undoubted manuscript of the Poet, the following words"—as above. See Mr. M'Robert, the librarian's information, Chambers, vol. iv., p. 33.

It seems in vain, after this, to say that Burns's fears of mischief in consequence of his political opinions were groundless.]

IN various departments of the foregoing Correspondence, as our readers are aware, not a few interesting and important documents have been recovered by us, and arranged as nearly as possible in their appropriate order. We regret to say that more than one series of letters is still imperfect, and that the missing letters are in many cases beyond all reasonable hope of recovery; among these are most to be lamented the letters to Muir and Aiken. Besides these, however, there was another important series addressed to Dr. George Grierson, an intimate friend of our Author's and also of the late Mr. William Reid's, of Brash & Reid, booksellers, Glasgow; in whose possession the lost letters to Muir also were. These valuable relics were almost all destroyed by the inundation of the Clyde in 1831, alluded to at p. 139. But although part of our Author's correspondence in this way perished, a document by Dr. George Grierson himself, in relation to Burns's West Highland Tour —letter (3) to J. Smith, p. 147—fortunately survives, in which many curious particulars about that hitherto mysterious excursion are narrated: and which, by the courtesy of our friend John Reid, Esq., we have the satisfaction of presenting now. In connection with which, another document relating to subsequent Northern Tour—see Appendix—by the kindness of our esteemed correspondent, George Manners, Esq., of Croydon, to whom we are indebted for many similar favours, is appended.

Besides these, some interesting quotations from our Author's manuscripts in the British Museum, in elucidation or correction of Letters hitherto imperfectly edited, most obligingly supplied to us by Robert Carruthers, Esq., of the *Inverness Courier*, and which may be here more appropriately introduced than elsewhere, are inserted, and close this department of our work.

West Highland Tour.

BURNS AT INVERARY AND DUMBARTON:

BY DR. GEORGE GRIERSON.

Whoe'er thou art that lodgest here,
Heaven help thy wofu' case;
Unless thou com'st to visit Him,
That King of Kings, his Grace.

There's Highland greed, there's Highland pride;
There's Highland scab and hunger;
If Heaven it was that sent me here,
It sent me in an anger.

N.B.—The above lines were written at the Inn at Inverary by R. Burns, on the pane of glass, in presence of George Grierson, in 1788.

Burns wrote an encomium on Mary M'Lachlan, the Inn-keeper's daughter, at Tarbert——ending with

To fair Maria add M'Lachlan,
Quod Burns, a rhymer lad frae Mauchlin.

George Grierson was with him when he wrote the stanzas on Miss M'Lachlan, in 1788; and he, a day or two after this, wrote an Invocation to the Sun, at Bannachra, on the banks of Lochlomond.—It was in June, 1788; when Burns made a young man, Duncan M'Lachlan, son of Mr. M'Lachlan of Bannachra, bring out the largest bowl of punch his house could furnish, and made all the ladies and gentlemen kneel down, till he would repeat *extempore*, at the dawn of Day, an Invocation to the Sun. The company were Dr. Grierson, Mr. M'Lachlan, junior, and the family, Mr. M'Farlan from Jamaica, Mr. John Sheddan, merchant, and Miss Sheddan of Glasgow, Mr. Gardner of Lady-Kirk, and the two Misses Butters from Edinburgh. Next day, Messrs. Grierson, Gardner and Burns left Arden in the evening, and in coming to Dumbarton met with a Highlandman riding with his bare-back —— on a bare-backed horse. Burns pursued the Highlandman, till he was thrown from his horse into a thorn tree, and Burns's face was all bloody, he having fallen from his horse and cut his face.—They came that night safe to Dumbarton—when the magistrates did them all the honour of conferring the freedom of their city [on them]; and Oliphant preached next day, being the Fast-day, against the parties foresaid, and found great fault [with] the magistrates for conferring honours on the author of *vile*, *detestable*, and *immoral* publications.

[From original, entitled "Hints respecting Burns the Ayrshire Poet, by G. Grierson," in possession of John Reid, Esq., Kingston Place, Glasgow.]

[On the above curious and plain-spoken document the following remarks, to make it perfectly intelligible, are required:—

(1.) Dr. Grierson, who seems to be accurate enough as to facts, has evidently been misled in recollection as to the exact year. This celebrated, but hitherto mysterious, excursion took place in the last week of June, 1787.

(2.) If the Tarbert here referred to was the Tarbert on Lochfine, as we suppose it was, then Burns and his friends must have approached Inverary from the south, most probably, as Mr. Chambers conjectures, from Greenock, by way of Bute or Cowal; of which latter district Mary Campbell was a native, and whose birth-place Burns might secretly desire to see.—Compare Chambers, Vol. II., p. 93. The only objection to this theory would be the difficulty of transporting so many horses across lochs and arms of the sea, with speed enough to accomplish the journey in so short a time as implied. If, on the other hand, it is only a mis-spelling for Tarbet on Lochlomond, then the party must have remained longer there than Burns's own letters—(1) to Ainslie and (2) to J. Smith—import; or they must have come from the east, and Burns wrote the complimentary lines to Miss M'Lachlan, on his way to Inverary—returning a day or two after on the same track, which seems very unlikely indeed. Nothing more of the encomium on Miss M'Lachlan, so far as we are aware, remains; or of the Invocation to the Sun either—which is to be regretted.

(3.) The inscription on the window-pane at Inverary, as our readers will perceive, differs, according to Grierson, from the edition usually given; and we are much disposed to believe that Grierson's edition is the correct one.

(4.) About the year 1770, George Buchanan, Esq., merchant, Glasgow, acquired by purchase the lands of Auchindennan-Denniestoun, and the adjoining lands of Bannachra, on the banks of Lochlomond. Mr. Buchanan fixed his residence at Auchindennan, converted by him into Arden—now the property and residence of Sir James Lumsden, Lord-Provost of Glasgow. The M'Lachlans at Bannachra, therefore, would be tenants of Mr. Buchanan's.

From Mr. Buchanan's hospitable board our travellers, in a state of high exhilaration apparently, issued eastward on their way to Dumbarton. The extravagant escapade which followed must therefore have occurred between the east gate of Arden and the west gate of Cameron House, most probably at the sharp turn of the road where it leaves the loch, at what was once the old Italian villa of Belretiro—where thorn trees and quickset hedges, if we remember rightly, used to be plentiful and rough enough,—see notes on "Merry Miniature"—Appendix.

(5.) Rev. James Oliphant, formerly of Kilmarnock, and of the strictest sect there, was translated to Dumbarton in 1773, in face of much angry opposition—the objectors having employed a man to traverse the streets of the burgh selling "The whole works of Rev. James Oliphant, preacher in this parish, for the small charge of twopence." Mr. Oliphant had already received a by no means pleasant recognition from Burns in his poem of the "Ordination"—hence these anathemas on the Fast-day? It was Oliphant's turn of reprisals, and there is every reason to believe that by his influence the honour just conferred on Burns by the magistrates was cancelled—no trace of it being found in the records of the burgh. For fuller details of this strange proceeding, see Reminiscences, Original, Part II., "Dumbarton"—Appendix.

For certain local information in the two last notes we are indebted to Irving's History of Dumbartonshire, and to the courteous assistance of John Denny, Esq., Town-Clerk of Dumbarton, in examining the records. Of Dr. Grierson we have hitherto learned nothing; or of the other parties more conspicuously mentioned in the narrative—although a little additional time, we have no doubt, would enable us to trace them all.]

North Highland Tour.

WILLIAM INGLIS, Esquire,

INVERNESS.

Dear Sir,

The gentleman by whom this will be delivered to you is Mr. Burns of Ayrshire, who goes on an excursion to the North personally unacquainted, excepting in so far as his elegant and simple poems may have caught your attention. To men of such liberal and disinterested feelings as I know the citizens of Inverness to be, little seemed necessary as recommendatory of the Bard of Nature. Yet I thought it unworthy of me to permit him to migrate without mentioning him to you as my friend, and consigning him to you for that civility and attention which distinguishes you among all ranks of subjects. I offer my best respects to Mrs. Inglis, and am always, dear sir, your most obedt. servt.,

WILL. DUNBAR.*

Edin., 24th Augt., 1787.

To William Inglis, Esquire.

INVERNESS.

Mr. Burns presents his most respectful compliments to Mr. Inglis—would have waited on him with the inclosed, but is jaded to death with the fatigue of to-day's journey—won't leave Inverness till Thursday morning.

Ettles Hotel, Tuesday evening.

* [The gentleman to whom this note of introduction is addressed was Provost Inglis of Inverness, by whom our Author was hospitably entertained on the Wednesday evening, on returning from his visit to the Fall of Fyers. The writer of the note was William Dunbar, Esq., W.S., "Colonel of the Crochallan Corps." From original in possession of George Manners, Esq., Croydon.]

Manuscripts in British Museum.

Our readers will find a reference to these under the head of Goss, in Appendix; and, knowing that no edition of our Author's works could be complete without consulting these documents, but despairing of being able to do this at a sufficiently early date to embody the result in its proper place, we made the reference above noted as distant as possible. By the most courteous attention of our accomplished correspondent, Robert Carruthers, Esq., of the *Inverness Courier*, this difficulty has in a great measure been obviated, and many of the variations and corrections required have already been incorporated in the text. The most important of these will be found in the supplementary letters to James Johnson, p. 130; in the letter to the Provost and Town Council of Dumfries, p. 109; and in some notes to the autobiographical letter to Dr. Moore, p. 75.

The variations thus obtained are, upon the whole, not extremely important; but they are all deserving of attention. "What a grief it is," says Mr. Carruthers, writing to us on this subject, "that out of the 78 lots of the Pickering Collection of Burns's MSS., only 10 should have been purchased by the Museum! Some of the best went to America. The late Alexander Hastie's bequest to the Museum has added some pieces of interest," &c. Of the variations deserving more particular notice, and that did not reach us in time to be placed in the text, the following are subjoined:—

AUTOBIOGRAPHICAL LETTER
To Dr. Moore. [*p.* 76.]

[Burns himself, according to Currie, corrected this autobiographical letter, and the corrected copy was used for the press; but the greater part of the alterations seem to Mr. Carruthers to be in the style of the Doctor himself: very likely. The following passage, for example, from the original, as compared with Currie's text reproduced in our own—p. 76, c. 2, near foot—shows a difference both of terms and substance in Burns's favour, and frees him from all grounds of censure as to mis-statements of fact, implied against him, as it appears, in Mr. Chambers's edition.]

A LETTER from Dr. Blacklock to a friend of mine overthrew all my schemes, by rousing my poetic ambition. The doctor belonged to a set of critics for whose applause I had not even dared to hope. His idea that I would meet with every encouragement for a second edition fired me so much that away I posted to Edinburgh, &c.

[Chambers, taking Currie's edition, as other editors have also done, for granted as correct, observes that "Blacklock said nothing of Edinburgh,"—which is true. But the reader will observe that Burns makes no such allegation in the Doctor's name, the allegation to that effect being by Currie, on supposition, and not by Burns.—Compare Chambers, vol. I., p. 312.]

(2.) To Lady W. M. Constable. [*p.* 56.]

[In this letter, *Mrs.* Miller should be *Mr.* Miller: and after the words "unfortunate Mary" the following appears in the original:—]

I enclose your ladyship a poetic compliment I lately paid to the memory of our greatly-injured lovely Scotish Queen.

I have the honor to be, my Lady, your Ladyship's highly-obliged and ever-devoted humble servant,

   ROBT. BURNS.

Ellisland, near Dumfries, 25th April, 1791.

[With respect to the date of this letter there seems to have been some confusion. It has hitherto been dated as on the 11th of April. The probability is that our editions hitherto have been from a rough draught with that date, and without the concluding passage above quoted. When the letter was copied out and finished, it would be dated on a later day accordingly. Lady Winifred, with whose fine title and hereditary distinction we are accustomed to associate many romantic ideas, is described by Sir Walter Scott in a letter to Lockhart, as "that singular old curmudgeon" to whom Burns played "high Jacobite."]

(9.) To Mrs. Riddel. [*p.* 61.]

[Concluding paragraph stands thus in British Museum copy:—]

When Anacharsis' Travels come to hand, which Mrs. Riddel mentioned as her gift to the public library, Mr. B. will thank her for a reading of it previous to her sending it to the library, as it is a book Mr. B. has never seen, and he wishes to have a longer perusal than the regulations of the library allow.

[Could this have been a rough draught by Burns, or was the printed version "dressed up?"—Carruthers. A rough draught, as in many other instances, we have no doubt.]

To Miss Fontenelle. [*p.* 58.]

[Letter to this lady begins otherwise, thus:—]

ENCLOSED is the Address, such as it is, and may it be a prologue to an overflowing house. If all the town put together have half the ardour for your success and welfare of my individual wishes, my prayer will most certainly be granted.

[Burns evidently re-wrote the letter to Miss Fontenelle: the copy with the above opening was warmer in expression. It belonged to Charles Mathews.—Carruthers.]

(10.) To Mr. Thomson. [*p.* 94.]

[Before last paragraph the following appears in original:—]

So much for an idle farrago of a gossiping letter. Do you know a droll Scots song, more famous for its humour than its delicacy, called "The Grey Goose and the Glede?" Mr. Clarke says that the tune is positively an old chant of the Romish church, which corroborates the old tradition that at the Reformation the Reformers burlesqued much of the old church music with setting them to [lewd] verses. As a further proof, the common name for this song is "Cumnock Psalms."

[In the last paragraph—]

Dr. Maxwell—the identical Maxwell whom Burke mentioned in the House of Commons—was the physician who seemingly, &c.

[Why this paragraph should have been mutilated by editors, we cannot imagine.]

(4.) To James Johnson. [*p.* 104.]

[In Chambers's edition of this letter—compare our own edition, p. 80, and Chambers's, as reproduced by us, p. 104—the following paragraph should be inserted at the asterisks placed by Mr. Chambers near the end.]

I do not, my dear Sir, wish you to do this; and I beg you will not hint it to Mr. Clarke. If we do it at all, I will break it to him myself.

[This most characteristic paragraph, so strangely omitted by Mr. Chambers, confirms, in a remarkable way, our own conjecture with respect to the whole of this letter, and more particularly with respect to this very reference of our Author's to the debt.—Compare note by us on the subject, p. 104, c. 2.]

DOMESTIC CORRESPONDENCE.

BIOGRAPHICAL REMARKS.

BURNS AS A DOMESTIC LETTER-WRITER.

SCOTCH people, as a rule, are frigid in their correspondence with their friends—that is, with their relations; and the nearer the relationship is, the less ostentation the most affectionate among them make of the love they cherish in their hearts. Passionate or cordial enough letters they can at any time indite, where love and manly brotherhood alone are the foundation of correspondence; but when consanguinity intrudes, the fervour of their diction at once abates and their reserve increases, until letters between the nearest relatives, especially of the men, look like formal business communications with "compliments" and "kind regards," when the truest and warmest love in reality is at bottom. They have an inward dread of being caught with sentimentalisms of affection on their tongue, much more of committing in appropriate terms such sentiments to paper; not because they less purely or profoundly entertain and cherish such affections, but because they universally hold them to be too sacred for utterance, and their expression therefore superfluous or profane. As between relations of opposite sexes—as of brother to sister, or of son to mother—they allow themselves occasionally, or dutifully, a little more license in the use of endearing terms; but as between father and son, or brother and brother, the slightest approach to mere tenderness, or

abandon of love in any way, would be a moral misdemeanour or breach of the tacit family compact of unspoken attachment, of which only a fool or scoundrel in their estimation would be guilty. It is with the utmost difficulty a father among them can address his son in writing, unless a mere boy, as "My dearest ———;" and a son, in addressing his father, if he be a genuine Scot, will cast about for days, or for minutes at least, beforehand, to get the truest relative forms—the least and yet the most expressive of what he inwardly feels—and will conclude at last by adopting the most formal, reverential, commonplace, distant, inexpressive, or absurd of all. Brothers, in like manner, are equally perplexed in corresponding with brothers, and subside by a sort of mutual convention into the plainest stereotype and the briefest forms. The more distant a Scotchman's relative is by blood, if he be worth writing to in reality at all, the greater show of cordiality he enjoys; but still with a certain amount of reserve infused—sufficient to remind him of the family bond, and to give zest to the freedom which is lawful under it, at such a remote degree.

Where a Scotchman, if he *pleases*, may indulge himself without reproach of weakness as a family correspondent, is in writing to a wife or a daughter. Nothing but want of language in such cases can interfere with, or prevent, the truest tenderness or the sweetest endearment of expression; where the best he can say in the way of love, or the handsomest in the way of compliment, cannot possibly expose him to the charge of fraud or folly. Even in such cases, however, the habitual reserve of his nature predominates, and very few letters by Scotchmen to their wives or daughters, we suspect, are all, in point of elegance or endearment, what their authors would like, and intend them to be. It is marvellous and beautiful to see a man like John Knox in this predicament.

In these respects, Burns was as much a Scotchman as his brethren; would not, could not, did not surmount the native reserve, or dissolve by his own stronger passion the domestic restraints of his people. His domestic correspondence, properly so called, is of necessity limited; but all that remains of it (if much more ever existed) is entirely characteristic of his constitution as a Scotchman. Readers of another kindred—warmer or more demonstrative—on comparing these scanty fragments of unimpassioned letter-writing to relatives, with the glowing eloquence and inspiration of his correspondence with strangers, may be disposed to question to some extent the depth or reality of his affections. His filial reverence has the look of awe, his fraternal hints the awkward formality of a semi-tutorial lecture; he begins stiffly, he writes unequally, carelessly, abruptly; he concludes formally with "compliments" and "respects," &c.; so unlike the man who addressed Mrs. Dunlop, Miss Chalmers, and Clarinda—or Thomson, and Ainslie, and Muir, and Cunningham, and Nicol, or even Hamilton, and Ballantine, and Dr. Moore. Can this be Burns, the son and the brother? some gushing Southern, or impulsive, excitable Western reader will exclaim. Be not offended, O gushing or impulsive Reader! It *is* Burns—Burns the Scotchman; but with the solemnity and reserve of Scottish domestic life in him, qualifying, almost extinguishing, the fire of passion and the flame of poetry.

To his cousin, as behoves, and as a sense of propriety and gratitude at the time, as well as the highest personal esteem required, he is a little more lavish of loving terms, and a little, or rather a good deal, more unrestrained in his confidences.

A real sense of obligation there, and of fraternal kindnesses received, or offered, and at last entreated, enforces the appropriate terms. But even here, the curious alternations between "Sir," and "Dear Sir," and "My Dear Sir;" "Dear Cousin," and "My Dear Cousin," and "Your most affectionate Cousin,"—sometimes in the same letter; and then "O James!" in an agony of pain and shame, betraying the latent love, and appealing to the latent sympathy—reveal more plainly than any remarks of ours could, not only the man, but the Scotchman as a correspondent. Such confession must, in fact, be extorted from him. The whole of this series, indeed, is very beautiful, and most characteristic, both of the individual writer and of his fellow-countrymen. To nearer kindred, with whom he corresponded less frequently, but whose blood was his very own, and who were bound, therefore, at once to comprehend and sympathise with him, no unnecessary word, or term of endearment is vouchsafed. Deeds alone, in their case, must answer for his love.

Addressed to his wife, only two short, significant fragments are to be found; one of these, in rich and loving confidence at their marriage, when he was still corresponding in high-flown questionable terms with Clarinda, has just been recovered, and appears in this edition for the first time. Along with which, although not to her, another about her wedding-dress, and dresses for his sisters, is now also for the first time made public; and, by beautiful juxta-position of time and circumstances, sets forth the lover, and the brother, and the bridegroom in such a light, that one would not, upon any consideration, lose it. The remaining letter to Jean, before his own return to die, and the letter to his father-in-law about her, in his prospect of immediate death, which is the last known to have been addressed by him to any earthly correspondent, require no commentary by us. He had no surviving daughter to whom he could have written had he lived; but if such relationship, or possibility of such correspondence had been permitted by heaven, the letters of Robert Burns to his child Elizabeth would certainly have been the most precious and beautiful of their sort ever indited by a Scotchman.

Robt Burns was born at Alloway in the Parish of Ayr—Jan.ʸ 25ᵗʰ 1759—

Jean Armour his wife was born at Mauchline Feb.ʸ 27ᵗʰ 1767—

Sept.ʸ 3: 1786 were born to them twins, Robert, their eldest Son, at a quarter past Noon & Jean, since dead at fourteen months old. — March 3, were born to them twins again, two daughters, who died within a few days after their birth. — August 18ᵗʰ 1789 was born to them Francis, Wallace; so named after Mrs Dunlop of Dunlop: he was born a quarter before seven, forenoon. — April 9ᵗʰ 1791. between three & four in the morning, was born to them William, Nicol; so named after Willm Nicol of the High School, Edinr —— November 21.ˢᵗ 1792, at a quarter past Noon, was born to them Elizabeth Riddel, so named after Mrs Robt Riddel of Glenriddel.——

James Glencairn born 12ᵗʰ Augᵗ 1794 named after the late Earl of Glencairn

Maxwell Born 26ᵗʰ July 1796 the day of his fathers funeral: so named after Dr Maxwell the Physician who attended the Poet in his last illness

Inserted by W. N. Burns 9ᵗʰ April 1867

CORRESPONDENCE.

[THE Domestic Correspondence, as here arranged, will be found to include one or two letters by friends or relatives to the Author, as well as those addressed to relatives by him; two concerning strictly domestic matters, but to persons not of his own household; and two in particular to Mr. A. Lawrie, so beautifully domestic in their tone, as being addressed to a correspondent much younger than himself, that they would have been lost or at least misplaced in any other connection.]

To William Burness.

Irvine, Dec. 27, 1781.

HONORED SIR,

I HAVE purposely delayed writing, in the hope that I should have the pleasure of seeing you on New-Year's-day; but work comes so hard upon us, that I do not choose to be absent on that account, as well as for some other little reasons which I shall tell you at meeting. My health is nearly the same as when you were here, only my sleep is a little sounder, and on the whole I am rather better than otherwise, though I mend by very slow degrees. The weakness of my nerves has so debilitated my mind, that I dare neither review past wants, nor look forward into futurity; for the least anxiety or perturbation in my breast produces most unhappy effects on my whole frame. Sometimes, indeed, when for an hour or two my spirits are a little lightened, I glimmer a little into futurity; but my principal, and indeed my only pleasurable employment is looking backwards and forwards in a moral and religious way. I am quite transported at the thought that ere long, perhaps very soon, I shall bid an eternal adieu to all the pains, and uneasiness, and disquietudes of this weary life; for I assure you I am heartily tired of it; and if I do not very much deceive myself, I could contentedly and gladly resign it.

> " The soul, uneasy, and confined at home,
> Rests and expatiates in a life to come."

It is for this reason I am more pleased with the 15th, 16th, and 17th verses of the 7th chapter of Revelations, than with any ten times as many verses in the whole Bible, and would not exchange the noble enthusiasm with which they inspire me for all that this world has to offer. As for this world, I despair of ever making a figure in it. I am not formed for the bustle of the busy, nor the flutter of the gay. I shall never again be capable of entering into such scenes. Indeed I am altogether unconcerned at the thoughts of this life. I foresee that poverty and obscurity probably await me, and I am in some measure prepared, and daily preparing, to meet them. I have but just time and paper to return you my grateful thanks for the lessons of virtue and piety you have given me, which were too much neglected at the time of giving them, but which I hope have been remembered ere it is yet too late. Present my dutiful respects to my mother, and my compliments to Mr. and Mrs. Muir; and, with wishing you a merry New-Year's-day, I shall conclude. I am, honored Sir, your dutiful son,

ROBERT BURNESS.

P.S. My meal is nearly out, but I am going to borrow till I get more.

[Burns, during his residence at Irvine, was remarkable chiefly for long continued fits of melancholy depression.—Mr. Carruthers is strongly of opinion that this letter should be dated 1782—but there seems to be arguments against that.]

(1.) To Mr. James Burness,
WRITER, MONTROSE.

Lochlea, 21st June, 1783.

DEAR SIR,

MY father received your favour of the 10th current, and as he has been for some months very poorly in health, and is in his own opinion (and, indeed, in almost every body's else) in a dying condition, he has only, with great difficulty, written a few farewell lines to each of his brothers-in-law. For this melancholy reason, I now hold the pen for him, to thank you for your kind letter, and to assure you, Sir, that it shall not be my fault if my father's correspondence in the north die with him. My brother writes to John Caird, and to him I must refer you for the news of our family.

I shall only trouble you with a few particulars relative to the wretched state of this country. Our markets are exceedingly high—oatmeal 17d. and 18d. per peck, and not to be got even at that price. We have indeed been pretty well supplied with quantities of white peas from England and elsewhere, but that resource is likely to fail us, and what will become of us then, particularly the very poorest sort,

Heaven only knows.* This country, till of late, was flourishing incredibly in the manufacture of silk, lawn, and carpet-weaving; and we are still carrying on a good deal in that way, but much reduced from what it was. We had also a fine trade in the shoe way, but now entirely ruined, and hundreds driven to a starving condition on account of it. Farming is also at a very low ebb with us. Our lands, generally speaking, are mountainous and barren; and our landholders, full of ideas of farming gathered from the English and the Lothians, and other rich soils in Scotland, make no allowance for the odds of the quality of land, and consequently stretch us much beyond what in the event we will be found able to pay. We are also much at a loss for want of proper methods in our improvements of farming. Necessity compels us to leave our old schemes, and few of us have opportunities of being well informed in new ones. In short, my dear Sir, since the unfortunate beginning of this American war, and its as unfortunate conclusion, this country has been, and still is, decaying very fast. Even in higher life, a couple of our Ayrshire noblemen, and the major part of our knights and squires, are all insolvent. A miserable job of a Douglas, Heron, and Co.'s bank, which no doubt you have heard of, has undone numbers of them; and imitating English and French, and other foreign luxuries and fopperies, has ruined as many more.† There is a great trade of smuggling carried on along our coasts, which, however destructive to the interests of the kingdom at large, certainly enriches this corner of it, but too often at the expense of our morals. However, it enables individuals to make, at least for a time, a splendid appearance; but Fortune, as is usual with her when she is uncommonly lavish of her favours, is generally even with them at the last; and happy were it for numbers of them if she would leave them no worse than when she found them.

My mother sends you a small present of a cheese; 'tis but a very little one, as our last year's stock is sold off; but if you could fix on any correspondent in Edinburgh or Glasgow, we would send you a proper one in the season. Mrs. Black promises to take the cheese under her care so far, and then to send it to you by the Stirling carrier.

I shall conclude this long letter with assuring you that I shall be very happy to hear from you, or any of our friends in your country, when opportunity serves.

My father sends you, probably for the last time in this world, his warmest wishes for your welfare and happiness; and my mother and the rest of the family desire to inclose their kind compliments to you, Mrs. Burness, and the rest of your family, along with those of, dear Sir,

    Your affectionate Cousin,

       R. B.

[The estimable relative to whom this series of letters is addressed, called by the writer 'cousin,' was, in fact, a cousin once removed—his *father* and Robert Burns's grandfather only being brothers. The propinquity, however, was as affectionately acknowledged on both sides as if it had been much nearer. The Montrose branch, indeed, ultimately incorporated by pretence (as Heralds say) the well-known armorial device of the Ayrshire Poet with their own, to testify the honour and the love in which they held it.—See also note on letter (6).]

* [The extraordinary famine here recorded prevailed also on the eastern coast of the Island, and the inhabitants of certain districts bordering on the Frith of Forth were saved from impending destruction by the very same means—the arrival of two or three ships at Grangemouth with cargoes of white peas from Holland. The cause of this dreadful scarcity, if we mistake not, was a storm of frost and snow in the month of June or July preceding; during which all fruit germs were destroyed, and the hopes of a harvest annihilated.]

† [Compare reflection in "The Twa Dogs."]

(2.)   **TO MR. JAMES BURNESS,**
MONTROSE.

      *Lochlea, 17th Feb., 1784.**

DEAR COUSIN,

I WOULD have returned you my thanks for your kind favour of the 13th of December sooner, had it not been that I waited to give you an account of that melancholy event, which, for some time past, we have from day to day expected.

On the 13th current I lost the best of fathers. Though, to be sure, we have had long warning of the impending stroke; still the feelings of nature claim their part, and I cannot recollect the tender endearments and parental lessons of the best of friends and ablest of instructors, without feeling what perhaps the calmer dictates of reason would partly condemn.

I hope my father's friends in your country will not let their connexion in this place die with him. For my part I shall ever with pleasure—with pride, acknowledge my connexion with those who were allied by the ties of blood and friendship to a man whose memory I shall ever honour and revere.

I expect, therefore, my dear Sir, you will not neglect any opportunity of letting me hear from you, which will very much oblige,

    My dear Cousin, yours sincerely,

       R. B.

* [In November, 1783, to provide against any painful contingency of debt or difficulty at Lochlea, the farm of Mossgiel, at Mauchline, was taken; but the family did not remove from Lochlea till March, 1784. During this interval, Burns and his brother Gilbert might have occasion now and then to visit Mossgiel, to make the necessary preliminary arrangements for their intended settlement there. Compare Memoir of the Poet by Gilbert Burns—Appendix, p. xv.; also, for death and funeral of William Burness, Biography, p. x.]

(3.)   **TO JAMES BURNESS,**
MONTROSE.

      Mossgiel, August, 1784.

WE have been surprised with one of the most extraordinary phenomena in the moral world which, I dare say, has happened in the course of this half century. We have had a party of [the] Presbytery [of] Relief, as they call themselves, for some time in this country. A pretty thriving society of them has been in the burgh of Irvine for some years past, till about two years ago, a Mrs. Buchan from Glasgow came and began to spread some fanatical notions of religion among them, and, in a short time, made many converts; and, among others, their preacher, Mr. Whyte, who, upon that account, has been suspended and formally deposed by his brethren. He continued, however, to preach in private to his party, and was supported, both he and their spiritual mother, as they affect to call old Buchan, by the contributions of the rest, several of whom were in good circumstances; till, in spring last, the populace rose and mobbed Mrs. Buchan, and put her out of the town; on which all her followers voluntarily quitted the place likewise, and with such precipitation, that many of them never shut their doors behind them; one left a washing on the green, another a cow bellowing at the crib without food, or any body to mind her, and after several stages, they are fixed at present in the neighbourhood of Dumfries. Their tenets are a strange jumble of enthusiastic jargon; among others, she pretends to give them the Holy Ghost by breathing on them, which she does with postures and practices that are scandalously indecent. They have likewise disposed of all their effects, and hold a community of goods, and live nearly an idle life, carrying on a great farce of pretended devotion in barns and woods, where they lodge and lie all together, and hold likewise a community of women, as it is another of their tenets that they can commit no moral sin. I am personally acquainted with most of them, and I can assure you the above mentioned are facts.*

This, my dear Sir, is one of the many instances of the folly of leaving the guidance of sound reason and common sense in matters of religion.

Whenever we neglect or despise these sacred monitors, the whimsical notions of a perturbated brain are taken for the immediate influences of the Deity, and the wildest fanaticism, and the most inconstant absurdities, will meet with abettors and converts. Nay, I have often thought, that the more out-of-the-way and ridiculous the fancies are, if once they are sanctified under the sacred name of religion, the unhappy mistaken votaries are the more firmly glued to them.

R. B.

* [The miserable fanatical delusion, above described, came, as might be expected, "to nought, and all, as many as obeyed it, were scattered." The last remaining representative of the sect, a tall melancholy personage, with a reddish white beard, and a peculiar hat and coat, we can remember in our own boyhood, forty years ago, to have seen wandering in silence about the streets of this city.]

(4.)　　　TO MR. JAMES BURNESS,
MONTROSE.

Mossgiel, Tuesday noon, Sept. 26, 1786.

MY DEAR SIR,

I THIS moment receive yours—receive it with the honest hospitable warmth of a friend's welcome. Whatever comes from you wakens always up the better blood about my heart, which your kind little recollections of my parental friends carries as far as it will go. 'Tis there that man is blest! 'Tis there, my friend, man feels a consciousness of something within him above the trodden clod! The grateful reverence

to the hoary (earthly) author of his being—the burning glow when he clasps the woman of his soul to his bosom—the tender yearnings of heart for the little angels to whom he has given existence—these nature has poured in milky streams about the human heart; and the man who never rouses them to action, by the inspiring influences of their proper objects, loses by far the most pleasurable part of his existence.

My departure is uncertain, but I do not think it will be till after harvest. I will be on very short allowance of time indeed, if I do not comply with your friendly invitation. When it will be, I don't know; but if I can make my wish good, I will endeavour to drop you a line some time before. My best compliments to Mrs ——; I should [be] equally mortified should I drop in when she is abroad, but of that I suppose there is little chance.

What I have wrote, heaven knows; I have not time to review it; so accept of it in the beaten way of friendship. With the ordinary phrase—perhaps rather more than the ordinary sincerity—I am, dear Sir,

Ever yours,

R. B.

[Written evidently in prospect of his departure for the West Indies.]

(5.)　　　TO MR. JAMES BURNESS.

Ellisland, 9th Feb., 1789.

MY DEAR SIR,

WHY I did not write to you long ago is what, even on the rack, I could not answer. If you can in your mind form an idea of indolence, dissipation, hurry, cares, change of country, entering on untried scenes of life, all combined, you will save me the trouble of a blushing apology. It could not be want of regard for a man for whom I had a high esteem before I knew him—an esteem which has much increased since I did know him; and this caveat entered, I shall plead guilty to any other indictment with which you shall please to charge me.

After I parted from you, for many months my life was one continued scene of dissipation. Here at last I am become stationary, and have taken a farm and—a wife.

The farm is beautifully situated on the Nith, a large river that runs by Dumfries, and falls into the Solway frith. I have gotten a lease of my farm as long as I pleased; but how it may turn out is just a guess, and it is yet to improve and enclose, &c.; however, I have good hopes of my bargain on the whole.

My wife is my Jean, with whose story you are partly acquainted. I found I had a much-loved fellow creature's happiness or misery among my hands, and I durst not trifle with so sacred a deposit. Indeed I have not any reason to repent the step I have taken, as I have attached myself to a very good wife, and have shaken myself loose of a very bad failing.

I have found my book a very profitable business, and with the profits of it I have begun life pretty decently. Should fortune not favour me in farming, as I have no great faith in her fickle ladyship, I have provided myself in another resource, which, however some folks may affect to despise it, is still a comfortable shift in the day of misfortune. In the hey-day of my fame, a gentleman, whose name at least I dare say you know, as his estate lies somewhere near Dundee, Mr. Graham, of Fintray, one of the Commissioners of Excise, offered me the commission of an Excise officer. I thought it prudent to accept the offer; and accordingly I took my instructions, and have my commission by me. Whether I may ever do duty, or be a penny the better for it, is what I do not know; but I have the comfortable assurance, that come whatever ill fate will, I can, on my simple petition to the Excise-board, got into employ.

We have lost poor uncle Robert this winter. He has long been very weak, and with very little alteration on him; he expired 3d January.

His son William has been with me this winter, and goes in May to be an apprentice to a mason. His other son, the eldest, John, comes to me I expect in summer. They are both remarkably stout young fellows, and promise to do well. His only daughter, Fanny, has been with me ever since her father's death, and I purpose keeping her in my family till she be quite woman-grown, and fit for better service. She is one of the cleverest girls, and has one of the most amiable dispositions I have ever seen.

All friends in this country and Ayrshire are well. Remember me to all friends in the north. My wife joins me in compliments to Mrs. B. and family.

> I am ever, my dear Cousin,
>
> Yours sincerely,
>
> R. B.

* [The Fanny here mentioned, we are informed by Cunningham, was subsequently married to James Armour, a brother of Mrs. Burns's. She settled with her husband at Mauchline, where they had a numerous family.]

(6.)

TO MR. JAMES BURNESS,
WRITER, MONTROSE.

Dumfries, [Brow,] 12th July [1796.]

MY DEAR COUSIN,

WHEN you offered me money assistance, little did I think I should want it so soon. A rascal of a haberdasher, to whom I owe a considerable bill, taking it into his head that I am dying, has commenced a process against me, and will infallibly put my emaciated body into jail. Will you be so good as to accommodate me, and that by return of post, with ten pounds? O James! did you know the pride of my heart, you would feel doubly for me! Alas! I am not used to beg! The worst of it is, my health was coming about finely. You know, and my physician assured me, that melancholy and low spirits are half my disease; guess then my horrors since this business began. If I had it settled, I would be, I think, quite well in a manner. How shall I use the language to you, O do not disappoint me! but strong necessity's curst command.

I have been thinking over and over my brother's affairs, and I fear I must cut him up; but on this I will correspond at another time, particularly as I shall [require] your advice.

Forgive me for once more mentioning by return of post;—save me from the horrors of a jail!

My compliments to my friend James, and to all the rest. I do not know what I have written. The subject is so horrible I dare not look it over again.

> Farewell!   R. B.

[The painful request of this letter, our readers are no doubt aware, was promptly and affectionately complied with. George Thomson at the same time sent £5. Compare letter (57) to him. The account in question, for which summary proceedings were apprehended, amounted only to £7, 9s. It was rendered officially through an agent, at a dissolution of co-partnership, and not with any immediate design, it may be hoped, of annoying the distinguished sufferer. At all events, his own nervous irritation undoubtedly magnified the evil.

The painful expression, indeed, employed by himself in this very letter with respect to his brother's affairs, and which was undoubtedly used by him to screen the humiliation of his own position by showing to his cousin James that he had a claim upon others, implied as much severity on his own part as that of which he was complaining towards himself—howbeit such sort of work was far from him, neither entered it into his mind. It was but sorrowful rhetoric with him; it was a legal application in the other case, to be sure, but might not after all have been much more. For a proof of his generosity in such circumstances, and how far he was from "cutting up" anybody, see letter (3) to J. Clarke, just sixteen days before—p. 193; also letter (5) to Gilbert himself, on this very subject.

The "James" referred to in conclusion was a son of Mr. Burness.—He was then a lad of sixteen or seventeen; married in 1800 a daughter of Provost Glegg, Montrose, and became the father of Sir Alexander Burnes, the distinguished scholar, diplomatist, and explorer of Hindostan, who, with his brother Charles, was cut to pieces by the insurgents at the beginning of the Affghan war,—November, 1841. James, who in turn became Provost of Montrose, was a man of the highest respectability. He died 1852, having seen his children's glory, and suffered so dreadful a calamity in their loss.]

To Mr. Archibald Lawrie.

Mossgiel, 13th Nov., 1786.

DEAR SIR,

I HAVE along with this sent the two volumes of Ossian, with the remaining volume of the Songs. Ossian I am not in such a hurry about; but I wish the Songs, with the volume of the Scotch Poets, returned as soon as they can conveniently be despatched. If they are left at Mr. Wilson, the Bookseller's shop, in Kilmarnock, they will easily reach me.

My most respectful compliments to Mr. and Mrs. Lawrie; and a Poet's warmest wishes for their happiness to the young ladies; particularly the fair musician, whom I think much better qualified than ever David was, or could be, to charm an evil spirit out of a Saul.

Indeed, it needs not the feelings of a poet to be interested in the welfare of one of the sweetest scenes of domestic peace and kindred love that ever I saw; as I think the peaceful unity of St. Margaret's Hill can only be excelled by the harmonious concord of the Apocalyptic Zion.

> I am, dear Sir, yours sincerely.
>
> ROBT. BURNS.

[There seem to be two editions of this letter, which vary to the extent of three words—the one having, and the other omitting, the word returned after Poets, and a before Saul.]

(2.)   MONSR. MONSR. ARCHIBALD LAWRIE.
COLLINE DE ST. MARGARETE.

Mauchline, 15th November, 1786.

DEAR SIR,

If convenient, please return me by Connel, the bearer, the two volumes of songs I left last time I was at St. Margaret's Hill.

My best compliments to all the good family.

A Dieu je vous commende.

ROBT. BURNS.

———

(3.)   TO [MR. ARCHIBALD LAWRIE.]

Edinburgh, 14th August, 1787.

MY DEAR SIR,

HERE am I—that is all I can tell you of that unaccountable being myself. What I am doing, no mortal can tell; what I am thinking, I myself cannot tell; what I am usually saying, is not worth telling. The clock is just striking one, two, three, four, —, —, —, —, —, —, —, twelve, forenoon; and here I sit, in the attic story, *alias* the garret, with a friend on the right hand of my standish—a friend whose kindness I shall largely experience at the close of this line—there—thank you—a friend, my dear Mr. Lawrie, whose kindness often makes me blush; a friend who has more of the milk of human kindness than all the human race put together, and what is highly to his honour, peculiarly a friend to the friendless as often as they come in his way; in short, Sir, he is, without the least alloy, a universal philanthropist; and his much-beloved name is—a bottle of good old Port! In a week, if whim and weather serve, I shall set out for the north —a tour to the Highlands.

I ate some Newhaven broth, in other words, boiled mussels, with Mr. Farquhar's family, t'other day. Now I see you prick up your ears. They are all well, and Mademoiselle is particularly well. She begs her respects to you all; along with which please present those of your humble servant. I can no more. I have so high a veneration, or rather idolatrisation, for the cleric character, that even a little *futurum esse vel faisse Priestling,* in his *Penna pennae pennae,* &c., throws an awe over my mind in his presence, and shortens my sentences into single ideas.

Farewell, and believe me to be ever, my dear Sir, yours,

ROBERT BURNS.

[First published in *Glasgow Citizen,* April 8, 1851.]

[The young gentleman to whom these letters were addressed became subsequently minister of Loudoun, in succession to his father, Rev. George Lawrie— see letter to him; and married the only sister of our Author's friend, Dr. James M'Kittrick Adair, husband of Charlotte Hamilton.]

———

(1.)   To Mr. Gilbert Burns.

Edinburgh, 17th September, 1787.

MY DEAR SIR,

I ARRIVED here safe yesterday evening, after a tour of twenty-two days, and travelling near six hundred miles, windings included. My farthest stretch was about ten miles beyond Inverness. I went through the heart of the Highlands by Crieff, Taymouth, the famous seat of Lord Breadalbane, down the Tay, among cascades and druidical circles of stones, to Dunkeld, a seat of the Duke of Athole, thence across Tay, and up one of his tributary streams to Blair of Athole, another of the Duke's seats, where I had the honour of spending nearly two days with his Grace and family; thence many miles through a wild country, among cliffs grey with eternal snows and gloomy savage glens, till I crossed Spey and went down the stream through Strathspey, so famous in Scottish music; Badenoch, &c., till I reached Grant Castle, where I spent half a day with Sir James Grant and family; and then crossed the country for Fort George, but called by the way at Cawdor, the ancient seat of Macbeth; there I saw the identical bed, in which tradition says king Duncan was murdered; lastly, from fort George to Inverness.

I returned by the coast, through Nairn, Forres, and so on, to Aberdeen, thence to Stonehive, where James Burness, from Montrose, met me by appointment. I spent two days among our relations, and found our aunts, Jean and Isabel, still alive, and hale old women. John Caird, though born the same year with our father, walks as vigorously as I can: they have had several letters from his son in New York. William Brand is likewise a stout old fellow; but further particulars I delay till I see you, which will be in two or three weeks. The rest of my stages are not worth rehearsing; warm as I was from Ossian's country, where I had seen his very grave, what cared I for fishing-towns or fertile carses? I slept at the famous Brodie of Brodie's one night, and dined at Gordon Castle next day, with the Duke, Duchess, and family. I am thinking to cause my old mare to meet me, by means of John Ronald, at Glasgow; but you shall hear farther from me before I leave Edinburgh. My duty and many compliments from the north to my mother; and my brotherly compliments to the rest. I have been trying for a berth for William, but am not likely to be successful. Farewell.

R. B.

[Compare notes on Northern Tour, at dates—Appendix.]

———

(2.)   TO MR. GILBERT BURNS.

Ellisland, 11th January, 1790.

DEAR BROTHER,

I MEAN to take advantage of the frank, though I have not, in my present frame of mind, much appetite for exertion in writing. My nerves are in a cursed state. I feel that horrid hypochondria pervading every atom of both body and soul.

This farm has undone my enjoyment of myself. It is a ruinous affair on all hands. But let it go to hell! I'll fight it out and be off with it.

We have got a set of very decent players here just now. I have seen them an evening or two. David Campbell, in Ayr, wrote to me by the manager of the company, a Mr. Sutherland, who is a man of apparent worth. On New-Year's-day evening I gave him the following prologue, which he spouted to his audience with applause.

> No song nor dance I bring from yon great city,
> That queens it o'er our taste—the more's the pity:
> Tho', by the bye, abroad why will you roam?
> Good sense and taste are natives here at home, &c.

I can no more.—If once I was clear of this cursed farm, I should respire more at ease.

					R. B.

<table><tr><td>(3.)</td><td>TO MR. GILBERT BURNS.</td></tr></table>

[*Sunday,*] 10th *July*, 1796.

DEAR BROTHER,

IT will be no very pleasing news to you to be told that I am dangerously ill, and not likely to get better. An inveterate rheumatism has reduced me to such a state of debility, and my appetite is so totally gone, that I can scarcely stand on my legs. I have been a week at sea-bathing, and I will continue there, or in a friend's house in the country, all the summer. God keep my wife and children: if I am taken from their head, they will be poor indeed. I have contracted one or two serious debts, partly from my illness these many months, partly from too much thoughtlessness as to expense, when I came to town, that will cut in too much on the little I leave them in your hands. Remember me to my mother.

					Yours,
					R. B.

[Gilbert Burns, next brother to the Poet, was born at Alloway, 1760; died at Grant's Braes, Lethington, 27th April, 1827, and was buried in Bolton church-yard; where his mother and several of his family, who predeceased or followed him, repose. He was a man in every relation of life—as son, brother, husband, and father—most exemplary and estimable. He removed from Mossgiel first to Dinning in Dumfriesshire, as a farmer, then to Morham Mains, near Haddington, as manager of that farm for a son of Mrs. Dunlop's, whose property it was, and subsequently became factor to Lady Blantyre, on her ladyship's estate of Leth-ington, in East Lothian. In these migrations his mother accompanied him; and with him she resided till her death—which occurred in 1820.

Gilbert, in the opinion of those who knew him best, was more a theoretical, than a practical farmer, and a great speculator in agricultural systems. On the other hand, he had gifts like his brother's, though not of poetry, that with proper cultivation would have made him a distinguished man in the world of letters—as his contributions to Dr. Currie's life of the Poet, partially quoted in our own edition, prove. In consequence of some dissatisfaction, expressed by him and other friends, with the manner in which Dr. Currie had edited the Poet's works or written his life, he was induced to undertake an edition himself, which appeared in 1820—but was not so successful as expected. For this he received from the publishers, Cadell and Davies, the sum of £250—out of which he discharged to the widow and family of the Poet the debt of £180 still due to them by him. Of this sum, however, it appears Mrs. Burns, with much generosity, did not personally avail herself, but applied it to relieve another member of the family.]

Gilbert had a family of six sons and five daughters.—Of these, James and John predeceased their father at short intervals—dying in succession of fever, of which he also died—the three being interred in the same churchyard within a space of as many months. James, his second son, died some eighteen or twenty years ago at Ewdine, where he was factor to Lord Blantyre; and Robert, the fourth son, died at Buenos Ayres, sometime before that. Thomas, the third son, formerly the esteemed minister of Monkton, Ayrshire, and whose fatherly affectionate bearing we shall long remember, is now spiritual head of the Free Church Colony of Scotchmen in Otago, New Zealand; William, the eldest, and present representative of the family, is still alive in Dublin; and Gilbert, of Kincar-mucron Lodge, the youngest, resides also in the neighbourhood of that city. For most of these particulars we are indebted to an esteemed friend and correspon-dent, a relative of the family.]

<table><tr><td>(1.)</td><td>## To Mr. William Burns.</td></tr></table>

Isle, 2d *March*, 1789.

MY DEAR WILLIAM,

I ARRIVED from Edinburgh only the night before last, so could not answer your epistle sooner. I congratulate you on the prospect of employ; and I am indebted to you for one of the best letters that has been written by any mechanic-lad in Nithsdale, or Annandale, or any dale on either side of the Border, this twelvemonth. Not that I would have you always affect the stately stilts of studied composition, but surely writing a handsome letter is an accomplishment worth courting; and, with attention and practice, I can promise you that it will soon be an accomplishment of yours. If my advice can serve you—that is to say, if you can resolve to accustom yourself not only in reviewing your own deport-ment, manners, &c., but also in carrying your consequent resolutions of amending the faulty parts into practice—my small knowledge and experience of the world is heartily at your service. I intended to have given you a sheetful of counsels, but some business has prevented me. In a word, learn taciturnity; let that be your motto. Though you had the wisdom of Newton, or the wit of Swift, garrulousness would lower you in the eyes of your fellow-creatures. I'll probably write you next week.—I am, your brother,

					ROBERT BURNS.

[Original in possession of Miss Begg.]

<table><tr><td>(2.)</td><td>TO MR. WILLIAM BURNS.</td></tr></table>

Isle, *March* 25th, 1789.

I HAVE stolen from my corn-sowing this minute to write a line to accompany your shirt and hat, for I can no more. Your sister Maria arrived yesternight, and begs to be remem-bered to you. Write me every opportunity—never mind postage. My head, too, is as addle as an egg this morning with dining abroad yesterday. I received yours by the mason. Forgive me this foolish-looking scrawl of an epistle. I am ever, my dear William, yours,

					R. B.

P. S.—If you are not then gone from Longtown, I'll write you a long letter by this day se'ennight. If you should not succeed in your tramps, don't be dejected, or take any rash step—return to us in that case, and we will court Fortune's better humour. Remember this, I charge you.

(3.)

TO MR. WILLIAM BURNS,

SADDLER,

CARE OF MR. WRIGHT, CARRIER, LONGTOWN.

Isle, 15th April, 1789.

My DEAR WILLIAM,

I AM extremely sorry at the misfortune of your legs; I beg you will never let any worldly concern interfere with the more serious matter, the safety of your life and limbs. I have not time in these hurried days to write you anything other than a mere how d'ye letter. I will only repeat my favourite quotation :—

" What proves the hero truly great
Is never, never to despair."

My house shall be your welcome home; and as I know your prudence (would to God you had *resolution* equal to your *prudence !*) if, anywhere at a distance from friends, you should need money, you know my direction by post.

The enclosed is from Gilbert, brought by your sister Nanny. It was unluckily forgot. Yours to Gilbert goes by post.—I heard from them yesterday, they are all well.

Adieu,

R. B.

(4.)

TO MR. WILLIAM BURNS.

Ellisland, 5th May, 1789.

My DEAR WILLM.,

I AM happy to hear by yours from Newcastle, that you are getting some employ. Remember

" On Reason build Resolve,
That column of true majesty in man."

I had a visit of your old landlord. In the midst of a drunken frolic in Dumfries, he took it into his head to come and see me; and I took all the pains in my power to please and entertain the old veteran. He is high in your praises, and I would advise you to cultivate his friendship, as he is, in his way, a worthy, and to you may be a useful man.

Anderson I hope will have your shoes ready to send by the waggon to-morrow. I forgot to mention the circumstance of making them pumps; but I suppose good calf shoes will be no great mistake. Wattie has paid me for the thongs.

What would you think of making a little inquiry how husbandry matters go, as you travel, and if one thing fail, you might perhaps try another ?

Your falling in love is indeed a phenomenon.* To a fellow of your turn it cannot be hurtful. I am, you know, a veteran in these campaigns, so let me advise you always to pay your particular assiduities and try for intimacy as soon as you feel the first symptoms of the passion: this is not only best, as making the most of the little entertainment which the sportabilities of distant addresses always gives, but is the best preservative for one's peace. I need not caution you against guilty amours—they are bad and ruinous everywhere, but in England they are the very devil. I shall be in Ayrshire about a fortnight. Your sisters send their compliments. God bless you.

ROBERT BURNS.

Mr. William Burns, Saddler,
At the shop of Mr. Nicholson, Saddler,
　　　Nowgate Street,
　　　　　Newcastle-on-Tyne.

* [Our Author seems not to have remembered his brother's youthful fancy for Nelly Miller at Mauchline—see Reminiscences Original : Appendix—or knew perhaps that it was not of a very serious character.

The above letter we print from *Newcastle Daily Journal,* to which it was contributed by Autograph Collector, March 19, 1865, with certain queries concerning William Burns, which will be found answered in the sequel.]

(5.)

TO MR. WILLIAM BURNS.

Ellisland, 14th August, 1789.

My DEAR WILLIAM,

I RECEIVED your letter, and am very happy to hear that you have got settled for the winter. I enclose you the two guinea notes of the Bank of Scotland, which I hope will serve your need. It is, indeed, not quite so convenient for me to spare money as it once was, but I know your situation, and I will say it, in some respect your worth. I have no time to write at present, but I beg you will endeavour to pluck up a little more of the man than you used to have.

Remember my favourite quotation—

" On Reason build Resolve,
That column of true majesty in man ;"

" What proves the hero truly great
Is never, never to despair."

Your mother and sister beg their compliments.—*A Dieu je vous commende,*

ROBERT BURNS.

[From *Banffshire Journal:* Original given by Mrs. Begg, the Poet's sister, when residing at Tranent, to a certain Mr. F., who had shown her no little kindness; and now in possession of Mr. F.'s son, Badenoch.]

(6.)   TO MR. WILLIAM BURNS.

Ellisland, 10th Nov., 1789.

DEAR WILLIAM,

I WOULD have written you sooner, but I am so hurried and fatigued with my Excise business, that I can scarcely pluck up resolution to go through the effort of a letter to anybody. Indeed you hardly deserve a letter from me, considering that you have spare hours in which you have nothing to do at all, and yet it was near three months between your two last letters.

I know not if you heard lately from Gilbert. I expect him here with me about the latter end of this week. * * * * My mother is returned, now that she has seen my little boy Francis fairly set to the world. I suppose Gilbert has informed you that you have got a new nephew. He is a fine thriving fellow, and promises to do honour to the name he bears. I have named him Francis Wallace, after my worthy friend, Mrs. Dunlop of Dunlop.

The only Ayrshire news that I remember in which I think you will be interested, is that Mr. Ronald is bankrupt. You will easily guess, that from his insolent vanity in his sunshine of life, he will now feel a little retaliation from those who thought themselves eclipsed by him; for, poor fellow, I do not think he ever intentionally injured any one. I might, indeed, perhaps except his wife, whom he certainly has used very ill; but she is still fond of him to distraction, and bears up wonderfully—much superior to him—under this severe shock of fortune. Women have a kind of sturdy sufferance, which qualifies them to endure beyond, much beyond, the common run of men; but perhaps part of that fortitude is owing to their short-sightedness, for they are by no means famous for seeing remote consequences in all their real importance.

I am very glad at your resolution to live within your income, be that what it will. Had poor Ronald done so, he had not this day been a prey to the dreadful miseries of insolvency. You are at the time of life when those habitudes are begun which are to mark the character of the future man. Go on and persevere, and depend on less or more success. I am, dear William, your brother,

R. B.

(7.)   TO MR. WILLIAM BURNS,

SADDLER, NEWCASTLE-ON-TYNE.

Ellisland, 10th February, 1790.

MY DEAR WILLIAM,

Now that you are setting out for that place [London], put on manly resolve, and determine to persevere; and in that case you will less or more be sure of success. One or two things allow me to particularise to you. London swarms with worthless wretches, who prey on their fellow-creatures'

thoughtlessness or inexperience. Be cautious in forming connections with comrades and companions. You can be pretty good company to yourself, and you cannot be too shy of letting anybody know you further than to know you as a saddler. Another caution. . . . . It is an impulse the hardest to be restrained; but if once a man accustoms himself to gratifications of that impulse, it is then nearly or altogether impossible to restrain it. . . . .

I have gotten the Excise division, in the middle of which I live. Poor little Frank is this morning at the height of the small-pox. I got him inoculated, and I hope he is in a good way.

Write me before you leave Newcastle, and as soon as you reach London. In a word, if ever you be, as perhaps you may be, in a strait for a little ready cash, you know my direction. I shall not see you beat while you fight like a man.—Farewell! God bless you.

ROBT. BURNS.

[The history and progress, somewhat sorrowful, of this younger brother, of whom our Author seems to have taken a sort of paternal care, is sufficiently manifest from the series of letters addressed to him and now for the first time completed and arranged. For an account of his premature and melancholy death, the reader is referred to Mr. Murdoch's letter at the close of this correspondence.]

To Mr. Samuel Brown.

Mossgiel, 4th May, 1788.[*]

DEAR UNCLE,

THIS, I hope, will find you and your conjugal yoke-fellow in your good old way; I am impatient to know if the Ailsa fowling[†] be commenced for this season yet, as I want three or four stones of feathers, and I hope you will bespeak them for me. It would be a vain attempt for me to enumerate the various transactions I have been engaged in since I saw you last, but this know,—I am engaged in a *smuggling trade*, and God knows if ever any poor man experienced better returns, two for one; but as freight and delivery have turned out so dear, I am thinking of taking out a licence and beginning in fair trade. I have taken a farm on the borders of the Nith, and in imitation of the old Patriarchs, get men-servants and maid-servants, and flocks and herds, and beget sons and daughters. Your obedient Nephew,

R. B.

* [Incorrectly dated in some editions 1789.]

† [That is, of the Solan Geese and other wild fowl on the Craig, of which there used to be, and perhaps still is, an annual slaughter.]

[It was with the uncle to whom this letter is addressed, a brother of his mother's, our Author resided at Kirkoswald.]

JEAN'S MARRIAGE DRESS
AND
JEAN'S HOME-COMING.

To Mr. Robert M'Indoe,
MERCHANT, GLASGOW.

Mauchline, 5th Aug., 1788.

MY DEAR SIR,

I AM vexed for nothing more that I have not been at Glasgow, than not meeting with you. I have seldom found my friend Andrew M'Culloch wrong in his ideas of mankind; but respecting your worship, he was true as Holy Writ. This is the night of our Fair, and I, as you see, cannot keep well *in a line*; but if you will send me by the bearer, John Ronald, carrier between Glasgow and Mauchline, fifteen yards of black silk, the same kind as that of which I bought a gown and petticoat from you formerly—Lutestring, I think, is its name—I shall send you the money and a more coherent letter, when he goes again to your good town. To be brief, send me fifteen yds. black Lutestring silk, such as they used to make gowns and petticoats of, and I shall chuse some sober morning before breakfast, and write you a sober answer, with the sober sum which will then be due you from,

Dear Sir, fu' or fasting, yours sincerely,

ROBT. BURNS.

Memorandum attached to letter—"Order complied with : price of silk from 4s. 6d. to 5s. 6d.—Ordered to be sent to Cross's, Trongate, before one o'clock at latest, with price stated—R. M'I. Addressed to Mr. Peter Buchanan. 7th Sept., 1788."

[From original in possession of John Reid, Esq., Kingston Place, Glasgow. By the memorandum affixed to this letter, it would appear that the merchant to whom the order had been intrusted was Mr. Buchanan. The previous order of the same material must either have been for an earlier present to Jean, or stuff for the dresses to his sisters with which the Poet complimented them on his first return from Edinburgh—see Mrs. Begg's statement in Chambers, vol. II., p. 90—where the material is said to have been of "made silk, sufficient to make a bonnet and cloak to each, and a gown besides to his mother and youngest sister." In the present instance, there can be no doubt, from the letter which follows, that the gift was for Jean—that this in fact was the order for Jean's MARRIAGE DRESS. In any view, the light which shines on the man's existence, through this piece of drapery, with the "baiveridge" of a kiss to follow, is exquisite. The reader may compare also song "The Bonie Lad that's far awa," stanza iv.—Poetical Works, p. 176.]

(1.)
To Mrs. Burns.

Ellisland, Friday, 12th Sept., 1788.

MY DEAR LOVE,

I RECEIVED your kind letter with a pleasure which no letter but one from you could have given me. I dreamed of you the whole night last; but, alas! I fear it will be three weeks yet, ere I can hope for the happiness of seeing you—My harvest is going on. I have some to cut down still, but I put in two stacks to day, so I [am] as tired as a dog.—

[You mig]ht get one of Gilbert's sweet milk cheeses [   ] and send it to [   ]. On second thoughts, I believe you had best get the half of Gilbert's web of table linen, and make it up; tho' I think it damnable dear, but it is no out-laid money to us, you know. I have just now consulted my old landlady about table linen, and she thinks I may have the best for two shillings per yard; so after all, let it alone until I return; and some day soon I will be in Dumfries and will ask the price there. I expect your new gowns will be very forward, or ready to make, against I be home to get the baiveridge. I have written my long-thought-on letter to Mr. Graham, the Commissioner of Excise; and have sent a shootful [of Poe]try besides. Now I talk of Poetry, I had [   ] strathspey among my hands to m[ake a song to] for Johnson's Collection which, I [   ]

[The original of above is in possession of Andrew Nicolson, shoemaker, Dumfries. The loyalty of this man's devotion to the memory of Burns is an honour to Dumfries and his native country. His wife was a servant in Mrs. Burns's house, and received the remains of parlour furniture originally in Ellisland, as plenishing for her own house, when she married. This fragment of a letter and several other papers were accidentally among the stuff removed from Mrs. Burns's house at the time, and were long afterwards discovered. The present possessor of these has been repeatedly offered large sums of money for them in vain. Compare letter to Morison, p. 175, with note upon.

In other respects this letter is most interesting. It was at this very moment, as we see, when "tired as a dog," that the Author was indicting his epistle to Graham of Fintray; and still more, the two immortal lyrics dedicated to Jean—"Of a' the airts the wind can blaw," and "Were I on Parnassus Hill"—which, together with this letter, demonstrate the genuineness of his conjugal affection. The idea, too, of consulting her about "shootfuls of Poetry," and "strathspeys" to be fitted with songs, most likely in honour of herself, for "Johnson's Collection"—blows the man! But the intermingling of such prosaic concerns as "cheese and table cloths," and the making of "new gowns"—that, by the bye, was not promise—with all this ecstatic woman-worship—is delightful in the extreme; and the appearance of old Nance Kelly as housewife on the scene, with her discussions on the Bible, her prayers and her "armfuls of riches,"—see Mrs. Burns's own Memoranda in Appendix—completes the picture. Mrs. Burns herself, however, was soon to arrive, and Nance's administration would terminate.

Mr. George Combe's verdict, on phrenological principles alone, that Acquisitiveness was largely developed in our Author's constitution, was doubted by many, and reported with astonishment by Mr. Combe himself; but the above letter, which Mr. Combe could not by possibility have seen, confirms the truth of that verdict indisputably.

So precious a little fragment—precious in every way—of a great existence, revealing or illustrating the secrets of a lifetime, we have scarcely ever seen. On same subject the reader may compare Gossip, 12, Mrs. Ma'r of Tarbolton—Appendix.]

To Dr. Mundell,
DUMFRIES.

Ellisland, Tuesday Morning.

DEAR DOCTOR,

THE bearer, Janet Nievison, is a neighbour, and occasionally a laborer of mine.—She has got some complaint in her shoulder, and wants me to find her out a Doctor that will cure her, so I have sent her to you.—You will remember that she is just in the jaws of matrimony, so for heaven's sake, get her "hale and sound" as soon as possible. We are all pretty well; only the little boy's sore month has again inflamed Mrs. B——'s nipples. I am, yours,

ROBT. BURNS.

[From fac-simile of original obligingly supplied by Dr. Grierson of Thornhill.]

* 2 E

(2.)　　　TO MRS. BURNS.

Brow, Thursday.

MY DEAREST LOVE,

I DELAYED writing until I could tell you what effect sea-bathing was likely to produce. It would be injustice to deny that it has eased my pains, and I think has strengthened me; but my appetite is still extremely bad. No flesh nor fish can I swallow: porridge and milk are the only thing I can taste. I am very happy to hear by Miss Jess Lewars, that you are all well. My very best and kindest compliments to her, and to all the children. I will see you on Sunday.

Your affectionate husband,

R. B.

———

To Mr. James Armour,

(1.)　　　MASON, MAUCHLINE.

July 10th, [1796.]

FOR Heaven's sake, and as you value the we[l]fare of your daughter and my wife, do, my dearest Sir, write to Fife to Mrs. Armour to come if possible. My wife thinks she can yet reckon upon a fortnight. The medical people order me, *as I value my existence,* to fly to sea-bathing and country-quarters, so it is ten thousand chances to one that I shall not be within a dozen miles of her when her hour comes. What a situation for her, poor girl, without a single friend by her on such a serious moment.

I have now been a week at salt-water, and though I think I have got some good by it, yet I have some secret fears that this business will be dangerous, if not fatal.

Your most affectionate son,

R. B.

———

(2.)　　　TO MR. JAMES ARMOUR,

MAUCHLINE.

Dumfries, 18th July, 1796.

MY DEAR SIR,

Do, for Heaven's sake, send Mrs. Armour here immediately. My wife is hourly expecting to be put to bed. Good God! what a situation for her to be in, poor girl,* without a friend! I returned from sea-bathing quarters to-day, and my medical friends would almost persuade me that I am better; but I think and feel that my strength is so gone, that the disorder will prove fatal to me.

Your son-in-law,

R. B.

* [Mrs. Burns not yet thirty years of age.—"It was an affecting circumstance," says Dr. Currie, "that on the morning of the day of her husband's funeral, Mrs. Burns was undergoing the pains of labour, and that during the solemn service we have just been describing [funeral service] the posthumous son of our Poet was born." Affecting and sorrowful it no doubt was, in the highest degree; but the beautiful dream she has personally described, like a revelation from Paradise, at that dreadful crisis, would soothe and cheer her.—See her own Memoranda-Appendix, p. xxv. This child, named Maxwell, in honour of Dr. Maxwell, died in infancy.]

AUTHOR'S ANXIETY

FOR THE EDUCATION AND WELFARE OF HIS CHILDREN.

[IF there was one moral instinct by which ROBERT BURNS was more conspicuously distinguished than another, it was that of Parental Affection for his children; which in the concluding years of his life, when sorrow and difficulties began to accumulate, and the horizon of their prospects was darkened, became almost overwhelmingly intense. This feeling is nowhere more clearly or affectingly exhibited than in the well-known letter to Erskine of Mar, written under the most painful apprehensions on that engrossing subject, and which we therefore here introduce as the most appropriate conclusion we can find for his entire correspondence. The citizen, the father, and the man, are all legible here. The interesting letter by his Widow, which follows on the same subject, and is now for the first time published, forms a natural and satisfactory pendant to the whole.]

To John Francis Erskine, Esq.,

OF MAR.

Dumfries, 13th April, 1793.

SIR,

DEGENERATE as human nature is said to be—and in many instances worthless and unprincipled it is—still there are bright examples to the contrary; examples that, even in the eyes of superior beings, must shed a lustre on the name of man.

Such an example have I now before me, when you, Sir, came forward to patronize and befriend a distant, obscure stranger, merely because poverty had made him helpless, and his British hardihood of mind had provoked the arbitrary wantonness of power. My much esteemed friend, Mr. Riddel of Glenriddel, has just read me a paragraph of a letter he had from you. Accept, Sir, of the silent throb of gratitude; for words would but mock the emotions of my soul.

You have been misinformed as to my final dismission from the Excise; I am still in the service.—Indeed, but for the exertions of a gentleman who must be known to you, Mr. Graham of Fintry, a gentleman who has ever been my warm and generous friend, I had, without so much as a hearing, or the slightest previous intimation, been turned adrift, with my helpless family, to all the horrors of want. Had I had any other resource, probably I might have saved them the trouble of a dismission; but the little money I gained by my publication is, almost every guinea, embarked to save from ruin an only brother, who, though one of the worthiest, is by no means one of the most fortunate of men.

In my defence to their accusations, I said, that whatever might be my sentiments of republics, ancient or modern, as to Britain, I abjured the idea!—That a CONSTITUTION which, in its original principles, experience had proved to be every way fitted for our happiness in society, it would be insanity to sacrifice to an untried visionary theory:—that, in consideration of my being situated in a department, however humble, immediately in the hands of people in power, I had forborne taking any active part, either personally, or as an author, in the present business of REFORM: But that, where I must declare my sentiments, I would say there existed a system of corruption between the executive power and the representative part of the legislature, which boded no good to our glorious CONSTITUTION; and which every patriotic Briton

must wish to see amended.—Some such sentiments as these I stated in a letter to my generous patron, Mr. Graham, which he laid before the Board at large; where, it seems, my last remark gave great offence; and one of our supervisors-general, a Mr. Corbet, was intrusted to enquire on the spot, and to document me—"that my business was to act, *not to think; and that whatever might be men or measures, it was for me to be silent and obedient.*"

Mr. Corbet was likewise my steady friend; so between Mr. Graham and him, I have been partly forgiven : only, I understand that all hopes of my getting officially forward are blasted.

Now, Sir, to the business in which I would more immediately interest you. The partiality of my COUNTRYMEN has brought me forward as a man of genius, and has given me a character to support. In the POET I have avowed manly and independent sentiments, which I trust will be found in the MAN. Reasons of no less weight than the support of a wife and family, have pointed out as the eligible, and situated as I was, the only eligible line of life for me, my present occupation. Still my honest fame is my dearest concern; and a thousand times have I trembled at the idea of those *degrading* epithets that malice or misrepresentation may affix to my name. I have often, in blasting anticipation, listened to some future hackney scribbler, with the heavy malice of savage stupidity, exulting in his hireling paragraphs—" Burns, notwithstanding the *fanfaronade* of independence to be found in his works, and after having been held forth to public view and to public estimation as a man of some genius, yet quite destitute of resources within himself to support his borrowed dignity, he dwindled into a paltry exciseman, and slunk out the rest of his insignificant existence in the meanest of pursuits, and among the vilest of mankind."

In your illustrious hands, Sir, permit me to lodge my disavowal and defiance of these slanderous falsehoods. BURNS was a poor man from birth, and an exciseman by necessity: but I *will* say it! the sterling of his honest worth no poverty could debase, and his independent British mind, oppression might bend, but could not subdue. Have not I, to me, a more precious stake in my country's welfare than the richest dukedom in it?—I have a large family of children, and the prospect of many more. I have three sons, who, I see already, have brought into the world souls ill qualified to inhabit the bodies of SLAVES.—Can I look tamely on, and see any machination to wrest from them the birthright of my boys—the little independent BRITONS, in whose veins runs my own blood?—No! I will not! should my heart's blood stream around my attempt to defend it!

Does any man tell me, that my full efforts can be of no service, and that it does not belong to my humble station to meddle with the concern of a nation?

I can tell him, that it is on such individuals as I that a nation has to rest, both for the hand of support and the eye of intelligence. The uninformed mob may swell a nation's bulk; and the titled, tinsel, courtly throng may be its feathered ornament; but the number of those who are elevated enough in life to reason and to reflect, yet low enough

to keep clear of the venal contagion of a court !—these are a nation's strength.

I know not how to apologize for the impertinent length of this epistle; but one small request I must ask of you further —when you have honoured this letter with a perusal, please to commit it to the flames. BURNS, in whose behalf you have so generously interested yourself, I have here in his native colours drawn *as he is;* but should any of the people in whose hands is the very bread he eats get the least knowledge of the picture, *it would ruin the poor BARD for ever !*

My poems having just come out in another edition, I beg leave to present you with a copy, as a small mark of that high esteem and ardent gratitude, with which I have the honour to be,

Sir,
Your deeply indebted,
And ever devoted humble servant,
R. B.

(The gentleman to whom this letter is addressed was the then representative of the ancient but attainted House of Mar, and was ultimately restored to its honours. Having heard that Burns was in danger of dismissal from the Excise for his politics, he handsomely came forward to inaugurate a subscription on his behalf in the event of such a contingency occurring. Hence the above letter to him of self-vindication and thanks by our Author. The letter, it appears, was carefully engrossed in the **Poet's** memorandum book, and the most emphatic words underlined as here represented. There seems to be very little doubt, therefore, that the writer had experienced official hints which rendered his further employment uncertain, and clouded his life to that extent with anxiety and gloom.)

THE POET'S FAMILY.

Mrs. Burns to Mrs. Riddel.

Dumfries, th, 1801.

MADAM,

MRS. SCOT was so good as call on me the other day, and informed me of your kind inquiry after my family, and that you wished to know what was become of Mr. Burns' children. We still live in the same house that you left us in, and William Nichol is the only child I have at home. Robert is at Glasgow College, and has been two winters; he was one in Edinr. It is reported, and I believe with truth, that he will be provided for in London by Mr. Addingtone, through the interest of Mr. Shaw the present Sheriff of London. Francis Wallace died last year—he was to have gone to the East Indies this spring had he lived : Mr. Shaw had got a cadet's place for him. James Glencairn is in the Bluecoat School in Newgate Street—he was also put there by Mr. Shaw. It is about 10 months since James M'Clure took him to London. He call'd with James on you at Mr. Banks, but you was in the country—He left his name and where James was to be found, but they had not told you. William is not settled yet—he is still at school. I return you my sincere thanks for your good wishes to my family, and believe me, Madam,

Your obliged and sincere well-wisher,

JEAN BURNS.

P.S.—Maxwell died 2 years and 9 months after Mr. Burns.

J. B.

* [Letter has been sealed with a large wafer, which destroys the date.]

[The above interesting document, which we print from the original holograph in possession of T. C. S. Corry, Esq., M.D., of Belfast, contains a much simpler and more graphic account of the Poet's family, with their prospective destinations, than anything we could put in its place; and we allow it, therefore, to remain as it is, without further commentary. The Mr. Addington referred to, afterwards Lord Sidmouth, was Prime-Minister; and the Mr. Shaw referred to was an Ayrshire man, afterwards Sir James, and Lord-Mayor of London. Some quotations from his life may interest our readers: he was elected Alderman, 1798; Sheriff, 1800; Lord-Mayor, 1805; M.P. for the City of London, 1806; created Baronet, 1809; Chamberlain of City, 1831. Died Oct. 22, 1843, aged 79. Sir James was the first Scotchman who filled the office of Lord-Mayor of London. He was most affectionately attached to his native country, and his benefactions to Kilmarnock in particular, where he spent his earliest years, have been commemorated by a marble statue in his honour there.

The James M'Clure referred to, as James Glencairn's guide to London, was Burns's personal attendant on his death bed.

It is obvious from the commencement of the above letter that Mrs. Riddel must have been calling for the family after the Poet's death: compare history of "Kerry Miniature," also letter (10) to her. It may interest our readers, as a matter of pleasant curiosity, to know, that, by the phonetic orthography of the original of this letter, Jean's pronunciation must have been of the broadest Ayrshire dialect.]

LETTERS,

FROM RELATIVES AND FRIENDS,

TO THE AUTHOR, &c.

(1.)　　## To Mr. Robert Burns.

Mossgiel, 1st Jan., 1789.

DEAR BROTHER,

I HAVE just finished my New-year's-day breakfast in the usual form, which naturally makes me call to mind the days of former years, and the society in which we used to begin them; and when I look at our family vicissitudes "through the dark postern of time long elapsed," I cannot help remarking to you, my dear brother, how good the GOD of SEASONS is to us, and that, however some clouds may seem to lower over the portion before us, we have great reason to hope that all will turn out well.

Your mother and sisters, with Robert the Second, join me in the compliments of the season to you and Mrs. Burns, and beg you will remember us in the same manner to William the first time you see him. I am, dear Brother,

Yours,

GILBERT BURNS,

[From Chambers's Edition, 1856.

(2.)　　　　　　TO MR. ROBERT BURNS.

Mossgiel, 4th Sept., 1790.

DR. BROTHER,

I HAVE got only about the half of my hay drove, and would have been the better to have had your horse another week, but as you need him yourself I must try to do without him. I have been much distressed with the bad weather; it has destroyed and rendered unsaleable not less than 300 stones of hay to me, besides extra wages endeavouring to save it, and my crop, which is but light, is all as green as leeks; so that if the season is not uncommonly favourable, you will have to serve me in seed-corn; but in this respect a number of my neighbours are no better than myself, and I will hope for the best. I do, indeed, foresee many difficultys, and partly feel them, and would gladly make use of a tocher to ward them off, but the only one I am certain of having in my power would in a few years involve me in much greater difficultys.

Monday morn. Already has the frost begun to allarm us. I hope it has not yet done the oats any hurt, but we have much to fear, for the earliest of mine will take three weeks of the best weather. I have this morning weighed 18 stones 3 pounds of cheese for you; which, with 6 st. 14 lb. before, makes 25 st. 1 lb. Be sure to warn all your friends to keep them in a dry cool place and turn them frequently.

Acct. curt. betwixt G. Burns and Robt. Burns.
Gilbt. Burns Dr.

	£	s	d
chestnut-coloured horse,	12	12	
new saddle and bridle,	3	19	
	£16	11	
balance due, 2　4　6,	2	4	6
	£18	15	6

Per Contra Cr.

	£	s	d
cash per Mrs. Burns,	9	9	
25 st. 1 lb. sweet milk cheese at 6s 6d,	8	2	10½
5 st. 2½ lb. scummed ditto at 4s,	1	0	7½
cash paid school wages for William Burns,		3	
	£18	15	6

The above is a state of accounts betwixt you and I, as far as I can recollect. The balance of £2 4s 6d I shall want, as I am scarce of money, and I hope when you have got in the price of the cheese it will be convenient for you to spare it. If you can give me a bed, I wish to spend a Sunday with you before I begin harvest, and I will write you that you may be disengaged, if I can possibly get away; but I am excessively hurried, and if the weather is bad it will not be in my power.

Samuel Ross wishes to know whether you will need his son, as he wishes him not to stay in your country if you do not need him, and will try to find a place for him in this. Tell Nanny that Bell is much better than she was once, but still

complains frequently of being out of order and want of digestion, and from the extreme delicacy of her nervous system is incapable of bearing any fatigue, either of body or mind. She wished to have wrote, but could not muster as much resolution. Farewell—wishing you guid furder, health and guid weather, I remain, dear Brother,

Yours, &c.,   G. BURNS.

[The letter is addressed to "Mr. Robert Burns, Ellisland, near Dumfries," and on the corner is marked, "Wt. 14 chances." The poet, at the date of the letter, had been settled about two years at Ellisland, and his prospects were at that time better than at any former part of his life, although, alas! few of them were destined to be realised.—*Elgin Courier.* Compare Account with D. Kelly—Appendix, p. xxvi.]

To Mr. Wallace,

(3.)   WRITER, DUMFRIES.

Mossgiel, 1st Jan., 1797.

MR. WALLACE,
   SIR,

I INTENDED to have been in Dumfries about this time, to have paid off my brother's debts; but I find much difficulty in sparing as much money. I think of offering Captain Hamilton and Mr. Williamson the half of their accts., and begging a little time to pay the other half. If Mr. Clark pay up his bill, I hope to be able to pay off the smaller accts. I beg you will write me your opinion immediately on this subject. Will you have the goodness to mention this to them, which will save me some uneasiness when I come to Dumfries, which I think will be in two or three weeks, unless I have occasion to delay it till Dumfries fair? I beg that you will smooth the way to me in this business as much as you can. I do feel much hurt at it; but, as I suppose the delay can be no great inconvenience to the gentlemen, I hope they will be indulgent to me.

I am, Sir, your most obedt. humble sert.,

GILBERT BURNS.

[From Chambers's Edition, 1850.]
[Compare note on letter (1) to Captain Hamilton; also on letter to Gilbert Burns himself.]

To Mr. George Thomson,

(4.)   TRUSTEES' OFFICE, EDINBURGH.

Dinning, 14th March, 1800.

   SIR,

I RECEIVED your very acceptable present of your songs, which calls for my warmest thanks. If ever I come to Edinburgh, I will certainly avail myself of your invitation, to call on a person whose handsome conduct to my brother's family has secured my esteem, and confirmed to me the opinion, that musical taste and talents have a close connection with the harmony of the moral feelings. I am unwilling, indeed, to believe that the motions of every one's heart are dark as Erebus, to whom Dame Nature has denied a good ear and musical

capacity, as her ladyship has been pleased to endow myself but scantily in these particulars; but "happy the swain who possesses it, happy his cot, and happy the sharer of it." To the sharer of yours, I beg you will present my most cordial congratulations. My sister-in-law begs me to present her best thanks to you for her copy, and to assure you that, however little she may have expressed it, she has a proper sense of the kind attention you have so kindly shown her.

I am, dear Sir, with the highest esteem,

Your most obedient humble servant,

GILBERT BURNS.

[From Chambers's Edition, 1856.]

To Messrs. Cadell and Davies,

(5.)   BOOKSELLERS, LONDON.

Grant's Braes, 19th February, 1820.

   GENTLEMEN,

I RETURN you the proof of the "Fete Champetre," with such corrections as it appeared to me to require, and such notes as I think will make it understood. The Title-page will do, but supposing it not necessary, and willing to prevent additional postage, have not returned it. As the publication may now I suppose be soon expected, I shall be much obliged to you to put me in possession of the copies I am to get, as early as any copies can be ready for delivery in this country, as I intend some of them as presents to people I am under great obligations to, and the value will be increased by being put as early into their hands as any other person can receive the volumes.

I remain, Gentlemen,

Your most obt. humble sert.,

GILBERT BURNS.

[The above letter, which refers to Gilbert's Edition of his Brother's Poems, we print from the original in possession of T. C. S. Corry, Esq., M.D., Belfast, to whom we are indebted for many similar obligations. The document enclosed a proof sheet, as stated; which, however, does not accompany the letter in our hands.]

To Mr. Robert Burns.

(1.)

Longtown, Feb. 15, 1789.

   DEAR SIR,

As I am now in a manner only entering into the world, I begin this our correspondence with a view of being a gainer by your advice, more than ever you can be by any thing I can write you of what I see, or what I hear, in the course of my wanderings. I know not how it happened, but you were more shy of your counsel than I could have wished the time I staid with you; whether it was because you thought it would disgust me to have my faults freely told me while I was dependant on you; or whether it was because you saw that by my indolent disposition, your instructions would have no effect, I cannot determine; but if it proceeded from any of the above causes, the reason of withholding your admonition is

now done away, for I now stand on my own bottom, and that indolence, which I am very conscious of, is something rubbed off, by being called to act in life whether I will or not; and my inexperience, which I daily feel, makes me wish for that advice which you are so able to give, and which I can only expect from you or Gilbert since the loss of the kindest and ablest of fathers.

The morning after I went from the Isle, I left Dumfries about five o'clock and came to Annan to breakfast, and staid about an hour; and I reached this place about two o'clock. I have got work here, and I intend to stay a month or six weeks, and then go forward, as I wish to be at York about the latter end of summer, where I propose to spend next winter, and go on for London in the spring.

I have the promise of seven shillings a week from Mr. Proctor while I stay here, and sixpence more if he succeeds himself, for he has only now begun trade here. I am to pay four shillings per week of board wages, so that my neat income here will be much the same as in Dumfries.

The inclosed you will send to Gilbert with the first opportunity. Please send me the first Wednesday after you receive this, by the Carlisle waggon, two of my coarse shirts, one of my best linen ones, my velveteen vest, and a neckcloth; write to me along with them, and direct to me, Saddler, in Longtown, and they will not miscarry, for I am boarded in the waggoner's house. You may either let them be given in to the waggon, or send them to Coulthard and Gellebourn's shop and they will forward them. Pray write me often while I stay here.—I wish you would send me a letter, though never so small, every week, for they will be no expense to me and but little trouble to you. Please to give my best wishes to my sister-in-law, and believe me to be your affectionate

And obliged Brother,

WILLIAM BURNS.

P.S.—The great-coat you gave me at parting did me singular service the day I came here, and merits my hearty thanks. From what has been said, the conclusion is this—that my hearty thanks and my best wishes are all that you and my sister must expect from

W. B.

(2.)　　　　　　TO MR. ROBERT BURNS.

Newcastle, 24th Jan., 1790.

DEAR BROTHER,

I WROTE you about six weeks ago, and I have expected to hear from you every post since, but I suppose your excise business, which you hinted at in your last, has prevented you from writing. By the bye, when and how have you got into the excise; and what division have you got about Dumfries? These questions please answer in your next, if more important matter do not occur. But in the mean time let me have the letter to John Murdoch, which Gilbert wrote me you meant to send; inclose it in your's to me, and let me have

them as soon as possible, for I intend to sail for London in a fortnight, or three weeks at farthest.

You promised me when I was intending to go to Edinburgh, to write me some instructions about behaviour in companies rather above my station, to which I might be eventually introduced. As I may be introduced into such companies at Murdoch's or on his account when I go to London, I wish you would write me some such instructions now; I never had more need of them, for having spent little of my time in company of any sort since I came to Newcastle, I have almost forgot the common civilities of life. To these instructions pray add some of a moral kind, for though (either through the strength of early impressions, or the frigidity of my constitution) I have hitherto withstood the temptation to those vices to which young fellows of my station and time of life are so much addicted, yet, I do not know if my virtue will be able to withstand the more powerful temptations of the metropolis; yet, through God's assistance and your instructions I hope to weather the storm.

Give the compliments of the season and my love to my sisters, and all the rest of your family. Tell Gilbert the first time you write him that I am well, and that I will write him either when I sail or when I arrive at London.

I am, &c.

W. B.

(3.)　　　　　　TO MR. ROBERT BURNS.

London, 21st March, 1790.

DEAR BROTHER,

I HAVE been here three weeks come Tuesday, and would have written you sooner but was not settled in a place of work:—We were ten days on our passage from Shields; the weather being calm I was not sick, except one day when it blew pretty hard. I got into work the Friday after I came to town; I wrought there only eight days, their job being done. I got work again in a shop in the Strand, the next day after I left my former master. It is only a temporary place, but I expect to be settled soon in a shop to my mind, although it will be a harder task than I at first imagined, for there are such swarms of fresh hands just come from the country that the town is quite overstocked, and except one is a particularly good workman (which you know I am not, nor I am afraid ever will be), it is hard to get a place: However, I don't yet despair to bring up my lee-way, and shall endeavour if possible to sail within three or four points of the wind. The encouragement here is not what I expected, wages being very low in proportion to the expense of living, but yet, if I can only lay by the money that is spent by others in my situation in dissipation and riot, I expect soon to return you the money I borrowed of you and live comfortably besides.

In the mean time I wish you would send up all my best linen shirts to London, which you may easily do by sending them to some of your Edinburgh friends, to be shipped from Leith. Some of them are too little; don't send any but what are good, and I wish one of my sisters could find as much time as to trim my shirts at the breast, for there is no such thing to be seen here as a plain shirt, even for wearing, which is what I want these for. I mean to get one or two new shirts here for Sundays, but I assure you that linen here is a very expensive article. I am going to write to Gilbert to send me an Ayrshire cheese; if he can spare it he will send it to you, and you may send it with the shirts, but I expect to hear from you before that time. The cheese I could get here; but I will have a pride in eating Ayrshire cheese in London, and the expense of sending it will be little, as you are sending the shirts any how.

I write this by J. Stevenson, in his lodgings, while he is writing to Gilbert. He is well and hearty, which is a blessing to me as well as to him: We were at Covent Garden chapel this forenoon, to hear the *Calf* preach; he is grown very fat, and is as boisterous as ever.* There is a whole colony of Kilmarnock people here, so we don't want for acquaintance.

Remember me to my sisters and all the family. I shall give you all the observations I have made on London in my next, when I shall have seen more of it.

I am, Dear Brother, yours, &c.,

W. B.

* [The Rev. James Steven : "The Calf"—Poetical Works, p. 24.]

From Mr. Murdoch to the Bard,

GIVING HIM AN ACCOUNT OF THE DEATH OF HIS BROTHER
WILLIAM.

*Hart Street, Bloomsbury Square, London,
September 14th, 1790.*

My dear Friend,

Yours of the 16th of July I received on the 26th, in the afternoon, per favor of my friend Mr. Kennedy, and at the same time was informed that your brother was ill. Being engaged in business till late that evening, I set out next morning to see him, and had thought of three or four medical gentlemen of my acquaintance, to one or other of whom I might apply for advice, provided it should be necessary. But when I went to Mr. Barber's, to my great astonishment and heartfelt grief, I found that my young friend had, on Saturday, bid an everlasting farewell to all sublunary things.—It was about a fortnight before that he had found me out, by Mr. Stevenson's accidentally calling at my shop to buy something. We had only one interview, and that was highly entertaining to me in several respects. He mentioned some instruction I had given him when very young, to which he said he owed, in a great measure, the philanthropy he pos-

sessed.—He also took notice of my exhorting you all, when I wrote, about eight years ago, to the man who, of all mankind that I ever knew, stood highest in my esteem, "not to let go your integrity."—You may easily conceive that such conversation was both pleasing and encouraging to me: I anticipated a deal of rational happiness from future conversations.—Vain are our expectations and hopes. They are so almost always—Perhaps (nay, certainly) for our good. Were it not for disappointed hopes we could hardly spend a thought on another state of existence, or be in any degree reconciled to the quitting of this.

I know of no one source of consolation to those who have lost young relatives equal to that of their being of a good disposition, and of a promising character.

*   *   *   *   *   *

Be assured, my dear friend, that I cordially sympathize with you all, and particularly with Mrs. W. Burns, who is undoubtedly one of the most tender and affectionate mothers that ever lived. Remember me to her in the most friendly manner, when you see her, or write.—Please present my best compliments to Mrs. R. Burns, and to your brother and sisters.—There is no occasion for me to exhort you to filial duty, and to use your united endeavours in rendering the evening of life as comfortable as possible to a mother who has dedicated so great a part of it in promoting your temporal and spiritual welfare.

Your letter to Dr. Moore I delivered at his house, and shall most likely know your opinion of Zeluco the first time I meet with him. I wish and hope for a long letter. Be particular about your mother's health. I hope she is too much a Christian to be afflicted above measure, or to sorrow as those who have no hope.

One of the most pleasing hopes I have is to visit you all; but I am commonly disappointed in what I most ardently wish for.—I am, Dear Sir, yours sincerely,

John Murdoch.

To Mr. Robert Burns.

Sir,

I received your favour of the 5th instant this day, containing a bill for the money expended in your deceased brother's sickness and funeral. Wishing you all health and happiness, I am, Sir, your very humble servant,

W. Barber.

Strand, Oct. 8, 1790.

[Found among the Poet's papers, and now in possession of our friend Thomas Thorburn, Esq., Ryedale, Dumfries.]

To the following most obliging and esteemed Correspondents our best acknowledgments are due, for original documents or valuable information contributed by them to the foregoing portions of our work, and for some information also contained in our Appendix—as under:

AIKEN, P. F., Esq., Wullcroft House, Durdham Park, Bristol;
> Letter (4) to Aiken; also Letter by Miss Grace Aiken, with interesting information relative, ...Prose Works, p. 116—119.

ALLAN, Mr. JOHN, Farmer in Smeeston, Tarbolton, and son of "Tibbie Lass;"
> Anecdote concerning heroine of that song; and also concerning "Death" in "Death and Dr. Hornbook," ....Poetical Works, p. 92 and 261.

BEGG, Miss, Niece of the Poet, Bridgehouse, Ayr;
> Copy of Letter to William Burns, with much valuable information relative to Poet's life and history.

BROADFIELD, Mr. EDWARD, Glasgow;
> Letter (1) to Aiken, revised verbatim; ....Prose Works, p. 115.
> Inscription on blank leaf of Hannah More's Works, revised verbatim.

BURNS, Col. W. N., Son of the Poet, Cheltenham;
> Register from Poet's Family Bible, photograph—see Illustration;
> also, Photographs from Nasmyth, &c.;

CARRUTHERS, ROBERT, Esq., *Inverness Courier;*
> Supplementary Letters (1), (2), (3), to Johnson, ...Prose Works, p. 130.
> Quotations from Manuscripts in British Museum,... do. p. 206.

CLARK, C. G., Esq., Dumfriesshire; through Dr. Grierson, Thornhill;
> Photograph Inscriptions on Young's Night Thoughts, to and by "Clarinda." ....Prose Works, p. 32.

CORRY, T. C. S., Esq., M.D., Belfast;
> Letters (10), partly (12), to Mrs. Riddel, ...Prose Works, p. 61;
> Letter by Mrs. Burns, widow, to Mrs. Riddel, do. p. 219;
> Letter by Gilbert Burns to Cadell and Davies, do. p. 221.

CRUM, Mrs. JAMES, Busby;
> Letter (3) to Aiken, do. p. 146.

CUTHBERT, THOMAS, Esq., Burnock Holms, Ochiltree;
> Information concerning composition of certain poems, "Soldier's Return," "On Destruction of the Woods at Drumlanrig," &c.

DENNY, JOHN, Esq., Town-Clerk, Dumbarton;
> Most courteous assistance in examining Burgh Records, anent Burns's Freedom of that town, ...Appendix, p. xxxviii.

EVERITT, Mrs. BURNS, Grand-daughter of the Poet, Ayr;
> Impression of Poet's seal in her possession, attached to this series; also Anecdote of Poet's humanity, ...Appendix, p. xxxix.

GEMMELL, GAVIN, Esq., Banker, Ayr;
> Various Readings, in "Vision," &c.; also most valuable and courteous assistance in obtaining original documents—as infra.

GEMMELL, THOS. M., Esq., *Ayr Advertiser;*
> Courteous information concerning John Ballantine, Esq.

GILCHRIST, Dr. JAMES, Crichton Institute, Dumfries;
> Courteous information concerning original manuscript of the "Whistle."

GLADSTONE, Mr. & Mrs. STEWART, Capenoch, Dumfriesshire;
> Letter (2) to Samuel Clarke, Jun., Dumfries............Prose Works, p. 196.

GLADSTONE, Miss MARY SELINA, Fasque, Laurencekirk;
> Letter to Blair, gunmaker, Birmingham; also, manuscript of "Lines Written in Friars-Carse Hermitage," ....Prose Works, p. 203.

GRIERSON, Mr. T. B., Surgeon, Thornhill;
> Photograph of Letter to Dr. Mundell, ...Prose Works, p. 217;
> Photograph of Excise Permit—see Illustration;
> Fac-simile of "Jolly Beggars" from which our edition is printed; also Fac-simile of Poet's Assignment, in Appendix; so admirable a fac-simile as to be mistaken by us at the time for a duplicate original by the Poet—See Note in Appendix, ...p. xii.

HOGG, Rev. DAVID, Manse, Kirkmahoe, Dumfriesshire;
> Original information concerning "Cutty Sark" in "Tam o' Shanter." [Poetical Works, p. 243;
> Original information concerning "Winsome Willie" and the Tailor, [Appendix, p. xiii.

HUTCHINSON, Mrs. BURNS, Grand-daughter of the Poet, Cheltenham;
> Much interesting and valuable information concerning his life, and certain of his poems.

JOHNSTON, Miss, Sanquhar, by G. Gemmell, Esq., Ayr;
> Memorandum for Provost Edward Whigham, ...Prose Works, p. 162.

LOGAN, Miss, Bishopsclough, by G. Gemmell, Esq., Ayr;
> Letter (1) to John Logan, Esq., Knockshinnoch,......Prose Works, p. 134;
> Do. (2) do. do. revised verbatim from original, p. 134;
> Kirk's Alarm, do. do. do. Poetical Works, p. 290.

MANNERS, GEORGE, Esq., F.S.A., Croydon;
> Letter (21) to Mrs. Dunlop, with Psalmody,............Prose Works, p. 18;
> Do. (34) to Clarinda, do. p. 49;
> Do. (13) to Mrs. Riddel, do. p. 61;
> Do. (2) to Robert Cleghorn, do. p. 170;
> Do. (1) to Captain Hamilton, do. p. 191;
> * Do. to William Inglis, Esq., Inverness, do. p. 205.
> N.B.—This last letter, we are requested by Mr. Manners to state, is from a copy obligingly afforded to him by a collector, and not in his own possession, as inadvertently stated by us. The original, we believe, is now the property of a gentleman in Glasgow.

M'DIARMID, WM. RITCHIE, Esq., *Dumfries Courier;*
> Letter to Provost Staig, Dumfries,............Prose Works, p. 190;
> Memoranda by Mrs. Burns,............Appendix, p. xli;
> Portrait of Mrs. Burns—vide Engraving.

M'DONALD, Mr. JAMES, Castle Street, Dundee;
> Valuable information with respect to manuscript documents, Pasque Manuscript, &c.

NICOLSON, Mr. ANDREW, Shoemaker, Dumfries;
> Letter (1) to Mrs. Burns,............Prose Works, p. 211;
> also, Information concerning Poet's Household Plenishing, &c.

PAGAN, GEORGE, Esq., Banker, New Cumnock, by G. Gemmell, Esq., Ayr.
> Letter to Messr. Thos. Campbell, Penches,............Prose Works, p. 155.

REID, JOHN, Esq., Kingston Place, Glasgow;
> Letter (4) to Muir,............Prose Works, p. 142;
> Do. (3) do. revised verbatim from original,... do. p. 144;
> Do. to Robert M'Indoe, do. p. 217;
> Do. by Dr. George Grierson, do. p. 208;
> Original Versions of Epigrams, &c.; also,
> Important information concerning Burns's first visit to Glasgow—See Appendix, ...p. xxxvi.

SIM, Sergeant JOHN, Bridge-end, Perth;
> Curious and important information concerning authorship of poem incorrectly ascribed to Robert Burns—"To my Bed."

STUART-MENTETH, Sir JAMES, Bart., of Mansfield House, Ayrshire;
> Three Documents relating to Contest for Whistle,... Poet. Works, p. 251;
> Photograph of Nursing Chair—see Illustration;
> Interesting information concerning Chrissy Flint; and
> Valuable information concerning Poet's life, availed of in Biography.

THORBURN, THOMAS, Esq., Ryedale, Dumfries;
> Inscription on Mason Apron—see letter to Charles Sharpe, Esq.—controverted,............Prose Works, p. 117;
> Notice of Clarinda—see Burns's Heroines.

WALLER'S, Mr. JOHN, Catalogue, of Fleet Street, London;
> Letters (1), (5), (14), (15) to Mrs. Riddel,......Prose Works, p. 20, et seq.

Besides the above original contributions in the form of Letters alone, amounting in all to upwards of fifty; all of less or more, and many of them of the greatest, importance, there are also a few Letters included in the present edition from the columns of newspapers or other public documents, which do not require to be here specified. Other contributors, whose valuable assistance has been availed of chiefly, or exclusively, in the Appendix, will find their names acknowledged with thanks, at the conclusion of that department.

APPENDIX:

CONTAINING

DOCUMENTS AND INFORMATION

SUPPLEMENTARY AND ORIGINAL.

NOTE.

The Reader, on examination, will find that this portion of our Work includes much more varied and extensive information than was originally promised or hoped for. The interest attaching to some of these new materials was such, in our opinion, as could not fail to render them most attractive to all readers; and the propriety of introducing certain others, for the more perfect elucidation of our Author's Life and Language, seemed to be also such as would justify the enlargement of this Department in proportion, to make the Edition itself as comprehensive and complete as possible.

The Appendix as now arranged, therefore, will include the following among other

GENERAL CONTENTS.

Author's Journals;

Sketch of Life and History of Poems, by Gilbert Burns;

Memoranda of Poet's Life, by his Widow,—now first published;

Original Authentic Reminiscences and Traditions collected by Editor,—now first published;

Gossip, Corrected or Enlarged by Editor;

Editorial Remarks on Scottish Language and Language of Burns;

History of "Kerry Miniatures," Phrenological Development of Burns, &c.;

Heroines of Burns;

Glossary, Terms and Phrases, Enlarged;

Index.

APPENDIX.

In the Name of the Nine, Amen.

[This document, although generally included in our Author's Correspondence, does not seem to us to be of such a character as properly to occupy a place there; we have reserved it, therefore, for the Appendix. The ballad alluded to was most probably "Holy Willie's Prayer."]

WE, ROBERT BURNS, by virtue of a warrant from Nature, bearing date the twenty-fifth day of January, Anno Domini one thousand seven hundred and fifty-nine, Poet-Laureat and Bard-in-Chief, in and over the districts and countries of Kyle, Cunningham, and Carrick, of old extent, To our trusty and well-beloved William Chalmers and John M'Adam, Students and Practitioners in the ancient and mysterious Science of Confounding Right and Wrong.

RIGHT TRUSTY:

Be it known unto you, that whereas, in the course of our care and watchings over the order and police of all and sundry the manufacturers, retainers, and venders of Poesy; bards, poets, poetasters, rhymers, jinglers, songsters, ballad-singers, &c., &c., &c., &c., male and female—We have discovered a certain nefarious, abominable, and wicked song or ballad, a copy whereof we have inclosed; Our Will therefore is, that Ye pitch upon and appoint the most execrable individual of that most execrable species, known by the appellation, phrase, and nick-name of The Deil's Yell Nowte:* and after having caused him to kindle a fire at the Cross of Ayr, ye shall, at noontide of the day, put into the said wretch's merciless hands the said copy of the said nefarious and wicked song, to be consumed by fire in the presence of all beholders, in abhorrence of, and terrorem to, all such compositions and composers. And this in nowise leave ye undone, but have it executed in every point as this Our Mandate bears, before the twenty-fourth current, when in person We hope to applaud your faithfulness and zeal.

Given at Mauchline this twentieth day of November, Anno Domini one thousand seven hundred and eighty-six.

GOD SAVE THE BARD!

* [Explained by Currie to be Old Bachelors; by Gilbert Burns, to be Sheriff-Officers.]

Tragic Fragment.

IN my early years nothing less would serve me than courting the tragic Muse.—I was, I think, about eighteen or nineteen when I sketched the outlines of a tragedy forsooth; but the bursting of a cloud of family misfortunes, which had for some time threatened us, prevented my farther progress. In those days I never wrote down any thing; so, except a speech or two, the whole has escaped my memory.—The following, which I most distinctly remember, was an exclamation from a great character:—great in occasional instances of generosity, and daring at times in villainies. He is supposed to meet with a child of misery, and exclaims to himself—

> "All devil as I am, a damned wretch,
> A harden'd, stubborn, unrepenting villain,
> Still my heart melts at human wretchedness;
> And with sincere tho' unavailing sighs,
> I view the helpless children of distress.
> With tears indignant I behold th' oppressor
> Rejoicing in the honest man's destruction,
> Whose unsubmitting heart was all his crime.
> Even you, ye helpless crew, I pity you;
> Ye, whom the scorning good think sin to pity:
> Ye poor, despis'd, abandon'd vagabonds,
> Whom vice, as usual, has turn'd o'er to ruin.
> —O, but for kind, tho' ill-requited friends,
> I had been driven forth like you forlorn,
> The most detested, worthless wretch among you!"

ADDITIONAL EXTRACTS

From Common-Place Book.

Edinburgh, April 9, 1787.

As I have seen a good deal of human life in Edinburgh, a great many characters which are new to one bred up in the shades of life as I have been, I am determined to take down my remarks on the spot. Gray observes, in a letter to Mr. Palgrave, that "half a word fixed upon, or near the spot, is worth a cart-load of recollection." I don't know how it is with the world in general, but with me, making my remarks is by no means a solitary pleasure. I want some one to laugh with me, some one to be grave with me, some one to please me and help my discrimination, with his or her own remark, and at times, no doubt, to admire my acuteness and penetration. The world are so busied with selfish pursuits, ambition, vanity, interest, or pleasure, that very few think it worth their while to make any observation on what passes around them, except where that observation is a sucker, or branch of the darling plant they are rearing in their fancy. Nor am I sure, notwithstanding all the sentimental flights of novel-writers, and the sage philosophy of moralists, whether we are capable of so intimate and cordial a coalition of friendship, as that one man may pour out his bosom, his every thought and floating fancy, his very inmost soul, with unreserved confidence to another, without hazard of losing part of that respect which man deserves from man; or, from the unavoidable imperfections attending human nature, of one day repenting his confidence.

For these reasons, I am determined to make these pages my confidant. I will sketch every character that anyway strikes me, to the best of my power, with unshrinking justice. I will insert anecdotes, and take down remarks, in the old law-phrase, *without feud or favour.* Where I hit on anything clever, my own applause will in some measure feast my vanity; and, begging Patroclus' and Achates' pardon, I think a lock and key a security at least equal to the bosom of any friend whatever.

My own private story likewise, my love-adventures, my rambles; the frowns and smiles of fortune on my bardship; my poems and fragments, that must never see the light—shall be occasionally inserted. In short, never did four shillings purchase so much friendship, since confidence went first to market, or honesty was set up to sale.

To these seemingly invidious, but too just ideas of human friendship, I would cheerfully make one exception—the connection between two persons of different sexes, when their interests are united and absorbed by the tie of love—

> "When thought meets thought, ere from the lips it part,
> And each warns with springs mutual from the heart."

There confidence, confidence that exalts them the more in one another's opinion, that endears them the more to each other's hearts, unreservedly "reigns and revels." But this is not my lot; and, in my situation, if I am wise (which, by the bye, I have no great chance of being), my fate should be cast with the Psalmist's sparrow, "to watch alone on the house-tops." Oh the pity!

   *   *   *

There are few of the sore evils under the sun give me more uneasiness and chagrin than the comparison how a man of genius, nay, of avowed worth, is received everywhere, with the reception which a mere ordinary character, decorated with the trappings and futile distinctions of fortune, meets. I imagine a man of abilities, his breast glowing with honest pride, conscious that men are born equal, still giving *honour to whom honour is due*; he meets at a great man's table a

Squire Something, or a Sir Somebody; he knows the *noble* landlord at heart gives the bard, or whatever he is, a share of his good wishes, beyond, perhaps, any one at table: yet how will it mortify him to see a fellow whose abilities would scarcely have made an *eightpenny tailor*, and whose heart is not worth three-farthings, meet with attention and notice that are withheld from the son of genius and poverty!

The noble Glencairn has wounded me to the soul here, because I dearly esteem, respect, and love him. He showed so much attention, engrossing attention, one day, to the only blockhead at table (the whole company consisted of his lordship, dunderpate, and myself), that I was within half a point of throwing down my gage of contemptuous defiance; but he shook my hand, and looked so benevolently good at parting. God bless him! though I should never see him more, I shall love him until my dying day! I am pleased to think I am so capable of the throes of gratitude, as I am miserably deficient in some other virtues.

With Dr. Blair I am more at my ease. I never respect him with humble veneration; but when he kindly interests himself in my welfare, or, still more, when he descends from his pinnacle, and meets me on equal ground in conversation, my heart overflows with what is called *liking.* When he neglects me for the mere caress of greatness, or when his eye measures the difference of our points of elevation, I say to myself, with scarcely any emotion, What do I care for him or his pomp either? * * *

It is not easy forming an exact judgment of any one; but, in my opinion, Dr. Blair is merely an astonishing proof of what industry and application can do. Natural parts like his are frequently to be met with; his vanity is proverbially known among his acquaintance; but he is justly at the head of what may be called fine writing; and a critic of the first, the very first rank in prose; even in poetry, a bard of Nature's making can only take the *pas* of him. He has a heart not of the very finest water, but far from being an ordinary one. In short, he is truly a worthy and most respectable character.

Ellisland, Sunday 14th [15th?] June, 1788.

This is now the third day that I have been in this country. "Lord! what is man?" What a bustling little bundle of passions, appetites, ideas, and fancies! And what a capricious kind of existence he has here! * * * There is, indeed, an elsewhere, where, as Thomson says, *virtue sole survives.*

>   ——"Tell us, ye dead;
> Will none of you in pity disclose the secret,
> What 'tis you are, and we must shortly be!
> ——————————A little time
> Will make us wise as you are, and as close."

I am such a coward in life, so tired of the service, that I would almost at any time, with Milton's Adam, "gladly lay me in my mother's lap, and be at peace."

But a wife and children bind me to struggle with the stream, till some sudden squall shall overset the silly vessel, or, in the listless return of years, its own craziness reduce it to a wreck. Farewell now to those giddy follies, those varnished vices, which, though half sanctified by the bewitching levity of wit and humour, are at best but thriftless

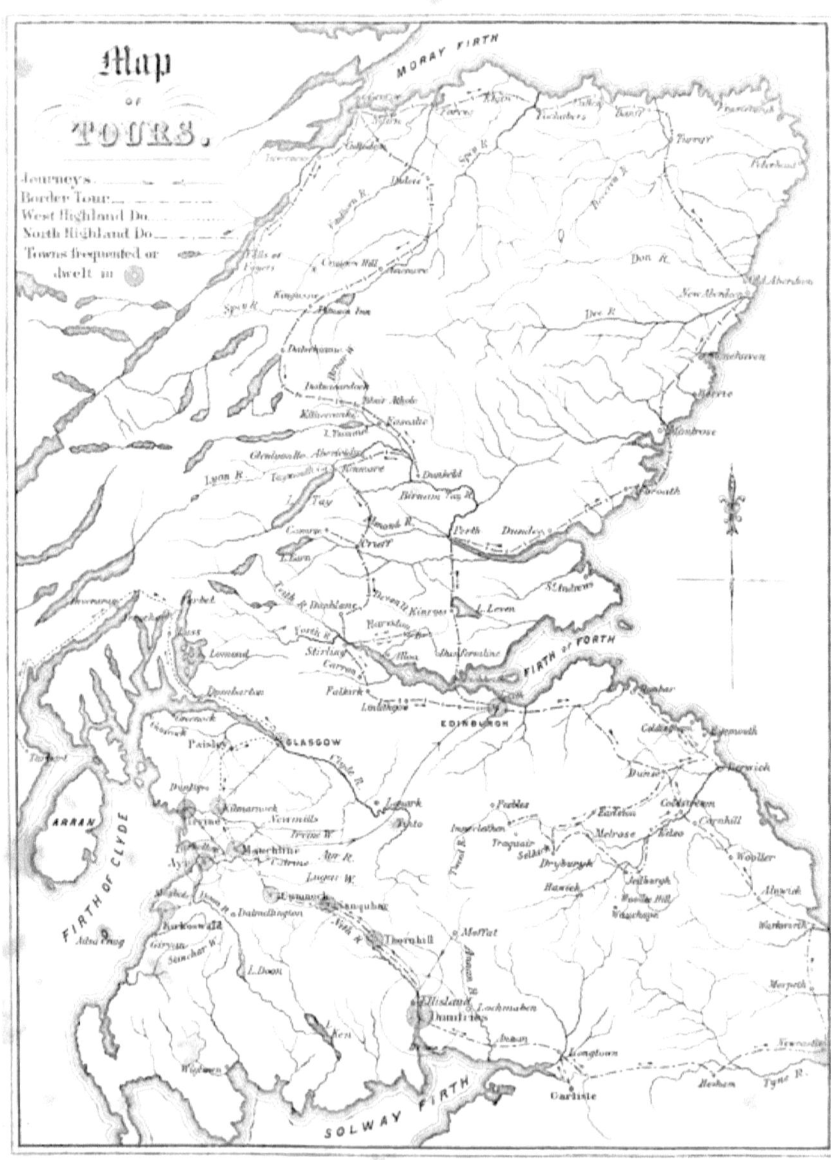

Map
of
TOURS.
Journeys
Border Tour
West Highland Do.
North Highland Do.
Towns frequented or
dwelt in
MORAY FIRTH
FIRTH OF FORTH
FIRTH OF CLYDE
SOLWAY FIRTH
ARRAN
GLASGOW
EDINBURGH
Paisley
Dumbarton
Greenock
Stirling
Falkirk
Linlithgow
Lanark
Peebles
Melrose
Kelso
Berwick
Dunse
Coldstream
Cornhill
Wooller
Alnwick
Hawick
Jedburgh
Selkirk
Dryburgh
Traquair
Moffat
Thornhill
Sanquhar
Dumfries
Lochmaben
Longtown
Carlisle
Hexham
Newcastle
Morpeth
Warkworth
Tyne R.
Wigtown
L. Ken
L. Doon
Girvan
Barskimming
Kirkoswald
Ailsa Craig
Ayr
Mauchline
Kilmarnock
Irvine
Dunlop
Tarbert
Loch Lomond
Crieff
Perth
Dundee
St. Andrews
L. Leven
Kinross
Dunfermline
Alloa
Dunblane
Dunkeld
Birnam
Kenmore
Taymouth Castle
Aberfeldy
Glenlyon Ho.
L. Tay
Lyon R.
Killiecrankie
Blair Athole
Dalnacardoch
Dalwhinnie
Pitmain Inn
Kingussie
Aviemore
Craig Hill
Carrbridge
Spey R.
Dulsie
Forres
Nairn
Inverness
Don R.
Dee R.
New Aberdeen
Old Aberdeen
Stonehaven
Bervie
Montrose
Arbroath
Peterhead
Fraserburgh
Turriff
Banff
Huntly
Keith
Almond R.
Devon R.
Forth R.
Clyde R.
Ayr R.
Nith R.
Annan R.
Dunbar
Coldingham
Eyemouth

idling with the precious current of existence; nay, often poisoning the whole, that, like the plains of Jericho, *the water is naught and the ground barren*, and nothing short of a supernaturally-gifted Elisha can ever after heal the evils.

Wedlock—the circumstance that buckles me hardest to care, if virtue and religion were to be anything with me but names—was what in a few seasons I must have resolved on: in my present situation, it was absolutely necessary. Humanity, generosity, honest pride of character, justice to my own happiness for after-life, so far as it could depend (which it surely will a great deal) on internal peace; all these joined their warmest suffrages, their most powerful solicitations, with a rooted attachment, to urge the step I have taken. Nor have I any reason on her part to repent it. I can fancy how, but have never seen where, I could have made a better choice. . Come, then, let me act up to my favourite motto, that glorious passage in Young—

"On reason build resolve,
That column of true majesty in man."

[Small remaining Fragments were incorporated in Author's correspondence, chiefly with 'Clarinda.']

The Border Tour.

[Our readers need hardly be reminded that this Tour is chiefly through that part of the country since known as the Land of Scott, and of which almost every spot here mentioned has in some way been immortalised by that Author. We attach a few notes to the text where absolutely necessary; the reader, for farther illustration, may compare the Author's letters, where dates correspond.]

LEFT Edinburgh [*May 5*, 1787]—Lammermuir-hills miserably dreary, but at times very picturesque. Langton-edge, a glorious view of the Merse—Reach Berrywell—old Mr. Ainslie an uncommon character;—his hobbies, agriculture, natural philosophy, and politics.—In the first he is unexceptionably the clearest-headed, best-informed man I ever met with; in the other two, very intelligent:—As a man of business he has uncommon merit, and by fairly deserving it has made a very decent independence. Mrs. Ainslie, an excellent, sensible, cheerful, amiable old woman. Miss Ainslie—her person a little *embonpoint*, but handsome; her face, particularly her eyes, full of sweetness and good humour: she unites three qualities rarely to be found together; keen, solid penetration; sly, witty observation and remark; and the gentlest, most unaffected female modesty. Douglas, a clever, fine promising young fellow.—The family-meeting with their brother, my *compagnon de voyage*, very charming; particularly the sister. The whole family remarkably attached to their menials—Mrs. A. full of stories of the sagacity and sense of the little girl in the kitchen. Mr. A. high in the praises of an African, his house-servant—all his people old in his service—Douglas's old nurse came to Berrywell yesterday to remind them of its being his birthday.

A Mr. Dudgeon, a poet at times, a worthy remarkable character—natural penetration, a great deal of information, some genius, and extreme modesty.*

* [Author of Scottish song " The Maid that tends the Goats."

Sunday.—Went to church at Dunse—Dr. Bowmaker a man of strong lungs and pretty judicious remark; but ill skilled in propriety, and altogether unconscious of his want of it.

Monday.—Coldstream—went over to England—Cornhill—glorious river Tweed—clear and majestic—fine bridge. Dine at Coldstream with Mr. Ainslie and Mr. Foreman—beat Mr. F——in a dispute about Voltaire. Tea at Lennel House with Mr. Brydone—Mr. Brydone a most excellent heart, kind, joyous, and benevolent; but a good deal of the French indiscriminate complaisance—from his situation past and present, an admirer of every thing that bears a splendid title, or that possesses a large estate— Mrs. Brydone a most elegant woman in her person and manners; the tones of her voice remarkably sweet—my reception extremely flattering—sleep at Coldstream.*

Tuesday.—Breakfast at Kelso—charming situation of Kelso —fine bridge over the Tweed—enchanting views and prospects on both sides of the river, particularly the Scotch side; introduced to Mr. Scott of the Royal Bank—an excellent, modest fellow—fine situation of it—ruins of Roxburgh Castle—a holly-bush growing where James II. of Scotland was accidentally killed by the bursting of a cannon. A small old religious ruin, and a fine old garden planted by the religious, rooted out and destroyed by an English hottentot, a *maitre d'hotel* of the duke's, a Mr. Cole. Climate and soil of Berwickshire, and even Roxburghshire, superior to Ayrshire—bad roads. Turnip and sheep husbandry, their great improvements—Mr. M'Dowal, at Caverton Mill, a friend of Mr. Ainslie's, with whom I dined to-day, sold his sheep, ewe and lamb together, at two guineas a piece.— Wash their sheep before shearing—seven or eight pounds of washen wool in a fleece—low markets, consequently low rents—fine lands not above sixteen shillings a Scotch acre —magnificence of farmers and farm-houses—come up Teviot and up Jed to Jedburgh to lie, and so wish myself a good night. [' To lie'—Ayrshire expression for to sleep.]

Wednesday.—Breakfast with Mr. —— in Jedburgh—a squabble between Mrs. ——, a crazed, talkative slattern, and a sister of her's, an old maid, respecting a Relief minister—Miss gives Madam the lie; and Madam, by way of revenge, upbraids her that she laid snares to entangle the said minister, then a widower, in the net of matrimony. Go about two miles out of Jedburgh to a roup of parks— meet a polite, soldier-like gentleman, a Captain Rutherford, who had been many years through the wilds of America, a prisoner among the Indians. Charming, romantic situation of Jedburgh, with gardens, orchards, &c., intermingled among the houses—fine old ruins—a once magnificent cathedral,

* [We find an anecdote in Chambers, relative to this part of the Journal, by Mr. Ainslie, to the effect—that, when on the English side of the river, Burns, with uncovered head, knelt down, and with uplifted hands, in a transport of solemn enthusiasm pronounced aloud, in tones of the deepest emotion, the two concluding stanzas of the " Cotter's Saturday Night," as a prayer for Scotland.
Patrick Brydone, Esq., was well-known as author of a " Tour in Sicily and Malta;" Mrs. Brydone was a daughter of Dr. Robertson, the historian; and Miss Brydone, their daughter, a woman of great accomplishments, became Countess of Minto.]

and strong castle. All the towns here have the appearance of old, rude grandeur, but the people extremely idle—Jed a fine romantic little river.

Dine with Captain Rutherford—the Captain a polite fellow, fond of money in his farming way; showed a particular respect to my bardship—his lady exactly a proper matrimonial second part for him. Miss Rutherford a beautiful girl, but too far gone woman to expose so much of a fine swelling bosom—her face very fine.

Return to Jedburgh—walk up Jed with some ladies to be shown Love-lane and Blackburn, two fairy scenes. Introduced to Mr. Potts, writer, a very clever fellow; and Mr. Somerville, the clergyman of the place, a man, and a gentleman, but sadly addicted to punning.*—The walking party of ladies, Mrs. —— and Miss —— her sister, before mentioned. —*N.B.* These two appear still more comfortably ugly and stupid, and bore me most shockingly. Two Miss ——, tolerably agreeable. Miss Hope, a tolerably pretty girl, fond of laughing and fun. Miss Lindsay, a good-humoured, amiable girl; rather short *et embonpoint*, but handsome, and extremely graceful—beautiful hazel eyes, full of spirit, and sparkling with delicious moisture—an engaging face *au tout ensemble* that speaks her of the first order of female minds —her sister, a bonnie, strappan, rosy, sonsie lass. Shake myself loose, after several unsuccessful efforts, of Mrs. —— and Miss ——, and somehow or other, get hold of Miss Lindsay's arm. My heart is thawed into melting pleasure after being so long frozen up in the Greenland bay of indifference, amid the noise and nonsense of Edinburgh. Miss seems very well pleased with my bardship's distinguishing her, and after some slight qualms, which I could easily mark, she sets the titter round at defiance, and kindly allows me to keep my hold; and when parted by the ceremony of my introduction to Mr. Somerville, she met me half, to resume my situation.——*Nota Bene.*—The poet within a point and a half of being d—nnably in love—I am afraid my bosom is still nearly as much tinder as ever.

The old, cross-grained, whiggish, ugly, slanderous Miss ——, with all the poisonous spleen of a disappointed, ancient maid, stops me very unseasonably to ease her bursting breast, by falling abusively foul on the Miss Lindsays, particularly on my Dulcinea;—I hardly refrain from cursing her to her face for daring to mouth her calumnious slander on one of the finest pieces of the workmanship of Almighty Excellence! Sup at Mr. ——'s; vexed that the Miss Lindsays are not of the supper-party, as they only are wanting. Mrs. —— and Miss —— still improve infernally on my hands.

Set out next morning for Wauchope, the seat of my correspondent, Mrs. Scott—breakfast by the way with Dr. Elliot, an agreeable, good-hearted, climate-beaten old veteran, in the medical line; now retired to a romantic, but rather moorish place, on the banks of the Roole—he accompanies us almost to Wauchope—we traverse the country to the top of Bochester, the scene of an old encampment, and Woolee Hill.

Wauchope.—Mr. Scott exactly the figure and face commonly given to Sancho Panza—very shrewd in his farming matters, and not unfrequently stumbles on what may be called a strong thing rather than a good thing. Mrs. Scott all the sense, taste, intrepidity of face, and bold, critical decision, which usually distinguish female authors. Sup with Mr. Potts—agreeable party. Breakfast next morning with Mr. Somerville—the *bruit* of Miss Lindsay and my bardship, by means of the invention and malice of Miss ——. Mr. Somerville sends to Dr. Lindsay, begging him and family to breakfast if convenient, but at all events to send Miss Lindsay; accordingly Miss Lindsay only comes.—I find Miss Lindsay would soon play the devil with me—I met with some little flattering attentions from her. Mrs. Somerville an excellent, motherly, agreeable woman, and a fine family. Mr. Ainslie and Mrs. S——, juurs., with Mr. ——, Miss Lindsay, and myself, go to see *Esther*, a very remarkable woman for reciting poetry of all kinds, and sometimes making Scotch doggerel herself—she can repeat by heart almost every thing she has ever read, particularly Pope's Homer from end to end —has studied Euclid by herself, and, in short, is a woman of very extraordinary abilities.—On conversing with her I find her fully equal to the character given of her.—She is very much flattered that I send for her, and that she sees a poet who has *put out a book*, as she says.—She is, among other things, a great florist—and is rather past the meridian of once celebrated beauty.*

I walk in *Esther's* garden with Miss Lindsay, and after some little chit-chat of the tender kind, I presented her with a proof print of my Nob, which she accepted with something more tender than gratitude. She told me many little stories which Miss —— had retailed concerning her and me, with prolonging pleasure—God bless her! Was waited on by the Magistrates, and presented with the freedom of the burgh.

Took farewell of Jedburgh, with some melancholy, disagreeable sensations.—Jed, pure be thy crystal streams, and hallowed thy sylvan banks! Sweet Isabella Lindsay, may peace dwell in thy bosom, uninterrupted, except by the tumultuous throbbings of rapturous love! That love-kindling eye must beam on another, not on me—that graceful form must bless another's arms, not mine!†

Kelso.—Dine with the Farmers' Club—all gentlemen, talking of high matters—each of them keeps a hunter from thirty to fifty pounds value, and attends the fox-huntings in the country—go out with Mr. Ker, one of the club, and a friend of Mr. Ainslie's, to lie—Mr. Ker a most gentlemanly, clever, handsome fellow, a widower with some fine children—his mind and manner astonishingly like my dear old friend Robert Muir, in Kilmarnock—everything in Mr. Ker's most elegant—he offers to accompany me in my En-

---

* [Dr. Somerville was distinguished as a literary man. It is said that after the appearance of this passage in Currie's life of the Poet, he entirely abandoned the habit of punning.]

* [Esther Easton, a woman of extraordinary gifts, was the wife of a common working gardener. She subsequently taught a school, and was ultimately dependent on charity.]

† [Isabella Lindsay, sister of Dr. Lindsay, we learn from Mr. Chambers, married afterwards a Mr. Adam Armstrong an employé of the Russian government. "She died young, leaving four children : the youngest is General Robert Armstrong, now (1856) Director of the Imperial Mint at St. Petersburg. Peggy, the youngest sister, died not long after the Poet's visit, at the age of twenty-two."]

glish tour. Dine with Sir Alexander Don—a pretty clever fellow, but far from being a match for his divine lady.[*]

A very wet day * * *—Sleep at Stodrig again; and set out for Melrose—visit Dryburgh, a fine old ruined abbey —still bad weather—cross Leader, and come up Tweed to Melrose—dine there, and visit that far-famed, glorious ruin —come to Selkirk, up Ettrick;—the whole country hereabout, both on Tweed and Ettrick, remarkably stony.

Monday.—Come to Inverleithing, a famous [Spa,] and in the vicinity of the palace of Traquhair, where having dined, and drank some Galloway-whey, I here remain till to-morrow—saw Elibanks and Elibracs, on the other side of the Tweed.

Tuesday.—Drank tea yesternight at Pirn, with Mr. Horsburgh.—Breakfasted to day with Mr. Ballantine of Hollowleet—Proposal for a four-horse team to consist of Mr. Scott of Wauchope, Pittleland: Logan of Logan, Fittiofur: Ballantine of Hollowlee, Forowynd: Horsburgh of Horsburgh.— Dine at a country inn, kept by a miller in Earlston, the birth-place and residence of the celebrated Thomas-a-Rhymer —saw the ruins of his castle—come to Berrywell.

Wednesday.—Dine at Dunse with the Farmers' Club—company, impossible to do them justice—Rev. Mr. Smith a famous punster, and Mr. Meikle a celebrated mechanic, and inventor of the threshing-mill.—*Thursday,* breakfast at Berrywell, and walk into Dunse to see a famous knife made by a cutler there, and to be presented to an Italian prince.—A pleasant ride with my friend Mr. Robert Ainslie and his sister, to Mr. Thomson's, a man who has newly commenced farmer, and has married a Miss Patty Grieve, formerly a flame of Mr. Robert Ainslie's. Company—Miss Jacky Grieve, an amiable sister of Mrs. Thomson's, and Mr. Hood, an honest, worthy, facetious farmer, in the neighbourhood.

Friday.—Ride to Berwick—An idle town, rudely picturesque.—Meet Lord Errol in walking round the walls— His lordship's flattering notice of me.—Dine with Mr. Clunzie, merchant—nothing particular in company or conversation.—Come up a bold shore, and over a wild country to Eyemouth—sup and sleep at Mr. Grieve's.

Saturday.—Spend the day at Mr. Grieve's—made a Royal-arch mason of St. Abb's Lodge.[‡]—Mr. William Grieve, the oldest brother, a joyous, warm-hearted, jolly, clever fellow —takes a hearty glass, and sings a good song.—Mr. Robert, his brother, and partner in trade, a good fellow, but says little. Take a sail after dinner. Fishing of all kinds pays tithes at Eyemouth.

Sunday.—A Mr. Robinson, brewer at Ednam, sets out with us to Dunbar.

The Miss Grieves very good girls.—My bardship's heart got a bruise from Miss Betsey.

Mr. William Grieve's attachment to the family-circle so fond, that when he is out, which by the bye is often the case, he cannot go to bed till he sees if all his sisters are sleeping well——Pass the famous Abbey of Coldingham, and Pease-bridge.—Call at Mr. Sheriff's, where Mr. A. and I dine.—Mr. S. talkative and conceited. I talk of love to Nancy the whole evening, while her brother escorts home some companions like himself.—Sir James Hall of Dunglass, having heard of my being in the neighbourhood, comes to Mr. Sheriff's to breakfast—takes me to see his fine scenery on the stream of Dunglass—Dunglass the most romantic, sweet place I ever saw—Sir James and his lady a pleasant happy couple. He points out a walk for which he has an uncommon respect, as it was made by an aunt of his, to whom he owes much.

Miss —— will accompany me to Dunbar, by way of making a parade of me as a sweetheart of hers, among her relations. She mounts an old cart horse, as huge and as lean as a house; a rusty old side-saddle without girth or stirrup, but fastened on with an old pillion-girth—herself as fine as hands could make her, in cream-coloured riding clothes, hat and feather, &c.—I, ashamed of my situation, ride like the devil, and almost shake her to pieces on old Jolly—got rid of her by refusing to call at her uncle's with her.[*]

Past through the most glorious corn-country I ever saw, till I reach Dunbar, a neat little town.—Dine with Provost Fall, an eminent merchant, and most respectable character, but undescribable, as he exhibits no marked traits. Mrs. Fall, a genius in painting; fully more clever in the fine arts and sciences than my friend Lady Wauchope, without her consummate assurance of her own abilities.—Call with Mr. Robinson (whom, by the bye, I find to be a worthy, much respected man, very modest; warm, social heart, which with less good sense than his would be perhaps with the children of prim precision and pride, rather inimical to that respect which is man's due from man)—with him I call on Miss Clarke, a maiden in the Scotch phrase, "*Guid enough, but no brent new;*" a clever woman, with tolerable pretensions to remark and wit; while time had blown the blushing bud of bashful modesty into the flower of easy confidence. She wanted to see what sort of *rare show* an author was; and to let him know, that though Dunbar was but a little town, yet it was not destitute of people of parts.

---

[*] [Lady Harriet Don, sister to the Earl of Glencairn. Compare letter (1) to Creech.]

[†] [Chambers reads 'Hollylee.']

[‡] [We quote following entry from Mr. Chambers's edition:—

"EYEMOUTH, 19th May, 1787.

At a general encampment held this day, the following brethren were made Royal-arch Masons—namely, Robert Burns, from the Lodge of St. James's, Tarbolton, Ayrshire, and Robert Ainslie, from the Lodge of St. Luke's, Edinburgh, by James Carmichael, Wm. Grieve, Daniel Dow, John Clay, Robert Grieve, &c., &c. Robert Ainslie paid one guinea admission dues; but on account of R. Burns's remarkable poetical genius, the encampment unanimously agreed to admit him gratis, and consider themselves honoured by having a man of such shining abilities for one of their companions."]

---

[*] [Ladies are sometimes persecuting; but we cannot help regretting our Author's want of gallantry in this case: it was unlike himself, and is one of a few things in this Journal we would rather had never been published.]

Breakfast next morning at Skateraw, at Mr. Lee's, a farmer of great note.—Mr. Lee, an excellent, hospitable, social fellow, rather oldish—warm-hearted and chatty—a most judicious, sensible farmer. Mr. Lee detains me till next morning.—Company at dinner—my rev. acquaintance Dr. Bowmaker, a reverend, rattling old fellow; two sea lieutenants; a cousin of the landlord's, a fellow whose looks are of that kind which deceived me in a gentleman at Kelso, and has often deceived me—a goodly handsome figure and face, which incline one to give them credit for parts which they have not; Mr. Clarke, a much cleverer fellow, but whose looks a little cloudy, and his appearance rather ungainly, with an every-day observer may prejudice the opinion against him; Dr. Brown, a medical young gentleman from Dunbar, a fellow whose face and manners are open and engaging.—Leave Skateraw for Dunse next day, along with Collector ——, a lad of slender abilities and bashfully diffident to an extreme.

Found Miss Ainslie, the amiable, the sensible, the good-humoured, the sweet Miss Ainslie, all alone at Berrywell. —Heavenly powers who know the weakness of human hearts, support mine! What happiness must I see only to remind me that I cannot enjoy it!

Lammermuir Hills, from East Lothian to Dunse very wild.—Dine with the Farmers' Club at Kelso. Sir John Hume and Mr. Lumsden there, but nothing worth remembrance when the following circumstance is considered—I walk into Dunse before dinner, and out to Berrywell in the evening with Miss Ainslie—how well-bred, how frank, how good she is! Charming Rachel! may thy bosom never be wrung by the evils of this life of sorrows, or by the villainy of this world's sons!*

Thursday.—Mr. Ker and I set out to dine at Mr. Hood's on our way to England.

I am taken extremely ill with strong feverish symptoms, and take a servant of Mr. Hood's to watch me all night —embittering remorse scares my fancy at the gloomy forebodings of death.—I am determined to live for the future in such a manner as not to be scared at the approach of death—I am sure I could meet him with indifference, but for "The something beyond the grave."—Mr. Hood agrees to accompany us to England if we will wait till Sunday.

Friday.—I go with Mr. Hood to see a roup of an unfortunate farmer's stock—rigid economy, and decent industry, do you preserve me from being the principal *dramatis persona* in such a scene of horror.

Meet my good old friend Mr. Ainslie, who calls on Mr. Hood in the evening to take farewell of my bardship. This day I feel myself warm with sentiments of gratitude to the Great Preserver of men, who has kindly restored me to health and strength once more.

A pleasant walk with my young friend Douglas Ainslie, a sweet, modest, clever young fellow.

---

* [Miss Ainslie died unmarried—a good-looking, elderly lady, of **very agreeable manners**.—*Chambers*.]

Sunday 27th May.—Cross Tweed, and traverse the moors through a wild country till I reach Alnwick—Alnwick Castle a seat of the Duke of Northumberland, furnished in a most princely manner.—A Mr. Wilkin, agent of His Grace's, shows us the house and policies. Mr. Wilkin, a discreet, sensible, ingenious man.

Monday.—Come, still through by-ways, to Warkworth, where we dine.—Hermitage and old castle. Warkworth situated very picturesque, with Coquet Island, a small rocky spot, the seat of an old monastery, facing it a little in the sea; and the small but romantic river Coquet, running through it.—Sleep at Morpeth, a pleasant enough little town, and on next day to Newcastle.—Meet with a very agreeable, sensible fellow, a Mr. Chattox, who shows us a great many civilities, and who dines and sups with us.

Wednesday.—Left Newcastle early in the morning, and rode over a fine country to Hexham to breakfast—from Hexham to Wardrue, the celebrated Spa, where we slept.

Thursday.—Reach Longtown to dine, and part there with my good friends Messrs Hood and Ker—A hiring day in Longtown—I am uncommonly happy to see so many young folks enjoying life.—I come to Carlisle. (Meet a strange enough romantic adventure by the way, in falling in with a girl and her married sister—the girl, after some overtures of gallantry on my side, sees me a little cut with the bottle, and offers to take me in for a Gretna-green affair.—I not being such a gull as she imagines, make an appointment with her, by way of *vive la bagatelle*, to hold a conference on it when we reach town.—I meet her in town and give her a brush of caressing, and a bottle of cyder, but finding herself *un peu trompée* in her man she sheers off.) Next day I meet my good friend, Mr. Mitchell, and walk with him round the town and its environs, and through his printing works, &c.—four or five hundred people employed, many of them women and children. Dine with Mr. Mitchell, and leave Carlisle. Come by the coast to Annan. Overtaken on the way by a curious old fish of a shoemaker, and miner, from Cumberland mines.

[*Here the Manuscript abruptly terminates. Journal includes period of twenty-six days.*]

The Highland Tour.

[*Saturday,*] *25th August*, 1787.

I LEAVE Edinburgh for a northern tour, in company with my good friend Mr. Nicol, whose originality of humor promises me much entertainment.—Linlithgow—a fertile improved country—West Lothian. The more elegance and luxury among the farmers, I always observe, in equal proportion, the rudeness and stupidity of the peasantry. This remark I have made all over the Lothians, Merse, Roxburgh, &c. For this, among other reasons, I think that a man of romantic taste, a "Man of Feeling," will be better pleased with the poverty, but intelligent minds of the peasantry in Ayrshire (peasantry they are all below the Justice of Peace) than the opulence of a club of Merse farmers, when at the the same time, he considers the Vandalism of their plough-folks, &c. I carry this idea so far, that an uninclosed, half improven country is to me actually more agreeable, and gives me more pleasure as a prospect, than a country cultivated like a garden.—Soil about Linlithgow light and thin.—The town carries the appearance of rude, decayed grandeur—charmingly rural, retired situation. The old royal palace a tolerably fine, but melancholy ruin—sweetly situated on a small elevation, by the brink of a loch. Shewn the room where the beautiful, injured Mary Queen of Scots was born—a pretty good old Gothic church. The infamous stool of repentance standing, in the old Romish way, on a lofty situation.

What a poor, pimping business is a Presbyterian place of worship; dirty, narrow, and squalid; stuck in a corner of old popish grandeur such as Linlithgow, and much more Melrose! Ceremony and show, if judiciously thrown in, absolutely necessary for the bulk of mankind, both in religious and civil matters.—Dine—Go to my friend Smith's at Avon printfield—find nobody but Mrs. Miller, an agreeable, sensible, modest, good body; as useful, but not so ornamental as Fielding's Miss Western—not rigidly polite à la Française, but easy, hospitable, and housewifely.

An old lady from Paisley, a Mrs. Lawson, whom I promise to call for in Paisley—like old lady W—— and still more like Mrs. C——, her conversation is pregnant with strong sense and just remark, but like them, a certain air of self-importance and a duresse in the eye, seem to indicate, as the Ayrshire wife observed of her cow, that "she had a mind o' her ain."

Pleasant view of Dunfermline and the rest of the fertile coast of Fife, as we go down to that dirty, ugly place, Borrowstounness—see a horse-race and call on a friend of Mr. Nicol's, a Bailie Cowan, of whom I know too little to attempt his portrait. Come through the rich carse of Falkirk to pass the night. Falkirk nothing remarkable except the tomb of Sir John the Graham, over which, in the succession of time, four stones* have been placed.—Camelon, the ancient metropolis of the Picts, now a small village in the neighbourhood of Falkirk.—Cross the grand canal to Carron.—Come past Larbert and admire a fine monument of cast-iron erected by Mr. Bruce, the African traveller, to his wife.

Pass Dunipace, a place laid out with fine taste—a charming amphitheatre bounded by Denny village, and pleasant seats down the way to Dunipace.—The Carron running down the bosom of the whole makes it one of the most charming little prospects I have seen.

Dine at Auchinbowie: Mr. Monro an excellent, worthy old man—Miss Monro an amiable, sensible, sweet young woman, much resembling Mrs. Grierson. Come to Bannockburn—Shewn the old house where James III. finished so tragically his unfortunate life. The field of Bannockburn—the hole where glorious Bruce set his standard. Here no Scot can pass uninterested.—I fancy to myself that I see my gallant, heroic countrymen coming o'er the hill and down upon the plunderers of their country, the murderers of their fathers; noble revenge, and just hate, glowing in every vein, striding more and more eagerly as they approach the oppressive, insulting, blood-thirsty foe! I see them meet in gloriously-triumphant congratulation on the victorious field, exulting in their heroic royal leader, and rescued liberty and independence! Come to Stirling.—*Monday:* go to Harvieston. Go to see Caudron Linn, and Rumbling Brig, and Diel's Mill.* Return in the evening. Supper—Messrs. Doig, the schoolmaster; Bell; and Captain Forrester of the castle—Doig a queerish figure, and something of a pedant—Bell a joyous fellow, who sings a good song.—Forrester a merry, swearing kind of man, with a dash of the sodger.

Tuesday Morning.—Breakfast with Captain Forrester—Ochel Hills—Devon River—Forth and Teith—Allan River—Strathallan, a fine country, but little improved—Cross Earn to Crieff—Dine and go to Arbruchil—cold reception at Arbruchil—a most romantically pleasant ride up Earn, by Auchterlyre and Comrie to Arbruchil—Sup at Crieff.

Wednesday Morning.—Leave Crieff—Glen Almond—Almond river—Ossian's grave—Loch Fruoch—Glenquaich—Landlord and landlady remarkable characters—Taymouth—described in rhyme—Meet the Hon. Charles Townshend.

Thursday.—Come down Tay to Dunkeld—Glenlyon House—Lyon River—Druid's Temple—three circles of stones—the outer-most sunk—the second has thirteen stones remaining—the innermost has eight—two large detached ones like a gate, to the south-east—Say prayers in it—Pass Taybridge—Aberfeldy—described in rhyme—Castle-Menzies—Inver—Dr. Stewart—Sup.

Friday.—Walk with Mrs. Stewart and Beard to Birnam top—fine prospect down Tay—Craigiebarns hills—Hermitage on the Bran Water, with a picture of Ossian—Breakfast with Dr. Stewart—Neil Gow plays—a short, stout-built, honest Highland figure, with his grayish hair shed on his honest social brow—an interesting face, marking strong sense, kind openheartedness, mixed with unmistrusting simplicity—visit his house—Marget Gow.

Ride up Tummel River to Blair†—Fascally a beautiful romantic nest—wild grandeur of the pass of Gillicrankie—visit the gallant Lord Dundee's stone.

Blair—Sup with the Duchess—easy and happy from the manners of the family—confirmed in my good opinion of my friend Walker.‡

---

* [According to Chambers, should be there.]

* [Compare letter (4) to Gavin Hamilton—Prose Works, p. 158.]
† [Residence of the Duke of Athole.]　‡ [Compare letter to—Prose Works, p. 195.]

Saturday.—Visit the scenes round Blair—fine, but spoiled with bad taste—Tilt and Garrie rivers—Falls on the Tilt—Heather seat—Ride in company with Sir William Murray and Mr. Walker, to Loch Tummel—meandering of the Rannoch, which runs through quondam Struan Robertson's estate from Loch Rannoch to Loch Tummel—Dine at Blair—Company—General Murray; Captain Murray, an honest Tar; Sir William Murray, an honest, worthy man, but tormented with the hypochondria; Mrs. Graham, *belle et amiable;* Miss Cathcart; Mrs. Murray, a painter; Mrs. King; Duchess and fine family, the Marquis, Lords James, Edward, and Robert; Ladies Charlotte, Emilia, and children dance; Sup—Mr. Graham of Fintray.*

Come up the Garrie—Falls of Bruar—Dalnacardoch—Dalwhinnie—Dine—Snow on the hills 17 foot deep—No corn from Loch-Garrie to Dalwhinnie—Cross the Spey, and come down the stream to Pitnain—Straths rich—*les environs* picturesque—Craigow hill—Ruthven of Badenoch—Barracks—wild and magnificent—Rothemurche on the other side, and Glenmore—Grant of Rothemurche's poetry—told me by the Duke Gordon—Strathspey, rich and romantic—Breakfast at Aviemore, a wild spot—dine at Sir James Grant's—Lady Grant, a sweet, pleasant body,—come through mist and darkness to Dulsie, to lie [sleep].

Tuesday.—Findhorn river—rocky banks—come on to Castle Cawdor, where Macbeth murdered King Duncan—saw the bed in which King Duncan was stabbed†—dine at Kilravock—Mrs. Rose, sen., a true chieftain's wife—Fort George—Inverness.

Wednesday.—Loch Ness—Braes of Ness—General's hut—Fall of Fyers—Urquhart Castle and Strath.

Thursday.—Come over Culloden Muir—reflections on the field of battle—breakfast at Kilravock—old Mrs. Rose, sterling sense, warm heart, strong passions, and honest pride, all in uncommon degree—Mrs. Rose, jun., a little milder than the mother—this perhaps owing to her being younger—Mr. Grant, minister at Calder, resembles Mr. Scott at Inverleithing. Mrs. Rose and Mrs. Grant accompany us to Kildrummie—two young ladies—Miss Rose, who sang two Gaelic songs, beautiful and lovely—Miss Sophia Brodie, most agreeable and amiable—both of them gentle, mild; the sweetest creatures on earth, and happiness be with them!‡—Dine at Nairn—fall in with a pleasant enough gentleman, Dr. Stewart, who had been long abroad with his father in [consequence of] the forty-five; and Mr. Falconer, a spare, irascible, warm-hearted Norland, and a Nonjuror—Brodiehouse to lie.

Friday.—Forres—famous stone at Forres—Mr. Brodie tells me that the muir where Shakespeare lays Macbeth's witch-meeting is still haunted—that the country folks won't pass it by night.

* [Compare letter (1) to Robert Graham, Esq.—Prose Works, p. 171.]
† [Story of the bed no doubt fabulous.]
‡ [Compare letter to Mrs. Rose—Prose Works, p. 51.]

*   *   *   *   *   *   *

Venerable ruins of Elgin Abbey*—A grander effect at first glance than Melrose, but not near so beautiful. Cross Spey to Fochabers—fine palace,† worthy of the generous proprietor—Dine—Company, Duke and Duchess, Ladies Charlotte and Magdeline, Colonel Abercrombie and Lady, Mr. Gordon and Mr. ——, a clergyman, a venerable, aged figure—the Duke makes me happier than ever great man did—noble, princely; yet mild, condescending, and affable; gay and kind—the Duchess witty and sensible—God bless them!

Come to Cullen to lie—hitherto the country is sadly poor and unimproved.

Come to Aberdeen—meet with Mr. Chalmers, printer, a facetious fellow—Mr. Ross a fine fellow, like Professor Tytler,—Mr. Marshall one of the *poetæ minores*—Mr. Sheriffs, author of "Jamie and Bess," a little decrepid body with some abilities—Bishop Skinner, a nonjuror, son of the author of "Tullochgorum," a man whose mild, venerable manner is the most marked of any in so young a man‡—Professor Gordon, a good-natured, jolly-looking professor—Aberdeen, a lazy town—near Stonhive, the coast a good deal romantic—meet my relations—Robert Burns, writer, in Stonhive, one of those who love fun, a gill, and a punning joke, and have not a bad heart—his wife a sweet hospitable body, without any affectation of what is called town-breeding.

Tuesday.—Breakfast with Mr. Burns—lie at Lawrence Kirk—Album library—Mrs. —— a jolly, frank, sensible, love-inspiring widow—Howe of the Mearns, a rich, cultivated, but still uninclosed country.

* [Should be Cathedral—plundered and destroyed, 1390, by Alexander Stewart, Earl of Buchan, otherwise known as the "Wolf of Badenoch."]

† [Castle-Gordon, residence of the Duke of Gordon.—Compare "Streams that glide," Posthumous Works, p. 326. We are informed by Allan Cunningham that her Grace had kindly planned a meeting at the Castle for Mr. Addington (afterwards Lord Sidmouth and Prime Minister) with Burns and Beattie. Mr. Addington unfortunately could not accept the invitation, but wrote and forwarded the following lines:—

> Yes! pride of Scotia's favoured plains, 'tis thine
>   The warmest feelings of the heart to move;
> To bid it throb with sympathy divine,
>   To glow with friendship or to melt with love.
>
> What though each morning sees thee rise to toil,
>   Though Plenty on thy cot no blessing showers,
> Yet Independence cheers thee with her smile,
>   And Fancy strews thy moorland with her flowers!
>
> And dost thou blame the impartial will of Heaven,
>   Untaught of life the good and ill to scan?
> To thee the Muse's choicest wreath is given—
>   To thee the genuine dignity of man!
>
> Then, to the want of worldly gear resigned,
>   Be grateful for the wealth of thy exhaustless mind.

The reader will find a similar sort of stanza adopted by our Author himself in his Sonnet on hearing a Thrush sing, also on Death of Robert Riddel, Esq.—Posthumous Works, p. 322.]

‡ [It was in Chalmers's house that our Author was introduced to the Rev. titular Bishop Skinner, son of the Rev. John Skinner of Linshart, author of Tullochgorum. Burns was now too far beyond Linshart—which lies to the west of Peterhead—and could not return; which, doubtless, he deeply regretted. Compare Rev. J. Skinner's Epistle to Burns—Prose Works, p. 132.

> O! happy hour for ever mair,
> That led my chiel up Chalmers' stair, &c.]   [t. my son]

Wednesday.—Cross North Esk river and a rich country to Craigow.

* * * * * *

Go to Montrose, that finely-situated handsome town—breakfast at Muthie, and sail along that wild rocky coast, and see the famous caverns, particularly the Gairiepot—land and dine at Arbroath—stately ruins of Arbroath Abbey—come to Dundee, through a fertile country—Dundee, a low-lying, but pleasant town—old steeple—Tayfrith—Broughty Castle, a finely situated ruin, jutting into the Tay.

Friday.—Breakfast with the Miss Scotts—Miss Bess Scott like Mrs. Greenfield—my bardship almost in love with her—come through the rich harvests and fine hedge-rows of the Carse of Gowrie, along the romantic margin of the Grampian Hills, to Perth—fine, fruitful, hilly, woody country round Perth.

Saturday Morning.—Leave Perth—come up Strathearn to Enkermay—fine, fruitful, cultivated Strath—the scene of "Bessy Bell, and Mary Gray," near Perth—fine scenery on the banks of the May—Mrs. Belches, gawcie, frank, affable, fond of rural sports, hunting, &c.—Lie at Kinross—reflections in a fit of the colic.

Sunday, [*Sep.* 16.]—Pass through a cold, barren country to Queensferry—dine—cross the ferry and on to Edinburgh.

Bachelor's Club.

[ATTRIBUTED TO BURNS.]

History of the Rise, Proceedings, and Regulations of the Bachelor's Club.

> Of birth or blood we do not boast,
> Nor gentry does our club afford;
> But ploughmen and mechanics we
> In nature's simple dress record.

As the great end of human society is to become wiser and better, this ought therefore to be the principal view of every man in every station of life. But as experience has taught us that such studies as inform the head and mend the heart, when long continued, are apt to exhaust the faculties of the mind, it has been found proper to relieve and unbend the mind by some employment or another, that may be agreeable enough to keep its powers in exercise, but at the same time not so serious as to exhaust them. But, superadded to this, by far the greater part of mankind are under the necessity *of earning the sustenance of human life by the labour of their bodies,* whereby, not only the faculties of the mind, but the nerves and sinews of the body, are so fatigued, that it is absolutely necessary to have recourse to some amusement or diversion, to relieve the wearied man, worn down with the necessary labours of life.

As the best of things, however, have been perverted to the worst of purposes, so, under the pretence of amusement and diversion, men have plunged into all the madness of riot and dissipation; and, instead of attending to the grand design of human life they have begun with extravagance and folly, and ended with guilt and wretchedness. Impressed with these considerations, we, the following lads in the parish of Tarbolton, viz., Hugh Reid, Robert Burns, Gilbert Burns, Alexander Brown, Walter Mitchell, Thomas Wright, and William M'Gavin, resolved, for our mutual entertainment, to unite ourselves into a club or society, under such rules and regulations, that while we should forget our cares and labours in mirth and diversion, we might not transgress the bounds of innocence and decorum; and after agreeing on those, and some other regulations, we held our first meeting at Tarbolton, in the house of John Richard, upon the evening of the 11th of November, 1780, commonly called Halloween, and after choosing Robert Burns president for the night, we proceeded to debate on this question—*Suppose a young man, bred a farmer, but without any fortune, has it in his power to marry either of two women, the one a girl of large fortune, but neither handsome in person, nor agreeable in conversation, but who can manage the household affairs of a farm well enough; the other of them a girl every way agreeable, in person, conversation, and behaviour, but without any fortune: which of them shall he choose?*—Finding ourselves very happy in our society, we resolved to continue to meet once a month in the same house, in the way and manner proposed, and shortly thereafter we chose Robert Ritchie for another member. In May, 1781, we brought in David Sillar,* and in June, Adam Jamaison, as members. About the beginning of the year 1782, we admitted Matthew Patterson and John Orr, and in June following we chose James Patterson as a proper brother for such a society. The club being thus increased, we resolved to meet at Tarbolton on the race night, the July following, and have a dance in honour of our society. Accordingly we did meet, each one with a partner, and spent the evening in such innocence and merriment, such cheerfulness and good humour, that every brother will long remember it with pleasure and delight.

Rules and Regulations to be observed in the Bachelor's Club.

1st. The club shall meet at Tarbolton every fourth Monday night, when a question on any subject shall be proposed, disputed points of religion only excepted, in the manner hereafter directed; which question is to be debated in the club, each member taking whatever side he thinks proper.

2d. When the club is met, the president, or, he failing, some one of the members till he come, shall take his seat; then the other members shall seat themselves, those who are for one side of the question, on the president's right hand; and those who are for the other side, on his left; which of them shall have the right hand is to be determined by the president. The president and four of the members, being present, shall have power to transact any ordinary part of the society's business.

3d. The club met and seated, the president shall read the question out of the club's book of records (which book is always to be kept by the president), then the two members nearest the president shall cast lots who of them shall speak first, and according as the lot shall determine, the member nearest the president on that side shall deliver his opinion, and the member nearest on the other side shall reply to him; then the second member of the side that spoke first; then the second member of the side that spoke second; and so on to the end of the company; but if there be fewer members on one side than on the other, when all the

---

* [To whom the celebrated Epistle was afterwards addressed.]

members of the least side have spoken according to their places, any of them, as they please among themselves, may reply to the remaining members of the opposite side; when both sides have spoken, the president shall give his opinion, after which they may go over it a second or more times, and so continue the question.

4th. The club shall then proceed to the choice of a **question for the subject of** next night's meeting. The president shall first propose **one, and any other** member who chooses may propose more questions; and whatever one of them is most agreeable to the majority of the members, shall be the subject of debate next club-night.

5th. The club shall, lastly, elect a new president for the next meeting; the president shall first name one, then any of the club may name another, and whoever of them has the majority of votes shall be duly elected; allowing the president the first vote, and the casting vote upon a par, but none other. Then after a general toast to the mistresses of the club, they shall dismiss.

6th. There shall be no private conversation carried on during the time of debate, nor shall any member interrupt another while he is speaking, under the penalty of a reprimand from the president for the first fault, doubling his share of the reckoning for the second, trebling it for the third, and so on in proportion for every other fault, provided always, however, that any member may speak at any time after leave asked, and given by the president. All swearing and profane language, and particularly all obscene and indecent conversation, is strictly prohibited, under the same penalty as aforesaid in the first clause of this article.

7th. No member, on any pretence whatever, shall mention any of the club's affairs to any other person but a brother member, under the pain of being excluded; and particularly if any member shall reveal any of the speeches or affairs of the club, with a view to ridicule or laugh at any of the rest of the members, he shall be for ever excommunicated from the society; and the rest of the members are desired as much as possible, to avoid, and have no communication with him as a friend or comrade.

8th. Every member shall attend at the meetings, without he can give a proper excuse for not attending; and it is desired that every one who cannot attend will send his excuse with some other member; and he who shall be absent three meetings, without sending such excuse, shall be summoned to the next club-night, when, if he fail to appear, or send an excuse, he shall be excluded.

9th. The club shall not consist of more than sixteen members, all bachelors, belonging to the parish of Tarbolton: except a brother member marry, and in that case he may be continued, if the majority of the club think proper. No person shall be admitted a member of this society without the unanimous consent of the club; and any member may withdraw from the club altogether, by giving a notice to the president, in writing, of his departure.

10th. Every man proper for a member of this society, must have a frank, honest, open heart, above anything dirty or mean; and must be a professed lover of one or more of the female sex. No haughty, self-conceited person, who looks upon himself as superior to the rest of the club, and especially no mean-spirited worldly mortal, whose only will is to heap up money, shall upon any pretence whatever be admitted. In short, the proper person for this society is a cheerful, honest-hearted lad, who, if he has a friend that is true, and a mistress that is kind, and as much wealth as genteelly to make both ends meet—is just as happy as this world can make him.

Author's Assignment
OF HIS WORKS.

[FROM ORIGINAL DRAFT IN POSSESSION OF DR. GRIERSON, THORNHILL.]

KNOW all men by these presents that I Robert Burns in Mossgiel: Whereas I intend to leave Scotland and go abroad, and having acknowledged myself the father of a child named Elizabeth, begot upon Elizabeth Paton in Largieside: and whereas Gilbert Burns in Mossgiel, my brother, has become bound, and hereby binds and obliges himself to aliment clothe and educate my said natural child in a suitable manner as if she was his own, in case her mother chuse to part with her, and that until she arrive at the age of fifteen years. Therefore, and to enable the said Gilbert Burns to make good his said engagement, Wit ye me to have assigned, disponed, conveyed and made over to, and in favors of, the said Gilbert Burns, his Heirs, Executors, and Assignees, who

are always to be bound in like manner with himself, all and sundry goods, gear, corns, cattle, horses, nolt, sheep, household furniture, and all other moveable effects of whatever kind that I shall leave behind me on my departure from the Kingdom, after allowing for my part of the conjunct debts due by the said Gilbert Burns and me as joint tacksmen of the farm of Mossgiel. And particularly, without prejudice of the foresaid generality, the profits that may arise from the publication of my Poems presently in the press—And also, I hereby dispone and convey to him in trust for behoof of my said natural daughter, the Copyright of said Poems in so far as I can dispose of the same by law, after she arrives at the above age of fifteen years complete—Surrogating and Substituting the said Gilbert Burns my brother and his foresaids in my full right, title, room and place of the whole Premises, with power to him to intromit with, and dispose upon the same at pleasure, and in general to do every other thing in the Premises that I could have done myself before granting hereof, but always with and under the conditions before expressed—and I obllidge myself to warrand this disposition and assignation from my own proper fact and deed allenarly—Consenting to the Registration hereof in the Books of Council and Session, or any other Judges Books competent, therein to remain for preservation, and constitute . . . . whereof I have . . . . Procurators, &c.

In witness whereof I have wrote and signed these presents, consisting of this and the preceeding page, on stamped paper, with my own hand, at Mossgiel, the twenty-second day of July, one thousand seven hundred and eighty-six years.

ROBERT BURNS.

Upon the twenty-fourth day of July, one thousand seven hundred and eighty-six years, I, William Chalmer, Notary Publick, past to the Mercat Cross of Ayr head Burgh of the Sheriffdome thereof, and thereat I made due and lawful intimation of the foregoing disposition and assignation to His Majestie's lieges, that they might not pretend ignorance thereof, by reading the same over in presence of a number of people assembled. Whereupon William Crooks, writer, in Ayr, as attorney for the before designed Gilbert Burns, protested that the same was lawfully intimated, and asked and took instruments in my hands. These things were done betwixt the hours of ten and eleven forenoon, before and in presence of William M'Cubbin, and William Eaton, apprentices to the Sheriff Clerk of Ayr, witnesses to the premises.

(Signed)   WILLIAM CHALMER, N.P.

WILLIAM M'CUBBIN, *Witness.*
WILLIAM EATON, *Witness.*

[The body of the above document has been written and signed by the Poet himself in a clear, plain, legible hand; and the copy from which we print seems to be a duplicate by the Author himself from the original. "Procutors" is a Scottish contraction for "Procurators," and has been mis-spelt in the original "Procutars." "Proceeding" is also thus spelt.

The implementing of this document in favour of "dear-bought Bess," became, as our readers are aware, unnecessary. The legal functionary by whom it is proved was the "Willie Chalmers" of our Author's epistolary and poetical notice; and to whom also, in his professional character, the burlesque Proclamation "In Name of the Nine" is addressed.]

Memoir of Poet

BY

GILBERT BURNS.

[FROM LETTER TO MRS. DUNLOP.]

*   *   *   *   *   *

WITH him [Mr. Murdoch] we learnt to read English tolerably well, and to write a little. He taught us, too, the English grammar. I was too young to profit much from his lessons in grammar; but Robert made some proficiency in it—a circumstance of considerable weight in the unfolding of his genius and character; as he soon became remarkable for the fluency and correctness of his expression, and read the few books that came in his way with much pleasure and improvement; for even then he was a reader when he could get a book. Murdoch, whose library at that time had no great variety in it, lent him *The Life of Hannibal*, which was the first book he read (the school-books excepted), and almost the only one he had an opportunity of reading while he was at school; for *The Life of Wallace*, which he classes with it in one of his letters to you, he did not see for some years afterwards, when he borrowed it from the blacksmith who shod our horses.

The farm was upwards of seventy acres (between eighty and ninety, English statute measure), the rent of which was to be forty pounds annually for the first six years, and afterwards forty-five pounds. My father endeavoured to sell his leasehold property,* for the purpose of stocking this farm, but at that time was unable, and Mr. Ferguson lent him a hundred pounds for that purpose. He removed to his new situation at Whitsuntide, 1766. It was, I think, not above two years after this, that Murdoch, our tutor and friend, left this part of the country; and there being no school near us, and our little services being useful on the farm, my father undertook to teach us arithmetic in the winter evenings, by candle-light; and in this way my two eldest sisters got all the education they received. I remember a circumstance that happened at this time, which, though trifling in itself, is fresh in my memory, and may serve to illustrate the early character of my brother. Murdoch came to spend a night with us, and to take his leave when he was about to go into Carrick. He brought us, as a present and memorial of him, a small compendium of English Grammar, and the tragedy of *Titus Andronicus*, and by way of passing the evening, he began to read the play aloud.† We were all attention for some time,

till presently the whole party was dissolved in tears. A female in the play (I have but a confused remembrance of it) had her hands chopt off, and her tongue cut out, and then was insultingly desired to call for water to wash her hands. At this, in an agony of distress, we with one voice desired he would read no more.‡ My father observed that if we would not hear it out, it would be needless to leave the play with us. Robert replied, that if it was left he would burn it. My father was going to chide him for this ungrateful return to his tutor's kindness; but Murdoch interfered, declaring that he liked to see so much sensibility; and he left *The School for Love*, a comedy (translated I think from the French), in its place.

Nothing could be more retired than our general manner of living at Mount Oliphant; we rarely saw anybody but the members of our own family. There were no boys of our own age, or near it, in the neighbourhood. Indeed the greatest part of the land in the vicinity was at that time possessed by shopkeepers, and people of that stamp, who had retired from business, or who kept their farm in the country, at the same time that they followed business in town. My father was for some time almost the only companion we had. He conversed familiarly on all subjects with us, as if we had been men; and was at great pains, while we accompanied him in the labour of the farm, to lead the conversation to such subjects as might tend to increase our knowledge, or confirm us in virtuous habits. He borrowed *Salmon's Geographical Grammar* for us, and endeavoured to make us acquainted with the situation and history of the different countries in the world; while from a book-society in Ayr he procured for us the reading of *Derham's Physico and Astro-Theology*, and *Ray's Wisdom of God in the Creation*, to give us some idea of astronomy and natural history. Robert read all these books with an avidity and industry scarcely to be equalled. My father had been a subscriber to *Stackhouse's History of the Bible*, then lately published by James Meuros, in Kilmarnock: from this Robert collected a competent knowledge of ancient history; for no book was so voluminous as to slacken his industry, or so antiquated as to damp his researches. A brother of my mother, who had lived with us some time, and had learnt some arithmetic by our winter evening's candle, went into a bookseller's shop in Ayr, to purchase *The Ready Reckoner, or Tradesman's Sure Guide*, and a book to teach him to write letters. Luckily, in place of *The Complete Letter-Writer*, he got by mistake a small collection of letters by the most eminent writers, with a few sensible directions for attaining an easy epistolary style. This book was to Robert of the greatest consequence. It inspired him with a strong desire to excel in letter-writing, while it furnished him with models by some of the first writers in our language.

My brother was about thirteen or fourteen when my father, regretting that we wrote so ill, sent us, week about, during a summer quarter, to the parish school of Dalrymple, which,

---

* [The celebrated "Cottage," with its adjoining garden grounds—since the object of so much interest, and of so many pilgrimages from all parts of the civilized world, as the scene of the Poet's birth.]

† [Currie naturally enquires "why this silly (he might have said revolting) play is still printed as Shakespear's against the opinion of all the best critics?" We may further observe, notwithstanding the high esteem to which Murdoch as a teacher was entitled, the melancholy want of taste and sense that could allow him to read in the hearing of children, or to offer to leave as a keepsake in their hands, a tragedy so horrible; and the divine protest uttered by a child of nine years old, himself destined to be the great rival of Shakespeare in every type of tenderness, against the folly of his teacher,—and unconsciously against the very authorship of such a work, if ascribed to the greatest dramatist of the world. In all senses here, undoubtedly,

"The boy was father of the man."]

---

‡ [The anecdote here related, so characteristic in its way, reminds us, by a sort of contrast, of Goethe and his sister in their childhood reading horrible forbidden plays, till they screamed with terror and betrayed their own secret.]

though between two and three miles distant, was the nearest to us, that we might have an opportunity of remedying this defect. About this time a bookish acquaintance of my father's procured us a reading of two volumes of Richardson's *Pamela*, which was the first novel we read, and the only part of Richardson's works my brother was acquainted with till towards the period of his commencing author. Till that time too he remained unacquainted with Fielding, with Smollett (two volumes of *Ferdinand Count Fathom*, and two volumes of *Peregrine Pickle* excepted), with Hume, with Robertson, and almost all our authors of eminence of the later times. I recollect indeed my father borrowed a volume of English history from Mr. Hamilton of Bourtree-hill's gardener. It treated of the reign of James the First, and his unfortunate son, Charles, but I do not know who was the author; all that I remember of it is something of Charles's conversation with his children. About this time Murdoch, our former teacher, after having been in different places in the country, and having taught a school some time in Dumfries, came to be the established teacher of the English language in Ayr, a circumstance of considerable consequence to us. The remembrance of my father's former friendship, and his attachment to my brother, made him do every thing in his power for our improvement. He sent us Pope's works, and some other poetry, the first that we had an opportunity of reading, excepting what is contained in *The English Collection*, and in the volume of *The Edinburgh Magazine* for 1772; excepting also *those excellent new songs* that are hawked about the country in baskets, or exposed on stalls in the streets.

The summer after we had been at Dalrymple school, my father sent Robert to Ayr, to revise his English grammar, with his former teacher. He had been there only one week, when he was obliged to return, to assist at the harvest. When the harvest was over, he went back to school, where he remained two weeks; and this completes the account of his school education, excepting one summer quarter, some time afterwards, that he attended the parish school of Kirk-Oswald (where he lived with a brother of my mother's), to learn surveying.

During the two last weeks that he was with Murdoch, he himself was engaged in learning French, and he communicated the instructions he received to my brother, who, when he returned, brought home with him a French dictionary and grammar, and the *Adventures of Telemachus* in the original. In a little while, by the assistance of these books, he had acquired such a knowledge of the language, as to read and understand any French author in prose. This was considered as a sort of prodigy, and, through the medium of Murdoch, procured him the acquaintance of several lads in Ayr, who were at that time gabbling French, and the notice of some families, particularly that of Dr. Malcolm, where a knowledge of French was a recommendation.

Observing the facility with which he had acquired the French language, Mr. Robinson, the established writing-master in Ayr, and Mr. Murdoch's particular friend, having himself acquired a considerable knowledge of the Latin language by his own industry, without ever having learnt it at school, advised Robert to make the same attempt,

promising him every assistance in his power. Agreeably to this advice, he purchased *The Rudiments of the Latin Tongue*, but finding this study dry and uninteresting, it was quickly laid aside. He frequently returned to his *Rudiments* on any little chagrin or disappointment, particularly in his love affairs; but the Latin seldom predominated more than a day or two at a time, or a week at most. Observing himself the ridicule that would attach to this sort of conduct if it were known, he made two or three humorous stanzas on the subject, which I cannot now recollect, but they all ended,

" So I'll to my Latin again."

Thus you see Mr. Murdoch was a principal means of my brother's improvement. Worthy man! though foreign to my present purpose, I cannot take leave of him without tracing his future history. He continued for some years a respected and useful teacher at Ayr, till one evening that he had been overtaken in liquor, he happened to speak somewhat disrespectfully of Dr. Dalrymple, the parish minister, who had not paid him that attention to which he thought himself entitled. In Ayr he might as well have spoken blasphemy. He found it proper to give up his appointment. He went to London, where he still lives, a private teacher of French. He has been a considerable time married, and keeps a shop of stationery wares.

The father of Dr. Paterson, now physician at Ayr, was, I believe, a native of Aberdeenshire, and was one of the established teachers in Ayr when my father settled in the neighbourhood. He early recognised my father as a fellow native of the north of Scotland, and a certain degree of intimacy subsisted between them during Mr. Paterson's life. After his death, his widow, who is a very genteel woman, and of great worth, delighted in doing what she thought her husband would have wished to have done, and assiduously kept up her attentions to all his acquaintance. She kept alive the intimacy with our family, by frequently inviting my father and mother to her house on Sundays, when she met them at church.

When she came to know my brother's passion for books, she kindly offered us the use of her husband's library, and from her we got the *Spectator, Pope's Translation of Homer*, and several other books that were of use to us. Mount Oliphant, the farm my father possessed in the parish of Ayr, is almost the very poorest soil I know of in a state of cultivation. A stronger proof of this I cannot give, than that, notwithstanding the extraordinary rise in the value of lands in Scotland, it was, after a considerable sum laid out in improving it by the proprietor, let a few years ago five pounds per annum lower than the rent paid for it by my father thirty years ago. My father, in consequence of this, soon came into difficulties, which were increased by the loss of several of his cattle by accidents and disease. To the buffettings of misfortune, we could only oppose hard labour and the most rigid economy. We lived very sparingly. For several years butcher's meat was a stranger in the house, while all the members of the family exerted themselves to the utmost of their strength, and rather beyond it, in the labours of the farm. My brother, at the age of thirteen, assisted in threshing the crop of corn, and at fifteen was the principal labourer on the farm, for we had no hired servant, male or female. The anguish of mind we felt at our tender years, under those straits and difficulties was very great. To think of our father growing old (for he was now above fifty) broken down with the long continued fatigues of his life, with a wife and five other children, and in a declining state of circumstances, these reflections produced in my brother's mind and mine sensations of the deepest distress. I doubt not but the hard labour and sorrow of this period of his life, was in a great measure the cause of that depression of spirits with which Robert was so often afflicted through his whole life afterwards. At this time he was almost constantly afflicted in the evenings with a dull headache, which, at a future period of his life, was exchanged for a palpitation of the heart, and a threatening of fainting and suffocation in his bed, in the night time.

By a stipulation in my father's lease, he had a right to throw it up, if he thought proper, at the end of every sixth year. He attempted to fix himself in a better farm at the end of the first six years, but failing in that attempt, he continued where he was for six years more. He then took the farm of Lochlea, of 130 acres, at the rent of twenty shillings an acre, in the parish of Tarbolton, of Mr. ————, then a merchant in Ayr, and now (1797) a merchant in Liverpool. He removed to this farm at Whitsunday, 1777, and possessed it only seven years. No writing had ever been made out of the conditions of the lease; a misunderstanding took place respecting them; the subjects in dispute were submitted to arbitration, and the decision involved my father's affairs in ruin. He lived to know of this decision, but not to see any execution in consequence of it. He died on the 13th of February, 1784.

The seven years we lived in Tarbolton parish (extending from the seventeenth to the twenty-fourth of my brother's age) were not marked by much literary improvement; but, during this time, the foundation was laid of certain habits in my brother's character, which afterwards became but too prominent, and which malice and envy have taken delight to enlarge on. Though when young he was bashful and awkward in his intercourse with women, yet when he approached manhood, his attachment to their society became very strong, and he was constantly the victim of some fair enslaver. The symptoms of his passion were often such as nearly to equal those of the celebrated Sappho. I never indeed knew that he *fainted, sunk, and died away:* but the agitation of his mind and body exceeded anything of the kind I ever knew in real life. He had always a particular jealousy of people who were richer than himself, or who had more consequence in life. His love, therefore, rarely settled on persons of this description. When he selected any one out of the sovereignty of his good pleasure to whom he should pay his particular attention, she was instantly invested with a sufficient stock of charms, out of the plentiful stores of his own imagination; and there was often a great dissimilitude between his fair captivator, as she appeared to others, and as she seemed when invested with the attributes he gave her. One generally reigned paramount in his affections; but as

Yorick's affections flowed out toward Madame de L—— at the remise door, while the eternal vows of Eliza were upon him, so Robert was frequently encountering other attractions, which formed so many under plots in the drama of his love. As these connexions were governed by the strictest rules of virtue and modesty (from which he never deviated till he reached his twenty-third year), he became anxious to be in a situation to marry. This was not likely to be soon the case while he remained a farmer, as the stocking of a farm required a sum of money he had no probability of being master of for a great while. He began, therefore, to think of trying some other line of life. He and I had for several years taken land of my father for the purpose of raising flax on our own account. In the course of selling it, Robert began to think of turning flax-dresser, both as being suitable to his grand view of settling in life, and as subservient to the flax raising. He accordingly wrought at the business of a flax-dresser in Irvine for six months, but abandoned it at that period, as neither agreeing with his health nor inclination. In Irvine he had contracted some acquaintance of a freer manner of thinking and living than he had been used to, whose society prepared him for overleaping the bounds of rigid virtue which had hitherto restrained him. Towards the end of the period under review (in his twenty-fourth year), and soon after his father's death, he was furnished with the subject of his Epistle to John Rankin. During this period also he became a freemason, which was his first introduction to the life of a boon companion. Yet, notwithstanding these circumstances, and the praise he has bestowed on Scotch drink (which seems to have misled his historians), I do not recollect, during these seven years, nor till towards the end of his commencing author, (when his growing celebrity occasioned his being often in company) to have ever seen him intoxicated; nor was he at all given to drinking. A stronger proof of the general sobriety of his conduct need not be required, than what I am about to give. During the whole of the time we lived in the farm of Lochlea with my father, he allowed my brother and me such wages for our labour as he gave to other labourers, as a part of which, every article of our clothing manufactured in the family was regularly accounted for. When my father's affairs grew near a crisis, Robert and I took the farm of Mossgiel, consisting of 118 acres, at the rent of £90 per annum (the farm on which I live at present), from Mr. Gavin Hamilton, as an asylum for the family in case of the worst. It was stocked by the property and individual savings of the whole family, and was a joint concern among us. Every member of the family was allowed ordinary wages for the labour he performed on the farm. My brother's allowance and mine was seven pounds per annum each. And during the whole time this family concern lasted, which was four years, as well as during the preceding period at Lochlea, his expenses never in any one year exceeded his slender income. As I was intrusted with the keeping of the family accounts, it is not possible that there can be any fallacy in this statement in my brother's favour. His temperance and frugality were everything that could be wished.

The farm of Mossgiel lies very high, and mostly on a cold

wet bottom. The first four years that we were on the farm were very frosty, and the spring was very late. Our crops in consequence were very unprofitable; and, notwithstanding our utmost diligence and economy, we found ourselves obliged to give up our bargain, with the loss of a considerable part of our original stock. It was during these four years that Robert formed his connexion with Jean Armour, afterwards Mrs. Burns. This connexion *could no longer be concealed,* about the time we came to a final determination to quit the farm. Robert durst not engage with a family in his poor unsettled state, but was anxious to shield his partner by every means in his power from the consequences of their imprudence. It was agreed therefore between them, that they should make a legal acknowledgment of an irregular and private marriage; that he should go to Jamaica to *push his fortune;* and that she should remain with her father till it might please Providence to put the means of supporting a family in his power.

Mrs. Burns was a great favourite of her father's. The intimation of a marriage was the first suggestion he received of her real situation. He was in the greatest distress, and fainted away. The marriage did not appear to him to make the matter better. A husband in Jamaica appeared to him and his wife little better than none, and an effectual bar to any other prospects of a settlement in life that their daughter might have. They therefore expressed a wish to her, that the written papers which respected the marriage should be cancelled, and thus the marriage rendered void. In her melancholy state, she felt the deepest remorse at having brought such heavy affliction on parents that loved her so tenderly, and submitted to their entreaties. Their wish was mentioned to Robert. He felt the deepest anguish of mind.* He offered to stay at home and provide for his wife and family in the best manner that his daily labours could provide for them; that being the only means in his power. Even this offer they did not approve of; for, humble as Miss Armour's station was, and great though her imprudence had been, she still, in the eyes of her partial parents, might look to a better connexion than that with my friendless and unhappy brother, at that time without house or hiding-place. Robert at length consented to their wishes; but his feelings on this occasion were of the most distracting nature; and the impression of sorrow was not effaced, till by a regular marriage they were indissolubly united. In the state of mind which this separation produced, he wished to leave the country as soon as possible, and agreed with Dr. Douglas to go out to Jamaica as an assistant overseer, or, as I believe it is called, a book-keeper, on his estate. As he had not sufficient money to pay his passage, and the vessel in which Dr. Douglas was to procure a passage for him was not expected to sail for some time, Mr. Hamilton advised him to publish his poems in the meantime by subscription, as a

* [This is manifestly a rehearsal by Gilbert Burns, from our Author's own account of the matter, when in a state of excitement on the subject, and perhaps labouring under false impressions with regard to it. At the utmost, the painful proceeding referred to was only a "wish," or proposal on Mr. Armour's part. There is no evidence whatever in this statement that it was actually adopted. Compare note on correspondence to Ballantine—Prose Works, p. 183.]

likely way of getting a little money to provide him more liberally in necessaries for Jamaica. Agreeably to this advice, subscription bills were printed immediately, and the printing was commenced at Kilmarnock, his preparations going on at the same time for his voyage. The reception, however, which his poems met with in the world, and the friends they procured him, made him change his resolution of going to Jamaica, and he was advised to go to Edinburgh, to publish a second edition. On his return, in happier circumstances, he renewed his connexion with Mrs. Burns, and rendered it permanent by an union for life.

Thus, Madam, have I endeavoured to give you a simple narrative of the leading circumstances in my brother's early life. The remaining part he spent in Edinburgh, or in Dumfriesshire, and its incidents are as well known to you as to me. His genius having procured him your patronage and friendship, this gave rise to the correspondence between you, in which, I believe, his sentiments were delivered with the most respectful, but most unreserved confidence, and which only terminated with the last days of his life.

Remarks

BY GILBERT BURNS ON POET'S AUTOBIOGRAPHICAL LETTER TO DR. MOORE.

I wonder how Robert could attribute to our father that lasting resentment of his going to a dancing-school against his will, of which he was incapable. I believe the truth was, that he, about this time began to see the dangerous impetuosity of my brother's passions, as well as his not being amenable to counsel, which often irritated my father; and which he would naturally think a dancing-school was not likely to correct. But he was proud of Robert's genius, which he bestowed more expense in cultivating than on the rest of the family, in the instances of sending him to Ayr and Kirk-Oswald schools; and he was greatly delighted with his warmth of heart, and his conversational powers. He had indeed that dislike of dancing-schools which Robert mentions; but so far overcame it during Robert's first month of attendance, that he allowed all the rest of the family that were fit for it to accompany him during the second month. Robert excelled in dancing, and was for some time distractedly fond of it.

I do not know how my brother could be misled in the account he has given of the Jacobitism of his ancestors. I believe the Earl Marischal forfeited his title and estate in 1715, before my father was born; and among a collection of parish-certificates in his possession, I have read one, stating that the bearer had no concern in the *late wicked rebellion.*

My brother seems to set off his early companions in too consequential a manner. The principal acquaintance we had in Ayr, while boys, were four sons of Mr. Andrew M'Culloch.

a distant relation of my mother's, who kept a tea-shop, and had made a little money in the contraband trade, very common at that time. He died while the boys were young, and my father was nominated one of the tutors. The two eldest were bred shopkeepers, the third a surgeon, and the youngest, the only surviving one, was bred in a counting-house in Glasgow, where he is now a respectable merchant. I believe all these boys went to the West Indies. Then there were two sons of Dr. Malcolm, whom I have mentioned in my letter to Mrs. Dunlop. The eldest, a very worthy young man, went to the East Indies, where he had a commission in the army; he is the person whose heart my brother says the *Mussy Begum sums could not corrupt*. The other, by the interest of Lady Wallace, got an ensigncy in a regiment raised by the Duke of Hamilton during the American war. I believe neither of them are now (1797) alive. We also knew the present Dr. Paterson of Ayr, and a younger brother of his, now in Jamaica, who were much younger than us. I had almost forgot to mention Dr. Charles of Ayr, who was a little older than my brother, and with whom we had a longer and closer intimacy than with any of the others, which did not, however, continue in after life.

History of Poems:

FROM LETTER TO DR. CURRIE BY GILBERT BURNS.

Mossgiel, 2d April, 1798.

Dear Sir,

Your letter of the 14th of March I received in due course, but from the hurry of the season have been hitherto hindered from answering it. I will now try to give you what satisfaction I can in regard to the particulars you mention. I cannot pretend to be very accurate in respect to the dates of the poems, but none of them, except *Winter, a Dirge* (which was a juvenile production), *The Death and Dying Words of poor Maillie*, and some of the songs, were composed before the year 1784. The circumstances of the poor sheep were pretty much as he has described them. He had, partly by way of frolic, bought a ewe and two lambs from a neighbour, and she was tethered in a field adjoining the house at Lochlie. He and I were going out with our teams, and our two younger brothers to drive for us, at mid-day; when Hugh Wilson, a curious looking awkward boy, clad in plaiding, came to us with much anxiety in his face, with the information that the ewe had entangled herself in the tether, and was lying in the ditch. Robert was much tickled with *Huoc's* appearance and postures on the occasion. Poor Maillie was set to rights, and when we returned from the plough in the evening, he repeated to me her *Death and Dying Words* pretty much in the way they now stand.

Among the earliest of his poems was the *Epistle to Davie*. Robert often composed without any regular plan. When any thing made a strong impression on his mind, so as to rouse it to poetic exertion, he would give way to the impulse, and embody the thought in rhyme. If he hit on two or three stanzas to please him, he would then think of proper introductory, connecting, and concluding stanzas; hence the middle of a poem was often first produced. It was, I think, in summer, 1784, when in the interval of harder labour, he and I were weeding in the garden (kail-yard), that he repeated to me the principal part of this epistle. I believe the first idea of Robert's becoming an author was started on this occasion. I was much pleased with the epistle, and said to him I was of opinion it would bear being printed, and that it would be well received by people of taste; that I thought it at least equal, if not superior, to many of Allan Ramsay's epistles, and that the merit of these, and much other Scotch poetry, seemed to consist principally in the knack of the expression, but here, there was a strain of interesting sentiment, and the Scotticism of the language scarcely seemed affected, but appeared to be the natural language of the poet; that, besides, there was certainly some novelty in a poet pointing out the consolations that were in store for him when he should go a-begging. Robert seemed very well pleased with my criticism, and we talked of sending it to some magazine, but as this plan afforded no opportunity of knowing how it would take, the idea was dropped.

It was, I think, in the winter following, as we were going together with carts for coal to the family fire (and I could yet point out the particular spot), that the author first repeated to me the *Address to the Deil*. The curious idea of such an address was suggested to him by running over in his mind the many ludicrous accounts and representations we have, from various quarters, of this august personage. *Death and Doctor Hornbook*, though not published in the Kilmarnock edition, was produced early in the year 1785. The Schoolmaster of Tarbolton parish, to eke up the scanty subsistence allowed to that useful class of men, had set up a shop of grocery goods. Having accidentally fallen in with some medical books, and become most hobby-horsically attached to the study of medicine, he had added the sale of a few medicines to his little trade. He had got a shop-bill printed, at the bottom of which, overlooking his own incapacity, he had advertised, that "Advice would be given in common disorders at the shop gratis." Robert was at a mason-meeting in Tarbolton, when the *Dominie* unfortunately made too ostentatious a display of his medical skill. As he parted in the evening from this mixture of pedantry and physic, at the place where he describes his meeting with Death, one of those floating ideas of apparition he mentions in his letter to Dr. Moore crossed his mind; this set him to work for the rest of the way home. These circumstances he related when he repeated the verses to me next afternoon, as I was holding the plough, and he was letting the water off the field beside me. The *Epistle to John Lapraik* was produced exactly on the occasion described by the author. He says in that poem, *On fasten-e'en we had a rockin* [p. 65]. I believe he has omitted the word *rockin* in the glossary. It is a term derived from those primitive times, when the country-women employed their spare hours in spinning on the rock, or distaff. This simple implement is a very portable one, and well fitted to the social inclination of meeting in a neighbour's house; hence the phrase of *going a rocking*, or *with the rock*. As the connexion the phrase had with the implement was forgotten when the rock gave place to the spinning-wheel, the phrase came to be used by both sexes on social occasions, and men talk of going with their rocks as well as women.

It was at one of these *rockings* at our house, when we had twelve or fifteen young people with their *rocks*, that Lapraik's song beginning—"When I upon thy bosom lean," was sung, and we were informed who was the author. Upon this, Robert wrote his first epistle to Lapraik; and his second in reply to his answer. The verses to the *Mouse* and *Mountain Daisy* were composed on the occasions mentioned, and while the author was holding the plough; I could point out the particular spot where each was composed. Holding the plough was a favourite situation with Robert for poetic compositions, and some of his best verses were produced while he was at that exercise.* Several of the poems were produced for the purpose of bringing forward some favourite sentiment of the author. He used to remark to me, that he could not well conceive a more mortifying picture of human life than a man seeking work. In casting about in his mind how this sentiment might be brought forward, the elegy, *Man was made to Mourn*, was composed. Robert had frequently remarked to me that he thought there was something peculiarly venerable in the phrase, "Let us worship God," used by a decent sober head of a family introducing family worship. To this sentiment of the author the world is indebted for the *Cotter's Saturday Night*. The hint of the plan, and title of the poem, were taken from Fergusson's *Farmer's Ingle*. When Robert had not some pleasure in view in which I was not thought fit to participate, we used frequently to walk together when the weather was favourable, on the Sunday afternoons (those precious breathing-times to the labouring part of the community), and enjoyed such Sundays as would make one regret to see their number abridged. It was in one of these walks that I first had the pleasure of hearing the author repeat the *Cotter's Saturday Night*. I do not recollect to have read or heard any thing by which I was more highly *electrified*. The fifth and sixth stanzas, and the eighteenth, thrilled with peculiar ecstasy through my soul. I mention this to you, that you may see what hit the taste of unlettered criticism. I should be glad to know if the enlightened mind and refined taste of Mr. Roscoe, who has borne such honourable testimony to this poem, agrees with me in the selection. Fergusson in his *Hallow Fair* of Edinburgh, I believe, likewise furnished a hint of the title and plan of the *Holy Fair*. The farcical scene the poet there describes was often a favourite field of his observation, and the most of the incidents he mentions had actually passed before his eyes. It is scarcely necessary to mention, that the *Lament* was composed on that unfortunate passage in his matrimonial history, which I have mentioned in my letter to Mrs. Dunlop, after the first distraction of his

---

* Currie observes, that in place of the exercise, which could not be enjoyed at Dumfries, he substituted morning and evening walks by the Nith. But the truth is, that a habit of solitary wandering was congenial to him, by woods, by streams, or in the fields—as is everywhere testified in his poems.

feelings had a little subsided. *The Tale of Twa Dogs* was composed after the resolution of publishing was nearly taken. Robert had had a dog, which he called *Luath*, that was a great favourite. The dog had been killed by the wanton cruelty of some person the night before my father's death. Robert said to me that he should like to confer such immortality as he could bestow upon his old friend *Luath*, and that he had a great mind to introduce something into the book under the title of *Stanzas to the Memory of a Quadruped Friend*; but this plan was given up for the *Tale* as it now stands. *Cæsar* was merely the creature of the poet's imagination, created for the purpose of holding chat with his favourite *Luath*. The first time Robert heard the spinnet played upon was at the house of Dr. Lawrie, then minister of the parish of Loudoun, now in Glasgow, having given up the parish in favour of his son. Dr. Lawrie has several daughters; one of them played; the father and mother led down the dance; the rest of the sisters, the brother, the poet, and the other guests, mixed in it. It was a delightful family scene for our poet, then lately introduced to the world. His mind was roused to a poetic enthusiasm, and the stanzas [Verses p. 55] were left in the room where he slept. It was to Dr. Lawrie that Dr. Blacklock's letter was addressed, which my brother, in his letter to Dr. Moore, mentions as the reason of his going to Edinburgh.

When my father *feued* his little property near Alloway-Kirk, the wall of the church-yard had gone to ruin, and cattle had free liberty of pasturing in it. My father, with two or three other neighbours, joined in an application to the town council of Ayr, who were superiors of the adjoining land, for liberty to rebuild it, and raised by subscription a sum for inclosing this ancient cemetery with a wall; hence he came to consider it as his burial-place, and we learned that reverence for it people generally have for the burial-place of their ancestors. My brother was living in Ellisland when Captain Grose, on his peregrinations through Scotland, staid some time at Carse-House, in the neighbourhood, with Captain Robert Riddel, of Glen-Riddel, a particular friend of my brother's. The antiquarian and the poet were "Unco pack and thick thegither." Robert requested of Captain Grose, when he should come to Ayrshire, that he would make a drawing of Alloway-Kirk, as it was the burial-place of his father, and where he himself had a sort of claim to lay down his bones when they should be no longer serviceable to him; and added, by way of encouragement, that it was the scene of many a good story of witches and apparitions, of which he knew the Captain was very fond. The Captain agreed to the request, provided the poet would furnish a witch-story, to be printed along with it. *Tam o' Shanter* was produced on this occasion, and was first published in *Grose's Antiquities of Scotland*.

This poem is founded on a traditional story. The leading circumstances of a man riding home very late from Ayr, in a stormy night, his seeing a light in Alloway-Kirk, his having the curiosity to look in, his seeing a dance of witches, with the devil playing on the bag-pipe to them, the scanty covering of one of the witches, which made him so far forget himself as to cry—*Weel loupen, short sark!*—with the melancholy catastrophe of the piece; is all a true story, that can be well attested by many respectable old people in that neighbourhood.

I do not at present recollect any circumstances respecting the other poems that could be at all interesting; even some of those I have mentioned, I am afraid, may appear trifling enough, but you will only make use of what appears to you of consequence.

* * * * * *

Poet's Early Friends and Patrons:

BY THE SAME.

THE farm of Mossgiel, at the time of our coming to it (Martinmas, 1783), was the property of the Earl of Loudoun, but was held in tack by Mr. Gavin Hamilton, writer, in Mauchline, from whom we had our bargain; who had thus an opportunity of knowing, and shewing a sincere regard for, my brother, before he knew that he was a poet. The poet's estimation of him, and the strong outlines of his character, may be collected from the Dedication to this gentleman. When the publication was begun, Mr. H. entered very warmly into its interests, and promoted the subscription very extensively. Mr. Robert Aiken, writer in Ayr, is a man of worth and taste, of warm affections, and connected with a most respectable circle of friends and relations. It is to this gentleman *The Cotter's Saturday Night* is inscribed. The poems of my brother which I have formerly mentioned no sooner came into his hands, than they were quickly known, and well received in the extensive circle of Mr. Aiken's friends, which gave them a sort of currency, necessary in this wise world, even for the good reception of things valuable in themselves. But Mr. Aiken not only admired the poet; as soon as he became acquainted with him, he shewed the warmest regard for the man, and did every thing in his power to forward his interest and respectability. *The Epistle to a Young Friend* was addressed to this gentleman's son, Mr. A. H. Aiken, now of Liverpool. He was the oldest of a young family, who were taught to receive my brother with respect, as a man of genius, and their father's friend.

The Brigs of Ayr is inscribed to John Ballantine, Esq., Banker in Ayr; one of those gentlemen to whom my brother was introduced by Mr. Aiken. He interested himself very warmly in my brother's concerns, and constantly shewed the greatest friendship and attachment to him. When the Kilmarnock edition was all sold off, and a considerable demand pointed out the propriety of publishing a second edition, Mr. Wilson, who had printed the first, was asked if he would print a second, and take his chance of being paid from the first sale. This he declined, and when this came to Mr. Ballantine's knowledge, he generously offered to accommodate Robert with what money he might need for that purpose; but advised him to go to Edinburgh, as the fittest place for publishing. When he did go to Edinburgh, his friends advised him to publish again by subscription, so that he did not need to accept this offer. Mr. William Parker, merchant in Kilmarnock, was a subscriber for thirty-five copies of the Kilmarnock edition. This may perhaps appear not deserving of notice here; but if the comparative obscurity of the poet at this period be taken into consideration, it appears to me a greater effort of generosity than many things which appear more brilliant in my brother's future history.

Mr. Robert Muir, merchant in Kilmarnock, was one of those friends Robert's poetry had procured him, and one who was dear to his heart. This gentleman had no very great fortune, or long line of dignified ancestry; but what Robert says of Captain Matthew Henderson might be said of him with great propriety, *that he held the patent of his honours immediately from Almighty God.* Nature had indeed marked him a gentleman in the most legible characters. He died while yet a young man, soon after the publication of my brother's first Edinburgh edition. Sir William Cunningham of Robertland paid a very flattering attention, and shewed a good deal of friendship for the poet. Before his going to Edinburgh, as well as after, Robert seemed peculiarly pleased with Professor Stewart's friendship and conversation.

But of all the friendships which Robert acquired in Ayrshire or elsewhere, none seemed more agreeable to him than that of Mrs. Dunlop of Dunlop, nor any which has been more uniformly and constantly exerted in behalf of him and his family; of which, were it proper, I could give many instances. Robert was on the point of setting out for Edinburgh before Mrs. Dunlop had heard of him. About the time of my brother's publishing in Kilmarnock, she had been afflicted with a long and severe illness, which had reduced her mind to the most distressing state of depression. In this situation, a copy of the printed poems was laid on her table by a friend, and happening to open on *The Cotter's Saturday Night*, she read it over with the greatest pleasure and surprise; the poet's description of the simple cottagers, operating on her mind like the charm of a powerful exorcist, expelling the demon *ennui*, and restoring her to her wonted inward harmony and satisfaction.—Mrs. Dunlop sent off a person express to Mossgiel, distant fifteen or sixteen miles, with a very obliging letter to my brother, desiring him to send her half a dozen copies of his poems, if he had them to spare, and begging he would do her the pleasure of calling at Dunlop House as soon as convenient. This was the beginning of a correspondence which ended only with the poet's life. The last use he made of his pen was writing a short letter to this lady a few days before his death.

Colonel Fullarton, who afterwards paid a very particular attention to the poet, was not in the country at the time of his first commencing author. At this distance of time, and in the hurry of a wet day, snatched from laborious occupations, I may have forgot some persons who ought to have been mentioned on this occasion, for which, if it come to my knowledge, I shall be heartily sorry.

Second Tour

BY STIRLING TO CLACKMANNANSHIRE.

[FROM LETTER BY DR. ADAIR TO DR. CURRIE.]

Burns and I left Edinburgh together in August, 1787.* We rode by Linlithgow and Carron, to Stirling. We visited the iron-works at Carron with which the Poet was forcibly struck. The resemblance between that place and its inhabitants to the cave of the Cyclops, which must have occurred to every classical visitor, presented itself to Burns. At Stirling the prospects from the castle strongly interested him; in a former visit to which, his national feelings had been powerfully excited by the ruinous and roofless state of the hall in which the Scottish Parliaments had frequently been held. His indignation had vented itself in some imprudent, but not unpoetical lines, which had given much offence, and which he took this opportunity of erasing, by breaking the pane of the window at the inn on which they were written.†

At Stirling we met with a company of travellers from Edinburgh, among whom was a character in many respects congenial with that of Burns. This was Nicol, one of the teachers of the High Grammar-School at Edinburgh—the same wit and power of conversation; the same fondness for convivial society, and thoughtlessness of to-morrow, characterized both. Jacobitical principles in politics were common to both of them; and these have been suspected, since the revolution of France, to have given place in each to opinions apparently opposite. I regret that I have preserved no *memorabilia* of their conversation, either on this or on other occasions, when I happened to meet them together. Many songs were sung: which I mention for the sake of observing, that when Burns was called on in his turn, he was accustomed instead of singing, to recite one or other of his own shorter poems, with a tone and emphasis which, though not correct or harmonious, were impressive and pathetic. This he did on the present occasion.

From Stirling we went next morning through the romantic and fertile vale of Devon to Harvieston, in Clackmannanshire, then inhabited by Mrs. Hamilton, with the younger part of whose family Burns had been previously acquainted. He introduced me to the family, and there was formed my first acquaintance with Mrs. Hamilton's eldest daughter, to whom I have been married for nine years. Thus was I indebted to Burns for a connexion from which I have derived, and expect further to derive, much happiness.

During a residence of about ten days at Harvieston, we made excursions to visit various parts of the surrounding scenery, inferior to none in Scotland in beauty, sublimity, and romantic interest; particularly Castle-Campbell, the ancient seat of the family of Argyle; and the famous cataract of the Devon, called the *Caldron Linn;* and the *Rumbling Bridge,* a single broad arch, thrown by the Devil, if tradition is to be believed, across the river, at about the height of a hundred feet above its bed. I am surprised that none of these scenes should have called forth an exertion of Burns's muse. But I doubt if he had much taste for the picturesque. I well remember that the ladies at Harvieston, who accompanied us on this jaunt, expressed their disappointment at his not expressing in more glowing and fervid language his impressions of the *Caldron Linn* scene, certainly highly sublime, and somewhat horrible.‡

A visit to Mrs. Bruce of Clackmannan, a lady above ninety, the lineal descendant of that race which gave the Scottish throne its brightest ornament, interested his feelings more powerfully. This venerable dame, with characteristical dignity, informed me, on my observing that I believed she was descended from the family of Robert Bruce, that Robert Bruce was sprung from her family. Though almost deprived of speech by a paralytic affection, she preserved her hospitality and urbanity. She was in possession of the hero's helmet and two-handed sword, with which she conferred on Burns and myself the honour of knighthood, remarking, that she had a better right to confer that title than *some people* * * *. You will of course conclude that the old lady's political tenets were as Jacobitical as the poet's, a conformity which contributed not a little to the cordiality of our reception and entertainment.—She gave, as her first toast after dinner, *Awa Uncos,* or Away with the Strangers—Who these strangers were, you will readily understand. Mrs. A. corrects me by saying it should be *Hooi,* or *Hoohi uncos,* a sound used by shepherds to direct their dogs to drive away the sheep.‖

We returned to Edinburgh by Kinross (on the shore of Lochleven) and Queen's-ferry. I am inclined to think Burns knew nothing of poor Michael Bruce, who was then alive at Kinross, or had died there a short while before. A meeting between the bards, or a visit to the deserted cottage and early grave of poor Bruce, would have been highly interesting.

At Dumfermline we visited the ruined Abbey, and the Abbey-church, now consecrated to Presbyterian worship. Here I mounted the *cutty stool,* or stool of repentance, assuming the character of a penitent for fornication; while Burns from the pulpit addressed to me a ludicrous reproof and exhortation, parodied from that which had been delivered to himself in Ayrshire, where he had, as he assured me, once been one of seven who mounted the *seat of shame* together.

In the church-yard two broad flag-stones marked the grave of Robert Bruce, for whose memory Burns had more than common veneration. He knelt and kissed the stone with sacred fervour, and heartily (*suum ut mos erat*) execrated the worse than Gothic neglect of the first of Scottish heroes."§

---

* [Dr. James M'Kittrick Adair was a young and fashionable friend of Mrs. Dunlop's—through whom he was introduced to Burns. Mr. Chambers, by a number of arguments which we need not here reproduce, distinctly proves that Dr. Adair, writing from memory at the distance of several years, makes an error of two months as to the date of this tour—which was certainly in the month of October. Dr. Adair, who was settled as a physician at Harrowgate, died in 1802, and his wife, in the bloom of her beauty, in 1808.]

† [It is said that the Poet dashed out this unlucky pane with his whip shaft. See Miscellaneous Poetical Pieces.]

‡ [The silence here complained of, we have no doubt, would be occasioned by the too great loquacity of Dr. Adair himself. Burns did not like too much prompting on such occasions, and never condescended to rival any enthusiast.]

‖ [There was surely a mistake here? Bruce was interred under white marble, within the church; where a pulpit now stands on his tomb.]

Mrs Burns,
Widow of The Poet.
(circa)
1826.
By most Obliging Permission of Mr ...
DUMFRIES

Memoranda:

BY MR. M'DIARMID, FROM MRS. BURNS'S DICTATION.

[The following most interesting Memoranda made by the late John M'Diarmid, Esq., of the *Dumfries Courier*, from Mrs. Burns's own lips, have been communicated to us, for the present work, by William Ritchie M'Diarmid, Esq., his son and successor. The order of Remarks and Anecdotes is slightly interwoven, as the reader will perceive; but we have judged it better to present so interesting a document exactly as it stands. Only two detached sentences which interrupted the commentary, and seemed to be a little out of place, have been arranged otherwise than in the manuscript—They will be found followed by a blank, thus, ——. The work to which so frequent reference occurs, and from which quotations are made, is "Lockhart's Life of Burns"—Constable's Miscellany, 1828. Where the quotations are not given in the original, they have been supplied by us from the volume itself (in brackets). On the general accuracy of Mr. Lockhart's work it would be impertinent in us to remark; but we must confess our astonishment that a gentleman of Mr. Lockhart's taste and judgment should have made so many statements calling for contradiction, when one of the parties most deeply interested, and whose personal feelings must have been most painfully affected, was still alive to hear them. It is fortunate that her protest has been thus recorded on the spot; and the public are indebted to Mr. M'Diarmid for having preserved such Memoranda. It was his own intention, we have been informed, to write a life of the Poet—a work which he did not live to accomplish. The present publication, however, will so far supplement this unfulfilled intention; and we have to record our best acknowledgments to Mr. William M'Diarmid, his son, for the privilege we enjoy of communicating it to the world.]

As there was no proper farm-house on Ellisland, the proprietor determined to build a new one for the accommodation of Burns. In the interim, he lived five months in the old house which was occupied by his predecessor in the farm, a man of the name of David Cullie. David was an antiburgher, and belonged to the congregation of the late Rev. Mr. Inglis, a clergyman for whom Burns contracted a great veneration. David by this time was about seventy years old, and had a wife nearly of the same age. He was well to live in worldly circumstances: his family were grown up and settled in the world, and therefore he declined the farm. Mrs. Burns joined her husband at Martinmas, and lived for about five months at the Isle—a place I know well. David Cullie used to visit at Ellisland farm-house; and tho' the cheese was Dunlop, Mrs. B. used to remark that he never took cheese but he took butter also. Burns used to laugh heartily at this.

About this time, Burns sometimes read books not always seen in people's hands on Sunday. Mrs. B. checked this—when the Bard laughingly replied, "You'll not think me so good a man as Nancy Kelly is a woman?" "Indeed, no." "Then I'll tell you what happened this morning: When I took a walk this morning by the banks of the Nith, I heard Nancy Kelly[*] praying long before I came till her. I walked on, and before I returned I saw her helping herself to an armful of my fitches." The parties kept a cow.

As David Kelly was one of the most respectable of Mr. Inglis's congregation, the examination for the district was held in his house. A dinner was always given on the occasion; and Mrs. B. and her husband were frequently invited. Here the Bard met with Mr. I., and was led to entertain so high an opinion of him, that he frequently attended his church afterwards. The rev. gentleman deserved all this admiration.

Before this time, Burns had written the "Holy Fair," and an impression had gone abroad that he was rather a scoffer or a free-thinker. D. Cullie and his wife were aware of this, and altho' they treated him civilly as the incoming tenant, during the five months he resided under their roof, still they felt for him as for one who was by no means on the right path. On one occasion, Nance and the Bard were sitting in the spence, when the former turned the conversation on her favourite topic—religion. Mr. Burns, from whatever motive, sympathised with the matron, and quoted so much Scripture that she was fairly astonished, and staggered in the opinion she formerly entertained. When she went ben [? but] she said to her husband, "Oh! David Cullie, hoo they have wranged that man; for I think he has mair o' the Bible aff his tongue than Mr. Inglis himsel." The Bard enjoyed the compliment; and almost the first thing he communicated to his wife on her arrival was " the lift he had got from auld Nance."[†]

Page 180—near bottom—

"Few housekeepers start with a larger provision of young mouths to feed than this couple."

So far from this, Mrs. Burns had only one child living; her first-born were twins—Robert, still alive, and Jane, who died in infancy at the age of seventeen months. The doctor would not allow Mrs. Burns to nurse both, and as the boy was stouter than the girl, he was sent to Mossgiel, and placed under the care of his grandmother. When Mrs. B., therefore, went to Ellisland, so far from having many mouths to feed, she had none at all; Robert, indeed, the survivor of her first, was brought to the place about half a year or more after his mother arrived.

"I suppose 'sonsy, smirking, dear-bought Bess' accompanied her younger brothers and sisters from Mossgiel."

So far from this, she never was in Burns's house. Mrs. B. saw her once at Mossgiel. When the child was between two and three years old, her father paid the mother a sum of money in acquittance of all claims. Her mother was leaving the country; hence the arrangement. Old Mrs. B., however, took a fancy to the child, and kept her for some years; for which the Bard's brother received a compensation. The name of this child's mother was Betty Paton. She had been shearing about Lochley, Ayrshire, where the Bard's father lived. This was before the Poet had seen his future wife. The girl afterwards lived with her mother, and gained a livelihood by tambouring and flowering. She was afterwards married to a servant of Sir Wm. Cunningham's, and died early, after giving birth to several children.

Page 181.—SERVANTS BREAKFASTING WITH THEIR MASTER.

["From that quarter also Burns brought a whole establishment of servants, male and female, who, of course, as was then the universal custom amongst the small farmers, both of the west and of the south of Scotland, partook, at the same table, of the same fare with their master and mistress."]

This is untrue. It was a custom of Burns's father to ask his servants to breakfast with him on New-year's-day morning; and this custom the son kept up. At every other time he and his wife ate alone, excepting when the Bard's sister formed part of their household.

---

[*] [There is a suspicious resemblance in the spelling of these names "Kelly" and "Cullie"—perhaps intentional, but sufficient at all events to perplex the reader, and to prevent identification of the parties. The name, we believe, is sometimes also spelt "Kailie." The same parties, we have no doubt, are indicated throughout. See business account with them, *infra*.]

Page 191—Vide Cunningham's information [to Lockhart].

["' Yes,' my father said, 'the walks on the river bank are fine, and you will see from your windows some miles of the Nith; but you will also see several farms of fine rich soil, any one of which you might have had. You have made a poet's choice, rather than a farmer's.'"]

This may be true.

Page 192.

["If Burns had much of a farmer's skill, he had little of a farmer's prudence and economy. I once inquired of James Corrie, a sagacious old farmer, whose ground marched with Ellisland, the cause of the poet's failure. 'Faith,' said he, 'how could he miss but fail, when his servants ate the bread as fast as it was baked? I don't mean figuratively, I mean literally. Consider a little. At that time, close economy was necessary to have enabled a man to clear twenty pounds a-year by Ellisland. Now, Burns's own handy-work was out of the question: he neither ploughed, nor sowed, nor reaped, at least like a hard-working farmer; and then he had a bevy of servants from Ayrshire. The lasses did nothing but bake bread, and the lads sat by the fireside, and ate it warm with ale. Waste of time and consumption of food would soon reach to twenty pounds a-year.'"]

This paragraph [still from Cunningham] is most untrue. Burns did work, and often like a hard-working farmer. Soon after he went to Ellisland, he was appointed an Exciseman in the same district, and his duties took him off a good deal. Mrs. B. has walked with a child in her arms on the banks of the Nith, and seen him sow after breakfast two bags of corn for the folk to harrow through the day. The best answer to this is to tell the establishment. The Poet had two women, one of whom was his own sister—who afterwards married and is now in Ireland [1828]. He kept twelve cows, and made butter and cheese. Cows beautiful, and sold very high at the roup. Had three horses, two for plough or cart, and one that rode, or harrowed occasionally. The former were a pretty grey team, and Mrs. B. regretted nothing so much as to see them parted—that is, go to different proprietors. Tho' the Bard was often from home, each of his servants had his or her assigned task; and the fact that the Bard's sister continued with him all the time he remained at Ellisland, and was not only respectable, but attached to [his*] interest, disproves of itself the stupid allegation. There was no waste: on the contrary, every thing went on on the principle that is observed in any other well regulated farm-house.

Page 93.—Mr. Lockhart alludes to the letter addressed by Mrs. Dunlop of Dunlop to Burns, and to his first visit to Dunlop House, near Stewarton, Ayrshire.

["At the residence of these new acquaintances, Burns was introduced into society of a class which he had not before approached."]

On reading this passage over to the widow, she remarked— "Aye, I have heard him say that he was so much embarrassed with ladies looking at him, that altho' at breakfast a grand egg-spoon was laid down to him, he used a knife, and never saw the other until after he had done."

Page 96.

["Mrs. Stewart of Stair, a beautiful and accomplished lady."]

This passage is egregiously incorrect. She was the reverse of beautiful. See Miss Dunlop respecting this, and also anent the "Lass o' Ballochmyle."—†

---

* [This word in the original, being apparently 'her,' renders the sense of the passage indistinct. There seems to be a mistake of the pen.]

† [This reference we have not been able to identify.]

Mr. Gavin Hamilton was a gentleman in every sense of the word. He was uniformly kind to the Poet, and his family have always paid attention to his widow.

Page 169, at the bottom.

["Burns's distresses, however, were to be still farther aggravated. While still under the hands of his surgeon [at Edinburgh], he received intelligence from Mauchline that his intimacy with Jean Armour had once more exposed her to the reproaches of her family. The father sternly and at once turned her out of doors; and Burns, unable to walk across his room, had to write to his friends in Mauchline, to procure shelter for his children, and for her whom he considered as—all but his wife."]

This is untrue. The father was no doubt angry that his daughter continued to correspond with the Bard—after he had written to her; but he had no opportunity of turning her out of doors. Her mother had warned her that her father was angry, and that she had better remain from home a little. She was then on a visit to William Muir, miller, Tarbolton Mill—the person who is alluded to in 'Death and Doctor Hornbook'—

"Dandering down by Willie's mill"—&c.‡

ELLISLAND: There is more said about the number of persons who visited Burns at Ellisland than hath warrant. Occasionally his friends from Dumfries visited him, chiefly on the Sabbath day: such as Mr. Findlater, Supervisor of Excise. The neighbouring gentry sometimes called, and sometimes the Bard visited them; but the influx of visitors was by no means overpowering.

Mrs. B. thinks that he was induced to give up the farm of Ellisland partly from despondency—Gilbert easily lost heart—and partly from his engagements as an Exciseman. Mr. Miller of Dalswinton made no objection to take the farm off the Poet's hand. Accordingly, he sold off both his stock and crop. The sale was a very good one, and was well attended. A cow in her first calf brought eighteen gns., and the purchaser never rued his bargain. Two other cows brought good prices. These had been presented to him by Mrs. Dunlop of Dunlop. Burns neither failed as a farmer, nor in any other capacity. At Martinmas, 1791, he repaired to Dumfries, and took up his abode in Bank Street. His salary as an Exciseman never exceeded £70, and that he only got as Port-officer. He did not enjoy the rise long.

Did not come empty-handed to Dumfries: brought a nice little braw cow, which was placed in a byre in the Globe Close; but as no proper grazing ground could be got, the cow was sold. Had three children living then—Robert, Francis, and William.——

Burns was not an early riser, excepting when he had anything particular to do in the way of his profession—such as stamping leather, measuring malt, &c. Even tho' he had dined out, he never lay after nine o'clock. The family breakfasted at nine. If he lay long in bed awake he was always reading. At all meals he had a book beside him on the table. He did his work in the forenoon, and was seldom engaged professionally in the evening. Dined at two o'clock, when he dined at home. Was fond of plain things, and hated tarts, pies, and puddings. When at home in the evening, he employed his time in writing and reading, with the children

---

‡ [Misquotation for ",As' tadlin doon on Willie's Mill," &c.]

playing about him. Their prattle never disturbed him in the least; and in this he resembled Robert Southey.[*]—

A country woman in Dunscore once remarked, who had seen Burns riding slowly among the hills reading, "That's surely no a good man, for he has aye a book in his hand!"[+]——

Resided in Bank Street nearly three years. Mrs. B. recollects Lady Winifred Maxwell calling at the house: when at Ellisland, Burns dined once or twice at Terreglea House. Family lived in great style, and Mrs. B. recollects Burns talking with wonder of the number of wax candles he had seen lighted at supper. Lady Winifred presented him with a splendid snuff-box supposed to have been of Indian manufacture, inlaid with gold, tortoise-shell, &c., and ornamented with a portrait of Queen Mary from the original portrait. This box was at once valuable and highly valued. It was taken by William Burns to India, and broken just as he landed, to the infinite regret of all the family.

Had but rarely company home in the evening. Was much occupied composing his songs—most of which he wrote several times over. "Had plenty of excise paper, and scrawled away." Mrs. B. thinks he chiefly composed while riding and walking, and wrote from memory after he came in. Was not a good singer, but had a very correct ear. Could "step a tune" rudely on the fiddle, but was no player. Sometimes took this method of satisfying himself as to the modulations of a tune. Was very particular with his letters when of any consequence; and uniformly wrote a scroll before the principal. Went to bed generally at eleven o'clock, and sometimes a little sooner. When at Ellisland, went pretty often to Dunscore Church, and occasionally dined with his friend Captain Riddel of Friars-Carse. The Captain was a very pleasant man, and was married to an amiable lady. They had no family. In Dumfries he went to church frequently in the forenoon: went oftenest to Mr. Inglis's, the dissenting clergyman. The family had one seat there. Sometimes went to St. Michael's Church, which the widow attends regularly. Was often out at dinner at Mr. Syme's, at Goldielea,[‡] &c. Mr. Findlater, Mr. Lewars, and Mr. Richardson sometimes looked in on him at home. Gave them a glass of toddy; never took supper, and never drank by himself at home. The drink then was chiefly rum and gin; very little whisky was used.

Mrs. Burns describes Grose as one of the funniest, laughing, fat, good-natured men she ever saw. When he called he took a glass of rum and water; never dined, "for they were always gaun to Captain Riddel's to their dinner." Remembers Burns writing to her [Mrs. B.'s] father to draw some antiquities about the west country; but was not present when the bargain was made about Alloway Kirk.

[*] [Robert Southey, rather, resembled him.]

[+] [Whether by this remark his simple neighbour meant only that the Poet was surely not a married man, or "gudeman" of a house, having apparently too much time on hand; or not a good man, from the questionable way in which he spent it, does not distinctly appear. The same habit, we have already elsewhere referred to, as characteristic of him from his boyhood.]

[‡] [Afterwards called Woodley Park, when occupied by the Riddels; and again Goldielea, when parted with by them.]

Page 198. David M'Culloch's [of Ardwell's] information.

"The farmer, if Burns was seen passing, left his reapers, and trotted by the side of Jenny Geddes, until he could persuade the bard that the day was hot enough to demand an extra-libation. If he entered an inn at midnight, after all the inmates were in bed, the news of his arrival circulated from the cellar to the garret; and ere ten minutes had elapsed, the landlord and all his guests were assembled round the ingle; the largest punchbowl was produced; and

'Be ours this night—who knows what comes to-morrow?'

was the language of every eye in the circle that welcomed him. The stateliest gentry of the county, whenever they had especial merriment in view, called in the wit and eloquence of Burns to enliven their carousals. The famous song of The Whistle of worth commemorates a scene of this kind, more picturesque in some of its circumstances than every day occurred, yet strictly in character with the usual tenor of life among this jovial squirearchy. Three gentlemen of ancient descent had met to determine, by a solemn drinking match, who should possess the Whistle, which a common ancestor of them all had earned ages before, in a Bacchanalian contest of the same sort with a noble toper from Denmark; and the poet was summoned to watch over and celebrate the issue of the debate."

There is undoubtedly much exaggeration here. "Burns," his widow says, "always kept good hours and was seldom out after dark." When later, he was accompanied by Mr. Findlater, Supervisor.

Mrs. B. remembers the circumstances about the Whistle—that, as she heard them related—the Bard, tho' present at the contest, came home in his ordinary trim. Tho' he drank, perhaps, like some others, he was not required to keep pace with the champions. The song was composed soon after the drinking bout; and Captain Riddel frequently called to see how he was coming on with it.[§]

Page 199.

"Nor, as has already been hinted, was he safe from temptations of this kind, even when he was at home, and most disposed to enjoy in quiet the society of his wife and children. Lion-gazers from all quarters beset him; they eat and drank at his cost, and often went away to criticise him and his fare, as if they had done Burns and his black bowl great honour in condescending to be entertained for a single evening, with such company and such liquor."

Great exaggeration here. Many called and went away; none but intimates staid and were entertained. Mr. Findlater, when he returned with the Bard from a long ride, sometimes staid all night, and then the black bowl was filled before they went to bed.

THE PUNCH BOWL. The Black Bowl, about which so much has been said, was not strictly "a nuptial present." Mrs. B.'s father assisted in building the Duke of Argyle's House at Inverary; and it was then he hewed the bowl out of a piece of black marble. Burns took a fancy to it on one of his visits to Ayrshire, and it was then his father-in-law gave it to him. Mrs. B.'s grandfather was a builder too. He built Auchencruive [House], Lord Dumfries's House near Cumnock, and various other mansions.

[Page 204.] STORY ABOUT THE BROAD-SWORD.

"The summer after, some English travellers, calling at Ellisland, were told that the poet was walking by the river. They proceeded in search of him, and presently, 'on a rock that projected into the stream, they saw a man employed in

[§] [That is, with the finished copy. On this subject, once more before us, we may quote the following attestation by Mrs. Begg, obligingly communicated to us by her daughter:—"My grandmother was at Ellisland when the 'Whistle' was contended for. In his letter of 14th August, 1789, to his brother William, the Poet mentions his mother; in another, 10th November, same year, he says, 'my mother is returned, now that she has seen my boy, Francis Wallace, fairly set to the world.' Now my mother (Mrs. Begg) always said her mother said that Robert was at the dinner, and that he returned quite sober from the contest."— After such accumulated evidence on this point, it may reasonably be hoped we shall hear no more to Burns's disadvantage on the subject.]

angling, of a singular appearance. He had a cap made of a fox's skin on his head, a loose great-coat, fastened round him by a belt, from which depended an enormous Highland broadsword. [Was he still dreaming of the Bruce?] It was Burns. He received them with great cordiality, and asked them to share his humble dinner.' These travellers also closed the evening they spent at Ellisland with the brightest of their lives."

Mrs. B. rather distrusts this story. He had a cap of the kind described, and two swords—one of them an *Andrea Ferrara*: but she never saw him so foolish as to put the sword on. He was no fisher, and never, as she thinks, tried.

[Page 206.] THE DUNSCORE LIBRARY.

"He was so good," says Mr. Riddel, "as to take the whole management of this concern; he was treasurer, librarian, and censor, to our little society, who will long have a graceful sense of his public spirit, and exertions for their improvement and information."

The books were kept at Burns's house, where the lads came and received them from the Bard. He was, in a word, the librarian.

Page 207. BURNS'S COMPANIONS, CALEDONIAN CLUB, &c.

"Burns knew more of the matter personally than any of the others, and his words are these :—' In Dumfries his dissipation became still more deeply habitual. He was here exposed more than in the country, to be solicited to share the riot of the dissolute and the idle. Foolish young men, such as writers' apprentices, young surgeons, merchants' clerks, and his brother excisemen, flocked eagerly about him, and from time to time pressed him to drink with them, that they might enjoy his wicked wit. The Caledonian Club, too, and the Dumfries and Galloway Hunt, had occasional meetings in Dumfries after Burns came to reside there, and the poet was of course invited to share their hospitality, and hesitated not to accept the invitation.'"

There is much nonsense here. Dr. Mundel, Dr. Brown, and occasionally Dr. Coupland, were the only professional gentlemen who were in the habit of looking in on him. As to writers' apprentices, the Bard had no occasion to associate with persons so juvenile. Mr. Kerr, afterwards clerk to the Justices, and Provost of Dumfries, was a friend of Lowars, and with him Burns might meet at times. But he was always respectable, and a fit associate for any man.

Had a Highland plaid of the Robinson tartan, a dirk, and a splendid silk waistcoat, which he got from Gilbert Stewart. [*]

Mrs. Burns thinks the excise rebuke was a mild one; recollects of his writing to Mr. Graham of Fintry, and Mr. Erskine of Marr; the latter of whom wrote the Bard a very handsome letter in which [he] offered to do something for him in the event of his being dismissed.

HIS BEARING TO HIS CHILDREN. On this important subject the amiable and excellent Mr. Gray has done the Poet merely simple justice. At the time of his death, Robert was only ten, Francis seven, and William five, and James two. When at home in the evening, he heard them their lessons, and took pleasure in explaining everything that they had difficulty in comprehending. Was most strict in impressing on their minds the value and beauty and necessity of truth. He would have forgiven them easily any slight fault, but to have told a lie was in his eyes almost an inexpiable offence. The children felt their father's death keenly; and William, the second surviving son, was dreadfully affected every time he saw a funeral. So obvious was this, that his mother knew by his white face that he had seen some mournful procession, when he came in at meal time.

He had formed no fixed plans as to what he would breed his sons to; but the widow has often heard him say, that unless he saw his way clearly he would rather make them good mechanics, than injure the family by making one a scholar with little prospect of getting forward. He used to read the Bible to William, Francis, and Robert: and William was in the habit of remarking after his death, "Mother, I cannot see those sublime things in the Bible that my father used to see!"[†]

"The Lassie wi' the lint-white locks." Her name was Jane Lorimer. She was the daughter of Wm. Lorimer, farmer at Kemishall; and in good circumstances. He had two daughters and three sons. His wife was given to drinking, and that injured her daughters. Jean used to visit at Ellisland: she had remarkably fair hair; and was perfectly virtuous. The song was written on her. She took the fancy of an Englishman at a Moffat Ball, and was married at Gretna Green. The man was a reprobate; but his mother allowed her an annuity. It is generally believed that Cunningham has borne too hard on this poor woman.

"Had we never met sae kindly."

The Nancy of the moving strain was no frail dame of Dumfriesshire. Mrs. B. thinks it was no one but Clarinda.[‡]

Burns thought himself dying before he went to the Brow. He seemed afraid however of dwelling on the subject, considering Mrs. B.'s situation. On one occasion he said distinctly "Don't be afraid: I'll be more respected a hundred years after I am dead than I am at present." He was not above a week at the Brow when he returned. Mrs. Burns was so struck with the change in his appearance, that she became almost speechless. From this period he was closely confined to bed, and was scarcely '*himself*' for half an hour together. By this, it is meant that his mind wandered, and that his nervous system was completely unhinged. He was aware of this infirmity himself, and told his wife that she was to touch him, and remind him that he was going wrong. The day before he died, he called very quickly and with a hale voice, "Gilbert, Gilbert!" Three days before he died, he got out of the bed, and his wife found him sitting in a corner of the room with the bed clothes about him. Mrs. B. got assistance, and he suffered himself to be gently led back to bed. But for the fit, his strength would have been unequal to such an exertion.

Dr. Maxwell was indefatigable in his attention; visited his patient frequently in the course of the day,[§] and was frequently in the house by six o'clock in the morning. The same attention he maintained to the family.

[Burns] read the big Bible frequently, and said once to his wife, "If the rest of them know that I was so religious, they would laugh at me"—meaning Syme, and Maxwell.

Soon after her husband's death, Mrs. Burns had a very remarkable dream. Her bedroom had been removed to the family parlour, when she imagined that her husband drew the

---

[*] [As a sort of costume, it may be presumed, for the Caledonian Club, &c.]

[†] [True and beautiful, as a fact—and older, as a theory, than Thomas Carlyle: "Blessed are your eyes, for they see!"]

[‡] [True. The simplicity of this conjecture is exquisite.]

[§] [That is, of any one day—every day.]

curtains and said " Are you asleep? I have been permitted to return and take one look of you and that child; but I have not time to stay." The dream was so vivid that Mrs. B[urns] started up, and even to this moment the scene seems to her a reality.[*]

[NOTES BY MRS. BURNS.]

" Three lawyers' tongues turned inside out
With lies seamed like a beggar's clout;
Three priests' hearts rotten, black as muck,
Lay stinking vile in every neuk "—

Somebody objected to this, but Burns would not alter it at the time; although it has been altered since.

He was fond of his ballad " The Soldier's Return "—the first verse stood originally thus—[see Text—Poetical Works, p. 202]. Mr. Thomson altered this, and, as I think, spoiled it. Would scarcely ever submit to Thomson's alterations.

Burns was remarkably fond of the air of the " Chevalier's Lament," " The Sutor's Daughter," " Coolen " (an Irish air), &c., &c.
Mrs. Burns can repeat a great many of the songs, and seems no bad judge of poetry.

The first time ever Mrs. B. saw the Bard was in Mauchline. His family then lived in Mossgiel, about a mile from the village. Mrs. B., then about seventeen, was spreading clothes in a bleach-green along with some other girls, when Burns passed in his way to call on Mr. Hamilton. He had a little dog which ran on the clothes. Mrs. B. scolded, and threw something at the animal. Burns said, " Lassie, if ye thought ocht o' me, ye wadna hurt my dog." Mrs. B. thought to herself " I wadna think much o' you at ony rate."—Saw him afterwards at a dancing room, and got acquainted.

[This, being from Mrs. Burns's own mouth, supersedes all other accounts of the incident.]

He never spoke English, but spoke very correct Scotch. The word " patent "—tell the story anent this.

[What story this was, we have no means at present of ascertaining.]

Burns admired Wilson's " Watty and Meg " greatly. On one occasion, Andrew Bishop, a well known ballad-crier, was going along crying " ' Watty and Meg,' &c., by Burns." The Bard was writing at his desk and exclaimed, " O Andrew, that's a d——d lie! but I would have been very proud to have acknowledged it."——

END OF MRS. BURNS'S MEMORANDA.

---

[*] [The man who can read this record without interest, or the concluding passages without the profoundest sympathy or reverence, is surely not to be envied in his moral nature or congratulated on his faith. The only parallel to it in sorrow we know, although essentially different from it in some important respects, is the death-bed scene of Lord Byron: which we epitomise, with a few extracts from Moore's Life of his Lordship, that our readers may compare the two.]

LORD BYRON'S DEATH-BED.

[At thirty-three, it appears, he began to have " an old face "—rheumatic fever, somewhat similar to Burns's, aggravated by exposure to cold and wet, followed:
Bleeding recommended, to which his Lordship at first would not submit for various strong reasons of repugnance—among others, a vow he had made to his mother never to allow it:
Finally, on being told that his *reason* was in danger, he acquiesced]—

" He cast at us both the fiercest glance of vexation, and throwing out his arm, said in the angriest tone, ' There—you are, I see, a d——d set of butchers—take away as much blood as you like, but have done with it !' We seized the moment (adds Mr. Milligan) and drew about twenty ounces." —*Moore*, vol. II., 766.

⁂

" In addition to the bleeding, which was repeated twice on the 17th (April, 1824), it was thought right also to apply blisters to the soles of his feet. ' When on the point of putting them on' (says Mr. Milligan), ' Lord Byron asked me whether it would answer the purpose to apply both on the same leg. Guessing immediately the motive that led him to ask this question, I told him that I would place them above the knees.' ' Do so,' he replied."

" It is painful to dwell on such details, but we are now approaching the close. In addition to most of those sad varieties of wretchedness which surround alike the grandest and humblest death-beds, there was also in the scene now passing around the dying Byron, such a degree of confusion and uncomfort as renders it doubly dreary to contemplate. —*Moore*, vol. II., 767.

⁂

" ' In all the attendants,' says Parry, ' there was the officiousness of zeal: but owing to their ignorance of each other's language, their zeal only added to the confusion. This circumstance and the want of common necessaries, made Lord Byron's apartment such a picture of distress and even anguish during the two or three last days of his life, as I never before beheld, and wish never again to witness."

[After rallying for a short interval, his strength again gave way, and after an affecting interview with his friends and attendants]—

" Almost immediately afterwards, a fit of delirium ensued; and he began to talk wildly, as if he were mounting a breach in an assault—calling out half in English, half in Italian— ' Forwards, forwards, courage, follow my example,' " &c., &c.—*Moore*, vol. II., 769.

⁂

" ' When he took my hand,' says Parry, ' I found his hands were deadly cold. With the assistance of Tita,[*] I endeavoured gently to create a little warmth in them; and also loosened the bandage which was tied round his head. Till this was done, he seemed in great pain, clenched his hands at times, gnashed his teeth, and uttered the Italian exclamation of ' *Ah Christi !*' He bore the loosening of the band passively,

---

[*] [Gondolier, who had followed him from Venice.]

and after it was loosened, shed tears; then taking my hand again, uttered a faint good night, and sunk into a slumber."

In about half an hour he again awoke, when a second dose of the strong infusion was administered to him. * * *

It was about six o'clock on the evening of this day, when he said 'Now I shall go to sleep;' and then turning round fell into that slumber from which he never awoke. For the next twenty-four hours he lay incapable of either sense or motion, with the exception of, now and then, slight symptoms of suffocation, during which his servant raised his head; and at a quarter-past six o'clock on the following day, the 19th, he was seen to open his eyes and immediately shut them again. The physicians felt his pulse—he was no more!—*Moore*, vol. II., 770, 771.

Among his last words were 'Augusta,' 'Ada,' 'Lady Byron'—'Poor Greece,' &c.—

He was universally mourned—the festivities of Easter were interrupted—and all amusements came to an end; by a public proclamation.

All public offices, even the tribunals are to remain closed for three successive days.

A general mourning will be observed for twenty one days.

Prayers and a funeral service are to be offered up in all the churches.—*Moore*, vol. II., 772.

Account with David Kelly.

[COMPARE WITH FOREGOING MEMORANDA.]

"THERE was handed to us this week a fragment of an account in the handwriting of Robert Burns, with an autograph letter sent to the poet by his brother Gilbert. Both manuscripts have for some time been in the possession of a London gentleman who has for many years been a diligent collector of everything that is curious and rare in literature. Any one who has seen a fac-simile of the Poet's handwriting will be satisfied at a glance that the fragment (would that it had been less prosaic!) was written by him. Here it is—matter-of-fact enough :—

D. KELLY DR. TO R. BURNS.

house and yard, . .	£1 3 0
2 cows—a year's pasture,	4 0 0

On the back of the slip there is part of what seems to be a *per contra* account. It is as follows :—

By Sandy's acct. of all the corn I bought from D. Kelly —it measures 780 bushels.

	Bush.
Milled, . .	283
To Mill, .	050

How the remaining 447 bushels were disposed of must remain a mystery until the lost half of the account is discovered; and

we must also wait till then before we can tell when the transaction took place, and how such an extensive corn merchant, as D. Kelly appears to have been, came to live in a house which was rented at so low a figure."—*Elgin Courier.*

[By comparing these curious fragments with the foregoing Memoranda by Mrs. Burns, our respected friend the Editor of *Elgin Courier* will find the mystery of D. Kelly's relationship as a grain dealer with Robert Burns easily solved. Burns, on succeeding to the farm, had simply purchased the last year's crop in stack or barn from, and sublet some cottage with cow's grass to, the outgoing tenant; or rather, received from the tenant so much in usage of rent for temporary accommodation at Ellisland itself. The story of the 'Bitches,' too, as our readers will remember, and 'the parties who kept a cow,' is now all clear: but the 'Bitches' are not changed in the account; the 'prayer' would be, *per contra*, enough for them. O Nance, Nance!]

(Gilbert's letter will be found in Domestic Correspondence.)

Reminiscences

ORIGINAL AND AUTHENTIC:

COLLECTED AND ARRANGED BY THE EDITOR.

PART I.

IN ILLUSTRATION OF BIOGRAPHY.

1.—BIOGRAPHY, p. xv. The entire contents of this page may be included under this reference, and illustrated by the following Memoranda taken from the lips of witnesses lately or still alive, by the Editor.

NANSE TANNOCK'S HOWF, at MAUCHLINE: 1784-6.

MRS. NELLY MARTIN or MILLER, who died December 22, 1858, aged 92, and was originally sweetheart to the Poet's brother William, was intimately acquainted also with the Poet himself, and confirmed in the most earnest and emphatic manner, as if living over again in his society the scenes of her youth, the rumours of the extraordinary gift of eloquence with which he was even then endowed. According to her account, to escape from his tongue, if once entangled by it, was almost an impossibility. "He was unco, by-ordinar ongangin in his talk." For which reason, he was an invaluable visitor at the change-house, where Nanse Tannock had a jesuitical device of her own for detaining him. Nanse carried a huge leather pouch at her side, slung from her waist (as old Scotch landladies used to do) filled with keys, pence, 'change,' and et ceteras. When application for Burns was made at her door—as was often the case, "for atweel he was uncolie in demand "—by personal friends of his, or rivals of her own—"Is Rab here?" or "Is Mossgiel here?" —Nanse would thrust her hand into the capacious leather pouch, and, jingling ostentatiously among keys and coppers, would solemnly and fraudulently declare "that he was na *there* (in her pouch) that night!"—"Rab," in reality, being most probably engaged at the very moment in rehearsing his last poetical effusion, "The Holy Fair," or "The Twa Herds," to an ecstatic audience in the parlour.

It was convenient for Nanse, as a discreet hostess, to say afterwards, when questioned about Burns's occasional visits to her spence, more particularly in reference to the "nine times a week" specified by himself in his "Earnest Cry and Prayer"—"that he might be a vera clever lad, but he certainly was *regardless*, as, to the best of her belief, he had never taken three half-mutchkins in her house in all his life." [*] He might not indeed be half as often as he 'regardlessly' himself alleged; but facts, we are afraid, are very decidedly against Nanse's allegation. It was in her own parlour, in fact, the first reading of "The Holy Fair" took place; when there were present Robert and his sweetheart, Jean Armour; William and his sweetheart, Nelly Miller; and "anither lad or twa and thar sweethearts. Robin himsel was in unco glee. He kneelit until a chair in the midds o' the room, wi' his elbows on the bak o't, and read owre the 'Holy Fair' frae a paper i' his han'—and sic laughin! we could hardly steer for laughin; an' I never saw himsel in sic glee." It must be observed, however, that both the quantity and the quality of 'refreshment' on this, as on similar occasions, were very moderate indeed—"three ha'penny yill—twa or three bottles for the company" being the average reckoning; with a glass or two of whisky at most.

His personal appearance then, as described by this eye-witness, was striking, and must have been attractive in no common degree; and his habits simple, gentle, gravely studious. "In a licht blew-coat o' his mither's makin and dyeing; ay, and o' his mither's sewin, I'se warrand, in thae days; and his bonie black hair hingin down, and curlin ower the neck o't; a buik in his han'—aye a buik in his han'—an' whiles his bannet aneath his tither ockster, and didna ken that he was barehended—gaun about the dyke-sides and hedges; an idler, ye ken—an idler just, that did little but read; and even on the hairst-rig, it was soup and soup and then the buik—soup and soup and then the buik! He was na to ca' a bonie man: dark and strong; but uncommon invitin in his speech—uncommon! Ye could na hae cracket wi' him for ae minute, but ye wad hae studen four or five!"—Behold, then, the rural Apollo, in coat of his mother's spinning and sewing, by day upon the hairst-rig, book in hand; by night among ecstatic admirers, transported they knew not how, dispensing his inspiration (thereafter destined for the world) from the humble chair-back orchestra of a village change-house floor!

"You and Willie then, it seems, didna mak it out?"—"No—Our sweetheartin some way fell through. He gaed awa some gate to the West Indies,—or doo'd; an' I was married on anither man."—William, as our readers are aware, did not accomplish such purpose of going abroad, if he ever seriously entertained it; but died, still a young man, at London.

Miss Brown, Mauchline, states that her father well remembered Robert Burns, and has seen him frequently at Nanse Tannock's after his marriage, carrying his eldest son

aloft on his hand, balancing and tossing the child, in paternal pride, towards the kitchen ceiling!—Very beautiful, indeed, is this homely picture; and Jean herself, undoubtedly, would be there.

2.—BIOGRAPHY, *p.* xviii. LOVE DISCUSSIONS, AMOROUS MADNESS, LIFE AT TARBOLTON—still pure: 1780-2.

(1.) MR. ANDREW HARVEY of Park Mill, a very shrewd intelligent man, relates many anecdotes of Burns, received from his (Mr. H.'s) father—one of these highly characteristic and beautiful. Mr. Harvey's father, then a youth, was a teacher of elementary branches, and also in those days professor of music, in the neighbourhood. Burns attended his music-class held at Lochlea, and was on intimate terms with Harvey. He was much addicted to discussions with his friend on all topics of interest, most frequently on that of love. In some light-hearted talk of this kind one afternoon, on their way to Mauchline, the question turned on the privileges of love-making in general: whether it were better to have a *number* of sweethearts "in hand," or only one at a time? "Mr. Burns, wha thocht nae man could kepp him in an argument," maintained the propriety or advantage of *indiscriminate* courtship, "But my faither keppit him wi' this—'If a flock o' bonie doos gaed by ye wi' a fluff, and ye played skelp amang them a' at ance, ye might wing and hurt half a dizzen o' them, and no kill ane.'" Burns was thoughtfully, affectionately silent on this: "he was keppit there;" and only a good and true nature after all would have been "keppit" with the force of such an argument. This, we may presume, was not a bad specimen of the sort of discussions that were carried on in the Bachelor's Club at Tarbolton.

Notwithstanding the passion which was then beginning to display itself—the "amorous madness," as he calls it, his life was still pure, and his affections uncontaminated; but his situation was not safe. The visit to Irvine, and the friendships he contracted there, proved injurious also. Shortly after his return home to Lochlea again, the first mistake, with bitter consequences, followed. The circumstances attending the birth of "black-eyed Bess" about this time have been distinctly verified to us—and by no means creditably to the mother; but "The bairn was like, oh, unco like the father—wi' wonderfu', big, bonie black een. He could never deny that wean!" He was very far, in fact, from attempting any such denial; but made the most affectionate legal provision for the child's support, in case of his own departure to the West Indies, as our readers are already aware.

(2.) MARKET-DAYS at AYR: 1785-6.
GILBERT BAIRD, Girvan, died *circa* 1861, aged 95; remembered distinctly seeing Burns on market-days at Ayr in his master's house, who was "cousin's-husband to Burns" —that is, cousin by marriage. Gilbert Baird was apprenticed to this man as a dyer, and had charge of the business when he was out—which was regularly every market-day after dinner, when Burns was there. He, the master, "went out with

------

* Mr. Chambers's Notes on Ayrshire.

Burns, and they whiles stoppet gey lang—it was the gloamin or they cam hame." G. Baird was then sixteen years of age: described Burns as a stoutish, lout-shouthered, good-looking, swarthy man; with large head and pock-marked face: being interrogated on the point, asserted this distinctly. His conversation most interesting and fascinating; "aye drew the master awa out." His age at that time seemed to be about twenty-five or twenty-six (that was, about the era of publication); and his dress, when thus visiting Ayr, was knee-breeches of corduroy, broad-tailed loose coat, with broad "penny buttons;" himself looked-on with suspicion by young people, as having been denounced by the clergy.

[For further information concerning Burns's personal appearance, pock-marks, &c., see Reminiscences, Part II.]

3.—BIOGRAPHY, p. xviii. GIFT OF ELOQUENCE AND STORY-TELLING: 1777-82.

(1.) MR. WILLIAM REID, of Burn, Stair, son of John Reid and Jean Ronald of Bennals, was born at Langlands, west of Tarbolton. His father was an intimate friend of Burns, and a constant companion of his on all opportunities. Rankine of Adam-hill was the senior of both, and often took young Reid along with him to carousals, but never allowed him to drink. [Mr. John Reid's name does not occur in the list of those who are mentioned as members of the Bachelors' Club, but from internal evidence following, he seems to have been one—perhaps a junior member.]

Mr. William Reid has heard innumerable anecdotes of Burns from his father, of which he has privileged us with the following—among others which will be found as we proceed.

Burns's powers of story-telling, even at that early period, were known to be superlative. Mr. Reid's father believed (as many other more accomplished judges also did) that his written works, wonderful as they are, were in reality nothing as compared with his speech and story-telling. On the nights on which it was known he was to be at the smithy, the whole "sukken" (neighbourhood thirled, or bound to support the smith) turned out and attended: and Mr. Reid used to declare that he had frequently seen not only the whole work of the evening stopped, but listeners in half dozens absolutely rolling on the floor in ecstasies of laughter—Burns himself, elevated on the forge, enchanting the company with some incredible fiction. He had also repeatedly seen a whole field of shearers—some twenty or thirty in number—"at a thrang o' wark," where Burns was obligingly *assisting*, interrupted and brought to a final unanimous pause for half an hour together, listening to his rhetoric; until the loss of time insensibly became so great, that his *assistance* was the most serious, although the most delightful, retardation of the whole business of the day.

On one of these occasions, in particular, when some ready-witted Irishman encountered him, the display of humour on both sides became so exciting, that the entire field of labourers was congregated to listen, many of them rolling on the shorn ridge in convulsions of merriment. In short, the work, for a considerable portion of the day, ceased.

In the same sort of way, when assisting in the mill at "hand-sifting" of the meal in trough, all hands got so absorbed in listening, that no sifting could proceed; in consequence of which the machinery in producing overtook the folks in removing, and a general block-up took place.

(2.) ROBERT GOWDIE, Esq., Ayr, during his apprenticeship at Mr. Hamilton's (son of Gavin's), writer, Mauchline, received from eye and ear-witnesses many interesting details of Burns's habits and history when at Mossgiel. His gift of extemporaneous eloquence, and fictitious narrative in particular, both humorous and pathetic, was at that time incredibly profuse; in so much, that his own friends esteemed his poetic only his *second* gift—an estimate which has been often since confirmed. He was in the habit, where people assembled together—as on the harvest field, at the smithy, or in the change-house—to select one sympathetic hearer, whose whole affections were very soon enlisted and absorbed; and from whom the infection of love, wonder, or pity, insensibly spread over the whole company, till the house was filled with roars of laughter or melted absolutely into tears.

His stories, on such occasions, were purely works of fiction, and extemporaneous efforts of imagination. The smithy was a frequent scene of such triumphs. Burns took his own plough irons to be repaired: and during this process the story-telling began. On one remarkable occasion, when a piece of iron was being welded, the man who plied the sledge hammer was so fascinated with the narrative, that he "stood with his hammer thus" above his head immovable till the iron had cooled, and the process was effectually interrupted. "Rab, Rab," cried the smith, himself as much absorbed as anybody else—"This 'ill never do: you and me maun gang for a drap yill, or deil ae steek o' graithen 'ill be mended this night!" The smith's name was Meiklo, and the accuracy of this statement is indubitable.

The above quotations from Mr. Reid refer principally, we presume, from his own date and residence about Tarbolton, to the era of the Poet's life at Lochlea. At that time, he would be from 19 to 24 years of age. Mr. Gowdie's recollections from Mauchline bring us a year or two further down. We have heard in fables—of Orpheus, with a lyre in addition to his voice, leading stocks and stones, as well as men, in captivity to his music; but to hear of a lad, within the memory of the last generation, interrupting hammers, sheathing sickles, and stopping the very machinery of mills, by the eloquence of his tongue alone—is finer than fable. Mercury fascinating Ceres, cajoling Vulcan, and beguiling Sisyphus in his endless toil, is scarcely up to it: but we have additional testimony to corroborate the fact, as an every-day occurrence, years afterwards, and in the highest circles of life.

4.—BIOGRAPHY, p. xviii. CONTROVERSIAL GIFTS: &c.

MR. WILLIAM REID of Burn, already quoted, states that in his father's opinion, Burns's powers of speech in debate, although good, were inferior to Gilbert's; who, in Mr. Reid's distinct recollection, was unquestionably the best speaker in their Young Men's Society—[or Bachelors' Club]—a great theoriser also, but a poor practical farmer. There was one scene of public display, however, in which Robert often attracted great notice, and acquired acknowledged repute.—This was in Sabbath-day discussions on divinity, during the interval of public worship. On such occasions, he would take his place on some grave-stone in the corner of the church-yard, and there, first by conversation, in which he so conspicuously excelled, and finally by direct discourse, attract an astonished congregation. In such harangues, the doctrines or lives of the clergy were the natural constant themes; and although his satires and criticisms were perhaps severe enough, no good or consistent man had ever anything to fear from his observations.

About this there can be no doubt; and the spirit of manly frankness in him, which showed itself in respectful silence, when he was fairly "keppit" by an honest antagonist, as we have already seen in Harvey's case, affords sufficient proof that, although discourse had natural fascinations for him, it was a much higher aim than the mere love of victory or display that predisposed him so often to these rural Socratic exercises. He seems indeed to have had a very strong natural tendency in youth to religious and even doctrinal controversy, and to have been more than usually eloquent in acts of family devotion, over which, after his father's death, he presided as a priest in the household. Very wonderful outpourings, unquestionably, those early prayers of his would be. Nor was it to mere formal acts of devotion, or of public controversy on such subjects, this gift of eloquence was confined. On the contrary, it took the highest practical and purest philanthropic Christian form—that of indirect, imperceptible, efficacious advocacy of the rights or interests of the poor; as the following testimony shows.

5.—BIOGRAPHY, p. xix. ELOQUENCE AND CHARITY:—1783—et seq.

EVERYWHERE throughout his writings the innate humanity of his constitution shows itself—not only in his concern for mice and birds in the waste inclemency of winter, which by some may be said to be partly a mere poetic sentiment, however touching; but in the truest heartfelt sympathy for the children of affliction among his fellow men. This too, indeed, might be represented by detractors as more sentimental than real, if we had not the clearest proof of its active reality. His own resources in wealth were never, by a hundredth part, equal to his desire of doing good and relieving distress, as we know by innumerable complaints in his letters; and in the comparative poverty of Lochlea and Mossgiel, funds for anything like the charity he would have dispensed were out of the question. But his benevolence was not to be baulked by that. What his purse *could* not, his tongue was bound to do; and that in such a position as the most suspicious "world's worm" should not be aware of it. Cases of distress being ascertained, he ascertained also the proper quarters from which relief should naturally come to

each, and these he made available at once by the magic of conversation alone; not directly, or even by implication, as if he were the advocate of poverty at the door of prosperous relationship, but by the mere force of casual, and apparently unconscious, representation to those who were bound by nature to sympathise with the sufferers, and enabled by providence to supply their wants.

ROBERT GOWDIE, Esq., whose name has already been quoted, states, on the authority of those who were personally acquainted with the fact, that "he exerted his gift of sympathetic eloquence in this manner so effectually to relieve the necessities of the poor, that in numberless cases supplies of food and clothing were regularly sent to them from prosperous relatives in consequence of Burns's indirect but resistless appeals, through *description alone*—the recipients of such charity being quite unconscious of their true benefactor's efforts to relieve them, and the donors themselves unaware that he knew anything of their relationship!"

This beautiful and Christlike way of going about doing good was habitual to him, and continued in operation to the end of his life—witness his letter to Ferguson of Craigdarroch [Prose Works, p. 190] on poor Robie Gordon's behalf; and the numerous instances recorded by Chambers and others, in which he saved helpless transgressors from judicial vengeance by not *allowing* them to transgress, or *punished* them for actual transgression by counting back two-thirds of their forfeit, with a solemn face, into their own pockets! God bless his memory!

6.—BIOGRAPHY, p. xix. ATTENDANCE AT DIVINE WORSHIP: Tarbolton, 1777—86: et seq.

ON this subject various authorities might be produced. We content ourselves with the following, which we have reason to believe has never hitherto been quoted.

MRS. "GRANNY" HAY, aged 94 in 1866, was a servant girl at "Willie's Mill" at the age of 14 to 15* Her sister also followed her in the same place and situation. She remembers Burns distinctly as a tall, swarthy, and at that time rather spare young man, with long black hair on his shoulders [compare Nelly Martin, or Miller's statement], accustomed to ride to Tarbolton from Lochlea or Mossgiel, on Freemason Lodge nights, or other special occasions. He rode booted: he used to stable his horse at the mill: was remarkably kind, pleasant and affable; and "straiket her head wi' his han'" on the last occasion when she was there." Her mistress, Mrs. Muir, was a shrewd superior woman; could read, write, and cipher easily; and was fit to maintain discourse with Burns on all ordinary topics, even on poems occasionally rehearsed by him at the tea-table at the mill: "aye took his tea, when he cam about four-hours,"†

---

* As Mrs. Hay's recollections include distinctly what occurred at Lochlea as well as at Mossgiel, she must either have been a little younger than she supposes when at Willie's Mill, or she must have heard part of what she relates from her mistress—or both.

† Mrs. Muir, it appears, was also considerably initiated in Masonic lore; a knowledge of which she turned adroitly to account on occasion of a misadventure which occurred to her on horseback, when riding alone through a country road to Irvine.

He [Burns] "was a great frequenter o' kirks and preachings, baith at Tarbolton and round about:" on which occasions he was often, almost invariably, accompanied by the "Miller himsel" [Mr. Muir] who had a taste for pulpit-oratory, and was "an unco judge o' doctrine." "Burns would speir in for him as he gaed, and the twa gaed thegither." On one special occasion, Granny Hay remembers well that Burns complained to the mistress of not being able to finish some song that had occurred to him on a Sabbath morning; in consequence of which he was afraid he could not attend church that day—"it would na be right: he could na hearken when he was fashed." In despair, he rambled out by some dykeside, where he strolled alone "till he got the sang a' right;" when he repaired to church as usual with the cheerfulness of relief and of a good conscience. This difficulty and deliverance, it appears, he related in Mrs. Hay's hearing with the simplicity of a boy, "that verra mornin at the mill, afore they gaed up to the kirk!" One would give much to know what very song that was. His conversation then and always was cheerful, entertaining, and correctly pure. Our readers will hear more of Mrs. Muir in our Gossip hereafter; in the meantime, on this subject of our Author's attendance at religious worship, they may refer also to note on the "Holy Fair"—Poetical Works, p. 99.

7.—BIOGRAPHY, p. xxxv. FAMILY BIBLE: Ellisland, 1788—89.

BURNS's intimate acquaintance with the Holy Scriptures, both in their historical and doctrinal contents, must be obvious to every reader of his works. Readers also must be aware, from frequent references in the Poet's correspondence—more especially in letters to Miss Chalmers (4), and to P. Hill (1)—that he was not only a great reader of the Bible from direct appreciation of its beauty as "a glorious book," but that he had also a great fancy to possess the best and handsomest copy of it. The copy to be provided for him at his own request by Mr. Hill, seems to have been a large folio edition, with notes by John Guise, D.D.; at least such is the editor's imprint on the title-page of the copy he made his family Bible, and from which the Register, already presented to our readers, was photographed. But before this Bible could have been received, as it came out in numbers, he must have had at least one other large copy (quarto) of the Bible in his temporary lodgings at the Isle, and which was probably the very copy borne before him, with a basin of salt upon it, by Betty Smith, in solemn procession to the new house at Ellisland [Chambers, vol. III., 51]. Our readers may remember also the amusing characteristic conversation between our Author and old Mrs. Kelly in the spence at Ellisland—or rather, as we presume, at the Isle—as narrated by Mrs. Burns in her Memoranda [p. xxi]; in which the Poet's knowledge of the Bible was so unexpectedly displayed to his hostess, and so favourable an impression produced by it on her mind. This curious incident seems to have been followed up on our Author's part by a

more decided act of propitiation, in presenting a copy of the Bible itself—the quarto copy above referred to, and possibly the same copy which did duty in the procession at entering the new house—as a peace-offering to Mr. Kelly, the outgoing tenant of the farm. The Bible, which originally bore an inscription on it to the above effect, after passing through the hands of several of his descendants, came at last into the possession of Dr. Grierson of Thornhill; by whom all that remains of the volume, now considerably decayed, has been placed in our own hands. "Oh, David Cullie, hoo they hae wranged that man!"

8.—BIOGRAPHY, p. xlv. BURNS AS AN EXCISE OFFICER:

(1.) WE have already adduced so many proofs from his own letters—to Graham, to Edgar, to Findlater, to Staig and others—not only of the carefulness and assiduity, but the thoughtfulness for public benefit, with which our Author discharged his laborious and often painful functions as a public servant; and have in the same manner, and from the same sources, given so many clear proofs of his diligence and honour in that capacity when challenged by superiors for seeming neglect, that farther evidence on the subject seems to be superfluous. It is true, as Mr. Chambers shows, by a quotation from Findlater's *Diary*, that two slight instances of apparent neglect in some trifling affair, of a small cleansing of ale or the like, were noted, and that "Mr. Burns was admonished" in consequence: but we do not hear, on the other side, of the explanations of apparent neglect which Mr. Burns might have had to offer. One such explanation has fortunately come to hand in the following extraordinary letter, read and published for the first time at Dumfries, on occasion of the 110th anniversary of the Poet's birth, by the Secretary of the Burns' Club there.

To Mr. Findlater.

DEAR SIR,

I AM both much surprised and vexed at that accident of Lorimer's stock. The last survey I made prior to Mr. Lorimer's going to Edinr., I was very particular in my inspection, and the quantity was certainly in his possession as I stated it. The surveys I made during his absence might as well have been marked "key absent," as I never found any body but the lady, who I know is not mistress of keys, &c., to know anything of it, and one of the times it would have rejoiced all Holl to have seen her so drunk. I have not surveyed there since his return. I know the gentleman's ways are, like the grace of G——, past all comprehension; but I shall give the house a severe scrutiny to-morrow morning, and send you in the naked facts. I know, Sir, and regret deeply, that this business glances with a malign aspect on my character as an Officer; but as I am really innocent in the affair, and as the gentleman is known to be an illicit Dealer, and particularly as this is the *single* instance of the least shadow of carelessness or impropriety in my conduct as an Officer, I shall be peculiarly unfortunate if my character shall fall a sacrifice to the dark manœuvres of a smuggler.—I am, Sir, your obliged and obedient humble servt.,

ROBT. BURNS.

Sunday even :

I send you some rhymes I have just finished, which tickle my fancy a little.

The above letter, remarkable in many ways as evidence at once of integrity and of charity on the writer's part, is not less remarkable for the insight which it affords into the state of social life at that date among persons of external respectability. Mrs. Burns, in her Memoranda, states that Mrs. Lorimer was given to drink, which injured her daughter's prospects. How charitably true does that statement appear after the above dreadful revelation !

On the other hand again, what beautiful proofs are extant of the generosity of the man, where selfish austerity in the officer, without much advantage to the public, might have been justified or extolled to his own advantage by the law. These, as they still float in the district and are reverently and affectionately handed down to posterity, are too numerous to be here recited. They have been variously chronicled by various biographers; and the reader will find affecting specimens enough in Lockhart, Cunningham, and Chambers. Of these, one alone, exemplifying many, must suffice for us here to quote for the reader's satisfaction.

"Mr. Maxwell of Terraughty," says Cunningham, in his information to Lockhart, "an old, austere, sarcastic gentleman, who cared nothing about poetry, used to say, when the Excise-books of the district were produced at the meetings of the Justices, 'Bring me Burns's Journal: it always does me good to see it, for it shows that an honest officer may carry a kind heart about with him.'" What a volume do these brief words contain of attestation at once to fidelity and kindness.

But of official integrity, the best voucher to be found is from the hand of an impartial witness in our own generation; and this, although not strictly of our own, has been obligingly communicated to us by an esteemed literary friend, the REV. WM. HOWIE WYLIE, to whom the fact is known, for insertion under our present reference :—

"HOW TO GET AT THE CHARACTER OF BURNS.—We have been told that an official gentleman in London, one of the chief officers of the Excise, recently went over all the papers in the office which bore the signature of Robert Burns. He is a gentleman of eminent piety, and when he set about the investigation, he had a prejudice against our national bard. When he closed his examination of the papers, his unfavourable estimate had undergone quite a revolution. The papers demonstrated that Burns was a conscientious servant and a first-rate business man. If you go carefully through the best biographers of Burns, and sum up his money transactions, you will be amazed at the demonstration which they supply of the Poet's noble independence, prudence, and generosity. Many who shake their foolish heads when Burns is spoken of, would not come out so clean if a similar test were applied to themselves."—*Greenock Telegraph.*

We entirely agree with our esteemed friend, and with this honest-hearted public official, whoever he might be, that all reports, surmises, insinuations, and suspicions, and even the worst prejudices included, notwithstanding—the test of impartial documents is paramount, and overrules all. No honest mind can resist it; no honourable man will question it; and how much the force of this testimony is increased, how overwhelmingly clear it becomes, when it may be shown to demonstration that the very prejudices and suspicions of the moment which opposed it were the result of the sheerest envy, or of the most contemptible political spleen: Nay, that the very rebukes themselves administered were a mystery, which their own authors were ashamed to publish, and their official descendants since have been ashamed to reveal. "That they were not severe," is Mr. Findlater's opinion, in which Mrs. Burns herself coincides. How could they be severe? one may now reasonably ask, being directed by political fear alone against a man who was the living wonder of his country, and who had offended even the most selfish authority in nothing but in magnanimity, courage, and truth !—

(2.) EXCISE REBUKE.—On this subject, however, and from one of the very documents most probably above referred to, now in possession of MOSES PROVAN, Esq., of Auchengillan, Stirlingshire, and of West George Street, Glasgow, we are fortunately enabled, by that gentleman's courteous assistance, to present our readers with the following additional information.

From A. FINDLATER'S ROUND DIARY, including 10th June and 21st July, 1792, in Mr. Provan's possession, we make the following important memoranda :—

LIST OF OFFICERS IN ROUND.

Robt. Burns—age 32; fam. 6; yrs. emp. 3; in pret. charge, 1; from Dfrs. 3d to 1st; surs. in this Rd., 5.
Jno. M'Quaker.
Geo. Gray.
John Grant.
John Lewars.
John Brown.
Wm. Penn.
Peter Warwick.
Jno. Gillespie, supernumerary.
Jno. M'Culloch, expectant.
Wm. Rowand.
Jas. Graham, supernumerary.
Alex. Findlater, Supervisor.
John Mitchell, Collector.

In the above Round we find Mr. Burns admonished—noted on margin thus—"Admonish: J. T. Done: J. C." The circumstances seem to be very trivial, and are thus commented on by the Supervisor: * * * * * "An increase of stock wanting permit on the first, of seven gallons; and on the second, of six gallons foreign red wine not seized—probably a miscalculation of this large stock, &c., &c., with some trivial inadvertencies which I marked with my initials. Mr. Burns

has but lately taken charge of this division, and from that cause, and inexperience in the brewery branch of the business, has fallen into these errors, but promises, and I believe will bestow, due attention in future; which indeed he is very rarely deficient in."

In the Scheme of Seizures and Frauds, however, attached to this report, our Author seems to have more than compensated for this casual neglect—being the only officer in the Round who had made any seizure of whisky for the period, 42 days:—"Robt. Burns—27 gals. Aq. seized;" a fact which, in his particular case, with so many surmises against him, speaks volumes for his honour and integrity.

Our Author, however, is by no means the only officer admonished on the Round; nor does he seem to have been the only literary official either. John Brown's irregularities or inattention had been serious, in so much, that "it may fairly be presumed that the duty of these two makings of malt is thereby lost," &c., &c.; on which follows "Admonish sharply: J. T.; Done: J. C.;" succeeded by the still more significant memorandum, "Since removed: J. B." To prevent this unpleasant catastrophe, Mr. Mitchell intercedes with a marginal note in his own hand on Brown's behalf in vain: "Mr. Brown promises every possible attention in future, now that his mind is somewhat relieved, as having finished his publications as an author, which it's gladly hoped will be the case.—J. M." What has become of this gentleman's authorship we are not aware. The above document is thus titled and noted:—

EXCISE, 85th Year.
Dumfries Colln.
Do.   District.
8th Rod. Diary.
A. FINDLATER.
Received, 12th Sept., 1792.—A. P.
T. W.
13 Sepr., read, and censures ordered.—J. T.
20th Septemr., 1792, Dispatched.—J. C.[*]

The paper, besides the incidental interest attaching to it, is of importance otherwise.

Our readers are already aware of the painful apprehensions excited in Burns's mind by some mysterious reports against him at head-quarters, as a revolutionary politician. The anxiety occasioned by these, and his dread of dismissal in consequence, are fully narrated by him in his letter (9) to R. Graham, Esq., of Fintry, December, 1792. The correctness of this apprehension on our Author's part, in so far as political convictions were concerned, is altogether impugned by Mr. Findlater in letters to the *Glasgow Courier*, March, 1834, and January 29th, 1835, in reply to Allan Cunningham's allegation on the subject.[†]

In the last of these letters, now also, through the courtesy of Mr. Provan, before us, but which it is unnecessary to quote at length, Mr. Findlater does not deny that an inquiry into Burns's political conduct had been ordered, but contends "that he overrated in some degree the consequences likely to result from the situation he found himself placed in; nor is it much to be wondered at, all things considered—he, the most irritable of the 'genus irritabile,' hitherto totally unaccustomed to official censure, and his very inexperience tending to increase his alarm." With respect to Cunningham's further allegation that Burns had received an "official letter with a large seal" in relation to this matter, Mr. Findlater states that of this he knows nothing, and has "only to observe thereon, that if the Board of Excise corresponded with Burns, it was a very singular and unique case, as in every other they have no correspondence whatever with that rank of officers, but through the medium of the superior officials." But more particularly [with respect to the complaint in question—letter to Graham], Mr. Findlater observes, "I hasten to remark, that the letter in question [to Graham of Fintry] was in all likelihood written by the Poet while still smarting under his castigation, and under mistaken apprehensions of impending disasters—I say *mistaken* apprehensions, because on grounds of this kind I am accused of giving Burns the lie. I deny," &c.

What "castigation," then, is here referred to?—the discussion comes to that. The reader will observe that Findlater's Diary, above quoted, was received at head-quarters, 12th September, 1792; read, and censures ordered, 13th September; these being administered or "done," it is "dispatched," 20th September; and Burns's complaint to Graham of Fintry is written in December—all of the same year: which concurrence undoubtedly affords *prima facie* evidence in favour of Findlater's supposition that Burns was merely irritated by a formal rebuke—the admonition, to wit, already quoted from his own Diary. But how could such an admonition be called a "castigation?" It was an admonition for trivial irregularities, apologised for by Findlater himself. Either, therefore, Mr. Findlater uses a most exaggerated term for that admonition; or Burns was most unreasonably "irritable;" or there was something far more serious unknown to Mr. Findlater—what Cunningham rather sublimely calls the "dark transaction," and what Findlater ridicules as such—connected with Burns's political conduct and the "official letter with the large seal," of which he confessedly "knew nothing," but which might nevertheless be a threatening reality. It is manifest, indeed, that something of this sort did exist, both from the letter itself to Graham, so explicit in its painful terms; and in the letter following, Jan. 5th, 1793, in which the whole subject is minutely detailed for Mr. Graham's satisfaction—a letter which Mr. Findlater could not have seen, inasmuch as it was not published till 1856, by Mr. Chambers; and also, we may add, in the celebrated letter to Erskine of Mar—[See Domestic Correspondence.] As for the "official letter with the large seal," we have very little doubt that it would be simply Mr. Graham's own letter in reply to Burns's of December, 1792, and referred to by Burns in his next; which Mr. Graham might have written and sealed with official materials at the office of the Board. Whether any rebuke was contained in that, or some succeeding letter, must now remain a mystery. Mr. Findlater at all events knew nothing of it.

---

[*] J. C., whose initials appear throughout, was Superintendent Crawford.
[†] Compare also letter to Donald Horne, Esq., W.S., Edinburgh, as quoted by Lockhart, p. 144, edition 1828.

EXCISE RETURN BY ROBERT BURNS,

FROM ORIGINAL,

BY KIND PERMISSION OF MOSES PROVAN, ESQ., OF AUCHENGILLAN.

[See p. xxxiii—Appendix.]

[The paper on which this fac-simile is printed is as like the original as could be procured.]

Alexr Robson
Bye Ales –
Excise
Tanners
Wm Kennedy & Co.
Thos & Olivr
Leather total
Maltsters
Robt Wallace
John Corrie
Mrs Riddel

James Semon
John Haining
W.m Lorimer, Cairnmill
Tho.s M.c Smath, Penpont
John Robson, Byrnflat
Tho.D Kevison, Thornhill

Ja.s Smith
Reob.t Edgar
John Brown

John Kellock, Thornhill
M.c Lawson, Kirkmaher

Ja.s Robson, Castlehill

Stamps ~ 8
57 . 3 . 9
25 . 1 . 8
32 . 2 . 4

4t year &c. 54th year 1791
Dumfries Collect.
Do. District —
Do. 1st Itin. Division —
Including 6th April & 24th May
7th Round, Abstract

Quantities	Qualities	Duties £ s d		
6.	Vict.ry		16	..
		..	..	..
	Excise	..	16	
1149	Tanned	7	3	7½
	Leather	7	3	7½

Jno Ferguson
£4.. 11.. 2

Mr Burns
Salary ~ 6
Bye as 15.4
Jno Mulloch ..5..6
£4.. 19.. 2

Mr Findlater
Reed Charges £1. 15.—

Before quitting this subject, in so far at least as the discussion between Cunningham and Findlater is concerned, we think it right to observe that Cunningham finally acquiesced in Findlater's position. From his edition of 1842 we extract the following paragraph :—

"The records of the Excise Office exhibit no trace of this memorable matter, and two noblemen, who were then in the government, have assured me that this harsh proceeding received no countenance at head-quarters, and must have originated with some ungenerous or malicious person, on whom the Poet had spilt a little of the nitric acid of his wrath."

In addition to the above Diary, we have been favoured by Mr. Provan with inspection of, and permission to fac-simile, an Excise Return by our Author, of considerably earlier date, which we have the satisfaction of presenting to our readers, and which they can investigate at leisure. As relics, these two documents are presumably now the only extant papers of their kind, all Excise and other Public Returns of the period having years ago been burned, by stringent Act of Parliament; from which official conflagration these solitary papers escaped by a discreet act of inadvertence, we presume, on the part of the officiating angel. By this personage they were afterwards bestowed in compliment on an English clergyman, from whom ultimately they came into the hands, by valuable exchange, of their present obliging possessor.

(3.) BURNS'S SALARY.—On this much controverted subject, definite intelligence may possibly never be attained. According to Mr. Chambers, "The stated official income of Burns was £50 a year, which usually became £70, in consequence of extra allowances for certain departments of business, . . There seem to have been other sources of official income of a more precarious nature: on the back of a song in his handwriting he has noted what follows—'I owe Mr. Findlater £6, 8s. 5½d. *My share* of last year's fine is £12, 2s. 1d. W. M., £14, 3s. 6d.' If this was anything like the average of some other perquisite, it would make up Burns's official revenues to something above £80 a year."—*Vol.* iv., p. 120. On the back of his own Return [see fac-simile illustration] a note will be found in a clerk's hand, by which Burns's monthly salary, it should appear, for 1791, is stated at £6— part of which had been advanced in exciseable commodities, and the rest in cash. At this rate, exclusive of perquisites, his income then seems to have been about £70. Any addition beyond salary and perquisites, therefore, must have been by a little land-surveying, as Mr. Chambers informs us; which our readers are aware the Poet, in his youth, had studied at Kirkoswald.

Cunningham [vol. v., p. 21] seems to imply that when in Dumfries the Poet "kept a horse," which Findlater expressly denies, and in the letter now before us ridicules the argument by which Cunningham supports the idea, viz., "that Burns, in proceeding to accompany some friends into the country, uses the expression, 'I took my horse,' as if any man when about to ride would not say the same thing, or use some such terms, were it the Pope's horse or the sorriest hack in Christendom." It seems incredible, indeed, that Burns should ever have been able to "keep a horse" in Dumfries; or that

he should even have attempted it. In his last letter to his friend Cunningham, from Brow, he thus laments this very inability, when exercise on horseback might have contributed to prolong his life—"The deuce of the matter is this: when an Exciseman is off duty his salary is reduced to £35 instead of £50. What way, in the name of thrift, shall I maintain myself and keep a horse in country-quarters, with a wife and five children at home, on £35"—implying thereby that he had not kept a horse, or at least had not one at the time to keep, whether he could have afforded it otherwise or not.

As for the occasional expense incurred for hiring a horse on official business at Dumfries, Mr. Chambers informs us that such expense was reckoned to the Board; and on the back of the Return already referred to we find, in the same clerk's hand, "Mr. Findlater, Ridg. Charges £1, 15s, W. P." —which confirms the statement.

———

9.—BIOGRAPHY, *p.* xlviii. POSTAGE, A DOMESTIC TAX ON BURNS: Ellisland, 1788—89, *et seq.*

FROM what our readers have already seen, they can be at no loss to understand that the letters received by Burns, as well as those written by him, during his residence at Ellisland, and subsequently at Dumfries, must have been very numerous; and consequently, as letters were then paid for on delivery, and at very high rates of postage, the expense incurred by such outlay alone must have been a very serious item in his expenditure. The subject, so far as we are aware, has never been specially adverted to, even by those who have been most censorious in their judgment of our Author's economy; and whilst Cunningham and Lockhart without hesitation adopt "James Corrie's" theory of "warm scones and ale" to account for a deficit at Ellisland, it seems never to have entered their imagination, although as literary men they might have surmised it, that postage alone, enforced upon the Poet by his admirers would more than account for ten or twenty pounds a year. It is the more surprising in Lockhart's case, for, according to his own account, the expense incurred by Sir Walter Scott in this particular of correspondence alone was something enormous, and with no possibility of escape or relief in any way. Had Burns then, the poor farmer at Ellisland, no correspondence? or did all *his* letters come free? Many doubtless did—but not all; to say nothing of the very time, abstracted from his labour, that was required to answer them. The facts of the case, however, have been commemorated by an eye-witness: Mr. William Reid of Burn, already quoted, assures us that an intimate friend of his father's, and a friend also of Burns's, having paid the Poet a visit shortly after his establishment at Ellisland, and being, on his return to Ayrshire, interrogated by old Mr. Reid on the subject of Burns's prospects in the farm, replied—"that the farm itself might do weel enough through time, but the postage would eat up a'. If letters cam aye, as they cam the twa or three days he was there, the postage would be mair than half the rent o' the farm." Mr. Reid himself, we must observe, does not endorse the correctness of this opinion, or affirm that the average supposed was justified by facts; but he relates the report given, and the impression produced on the visitor's mind, as realities to the narrator: and as the rent of the farm at that time was to be £50 per annum, considering the number of letters he saw received and the rate of postage then paid, his calculation might not be very far from the truth.

10.—Biography, p. liii. Dr. Maxwell—Burns's Pistols, Bishop Gillis, Letter to Blair, &c.

Dr. William Maxwell: This gentleman, brother to the then Laird of Kirkconnell, a Roman Catholic by religious persuasion, but far from being stringent in his orthodoxy, was a gentleman remarkable in many ways, and enjoyed especially the highest reputation as a physician—the highest probably at that time in the south of Scotland; all difficult and dangerous cases being brought to him from far and near. He received his diploma from Edinburgh College the very year that Robert Burns was so distinguished a guest in that capital; and after a while's experience of Continental life as a student, during the Revolutionary crisis at Paris, returned to practise in his native county, and to attend the death-bed of the Poet, in poverty, whom he had seen in the blaze of his fame ten years before. His diploma, which we have examined (now in possession of Dr. Grierson, Thornhill), is subscribed as under, by a constellation of authorities in Literature and Science of which any nation, much more any single university, might well be proud; and by the highest and best of these Dr. Maxwell was esteemed a valuable professional brother.[*]

To this gentleman Burns, on his death-bed, bequeathed in his own characteristic way of proud affectionate regard, with its inseparable constituent element in him of gratitude for kindness received,

The Pair of Pistols presented to himself by Mr. Blair

[*] Gul. Robertson, S.T.P., Primarius.
Jacobus Gregory, Med. Theor: P.
Gul. Cullen, Med. Pract: P.
Joh. Walker, Hist. Nat. Prof.
Alexr. Hamilton, Art. Obst. P.
Fra. Home, M. and MM. P.
D. Rutherford, M. and Bot. P.
Alexr. Monro, Med. Anat. et Chir. P.
Joseph Black, Med. and Chemiæ, P.

A. Hunter, S.S.T., and H.E.P.
Al. Maccowochie, Jur. Pub. P.R.
Jacobus Robertson, S.T.O., LL.OO.P.
Robertus Dick, Jur. Civ. P.

Hugo Blair, Rhet. and Litt. Elegant. P.
Jac. Finlayson, Log. and Litt. Elegant. P. Emeritus.
Gul. Greenfield, Rhet. and Litt. Elegant. P.
Robertus Blair, Astron. P.
Joht. Robertson, Phys. P.
And. Dalzel, Litt. Gr. P. Acad. Sec. et Biblioth.
For William Maxwell, Scotus; 12 Sept., 1787.

N.B.—Dugald Stewart's name is here awanting; he had retired from the Chair of Moral Philosophy in the interval, and was not succeeded by Brown till the Session following—viz. 1788-9.

of Birmingham. These valuable reliques came through the hands of Dr. Maxwell's daughter into the possession of the Right Rev. Bishop Gillis of Edinburgh, by whom they were presented to the Society of Scottish Antiquaries, 19th April, 1859. By an awkward mistake, the Right Rev. Gentleman, at the celebration of the centenary of the Poet's birth, produced as *Burns's* a wrong pair of pistols, which were not only not his, but had no other historical value attachable to them at all—an accident which occasioned a good deal of annoyance to his Reverence at the time, and occasioned, moreover, the appearance of other authorities asserting for themselves, or rather for their friends, possession of the envied reliques, and indicating distinctly their whereabouts. In reply to these claims, the Bishop, without much delay, produced the VERITABLE OBJECTS, with a satisfactory explanation of his own mistake, and a triumphant refutation of every other claim. A copy of the paper read by him on this interesting subject to the Society of Antiquaries is now before us, by the polite attention of Dr. Maxwell's nephew, R. Maxwell Witham, Esq., of Kirkconnel, to whom our best acknowledgments for the favour are due. From this document we read as follows—

1st. That a pair of pistols purchased by Provost Fraser of Dumfries, at sale of Dr. Maxwell's effects, May, 1834, for £2, 6s., and through him in possession of his grandson Mr. Alexander Howat, now in America, are not the pistols known as Burns's Pistols at all.

2d. That another pair of pistols purchased by, or for the late Allan Cunningham, in the same year, from John Brodie, dealer, about half an hour after the sale referred to, for £5; and spoken of by Mr. Cunningham somewhat unguardedly in his Life of Burns, 1835, as the Poet's Pistols properly so called —viz., those which had been bequeathed by him to Dr. Maxwell—are not the genuine weapons either.

3d. That some Highland broadsword accompanying these, in Allan Cunningham's possession, is of an apocryphal pedigree also.

4th. And finally, that the veritable pistols presented on his death-bed by Burns to Dr. Maxwell, as a memorial of their friendship and of the Doctor's kindness, were carefully reserved by Miss Maxwell's orders from the sale of her father's property in May, 1834; were reverentially preserved by her during her own remaining lifetime—a period of twenty-four years—and subsequently bequeathed, with other property, by her to the Right Rev. Bishop Gillis, in whose arms, or at least in whose presence, Dr. Maxwell himself expired on 13th of October, that year.

About Cunningham's connection with the pistols that were purchased for him, however, there is something more to be investigated—in which the shrewdness of the Bishop conspicuously appears. We quote now verbatim from the Bishop's paper before us; who himself in the first place quotes from Allan Cunningham's Life of Burns, 1835, with reference to

Burns's Letter of Thanks, as follows—

p. 312. "A handsome pair of Pistols [says Allan Cunningham] with latchlocks, brass-barrelled and screwed, were at this time given to the Poet by Blair of Birmingham. His acknowledgments were brief and Burnslike—'Sir, I have received and proved the pistols, and can say for them what I would not say for the bulk of mankind—they are an honour to their maker.'"

"Now [says the Bishop], although I am ready to admit

that the above laconic epistle is exceedingly "Burns-like,"
if supposed to have been written to a gunsmith from whom he
had *purchased* the weapons; I very much demur to the likeness, if it is to be palmed upon me without further proof than
Allan Cunningham's own authority, as a letter of acknowledgment from a man of Burns's nature, for a gift to him
so valuable in the vocation he was then pursuing, of an
officer of Excise; for anything more unlike a letter of
thanks never was penned."——

Well said, Bishop. It was, in fact, no letter of thanks,
from Burns or from any man; certainly not *the* letter of
thanks, nor anything like it but in a single expression,
that was actually written and sent. In point of fact, without any other evidence to guide him than Cunningham's
own text, the Bishop demonstrates that the pistols referred
to by Cunningham must have been purchased by Burns from
one Johnson in the year 1795; to whom the brief characteristic note, of proof and satisfaction with the purchase, was
no doubt addressed; and this was Cunningham's own view
of the subject in 1834, before any personal consideration to
adopt another view existed with him. When such consideration arose after Dr. Maxwell's sale, BLAIR, the *Maker's* name,
was substituted for JOHNSON, the *Seller's* name, in Cunningham's next edition, and the letter of acknowledgment a little
altered to suit the emergency, and thus an interesting fictitious
narrative was constructed about imaginary reliques!

But further, Bishop Gillis most shrewdly conjectures that
the real pistols must have been much longer in Burns's possession, from the necessity of the case and from the appearance of the weapons themselves, than from 1795. He guesses
the date of their acquisition, by gift from the maker himself
or by purchase, to have been as far back as the year 1788,
immediately after the Poet had entered on the troublesome
and often dangerous office of Excise. That such was actually
the case, and that they came into our Author's hands by
gift from the maker in the month of October, 1788, we are
fortunately able to prove. The reader has already seen the
letter of thanks for this valuable present in its place at the
end of General Correspondence—Burns to Blair, 23d January,
1789, two days before his own birth-day—apologising for
delay, in which his "honour had lien bleeding for two
months past," and offering in every way to testify his gratitude as a poet, by a packet of rhymes, for the handsome gift
of the gunmaker. The reader can judge for himself whether
the Bishop was not right in his generous estimate of our
Author's character as a gentleman and a man of honour,
lavish to the last extreme, and beyond all reasonable bounds,
in gratitude for favours.

That Burns may have had another pair of pistols afterwards,
with the same maker's name on them, by purchase, is quite
possible; and that he may have used the same sort of com-
mendation of them, for that very reason, seems to be true;
but where these other pistols are, if they ever existed as his,
there is now no evidence to show. That Dr. Maxwell may
have had several such pistols of his own, is also quite possible
(as the reader will immediatly see); and that a pair of these
by Blair, with whom Maxwell had dealings, may have been
mistaken by our friend "Jock Brodie" at the sale for Burns's,

and subsequently disposed of by him, at a premium of four
guineas or so, to Allan Cunningham, is probable enough;
with which Mr. Cunningham's representatives in this discussion must be content. As for the Highland broadsword,
it must be laid aside, we are afraid, among the rest. Dr.
Maxwell, indeed, seems to have been a collector of such
objects, of which several were disposed of at his sale. But
he had far too profound a sense of honour and friendship,
and too much love and veneration in him for the immortal
dead, to allow a gift from Robert Burns in the prospect of
death, and in affectionate requital of his own services, to be
knocked down to a public bidder at any sale of his.

DR. MAXWELL AND THE FRENCH REVOLUTION: It appears
from the same paper by Bishop Gillis, that Dr. Maxwell in
his early enthusiasm for Revolutionary ideas in France "incurred heavy responsibilities with Blair of Birmingham for
the manufacture of fire-arms"—but that ultimately he returned "to the religious conviction of his earliest years, and
to the practice of a truly Christian life." The Reverend
Father then enters an eloquent protest against the scandalous
report that the Doctor as a gendarme "had dipped his handkerchief in the royal blood" at the execution of the "virtuous
and unfortunate Louis XVI." The fact that Dr. Maxwell
so did, and that the handkerchief itself was preserved by him
as a sacred memorial of that terrible event of which he was
an eye-witness and an involuntary partaker, has been solemnly affirmed by persons who assert that they saw the
souvenir—which we happen for ourselves to know, on independent testimony. We are far from believing, however,
that such an act—as that of dipping the handkerchief—was
"exclusively within the province of savage brutality," as the
Bishop did. On the contrary, we can imagine a totally
different motive altogether in Dr. Maxwell's mind for taking
so strange a note of so impressive a circumstance. Not
"brutality" at all, but profoundest sympathy, we can believe
to have been the prevailing sentiment of the youthful Scotsman's heart that morning: and can understand without difficulty how he should never have been able to refer to such
a scene afterwards but with tears in his eyes.

Miss Maxwell, who constituted Bishop Gillis her heir, died
September 12th, 1858: Bishop Gillis himself died February
24th, 1864.

————

We ought, perhaps, to remind our readers, before dismissing
this reference, that Burns himself, stimulated by his political
enthusiasm, sent a present of four carronades to the French
Revolutionary Government, which were intercepted by the
Custom-house authorities at Dover. These guns had been
purchased by him for £3, at the confiscation of a smuggler
which he had himself captured on the coast. Lockhart con-
demns this attempt of his to subsidize the French "as a
most absurd and presumptuous breach of decorum," seeing
that we either were, or were upon the point of being, at war
with France: but Mr. Chambers, who more carefully ex-
amines the dates, defends our Author from any such charge,
as no threatening of war had then been heard; on the con-

trary, the most pacific relations between that country, even in a state of revolution, and our own then existed, and were expected to continue. That Burns could have had no serious intention of offending Government by any such chivalrous munificence to Revolutionary France is clear enough from the fact, that at the very same moment—it is said by some at the time he was actually pacing up and down the beach discontented at the delay which occurred in the capture of this prize, he was occupied in ridiculing his own profession by composing the well known song of "The Deil's awa wi' the Exciseman!"

Reminiscences Original:

PART II.

MISCELLANEOUS.

A.—Mr. WILLIAM REID of Burn: his own and his Father's Recollections continued.

(1.) BURNS'S DISCRIMINATION OF CHARACTER. In Mr. Reid's own possession, long after his father's death, remained a large collection of the Poet's letters, chiefly on religious topics, addressed to Miss Jean Ronald—Mr. Reid's mother. These documents, which were long carefully preserved, were by some unfortunate accident recently lost or destroyed. They seem to have originated thus: Mr. Reid's mother, when Miss Ronald, having some time rallied Burns on his indiscriminate courtship to her own sisters and other girls in the neighbourhood (compare "Tarbolton Lasses," "Ronalds o' Bennals," &c., Posthumous Works), and laughed in his presence at their mutual credulity and impositions, affirmed that it was impossible for him to impose on her. He declared he had no such intention; but that, if he had, it might be easily accomplished by a serious profession of piety; after which her faith in himself and in his devotion would be as implicit as that of her neighbours in credulity. Miss Ronald's good faith in this aspect of the Poet's character seems to have been implicit enough, after all this warning, as her correspondence with him showed. We have seen also a long and very elaborate religious correspondence between this lady and her minister, and a considerable number of pious metrical effusions of her own—all accumulated about and after the date of Burns's acquaintance with the family; a singular incidental proof of his acuteness in discrimination of character.

He was a frequent evening visitor also in Mr. Reid's paternal grandfather's. The old gentleman, who enjoyed Burns's story-telling and drollery immensely, encouraged his visits—much to the scandal of his own wife, a serious and quiet person; who rebuked the whole household, old and young, for being led away by such an idle, gossiping, foolish lad, who had neither sense nor seriousness in her estimation. This unpleasant impression having reached Burns's ears, the next time he visited Boghead a most edifying inci-

dental discussion arose, into which Mrs. Reid was quietly and unconsciously betrayed. By imperceptible degrees it changed its character, and the good woman very soon found herself involved in the general interest excited to such an extent, that she not only laughed outright, but clapped her hands in ecstasy before the whole circle. When Burns retired, universal recriminations from the gudeman and family followed, at her sinful acquiescence who had so often rebuked others: "That's the awfu'est body"—was her contrite defence—"that's the awfu'est body, that Burns, I e'er heard. I'm sure I set mysel wi' a' my micht to gainstan him, but it's perfect impossible!"

(2.) HIS GALLANTRY. His admiration of the sex and delicate sense of gallantry were capable, according to old Mr. Reid, of endless illustration. One instance of this we have already quoted in our notes on the "Holy Fair," and need not here reproduce. One other shall suffice: On the harvest field, where any Beauty or Beauties were within sight, he was constantly getting real or imaginary thistle-thorns into his hands, which no masculine fingers—neither his own nor any other man's—could possibly remove; and no masculine eye could ever see. Therefore, as a matter of necessity, half-hours were every now and then consumed in fruitless search by feminine fingers and feminine eyes for these inscrutable tormentors! How handsomely and devoutly he would repay such trouble by similar services for them, we are already made aware of by his own confessions on the subject.—Letter (4) to Dr. Moore—Prose Works, p. 74, c. 1.

(3.) DISTRIBUTION OF HIS MANUSCRIPTS. His carelessness in this respect, or possibly intentional device by careless distribution to secure local publicity for his poems, before the idea of printing them occurred—or even before his authorship in certain cases was known—to ascertain public opinion concerning them, was well authenticated by Mr. Reid's father. Burns's poetical effusions, being suggested by the incident of the moment, were not only distributed in copies among friends with utter disregard of their fate, to be rehearsed or circulated at discretion; in which way their possession by so many unlikely parties is to be accounted for: but Mr. Reid used distinctly to assert that he had frequently found anonymous copies of them lying on the roads, or on the pathways of the fields, dropped apparently on purpose by their author to be so found by strangers, and provoke impartial criticism or applause. Old Mr. Reid had accumulated a considerable number in this very way—some of which he retained; others, when their publication was resolved upon, he returned. A stray copy of the "Holy Fair," having thus got abroad, was read and rehearsed freely over the whole country. One reverend gentleman, Mr. Reid of New Cumnock, who might assist now and then at Mauchline, and who was slightly lachrymose in his oratory, having heard of the celebrated performance, expressed a desire to read it. A copy was accordingly furnished. Having carefully perused it, he put his hands on his eyes in his usual pathetic fashion, and declared "that the warst thing about it was, that it was just owre true!"—Compare notes on "Holy Fair"—Poetical Works, p. 89.

(4.) His Natural Disposition was extremely warm, buoyant, and sprightly—except when afflicted with his deep periodical fits of melancholy. Drollery, mirth of every kind, sociality, frolic, and even practical joking—at the expense occasionally of intermeddling, sanctimonious, or too officious persons—were natural to him. His love of dancing was very strong; so much so, that when a full-grown young man he has been known to indulge in that amusement among the boys and girls in the dancing school—the only grown person, but the teacher, present. His eye indicated not only eloquence but incredible penetration. The glance with which he examined a stranger, or any questionable person, and seemed to see, or rather read them through instantaneously, is said to have been something almost miraculous.

(5.) Kirk-Session at Mauchline. About the time at which Burns's conduct attracted the unfavourable notice of the church, the Session at Mauchline consisted of but three active members—Rev. Mr. Auld, "Holy Willie," and John Sillars. The mode of conducting business and administering discipline in that select court was uniform. The reverend incumbent, as moderator, first expressed his opinion and foreshadowed judgment; "Holy Willie," in the character of obsequious retainer, acquiesced—"I say wi' you, Mr. Auld: but John Sillars, what say you?" John Sillars might dissent from the decision proposed or not, and very often did, as he pleased; but John Sillars in a court like that was an inevitable and hopeless minority; and so the discipline and morals of the parish progressed together in sad conformity.

Whatever may be thought in other respects of "Holy Willie's Prayer," its truth, as the delineation of a time-serving, sycophantish impostor, emptying a cart-load of unconscious blasphemies at the throne of the Eternal, is indubitable.

————

B.—Burns's First Visit to Glasgow. Our readers, by referring to the "Epistle to J. Smith," Poetical Works, p. 28—also to note on the same, p. 96—will observe that previous to the date of said Epistle, 1785, the Author had had some indeterminate idea of publication—

> "Th's while my notion's taen a slsent,
> To try my fate in guid, black prent;" &c.—

and also that we hoped, when then writing, to be able to throw some new and interesting light on that subject. We are indebted for the following almost romantic particulars to our esteemed friend and class-fellow, John Reid, Esq., Kingston Place, Glasgow.

Mr. Reid's father, the late William Reid, Esq., of Brash and Reid, booksellers, Glasgow, served his apprenticeship with Messrs. Dunlop and Wilson, the most extensive bookselling, publishing, and printing firm in that city, or indeed in the west of Scotland. Mr. Reid himself, then a very young man, had already begun to cultivate the muses, and was even projecting little literary ventures of his own unknown to his employers. One of his correspondents at the date of which we speak, from 1785 to 1788, was Gavin Turnbull of Kilmarnock, who was a correspondent also of Robert Burns's, and perhaps a little overrated by him.—Compare letter (34), containing specimens of his poetry, to Thomson. On one occasion, precise date now unknown, a stranger of most remarkable aspect, of rustic appearance and with a shepherd's plaid on his shoulders, presented himself to Mr. Reid on Dunlop and Wilson's premises—with an introduction to him, it is believed from his friend Gavin Turnbull. This stranger's errand was two-fold—first to obtain publication, or more extensive publication, for a volume of poems, which he had in manuscript or in printed sheets—uncertain which—in his hand; and second, an introduction through Mr. Reid or his employers to some of the wealthiest merchants in Glasgow, with a view to obtain a settlement for himself in the West Indies. He looked and spoke in the deepest distress—in distress approaching to despair, and was occasionally moved even to tears. The poems he produced at the same time were of so great beauty, that, between sympathy and admiration, Mr. Reid was at a loss what to do. Finally, after discussing all the circumstances of the case and carefully scrutinising the poems, Mr. Reid, though a much younger man, affectionately struck his visitor on the shoulder and said, "Your country, Sir, cannot afford to send you to the West Indies: you must go to Edinburgh and not to Jamaica." This stranger, we need hardly say, was Robert Burns. It was not in Messrs. Dunlop and Wilson's line to publish volumes, much less small volumes, of poetry; but Mr. Reid, though still a youth, gave the unknown Poet a letter of introduction to Mr. Creech, with whom he was personally acquainted, and the interview for the present terminated.

It is unfortunately now impossible to determine exactly the very date of this most interesting event. All the circumstances narrated, and which Mr. Reid himself used frequently to rehearse in presence of his family, seem to indicate the very earliest attempt of our Author to obtain publication for his works or a speedy escape from the country. No such distress could possibly have been manifest six months later; besides, it is certain that, on his first visit to Edinburgh, he did not travel by Glasgow. This remarkable interview, therefore—remarkable in every way—must have occurred early in 1786; and if so, the poems submitted to Mr. Reid's examination must have been still in manuscript. The idea of proceeding to Edinburgh on the recommendation of so young a man, and with no funds of his own to support him, would most naturally be abandoned by Burns as impracticable; and so the first publication of his muse was reserved for Kilmarnock: and when afterwards he did go to Edinburgh, it was under much higher auspices—so that his young friend's introduction to the great metropolitan bibliopole would not be required. Burns, however, never forgot this kindness. On his first visit to Glasgow, after his triumphant reception at Edinburgh, in 1787, Mr. Reid was among the first persons, if not the very first, on whom he called; and a copy of Beugo's engraving, water-coloured and framed, presented by the Poet to Mr. Reid on that occasion as a memento of their friendship, is still in possession of the family. At a later date, and when most probably for the last time he again visited Glasgow, he was accompanied out of the city by Mr. Reid, along the south bank of the Clyde as far as a stone which then stood by the brink of the river, in a line due north from the parish church at Govan. At this point the friends finally took farewell; Burns proceeding towards Paisley, where we find him hospitably entertained by Mr. Pattison, on his way homewards by Kilmarnock. Mr. Reid, of course, returned to Glasgow; but for thirty years afterwards used to visit that spot with his children, and relate to them the circumstances of his last interview and farewell with his illustrious fellow-countryman. This simple monument of so pleasant and honourable a friendship has long since been removed in process of widening the river, but we remember very well to have seen that stone, and to have rested or played about it in our boyhood.

Burns afterwards honoured Mr. Reid not only with his correspondence, but with permission to make additional verses to some of his own songs—"John Anderson, my jo," for example—which were published by Mr. Reid in a collection of poetry by himself in 1795, entitled, Poetry, Original and Selected; in four volumes. This correspondence, as our readers are aware, with much else of our Author's in Mr. Reid's possession, was irrecoverably lost by an inundation of the Clyde, 1831—Prose Works, p. 139. The following memorandum, in Mr. Reid's own hand, will testify his anxiety on the subject:

"Burns's letter [to Muir], in which he gives his opinion on the immortality of the soul, seems not to be here. I must have it among my other papers; as also the letter or letters to Dr. Grierson from Burns, which Dr. Grierson gave to me. Get these, and put them all together in a tin box."

These documents were only partially recovered. The letter to Muir on the immortality of the soul, which had already been published, is still in possession of Mr. Reid's son; but the letters to Grierson seem to be entirely lost. A letter, however, by Dr. Grierson himself, giving a detailed account of the Inverary Tour, on which he accompanied Burns, is already before our readers; and will be supplemented with some curious details in the following paragraph. How Mr. Reid came to be possessed of so many, and so valuable letters—one of them of the very highest value—to Muir, has not been explained to us. Our conjecture on the matter is, that as both Muir and Gavin Turnbull were Kilmarnock men, and both friends of our Author's, and as Gavin Turnbull was the man who most probably first introduced Robert Burns to Mr. Reid, the letters found among Muir's papers after his death would be transmitted as objects of interest for Mr. Reid's perusal, and so bequeathed to, or left in his custody.

Lest it should be thought presumptuous in Mr. Reid, being so young a man, to have offered Burns a letter of introduction to so exalted a personage as Provost Creech of Edinburgh, we may mention that Mr. Reid, notwithstanding his youth, was then personally intimate with Creech, and that their friendship ultimately became so cordial, that Mr. and Mrs. Reid spent a fortnight of their "marriage jaunt" at Edinburgh as Mr. Creech's visitors.

[See confirmation of above narrative, in statement by Robert Hedderwick, Esq.—Supplementary Gossip, infra.]

———

C.—BURNS A FREEMAN OF DUMBARTON: 1787. General Correspondence, p. 205.

On examining the Burgh Records in presence of John Denny, Esq., Town-Clerk—it appears

(1.) That the last meeting of Council before Burns's visit was May 8th, 1787:

(2.) Next meeting was Augst. 11th, 1787: Burns's visit having occurred June 28th or 29th of said year.

(3.) At meeting of Council, Augst. 11th, the only burgesses admitted were as follows—

> James Hall, print-cutter, Dalquhurn;
> Thos. Whyte, skinner, Dumbarton;
> John M'Naught, ship-carpenter, Dumbarton;
> James Reid, smith, Dumbarton.

At this meeting of Council were present—

> James Colquhoun, Provost,
> Bailie Niel Campbell,
>   ,, Robert Gardner,
> Messrs. Robert M'Lintock, Dean of Guild,
>   John Jardon, Treasurer,
>   Stewart Robertson,
>   Robert Martin,
>   John Napier,
>   John Key,
>   Robert Davidson, Councillors.

And among members absent was John Gray, writer.

The Town-Clerk at this date was John M'Auley, Esq., who would no doubt be officially present at all such meetings.

At the above meeting of Council, the names of Robert Burns, George Grierson, and ——— Gardner of Ladykirk, should undoubtedly have been entered as honorary burgesses, if such honour had been conferred upon them in the interval. That it had been so conferred Dr. Grierson in his letter to Mr. Reid—Prose Works, p. 205—distinctly affirms, and states, as a consequence of that honour being conferred, that Rev. Mr. Oliphant had next day preached against the foresaid, and severely blamed the magistrates for so prostituting the freedom of the burgh. That Mr. Oliphant did so preach on the day in question, and on that subject, is a distinct tradition in Dumbarton—and that he was very bold and bitter on the occasion. The fact, therefore, has not been exaggerated by Dr. Grierson, and the cause of this public rebuke to the magistrates must have been well known, or the rebuke itself would have been uncalled for. Why then does not Burns's name, with those of his companions, appear on the Records? The explanation seems to be very natural: Niel Campbell, Esq., then or subsequently Sheriff-Substitute; and John Gray, Esq., writer, Mr. Campbell's successor as Sheriff, were two of the most influential members of the Council; but these gentlemen were also, or one of them at least, nearly related to Rev. Mr. Oliphant by marriage; and both were very intimate with him, and much under his influence. Whatever the Provost and Mr. M'Auley, the Town-Clerk, therefore, might think or say on the subject, there can be very little doubt that their wish to honour Burns was overruled by these gentlemen, and that the meeting at which the freedom of the burgh had been conferred upon him was quashed or ignored, by non-recording. Such was clerical influence at that date in Dumbarton. Mr. Oliphant, it must be farther remembered, was the nominee of the Town Council, and thrust by them on a protesting population; so that other members of the magistracy as well as his own relatives, might for appearance' sake acquiesce in their suggestions. The reverend gentleman would therefore be sole dictator in the municipality, and seems to have exercised his prerogative with a high hand.

But it may seem strange that no reference to such a singular and humiliating act of despotism should ever have been made by Burns in any of his correspondence. It might be beneath his dignity to speak of it much, and in consideration for others he might be still more reticent: but that he *did* speak of it, and perhaps strongly, we have no manner of doubt. In his letter to M'Auley—Prose Works, *p.* 187—whose personal kindness he remembers with gratitude, there are numerous references to religion, to Presbyterian discipline, to family worship and psalm-singing, which seem to be only half serious, and entirely uncalled for in any ordinary case. But what is more significant, at the conclusion of said letter there is a great gap, supplied from the first appearance of the document in Currie by * * * *. What that gap contained can now only be conjectured. That it referred to Mr. Oliphant, and the proceedings of the Council, we, for our own part, have no doubt whatever. Dr. Currie at the moment might wisely suppress such a paragraph in the letter; and perhaps it could not with propriety be published during Mr. Oliphant's life. That reverend gentleman survived with increasing honours till 1818; and then the subject of the letter to M'Auley would be forgotten. But murder will out; and even clerical autocracy and magisterial subserviency cannot be hidden.

We should like much to see the original of that letter, wherever it now is, as a matter of mere curiosity.

D.—BURNS'S PERSONAL APPEARANCE, POCK-MARKS, &c.

THE circumstance so emphatically stated by Gilbert Baird —*p.* xxviii—of Burns being much pock-marked on the face, we had never heard alluded to before; but since that date, it has been confirmed to us by the testimony of a lady who was familiarly acquainted with him from an early period of her life.

MRS. MARION HUNTER, aged 97, formerly of Dumfries, now resident at Mr. Robert Hedderwick's, in Glasgow, the venerable party referred to, thus dictates her affidavit on the subject—"Burns was *pock-pitted*, and 'no mistake;' for I hae seen him just as near as you are to me at this moment o' time. His brow was weel covered wi' the holes—gey braid and deep they were; and the taps o' his cheeks—a' about here (pointing to the cheek bones), had a wheen, but no monie. He was a dark, swarthy chiel, gey broad and gross about the chin—no to ca' guid-lookin, and loutit a wee—but oh! he had a fine pair o' een, lairge, dark, lustrous; for a' tho worl' like lowin coals, that glower'd as if they'd pierce ye thro' and thro'! But for a' that, he was pock-marked—as every one

know that kent ought about him. A' folk were pock-marked in thae days, and what for no Burns? I'll tak my '*affidavy*' on that, I'll swear to't ony day!"[*] It is singular enough that a fact so palpable should not hitherto have been noticed; unless Allan Cunningham's observation, that his face was "deeply marked" after death, referred to it.

[*] [See curious anecdote of Burns by Mrs. Hunter.—Supplementary Gossip, *infra.*]

E.—AN INTERESTING MEMORIAL of our Author's personal

friendship for one of his correspondents we have lately seen in a copy of his first Edinburgh Edition, now in possession of J. BARCLAY MURDOCH, Esq., Lynedoch Street, Glasgow. This volume bears on corner of the fly-leaf the words ROBERT AINSLIE in a strong plain hand, manifestly autograph; and throughout has all the blanks and omissions in the letterpress, of names and designations of persons referred to in the poems, minutely and carefully filled up in the Poet's own handwriting. The volume has been bound with a few blank leaves at beginning and end, to receive notes from the Author undoubtedly; but these have not been added. It may seem strange, perhaps, that such a memorial of his friendship should have been picked up for a few shillings—less than the price of the volume—on a book stall in London, where its value was not known; but when we observe that several LETTERS by our Author to the same correspondent, intended always to be strictly private, have in like manner found their way to the world, nobody knows how, our surprise will be considerably abated. There has been a want of sense or sympathy somewhere.

F.—HIS HUMANITY.

With one anecdote more, which we have indirectly on the authority of an eye-witness, but more immediately from a lady, Mrs. EVERITT of AYR, the Poet's own grand-daughter, who is aware of the fact, we shall conclude. Returning home to his house in the Wee Vennel, one stormy wet night after dark, he discovered a poor half-witted street-strolling beggar woman, well known about Dumfries, half-naked, drenched and shivering, huddled together almost insensible on his own door-step. In those days there was no shelter of a police-office to which such a helpless vagrant could be removed, nor was there any house open at the moment to which she could be carried, but his own. Mrs. Burns might perhaps be excused for hesitating to receive such an inmate even for the night; but remonstrance was in vain. The miserable outcast, motionless, presumably unconscious, was carefully lifted in, and housed and sheltered under the Poet's hospitable roof till morning, when, not without breakfast we may be sure, she was enabled to pursue her way. "Then shall the king say unto them on his right hand, Come, ye blessed of my Father, inherit the kingdom prepared for you from the foundation of the world; For I was an hungered, and ye gave me meat: I was thirsty, and ye gave me drink: I was a stranger, and naked, and sick, and ye visited and took me in."

Amen!

Gossip:

CORRECTED OR ENLARGED BY EDITOR.

1.—BIOGRAPHY, *p.* xii. To avoid the necessity of several References on the same page, the following distinct particulars have been included under one head:

(1.) RESIDENCE AT KIRKOSWALD. This interesting, and in some respects eventful, sojourn took place in the summer of 1775, when the Poet was in his seventeenth year—see note on letter (4) to Dr. Moore, Prose Works, *p.* 75—a fact which gives a much greater significance to every manifestation of genius and character referable to the period. The study of mathematics, interrupted by love and the cultivation of poetry; experience and observation of life in its rudest forms, among smugglers and smuggling farmers; contests for intellectual superiority with the schoolmaster, and voluntary competition in letter-writing with schoolfellows, have all a new sort of meaning in the untutored lad of seventeen. Besides, the imaginary interruption of rural occupations at Lochlea in 1777 no longer requires to be taken into account, since the residence at Kirkoswald was past and gone fully two years before that.

The relative with whom he resided there, Samuel Brown, a brother of his mother's, and with whom he afterwards corresponded, seems to have been not altogether unobservant of his disposition at that early date; for on one occasion, when the boy remarked—"Weel uncle, ye're gaun awa to get that ravelled hasp reel'd?" the uncle replied—"My lad, if ye dinna tak anither way o't, yours will be waur to reel nor ye think!"—The teacher at Kirkoswald, who had some reputation in his day for mathematical attainments, was a Hugh Rodger, and grandfather to our informant; who stood also in the same sort of relation to Samuel Brown as Burns himself did.

(2.) "HALLOWEEN"—"TAM o' SHANTER"—"BRUCE'S ADDRESS," &c. To the north-east of Kirkoswald, at a few miles' distance, on the Carrick Shore, are first the celebrated Coves, or Caves of Colzean, from which that ancient Baronial stronghold was originally designated the Cove—said to be frequented by fairies; second, a little to the west of these, a beautiful smooth-sanded creek, identified as the spot at which Robert Bruce effected his landing, when disappointed of access at Turnberry on his eventful voyage from Arran; third, a little farther to the west still, and nearly due north from Kirkoswald, was the farm-house of Shanter, occupied then by Mr. Douglas Graham, now marked only by a grass-covered mound of ruins; and at the extreme point westwards, in direct view of Ailsa Craig, is Turnberry itself, surmounted by the Castle—ancient hereditary residence of the Earls of Carrick, and from which the second title of the Scottish Crown is still derived.*

---

* The whole of this coast, we may inform the geologist, abounds in beautiful varieties of pebbles and jaspers. We know of one magnificent heart-shaped jasper discovered at Turnberry by our old, long-deceased friend, Sandy M'Callum, Girvan—whose indefatigable researches in that region were all too ill-requited, or even acknowledged, during his lifetime.

With all these localities, occupied chiefly, or at least frequented, in those days, by smugglers, Burns as a youth, during his residence at Kirkoswald, was familiar; was well acquainted with every tradition of the neighbourhood; was an acute observer of the manners of the inhabitants; is said even to have overheard at Shanter door a conjugal lecture administered by Helen M'Taggart to her delinquent spouse; and was no doubt also acquainted with the reputation for witchcraft that attached to some of the poorer female residents on that stormy and sequestered coast. From this early groundwork of observation and tradition on the soil, rose ultimately the most wonderful and impressive of his poetic creations.—Compare notes on "Halloween" and "Tam o' Shanter"—Poetical Works, *p.* 100; *p.* 244.

(3.) WILLIAM NIVEN, Esq., late of KILBRIDE, Maybole, was at that period a schoolfellow of the Poet's at Kirkoswald, though somewhat younger; and seems to have manifested the prudential money-making faculty at an early age. By the successful cultivation of that faculty, indeed, he was distinguished to his latest hour. He realised a handsome fortune in the way of trade, chiefly, if we mistake not, at the building of a harbour on the coast, by which the proprietor himself, it is said, was all but ruined; and this fortune, by judicious investment, made him a landed proprietor in the district, where he officiated as magistrate for many years, with an assumption of importance that exposed him occasionally to not a little popular ridicule.

Mr. Chambers mentions his name as a claimant for the honour of having been really first intended in the Epistle ultimately addressed to Andrew Aiken. The gentleman, doubtless, had confidence enough to claim any sort of moral or social relationship to Burns that would exalt himself; but how he could ever be the bosom-friend of such a man, or entitled to the honour of an endearing Epistle from him, is to us incomprehensible, except on the principle of some involuntary assimilation of antipathies.

(4.) THE DANCING SCHOOL ERA, according to our Author's own account, was about this time also, but probably in the winter; according to Mrs. Begg's account, as in Chambers, it was a year or two later—probably after the removal of the family to Lochlea; at which time, if we are not misinformed, there was also a singing-school, or a singing-class at least, among the young folks there. However this may be, and both accounts may perhaps be true, Burns had undoubtedly a great taste, and a great passion for dancing, as is evidenced both by the tradition of his contemporaries and the direct statement of his relatives. The love principle lay unquestionably at the bottom of this; but the exercitation itself, the excitement, and the music, gave this popular accomplishment additional attractions for him, and the idea of dancing seems to have been perpetually present in his imagination as a poetical figure. We find it everywhere, with obvious pleasurable emotion, introduced in his poems, from the exquisite love-song of "Mary Morison"—

> Yestreen, when to the trembling string,
> The dance gaed thro' the lighted ha',

to the end of his career, when

> 'Twas pibroch, sang, strathspey, or reels—
> She dird'd them a' in' clearly, O;

or

> By my soul I'll dance a dance with you, Dumourier.

In short, the instinct was irrepressible.

His father's want of sympathy in such excitement seems to have been misconstrued by Robert as an aversion to dancing itself, and to him even personally, in consequence, whose own passionate propensity towards it could brook no restraint. But this view of his father's reluctance to patronize it much, much more of any aversion to him on account of it, is expressly disavowed by Gilbert in his Memoir; where he maintains, on the contrary, his father's special love of Robert, and willingness to indulge all the family as well as him in that innocent pastime, within reasonable bounds. The only fear their father seems to have had was, that Robert, with his love of society and disposition to gaiety, if not to gallantry, might be exposed to risks of dissipation there that would have been injurious to himself as well as distressing to his family.

2.—(5.) BIOGRAPHY, p. xiii.—ITINERANT RECITERS; once a most important class of public instructors among the peasantry of Scotland, and in very remote times with much higher qualifications as minstrels than that of mere recitation. The "Betty Davidson," with her "l'ammer beads" (necklace of amber), who was so affectionately cared for by our Author's family, and signalised by the Poet himself in his Autobiographical Letter to Dr. Moore, would have been one of the most popular reciters had she been compelled to exercise the faculty for a livelihood; and as a mere narrator, we have no doubt, would be as entertaining and recondite as a black-letter chronicle. Her gift, however, seems to have been consecrated entirely to one circle of indulgent friends; and the result of her unconscious tuition, in storing the youthful imagination of so great a poet as Robert Burns with the rudiments of ghostly lore, has made her immortal in her humble sphere, as the dependent of a peasant's household. With such a father, and such a mother, and such a nurse, was this great teacher of the people provided in the quiet munificence of God.

But at a much later period, these itinerant reciters, who lived entirely by their art, were still popular and numerous in the district. Male and female, they were received with joy, and liberally entertained at every "stead" or "toon" in Ayrshire. The enthusiasm with which the periodical visits of the most celebrated were welcomed by young and old in the remoter rural regions, to which they brought both intelligence and amusement, can scarcely now, in these days of penny newspapers and broad-sheets of foolish songs, be credited. Writing of those who frequented the country of which we now speak—that is, of Kyle and Carrick, but whose perambulations extended far beyond, an esteemed correspondent says:—

"I well recollect that we thought the beggars were the happiest mortals in the world. I mind well of going out in the dusk to see if any were coming. When any did come, our first question was 'Can you sing or tell stories?'—if they were strangers; but if they were known to us, there were no questions, but a corner was made for them in the house. We had names for them (from the stories they told, or the songs they sang) such as 'Pea-straw,' 'Eglinton Castle,' 'Duke of Gordon's Daughter,' 'Bush of Blackberries,' and so on. The one that repeated 'Turn gentle Hermit,' we called her 'Angelina.' I do not mind any incident,—only we made them so comfortable, and they were all so jolly with their songs and stories, that I deliberately set to and learned the whole of the 'Hermit of Warkworth' for the very purpose of procuring me comfortable lodgings by the Farmer's fireside when I would be an old beggar wife—not very aspiring, you will say. Beggars have no such treatment now-a-days. We had three grades:—the strangers were put in the barn; another set in the corner of the byre beside living things, but in a railed-off place, where they were safe from accident; and the honoured ones got a hassock in the kitchen corner. After I came to G——, I saw the 'Duke's Daughter' sitting with her back to the wall, and a parcel of boys playing pranks about her; and for old and happy days' sake, I sent out two of our men to carry her in, and put her in a back house till morning. This would be twenty years or more after I first knew her. Beggars in these days were not old frail folk, but maybe women that wrought in the field in the summer, and took their tramps in the winter," &c.

The reader may compare jocular letter by our Author (I) to M'Murdo, on the habits and privileges of strolling beggars, poets, &c.—Prose Works, p. 185.

6.—BIOGRAPHY, p. xxii.—LORD AFFLECK.

Alexander Boswell, Esq., of Auchinleck, or Affleck, representative of a very ancient Scottish family long settled there; Lord of Session by that title, and father of the celebrated James Boswell, was a man of great sagacity, scholarship, and humour—sometimes rude, but always racy.

Auchinleck House, at which Dr. Johnson was so hospitably received, was built by him, and the country around enriched and beautified with extensive plantations—some of them in broad belts along the parish roads. One of these described by Boswell in his Tour, and leading to the parish church, was not less than three miles long. It was a favourite walk of his Lordship's, and called by him jocosely the via sacra. Till his time, the district was comparatively destitute both of woods and mansions; but the building of Auchinleck House by him, and of Dumfries House by the Earl of Dumfries—Mansions of rival elegance and splendour, and the cultivation of wood in such extensive ranges by the gentry of the day, in a great measure redeemed it from this reproach. Jean Armour's grandfather was the contractor for and builder of Dumfries House, and of Auchincruive, as well as other mansions, in the neighbourhood [see Memoranda by Mrs. Burns].

and these certainly reflect great credit on his workmanship as a practical architect. Whether he was also the builder of Auchinleck House, we are not aware.

His Lordship had collected a most valuable library, including many important manuscripts, at Auchinleck, and spent every hour of his life not occupied by professional business at Edinburgh, in planting his wood and studying these literary treasures. He delayed his periodical departures again to Edinburgh till the last moment, and took leave of his privileged domestics, coachmen, or ploughmen, with some characteristic pleasantry, to which they were at liberty, in the same vein of humour, to reply. His Lordship, who was a devout Presbyterian, was of course an elder in the Kirk, and exemplary in the discharge of his Presbyterial duties. He was far from being bigoted, however, and took advantage of all opportunities to hear a stirring sermon elsewhere, by whomsoever preached. He was a frequent attender of Whitfield's ministrations when in that neighbourhood; too frequent, it would appear, to be overlooked as a defaulter by his own minister, Mr. Dun, who undertook to expostulate with his Lordship on the bad effect such open defection from the church was likely to produce. When the head and front of his Lordship's offence, which had been very obliquely implied at first, was at last clearly stated, and a reason for such dangerous proceedings requested, the reason was very quietly and effectively assigned—"Ye see the truth is, Maister Dun, when I gang to hear the like o' Mr. Whitfield preach, I maun hearken till the Word, will I, nill I; but in the Kirk here at hame, when ye're in the pulpit yersel, as ye oftenest are, as lang as ye preach I'm thrang planting, till I ha'e planted a' the trees in Affleck owre again—and that maks a difference." No farther reason, we believe, was ever required for his Lordship's occasional absence. This anecdote, which we have heard before from a very old friend long resident in the family, has been confirmed to us as genuine by Mr. Cuthbert of Ochiltree. The Rev. John Dun was the same minister of Auchinleck whose conversation was so disagreeable to Johnson, and whose ignorance of Episcopal affairs was so unceremoniously rebuked by the equally intolerant Doctor—"Sir, you know no more of our church than a Hottentot."

Lord Auchinleck died in 1782, that is four years before the publication of Burns's Poems, and a year before the Poet himself had come to live at Mossgiel; when, indeed, he was comparatively unknown, except among his companions at Tarbolton, as a poet at all. No communication, therefore, was likely ever to have occurred between them. Indeed, no communication seems ever to have taken place between this influential family and their illustrious neighbour at all; which is more to be regretted, considering the immense advantage such a library as that at Auchinleck House would have conferred on him. James was all his life absorbed in Paoli or Johnson, and could not credit the existence of such a giant at his own door. His son, Sir Alexander, himself a poet and a man of letters, who established a printing press at Auchinleck for his own amusement, was indeed an ardent admirer of Burns's—but came much too late upon the scene to be of any service to him; and so all dreams of any possible interest, influence, or friendship there, end in nothing: but

that Burns was well aware of the literary treasures accumulated at Auchinleck, and of the classical repute conferred upon it by Johnson's visit, is manifest from additional stanzas of "Vision"—*Posthumous Works, p. 409.*

7.—BIOGRAPHY p. xxiii.—" WINSOME WILLIE."

Our readers are already in possession [note on Epistle to W. S[impson], Poetical Works, p. 106] of much that might otherwise have been inserted here, as information concerning him. He was the first, so far as we are aware, who ventured to attempt a direct imitation of, and inasmuch as he attached our Author's own name to the fabrication, it might have been called a forgery on Robert Burns, if he had not himself communicated the fact to Burns, as a joke. The joke, however, not having been explained to the world, the fabrication itself was long accepted by many as a genuine production, and passed with a sort of half sanction into several early editions of the Poet's works. Of such spurious pieces, there are still several current, and it is perhaps the most questionable sort of compliment to his great genius, that a "discerning public," with all its just admiration of him, does not detect their falsehood. One of the most absurd of these is a certain " Address to the Potato," said to have been recited by Burns himself long ago to a very aged lady still living, and which recently appeared, from her dictation to a correspondent, in *Notes and Queries* [4th S., II. 41]. To spend time in critical refutation of such alleged authorship would be an insult to Burns; and whoever is so imperfectly acquainted with the internal characteristics of his writing, as to accept such verses in his name, would hardly be convinced by any more critical evidence to the contrary.

By far the best of these imitations, however, was the first— the " Epistle to a Tailor "—by " Winsome Willie; " but even that, on careful reading, is found to be intrinsically defective. This " Epistle," which appeared for the first time, along with " The Kirk's Alarm," " Holy Willie's Prayer," &c., in Stewart's piratical edition—Glasgow, 1801—and has been quoted with great and strange admiration since by Cunningham and others, as being, if not genuine, at least worthy of Burns, originated in this wise, as we learn from the unquestionable authority of an esteemed friend, Rev. Mr. Hogg of Kirkmahoe, in whose hands a whole MS. volume of Simpson's poetry and all the documents more particularly in question, we believe, are now to be found. Simpson, it appears, when teacher at Ochiltree, had a rhyming neighbour, Thomas Walker by name, and a tailor by trade; who, besides a little metrical correspondence with Simpson himself, was extremely anxious to have the honour of an " Epistle " from Burns. To procure this, he addressed a somewhat verbose, although laughable enough complimentary letter to Burns, in the favourite epistolary rhyming style then common in Scotland —to which, however, no reply was received. This neglect on our Author's part gave offence to the ambitious artist, and another epistle, not quite so respectful, and intended of course to be very witty, was despatched. This document may be found also in Stewart's edition. "No answer was received to this letter either," says our reverend correspondent, "and the poor tailor was sadly grieved, and almost demented, at the seeming slight. Day after day did he make his complaint to Simpson of Burns's unkindness in not writing him. To gratify Tom's ardent longings, Simpson wrote in Burns's name the poem entitled 'Epistle to a Tailor,' and sent it to Pool (the cottage where Tom resided). Almost half naked, and ecstatic with joy, Walker rushed into Simpson's school crying 'O Willie, Willie, I hae got ane noo; a clencher: read it man, read it!' With ill-restrained laughter he read it, and returned it to the tailor, who religiously preserved it till the day of his death, without ever discovering the hoax. A few days afterwards Simpson met Burns, and reproached him for not writing to the Tailor. Burns said 'Man, Willie, I aye intended to write to the bodie, but never got it dune.' Simpson then told the whole story, and read to him the answer he had sent in his name. Burns gave him a thump on the shoulder and said, 'Od, Willie, ye hae thrashed the tailor far better than I could hae dune.'" This anecdote serves at least to show the high estimation in which Burns's genius and the honour of his correspondence were held, at a date when his name was entirely unknown in the world. From all that we have seen either of Simpson's, or Sillars', or Lapraik's, our Author seems greatly to have overrated their gifts; and it appears to us one of the many proofs of his own innate generosity, that he should have so highly honoured and exalted any one of them.

8.—BIOGRAPHY, *p.* XXV.—MARY CAMPBELL :—

9.—BIOGRAPHY, *p.* xxxii.—MRS. M'LEHOSE :—

The reader is referred for particulars under these two heads to what is judged, on reconsideration, a more appropriate section of this work for such details—THE HEROINES OF BURNS: *infra.*

10.—BIOGRAPHY, *p.* xxxiv. REMOVAL TO ELLISLAND, DOMESTIC RELATIONSHIP, &c.

For full illustration of this topic, and the correction of many misrepresentations concerning it, the reader is referred to Mrs. Burns's own Memoranda—Appendix, *p.* xxi., &c.

11.—BIOGRAPHY, *p.* xxxv. FACTS AND OPINIONS: BURNS IN PROSPERITY.

With even so brief a summary of acknowledged facts in the case, as that in the text purports to be, it is strange to contrast the multitude of compassionate reflections that have accumulated on the extravagance of Robert Burns; and passing strange, to hear one most respectable conscientious biographer among the crowd record his own deliberate con-

viction, that a success of £500 at the moment, as a revenue from his works, was as much perhaps as Burns could enjoy "with equanimity." The most unconscionable speculator in the world, or the most mischievous madman (a Law, for example, of Stock-jobbing notoriety in Paris, or a Captain Macmo of Holmains, with homicidal duelling propensities, conspicuous enough in Edinburgh at the time), being raised out of equal obscurity in an instant, the one by a public imposture, and the other by the generosity of an unknown friend; and invested, without personal desert or worth of any kind, with the possession or disposal of hundreds of thousands of pounds, shall henceforth be respectable enough in the eyes of men and editors; and shall be suffered without serious reflection to do whatever they please with their own, although it should be at the risk of life and happiness to hundreds of their fellow-beings: but one of the most gifted souls in the universe shall not be entrusted with more than £500, the reward of his own labour, by a virtuous and considerate world, to whose welfare and delight he has contributed a hundred thousand times more; lest, having gifted away one half of said sum in filial or in fraternal duty, he may ruin or disgrace himself, through sheer want of management or "equanimity," with the other! Such an assumption—is it sorrowful? or is it laughable? Yet God, who gave little, know best.

But since this matter, like other gossip, must and will be talked about, we may further add, on incontrovertible authority, that Burns's upbringing and experience of social comforts in early life were by no means so depressing as many have imagined, and as some have represented: and that he was not therefore, on that account, so likely utterly to ruin himself, like a beggar on horseback, by the mismanagement of five hundred pounds. He belonged to a poor, but a thrifty, self-denying, economical and dignified household. The story for example, to'd by the man Blane, then goodman, or driver of the horses when ploughing, at Mossgiel, and on his authority circulated by others as a verity, as to his (Blane's) sleeping with Burns in the stable loft, and hearing and correcting his poems, is a piece of utterly unfounded gossip. Burns, indeed, to gratify, or rather to instruct the boy, whose wish to destroy the fugitive outcast he had restrained, might read the poem on the Mouse to him that evening as a lesson of charity. But as for sleeping in the stable loft with this lad, and consulting him about his poetry—we hope not many intelligent readers can believe that. The man himself, being cross-questioned by Mrs. Begg on the subject, could not substantiate his own statements, which were known on other evidence to be entirely false. Mrs. Burns's notions, in fact, both of morality and of social decorum were of the very strictest and most dignified character, and it certainly would not have been with her knowledge or permission that any such domestic accommodation was adopted by, much more provided for, her eldest son and the then head of her family, under her own roof; and whatever condescension Burns himself might occasionally show to his inferiors, he knew better perhaps his own rank, and was better able, than any man then living, to maintain that rank in the presence of the highest as well as of the humblest associates.

12.—Biography, p. xxxvi. Mrs. Muir of Tarbolton Mill; House-Heating at Ellisland, &c.

Our readers are already aware of the great friendship which had long subsisted between the Muirs of Tarbolton Mill and our Author; and of the fact also that, when Mrs. Burns's relation to the Poet had occasioned offence at home, she was affectionately received, and it may be said sheltered, by them, until the family quarrel was adjusted. Mrs. Muir, indeed, besides being a friend of the Poet's and an ardent admirer of his gifts, was really just such a matron as would be extremely glad to assist in such a difficulty. It was a sort of domestic trouble that she would rejoice very much to have the righting of, and an occasion for maternal patronage entirely to her mind. Accordingly, it appears, that most seasonable and acceptable assistance in the hour of greatest need by no means exhausted her liberality or friendship. On the contrary, it was but the occasion for her to pledge herself to more—viz., that when Jean's marriage had been publicly avowed and the home-coming was to be celebrated, she (Mrs. Muir) would be present on the occasion, wherever it was, and "brew the first peck o' maut" for the family. This the lady accomplished in rather difficult circumstances. She had not anticipated, perhaps, that the scene of such festivity was to be so distant as Ellisland, or that she would be detained more than a day at the utmost in fulfilling her pledge. But she was not to be baulked by any consideration of time or place: she went to Ellisland, according to promise; she welcomed the bride, and she "brewed the maut."

Mrs. "Granny" Hay of Tarbolton, whose name has already been quoted by us, in describing this strange adventure, informed us also that the visit was protracted for a fortnight, and was the cause of much offence to the old miller, who did not know of his wife's departure and threatened "to ding her wi' a stick when she cam hame. Na, he keepit his stick by the chimla-lug, for twa or three days, on purpose; but when he saw her comin down the road his han' trummlit and he set by the stick, and didna ken what to do wi' her when she cam ben. But she was angry when he spier'd at her afterhin, what way she gaed awa without tellin him or askin his leave; and syne mair angry words cam, on baith han's—and she wadna speak to him ony mair that night, but she spak to me; and they war never sic guid friends after."

The miller, in fact, was much older than his wife, and her conduct in undertaking such a visit without his knowledge or permission was decidedly reprehensible. She left the mill, it appears, one afternoon, when the old gentleman was asleep on the 'deas,' "for fear he wad hinder her frae gangin, if he waukenit." Granny Hay, who was an accomplice in the 'mistress's' manœuvre, was charged with the responsibility of appeasing his wrath when he awoke, and "had ill doin o't!"

Whether the solemn procession with the Bible and the basin of salt, from the Isle to Ellisland, described by Mr. Chambers as having preceded the formal occupation of Ellisland by the family, took place before or after Mrs. Muir's visit, we are not aware: but the probability is that that solemnity was observed just at the time, and that Mrs. Muir would be in Ellisland to open the door and welcome the approaching party.

13.—Biography, p. liv. Death of Burns: Various Authorities.

DEATH.

Currie, Edition 1801, vol. i., pp. 220, 223.

It was hoped by some of his friends, that if he could live through the months of spring, the succeeding season might restore him. But they were disappointed. The genial beams of the sun infused no vigour into his languid frame; the summer wind blew upon him, but produced no refreshment. About the latter end of June he was advised to go into the country; and impatient of medical advice, as well as of every species of control, he determined for himself to try the effects of bathing in the sea. For this purpose he took up his residence at Brow, in Annandale, about ten miles east of Dumfries, on the shore of the Solway-Firth.

.   .   .   .   .   .

At first Burns imagined bathing in the sea had been of benefit to him: the pains in his limbs were relieved; but this was immediately followed by a new attack of fever. When brought back to his own house in Dumfries, on the 18th of July, he was no longer able to stand upright. At this time a tremor pervaded his frame: his tongue was parched, and his mind sunk into delirium, when not roused by conversation. On the second and third day the fever increased, and his strength diminished. On the fourth, the sufferings of this great but ill-fated genius were terminated, and a life was closed in which virtue and passion had been at perpetual variance.

Cunningham, Virtue's Edition: p. xliii.

A tremor pervaded his frame; his tongue grew parched, and he was at times delirious: on the fourth day after his return, when his attendant, James Maclure, held his medicine to his lips, he swallowed it eagerly, rose almost wholly up, spread out his hands, sprang forward nigh the whole length of the bed, fell on his face and expired. He died on the 21st of July, when nearly thirty-seven years and seven months old.

Chambers, vol. iv., pp. 209, 210.

Before leaving Brow, Burns experienced a new attack of fever. According to Allan Cunningham, who was living in Dumfries at the time, the poet "returned on the 18th, in a small spring-cart. The ascent to his house was steep, and the cart stopped at the foot of the Mill-hole-brae; when he alighted, he shook much, and stood with difficulty; he seemed unable to stand upright. He stooped as if in pain, and walked tottering towards his own door: his looks were hollow and ghastly, and those who saw him then expected never to see him in life again." Dr. Currie, who probably had exact information regarding the case from Maxwell, says: "At this time a tremor pervaded his frame; his tongue was parched, and his mind sunk into delirium when not roused by conversation."

.   .   .   .   .   .

The life of Burns was now to be measured by hours rather than days. To secure the quietness demanded at such a time, his four little boys were sent to the house of Mr. Lewars. Jessy hovered by his couch with her usual assiduity. Findlater came occasionally to soothe the last moments of his friend. Early in the morning of the 21st, Burns had sunk into delirium, and it became evident that nature was well-nigh exhausted. Dr. Maxwell, who had watched by his bed the greater part of the night, was gone, and the only persons who remained in the room were a pair of humble but sympathising neighbours. The children were sent for to see their parent for the last time in life. They stood round the bed, while calmly and gradually he sank into his last repose. The eldest son retained a distinct recollection of the scene, and has reported the sad fact, that the last words of the bard were a muttered execration against the legal agent by whose letter, wittingly or unwittingly, the parting days of Burns had been imbittered.

For further particulars on this profoundly interesting subject, we need only refer our readers to Mrs. Burns's own statement in Memoranda, p. xxiv., *supra:* and with respect to the last words of Burns as reported by his eldest son, we may mention, that although Mr. Burns distinctly adhered to his recollection of the fact, Mrs. Thomson (Jessie Lewars) made no such report as within her own knowledge or hearing, and when spoken to on the subject used simply to observe that Mr. Burns "was but a bairn when his father died, and *might* be mistaken."

AFTER DEATH.

LOCKHART, Edition 1828: *pp.* 280, 281.

"I went to see him laid out for the grave," says Mr. Allan Cunningham; "several elder people were with me. He lay in a plain unadorned coffin, with a linen sheet drawn over his face; and on the bed, and around the body, herbs and flowers were thickly strewn, according to the usage of the country. He was wasted somewhat by long illness; but death had not increased the swarthy hue of his face, which was uncommonly dark and deeply marked—his broad and open brow was pale and serene, and around it his sable hair lay in masses, slightly touched with grey. The room where he lay was plain and neat, and the simplicity of the poet's humble dwelling pressed the presence of death more closely on the heart than if his bier had been embellished by vanity, and covered with the blazonry of high ancestry and rank. We stood and gazed on him in silence for the space of several minutes—we went, and others succeeded us—not a whisper was heard. This was several days after his death."

.   .   .   .

On the 25th of July, the remains of the poet were removed to the Trades' Hall, where they lay in state until next morning. The volunteers of Dumfries were determined to inter their illustrious comrade (as indeed he had anticipated) with military honours. The chief persons of the town and neighbourhood resolved to make part of the procession; and not a few travelled from great distances to witness the solemnity. The streets were lined by the Fencible Infantry of Angus-shire, and the Cavalry of the Cinque Ports, then quartered at Dumfries, whose commander,* Lord Hawkesbury (now Earl of Liverpool), although he had always declined a personal introduction to the poet, officiated as one of the chief mourners.

CUNNINGHAM, Virtue's Edition: p. xliv.

The burial of Burns, on the 25th of July, was an impressive and mournful scene; half the people of Nithsdale and the neighbouring parts of Galloway had crowded into Dumfries, to see their poet "mingled with the earth," and not a few had been permitted to look at his body, laid out for interment. It was a calm and beautiful day, and as the body was borne along the street towards the old kirk-yard, by his brethren of the volunteers, not a sound was heard but the measured step and the solemn music: there was no impatient crushing, no fierce elbowing—the crowd which filled the street seemed conscious what they were now losing for ever. Even while this pageant was passing, the widow of the poet was taken in labour; but the infant born in that unhappy hour soon shared his father's grave. On reaching the northern nook of the kirk-yard, where the grave was made, the mourners halted; the coffin was divested of the mort-cloth, and silently lowered to its resting-place, and as the first shovel-full of earth fell on the lid, the volunteers, too agitated to be steady, justified the fears of the poet, by three ragged vollies. He who now writes this very brief and imperfect account, was present: he thought then, as he thinks now, that all the military array of foot and horse did not harmonise with either the genius or the fortunes of the poet, and that the tears which he saw on many cheeks around, as the earth was replaced, were worth all the splendour of a show which mocked with unintended mockery the burial of the poor and neglected Burns.

DUMFRIES JOURNAL, Tuesday, 26th July, 1796.

Died here on the morning of the 21st instant, and in the 38th year of his age, ROBERT BURNS, the Scottish Bard.

His manly form and penetrating eye strikingly indicated extraordinary mental vigour.

For originality of wit, rapidity of conception, and fluency of nervous phraseology, he was unrivalled.

Animated by the fire of Nature, he uttered sentiments which, by their pathos, melted the heart to tenderness, or expanded the mind by their sublimity. As a luminary emerging from behind a cloud, he arose, at once, into notice; and his works and his name can never die, while divine Poesy shall agitate the chords of the human heart.

Actuated by the regard which is due to the shade of such a genius, his remains were yesterday interred with military honours, and every suitable respect. The corpse, having

----

* [A mistake on Mr. Lockhart's part: His Lordship was not commander, but only a junior subaltern officer—vide *Dumfries Journal, infra.*]

been previously conveyed to the Town Hall, remained there till the following ceremony took place.

The military here, consisting of the Cinque Port Cavalry, and the Angus-shire Fencibles, having handsomely tendered their services, lined the streets on both sides to the burial ground. The Royal Dumfries Volunteers, of which he was a member, in uniform, with crapes on their left arms, supported the bier. A party of that corps, appointed to perform the military obsequies, moving in slow solemn time to the Dead March in Saul, which was played by the military band, preceded in mournful array, with arms reversed. The principal part of the inhabitants of this town and neighbourhood, with a number of the particular friends of the bard from remote parts, followed in procession, the great bells of the churches tolling at intervals. Arrived at the churchyard gate, the funeral party, according to the rules of that exercise, formed two lines, and leaned their heads on their firelocks pointed to the ground.—Through this space the corpse was carried, and borne forward to the grave. The party then drew up alongside of it, and fired three volleys over the coffin when deposited in the earth.—The whole ceremony presented a solemn, grand, and affecting spectacle; and accorded with the general sorrow and regret for the loss of a man, whose like we scarce can see again.

[On same paper appear the following Notices:—]

THE ROYAL DUMFRIES VOLUNTEERS take this mode of returning their best acknowledgments to Major FRASER and the Officers of the Angus-shire Fencibles; and to Captain FINDLAY and the Officers of the Cinque Port Cavalry, for the very obliging and distinguished compliment rendered to them at the funeral.

☞ The friends of the late Mr. BURNS are requested to meet in the King's Arms here, on Thursday the 28th instant, at Noon.

FROM DIARY OF THE LATE MR. WILLIAM GRIERSON, Dumfries, an Eye-Witness: July, 1796.

Monday, 25th.—Showery forenoon, pleasant afternoon, wet evening and night. This day, at 12 o'clock, went to the burial of Robert Burns, who died on the 21st, aged 38 years. In respect to the memory of such a genius as Mr. Burns, his funeral was uncommonly splendid. The military here, consisting of the Cinque Port Cavalry and Angus-shire Fencibles, who, having handsomely tendered their services, lined the streets on both sides from the Court-House to the burial ground. (The corpse was carried from the place where Mr. Burns lived to the Court-House last night.) The firing party, which consisted of 20 of the Royal Dumfries-shire Volunteers, of which Mr. Burns was a member, in full uniform, with crapes on the left arm, marched in front with their arms reversed, moving in a slow and solemn time to the Dead March in Saul, which was played by the military band belonging to the Cinque Port Cavalry. Next to the firing party was the band, then the bier, or corpse, supported by six of the Volunteers, who changed at intervals. The relatives of the deceased, and a number of the respectable

inhabitants of both town and country, followed next. Then the remainder of the Volunteers followed in rank, and the procession closed with a guard of the Angus-shire Fencibles. The great bells of the churches tolled at intervals during the time of the procession. When arrived at the churchyard gate, the firing party formed two lines, and leaned their heads on their firelocks, pointed to the ground. Through this space the corpse was carried, and borne forward to the grave. The party then drew up alongside of it, and fired three volleys over the coffin when deposited in the earth. Thus closed a ceremony which, on the whole, presented a solemn, grand, and affecting spectacle, and accorded with the general sorrow and regret for the loss of a man whose like we can scarce see again.

[The reader will observe a strong resemblance between this account and that which is quoted from the *Dumfries Journal*.]

MONUMENT, SECOND INTERMENT, &c.

CHAMBERS, VOL. IV., p. 235.

After many years had passed without bringing the public to the raising of a monument over the remains of Burns, his widow, out of her small means, placed an unpretending stone upon his grave, merely indicating his name and age, and those of his two sons interred in the same spot. At length, Mr. William Grierson, who had been acquainted with Burns, and had attended his funeral, succeeded in getting a few gentlemen together, by whom a committee was formed for the purpose of collecting subscriptions for that object.

Money was speedily obtained; a plan was selected, and the foundations of a mausoleum were laid in St. Michael's Church-yard, at a little distance from the angle where the remains of the poet had been originally placed. On the 19th of September, 1815, the coffin of Burns was raised from its original resting-place, that it might be deposited in the new monument. On the lid being removed, "there," says Mr. M'Diarmid, "lay the remains of the great poet, to all appearance entire, retaining various traces of recent vitality, or to speak more correctly, exhibiting the features of one who had recently sunk into the sleep of death. The forehead struck every one as beautifully arched, if not so high as might reasonably have been supposed, while the scalp was rather thickly covered with hair, and the teeth perfectly firm and white. Altogether, the scene was so imposing, that the commonest workmen stood uncovered, as the late Dr. Gregory did at the exhumation of the remains of King Robert Bruce, and for some moments remained inactive, as if thrilling under the effects of some undefinable emotion, while gazing on all that remained of one " whose fame is wide as the world itself." But the scene, however imposing, was brief; for the instant the workmen inserted a shell beneath the original wooden coffin, the head separated from the trunk, and the whole body, with the exception of the bones, crumbled into dust. The monument erected on this occasion is an elegant Grecian temple, adorned with a mural sculpture by Turnerelli, descriptive of the idea of Coila finding Burns at the plough, and flinging her inspiring mantle over him.

BURNS' MAUSOLEUM.
From the Yard of St. Michael's.
DUMFRIES.

LOCKHART, Edition 1828: *pp.* 283, 284, 285.

There was much talk at the time of a subscription for a monument; but Mrs. Burns beginning ere long to suspect that the business was to end in talk, covered the grave at her own expense with a plain tombstone, inscribed simply with the name and age of the poet. In 1813, however, a public meeting was held at Dumfries, General Dunlop, son to Burns's friend and patroness, being in the chair; a subscription was opened, and contributions flowing in rapidly from all quarters, a costly mausoleum was at length erected on the most elevated site which the churchyard presented. Thither the remains of the poet were solemnly transferred on the 5th June,[*] 1815; and the spot continues to be visited every year by many hundreds of travellers. The structure, which is perhaps more gaudy than might have been wished, bears this inscription:—

IN AETERNUM HONOREM
ROBERTI BURNS
POETARUM CALEDONIAE SUI AEVI LONGE PRINCIPIS
CUJUS CARMINA EXIMIA PATRIO SERMONE SCRIPTA
ANIMI MAGIS ARDENTIS VIQUE INGENII
QUAM ARTE VEL CULTU CONSPICUA
FACETIIS JUCUNDITATE LEPORE AFFLUENTIA
OMNIBUS LITTERARUM CULTORIBUS SATIS NOTA
CIVES SUI NECNON PLERIQUE OMNES
MUSARUM AMANTISSIMI MEMORIAMQUE VIRI
ARTE POETICA TAM PRAECLARI FOVENTES
HOC MAUSOLEUM
SUPER RELIQUIAS POETAE MORTALES
EXTRUENDUM CURAVERE
PRIMUM HUJUS AEDIFICII LAPIDEM
GULIELMUS MILLER ARMIGER
REIPUBLICAE ARCHITECTONICAE APUD SCOTOS
IN REGIONE AUSTRALI CURIO MAXIMUS PROVINCIALIS
GEORGIO TERTIO REGNANTE
GEORGIO WALLIARUM PRINCIPE
SUMMAM IMPERII PRO PATRE TENENTE
JOSEPHO GASS ARMIGERO DUMFRISIAE PRAEFECTO
THOMA F. HUNT LONDONENSI ARCHITECTO
POSUIT
NONIS JUNIIS ANNO LUCIS VMDCCCXV
SALUTIS HUMANAE MDCCCXV.

The original tombstone of Burns was sunk under the pavement of the mausoleum; and the grave which first received his remains is now occupied, according to her own dying request, by a daughter of Mrs. Dunlop.

Immediately after the Poet's death, a subscription was opened for the benefit of his family; Mr. Miller of Dalswinton, Dr. Maxwell, Mr. Syme, Mr. Cunningham, and Mr. M'Murdo, becoming trustees for the application of the money. Many names from other parts of Scotland appeared in the lists, and not a few from England, especially London and Liverpool.

---

[*] [This date, which is somewhat carelessly stated by Mr. Lockhart, refers only to the laying of Foundation stone for Mausoleum.]

Seven hundred pounds were in this way collected; an additional sum was forwarded from India; and the profits of Dr. Currie's Life and Edition of Burns were also considerable. The result has been, that the sons of the poet received an excellent education, and that Mrs. Burns has continued to reside, enjoying a decent independence, in the house where the poet died, situated in what is now, by the authority of the Dumfries Magistracy, called Burns' Street—*p.* 285.

IN SHORT, for this honourable object, which in plain terms was but the voluntary liquidation of a national debt long over due to one of the nation's greatest benefactors and proudest creditors, more than one effort, at different times and in different places at home and abroad, was made—the result of which was the realisation of a sum amounting to £1200; of which £800 was invested for the use of Mrs. Burns and her three sons, and £400 to be apportioned equally between two other children, daughters of the deceased. This trust was lodged in the hands of the Provost and Magistrates of Ayr; and it is right to mention that in the whole of these proceedings, both in subscribing to and in investing the funds, Alderman, afterwards Sir James Shaw, of London, took a prominent, honourable, and most efficient part.

In addition to the sum above specified, there was also, as Mr. Lockhart states, a considerable amount realised by the sale of the Poet's works, as edited by Dr. Currie for behoof of the family. What the precise sum so realised was, seems to be uncertain; Mr. Chambers, on good authority, estimates it at from £1200 to £1400; and whether it was all invested, or otherwise applied at the moment, and to what extent, is also doubtful. On this subject, we quote in conclusion a letter from Mrs. Burns herself to her friend Mrs. Perochon, detailing the circumstances of her family in 1816; with a copy of which we have been favoured by Mr. M'Diarmid, of Dumfries, and which is the only document accessible to ourselves in relation to this matter.

LETTER FROM

Mrs. Burns to Mrs. Perochon.

2nd Feby., 1816.

MY DEAR MADAM,

I WAS most agreeably surprised by the contents of your letter, and as the idea of ever receiving any augmentation to my income had never before been suggested, I had learned to confine my wants to its present limits. Most gratefully do I enter into your present views, for that effect—and whether or not they are successful, will ever feel a high sense of your goodness. Much, indeed, do I already owe to your disinterested friendship; and while a generous public are anxious to do justice to the genius of my husband, by building so superb a monument to perpetuate his memory, you have paid the best tribute of your regard by so warmly interesting yourself in the behalf of his *widow and his children*. In this you follow the example of her whose virtues you inherit, and who so highly distinguished Mr. B. by a friendship which formed one of his first enjoyments.

I shall now endeavour, as you request, to give you all the information in my power of my affairs. After the sale of Mr. B.'s works, a fund was sunk for my use, to the amount of £1000—since when I have received regularly, annually, £60, with the addition of having my rent paid, which is £8; as this my yearly income amounts to more than the interest of the thousand pounds, I cannot exactly say from what source the odds is derived, unless from the remains of a sum of money placed in security by Sir J. Shaw—part of which was taken up to fit out one of my sons. This, then, is an exact statement of what I now possess, which, while my family were with me, was scarcely sufficient for our wants, and I own after they were provided for, I did not expect a continuance of the same sum. You desire me to give you freely my own ideas on the subject of an application being made to either of the respectable personages you mention. I can have no objections to a plan formed so much for my advantage, and beg that since it has been begun under your auspices, you will conduct it in whatever manner your own superior judgment directs. I would consider it a mark of unthankfulness were I to plead poverty, and equally as ungrateful were I to refuse an honorable addition to my comforts. Follow then, my dear Madam, the dictates of your own judgment, and I will contentedly await the result.

Will you make my best wishes acceptable to Mr. P—— and to your young friend when you write? I shall hope to have the pleasure of meeting you next week. Till then, accept of the assurance of the gratitude and esteem with which I am,

Dear Madam, Yours, &c.,

J—— B——.

Shortly after the writing of this letter, it should appear, and most probably in consequence of it, Mr. Maule, afterwards Lord Panmure, in 1817 settled a pension of £50 a year on Mrs. Burns, "which she enjoyed about a year and a-half," says Mr. Chambers, "when her son James, having obtained a place in the Commissariat, was able to relieve her from the necessity of being beholden to a stranger's generosity. Mrs. Burns, through the liberality of her children, spent her latter years in comparative affluence, yet "never changed, nor

---

* The lady to whom this letter is addressed was a daughter of Burns's good friend Mrs. Dunlop, and it was her remains which were interred, at her own special request, in that portion of St. Michael's churchyard which was the Poet's first resting place. The inscription on her tombstone is as follows:—

SACRED TO THE MEMORY OF

AGNES ELEANOR DUNLOP,

WIFE OF JOSEPH PEROCHON, ESQ., AND DAUGHTER OF THE LATE MRS. FRANCES WALLACE DUNLOP, THE ONLY DAUGHTER AND WORTHY REPRESENTATIVE OF SIR THOMAS WALLACE OF CRAIGIE, BART.,

WHO DIED 16th OCTOBER, 1825.

Mr. Perochon, like Mrs. Dunlop's other son-in-law, Mons. Henri, was a Frenchman. He survived his wife several years, but had lost his eyesight. He resided at Castlebank, Dumfries, and kept up friendly relations with the Poet's widow and family as long as he lived; Mrs. Burns used to dine with him every Sabbath afternoon. For these particulars we are indebted to the courteous attention of Mr. M'Diarmid and of Mrs. Burns Hutchinson.

---

wished to change her place."—In March, 1834, at the age of sixty-eight, she closed her respectable life in the same room in which her husband had breathed his last thirty-eight years before."

•

Phrenological Development of Burns.

This important subject we propose to treat more at length in our remarks on the "Kerry Miniatures" following: but for the present we subjoin some details of measurement, as we find them quoted by Mr. Chambers, vol. IV., *pp.* 309, 310.

THE CRANIUM OF BURNS.

CHAMBERS, VOL. IV. *pp.* 309, 310.

At the opening of the Mausoleum, March, 1834, for the interment of Mrs. Burns, it was resolved by some citizens of Dumfries, with the concurrence of the nearest relative of the widow, to raise the cranium of the Poet from the grave, and have a cast moulded from it, with a view to gratifying the interest likely to be felt by the students of phrenology respecting its peculiar development. This purpose was carried into effect during the night between the 31st March and the 1st April, and the following is the description of the cranium, drawn up at the time by Mr. A. Blacklock, surgeon, one of the individuals present:—

"The cranial bones were perfect in every respect, if we except a little erosion of their external table, and firmly held together by their sutures; even the delicate bones of the orbits, with the trifling exception of the *os unguis* in the left, were sound, and uninjured by death and the grave. The superior maxillary bones still retained the four most posterior teeth on each side, including the *dentes sapientiæ*, and all without spot or blemish; the incisores, cuspidati, &c., had in all probability recently dropped from the jaw, for the alveoli were but little decayed. The bones of the face and palate were also sound. Some small portions of black hair, with a very few gray hairs intermixed, were observed while detaching some extraneous matter from the occiput. Indeed, nothing could exceed the high state of preservation in which we found the bones of the cranium, or offer a fairer opportunity of supplying what has so long been desiderated by phrenologists—a correct model of our immortal Poet's head: and in order to accomplish this in the most accurate and satisfactory manner, every particle of sand, or other foreign body was carefully washed off, and the plaster of Paris applied with all the tact and accuracy of an experienced artist. The cast is admirably taken, and cannot fail to prove highly interesting to phrenologists and others.

"Having completed our intention, the skull, securely enclosed in a leaden case, was again committed to the earth, precisely where we found it.   ARCHD. BLACKLOCK."

A cast from the skull having been transmitted to the Phrenological Society of Edinburgh, the following view of the cerebral development of Burns was drawn up by Mr. George Combe, and published in connection with four views of the cranium (*W. & A. K. Johnston, Edinburgh*):—

I.—DIMENSIONS OF THE SKULL.

	INCHES.
Greatest circumference,	22½
From Occipital Spine to Individuality, over the top of the head,	14
" Ear to Ear vertically, over the top of the head,	13
" Philoprogenitiveness to Individuality (greatest length),	8
" Concentrativeness to Comparison,	7½
" Ear to Philoprogenitiveness,	4¾
" " Individuality,	4¾
" " Benevolence,	3¾
" " Firmness,	3½
" Destructiveness to Destructiveness,	5¾
" Secretiveness to Secretiveness,	5¾
" Cautiousness to Cautiousness,	5½
" Ideality to Ideality,	4½
" Constructiveness to Constructiveness,	4½
" Mastoid Process to Mastoid Process,	4¾

II.—DEVELOPMENT OF THE ORGANS.

	SCALE.
1. Amativeness, rather large,	16
2. Philoprogenitiveness, very large,	20
3. Concentrativeness, large,	18
4. Adhesiveness, very large,	20
5. Combativeness, very large,	20
6. Destructiveness, large,	18
7. Secretiveness, large,	19
8. Acquisitiveness, rather large,	16
9. Constructiveness, full,	15
10. Self-esteem, large,	18
11. Love of Approbation, very large,	20
12. Cautiousness, large,	19
13. Benevolence, very large,	20
14. Veneration, large,	18
15. Firmness, full,	15
16. Conscientiousness, full,	15
17. Hope, full,	14
18. Wonder, large,	18
19. Ideality, large,	18
20. Wit, or Mirthfulness, full,	15
21. Imitation, large,	19
22. Individuality, large,	19
23. Form, rather large,	16
24. Size, rather large,	17
25. Weight, rather large,	16
26. Colouring, rather large,	16
27. Locality, large,	18
28. Number, rather full,	12
29. Order, full,	14
30. Eventuality, large,	18
31. Time, rather large,	16
32. Tune, full,	15
33. Language, uncertain.	
34. Comparison, rather large,	17
35. Causality, large,	18

The Scale of the Organs indicates their relative proportions to each other: 2 is idiocy; 10, moderate; 14, full; 18, large; and 20, very large. According to above measurements the skull of Burns indicates a large brain. The length is eight, and the greatest breadth nearly six inches. The circumference is 22½ inches. These measurements exceed the average of Scotch living heads, *including the integuments*, for which four-eighths of an inch may be allowed. [See remarks on "Kerry Miniature."]

14.—BIOGRAPHY, *p.* lix. BURNS'S MANUSCRIPTS IN BRITISH MUSEUM.

The reader is referred for information on this subject to notes and quotations, Prose Works, p. 206.

Supplementary Gossip.

A.—BURNS'S HATRED OF IMPOSTURE.

MRS. MARION HUNTER, whose deposition we have already quoted, was a girl of eighteen when Burns had newly entered on his professional duties. He had then Cumnock, Muirkirk, and Douglas in his rounds. She remembers distinctly that when he came to Muirkirk on one of his professional visits, "a great, strong, deaf-and-dumb man, that spaed fortunes and could do naething but blutter and gurl," was at one of the public-houses in that village, practising his art and fleecing the natives. "Mr. Burns," on being informed of this worthy's presence in good faith by the inhabitants, expressed the greatest pleasure at the prospect of an interview; and, with two friends, repaired at once to the upstairs room where the astrologer was seated. Having called for some refreshment at a small table in the other end of the room, and having duly discussed it, first one and then the other of our Author's friends, by preconcerted arrangement, retired, and left him alone with the soothsayer. He thereupon indignantly struck the table, and demanded with vehemence whether the folks about Muirkirk were accustomed to treat strangers after such an unfriendly fashion by leaving them thus uncivilly to discharge the reckoning? No reply having been vouchsafed by the only other party in the room, the demand was repeated in a louder and more indignant tone—'blutter and gurl' being now the rejoinder, but no articulate syllable. Burns then advancing with an incredulous air inquired how his companion was so deaf or dumb, or both? Did he not hear him? Could he not speak? Still no articulate reply: on which the indignant Exciseman "gied him a clank on ae side o' the head wi' ae han', and keppit him on the ither side wi' the ither han', and then a ding on the back o' the head after a'. Then the dumb man opened his mouth, and loused his tongue, and swoor like ony dragoon—ye never heard as he swoor! But a' was na by. Burns syne took him by the neck aneth the chafts, and gied his napkin a bit twist wi' his fingers, and haurl'd him to the door o' the room, and pat his fit till the spaeman's back, and gart him shine down the stair wi' a hurl!"—A short and summary process of conviction and ejectment certainly, which cleared the neighbourhood, however, of one nuisance for a year; for "the creatur took to some ruined chapel about the place for that nicht, and the laddies chased him awa next mornin."

[In connection with this anecdote, let our readers glance for a moment at the "Kerry Miniature," and they will understand how Burns might possibly have looked on such an occasion.]

B.—BURNS'S FIRST AND FOLLOWING VISITS TO GLASGOW: See Appendix, p. xxxvii.

WITH reference to the friendship which subsisted so long between our Author and Mr. William Reid, of Messrs. Brash & Reid, booksellers, Glasgow, Mr. ROBERT HEDDERWICK, Garden Place, in that city, whose father was, when a boy, in the employment of that respectable old firm, informs us that he has heard his father again and again allude to the intimacy referred to. Mr. Reid's shop was Burns's first place of call when he visited Glasgow, and Mr. Reid was the special friend with whom his whole leisure was spent whilst he remained in the city. Mr. Brash, who was a matter-of-fact business man, and altogether devoid of poetical sympathy, disliked those visits; but Burns's appearance was Mr. Reid's signal at once to put on his hat and leave the shop; when the two friends disappeared—in plain terms, 'dived'—spending generally not a few hours together, in some snug retreat.

> [To] gie ae night's discharge to care,
>
> . . . .
>
> An' hae a swap o' rhyming ware
> Wi' ane anither.

But however this might be, Mr. Reid, so far as business was concerned, was *non est* until Burns had left the city. Thus far Mr. Hedderwick's relation:—but an intimacy of this kind, it is obvious, could not possibly have originated between persons of unequal age, without some considerable foundation of kindness on the younger, and of gratitude on the elder side, to begin with; nor could it have continued without a large measure of kindred feeling and mutual respect to sustain it; and by Mr. Hedderwick's spontaneous collateral testimony to this effect, the circumstances related by us on Mr. John Reid's own authority, of Burns's first visit to Glasgow, are sufficiently corroborated and confirmed.

Obituary Notices, &c.,
OF THE
POET'S FAMILY.

DUMFRIES COURIER, Tuesday, 19th May, 1857: Abridged.

DEATH OF ROBERT BURNS, ESQ.—We have to announce the demise of Mr. Robert Burns, which melancholy event occurred on the afternoon of Thursday, the 14th instant, at his residence in English Street here. Mr. Burns was born at Mauchline in September, 1786, so that he had nearly completed his 71st year. In several respects in point of intellect, the deceased was no ordinary man, but yet he was chiefly remarkable throughout life as being the oldest son of Robert Burns, the national poet of Scotland. Burns died in 1796, and his oldest boy was nearly ten years of age at the time of that premature decease. Of the father the son preserved a vivid remembrance, and was wont to describe their walks taken together on the banks of the Nith. Mr. Burns was educated at the Dumfries Academy, where he distinguished himself, especially in the classics; even before his father's death he gave promise of ability which filled the parental heart with pleasure, while the poet did not fail to lend a helping hand in the preparation of the school tasks of his son, as was discovered by Doctor Gray from the eloquence of the language in which his youthful pupil's translations from the Latin were couched. After completing the curriculum of the local seminary, Mr. Burns prosecuted his studies both at Glasgow College and the University of Edinburgh, becoming an excellent classical scholar, as well as an advanced mathematician. His own natural bent was for tuition, and his highest ambition to become rector of the academy in which he had been educated. But an appointment to a clerkship in the stamp office having been offered him by the prime minister, Mr. Addington, he proceeded to London in 1804 and entered upon his duties at Somerset House, where it was anticipated that a prosperous career had been opened up for him. For the work of a public office, however, he was not well suited, and indeed throughout his life he continued comparatively a child in matters of business; he was besides a man of strong passions, and the temptations of the metropolis were not resisted; from these reasons he did not rise to the position which his abilities and influence would otherwise have commanded. He remained in London, and at Somerset House, until 1833, a period of nearly thirty years, during which he had eked out a limited income by his favourite occupation of tuition; he retired at that time on a pension, and returned to Dumfries, where he has since resided almost constantly.

Mr. Burns, as we have already mentioned, was an accomplished scholar. Endowed with a prodigious memory and great powers of application, he had amassed a vast quantity of knowledge on a great range of subjects. His enthusiasm in the acquisition of information continued to almost his last days, and for some years he had been almost passionately attached to the study of the language of the Gael. In music he was a proficient student, possessing both a theoretical and practical knowledge of the art. A portion of the father's poetic mantle had fallen upon the son, and in his earlier years he composed verses of considerable intrinsic merit.

His vision, save for objects brought into close proximity with his eyes, was very indistinct, which rendered his appearance and manner somewhat awkward; but he always preserved the bearing of a gentleman in society, and the kindness and sweetness of his temper secured for him many warm friends, independently of the interest which attached to him as the eldest son of Scotland's poet.

His remains will be laid to-day beside those of his father, in the Mausoleum, St. Michael's Churchyard, the vault of which has not been opened for upwards of twenty years.

To the above notice we may add, that Mr. Burns, as eldest son of the family, was among themselves affectionately styled the 'Laird;' and besides being near-sighted, was also a little absent-minded, which would now and then occasion laughable jokes at his expense.

Mr. Burns married at St. Mary-le-bone Church, London, March 24th, 1809, Miss Anne Sherwood; who died at Dumfries, July 16th, 1835, and was interred in the Mausoleum. Of this marriage there were three children; the third and only surviving child of which family is Eliza, born in London, 1812, and married, 1836, at Bangalore, to Bartholomew Jones Everitt, Esq., Assistant-Surgeon, 12th Native Infantry, East India Company's Service, Madras Establishment. The eldest son of this marriage, Robert Burns Everitt, born at Penang, died an infant, at sea, in the return of his parents from India in 1830. Martha Burns Everitt, who was born in London, is the sole surviving child of this family. Mrs. Everitt has been for many years a widow. These two ladies, for some time resident at Belfast, now at Ayr, are the nearest lineal descendants in the third and fourth generation from Robert Burns.

DUMFRIES COURIER, Tuesday, 28th Nov., 1865: Abridged.

DEATH OF LIEUT.-COLONEL JAMES GLENCAIRN BURNS.—Colonel James Burns was born at Dumfries on the 12th August, 1794, and he had consequently more than completed the span of life allotted to man by the Psalmist. He was educated at the Dumfries Academy, and at Christ-Church, London, better known as the Blue-coat School; and having received a cadetship in the service of the East India Company, through the influence of a fast friend of his father's family (Sir James Shaw, Chamberlain of the City of London), he set sail in June, 1811, for the far East, and in due time arrived in Calcutta. He joined the 15th Regiment of the Bengal Native Infantry, and devoted himself to his military duties until 1817, when, by which time he had become a lieutenant, he was appointed by the Marquis of Hastings, then Governor-General of India, to an important post in the Commissariat Department. In the following year he married Miss Sarah Robinson, who died at Neemuch in November, 1821, in her 24th year, leaving three children, one of whom, a son named Robert, in a few weeks followed his mother to the grave: two daughters, Jean and Sarah, sailed for Britain in 1823, the elder to be placed under the care of her maternal grandmother in Sunderland, and the younger under that of the widow of the poet, residing in Dumfries. The elder daughter never reached the British shores, having died at sea on the 5th of June, in her fifth year, and an affecting account of the interest excited by the illness and death of a grand-daughter of the great poet among the passengers and ship's company will be found in the pages of the *Dumfries Magazine*. The younger daughter, Sarah, arrived safely in Dumfries, and remained with her grandmother, of whose declining years she was the solace, until the death of the poet's widow in 1834. In 1828 James Burns married Miss Mary Beckett, and remained in Bengal until 1831, when he, then Captain Burns, with his wife, revisited their native country. He spent a considerable portion of his furlough with his mother. Before his departure the whole country became alarmed at the progress of cholera (about to attack Dumfries with great virulence), and the coolness with which he regarded the malady, in consequence of his experience in India, infused courage into not a few trembling hearts. One incident of this visit was interesting, and is fully described by J. G. Lockhart, in his life of Sir Walter Scott, who at this time (1831) was about to seek—alas! in vain—the restoration of his wearied brain by a tour in the south of Europe:—"On the 17th September the old splendour of Abbotsford was, after a long interval, and for the last time, revived. Captain James Glencairn Burns, son of the poet, had come home from India on furlough, and Sir Walter invited him (with his cicerones, Mr. and Mrs. M'Diarmid of Dumfries) to spend a day under his roof. The neighbouring gentry were assembled, and having

his son to help him, Sir Walter did most gracefully the honours of the table."

[Complimentary verses by Lockhart in honour of the visitor were then sung—Mrs. Lockhart, Sir Walter's daughter, and Captain Burns himself, being the performers.]

Captain Burns returned to India in 1833, and soon after his arrival in Bengal he received from Lord Metcalfe the important appointment of Judge and Collector of Cachar, which he held until 1839, when he retired from active service with the rank of Major, and on his return to Britain resided for several years in the vicinity of London. For a portion of this period he was engaged as a Government Commissioner in an enquiry into the condition of operatives in paper mills, on which he presented a valuable report. He became a second time a widower in 1844, his wife dying at Gravesend in the end of that year, leaving an only daughter. In the same year, his brother, Colonel William Burns, retired from the East India Company's service, and soon afterwards the two brothers took up their joint abode at Cheltenham, where for twenty years they lived, almost without separation, on terms of brotherly affection and kindness, to a degree rare in family life. Some years afterwards, at the general brevet in the Indian army, he obtained the brevet rank of Lieutenant-Colonel. He had been qualified in languages before receiving a civil appointment, and he was skilled in the eastern tongues. On several occasions during his residence in Cheltenham he acted as examiner in Hindustani at the Cheltenham College.

.   .   .   .

His overflowing gaiety of spirits, his sweetness of temper, and his musical accomplishments, rendered him a universal favourite in society, and it was there and in the smaller family circle that he was most appreciated. In his hands the flute and violin discoursed sweet music, but the chief charm lay in the exquisite taste and feeling with which he trilled his father's songs and other melodies of Scotland. His histrionic powers were considerable, and his aid was most valuable in the private theatre. For twenty years he had suffered occasionally but severely from rheumatism, and latterly was sorely crippled by this painful malady, but his heart was buoyant to the last, and his general health so good that his life might have been extended for years, but for a sad accident: on the afternoon of the 15th instant, while proceeding to his drawing-room, he missed his footing and rolled down a long flight of stairs, receiving injuries which had a fatal effect on the following Saturday (18th November).

At his own request his remains were brought to Dumfries, and were interred the following Saturday, in the Mausoleum, St. Michael's Churchyard, beside those of his illustrious father. The surviving children of Lieut.-Colonel J. G. Burns are his daughter Sarah, the surviving child of his first marriage, married to Dr. Berkeley Hutchinson, with four children, a son and three daughters: and Miss Burns, the only child of his second marriage.

LIEUTENANT-COLONEL WILLIAM NICOL BURNS, the only surviving son of the Poet, is a widower without family.

———

Editorial Remarks

ON THE

SCOTTISH LANGUAGE AND LANGUAGE OF BURNS.

PART I.

THE SCOTTISH LANGUAGE.

Homer never wrote in Latin, because he was a Grecian; nor did Virgil write in Greek, because Latin was the language of his country. In short, all your ancient poets wrote in their mother tongue, and did not seek other languages to express their lofty thoughts. And thus, it would be well that custom should extend to every nation; there being no reason why a German poet should be despised, because he writes in his own tongue; or a Castilian or Biscayner, because they write in theirs.—CERVANTES.

> Prudent Sanct Paul doith mak narratioun,
> Twychyng the divers leid of every land;
> Sayand thare bene mair edificatioun
> In fyve wordis that folk doith understand,
> Nor to pronounce of wordis ten thousand
> In strange language, syne wait not quhat it menis:
> I think ale puttryng is not worth two praiis.—LYNDSAY.

ORIGIN.

IN tracing the origin and development of a language so rude and simple, yet in many of its forms so distinct and varied, with so much idiomatic force and so many grammatical irregularities as the Scotch, a mere philological discrimination of roots and derivatives would be entirely insufficient. Somewhat in this way has already been done by the most learned archæologists of the nation, and somewhat more, of our own observation, we shall presume hereafter to add; but our remarks must necessarily be of a mere general character, on the structure and development of the language itself.

As to derivation, however, in the meantime, which is a matter of much importance, we may mention that Horne Tooke, in his celebrated treatise on grammatical forms, quotes, without hesitation or apology, from Scottish writers in illustration of his own theories of the Anglo-Saxon, or Old English tongue—thereby implying the radical identity of the Scotch and English languages. Of Scottish authorities on the same subject we may particularise as the most distinguished, George Chalmers, who, like Horne Tooke, derives our language almost exclusively from the Anglo-Saxon; J. Sibbald, who traces it to the Belgic; Pinkerton and Jamieson, who seem to agree in referring it to the Gothic chiefly. Of these accomplished scholars, we may add that

Sibbald treats this difficult topic with ingenuity;

Pinkerton, with learning and vehemence;

Chalmers, reviewing both, with petulance;

Jamieson, with composure and modesty.

As between names, undeniably so great in this field, we do not presume to decide. Some deductions, indeed, must be made on all hands from their absolute conclusions. Sibbald, for example, in theory maintains the Belgic origin, but derives a great majority of words notwithstanding from the Teutonic proper; he carries ingenuity also, it must be allowed, to the verge of imagination in support of his theory. Pinkerton, a most accomplished but also crotchety man, maintains that the tongue of 150,000 captive English or mercenary soldiers, supposed at one time to have been distributed over Scotland, could have had no effect on the language; which is unreasonable. Their speech, indeed, would never supersede the language of the natives, but it would certainly modify it locally—as witness the case of Inverness, where a garrison of Cromwell's soldiers, for some time resident there, has affected the language of the inhabitants to the present day. He admits also that the grammar of the Scottish language has been affected by the Italian, through the French, through the English, which is partly true, but at variance with his own theory. Further, he has been contemptuously charged by Chalmers with incorrectly quoting, or wilfully perverting the text of his old authorities to maintain his theory—a very serious fault, if he be guilty of it. Chalmers, on the other hand, the very impersonation of learned arrogance, contradicts himself whilst contradicting others. He maintains, for example, that our ancient Scottish authors spoke uniformly of their language as the "Inglis tongue," but he forgets that this was in contradistinction to the Latin and the Gaelic tongues, then common in Scotland; and that English authors of that very period distinguish between their own and the Scottish tongue, to the extent of *translating* Scottish works into their English tongue. Besides, he himself quotes an Act of Parliament, March 1542-3, being the first parliament after the demise of James V., " That it sall be loful to all the lieges to haif the Holy Writ, to wit the New Testament and the Auld, in the vulgar tung, in Inglis or Scottis, of an good and true translation "—which would never have been thought of, if the Scotch and English languages then, or at any previous time, had been the same. Jamieson, a modest and laborious student, leans a little too much to the authority of others in maintaining the Gothic theory; but he derives a multitude of terms in his celebrated dictionary from other sources than Gothic, and leaves a vast number apparently without any derivation at all —as the reader will hereafter observe in our classified Tables of Derivation.

There seems, in short, to be a portion of truth in all these theories, as is manifest from the fact alone that four such eminent antiquarian philologists should have differed so decidedly on the subject; and the probability is, that the Scottish language, as in Burns's day, was made up of contributions from the various kindred sources above indicated, modified by accident, custom, or, more than all, by climate, as the case might be. In these circumstances, we judge it best to pursue our own investigations as independently as possible, availing ourselves of whatever light has been thrown on the subject by authorities so distinguished as the preceding.

The fact seems to be that the materials of the language are miscellaneous—Anglo-Saxon, Dutch, Danish, and Norwegian more directly predominating; that its modifications in structure and orthography have been the imperceptible growth of time; and that its idioms are constitutional or geographical, referable on the one hand to the very idiosyncrasies and

habits of the people, or on the other, to the accidental influences and associations of scenery, climate, family relationships, and soil. That a language so originating, and deriving its constituent elements from various sources in surrounding cognate or intermingling tongues, and so built up into strange irregular and yet harmonious forms—more regular and harmonious than many of those from which its elements were borrowed; and ultimately enriched with idioms of singular significance, with terms of most pregnant force, with syntactical arrangements most perfect, and with an accentuation so expressive of every emotion in the speaker as not to be surpassed by any language in the world; should have claims of individuality and distinction among other tongues advanced on its behalf, is not more wonderful than that French, Italian, and Spanish—all sister tongues, should have dictionaries and grammars of their own. Much of this individuality is doubtless due to geographical limitations and influences, and to the periodical influx and absorption of colonists, with their own terms, from neighbouring soils; or the frequent intermingling by commerce or otherwise, of the people of the land with various foreign representatives of the common stock. This may all be conceded; but the philological certainty remains, that every one of these linguistic contributions has been adopted and modified by the natives of the soil, and so blended with their own peculiar forms of speech, as to become integral parts of an independent whole—no longer Anglo-Saxon, Dutch, Danish, or Norwegian, but intrinsically and properly Scotch.

The Gothic and Teutonic tongues, in their various most important modifications, are undoubtedly the fountains of all: and the principal contributions from those quarters would come inland to the bulk of our people from their brethren who were located on the seaboard of the German Ocean. The Danish element, in particular, must have come abundantly with colonists, or shipwrecked pirates, or vanquished soldiers, or stranded fishermen, on the north-east coast of the island; whilst an infusion of Norwegian and Icelandic would occur in similar circumstances, still farther north. In the west and north-west, the Celtic element remains as a groundwork, from aboriginal tribes; and these all have by degrees been amalgamated, and wrought out into a uniform whole, with its several distinguishable dialects, as plainly as a coat of many colours, diversified but harmonious, for the use of a beloved and highly favoured people. The language may be thus geographically, as well as nationally or dialectically, disseminated; but that it is still one and not many, is demonstrable by the fact, that the speech of Ayrshire, as represented in its purest utterances by Montgomery and Burns, is as intelligible at Aberdeen as at Kilmarnock, and was as heartily appreciated at the time by the best writers of the north, as if they had been natives of the same parish with their distinguished brethren in the south, and yet their dialects were conspicuously different.

It is no part of our present performance to trace these radical contributions of speech beyond the limits of the island, much less to enter into profound philological investigations of their origin in the distant East; but it would be no difficult task to produce many a term from Lowland speech of Shemitic origin. How these have been imported, is another question: but whether by some stray Phœnician merchant-mariner penetrating or coasting northward from Cornwall; or more probably, by some hidden, long-lost route of emigration through central Europe westward—signifies not. Such terms as *yar*, in Yarrow, to flow; *coo* or *cow*, to rise; *sugh*, loud waste sound, travelling overhead; *oïa*, or *een*, the eyes, also a spring of water, Scotticé a 'wal-e'o;' *aïn*, name; *reik*, in Hebrew, vanity or emptiness, in Scotch, smoke; *pars* or *phars*, to break or bruise, Scotticé *frush* or to *frush*—the very word that Daniel translated at Babylon, and travelling to-us-ward undoubtedly through the French *froisser*, to bruise; these and many others, with idioms also to correspond, are not more truly Scotch than Hebrew, and could never be more perfectly translated from Hebrew than as they already stand in Scotch: and it is worthy of observation, in passing, that such terms are more perfectly preserved in Scotch than they seem to be in any intermediate dialect through which they may have passed to us. It is enough for our present purpose, that we discover the various constituent elements of speech above referred to here, and can trace their circulation with peculiar characteristic significations for centuries. Gothic or Teutonic, Celtic or Shemitic, they have long been incorporated in a certain tongue, associated with certain ideas, and identified with the history, the literature, and the very existence of certain people. These circumstances constitute their use, and the words which originate in them, a language. It is with the history and development of that language we are now immediately concerned, and to demonstrate the difference between that language and any mere provincial dialect of another tongue.

That several provincial dialects, particularly in the North of England, resemble the Lowland Scotch, and that the oldest English works in a perfect form resemble Scottish writings of their own period, is certain: but the distinction which makes the difference, as between mere dialects, can be easily pointed out; or the cause of the resemblance, as between authors of different nations, can be specified. So far as the resemblance in authorship, and the language employed by the respective authors of the earliest dates in the contiguous countries, is concerned, it is enough to observe—

(1.) That, besides the inevitable occurrence of certain words common to both, the English writers were earlier in the field, and so became models for their northern brethren, whose phraseology as authors came insensibly thus to resemble theirs, although their own proper speech and the speech of their nation remained unchanged. These English works became in fact models for them in so much, that one exquisite performance, the Cresseide of Henryson, is but a continuation of Chaucer; although Henryson otherwise is a purely Scottish poet, and author of the first and two of the finest pastorals ever written in that or any other language.

(2.) That some of our Scottish authors—as James I., for instance, whose "Quair," if not written, must at least have been imagined there—lived, studied, and wrote in England, thus of necessity imbibing both words and sounds in the very process of composition.

(3.) That some of the most influential of these elder Scottish Poets were academical, ecclesiastical, or courtly men; who had a language of their own, partly native and partly foreign, distinct from the language of the common people, but deemed most appropriate nevertheless for the peculiar field of letters in which they all desired to shine, and which was nearly, if not entirely the same in both countries. This language was acquired at Colleges, in Monasteries, in Ecclesiastical studies, in the reading of mediæval romances and other works popular among scholars, and which could never reach the common people except through their means. In what may be called the translation or adaptation of these mediæval works, the style was nearly uniform among authors of both countries, but the people of Scotland at large never adopted that style; and it is a remarkable, but most natural fact, on the supposition that they had a language of their own, that the most accomplished of these half-foreign writers had no corresponding influence or immortality among the people, and that the simplest and rudest productions of their pens were always more acceptable and endearing than the more scholarly labours of their muse. The supremacy of Sir David Lyndsay for a while was due to the political and religious character of his writings, as much as to his language: his language, in fact, was rather detrimental to his fame. But the supreme favourite, and to this day the grandest type of national epic minstrelsy, Blind Harry, was not only a Scotchman in sentiment and genius, but as a poet of the people accommodated his theme to their accustomed speech more, and has actually a larger amount of unmixed Scotch in his phraseology than any other writer of his nation for centuries.

(4.) Notwithstanding this well-known correspondence in style between Scotch and English writers of the period referred to, in which a crude mixture of Anglo-Saxon, French, and Latin prevailed, the presence and even the prevalence of the Scottish tongue—in its terms, in its idioms, and in its grammatical arrangement—in the Scottish writers, is most obvious to any attentive reader of both; and was so obvious at the time, that English translations or imitations, sometimes in compliment and sometimes in banter, of Scottish effusions occurred, which were as different from the original as translations in a cognate tongue could be; even as renderings by Burns and others in later times, from English into Scotch, made the original a new, almost another work.

(5.) And finally, under this head, it is impossible for a scholar, or even a shrewd cursory reader, if his attention is directed to the subject, not to discover innumerable instances in which certain old forms, *apparently* the same in Scotch and English at the period of their earliest use, have nevertheless a peculiar radical distinguishing difference, which, if cultivated honestly and freely—that is naturally, and without constraint of education or authority—would end in a wide and irreconcilable divergence. Such forms stand apparently together at a point, but it is with their voices in opposite directions. The attentive observer might even mark the very point of that divergence in their tone by a letter adopted on the one side or rejected on the other, and prophesy the appearance of two separate languages from the weight of a syllable peculiar to each. He could detect a different motion of the lips, a different construction of the larynx, a different vibration of the tongue—and, if he could look deep enough, a different pulsation of the blood, implying a different constitution, physical and moral, in the speakers, which must inevitably result in different languages, and which would enable him to predict the whole. Such are the germinal forms and accents, with distinct ideas or emotions attached, which, distributed broadcast for centuries among their respective peoples, produce at last such varieties as Burns and Shakspear.

These arguments will receive additional force from practical illustrations hereafter. In the meantime, as to the resemblance of certain dialects of the English language to the language of Scotland, and the necessity of discriminating between them, it remains farther to be observed—

(1.) That if dialects and languages are to be distinguished from one another at all, then it is of importance to determine first whether the northern dialects of England are not in reality the fragments of an original tongue which has degenerated by neglect into vulgar provincialism, as of Lancashire and Yorkshire, on the one hand; and has been changed by cultivation and the introduction of foreign elements into two distinct tongues, as of England and Scotland, on the other—which, to a certain great extent, is doubtless the case. In England, the occupation by the Romans, the invasion by the Danes, the settlement of the Saxons, and the final supremacy of the Normans with the right of dictating terms of law and the use of language to the vanquished, determined this. In those circumstances, the inhabitants of those remoter districts which escaped the influence of invasion would retain their language also without change; but being beyond improvement, as they were beyond invasion, and having neither national independence on the one hand nor intercourse with the world on the other, the language they thus retained intact would degenerate from want of cultivation, and remain unfruitful from ignorance; would end at last in boorish slang, or never rise at least above the level of the rudest dialect. In Scotland, on the other hand, many of the very same elements of speech by free cultivation would assume regular linguistic forms, by external additions would be modified and extended, by public use in state documents and decrees would acquire authority, by circulation in authorship would rise in dignity; and being thus adapted, with all necessary conditions, to the constitution, the character, and the habits of the people, acknowledged by their lawgivers, and above all, made the popular vehicle of passion, of sentiment, and of humour, in poems and songs—would cease to be the fragments of a dialect any longer, and assume the appropriate rank of elements in an independent tongue. In so far as they predominated, they would influence the tongue, and pass by degrees from a dialect altogether to the power and dignity of a language. If such then be the facts of the case, the distinction between dialects and languages is more a question of degree, with certain conditions, than of any radical difference on either side; and the original rudimental forms both of the Scotch and of the English language may lie still uncultivated and unclaimed, among the boors of Lancashire and Yorkshire.

(2.) But at the crisis of separation we have just now supposed, certain external conditions were absolutely necessary for success. Could the people so adopting or adhering to this language maintain their own independence ? could they provide for their own existence ? could they educate their own children ? could they enact their own laws ? could they choose their own allies ? could they elect their own kings ? could they protect their own clergy ? above all, so far as language was concerned, could they produce their own authors ? These conditions being possible, the language would be safe ; these conditions failing, the language, of inevitable necessity, would cease, and die away in its very utterance from the tongues of men. A nation is required for a language. No mere province can represent it, nor any country of slaves long maintain it. Its forms demand for growth the intellect of a free people ; its continuance is in their uncontaminated breath ; its dignity in their self-assertion ; and its triumphs in the inspiration of their unfettered genius. Such conditions, so far as Scotland is concerned, were all miraculously fulfilled, and the language accordingly survives. But if France by intrigue, or England by conquest, had subjugated Scotland, the language, if not the people, would have perished. Men like Scott and Burns would then have been impossible ; and if by any untoward circumstances of neglect or worldly-wise surrender of this native speech in succeeding generations, it should lapse, and be absorbed or forgotten, such men will never be possible again without a revolution in nature.

(3.) It may militate against this whole theory of an independent language, to acknowledge that it was either so little cultivated by its own most popular authors as to be almost useless in prose for anything beyond a satire or a chronicle ; or that being cultivated by them, it was found altogether unsuitable for subjects of philosophical or historical importance, and in relation to these was no better than a dialect. Such admissions, nevertheless, must so far be made. There are, indeed, many prose compositions, partly legal, partly philosophical, and partly historical, of great interest and beauty—undertaken in some instances by express command of the king—in which the original Scottish element of speech, in picturesque and unadorned simplicity, appears. But these are not sufficiently numerous or important to be classed in competition with other works of a similar character ; and we refer to these specimens of Scottish prose simply to remind our readers that such works exist, and that if the language had been cultivated with such an object in view, it had capabilities of application to themes of that kind far richer and more varied than is commonly supposed. The chief reason, however, why the language was abandoned in this particular field was not its own inadequacy or unsuitableness, but the long continued national distress by wars of defence and civil wars of dissension, which rendered its cultivation and development for such purposes an impossibility ; which extinguished, indeed, the very idea of such studies altogether at the time. There was the prevailing custom, also, in Scotland as well as in England, and in every continental country, of discussing such subjects and composing such treatises in the Latin language, that they might be accessible to the scholars of all nations alike, whom distance or military feuds might so far separate as to render them practically unacquainted with each other's tongues. This universal medium of intelligence and

civilization was justly called Humanity ; and in this sort of literature the Scots themselves so far excelled all others as to become preceptors in Europe—to the neglect in some measure of their own mother tongue. Besides all which, as we have already intimated, the progress of authorship in England having been more fortunate, and the translation of the Bible into the language of that country by authority having made the circulation of it more general, anything which was intended for public use in both countries, or which required to be treated of in regular forensic or philosophic style, would naturally fall to be treated of in that tongue. But it was not till a comparatively recent date, that works of much importance in that department of literature appeared in Scotland at all. In these circumstances, therefore, the use of the native tongue was practically confined to poetry ; and even in the earliest poetry of the nation, a considerable infusion of Latinity and of the oldest English appears.

(4.) But in conclusion of this inquiry, and from a moral point of view, it must be observed, that the people of Scotland have invariably refused to acknowledge, as of permanent authority, anything even in poetry which was not of sterling value, in their native tongue. If that tongue had been a mere dialect, cultivated only for amusement at the moment, and not worthy of recognition for any higher purpose ; if it had been only the slang of a region, like the dialect of Lancashire, or the corruption of a purer language by ignorance and vulgarity, like the mis-spelt speech of America, or the mis-spelt Scotch of magazine literature at the present day—then such works as those of Tim Bobbin, or Sam Slick, or Artemus Ward—caricatures in language, although otherwise works of genius—would have been sufficient, and more than sufficient, to illustrate its peculiarities. But such works as these in their native tongue have never been recognised by the Scottish people ; and even second or third-rate poets, of whom so many might be named, who have chosen the dialect of Scotland in its feeblest forms to represent her genius, have been rejected by the people as unworthy to typify her language. The very best of her earlier representatives, and the most popular of their time, have gradually been forgotten or regretfully relinquished because they were not equal to this sacred task. They may be looked at still as curiosities, or venerated as interesting reliques, but their influence on the Scottish people is gone ; not because they were not beautiful, but because they were not beautiful enough. Nothing but the purest, nothing but the wisest, nothing but the truest, the simplest, the grandest, and the best, can be recognised as immortal in that beloved tongue. So sharp and clear a discrimination as this, between the false and the real ; between the tawdry talk of a neighbourhood, with its vulgarities and emptiness, and the speech of a people communing with nature and with God, and commissioning their thoughts to travel in the guise of the homeliest revelation to the ends of the earth, is a sort of argument against which all the sneers and sophistications of imperfect scholarship, about dialect and provincialism, are in vain.

———

At this point in our remarks, the following tabulated summaries of Derivation, to inform the reader to some extent of the various sources from which the language is drawn, and to enable the student at leisure to investigate and determine for himself, may, with some advantage perhaps, be introduced.

According to JAMIESON, our great Scottish lexicographer, who modestly but decidedly maintains the theory of Gothic derivation in chief, we have been indebted for the original elements of our language to the following sources.

	WORDS.	
GOTHIC, varieties of—		
Gothic proper,	37	
Moeso-Gothic,	194	
Swedo-Gothic,	1976	
Swedish,	391	
Danish,	550	
Islandic,	2830	5,978
TEUTONIC, varieties of—		
German,	601	
Belgic,	629	
Anglo-Saxon,	2263	
Theodisque (Tietish),	21	3,514
CELTIC, varieties of—		
Welsh,	350	
Gaelic,	488	
Irish,	186	983
FOREIGN, varieties of—		
Latin,	1020	
French,	2342	
Italian,	110	
Spanish,	15	
Greek,	55	
Hebrew,	8	3,550
OLD ENGLISH,		1,801
SCOTS Words referred to Local use, without special derivation,		11,385
Total of Derivations,		27,202
Words in Dictionary estimated at		31,287
Words without any assigned derivation,		4,085

According to SIBBALD, a learned and ingenious, in some respects too ingenious, philologist, who, on the other hand, maintains the Belgic theory; and whose vocabulary, although valuable, is by no means so extensive as Jamieson's, the following proportions are found.

	WORDS.	
TEUTONIC, varieties of—		
Teutonic proper,	1065	
Saxon,	662	
Belgic proper,	36	
German,	9	
Old English,	21	
Theodisque (Tietish),	50	1,863
GOTHIC, varieties of—		
Gothic proper,	192	
Swedish,	260	
Danish,	126	
Islandic,	161	
Scandinavian,	32	780
CELTIC, variety of—		
Gaelic,		91
FOREIGN, varieties of—		
Latin,	218	
French,	716	
Italian,	11	
Spanish,	4	
Greek,	3	952
Total of Derivations,		3,686
Words in Vocabulary estimated at		5,316
SCOTS Words without special derivation,		1,690

In consequence of so great a difference in extent between these tables as to the number of words, it is necessary, for accurate comparison, to estimate the percentage in both; which seems to be as follows. According to Jamieson, the percentage of

Gothic terms is	21·94
Teutonic do.	13·92
Celtic do.	3·61
Foreign do.	13·05
Old English do.	6·03
Scots, underived do.	41·45

According to Sibbald, the percentage of

Teutonic (including Old English) terms is	50·4
Gothic do.	21·1
Celtic do.	2·46
Foreign do.	26·03
Scots, underived do.	43·83

It thus appears that words of Teutonic origin, according to Sibbald, amount to more than half of the whole language, although the proportion of Belgic-proper terms in that department is comparatively very small. By "Belgic" origin, therefore, so earnestly contended for by him, we must understand that not Belgic-proper, but Teutonic at large, is intended by Sibbald. According to Jamieson, on the other hand, who represents the Gothic theory, a comparatively small proportion of derivations is allotted to that source— very little larger, indeed, than Mr. Sibbald himself allows; whilst Teutonic and Old English together, according to him, being = 19·55, do not amount to half the proportion allowed them by Sibbald. There is a curious correspondence, however, between their Gothic, Celtic, and Foreign Derivatives, and words underived by them, respectively, which seems to attest the accuracy of their investigations there. As a matter of curiosity, although not affecting the theories in question, we may add that, according to Jamieson, the percentage of

Latin terms is	3·75
French do.	8·01

whilst according to Sibbald the percentage of

Latin terms is	5·9
French do.	19·64

which shows considerable diversity; and these percentages throughout must be understood to relate not to the entire number of words in the Dictionary on the one hand, or in the Vocabulary on the other; but only to the total number of derivations given in each, from which alone, of course, they could be properly ascertained.

In the above summaries, particularly in those of Sibbald, a considerable allowance, perhaps of ten per cent., must be made, for double, and sometimes triple, derivations of the same word; and in leaving the reader thus to choose for himself, that ingenious philologist displays the greatest candour. It must be remembered, however, that various forms of the same word are actually to be found in the language, which were therefore derived from as many independent sources, so that the proportion after all remains the same; whilst this very fact, of several words in various forms being derived from as many independent sources, indicates

a still remoter source from which they all originally flowed. To such distant comprehensive relationships, however, our present inquiries do not extend; but to verify in some measure the correctness of the foregoing deductions, we have made a separate analysis of the Belgic language proper, as represented in Sewel's and Buys', one of its best and largest dictionaries. From that authority, without consulting either Jamieson or Sibbald on the subject, we have noted down every Dutch word which had a manifest and undeniable correlative in the Scottish language—whether by affinity or by actual derivation, we do not for the present inquire; but in the great majority of instances, we believe, by derivation—and the number of terms in the Scottish language thus closely related to the Dutch appears to be . . . 768; which, in proportion to the total number of derivations in Jamieson, will give a percentage of only 2·86, almost identical with Jamieson's own—which is 2·31—and seems, therefore, to be a very strong corroboration of his theory. It is fair, however, to state, that if the number of corresponding *phrases* in the two languages, or of individual terms common to both Scotch and English, were also included, the proportion would be considerably greater; and many may have escaped our notice, which would have required minute investigation to trace.

ORTHOGRAPHY.

ONE of the most remarkable characteristics of the Scottish language in a written form is the provoking irregularity of its orthography; and this by no means only as between the ancient and modern forms, but as among the ancient forms themselves, which vary in almost every author and in the same author, on every page and in the same page, without end. In this respect the language is not altogether different from other uncultivated vernaculars—as old English, French, and Italian—and corresponds not a little to old Hebrew itself in this very point. But the origin of such irregularity is an interesting subject of inquiry.

(1.) It may be traced with obvious reason to the various sources of derivation, already indicated, in cognate languages from which the same words are drawn, but in which the same words are differently spelt. Thus the same words from the German, Dutch, Danish, Swedish, Islandic, or other tongues, being differently spelt in each, would be differently spelt also by the various authors through whom they were imported into Scots. If the sounds only were retained, the exact uniformity so desirable in a finished language would seem of secondary importance to the earliest writers, who had no common standard as yet to guide them, and observed only the dialect of their own immediate neighbourhoods. Where such diversity of form, however, implies any fundamental diversity of sound, it is valuable to the philologist as a key to derivation, and points with tolerable accuracy to the very source among many from which the same word, or word signifying the same thing, may have been imported into the language.

For evidence and illustration of this, consult examples and quotations, *infra.*

(2.) Besides this diversity of origin, however, there was the want of a written standard to rule the spelling of those very writers. Most of our earliest works were traditional, or in the rudest manuscript, and either by rehearsal or transcription varied in syllabic forms so much as sometimes not merely to affect the spelling, but, where letters occurred of similar forms, to change the very meaning and destroy the sense of words. In the case of rehearsal, for example, the variation would be double or triple—first in the pronunciation of the various rehearsers, second in the use of different letters by different amanuenses to express the same sound, and finally in the reading or rewriting of this very work of theirs when finished—to which the errors of printers, and the emendations of editors may be added, as aggravations of the original evil. The Maitland Poems present, perhaps, the most remarkable illustration of these accumulated corruptions extant. In the case of rude manuscripts, besides the occasional errors of inadvertency in the position, or the doubling or dropping of letters that had the same sound—or the mistaking of one letter for another to the injury of mere form—the same and even much more serious irregularity, with damage or destruction to the sense, would accrue, than in the case of mere rehearsals where there could be no mistake.

(3.) In addition to these two natural, and perhaps inevitable causes of orthographical irregularity, a fine contemptuous superiority to all rule, and arbitrary self-indulgence in the utmost freedom of form on the part of our authors themselves—who wrote as they spoke with a characteristic individuality of their own, according to the humour or convenience of the moment, must be taken into account. The extent to which this license of theirs was carried, by individual authors, can only be understood by those who are acquainted with the earlier specimens of composition in the language, and can neither be explained nor justified on any ordinary principles of phonetic propriety. It was heterography, in fact, and not orthography at all—a sort of phonetic eccentricity, originality, and self-contradiction in the use of letters, in which Scotchmen above all other writers in the world were likely to assert themselves. Even Burns, in this respect, is by no means an exception to the established disorder, as the text both of the "Jolly Beggars" and many other pieces, still untouched by editorial pens, is enough to testify; although by degrees this confusion was mitigated, partly by his own and partly by editorial revisions.

(4.) In these circumstances, and long before his appearance, a final cause began to operate, the effect of which was more injurious to the character of the language than any eccentricity that could occur from native sources. The art of printing was first introduced into Scotland in 1507, but seems to have collapsed in less than a generation. In 1540 it was revived by Thomas Davieson "Printer to the Kingis nobill Grace;" but before 1551, it had become licentious, and required restraint. In the meantime, however, one Johnne Skott, an Englishman and a printer, had been transplanted from London to St. Andrews by Archbishop Hamilton, no doubt with royal sanction, and was employed by the Archbishop in printing his Grace's catechism—1551. Among other national works of importance subsequently undertaken by him were the Poems of Sir David Lyndsay, some of which appeared with his imprint or initials in 1552. As was natural enough in the circumstances, much of Sir David's orthography was altered by this London craftsman from "Scottis to the Inglis dialect;" besides which, Sir David himself was afterwards (1565–6) done "both in Englessho and Skottessh" for William Pekeryng; and at a still later date (1581, with intervening editions in 1575, for the same gentleman's commercial benefit) the works of Lyndsay, compiled in the Scottish tongue were "first turned and made perfect Englisho, pleasant and profitable for all estates." Of these "pleasant, profitable, and perfect turnings" no fewer than seven editions were printed—"five in Scotland, and *three* (? two) in England." Of the "Englessho and Skottessh" printed in Scotland, one was by Skott of St. Andrews in 1568—which was probably a model for the final "English turning;" but the "door of the English book not only translated the Scottish into perfect Englisho, but *altered* the words, changed the sentiments, and twisted the language; so that the English editions cannot be regarded as the works of Lyndsay at all." This information we obtain chiefly from Chalmers, who strangely enough, in face of it all, insists that the Scotch and English languages are but slightly different modifications of one mother tongue. When we remember, however, that the London printer produced a national catechism for Archbishop Hamilton, and some other works of national importance as well as the poems of Sir David Lyndsay, it is not difficult to see how the last grand corruption was publicly engrafted on the language of the people, and how they were doomed to read and spell, and consequently to write, if not to speak, in an incorrect form "the tongue wherein they were born," simply because the printer of the day in their own country refused to supply them with it as it should have been read. They were thus forcibly subjected to an education in error, which has damaged the purity, and the very force of their language ever since. This corruption, of course, was not universal. Words which could not be so modified or tampered with would remain as they were, but the language had suffered violence; its integrity was openly infringed; and not only English spellings, but English words, were at last adopted and established where Scottish words alone would otherwise have appeared. Ramsay and Fergusson both patronised this bastard style, and Burns himself, in so far as he made their language his model, in deference to the habits of the people, tampered with the purity of his native tongue and confirmed the error.

With respect to this last and worst of all innovations on its integrity as a written language, it may be inquired whether the Scottish tongue did not become a mere dialect of the English? To some extent it did; but not to the same extent as might be supposed. The integrity of a language lies more in the sense and application of its words, than in the mere form of its syllables. Scottish senses and Scottish sounds were still retained by the very words whose external forms were thus violently or insidiously altered: and to this extent the language remained inviolate. Words of Scottish origin, and with Scottish significations, preserve to this hour their original articulation and also their original sense, although printed or written in an English form; and what is thus true of words and syllables is truer still, if possible, of all idiomatic expressions. No SCOTTISH IDIOM, any more than

French, or German, or Hebrew idiom, can lose its original application by any amount of mere typographical violence, or even of translation. If wrongly printed, it asserts its individuality; if wrongly translated, it disappears entirely, as under protest: but even where it remains, this immense disadvantage has accrued to readers in both languages—that the Scotchman is betrayed into mis-pronunciation and the corruption of his own most expressive tongue by the bastard form; and the Englishman, or foreigner approaching through an English channel, is disappointed and bewildered, nay, provoked to find a meaning in the terms before him entirely different from that which he is accustomed to attach to them, and to find himself utterly unable to read, or at least to articulate with satisfaction the very syllables he seems to see on the page. The syllables seem to be English, but they are not; and the sense should be English, but it is not: a double disadvantage to both author and reader thus occurs, which might have been entirely avoided if the first printer at St. Andrews had been kept sternly to his text, or if the authors of the period themselves had had dignity enough to assert the integrity and independence of their mother tongue.

Attempts to remedy this mischief are now being made in a sort of feeble or licentious way, almost as objectionable as the error itself, by arbitrary, vulgar English *mis*-spellings in imaginary Scotch phraseology—borrowed with a thousand distortions, and almost idiotic combinations of letters, in imitation of the lowest slang—no more to be compared with the Scots of our forefathers' day than schoolboy orations of Eton are with the simplicity of Lucretius. This newspaper and magazine style of so-called Scotch, which every Englishman imagines to be an authentic reproduction of the language in which a James and Mary, a Buchanan, a Robertson, an Erskine, a Scott, or a Wilson wrote and spoke, is setting in among the forms of their grand old simple language like an inundation of Cockneyism among the terms of Shakespear: concerning which only one hope can be expressed, that in the course of a generation or less it will sink, like a residuum of grammatical rubbish, and be finally forgotten. Let no English reader, in the meantime, mistake it for anything else; and let no Scotchman delude himself with the idea that such mis-spelt enormities are, or were, or can be, the language of his country. Not Scotch words are these, most intelligent friends, which you thus vainly employ; but only English words with a miserable mis-pronunciation, and incomprehensible mis-spelling to the bargain.

(5.) There was yet one other source of complication in the midst of these, which, originating in high quarters, spread its injurious influence with amazing rapidity through the entire language. This was the introduction by priests, lawyers, clerks, schoolmasters, and courtiers, of new words for old ideas, with slightly modified accentuation from the Latin language. In law processes and in scholastic forms, such an addition to the terminology of the language might be reasonable enough, as we see it universally adopted in other modern tongues; and the manner in which it has been applied in our own language is so far unobjectionable, inasmuch as the foreign terms have been almost invariably adapted to the vernacular. But it is to be regretted, notwithstanding, that such terms have often been employed where a judicious combination of native terms would have been equally easy and far more expressive, if the pride and ostentation of learning had not disdained their use. And it is not less to be lamented, that in writing or printing in such foreign terms, a peculiar typography had not been insisted on as it has been in Dutch and German authors, to mark out distinctly the foreign root or compound, that the borrowed syllable might never be confounded with any portion of the native tongue. This precaution, however, seems to have been entirely neglected, and Greek and Latin words are now so completely amalgamated with the broadest Scotch dialects as to read and almost sound like the vernacular itself. Our chief transgressors in this respect were the scholarly writers, who, from taste or profession, desired to exhibit their Latinity, and who made ancient authors their exclusive models; and chief among these was Sir David Lyndsay himself, both scholar and courtier, whose poems, in many of their finest passages, are but Scottified Latinity—a circumstance which made them acceptable to the highest class of readers at the time, but tended inevitably to their disuse and ultimate disappearance. The almost total absence of this learned affectation in Burns is one among the many natural charms which ensure perpetuity to his writings. It was fortunate in this respect, for himself as well as for the people, that he was not a scholarly man, but confined, or at least predisposed by the very circumstances of his education, to the use of the homeliest vernacular.

But although such orthographical irregularities in the native tongue (for we do not longer speak of English interpolations) are both arbitrary and capricious in style, and innumerable in extent, there is hardly, so far as we recollect, a single instance of vulgarity or stupidity among them. They were founded all on the simple principle of obtaining length and force for the syllables, in natural conformity with the origin of the words. The modes of accomplishing this object were no doubt varied according to the judgment of the writer, or the prevailing fashion of his local dialect, as already explained; but in every case EMPHASIS and FULNESS were to be preserved by some reasonable process, and all letters, both consonants and vowels —but vowels especially—were to be fortified or supplemented, and trained out in one way or another, where they were in danger of collapsing, to do twice their apparent natural work in a syllable. Where one consonant or one vowel of the same order is stronger or broader than another, the strong and broad are instinctively preferred; where no such choice is available, another consonant or another vowel of cognate sound is added to the first; and where such expedients fail, or are not considered satisfactory, an entire additional syllable is subjoined, or what would otherwise be a natural diphthong is divided into two. Thus—

born	is made	borne,	almost	bhorne;
corn	,,	korn	,,	khorne;
sworn	,,	shorn	,,	shorne;
school	,,	skull	,,	lshule,

afraid	is made	affrayed,	almost	affrayet;
live	,,	leve,	,,	lleve;
wine	,,	wyne,	,,	wine;
yell	,,	yend	,,	youle, &c.

As a general rule, it may be assumed that all consonants are naturally strong and rough, all sounds long and broad, and all syllables available; all words which can be divided in pronunciation are to be so divided, and all component parts of them made articulate, in the Scottish language.

Had such general principles been recognised from the first, so many variations and arbitrary attempts to enforce them in writing would have been unnecessary; but even now, with all those forms to help us, we seem to have lost the native articulation of our tongue, and are only driven back to it by the sheer impossibility of reading its very finest poetry otherwise. Mere typographical devices—as by printed accents, *ostled*, *horid*, *sweed*, and horrid orthographical devices—as *oo's*, and *boo's*, and *soo's*, are all equally unnecessary. The language, when rightly spoken, or correctly written, has resources in itself above all those, and should never be encumbered with such enormities.

Among forms which occasion the greatest difficulty, as between typography and pronunciation, are the combinations of *o*, *e*, *i*, with *u*, *w*, *e*.

ou and *ow*, which are but one and the same sound, under different forms of typography, = *oo* in English.

e, *ei*, *ie*, which alternate according to derivation or caprice, = *ee* in English; and where *ei* in modern orthography has been substituted for them, it should not be pronounced otherwise than as *ei*

i, itself, is one of the most arbitrary, being sometimes equivalent to English *i*, *y*, or the longest *e*. These variations are to be accounted for partly by abbreviations in typography, and partly by rules of the language, which from continued negligence have been overlooked and forgotten. For example, where *i* is now equivalent to *y*, the original orthography of the word where it so occurs has been with double *i*—thus *ij*; gradually, as in Dutch typography, superseded by *y*. In Dutch, the *y*, being printed, asserts its own sound; in Scotch, the *j* being dropped, and only the *i* left, the sound alternates from one side to the other until its original value is destroyed—and this, it must be obvious, through typographical carelessness alone, not through any imperfection of the language. Thus *prisin*, *risin*, *rivin*, &c., sound and should be printed *prysin*, *rysin*, *ryvin*, &c., as we frequently find them both in Burns and in earlier writers.

Where *i*, on the other hand, is equivalent to long *e*, it has been originally in combination with another vowel, or separated from *e* final by a single consonant only, which in process of time has been struck out; or it has been followed by certain softer consonants, which in like manner have disappeared. Thus—*dive* remains for *leive*, *gie* for *give*, *hie* for *high*, and *wi'* for *with*; in all which cases the inviolable sound = *ee*. In such cases as these also, where the vowel *i* occurs in participial forms, it sounds emphatically *ee*; nor is any alteration in orthography required to announce this. Thus, that one example may suffice—*livin* is not *livvin*, but *leevin*, and should be invariably so pronounced although not so printed; whereas *livin'* for *living*, might be either Scotch or English, and pronounced accordingly.

With respect to consonants, the chief varieties are in the exchange of *k*, *ck*, *ct*, indifferently, as equivalent to double *kk*;

in the use of *gh*, which is occasionally soft, but most frequently hard; or of *ch*, which is also sometimes soft, but most frequently hard, as in other northern tongues; and finally, in the dropping of *g*, *d*, or any other final consonant—the effect of which is invariably to lengthen or broaden, as the case may be, but always to intensify the natural sound of the syllable preceding, or sometimes even of the two preceding syllables, where there are more than one or two.

Mr. Sibbald, in a curious learned passage of his Glossary, traces with much ingenuity the origin of the Scottish *qvh* to the ancient obsolete Gothic letter O with a point in the middle of it, invented by Ulphilas as an equivalent for *Qu*, or *Hv*, or *Gv*; and supposed by him (Mr. Sibbald) to have been derived in sound at least from the old Greek *digamma* with a different form, or the older Hebrew *Ain*, with a more similar form. His conjectures on the subject have probability enough to support them; but our own *qvh*, however ancient it may thus have been, has also disappeared, having been almost universally since Burns's day superseded by *wh*; which however does not, and never will, express the peculiar force of the original strong combination: *qvhilk*, *qvhan*, &c., are qvhilk and qvhan still, however *whilk* and *whan* may be supposed to have filled their places.

To illustrate in its whole extent, however, the want of conformity we have thus been endeavouring to explain would be impossible here. All we can now afford to do, in conclusion of this department, is to quote a specimen or two of such irregularities to support our remarks. Many others equally good might be selected, and innumerable others of the same sort, although not so conspicuous, may be found in any of our ancient Scottish authors. We may classify these as follows:

I.—Variations illustrating the Process of Lengthening Syllables.

frammyt, fremit, frem'd, frem,	strange:
glowming, glooming, gloaming, gloamin,	twilight:
lown, lowne, lonne, lound,	sheltered
met, mat, moet, myt, micht, might,	might:
schregh, schriegh, schraigh,	to cry out:
sir, schir, schyr, schyir, syr,	sir, sire:
skiegh, skeich, skiegh, skygh,	proudly shy:
sprach, sprech, spraich,	howling:
sprengis, sprulngs, sprayings, spreyings,	shreds:
spruttit, spruttlit, spurtted, spreuttillit, } spreckled, sprackled, sprinkled,	spotted:
yed, yede, yeid, yude, yheid, yhude, ga'ed,	went:

in all which cases, taken at random, the length of the syllable not only increases, but increases in the order of time by usage in which it is thus represented.

II.—Variations by Difference of Derivation.

Mesell, meseal, meslin, mashlum, mashlam;
 French, *meslis*; Teutonic, *mesen*; mixed or spotted.
Practik, prattik, praktique, praktikos—pravtik, pevttis, prvtts, pratts;
 Greek, *praktikos*; Teutonic, *practicke*; French, *pratique*; Islandor, *prettid*; sharp practice, underhand dealing.
Rak, rock, roak, rawk, ruk;
 Saxon, *rocu*; Danish, *rackis*; Teutonic, *roock*; fog, mist, vapour.
Reik, reee, rek, roek;
 Islandic, *reiker*, Saxon, *rec*; Goruic, *ripuis*; Teutonic, *reicken*; smoke, darkness, breath; to which we may add the Hebrew *reik*, emptiness or vanity—"the people imagine reik."—Ps. II.
Scho, sche, she; Saxon, Swedish, Gotuic.
Scorp, Scarp; Skrupp, Skripp, Skrypp; to sneer at or deride;
 Danish and Swedish, alternately; &c., &c.

Flogget, fleyed, flelt;	Afflicked, afflixit, afflicted;
Live, laive, leve;	Publick, publlet;
Quit, quat, quite;	Respek, respeck, respect; &c.

Ower, owre, ouer, ouir, contracted as under—
O'er, o' re, o'er; thus, owtowring, owtane, owrelod, owsprod, &c.

and these we call arbitrary or accidental, not because there may be no reasons for them, but because they are to be found in use not only by the same author or authors, but sometimes even on the same page.

SYNTAX.

I.—Grammatical Peculiarities in Parts of Speech; which are not Improprieties, but Idiomatic Forms.

1.—Nouns:

Nouns are occasionally used for verbs, and verbs also are occasionally used for nouns, with intensified signification in both cases—as *lair* for *learning*, thus—

> A lesson worth the lair;—Montgomery's *Cherry and Slae*:

or *live* for *life*, thus—

> Last on live;—come on live;—

examples which show also the occasional double long sound of *i*.

2.—Pronouns:

(1.) Emphatic use of, along with and in addition to their own nouns; in Burns very frequent, both in prose and verse. At random, thus—

> The morn, it is my parting day;
> Jockey, he gaed to the fair;
> The lady, she cam glancin ben; &c.

corresponding to the use of the pronoun *ille* in Latin, and of the French *ce*.

(2.) Use of 2nd person plural instead of singular—*ye*, for *thou*; as in Dutch precisely, *gy lieden* for *gy*, *you folk* for *you*: and *illa*, which is singular, is in like manner not unfrequently used in the plural.

(3.) Accusative absolute of pronouns used, where nominatives would be used in English—thus *me*, *him*, *her*, *them*, as the French emphatically use *moi*, *lui*, &c.: which forms are sometimes used even as nominatives to verbs—

> What that *them* thought was best to do;—Barbour's *Bruce*.

(4.) Relative Pronoun is often and elegantly used to include its own antecedent, precisely analogous to the Latin usage. Examples of this are so numerous that one alone must suffice—

> To whom has much shall yet be given;—Burns, on *Thomson*:

a pronominal ellipsis far too strong to be used with propriety in the English, or perhaps in any other language.

3.—Verbs:

(1.) Orthographical Forms.
(a) 2nd sing. pres. indicative, same as 3d sing., where 3rd sing. ends in *s*, *s* being its own invariable termination: except

in *can* or *have* as helping verbs, in which it is occasionally found as *canst* or *hast*, thus—*canst gang*, *hast* tauld. Same general rule holds with respect to 2nd sing. past indicative, in which 2nd and 3rd are the same. It is observed in the subjunctive mood also, as—thou *would* deny. There seems, in fact, to be an idiomatic aversion in the language to the use of '*st* in 2nd sing., and even to the frequent use of *thou* itself: and where *thou* occurs with a verb, the '*st* which belongs naturally to that person is forcibly dropt, and a simpler, stronger form substituted. This peculiarity is by no means restricted to old writers; it occurs constantly in Burns—

> And far he thou distant, thou reptile that seious;—*Death of the Daisie*.
> [Compare "Scotch Drink," "Auld Farmer's Salutation," &c.]

(*b*) Past tense ends in *ed*, *et*, *it*; for which reason alone that syllable is emphatic, and when not required is always struck out, thus—'*d*, '*t*, '*t*.

(*c*) Participle ends in *and*, *end*, *an*, *en*, *in*; and where emphasis against the next word is required, the other form of *ing*, which seems to come from the Islandic *ena* and is equivalent to *yagd*, is employed. The termination *and* or *an*, so far from being a mere arbitrary peculiarity, or confined to a local dialect, is the oldest and most accredited form of that syllable in the Scots language, and was almost invariable in all Parliamentary, Ecclesiastical, and other public documents, as well as in the best authors throughout the kingdom. The form itself seems to have originated (but this we hazard only as a conjecture of our own) from the dis-syllable *ende* added to verbs in the Dutch, expressing continuance and conclusion, the action so represented being carried out or prolonged to the *end*, thus—*love-end*, or *love-and*; shortened by degrees to *an*, *en*, or *in*.

(2.) *To*, sign of the infinitive mood, is often dropt after *seen*, and some other verbs than those after which it usually disappears in English, thus—

> The furrowed, waving corn is seen
> Rejoice in fostering showers; *i.e.* to rejoice.—BURNS.

(3.) *If*, sign of the subjunctive mood, is, for conciseness' sake, sometimes omitted also—

> If] Sa Minerva would me Sapience lend;—LINDSAY's *Squire Meldrum*.

(4.) Even '*s*, for *is* or *has* of the 3rd sing. pres. indicative, is sometimes omitted—

> Our maistres and goddes [is
> Venus that lusty quene;—BELIN'S *Pilgremer*

Of which we have numerous examples in Burns also, as—

> An' wight an' wilfu' a' his days' [has] be-n;—*Inventory*.

(5.) The common use of Negative particle when joined as a syllable to the verb—whether helping or principal—as in *canna*, *couldna*, *didna*, *havina*—must be distinguished from emphatic use of the same particle when separate—as *can na*, *could na*, *did na*, *heard na*; which are all equivalent to *can nane*, could *nane*, did *nane*, heard *nane*, &c.

(6.) The Participle is sometimes used conditionally as a sort of conjunction—*sae being*, *sae bound*, *heard sae*; equivalent to *such being the case*, or *if so be*.

(7.) The Infinitive itself is sometimes, though rarely, used as a participle; thus—

> Gae hame, puir tuke, while I have done indyte—*i.e.* indyting;—LINDSAY.

(8.) Certain Prepositions, in Scots as well as in other languages, and in Scots with great force—are frequently used as verbs, where much emphasis is required—as *on*, *up*, *after*, *aff*, *awa*; which are illustrations of the strongest and briefest form of Ellipsis.

4.—CONJUNCTIONS:

Two of the most important conditional conjunctions in the Scots language, *gif* and *gin*, are but contracted forms of the same verb in different moods of it—*gif* being *give*, and *gin*, *gien* or *given*, implying certain conditions or postulates of action. They are nearly synonymous, signifying *if*—which indeed is but *gif*, still more abbreviated, but they have a fine distinction too, as to the time of condition, which only the initiated in the language can appreciate. *Gif* implies a proposal or demand to be made; *gin* implies a condition already demanded or done.

> O gin ye were dead, gudeman, ... is right;
> O gif ye were dead, gudeman, . . . would be wrong.

An, another conditional conjunction, which has the same meaning as *gin*,

> O an ye were dead, gudeman,

must be carefully distinguished from *an'*, which is an abbreviation of *and*. *And* itself, or *an'*, seems to be of the same origin as—*and* or—*end* in the participle, and signifies the last or concluding addition, thus—John, Peter, James, Thomas, *end* or *and* Paul. *And*, however, is sometimes, but very rarely and we suspect by mistake, substituted for *an*, thus—

> An we smell, thou shalt yell, little custron cuist;
> And we smell, thou shalt yell, little custron cuist;—MONTGOMERY's *Flyting*.

II.—GRAMMATICAL PECULIARITIES IN SYNTAX.

1.—REDUNDANCIES in the use of Terms.

(1.) Of Prepositions—*for to*, or *for till*, thus—

> Which is in time for to tak tent;—MONTGOMERY's *Cherry and Slae*.
> Which late is, and that is,
> For to cut off the head;   do.   do.

(2.) Of Double Negatives, very frequent; thus—

> Then shrink not for no shower;—MONTGOMERY's *Cherry and Slae*.
> Was never sene sle justing in na landis;—LINDSAY's *Justing*

2.—ELLIPSIS: most frequent and expressive, of various kinds, as—

(1.) Of several words or great part of a sentence, amounting to aposiopesis—common enough in every language, and equally expressive in Scotch as in any other; thus—

> My Lady's gown, there's gairs upon't;—BURNS:

i.e. My lady's gown—as for that, there are gairs upon it; analogous to Latin form *cinctus tempora lauro*, bound as to his temples with laurel; but much more expressive.

Again—

> I red us put upon the king,
> And walkin him of his skiping ;—LYNDSAY's *Thrie Estaitis* :

a most singular form, strongly analogous to Latin, exemplifying both a strange grammatical construction and double ellipsis at the same time, being equivalent to

> I red (or advise) that we should put upon the king,
> And walkin him out of his skiping.

We hardly know in what other language but Latin so strange and concise an expression could occur.

(2.) Of single words, adverbs and prepositions, thus—

> Advise thee it lies thee
> On no less than thy life ;—MONTGOMERY's *Cherry and Slae*.
> As wise as ye are may ye gae wrong ;   do.   do.
> I put the case thou not prevailed ;   do.   do.
> I was that na man durst com neir me ;—LYNDSAY's *Bautie and Bauche*.

(3.) Of the article alone, elegantly, thus—

> Quhare mony lustie lady micht be sene ;—LYNDSAY's *Justing*.
> And sumtymes stridlinge on my neck,
> Demand wi' mony bend and beck ;—LYNDSAY's *Complaint*.

(4.) Of syllables, thus—

> Oft times deferring of a day
> Might not be mend the morn ;—MONTGOMERY's *Cherry and Slae*.

(5.) Ellipsis and Redundancy in one, thus—

> Adulterers and dinners,
> Backbyters, misbehavers,
> Stand sure for till offend ;—BURNE's *Pilgremer*.

3.—INVERSIONS, often very elegant, and PECULIAR FORMS abound—including such varieties as unusual arrangement of words ; superseding of ordinary words ; interrogatory forms instead of direct affirmation ; interrogation and ellipse combined, with immense force ; use of common words in an entirely strange sense, with much beauty ; and the combination of two separate forms in one expression : In all which peculiar variations the reader will easily perceive that there may be both much force and a certain beauty combined, which would distinguish at once between a vulgar contempt or ignorance of grammar, and genuine originality of speech. Such varieties it would be impossible for us here to illustrate by quotations in full, but one or two may serve to indicate what we mean.

(1.) Inversions, thus—

> For fear and quhat for lak of fude,
> My body empty was of blude ;—BURNE's *Pilgremer*.
> As burnt halgts with fire the danger dreads ;—MONTGOMERY's *Cherry and Slae*.

(2.) Inversion and Ellipsis in one, thus—

> Nild nakit man gars ryne ;—BURNE's *Pilgremer* :

and most remarkable of all, under the same category—

> Be na dainger, for this dangeir
> Of you be tane an ill conseil ;—MAITLAND's *Satyre of Ladies*.

that is—

> Be no danger, for this danger—
> That an ill conseit may be taken of you.

(3.) Interrogatory forms instead of direct affirmation, thus—

> And wha but my fine fickle lover was there ?—BURNS's *Last May, &c.*
> Gat ye me, O gat ye me,
> O gat ye me wi' naething ?   do.   *Lass o' Ecclefechan.*

(4.) Interrogation and Ellipsis combined, thus—

> Sic twa, O do I live to see 't—
> Sic famous twa should disagreet ?   do.   *Twa Herds* :

than which, no form of language could be imagined more powerful or suggestive.

On this subject of Ellipsis we have only farther to remark, that both in Scottish speech and writing a peculiar and not ungraceful form of it prevails, especially in verse—where brevity and emphasis are required. It corresponds to the Latin ellipsis of the antecedent, and may have been adopted unconsciously from that language ; but it is in fact the very converse, and may therefore be original in our tongue—being the ellipsis not of the antecedent at all, but of the relative. The effect produced by this omission may be perplexing to a foreign reader, and may even mislead a native till he becomes acquainted with the form. Whole sentences may thus be darkened and confused for the moment, and the strangest misapprehensions raised about the syntax and very meaning of the author ; which nothing but patience and experience will enable the reader to interpret. But, the peculiarity of this form once recognised, a certain beauty appears in connection with it also, and great additional force is communicated by it to every sentence in which it occurs. We have specimens in Alexander Scott's Welcome to Queen Mary—on her arrival in Scotland, thus—

> To mend that menyé [which] hes so monye shangit,
> Now to forbid this grit abuse [which] hes bene,
> Now to expell that idoll [which] standis up plane, &c.,

in which quotations, the words in brackets are not found in the original. In Ramsay the same occurs :—

> Sooner a mother shall her fondness drap,
> An' wrang the bairn else smiling on her lap ;—*Gentle Shepherd*.

In other writers of the same period before and after, if we mistake not, this form may be found also ; and in the speech of the common people themselves, who may either have borrowed it from these, or used it instinctively—which is perhaps the more natural supposition—it is very frequent : but in Burns it does not occur so frequently as to be a very noticeable peculiarity. His immense power of language otherwise, and ease of adaptation, may explain this.

4.—PECULIAR FORMS—VULGAR OR OTHERWISE.

Finally, in this department of our remarks, we may observe that there are certain forms of the language vulgar ; whilst others, in which the same words occur, but otherwise arranged, are legitimate or classic. This difference of form is no mere irregularity, originating in careless disregard of consistent speech, but is founded on a certain philosophical relation of words to ideas, which is more exact or otherwise in the mind of the speaker, and illustrates, perhaps as distinctly as any other circumstance could, the originality and syntactical independence of the language. Thus—

I dinna, or I div'na ken—&	vulgar ;
I kenna, or I ken nocht—	classic ;
Af'weel I wat—	vulgar ;
Weel wat I that—	classic ;
Were ye seekin for me ?—	vulgar ;
Socht ye for me ?—	classic ;
Did ye get me wi' naething ?—	vulgar ;
Gat ye me wi' naething ?—	classic ;
Dinna cast a cloot till May be out—	vulgar ;
Cast na a cloot till May be out—	classic ;

In which, and in all similar cases, the reader will observe, it is not the introduction of new, but the appropriate collocation of old words, more correctly and carefully defining the idea, which makes all the difference; and it is impossible to compare these various forms of expression for what is apparently the same idea, without perceiving the difference, and the superior elegance or significance of one form as compared with another on the very simplest topics. No language that was a mere vulgar dialect could supply or would admit of such varieties.

PART II.

LANGUAGE OF BURNS, &c.

BEFORE arranging our remarks on the speech of Burns, whose sole use of the Scottish language has constituted an epoch in its history, we shall present our readers with a brief tabulated analysis of its progress as it was represented before his time by some of the most influential writers in the country. This analysis, as a matter of course, can only be approximate, but it will enable the reader in some sense to judge. We have selected at random a passage (or two half passages) from each of the authors named, including exactly 205 words; and these words we have subdivided as the table shows. In discriminating between Scotch and English, we have set all doubtful terms to the credit of the English, and these are summed up under the head of Common. French and Latin terms have been as rigorously set apart as possible; words from Latin and French so much assimilated to Scotch or English as to have become part and parcel of either language, have been counted Scotch or English accordingly, whatever their derivation might be; and only those which retained their French or Latin forms distinctly have been classified under these heads. Proper names, of course, should count for nothing in the analysis, but they have been enumerated where they occur.

AUTHORS.	WROTE.	WORKS QUOTED.	PROPER NAMES.	FRENCH.	LATIN, GREEK.	NATURAL-IZED.	COMMON.	SCOTCH.	TOTAL WORDS.
JOHN BARBOUR,	1316—75	"Bruce,"	0	6	1	3	105	87	= 205
JAMES I.,	1405—24	"Quair," &c.	0	4	1	0	140	50	= 205
ANDREW WYNTON,	1420	"Sanct Serf,"	4	1	5	1	107	84	= 200
ROBERT HENRYSON,	1417—60	"Fables,"	0	3	0	0	132	69	= 200
BLIND HARRY,	1450—60	"Wallace,"	3	3	Grk. 2, 3	3	90	99	= 205
HOLLAND,	1453	"The Houlet,"	2	4	5	1	124	69	= 205
WILLIAM DUNBAR,	1465—1515	"Friar,"	3	1	5	0	119	77	= 205
GAVIN DOUGLAS,	1485—1513	"Winter,"	7	1	4	0	125	68	Aver. } = 205
Do. Do.	Second Selection,	Do.	0	0	2	0	73	130	99 } = 205
QUINTYNE SCHAW,	1468—1513	"To a Courtier,"	3	0	3	0	96	101	= 205
ARCH-DEAN BELLENDEN,	1518—42	"To his Buke,"	5	0	3	0	103	94	= 205
STEWART OF LORN,	1513—42	"To James V.,"	1	1	3	0	148	52	= 205
SIR DAVID LYNDSAY,	1513—58	{ "Bauchie and Bawtie"— Scottish style,	3	0	1	0	133	68	= 205
Do. Do.	Second Selection,	{ "Three Estatis,"— Scholarly style,	1	0	26	0	128	50	= 205

On the above analysis we have only further to remark—

(1.) That by far the most powerful and popular author in the list, Blind Harry, has also the highest general average of Scottish terms; and the average in his case would be still greater, if the unusual number of proper names and foreign terms which accidentally occur in the passage selected were reduced in proportion to the rest.

Barbour, who wrote on an equally popular subject, and who may be called the chronicler of national romance, has also a considerably high average of the native tongue, and in his sentiments, ideas, figures, and phraseology, is entirely Scotch. But he has too many philosophical digressions in the old English tongue, and upon the whole admits too many English terms to be ranked altogether as a writer in the Scottish language.

(2.) The average in Gavin Douglas's case is unequal, being 68 in one instance and 130 in another; and this inequality prevailing throughout, as well as the character of his work— it being chiefly a translation of Virgil—seems to have injured his popularity.

(3.) Arch-Dean Bellenden, or Ballentine, who has a very high average of Scottish terms, was an accomplished scholar, and wrote by command of King James V. for the use of the Court when he desired to restore the cultivation of the Scottish language.

(4.) Stewart of Lorn affected a curious ornate style, with frequent pedantic repetitions, and an immense infusion of the English tongue, as the average obtained from him proclaims—and which constitutes him an exception.

(5.) Quintyne Schaw, who has the highest average, was an Ayrshire man who had studied on the Continent. The oldest forms of the Ayrshire dialect—as ei for et, owr his, owr law, &c.—such precisely as Burns used about 300 years after him, occur throughout the piece; but as he wrote very little, and all that now remains to us is the above solitary production of his "Advice to a Courtier," consisting of 30 lines, his name goes for nothing, except as a type of Ayrshire in the calendar.

(6.) Of the last, and in his own day the most popular and fashionable of them all, the great satirist of corruptions both in church and state, and forerunner of the Reformation, Sir David Lyndsay, we have only to observe, as the reader will see, that he cultivated two distinct styles—one of which had a reasonably high average of Scottish terms, but nothing as compared with Blind Harry; the other has the lowest average of native terms, and an overwhelming preponderance of Latin. It was this scholarly, or rather scholastic ingredient that insensibly wearied the people—who craved simplicity as well as truth, and loved their own language even better than the most pungent satire.

By the table which now follows, the lowest ebb and gradual

rise again of the language is illustrated. It is not affirmed that such averages—either those which are given above or those which follow—are absolutely reliable as tests of its progress; but taken together, they are certainly reliable so far. They indicate at least in a general way the fluctuations of the language as faithfully almost as the mercury in a weather-glass represents the atmosphere, or the rise and fall of vapour in a steam gauge intimates the expansion of fluid.

AUTHORS	WROTE.	WORKS QUOTED.	PROPER NAMES.	FRENCH.	NATURALISED.	COMMON.	SCOTCH.	TOTAL WORDS.
Sir Richard Maitland,	1342—86	"Satire,"	0	2	0	115	88	= 205
John Burel,	1570—16—?	"Pilgremer,"	0	0	6	136	63	= 205
Alexander Montgomery,	1570—1605?	"Cherry and Slae,"	2	0	0	150	53	= 205
James VI.,	1584—1614	"Phoenix,"	2	0	0	152	51	= 205
Allan Ramsay,	1715—86	"Gentle Shepherd," mixed style—average of four passages,				169½	35½	= 205
Do. Do.		Epistolary style,	3	0	0	153	49	= 205
Do. Do.		Familiar do.	1	0	0	143	61	= 205
Robert Fergusson,	1750—74	"Election," mixed style,	1	0	0	124	76	= 205
Do. Do.		Pastoral style,	0	0	0	124	81	= 205
Do. Do.		Do. do.	0	0	6	115	90	= 205
Robert Burns,	1783—95	"Cotter's Saturday Night," mixed style,				145	60	= 205
Do. Do.		"Farmer's Salutation," familiar style,				115	90	= 205
Do. Do.		"Halloween," scotch style,				104	101	= 205

The most obvious remark on the information afforded by the above tables is, that the foreign element gradually disappears—French, Latin, and even naturalised terms fade away from the columns, and nothing but Scotch and English remains; of which two grand constituent elements the English itself seems to predominate. On this, however, it must farther be observed, that in the aggregate of terms called COMMON, there is an immense proportion of small words, such as *I, he, she, it, we, you, they; a, an, the; to, in, on, or; has, was, were; am, will, be,* &c., &c., and these frequently repeated—terms which afford little or no criterion of the character of the language, and which, being always credited to the common English or Anglo-Saxon side, swell the aggregates in their own column. Fifty per cent. at least would be a moderate allowance for these words; so that the apparent average of Common terms as against the actual average of Scottish terms should be reduced one half, thus—103 should be only 51·50 as against 94; which turns the balance entirely on the other side.

The gradual disappearance of French and Latin elements dates, as our readers will observe, from the removal of the Court to England, and the disappearance of Court Poets from the North. The cessation of our alliance with France, also, no doubt contributed, as a matter of course, to this result. Not that French terms disappeared entirely from the Scottish tongue, either written or spoken, by any means; but that they were comparatively so seldom employed by writers at least, as in a random selection of any 205 words to disappear totally.

Among the names above selected, those of Maitland and Burel, the reader ought to be informed, were scarcely ever known to the public, and could therefore exert no influence on the speech of the nation. Maitland, grandfather to the first Earl of Lauderdale, was indeed a courtier, but his poems were not discovered or published till 1786; whilst Burel's, a burgess of Edinburgh, seem not to have appeared till 1709. Ramsay, who has been called the great restorer of the Scottish tongue, had in fact three styles—1st, what he intended to be pure English, and which might be English in so far as the mere words were concerned, but was never very good or classic English; 2d, a quiet mixture of Scotch and English, in which Scottish and English terms were about equally balanced, but Scottish idioms prevailed throughout, as in the "Gentle Shepherd;" 3d, the familiar, colloquial, and sometimes vulgar Scotch; in which either a good deal of English, adapted or harmonised, is to be found, or a good deal of Scots corrupted, and by careless orthography confounded or identified with English. The truth is, Ramsay was the reviver of the Scottish Language, not so much in its vocabulary, which he remodelled, indeed, but often spoilt, as by the restoration of Scots ideas, and of Scots idiomatic phraseology in the use of terms. His chief merit was to restore simplicity and to banish learned affectation; and so far to adapt the language of England itself to Scottish themes, as to make it seem almost natural and appropriate. His "Gentle Shepherd" is one of the most perfect illustrations that could well be imagined of such difficult workmanship.

In another respect, Ramsay was also a restorer of the language, inasmuch as by reading and quotation he collected a larger number of genuine Scottish terms than the people for a long time had known, and their frequent, or at least occasional use in poetry by him gave them a place once more in the literature of the country. These terms were accumulated by him not only from the oldest authors then extant, but from manuscripts unknown to the people; which he often corrupted as well as quoted, and plagiarised or imitated with consummate skill. He thus did service in one way, but mischief in another. He was a dictionary or a vocabulary in verse for the people, as Hamilton of Bangour, in one of his Epistles, almost expressly calls him; but his popularity was abused and converted by himself into literary license.

From such a repertory of mere terms as his works thus supplied, Robert Burns himself was largely equipped with phraseology, and even with trite sayings, engrafted here and there imperceptibly in his writings. But in so far as Burns neglected to repair the violations of Ramsay, he was himself a contributor to the irregularities of the language—a fact which Burns, in reviewing Ramsay, seems tacitly to acknowledge. Fergusson, who immediately preceded Burns, had a much more copious natural acquaintance with, and easier use of the language than Ramsay. He was not so much a poetical dictionary as he was a vital, articulate-speaking man; and

Burns's own great preference for Fergusson, on this ground alone, demonstrates not only Fergusson's superiority in this respect but Burns's instinctive appreciation of the difference between them.

The language of Scotland then, after a long period of decay, was thus beginning to be revived when Burns appeared, who was destined to present it in the most attractive poetical form for the use of the people in which it had ever been known; and not only so, but to unite it, to a certain extent, with the English language so perfectly, that it would perhaps be impossible to adjust the two with more harmony and beauty. To his immediate predecessors he had a close affinity, and was to them both the grand supplement and climax. Ramsay to him was a quarry for words and a model for epistolary style, with this difference, that every word in Burns was a living stone in the temple of language, and every epistle a volume of humour, wisdom, and love—which was far from being so in either case with Ramsay. Fergusson was also a model for style to Burns, but suggested therein, and supplied a sort of inspiration besides, with this difference in his case, that the range of Burns's intellect and capacity was a hundred times greater, and his taste, to the utmost minutiæ of execution, infinitely fine.*

We have already, as our readers will find at the commencement of our Notes on Poetical Works [p. 81], adverted to the peculiar difficulties which lie in the way of faithfully reproducing the text of Burns. These we need not now recapitulate. They are of various sorts; but those alone which arise from linguistic irregularities in the Poet's own editions require illustration here: and such irregularities in Burns are by no means less frequent than in older authors. Besides all the variations of later editions, and the errors which arise from mere typographical remissness, the following examples may be found in the original and earliest copies of our Author's works—

—aid	or —end ;	
—aidie	—aidie ;	
—aip	—ape ;	
—act	—act ;	
aff	aff ;	
—ass	—ssn ;	
an'	and ;	
—an	—en ;	
—in	—in ;	
—ang	—ang ;	
—are	—aur	—ere ;
—ano	—a'e ;	
—oon	—an'	—and ;
—ousie	—usie	—ony ;
—ou	—ow	—ou ;
—uwsie	—uwsie ;	
—ee	—ey ;	
—e'en	—e'n ;	
—ere	—e'er ;	
—ei	—li	—ed ;
—ither	—ither ;	
—eigh	—egh ;	

Of special words, the following may be selected as illustrative of such irregularities: *brimstone, branstane; swoor—swer—ore; tries* or *frees; rantou, rantin, ranting, once ranton; druken, drucken, drukken; to* se *t'* or *te, once* sae; *pu'pit—with rupit; poupit—with roupit; stint, stent; fight, feght, faght, fechtin; gane, ga'en, gaun; gies* or *ies; newlin,* properly *newling;—similar form to* angiblins; *&c.* To attempt to produce harmony among these variations would be a liberty, we presume, beyond the sphere of any editor, more especially as they occur chiefly in familiar epistles, ludicrous descriptions, inventories, &c., where the utmost license both of speech and of orthography is intended; although in some rare cases, where variations in the same word occur close to one another, and so would offend both the eye and the ear—in which cases we may justly assume the difference to be an oversight—a uniform standard founded on the Author's own general usage may be adopted with advantage; and in such rare cases only have we attempted it. On the other hand, where the variation occurs through the appearance of some decidedly ancient form, as *—an* or *—en,* for *—in,* we have been scrupulously careful to preserve such form, as a relique of the antiquity that was dear to Burns, and a connecting link between his own and the speech of by-gone generations.

In attempting farther to harmonise the orthography of Burns, an editor will find that, in terminating lines with a present participle active, the Author almost invariably prefers the form *in,* even where the word otherwise might end in *ing;* and that where *ing* itself does appear, there is generally some special reason for its appearance. A few solitary exceptions are to be found without any apparent reason, which seem to be oversights in the original, and which therefore ought to be harmonised. Thus—

browin,		coxin,	
growin		beltin,	
vowin,		flatterin,	
once spewing,	should be spewin :	phrasin,	
sawin,		once pleasing,	should be pleasin :
mawin,		" sweit'ring	" sweit'rin :
thrawin,		" bickering	" bickerin :
once drawing,	should be drawin :	tyin,	
rockin,		peyin,	
stockin,		tryin,	
jokin,		seyin,	
yokin,		once frying,	should be fryin :
once provoking,	should be provokin :	&c.	&c.

more especially as we find the words here harmonised for certain passages used by the Author himself in such harmonised form in other passages—thus clearly showing that the irregularities were an oversight. In certain cases, this apparently slight process is of the utmost importance to the language—viz., those cases in which retaining the *g* would convert a Scotch into an English word entirely. As a general

---

* In certain other gifts—those of convivial humour and colloquial eloquence—Fergusson seems also to have been the prototype of Burns. Mr. Stuart of the Star in acknowledging receipt of Burns's letter to him with respect to Fergusson's tombstone [Prose Works, p. 124]—thus affectionately, but rather obtrusively, refers to these gifts.

"That Mr. Burns has refined in the art of poetry must readily be admitted; but, notwithstanding many favourable representations, I am yet to learn that he inherits his [Fergusson's] convivial powers. There was such a richness of conversation, such a plenitude of fancy and attraction in him, that when I call the happy period of our intercourse to my memory, I feel myself in a state of delirium. I was then younger than he by eight or ten years, but his manner was so definitive, that he enraptured every person around him, and infused into the young and old the spirit and animation which operated on his own mind."

In addressing such a eulogium on Fergusson to Burns himself, whom the writer had neither seen nor heard, Mr. Stuart's enthusiasm was certainly by no means transmitted with reserve. But however exaggerated his boyish estimate of Fergusson's powers may have been, it seems to be indisputable that they were of a very high order.

rule, to drop the *g* final lengthens or broadens the penultimate syllable in Scotch, sometimes even the antepenult. To retain that letter, therefore, in a Scottish term, would be in a great measure to destroy the character of said term; thus—

laughing	sounds	luffing	mortgaging	sounds	mortgaging
laughin	"	law ghin	mortgagin	"	mortgawgin
making	"	making	parliamenting	"	parliamenting
makin	"	maukin	parliamentin	"	paaliamentin, &c.

In which and similar cases, therefore, unless there be some distinct reason to the contrary—unless *laughing* is to rhyme with *quaffing*, for example, as in the " Jolly Beggars " it does —the *g* should undoubtedly be dropped. We are enjoined by the Author himself so to drop it; and where it appears contrary to this rule of his own, and contrary to the very character of the language, we are justified in dealing with it as with any other typographical imperfection.

In pursuing further the development of the Scottish language, as it is illustrated in Burns, the reader who follows the progress of his authorship attentively cannot fail to observe that there is a gradual change from long to short, and from broad to contracted forms. This process is not so perceptible in previous editions of his works as in that now before the reader. One great object of this edition has been to illustrate such changes, by the faithful reproduction of originals from the earliest dates onward; and by comparing these as they successively appear, the reader will find that in all our Author's earliest writings, whether published by himself or discovered only after his death, the longest and the broadest forms occur; and that in most of those which date from after his visit to Edinburgh and during his residence at Dumfries, the shorter and more contracted types of the same words appear. Thus—

—an	originally	—and,	becomes	—es,
—en	"	—an	"	—in,
—in	"	—en	"	—ing.

—anie	becomes	—any,	—et	becomes	—it,
—any	"	—annie,	—it	"	—ed,
—eny	"	—any,	i'	"	in,
—onie	"	—onny	wi'	"	with, &c., &c.

illustrations of which might be multiplied indefinitely; besides which, the substitution of actual English forms for Scottish forms is perceptible, and the gradual decay of original breadth and force and individuality of articulation is undeniable. In these changes, all insignificant as they seem, and hardly worth recording in a tabulated form, the reader will nevertheless perceive, on reflection, indications of a much more important change that any more syllabic transition from length to brevity, or from force of articulation to comparative weakness. Such changes, however rapidly they were accomplished, could never occur without previous corresponding modification in the national life and habits. They point, in fact, like an incontrovertible index, to the transitions both of life and utterance at the moment, and of our Author's relationship to both. The modification thus ultimately attained may have been in progress for a longer period than the authorship of a single lifetime indicates; but the adaptation of that authorship in its published form to the change that was in progress is indubitable evidence of the change itself. The world of Burns's earlier life must have been a broader and homelier, stronger and perhaps tenderer, if sometimes rougher and ruder world— for it delighted in broader, stronger, and plainer syllables— than the world into which his popularity thrust him, and that was hurrying, justling, bustling, dissipating its energies, adjusting or curtailing its articulation, and contracting its sympathies all round. The speech it employed was a different speech, more economical, more formal, more artificial; easier, shorter, sharper, and quicker. Its habits, therefore, intellectual and social; its ideas, its sentiments, its sympathies, must of necessity have been different also. Its time was more occupied, and its tongue must go swifter through its work; or its relationships were more refined, and its language must be trimmed to suit. It was not in Burns, by any means, this change originated. On the contrary, we have the clearest evidence that he clung affectionately, as long as he could cling, to the rich old significant and persuasive forms of the mother tongue. But the change was imperative, and it was finally acquiesced in and confirmed by him. At the bidding of the world, which, as we see, had reasons of its own for the change, his mother tongue in such forms must be abandoned, and his own articulation to that extent reformed. But this behest was not publicly complied with without the enduring impress of his own authority. The speech as it alters is associated by him with the most attractive sounds, and glides thus with the accompaniment of music in a finished form over all the land. So trivial a distinction of accents, so small a change of letters, like the evanescent breath of centuries, is thus caught up and registered, not to be altered again for centuries to come, but by the express consent of the people themselves—a process in which still deeper mysteries than that of speech are involved.

The change thus recorded has been gradually, and, it seems to us, unfortunately extending since his day; and although the vital energies of the people are by no means exhausted— which God forbid!—their social relationships have been contracted, their characteristic individuality has been diminished, and their entire national existence seems to be tending rapidly to assimilation, in some respects not for the better, but much otherwise, with the indiscriminate surrounding world. In this continuous, and perhaps resistless change, the influence of Burns, if Burns were but honestly printed and faithfully studied, in stimulating their latent vitality, in refreshing their memories, in renewing their affections, and in recalling their lives—may be of inestimable service.

٭ The following note should have been added in page lxi., column 1 :

And far be thee distant, thou reptile that seizes; *—Banks of the Devon.*

* That is, according to Cunningham and Chambers. If such reading is correct, then the form so employed illustrates not only a Scottish idiom, but a Scottish idiom carried forcibly into the English language; which we very much doubt. Burns would not have been guilty of such an impropriety; nor does his own text, as preserved by Johnson in the " Museum " and confirmed by Currie in his edition, justify that reading. Compare " Banks of the Devon," p. 181 of present edition, with our own note on the subject, p. 269.

At p. lxiv., c. 2, near foot, for Hangour, read **Gilbertfield.**

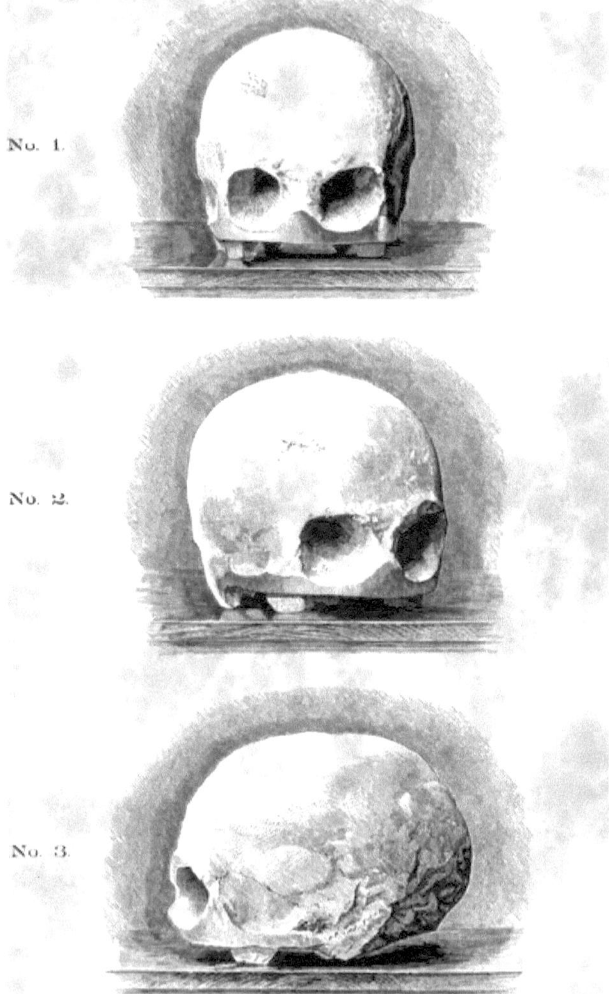

FROM A CAST MOST COURTEOUSLY PRESENTED BY JAMES FRASER. ESQ
DUMFRIES.

The Kerry Miniatures;

OR, THE

ROMANCE AND PHILOSOPHY OF TWO PICTURES.*

I.—THEIR DISCOVERY.

IN presenting these two interesting relics to the world, some account of their discovery is required, before any theory can be founded on them; to which, therefore, in the first place, as a necessary preliminary, we shall address ourselves.

In Chambers's Edition, vol. iv., p. 161, a letter from Burns (50) to Thomson will be found, May, 1795, with reference to the portraits by Nasmyth and Allan then extant; in which the following passage is introduced in brackets, as having been omitted by Dr. Currie and all succeeding editors of the Poet's works: ["Several people think that Allan's likeness of me is more striking than Nasmyth's, for which I sat to him half-a-dozen times. However, there is an artist of considerable merit just now in this town, who has hit the most remarkable likeness of what I am at this moment, that I think was ever taken of anybody. It is a small miniature, and as it will be in your town getting itself be-crystallised, &c., I have some thoughts of suggesting to you to prefix a vignette taken from it to my song, *Contented wi' Little, and Cantie wi' Mair,* in order the portrait of my face and the picture of my mind may go down the stream of Time together." . . . .]

No other notice of, or reference to, this miniature, so far as we are aware, anywhere else occurs. The probability therefore is, that it never was sent to Edinburgh at all; domestic difficulties and declining health being reasons sufficiently strong to interfere with that design. If it ever was sent there, it seems incredible that the Poet's wish, sacred and imperative in the circumstances, regarding it, should not instantly have been complied with. In this picture, however, three points of identification are conspicuous: 1. It is a small miniature portrait by some travelling artist on the spot, that is, at Dumfries, in the end of April or beginning of May, 1795; which must have been in the very beginning of May, for Thomson's reply to the letter above quoted from is dated the 13th of that month. 2. It represents him as he then was, in the 37th year of his age, prematurely old, as we know; and with health already declining. "I am beginning," said he to a friend that very spring, "to feel as if I were soon to be an old man." In a letter to Mrs. Dunlop, of 25th June the year before, referring to the same subject, he says, "To tell you that I have been in poor health will not be excuse enough, though it is true. I am afraid that I am about to suffer for the follies of my youth. My medical friends threaten me with a flying gout; but I trust they are mistaken." "The fact is," says Chambers, commenting on the above, "that Burns had lived too fast to be what most men are at seven-and-thirty." 3. Although done by an unknown artist, it is, in Burns's own opinion, one of the most remark-

---

* All references to these Miniatures occurring in previous parts of this work will be found answered in the following remarks, although not severally specified.

able hits in the way of a likeness, that was ever made of anybody; and such as he himself should desire to be known by among his fellow-men, on "the stream of Time" for ever.

The passage above quoted, which occurs only in Chambers's Edition, had almost entirely faded from our recollection, when the following letter reached us; and it was not for some time after we could remember exactly where it was to be found.

THE O'CONNOR-KERRY TO REV. P. HATELY WADDELL.

Hermitage, Listowel: September 13th, 1866.

REVEREND SIR,

I HAVE in my possession over forty years two portraits—one is a likeness of the immortal bard Robert Burns, and the other is, I believe, a likeness of one of his sons. These pictures are painted on mahogany panels, and are of an oval shape. The Bard's picture is eight inches and three-quarters high and seven inches broad. The panel on which the boy's picture is painted is seven inches high by five and half inches broad. I am fully of opinion that they were painted a short time before the Bard's death, as he looks to be forty years of age. The pictures are creditable works of art. The heads are well drawn, and painted in a free and bold manner. I received them in exchange from Major Robert H. Maunsell of Scallaheen in the county of Tipperary. I gave him for them a valuable old marine picture painted on an oak panel. The Major is alive. On the 20th of June, 1865, my abode called Hermitage was burnt to ashes—also a large portion of my effects. I have been struggling under adverse circumstances for a considerable time, but the burning reduced me to a low ebb, and to support myself and family I am compelled to sell articles I hold in veneration—the picture of Robert Burns is one of these. I am fully of opinion that these pictures are original portraits, and were in the possession of Robert Burns to the time of his death. Also I am of opinion that Major Maunsell told me he bought them of a member of the Poet's family. I am not acquainted with the works of Raeburn or Nasmyth, but I am certain the pictures of Burns and his son were painted by either of those artists, as you had not at the close of the Poet's life another portrait painter in Scotland of sufficient repute to produce a work equal to those I have. . . . . . . I shall send the pictures to a person in Dublin, as it is more than probable you have a friend there who would take the trouble of getting one or more competent judges to inspect the pictures, and give you their opinion as to their merits in every way. The boy's picture has a crack in it running between his right ear and eye, and severs from his right hand a bunch of flowers: but the likeness is not injured in the smallest degree. . . . The boy appears to be about ten years old. . . . . . Now the fact of having with a picture of Burns a likeness of one of his sons goes to prove almost to demonstration that my pictures are originals; as I may fairly conclude that the greatest admirer of Burns, not of his kindred, would not think of getting a copy of one of his sons with a copy of the father: and that the boy I have is a likeness of one of the sons there cannot be the slightest doubt. The Bard's picture is not in any way injured.—Neither the picture of father or son were cleaned, ... as sad experience taught

me not to depend on the great majority of those who profess to clean pictures without injuring them. I pray you to favour me with an answer, and you will oblige your humble servant,   THE O'CONNOR-KERRY.

Addressed "to the care of the Editor of the 'Scotchman,' [sic] Edinburgh."

In reply to further inquiries on the subject, the following additional information was received :—

Hermitage, Listowel, September 22d, 1866.

REVEREND DEAR SIR,

. . . . In reply to your queries I have to state that I cannot give authentic information that the pictures I have of Burns and his son are genuine or original; nay, I am not certain that the boy represents a son of the Bard—but I firmly and fully believe it, as the panel on which his picture is painted is mahogany, the same *exactly* as that on which the picture of Burns is painted. The oval shape also helps to corroborate my belief, and the pictures were, as I believe, painted by the same artist; to which I can safely add that there is a visible likeness between the man and the boy. I can vouch that the pictures are in my possession forty-five years, or nearly so long; as I am of opinion that I received them from Major Maunsell whom he was a banker at Lime-rick. I cannot bind myself exactly as to time, but I am certain I had them from him long before he went to live to Scallaheen in the county Tipperary, and that is close on forty years ago. I do not know how long Major Maunsell had the pictures before they became mine. . . . . I admit that it is not usual with portrait painters who paint in oil colours, to execute miniature pictures in the same way. I have a family picture of a female painted in oil colours on copper, and it is only two inches high by one inch and half broad. . . . . It is quite possible that neither Raeburn nor Nasmyth painted the portraits of Burns or the boy which I have. The pictures were not framed when Major Maunsell gave them to me. He had them hung in his library by strings which went through holes perforated in the tops of the panels, and I suppose they were suspended in the same way from the time they were first hung up. . . . . The pictures were, I believe, never cleaned, and are free from injury, except the crack in the boy's picture which I alluded to before, and the holes through which the strings went. I did not see or hear of any engraving from these pictures—nay, I did not see any picture like them. Four or five years ago I bought at Dublin the songs of Burns set to music, and there was a picture of the Bard on the first sheet; but mine is not at all like it. In the print to which I allude, Burns is repre-sented as a young, dashing, handsome fellow—The picture displays much of the parade of art*—Mine is a plain un-sophisticated picture with a thoughtful, care-marked face. The music was lost in the burning of my abode. If I had it, I would send you the portrait—But if it is like Burns, mine is of little or no value as a likeness or in any other way. . . .

I assure you, Reverend dear Sir, that I am with great sincerity, your grateful humble servant,

THE O'CONNOR-KERRY.

* [Nasmyth's portrait, presumably.]

With reference to the above letters, and in so far as they refer to the Portrait of Burns, the reader will perceive at once, first, the singular, indeed absolute correspondence between the description here given of the likeness in question and the portrait spoken of by the Poet himself in circum-stances already known; and second, the entire unacquainted-ness of the venerable and accomplished writer with the reference above quoted from Chambers's Edition to any such picture at all. The picture he speaks of is a small miniature; but he recognises Robert Burns in that miniature distinctly as a man about forty years of age, with a thoughtful, care-marked countenance, yet does not seem to be aware that Burns in reality never reached that age. The artist's name he does not know, but as a connoisseur, conjectures from the style that the work must be by Nasmyth or Raeburn, or some other painter of repute, which it could not be; and lastly, he values it so highly as the most expressive likeness of Burns, that he has cherished it for nearly half a century with affectionate veneration, and parts with it at last in con-sequence of misfortunes that will not permit him to retain it longer. This was surely one of the most singular com-mentaries by an unconscious hand on an unknown and long-lost document that could well be imagined. The two men, Burns and the O'Connor, seemed manifestly to speak of one and the same object. In addition, it was to be observed that the picture itself now spoken of was in the same *unfinished* state as that which the Poet proposed to send for decoration to Edinburgh; and had been hanging in that state during so long a period (how much longer, the writer did not know), suspended by a simple cord, along with its pretty pendant, among magnificent works of art on the walls of ancient or palatial residences—itself the most highly valued of them all. These circumstances, we confess, seemed to ourselves at the time very nearly conclusive. As for the miniature of the boy with flowers—we know of nothing as yet on record con-cerning it. Its authenticity and its relationship to the other portrait, or that of its subject to Burns, would remain to be determined on independent grounds. The very character of the flowers themselves, as indicating the season of the year, might be important. The boy's age alone, guessed by the writer to be "about ten" years, as the other had been guessed at "forty years"—a little too much—and his re-semblance to the Poet, were in favour of it. To satisfy ourselves, however, most fully on the subject, we again communicated with the O'Connor, making certain additional inquiries and suggesting certain natural doubts; in reply to which we received the following rejoinder :—

Hermitage, Listowel, October 22d, 1866.

MY DEAR REVEREND SIR,

. . . . YOUR note of the 19th instant warrants me to hope that the pictures will be your property. To render any misunderstanding impossible between us on the subject of the pictures, I consider it my duty to lay before you in this document, as far as memory now serves, all the particulars of my former correspondence as to the length of time they are in my possession, and the person who gave them to me. If it should so happen that I do not now allude to any matter you consider of importance in my former notes, by stating it in reply to this, I will cheerfully subscribe to it, as I feel perfectly satisfied that I did not write one word to you on the subject of these pictures but what I believe perfectly correct. [Particulars here recapitulated.] I am induced to hope that I can yet get the information you wish for as to the age of Major Maunsell—how long he was a banker at Limerick before he gave the pictures to me—and whether he was in Scotland before that. To accomplish this work I shall make inquiries of those I may consider capable of answering them, and transmit their answers to you. But if I do not succeed to your satisfaction, my want of success is not to be a cause of empowering you to return the pictures. Nay, anything is not to be required of me beyond what this note contains—further than this, that if my veracity as to the contents of this note be impeached by any person who would have the hardihood to say or to write that I have made a wrong statement in this document, or in any of those of mine you hold, I would feel bound to adopt the strongest and most decided course that my friends would recommend, and I would take the liberty of appointing you one of my advisers.

    I am,

        My dear Reverend Sir,

           Your faithful humble servant,

              THE O'CONNOR-KERRY.

In the above document the following additional particulars are contained: 1. That the pictures, on more exact measurement, were found to be a trifle—one quarter of an inch—smaller each than as originally reported; a fact in corroboration of the theory that the portrait of Burns must be the Dumfries miniature. 2. That the oval form of the panels on which they were painted was the same, "which I consider peculiar." 3. That the miniature of Burns was "a large bust, as there are five buttons of his coat painted. It appears to me that he looks to be at least forty years of age." 4. That the boy's picture was full length—"he holds a bunch of flowers in his right hand." 5. That the marine view "which I gave the Major in exchange for the pictures of Burns and the boy" was "very old, and painted on an oak panel, which I valued highly." 6. That although, in consequence of misfortunes, the writer had "disposed of a valuable collection" previously, he could not up till the present moment bring himself "to dispose of Burns." And finally, that "these pictures of Burns and the boy were not out of my possession since I received them from Major Maunsell. I pledge myself that photographs, or copies of any kind, were not taken by any one since they became my property," . . . . &c.

In this correspondence, the same simplicity, dignity, and gentlemanly candour characterise the letters of the O'Connor throughout. The terms of love and of affectionate regard for Robert Burns, which occur in some of the passages necessarily omitted, were indeed refreshing to read; and it was altogether a luxury, which one does not often casually enjoy, to protract such a correspondence on any reasonable plea for the more satisfaction it afforded.

The result was, that a transfer of these interesting objects was willingly negotiated by us on the O'Connor-Kerry's own terms, and their transmission by post agreed upon. With respect to Major Maunsell, however, it appeared, on further inquiry, that he was no longer alive; but of his history, and the date of his death, particulars will be given hereafter.

II.—THEIR APPEARANCE AND CONDITION.

THAT the appearance of these pictures was anxiously looked for, our readers, we presume, will hardly doubt. They arrived in safety, and on examination proved to be exactly as described, both in size and character. They were two first-rate works of art, and would have done no discredit to Nasmyth or Raeburn—in proof of which it may be stated, that in the opinion of one of the most accomplished restorers in this country, who had occasion to inspect them, but who did not know their history, they might have been done by Nasmyth. "To me," says this gentleman, "the portraits looked very like Alexander Nasmyth. They were quite of the same character of handling as Nasmyth's small portraits; but whether they may be painted by him I cannot say." They could not be by Nasmyth, as the reader will by and by see.

The pictures were on mahogany panels of the same wood; the larger on what seemed to have been the butt end, and the smaller on what seemed to have been the thin end of the same slab, cut in two and roughly ovalled for the easel. The ovals were the same, or nearly so.

The pictures were manifestly by the same hand, in the same style, with an appropriate difference for youth and age, and of the same date—the dresses being those worn at the end of last century, and, according to one of the oldest tailors in Dumfries (now or lately residing in Burns's first house), the very colour, cloth, and fashion then popular in Dumfries.

The central point of the largest picture was the right eye, which seemed to shine like a lamp irradiating everything; the coat dark brown with bright fancy buttons; the waistcoat double-breasted, of a quiet pattern; the neckcloth of white cambric, rolled carelessly about the throat—the whole being in comparative _deshabille;_ the background aerial, dark and cloudy, indicative of passion and storm.

The picture of the boy was a pretty bagatelle, a family bijou of its sort—precisely what a parent would love to treasure. The figure short, erect, and jaunty, in full-dress schoolboy costume of green corduroy suit with bright "bowl buttons," and an elaborate white "point" French Revolution collar; the left hand in the jacket pocket, in the right hand a bunch of wild-flowers by the root and stem; the head with an immense shock of dark brown hair, done as nearly as possible in the style of the elder figure; the face and features most accurately and beautifully painted, much resembling the elder head; the feet in plain blunt black shoes with broad bright buckles—the right displayed; and the whole posed handsomely on an elevated plank, as in the neighbourhood of a garden, to give effect to the figure; with a pleasant aerial background, indicative of boyhood and hope—a thing to be treasured, as we have said; to be looked at again and again, to be affectionately laughed at, to be carried in the pocket, to

be exhibited to loving friends; in a word, to be cherished in a household for ever.

Both pictures had been rudely pierced at the top with the same sort of instrument—apparently a nail; both had been covered unwisely, and much obscured, with a double coat of common varnish of turpentine and oil, such as was used for furniture long ago; the two had been always together, as principal and pendant—insomuch, that the smaller had been laid face to face upon the larger at one time, before the varnish was firm, and had left the outline of its own oval on the surface. All idea of framing or glazing or "be-crystal-lising" these pictures had been abandoned—there were even several slight pin scratches on the surface of the varnish, apparently very old. The smaller panel was of thinner wood than the larger, being the light end of the slab; it had been cracked, in consequence, from head to foot, by the corner of the right eye and between the right hand and flowers, but not seriously damaged. The larger panel was entirely sound and very strong, but the surface had been slightly blemished by a nail scratch.

About the originality of both, there could be no doubt whatever, and about their truthfulness to nature as works of art, if possible, still less. There was not the slightest trace of copying, or of fiction, or of patching on either of them. They had been done, and done rapidly and well, without hesitation and by a skilful hand, from two living originals, a father and a son manifestly. The father, with some traces of anxiety and pain, was prematurely old at forty—he could not be so old. The child, with vivacity and confidence, looked precocious also; his probable age at the date of the portrait might be between eight and ten.

In conclusion of our survey we may add, that the external aspect of both pictures, as regarded the varnish and the crack, was somewhat discouraging—but it was a satisfaction at least to see, that beyond the inconsiderate double oil-varnishing by some homely hand, they had never been tampered with or "cleaned." The first thing, therefore, to be done, was to attempt to clean them; and this, after much deliberation, with the utmost care, and with entire success—with a success, indeed, beyond all our anticipations—was accomplished. The miniature of the boy, too, we had accurately repaired and fortified against similar mischances in future. So perfectly, indeed, was this repair executed, that the crack became invisible. On communicating these results to our venerable and esteemed correspondent, which we could not then refrain from doing, we received an answer of congratulation which we can as little now refrain from publishing; and this document we give entire.

Hermitage, Listowel, January 16th, 1867.

MY VERY DEAR, DEAR FRIEND,

YOUR to me most interesting note of 29th ult. I could not well answer before now. I am still labouring under a seriously deranged state of the bodily system. Cold and a troubled mind help to keep me down. I really could not tell the number of readings your last favor underwent both by myself and those about me for my gratification. I wriggled and shrunk when I in fancy saw you pouring a strong acid on the face of Robert Burns. It must be a powerful acid to remove *an old coat of oil*, and to do so without injuring your picture bewilders me. You must have great nerve to undertake the work; you must have great confidence in your acids and alkali. You must have given the matter great consideration before you attempted the great work—if you did not, I am egregiously mistaken. You accomplished the wonderful work in a satisfactory manner, and this fact is to me a source of real happiness. I congratulate you—again and again I congratulate you, on the accomplishment of your great and dangerous undertaking.

You express a wish to know how the pictures of Burns and his son escaped the burning of my house, furniture, and many valuable articles—such as books, jewellery, &c., &c. On 29th of June, 1865, I was at Listowel, which is about one and half miles from my house. I was returning about seven o'clock in the afternoon, and when within a quarter-mile of my home I saw fire burst out of the roof of the east wing. I rushed forward, but fell frequently before I reached my hall door: my servants and nieces were in an awful state. I called on them to drag out all they could as quick as possible. Little was done until help arrived. The first object with me was to save my pictures, books, a small share of family plate and jewellery. I removed the pictures first: the rest followed through the aid of the people, which I wanted much, as I was nearly suffocated. The fire spread with wonderful rapidity and devoured everything within its frightful range. I placed the pictures on the lawn a considerable distance from the fire, with other articles of value. The scratch on Burns' picture that you alluded to was on it many years—I believe it was on it when it was given to me. The picture of the boy was cracked and glued up when I got it, but the crack was opened at or after the burning, as I pasted paper on the back to keep it together. It has occurred to me that the hanging of the pictures of Burns and his son by strings, which was evidently the first adopted, goes to prove almost to demonstration, that they were in the possession of the immortal Bard.

I beg you to favour me with the result of your inquiries respecting the place at which the 39th were stationed at or about the time of the death of Burns, or after his death—say, two, three, four or five years.* I have many questions to put to you respecting the cleaning process, but my poor old head is not in working order. Health, peace, happiness both spiritual and temporal to you and yours, is the earnest wish and prayer of your faithful   O'CONNOR-KERRY.

[P.S. on envelope:] Robert Burns was a Freemason, the O'Connor-Kerry is a Mason also.

III.—THEIR POSSESSORS.

MAJOR ROBERT HEDGES MAUNSELL (son of Dean or Arch-Dean Maunsell of the Irish Episcopal Church, resident at Scallahoon, and member of a highly aristocratic family) was

---

* [We regret to state that our inquiries on this subject have hitherto been unsuccessful: *vide infra.*]

born in the year 1780. At the age of *fourteen* he entered the army, as Ensign in the 39th Regiment of Foot. In the year 1813 or 1814 he took the place of his father-in-law and uncle, as head of the banking firm of Thomas and Robert Maunsell, and John Kennedy, Limerick—the oldest banking establishment in that city. Thomas Maunsell was both the father-in-law and uncle of Major Maunsell. That the Major should have been an officer at so very early an age, may perhaps seem strange; such, nevertheless, was the fact. But the early date of the young man's commission and the rapidity of his promotion were alike due, we have no doubt, to the influence of some relative then at Court or in the Government. "Major Maunsell died at South Abbey, Youghal, on the last day of February, 1865. He had been living there for three years or thereabouts. Previously he had been living at Beakstown in the Co. Tipperary, but on his son's marriage he gave him up the latter place, and went himself to reside at Youghal." This gentleman, therefore, was eighty-five years old at the time of his death.

The Major's family mansion, called Plassy, is in the neighbourhood of Limerick—about two miles distant. It was occupied by the O'Connor's brother first, immediately after the Major himself left it; by Colonel Sir Guy Campbell next —whose regiment was quartered at Limerick, and who was married to a daughter of Lord Edward Fitzgerald. Reuben Harvey, Esq., occupied it after Sir Guy; and it is now, or was in 1866, in the possession of a Mr. Russell—"the great miller of Limerick"—a gentleman of much influence and wealth. It has been described to us as a princely or palatial residence. Mr. Russell "gave an enormous sum of money and is subject to a heavy yearly rent for a long lease of the house and demesne." It was in the innermost sanctuary, then, of such an abode, in the proprietor's own library, that these two miniatures of Burns and his son were suspended " by strings in the same way as they were first hung up," and where they hung for ten or fifteen years, objects of interest and veneration to this military millionaire, who was not very likely to admit impostures into his cabinet, and who certainly did not deceive himself in the acquisition of such valued objects.

From this dignified seclusion they passed, as we have seen, not by purchase, but by exchange for another object of the highest artistic value, into the hands of a still devouter worshipper of Burns, of higher birth if not of such princely fortune ; and who, we may be equally well assured, would make certain of their authenticity at the time of such exchange. At the Hermitage of Listowel they were again enthroned, as we may truly say, above the most venerated memorials and relics of the O'Connor's own family.

Maurice M'Namara O'Connor, our readers must now be informed, claimed to be, and was, of royal descent in Ireland. In reply to some inquiries on this subject we received the following explanation—which is too characteristic in every way to be abridged by the omission of a single word.

"To your query as to the nature of my title, and if it is equal to that of the O'Connor-Don or the Knight of Kerry. I have to state that mine is not in any way equal to either.

The term Don is, as you know, the Spanish title for gentleman. The late O'Connor-Don was the first of his family who took this to me extraordinary title. Before his time the heads of his House were known as the O'Connor-Sligo. The last O'Connor-Don was a perfect gentleman in habits and manners ; but I cannot understand his motive for making these facts known as he did, by appending Don to his name—nay, the word gentleman in the olden times embraced nearly all the grand traits which should characterise a truly good man.

The father of Fergus, the first King of Scotland, was O'Connor, King of Ulster. This King of Ulster had three sons by Meva, Queen of Connaught—these three sons were step-brothers of your Fergus. The names of these three brothers were Ciar, Lainne, and Coro. Ciar became King of this country, and from him it was called Kerry. I am the acknowledged, the undisputed lineal descendant ; and am called as my ancestors were, since the penal laws compelled them to give up their ancient title of Prince.

I am, my dear and Reverend Sir, your truly humble and obliged servant,　　　　THE O'CONNOR-KERRY.

Writing further on the subject, our highly-descended and accomplished correspondent says—

" I have many family miniature pictures, and I assure you Burns overtopped all. My grandmother, Mary M'Namara, was under Burns. She was a poetess—she was the "blue stocking" of my mother's family. She wrote seventy-five songs, ditties, and lamentations in the Irish language : perhaps more than seventy-five ; but I had this number, and I was during many years trying to get a person to please me who would translate them into English. In this I failed, and they are lost for ever [having been consumed at the burning of the Hermitage.] They were smooth and harmonious."

To any one who knows the pride of birth, the jealousy of wealth, and the importance of position, it must be altogether superfluous to say a word more as to the historical authenticity of the miniatures in question. That two such men, in every way qualified to judge, entitled by their respective positions to be fastidious as well as jealous in their tastes, and having the fullest opportunities at the time to verify everything, should wilfully deceive themselves, or be deceived, about two portraits of Robert Burns and a boy, and should exalt these portraits above all other similar objects in their possession, is incredible. Our readers have already evidence before them both of the O'Connor's interest in these pictures and in all that befel them, and of his practical acquaintance with art in several departments. How well he was able to appreciate a work of art is clear, and how deep his interest in these two objects in particular, or in one of them rather, must have been, will be equally clear from the terms of the letter which accompanied them back to Scotland.

" I am greatly excited. . . . I must derive consolation by and by for the loss of Burns, as I am now certain he has fallen into hands worthy of him. Alas ! alas ! you cannot conceive how acute my sorrow was at parting with Robert Burns. Be assured that I shall do all in my power to give you the most satisfactory information on every point calculated to make your pictures a real treasure to you." And again, when we had communicated to him our own convictions on the question of their authenticity, he replies—

"I never had the slightest doubt on my mind respecting the pictures of Burns and his son. There is not the slightest mark visible to warrant a truly skilful connoisseur to doubt of their being originals—nay, they bear marks amounting to almost positive proof that they were in possession of Robert Burns—but *please goodness, I will not be at ease* until I make all as clear as light emanating from a bright sun."

This the dear old gentleman did not live to do. Major Maunsell's death had interfered with this object in the first place—and his own death put an end to all inquiries in the second. Borne down by distress and suffering, and by ejectment, on some legal plea of sub-letting, "from land that had been the property of his kindred two thousand years ago," the O'Connor-Kerry died at the house of his dear and valued friend Joseph Phelps Newsome, Esq., Thomas Street, Limerick, on the 2d of November, 1867—universally respected, and beloved by *all* who know him.

Having had our own interest, as may be supposed, not a little excited in such a correspondent, we had the strongest desire to see him; and as a personal interview at the time was impossible, we earnestly begged, as a special favour, the transmission of his likeness by photograph. To this application the following reply was received—"All the photographs of my family and friends were lost when my place of abode was burnt—but please goodness, when I am able to go to Limerick, Cork, or Dublin, the journey shall be undertaken for the purpose of having a likeness of my old Celtic head placed on paper, and I shall do myself the high honor of presenting it to you for acceptance. The O'Connor who wrote on Irish antiquities was not in any way related to me. He descended from Roderick, King of Connaught.* The Ulster and Connaught O'Connors were quite distinct [that is, in the male line]. I had O'Connor's history, but it went in the burning. I shall do my utmost to make out a copy of it for you." . . . . &c.

Never having been able to accomplish such a journey in health, no photograph, so far as we are aware, was ever taken of this interesting type of a genuine Celtic nobleman. His correspondence extended to some fifteen or sixteen letters in all—the pleasantest, the truest, and the most endearing of their sort we ever received. We seem to have lost in this man, whom we never saw, one of the most intimate friends, and one of the most honourable acquaintances; and with profound affectionate salutations make adieu to his memory.

In compliment to him we have designated these pictures the "Kerry Miniatures."

But although Major Maunsell and the O'Connor-Kerry are now both gone, evidence of a still more convincing nature than any mere oral tradition as to the identity of the objects is at hand. Any evidence, indeed, which could have been afforded by these gentlemen, although they had both survived, might have had no bearing at all on the *date* at which the portraits were done; which, however, is a matter of the first importance, and must be determined by evidence deducible chiefly from the miniatures themselves—and this we proceed to supply as follows.

IV.—THEIR DATE AND HISTORY.

THAT these pictures were portraits of Robert Burns and his oldest son in 1795, we did not, and could not, for a moment doubt; but to demonstrate that this picture of him was the very picture referred to by himself at that date required careful investigation. Having bestowed such investigation, we are now fully satisfied of this important fact, and shall lay the evidence for that conclusion in detail before our readers.

With continued reference to Burns's own letter on the subject, as already quoted by us at the commencement of this narrative, and more fully recorded in his correspondence, letter (50) to Thomson, we remark—

1. That the picture itself is a miniature portrait as described by him, and not a profile; so that all profiles whatsoever are excluded from consideration: and it is a comparatively small miniature, considering the size of the subject —being a full bust of only 6½ by 5 inches at the broadest, on a panel of 8½ by 6½ inches, or thereby.

2. The panel on which it is painted is roughish and rudely hewn, precisely such as an itinerant artist might carry in his kit, or block with his chisel at the moment.

3. The sitter himself is in a sort of *deshabille*—and not in dress, as if he were honouring some distinguished master with whom he was on ceremony; but is at his ease indifferently, in his every-day style, with sufficient attention only to his external appearance to ensure respectability, and exactly as he might appear before an unknown artist without disrespect or impropriety. The child, on the other hand, is handsomely dressed—not only as for a great occasion to him, but as if the artist had already proved his power and was entitled to more deference on his second engagement for the family. These points, the reader will observe, as presumptive proof, are all in harmony. But—

4. Assuming that this miniature is at least intended to be a portrait of Robert Burns—when, how, or by whomsoever executed—we ascertain by impartial medical testimony that it must have been painted when the health of the sitter himself had begun to be impaired by passion or by dissipation, or by both, for that symptoms of injury to a strong constitution by such causes are manifest, especially in the cheeks. Without admitting this verdict in full (for we are convinced that care and anxiety and internal conflict had as much, if not more, to do, than any variety of excess whatever, in weakening the Poet's constitution), the effect, we must admit, is still undeniable; and a little bloodshot in the right eye, which would never have been introduced if it had not been there, seems to corroborate the medical view. Such symptoms, however, could not be apparent till the end of 1794, for it was only in the end of June of that year [letter (37) to Mrs.

---

* By a curious coincidence we note the following in a London paper—*Daily News*, 1868—"May 5, at the residence of his parents (Patrick Henry and Sophia), Notting Hill, Charles Owen Ossian Ossor O'Connor, the hereditary Prince of Connaught." Such intimations, at the present crisis of British history, have a meaning of their own, not altogether obscure.

Dunlop] he first glances at the subject, and not till December that he seriously complains [letter (38) to the same]. Even in 1795 he did not believe they were conspicuous, or even visible, or he would never have desired his own portrait of that year to be preserved in memory of his existence. Both the painter and the world, however, might have seen what the illustrious sufferer himself was not fully aware of. At all events, this portrait, so obviously and literally true to nature, could not have been painted before the spring of 1795.

5. The portrait of the boy, which has always gone along with it, which must have been varnished and hung together with it by the same hand and in the same house, is the portrait of his eldest son. This requires no attestation to any one who has seen that gentleman, and has been unanimously attested by all to whom it has been shown that had seen him, including parties of the best critical judgment, and who were intimately acquainted with the deceased. " With respect to the second of the Kerry Miniatures engraved in Waddell's Burns, it represents a stout, serious-looking, short-legged little fellow of nine years, with a rose in his right hand. It is an undoubted likeness—the child was father of the man." *Inverness Courier*. It is further attested by other pictures extant of the Poet's eldest son even in old age; by the resemblance of the picture itself to the accompanying miniature of his father; and finally, by the living likeness, in face and figure, of his own immediate descendants. This picture represents a child between eight and ten years of age—but precocious for that age. The O'Connor, from the portrait, guesses him " about ten;" the *Inverness Courier*, from the engraving alone, at " nine"—but describes him as " serious-looking." He was in fact a precocious child, in so far as to become his father's idol and the wonder of his family for that very reason —a sort of premature man, in short, and much in his father's confidence: but he was precisely eight years and eight months old—that is, completing his ninth, and verging on his tenth year in reality, at the supposed date of this painting. No correspondence, therefore, between the facts of the case and the testimony of two independent, we may almost say unconscious, witnesses, judging from a picture now seventy-five years old, could possibly be more exact. Yet greater exactness still is attainable.

6. It is well known that this boy was his father's constant companion in his early morning walks, by the Nith and in the woods about Dumfries. Indeed, it was one of the pleasantest recollections of Mr. Burns's own life to recall these wanderings with his father among the woodland solitudes where wild-flowers were to be gathered, and all beautiful objects in nature were to be seen. In the boy's hand here represented is a bunch of wild-flowers, gathered doubtless in one of these very rambles—one torn off from some shrub, the other plucked clean by the roots. In the engraving, this flower by the root, from its want of colour, looks something like a rose—and is so described by the *Inverness Courier* as " a rose in his right hand." But in the picture, so far as can be distinguished—it is an anemone, or some flower of that genus —the *anemone nemorosa* apparently, or wild anemone of the woods. Where, and at what season of the year, then, is the flower so represented to be found in bloom? The wild anemone is abundant in every grove in Scotland, more especially by our river-sides, and is in perfect bloom—when it may be seen in myriads—between the middle of April and the beginning of May. But according to the Poet's letter (50) to Thomson, quoted by Mr. Chambers, his own picture must have been painted in the end of April, for he refers to it as a finished work in the beginning of May, 1795. Whether the boy was painted before, or immediately after, the flower in question would still be in bloom among the groves or by the banks of the Nith. Its appearance, therefore, by the roots in the child's hand fixes the date of that picture, and by consequence, within a very few days, the date of the other also; so that the miniature before us must have been painted not only at the time, but on the very week in question; and unless there were *two* portraits of the Poet painted at the same moment and by the same man, this must be the only and the identical likeness referred to by Burns—in short, the miniature of April or May, 1795.

In addition to all which, the beautiful trait of domestic life here so unexpectedly and distinctly brought before us—of the father and the child wandering through the woods for a nosegay to grace the intended portrait, or the sweet memorial of those pleasant walks designed by the father himself to be looked at and cherished when he was no more—is valuable beyond all estimation. It would be sacrilege to doubt it. Yet Burns, it may be said, never refers to this portrait of his boy, which looks as if he had not felt much interest in it after all. On the contrary, he does refer to it, and was not altogether satisfied with it as a likeness, beautiful and true as it is. For some time after receiving those portraits we were in total ignorance of this fact; but in the course of our inquiries, we found a letter elucidating the whole matter. This letter, most courteously forwarded to us for publication by Dr. Corry of Belfast, who knew nothing of its subject, is addressed—letter (16)—to Mrs. Riddel, 1795; and in it the Poet speaks of a likeness which he carried in his pocket, and which he calls " the bagatelle," but which in his opinion the painter had spoilt. The precise date of the letter, unfortunately, is not now known; but that the pain and irritation of which symptoms are manifest in his own picture were increasing is obvious, for he speaks of himself as being too " miserable" almost to hold pen to paper; the date may therefore have been towards midsummer or autumn of that year. But that he does refer to this picture of the boy, and that he had been speaking to Mrs. Riddel on the subject before, is also obvious. There was no other likeness, indeed, than this, to which such reference could apply. He could never refer to his own likeness as a " bagatelle," for it was a serious affair; and it could not have been carried in a book in his pocket—being too large for that; nor could the man himself be suspected of such childish egotism. But this likeness of his boy *was a " bagatelle"*—and a beautiful bagatelle— which could easily be carried in his pocket, or enclosed in an exciseman's note-book; and it was supremely natural for him, as we have already said, if he admired it, so to carry it. But what parent was ever satisfied with a likeness in such circumstances? The likeness speaks for itself, and the workmanship is admirable; and that Burns was really proud of it,

k

and pleased with it after all, is clear. Why otherwise did he thus carry it about with him in his pocket, or despatch it to the country for ladies to admire? His action, like any other parent's in such a case, spoke a great deal louder than his words. That portrait, as our readers may remember, was cracked from top to bottom at some distant unknown date. For our own part, we can easily understand how that misfortune was occasioned. To carry a slight mahogany panel in a heavy note-book from day to day in an exciseman's pocket (however natural it might be for such an exciseman to do it), or to despatch it to the country in charge of some clown on horseback, was the most likely process imaginable to insure such a result; and in some such manner, undoubtedly, if not on this very occasion, the accident we have just specified occurred.

7. But how did these pictures, it may be inquired, reach Ireland? We have already seen that they were the most valued objects in two private collections in the highest families there, for sixty-five or sixty years at least; and that during all that period they changed places only from the library of a millionaire to the cabinet of a *ci-devant* hereditary native prince—neither of whom was likely, on any consideration, to admit doubtful or inferior objects into his keeping, much less into his most sacred keeping among the relics of his family. Beyond this we cannot trace their history backwards with certainty, nor is it requisite. The pictures themselves were but seventy-one years old when we received them, and we have documentary evidence of their history to within ten years of that date. That they were in Robert Burns's own possession, and hung by himself in such rude fashion as we have described, on his own parlour walls, is morally almost as certain as that they were for forty years in the possession of the O'Connor-Kerry. No other person who had got such portraits painted in honour of the Poet and his eldest son would or could have pierced them with a nail, or hung them like sign-boards with a piece of string, as these pictures were originally pierced and hung. Every principle of reverence and love in our nature is against such a presumption; but that he himself, distressed and sorrowful, in haste or in vexation, might have done it, is probable enough. That they were never sent to Edinburgh, is equally certain—first, because there is no reference to their appearance there in any letter of Thomson's; and second, because, if they had been sent, the portrait of the Poet most assuredly would have been engraved, or some reason assigned for not engraving it. Indeed, Currie's deliberate omission of the very passage referring to it, because that passage contained a derogatory reference to Nasmyth's portrait, and the engraving of a new copy from Nasmyth by Neagle for Currie's own edition, are sufficient evidence that neither Currie nor Thomson had ever seen the miniature. Two such judges could not have forgotten or undervalued it.

We may reasonably assume, therefore, that from 1795 till 1798 or thereby, they were in possession of the Poet's family —which leaves only some six or seven years to be accounted for. That they came from Scotland or from England in Major Maunsell's own possession, when he left the army and retired to his uncle's establishment at Limerick in 1813-14, is evident; and that Major Maunsell had them from some friend

or relative of the Poet's, is affirmed on the best authority, and there is no evidence whatever to invalidate that affirmation. Who this friend or relative was is another question. Our own opinion is that the friend was no other than Maria Woodley Riddel. That lady, as we have just seen, was in temporary possession of a picture belonging to the Poet, and which was doubtless the miniature of his son. It was sent to her in the country to examine; but how, when, or in what condition returned, we do not know. That Mrs. Riddel visited the Poet's widow and family, and was *in their house*, sometime after his death, about or before the year 1798 apparently, when she seems to have gone to London; and that she continued to make personal inquiries about all his children by name, through her friends the Scots at Tinwald House, where she was living in 1795 when the "bagatelle" was sent to her— and that she desired to see any of them when in London, we do know by a letter [Mrs. Burns to Mrs. Riddel, *p.* 219] now for the first time published; that she took a most affectionate interest in the Poet's memory, and wrote an eloquent panegyric on his genius, is certain. Having seen the one picture already, therefore, nothing was more natural than that she should desire to see and to possess the other, or both, if she could, and might even ask them as a memorial of the Poet as they hung there together on his parlour wall, when she took farewell of his family. We venture even to surmise, without any offence to her memory, that she called expressly on purpose. To suppose that Mrs. Burns sold the pictures to this lady for money would be an enormity; but to believe that she gifted them in gratitude, or on special request, would be right. Mrs. Riddel, as we learn, was subsequently married to an Irish gentleman about Court of the name of Fletcher, and as Mrs. Fletcher she lived, or at least died, in State apartments at Hampton Palace, 1820. That Mrs. Riddel, even when in Dumfries, had military acquaintances from Ireland in her retinue is also certain, and that these gentlemen were objects of jealousy to Burns is obvious from the "Epistle of Esopus to Maria." That Major Maunsell afterwards, whilst still a very young officer, and indebted for his rapid promotion undoubtedly to friends about Court, if not actually in the Government, might thus be introduced to Mrs. Riddel or Fletcher, is highly probable; and it is not unreasonable at least to suppose that through her also, not a relative, indeed, but a very devoted friend of the Poet's family, these most interesting objects came at last into his possession, and were by him conveyed to Ireland, on his return home.

8. We have only further to add, that the author of these pictures was most probably a wandering artist of the name of Jamieson; a man of genius who had studied at Rome, but of a restless disposition, who could settle nowhere, and hitherto unknown to fame. This man, so far as we can gather, was about that very date itinerating in the south of Scotland, and painting at Dumfries. Whether any specimens of his art are still to be found there, we have not as yet been able to ascertain; but if such should appear, a comparison of them with the miniatures of Burns and his son, now before us, might enable us to determine the authorship of these paintings.

But much higher questions than that of mere identity are connected with one of these pictures. As a matter of curiosity, it would be interesting at any length to determine the identity of both, as we have now endeavoured to do; but as regards the miniature of Burns himself, which purports to be a true, and the truest, delineation of the man extant, two questions of far greater importance originate. First, is it a reliable study of the Poet's head and features? and second, is it a true moral representation of the Man? To the consideration of which topics, therefore, which involve also the consideration of his phrenological development, we now proceed, as V., VI., and VII., in our inquiry.

V.—PORTRAIT IN RELATION TO HEAD,

AS REPRESENTED IN ACCOMPANYING ENGRAVINGS FROM PHOTOGRAPHS.

OUR readers, we presume, need hardly be informed that the photographs taken to illustrate these remarks represent the head of Robert Burns. That is, of course, the case: they have been taken, and engraved with much care, from a cast of his skull. But our object is to show, by anatomical comparison, that whatever head such photographs do represent must be the very head represented in the miniature.

It is necessary, however, to observe, in the first place, that from the style in which the cast has been taken, viz., from occiput forward to spring of the nose and not lower, it was impossible with propriety to place it *exactly* in the same position as the head in the miniature. The cast inclines forward, and slightly down to left; whereas the whole head in the miniature, for pictorial effect, is erect or inclining slightly backwards: for which difference of position allowance must be made in comparing the two—more especially Nos. 1 and 2 —with miniature. In the second place, although the miniature represents a slightly attenuated countenance, it is not by many degrees, in this respect, to be measured by the naked bone, from which all the remaining integuments of life together—amounting to not less than half an inch all round, in some places more—have been stript. Some allowance for this inevitable difference has already been made in estimating the size of the photographs, that the miniature and these might correspond in dimensions as far as possible; a good deal, however, must still be allowed by the observer on this ground—especially in computing the eyebrows and the mass of hair on the crown and at the back of the head, where the covering is manifestly thickest—if he desires to make a just comparison. Only the foundation of all developments, and the rigid scope of the outlines, can be expected here; and these will be found to correspond exactly.

With such simple proviso, it cannot fail to strike the most inexperienced observer—

1. That the entire mass of skull, as represented both in No. 2 and No. 3, has been literally reproduced in the miniature; so literally, that if any competent artist should now set himself honestly to work to reclothe that skull, the result of his labour would be precisely in that respect the miniature before him: the curl at the back of the head could not be otherwise than as it is, the eyebrows would project as they now do, and the flattened semicircle of the crown, loftiest over

the right eye, would be identically as represented in the engraving—insomuch, that although no face were seen at all, the head, with its wonderful development, would still be the head of Robert Burns, distinguishable among a thousand as his, and his alone.

2. It must appear, also, that the immense projection of the eyebrows is amply provided for in the natural development of the superior orbital bones, which are remarkably distinct in the photographs; and more especially the greater elevation of the left eyebrow as compared with the right. This remarkable difference is more conspicuous in the original than in the engraving, where the want of colour diminishes the striking effect. In point of fact, the left eye in the original is considerably higher than the right, both in its axis and in its surroundings; and in this particular beyond others, that the highest elevation of that eyebrow is nearest the nasal bone, and the greatest flatness of the other eyebrow is farthest from that bone—precisely as these points are shown in the photographs, and perceptibly enough also, although not so decidedly, in the engraving. The comparative flatness of the right eyebrow bone, indeed, is so great, that it might be supposed to have been an accidental abrasion after death, or of the cast after it was taken: but the picture corresponds. This flatness in the picture, again, might have been taken for an error on the painter's part: but the cast corresponds. These two unconscious and independent witnesses, one before death and the other long after, confirm each other; and "in the mouth of two such witnesses every word," concerning the man and concerning his likeness, is thus established. The living gaze, however lamp-like and fascinating it was, must in this respect have been slightly unequal.

3. It must also be obvious, that the slight apparent recession of the forehead, which is observable both in the photographs and in the miniature, is due not to any real deficiency of development there, but to the unusual projection of the eyebrow bone below it; and that this apparent recession of the forehead should seem to be greatest over the left eye, because the left eyebrow encroaches farthest on the head: which, in point of fact, is most clearly attested by the miniature. That this remarkable peculiarity should not have been observed during life, even by such a painter as Nasmyth, is singular but not unnatural. We attribute such oversight to the fascinating brilliancy of the eyes themselves, which diverted attention from the head; because, after death, when the eyes were gone, the peculiarity was noticeable at the first glance. Witnessing his disinterment in 1815, Mr. M‘Diarmid observes, that "the forehead struck every one as beautifully arched, if not so high as might reasonably have been supposed" [Appendix, p. xlvi]. But why "not so *high* as might reasonably have been supposed?"—Because in twenty years the public had forgotten the exact reality, and had taken their measurements in imagination from Nasmyth's exaggerated representation, who had unduly exalted the arch to please himself, and had diminished the buttresses. The head was arched by Nature, who could make no mistake, and did not need to flatter; and it was sufficiently high for all God's purposes—although not for Nasmyth's; but it was buttressed and backed with more than ordinary weight, which seemed to

diminish the elevation, whilst the lights that burned below, and the dark waving locks that overhung it above, attracted and deceived the spectator. There was one honest artist, however, with an eye for realities in his own head, who fortunately could represent the whole of it; and in the miniature, even in the engraving itself, now before us, the central lamp which shines there, and the overhanging eyebrows—all the more that the waving locks themselves are partially gone—explain everything. The head, as we see it there, is well formed, and high enough; but no higher than it was in reality, or than it should be.

4. As a concluding point of mere superficial resemblance between photographs and miniature, much more between the cast and the painting, it is scarcely necessary almost to direct the observer's attention to the origin and development of the nasal bone. The spring of the nose and the character of the region immediately above it are both as truly and perfectly represented and developed in the miniature as if they had been reflected on the panel from a mirror, or as if the panel itself had been a mirror to retain the living reflection.

So much for details of exact resemblance. What the face should have been to correspond with such a head, we can only for the present conjecture; for the miniature itself is on trial, and cannot be quoted as a witness: but with so much fidelity in points where comparison is open, and where painters most of all are disposed to be negligent (as if masses of hair or fictitious attitudes should cover or disguise a fallacy), we may reasonably conclude that every other detail has been rendered with equal adhesiveness to reality, which is but another name for truth. This truthfulness we can trace with certainty no farther than the outline of the nose; but the nose, as represented in the miniature, is the very nose of which we see the rudimental origin in the skull, and could not, without violence, have had any other shape than it has. The cheek bones correspond to the eyebrows, and the jaws and the chin exactly to the back part of the head. The whole contour, therefore, is in harmony, and we may safely affirm that no other facial development could possibly appertain to such a head. There would have been physical incongruity otherwise. The only features, therefore, which remain undetermined, are the eyes and lips; but after so much fidelity elsewhere, and everywhere else, we are warranted to credit both the skill and fidelity of the artist in these portions of his work also, even although they are the most difficult. Certainly no other painter of Robert Burns, in this respect, has a twentieth part of the same credit to support him. Nasmyth's head of Burns, in fact, is not Burns's head; Skirving, who never saw Burns, imagined a head, which Burns's own skull impugns and sets aside; Taylor, who could not perhaps have drawn the head, substitutes a hat, so we cannot judge what the head itself, in his hands, would have been. But in the picture before us there is neither pretension, nor falsehood, nor disguise. This painter, in short, this itinerant artist, is the only man who has approached, or even attempted, a real Head of Burns: and for the rest, we may simply affirm that it corresponds. The lips in the engraving are by no means what they should be, and no engraving will ever render them truly; but in the original they seem almost to vibrate and speak. As for the

eyes, we shall without ceremony say, that no two eyes could be imagined for splendour, depth, and passion, for latent fire of love and rage, for eloquence, for fascinating power, and for the most exquisite truthful tenderness, more perfectly in consonance than these two eyes—right and left together—are with the amazing skull which lies behind them. It seems to us, indeed, morally impossible that any man could have imagined these eyes who did not see them; and equally impossible that any competent critic should allege that the painter who represented them was a dauber, or an impostor, or a fool. Any other sort of eyes set in such a head would have been idle fallacies—tapers imperceptible, or lying lights, in the vestibule of a dome where all that was angelic and all that was animal in our common constitution, with scarce a curtain to divide them, were at perpetual war for supremacy.

5. Beyond what appears, however, in the mere engraving, as compared with the photographs, two singular coincidences between the cast and the portrait remain to be noticed. One of these refers to the general attitude of the figure in connection with the head; the other to a minute correspondence in the original which could scarcely be made perceptible in the engraving, or would not have been understood there if it had.

(a) Burns's ordinary lounging attitude, "with his head leaning forward and his hands behind his back, like a thinking man," is well known, and has already been commented on in this work—[Biography p. xxiii]. That attitude, of course, could not be permitted in a portrait where the face and head were to be well seen. It is manifest, notwithstanding, that the figure inclines to the left hand, and that the head itself has been gently erected on purpose to be represented in full. We can easily demonstrate that this inclination of the figure must have been, as represented, to the left, and that the lean in that direction must in general have been rather conspicuous. In walking at the plough, the man who guides it must necessarily stoop towards the left, inasmuch as the unploughed land and the straight edge of the plough by which the furrow is directed are both on that side. In stooping thus, the head acquires, by physical development of the muscles on one side and contraction on the other, a fixed position in the same direction; which, perpetuated for generations, will become congenital. But in so stooping to direct the furrow, the left eyebrow must be forcibly and continually, although at the moment imperceptibly raised, or the range before the plough, which is essential to direct its course, would be lost. Any one who chooses to place himself for a few minutes in this position, and attempt to look before him straight, will find the necessity of thus elevating the eyebrow referred to, and of changing occasionally, as ploughmen do, to relieve the head. This also, in the lapse of generations, will become a fixed characteristic; as sportsmen and the children of sportsmen attain unconscious facility in winking, and even contract an irresistible propensity to wink, with the same eye.

This peculiarity, however, is by no means confined to any class. The very same elevation of the left eyebrow is most conspicuously manifest in the common portraits of Shelley, in whose case no such physical cause could be assigned for it. In this respect decidedly, and somewhat also in the formation of the jaw-bone and chin, the portraits of Shelley resemble

this miniature of Burns. But it is necessary still farther to observe, that the external balance bones and internal pivot bones of Burns's skull, the bones on which the skull rests and moves from one side to the other, are most distinctly of unequal lengths, and that they diminish in regular gradation to the *left* side—the " mastoid process," as it is called, on the left side being at least half an inch shorter than the corresponding bone on the right side, and the two intervening pivot bones shorter in proportion. The head must therefore, of physical necessity, have inclined both forwards and towards the left not a little, both pivots and levers falling equally away in that direction. This inclination indeed is so great, that a considerable portion of the right mastoid process and pivot bone adjoining had to be shorn off in the plaster, before the cast itself would stand. If placed on its natural foundation without this precaution, it would either require to be propped up, or it would certainly topple over to the left. By comparing the level of the mastoid process (small depending pointed bone behind position of the ear) in profile photograph No. 3, where it does not touch the table at all, with corresponding bone on opposite side in photograph No. 2, which not only touches the table but has been shorn off square to a level with the artificial plaster props in front, to enable the skull to stand fair—the student will easily be able to compute the real difference between them, and consequent inclination of the head. This fact may be still more distinctly realised by observing the two " condyloid processes," or pivot bones as we prefer in common terms to call them, which appear like two dark knobs in figure No. 1, touching the table, one under each eye, adjacent to the props, and which most clearly indicate the inclination of the head to the left.

It must have been natural for Burns, therefore, at all times to carry his head downwards in this direction; and to sit for a portrait, as he sometimes did, would require a certain strain on the muscles for the moment—a sort of constraint which is most wonderfully and truthfully represented in the miniature before us. The same stoop is manifest in Taylor's picture, in which respect it is faithful. But in this respect, also, the portrait now under consideration displays greater artistic skill than any other portrait of the Poet extant. All other portraits, except Allan's imaginary one, are taken from the left side, from which no portrait at once truthful and effective *could* be taken of a man whose head and shoulders were so distinctly inclined downwards and towards that side. Shelley's portrait, indeed, was taken from the left, and is certainly effective, whether truthful or not. But Shelley's neck was long and taper, and the style of his dress entirely different from Burns's, which justified the painter in his case. Burns could be faithfully and well represented only from the right side, in which position the slightest constraint of the figure was required, and the range of the eyebrows was most easily adjusted consistently with truth, and by this artist alone has he been so represented. The same physical conformation implied also a certain shortness of the neck, which we know was manifest in Burns's figure, and which has been most truthfully, yet by no means disagreeably, represented in the miniature. There is not one point, in fact, anatomically, in which the picture fails. If it should still be objected, how-

ever, to the whole of this argument, that the bones on the left side of the skull have been accidentally wasted away, and that the head did *not* lean to that side at all, we have simply to reply that they are all perfect.

(*b*) Notwithstanding the many points of obvious undeniable physical correspondence between the cranium and the miniature thus anatomically compared, it might still be possible for a sceptic to allege that some other man than Burns, with a head the very same as his, was represented here, and that this was not Burns after all. Taking such an extreme objection on moral grounds, we might dismiss it summarily as unworthy of attention, and affirm categorically that no other Scotchman known, dead or alive, had ever such a head on his shoulders; but we prefer to entertain the objection, and to produce a seal of identity more unquestionable than Burns's own signature would have been to his last will and testament. On the outer edge of the right brow, about half way up the head, is a triangular flesh-mark or cicatrice underneath the hair, but quite discernible through it, most artistically painted in the miniature, representing a deep wound there. This scar could not be seen in Nasmyth's work for two reasons—first, because no wound had been received there when Nasmyth's portrait was painted, and second, because that part of the head in his portrait is both averted and covered with hair. It could not be seen in Skirving's for two reasons also—first, because Skirving never saw the man, and second, because the head as done by him is from the other side. It could not be seen in Taylor's, because in Taylor's portrait the head is shaded with a hat. In the Kerry Miniature it is distinct— first, because it was on the living subject undoubtedly, or it would never have been inserted; second, because the hair on the forehead at the close of the Poet's life was beginning to disappear, which revealed it; and third, because the right forehead is conspicuously displayed in the miniature, and the scar could not be hidden. But on the skull itself the foundation of a wound, by a welt in the bone, is manifest, of the same shape, of the same size in proportion, and on the same spot exactly. This mark is not represented in the engraving, but is traceable in the woodcuts Nos. 1 and 2. From such evidence there can be no appeal. It testifies alike to the identity of the portrait and to the fidelity of the artist, and leaves no doubt whatever not only that this is the picture of Robert Burns, but that Robert Burns must have received a wound on his forehead in the concluding decade of his life. We learn from his own and other letters, first, that he was thrown from his horse in a mad freak on Lochlomondside in 1787, when he was lifted, or rose, with his face " cut " and bleeding [pp. 148, 205]: and again, that his horse came down with him at Ellisland, as he was returning from a circuit in 1791 [p. 23], on which occasion he fell on his right side and broke his right arm, in attempting doubtless to save his head. But the arm giving way, the head would suffer; and a wound precisely similar to that here represented would or might easily, if not necessarily, be inflicted on the very place. On whichever of these two occasions this wound was received, the trace of it must have been visible externally in 1795, as thus represented; and the proof of it was legible for forty years afterwards, indented on the bare bone. Any further evidence,

we presume, before the most prejudiced jury of objectors, as to identity in this case, would be superfluous.

But the identity of the portrait being admitted or proved. Is it artistically good ? Is it morally faithful ? Does it do justice to the man ? And was the man himself justified in declaring, as he did, that it was the most wonderful likeness of himself that had ever been taken of anybody ? That it represented him, in short, as he then was, so faithfully, that he should desire it to go down the stream of Time in connection with his works, as the type of himself for ever ? These are different questions, and must be answered affirmatively, or otherwise, from another point of view.

VI.—MINIATURE OF BURNS IN ITS MORAL ASPECT.

On this subject, the first observation which naturally occurs is that no other portrait does represent him faithfully—most of them not at all. We shall put his own testimony for the present out of question, and with respect to Nasmyth's in the first place, have only to remind our readers that Sir Walter Scott, who had seen the man, declared it to be radically deficient as a picture of Robert Burns. It had neither substance nor character enough for him, in Sir Walter's opinion; and independently of such testimony the portrait is manifestly deficient. It is a showy performance, painted by a man who was not a portrait painter, and who certainly did not understand *this* sitter. It represents a flourishing country lad, in glowing colours, set off to advantage, who was not a gentleman, far less an intellectual giant ; who was not likely to live as Burns lived, who could not speak as Burns spoke—had not a mouth for that, and who could not have written the works which Burns wrote, if he had received the world in exchange for them. All this is clear, although Walter Scott had been silent on the subject : and one of the greatest causes of public misapprehension about Robert Burns, his life, his letters, and his poems, has been the falsehood of this very likeness. The public sees in that likeness, as commonly engraved by the best engravers, an affable easy-going Ayrshire swain, and cannot comprehend the lightning of his rage or the tornado of his passions. Compared with this portrait, the living man seems to belie himself; he writes down his own likeness; he becomes an enigma to his readers from the first, and is an enigma to the last, darker and darker, with contradiction and blasphemy combined—not because there was contradiction or blasphemy in reality, but because a portrait painter had misrepresented him in their eyes. Beugo's engraving from this likeness was said to be an improvement. We doubt this very much, except as regards the forehead and the chin, which are a little more according to nature. The grossness of the jawbone, the simper of the mouth, the squareness of the nose, the glimmer of the eyes, and above all, the deficiency of background in the head, are irredeemable errors. Allan's guess-work in his Cotter's Saturday Night is declared by Burns himself—although we do not at present rely on his testimony—to be better than both of them. The engraving by Neagle from Nasmyth, prefixed to Currie's edition, 1801, is in our opinion much

better. As regards the prominence of the left eyebrow, in fact, it is very near the truth. As for Skirving's, it cannot be taken into account, because it is now ascertained that he never saw the man and wrought only from description; which is evident enough—for the skull is a mistake, with fictitious developments, and the face is a woman's face, soft and quiet, as incapable of Burns's rage, or transport of any kind like his, as a plaster cast would be of animation ; whilst the fleshy jaw and enormous chin are in direct contradiction to the whole assumed phrenological development : both cannot be true, and neither is real.* Taylor's has something of the general outline, but no eyes or mouth of Burns—small eyes and a round mouth !—nor fire that would irradiate his countenance, whilst the head is entirely hidden. Let our readers refer for a moment to the anecdote recorded of Burns at Muirkirk [Appendix, p. xlix], or the accounts of his fury and suppressed rage on many similar occasions of imposture, or of cruelty, especially to the lower animals, related by eye-witnesses or recorded by himself—"Lines on the Wounded Hare," for example, with Thomson's own story attached—and endeavour to reconcile such paroxysms with the portraits above quoted, and they will find how imperfect they must be. The truth is, these painters never saw their subject in double lights, and could not comprehend, much less represent, the tremendous antagonisms of his moral nature. As for certain profiles we have seen—Silhouettes and others—these may give some outline, but the soul is not there. One of these indeed, for a while at Dalswinton or in that neighbourhood, and which we have seen, so far from giving even an outline, represents the Poet with a nose turned up at the point, and the back part of his head perpendicular !

Although the miniature now in question, therefore, should not be absolutely true ; and although the mere engraving should err a little on the dark side, which it unfortunately does, still, in its moral effect, it would be no less reliable than others, and would have accuracy of detail besides. But we believe it to be morally true, inasmuch as the face and head correspond, whilst the head is incontrovertibly true. At first sight, indeed, the effect is a little painful ; and in the engraving, where the beauty of the original cannot be so well seen, this bad effect is more sensible. But even thus, the picture

---

* " According to the best information we have been able to gather on the subject," say the publishers of Blackie's Edition, in which this portrait first appeared, " we learn that Burns never gave Mr. Skirving any sittings for his portrait. The Poet and artist were intimately acquainted, and thus Mr. Skirving enjoyed much better opportunities of observing his friend under the influence of the varied expressions which so frequently and changefully flitted across his countenance, than could be possessed by any other artist to whom he merely gave sittings," &c., &c. With respect to this announcement, no doubt made in good faith, we have simply to state, on the most unquestionable authority, that no such intimacy existed between the Poet and the artist, or could exist.

" There is a mistake about Skirving," says our correspondent, a person most intimately acquainted with all the relationships of the Poet's family—" I am very sure he never saw Robert Burns. He lived some years beside Gilbert Burns, and was in the habit of seeing him and his sisters frequently ; but never saw Robert." This information our correspondent had from Gilbert Burns himself ; and that the statement must be correct is obvious, for Archibald Skirving, being a genuine artist, and having once seen Robert Burns, could never have painted such a head. The whole theory, therefore, with respect to this portrait being the successful embodiment of vivid recollections on the artist's part, is a dream. It has no claim to any higher rank than that of an imaginary likeness, founded on the representations or the recollections of others.

represents a giant in pain, a gentleman in *deshabille*, a genius in commingled tenderness and scorn. On looking into it more narrowly, it improves, as all genuine works of art do; all mere painful impressions die away; sympathy and love succeed—the true character of the subject unfolds itself; the hand of a real artist is manifest in the work, and the soul of a great man in the sitter. The picture then becomes a study, in which days and nights might be spent with satisfaction and profit. You care no longer any more about external evidence; the evidence of the work is in itself, and in the life of the man it brings thus vividly before you. The portrait is a massive, solemn, and profoundly suggestive theme. The predominating expressions are various, but all characteristic: subdued passion, intense vehemence, sorrow conquered, and intellect over all animal propensities, over all grief and trials, over all bodily anguish (of which manifestly there has been much), triumphant. Thoughtful resignation pervades the whole—the "Contented wi' Little" apparent, the "Cantie wi' Mair" just possible. The man, you perceive, has been weather-beaten, both morally and physically, accustomed to storms and to hard usage within and without, but equal to, or above them all. The craniological development, as we have already seen, amazing, and so accurate withal, that a phrenological analysis might have been written from this head alone. The whole aspect unsophisticated, simple in the last degree, and grand beyond the showiest likeness ever executed in his honour. In a word, it is a portrait that absorbs the imagination and affects the soul at once; which could be gazed at for hours without weariness, and which will never be forgotten by any judge of the human countenance that once seriously looks at it. You involuntarily subscribe to his own declaration about the miniature, that this is "the most remarkable likeness of what he must have been in 1795, that ever was taken of anybody." With a dark flowing beard, this portrait might represent a Hebrew Seer or Psalmist: but it is Robert Burns; and all that Burns ever wrote or said, or thought or did, is represented here. His works have now another sense for you; and neither contradiction, nor blasphemy, nor falsehood is traceable in them all. They are natural, consistent, articulate expressions of a profound and tender, of a deep and strong, perhaps terrible, nature, but reliable as a rock, represented here by truth-speaking tints and shadows on the silent wood. These are by no means exclusively our own personal impressions. They have been shared in, less or more, by all who have dispassionately looked on this picture. Let one witness among many, who could have no prepossession to gratify or personal interest to serve, speak for all. From a discriminating article, by an editorial pen, in the *Glasgow Herald*, March 30, 1868, we extract the following.

"We have already published some interesting remarks on an engraving of the portrait from the *Inverness Courier*, and since then we have had, through the courtesy of Mr. Waddell, an opportunity of seeing and studying the original. What we have to say of the picture is derived entirely from itself, because we know nothing of its history, or the evidence by which it is traced back to the man whom it is supposed to represent. A single glance at it shows its truthfulness, its honesty—one might almost say its savage honesty. There are some portraits that we know cannot be untrue, they reveal so much of the whole soul of the original. The picture of Dante is an example. We could scarcely conceive of the poet who passed through the 'Inferno' having been unlike in feature that painfully suffering, clear cut face, with the untroubled far-reaching eyes. No painter can lie with his brush in such a fashion, and we instinctively say of a portrait like this—'It is true.' The supposed portrait of Burns in Mr. Waddell's possession is of this character. Be it Burns's likeness, or the likeness of some other individual, it is the portrait of a man who must have so looked when it was painted, and of a man of great intellect, of strong passions, of suffering, of a sort of faded splendour and yet undiminished intellectual power, and of subdued but unextinguished passion. It is the true portrait of no ordinary man—that one can see from the hastiest look. On gazing a little more attentively at this miniature one begins to see some of the characteristic Burns' features of the younger portraits; but there is over, and somewhat veiling them all, those ten hard years of mental toil and struggle, and occasional debauch. There is the rounded, full forehead—not very high, but deep, with the lines above the nose deepened upwards, and indenting the space between the eyebrows. The hair falls short and careless over the front, and gives at the first look rather a savage sort of expression to the face. The distance between the temples and the back of the head is very great, and with the large mass of brain shown behind corresponds with the cast taken of the skull. The eyes are larger, and infinitely more intense in their gaze, than in any other of the portraits. The painter shows us in those eyes most extraordinary slumbering power and passion; and if they were not, they deserved to have been, the eyes of Burns. The nose is large, prominent, and powerful, and the lips and mouth have quite an indescribable character, so flexible do they appear, and so ready to express any mood of the Poet's mind. This is a mouth which could utter ribald jokes or quiver with the tenderest emotion. The cheeks and chin are full, brown, and somewhat gross, giving a background of earth and power to the suppressed fire of the eye and the splendid sensibility of the mouth. But it is in vain to dwell upon separate features in order to give the reader any idea of this wonderful picture—for wonderful it is, whoever it represents. It is enough to say that to our mind it seemed not only a likeness of Burns, but a biography of him, telling, perhaps, rather too much of his suffering and his sins, disclosing his genius, and not hiding either—his heart full of all the humanities."

VII.—PHRENOLOGICAL SUMMARY.

BUT if these things be so, is it not painful to contemplate such a representation, or to dwell on it as a reality? Not necessarily painful; but solemnising and instructive in the highest degree. Burns, in truth, has been more misunderstood in these respects than most other men, and very much in consequence of pictorial misrepresentations. He has been thought of almost universally as a kind-hearted, light-hearted, richly-gifted, reckless moral profligate, squandering his gifts and abusing his opportunities; whose levity bordered on wilful profanity, and his love on licentiousness. He was in reality a son of sorrow, an overburdened wayfarer, and a soldier in perpetual conflict with himself and with the world, from his youth up; equally gifted with good and encumbered with evil; who bore this load of sorrow on his soul, and passed through these fires of temptation buffetting the flames in silence, as his countenance declares, with the fortitude and heroism of a martyr, to the end. And why should he not so be contemplated even by those who admire and love him most? Why should they not now see him as he was?

His head, as the most careless observer must perceive, is equally divided. It consists, in fact, of two unusually great but equal hemispheres, which meet together upwards in a plane, where firmness and veneration that would have been full enough in other men are comparatively deficient in him. With veneration and firmness more fully developed, one could hardly imagine the greatness of this man. But God had willed it otherwise. His veneration, such as it was, united with his goodness constrained him to adore all human excellence; his comparative want of veneration, united with his destructiveness, inclined him, in like manner, to ridicule and to trample on every base and vicious counterfeit. From this one faculty alone, thus doubly and doubtfully allied, came such hymns as that "To Mary in Heaven," and such satires as "Holy Willie's Prayer." His want of firmness, on the other hand, was pretty well compensated by immense general power of concentration, and his comparative want of self-esteem by his love of approbation; and the perpetual oscillation of his life between these extremes corresponds. No less than twelve times does he quote, separately or together—eight times the one, and four times the other—the celebrated passages from Young and Thomson as to the advantages of courage and resolution—" Resolve, that column of true majesty in man"—or as he himself in his Epistle to Blacklock much more emphatically calls it by apostrophe,

Thou stalk o' carl-hemp in man!

as if he knew its moral value well, and felt the want of it; yet every day of his life was this very column of resolve—of firm, conscientious resolve—overthrown by indecision: whilst the modesty of his own estimate of most of his own doings, and the almost childish anxiety he felt about the good opinion of even the humblest, and the vexation he endured under the neglect of the most contemptible, were manifest through life. In other respects the antagonism of his constitution must be equally obvious. His cautiousness, which even for a Scotchman was large, and his acquisitiveness, which was very decided [letter (1) to Mrs. Burns], must have been entering daily vexatious protests against the occasional extravagance or recklessness of his career, and the general want of aim in his existence. His essential goodness, which is like an angel's in front, must have been strained often to the uttermost to keep the destructiveness and other dangerous elements of the background in check; whilst these together, at intervals, must have generated uncontrollable paroxysms of rage against falsehood and cruelty. For the rest, it is enough to observe, that the principle of love and the purest love of off-

spring combined—the love of offspring, however, as strong as in a woman, far predominating over the other—must have plunged him incessantly into whirlpools of passion which the frigid commonplace observer can have no idea of, and which the more licentious ruffian would only laugh to scorn. But who could alter these things? "Shall the clay say to him that fashioneth it, What makest thou? or thy work, He hath no hands? Yea, let the potsherd strive with the potsherds of the earth; but woe unto him that striveth with his Maker!"

This head, in fact, to whomsoever it might belong, is the truest type in nature of what St. Paul long ago announced in doctrine—"that the flesh lusteth against the spirit, and the spirit against the flesh; and that these are contrary the one to the other, so that we cannot do the things," on either side, "that we would;" and if any man since the days of the Apostle was more truly entitled than another to exclaim in an agony of distraction, "O wretched man that I am! who shall deliver me from the body of this death? I thank God, through Jesus Christ our Lord!"—that man was Robert Burns. That he was himself fully sensible of all this—realised it clearly, and endured it with heroic patience; nay, that he understood his own moral development as well as if the most accomplished phrenologist had provided him with a chart of it all—is demonstrated by his own confessions, in letter after letter, to both men and women, with the frankest, the most unreserved, almost childlike affability. In proof of which, the reader may glance among others at letters to Miss Chalmers, (3), (4), (5), (7), (9); and to Clarinda, (37); also at several to Mrs. Dunlop, not a few to Hill, (3) to Cunningham, and others. But a life like this could not be lived, or temptations like these endured, without destructive consequences. The shortness of his life, indeed, has been a cause of regret, of astonishment and complaint, and even of reproach against himself, to many. To ourselves it seems natural enough, and his death very little earlier than it would have been in any circumstances. The supply of vital energy required for such a head, and the sort of life that head implied, would have exhausted any average constitution prematurely. Whatever our regretful moralists may think or say, Burns could not have survived with credit or satisfaction his fiftieth year; and this from no wilful error of his own. His doom and destiny alike were in him, and the irrevocable seal of God imprinted on his forehead.

But could all this be, we ask, without some traces of it on his countenance? Can a man, heavy laden, run without being wearied, or walk without being faint, in this world of infirmity and sin? Can he pass through the deep waters without danger to his soul? or through the seven-times-heated furnace without feeling its glow? Then might Robert Burns to his dying day have had no trace of such trials about him. But the supposition is incredible: it is contrary to fact, and to the testimony of eye-witnesses at a much earlier date than his death. "Burns had just come to Nithsdale," says Allan Cunningham; "and I think he appeared a shade more swarthy than he does in Nasmyth's picture, and at least ten years older than he really was at the time. His face was deeply marked by thought, and the habitual expression intensely melancholy. . . . . . He had a very manly face and a very melancholy look; but on the coming of those he esteemed, his looks brightened up, and his whole face beamed with affection and genius." This was in 1788, only a year after Nasmyth's performance: how much more, then, might this expression of sorrow and premature age have increased by 1795? No reasonable person reflecting on the subject, even with the delusive shadow on Nasmyth's canvas before him, can doubt it for a moment; and any picture which represented this mighty wrestler, self-reliant, self-sacrificing, and triumphant, without some traces of such conflict on him at the close, would have been a worthless and contemptible falsehood.

P.S.—Among other little marks indicating that the pictures must have been in the possession of the Poet's family, may be mentioned, as a matter of curiosity, that there is a small round spot on the lapelle of his waistcoat, which seems to have been made by a drop of soap or soda. This must have been before the picture was varnished, and was probably from Mrs. Burns's own finger when removing it from one spot to another—for an accident of that kind was by no means likely to occur in anybody's hands but her own, or at least elsewhere than in her own house.

Heroines of Burns.

(Where Letters are referred to in these Notes, the pages will be found in Prose Works.)

"ANNA."—Helen Ann Park, of "the gowden locks," celebrated in the song "Yestreen I had a pint of wine," p. 379, was barmaid at the Globe Hotel, Dumfries, and sister to the landlady (Mrs. Hyslop) there; said to have been a person of very ordinary attractions, with coarse red hair.

"ANNIE."—Anne Rankine, afterwards Mrs. Merry, celebrated in song "The Rigs o' Barley," p. 74, was the youngest daughter of J. Rankine of Adamhill. As Mrs. Merry, she resided long at New Cumnock, where her husband kept a public-house. Other claimants for the honour of this song have been named—Anne Ronald and Anne Blair, p. 108;*—but Mrs. Merry was unquestionably the heroine. At her house, as an old acquaintance, the Poet indited a letter to Mr. Thomas Campbell of Pencloe, August, 1786 [Prose Works, p. 155]; and at a subsequent date he presented her with one of his miniature likenesses (most probably Beugo's engraving coloured) as a token of their friendship—which gift is still religiously preserved by her son, Dr. J. Merry, Edinburgh. Mrs. Merry is said to have been of a tall, commanding aspect; and her favourite song to the end of her life was that in which her own name was celebrated.

"BELLES" OF MAUCHLINE—celebrated in song, p. 350, may be thus briefly distinguished: Miss Helen Miller married Burns's friend, Dr. Mackenzie; Miss Markland married also another friend of his, Mr. Finlay of the excise, first at Tarbolton, then at Greenock; Miss Jean Smith married a third friend, Mr. Candlish [see correspondence with whom], and became the mother of Rev. Robert S. Candlish, D.D.; Miss Betty Miller (sister to Miss Helen Miller) became a Mrs. Templeton, but died early in life; Miss Morton became the

*The reader of first edition of this work will observe that Anne Blair's name has, by inadvertence, been substituted for Anne Rankine's.

wife of a Mr. Paterson, merchant in Mauchline, and was among the last of the survivors. Jean Armour was Mrs. Burns, and the most favoured. Mr. Chambers, to whom we are indebted for certain of the above particulars, further informs us, that in 1851 no fewer than three of these ladies survived—Mrs. Finlay, Mrs. Paterson, and Mrs. Candlish; but before 1854 they had all departed.

"BLUE-EYED LASSIE"—celebrated in song of that name, p. 141—was a Miss Jeffrey, daughter of Rev. Mr. Jeffrey of Lochmaben, and subsequently married to Mr. Renwick of New-York. From edition of Thomson's Melodies, 1830, we learn that in 1822 she was a widow, but still with the same "twa sweet een that gave the Poet his death, clear and full of expression." Her description of Burns's visits to her father's manse, as recorded by Mr. Thomson's son in the edition referred to, conveys the highest idea of his affability, simplicity, and attractiveness of manner. "Everything he said or did had a gracefulness and charm that was in an extraordinary degree engaging." She is said by New-York Mirror (1846) to have been celebrated also in another song, "When first I saw fair Jeanie's face," p. 425. Her mother, Agnes Armstrong, is said to have been the heroine of the well-known beautiful song, "Roslin Castle."

"BONIE ANN"—daughter of Allan Masterton of the High School, Edinburgh; celebrated in the song bearing her name, p. 171. "Miss Masterton afterwards became Mrs. Derbishire, and was living in London in 1834."—Chambers.

"BONIE LASS OF ALBANY."—Acknowledged by Prince Charles Edward to be his sole legitimate daughter, by title of the Duchess of Albany. Her mother, with whom the Prince long cohabited as his wife, was Miss Clementina Walkinshaw, and the child here celebrated was their only offspring. A son, or grandson, of the "Lass of Albany's," we believe, visited Glasgow some years ago to inquire for his grandmother's family; who, however, did not reside in that city, being the Walkinshaws of Walkinshaw. He has been described to us as a very fine looking man, of military bearing.

"BONIE LESLEY BAILLIE,"—celebrated in song, p. 205, was daughter of Mr. Baillie of Mayfield. For description of this remarkable beauty, see letter (32) to Mrs. Dunlop, (5) to Thomson, and (7) to Cunningham. Miss Baillie became Mrs. Cumming of Logie, and died in Edinburgh, July, 1843.

"BONIE JEAN."—See "PHILLIS."

BURNET, ELIZA.—"Fair Burnet," celebrated in the "Address to Edinburgh," p. 64, and lamented in the "Elegy," p. 331, was, at the date of our Author's visit to the capital, a paragon of beauty and grace in female society there. She was the daughter of James Burnet, the celebrated, accomplished, and eccentric Lord Monboddo. Burns enjoyed his lordship's special patronage when in Edinburgh, and was thus privileged to be frequently in Miss Burnet's company. After one of these visits, according to Cunningham, being interrogated by his friend Mr. Geddes, "whether he admired the young lady?" the Poet replied, "I admire God Almighty more than ever! Miss Burnet is the most heavenly of all his works." In the same strain he refers to the lady in his letter to W. Chalmers, p. 155. Miss Burnet, confessedly supreme in beauty, was equally amiable and good. Notwithstanding the many attractions which entitled her to a place of her own the most enviable in society, she devoted herself almost exclusively to attendance on her aged father. She died of consumption at the early age of twenty-three, June, 1790.

CHARLOTTE HAMILTON—celebrated in the "Banks of the Devon," p. 132, also in "Fairest Maid on Devon Banks," p. 222—half-sister to Gavin Hamilton by the father's side, and full cousin to Miss Margaret Chalmers; resided for some time with other cousins of their own, the Taits of Harvieston, at their home in Clackmannanshire. She is described by our Author, in letter (4) to Gavin Hamilton, as a girl of extraordinary beauty. On his second visit to Harvieston, October, 1787, Burns was accompanied by Dr. J. M'Kittrick Adair, a relative of Mrs. Dunlop's, who describes the circumstances of his own introduction to the family on that occasion, with many interesting and amusing details. The ladies at Harvieston, in fact, had a great washing-day when the Poet and his young friend arrived, but contrived, notwithstanding, to do the honours of hospitality with grace: the result of which was Charlotte's marriage to Dr. Adair in 1789. Dr. Adair died in 1802; Charlotte followed him, prematurely, in 1806. In her hands were left a number of letters addressed to her cousin, Margaret Chalmers—which, most unfortunately, for what reason or caprice unknown, were by her destroyed.

"CHLORIS," "Jeanie," "Lassie wi' the lint-white locks," celebrated in no fewer than ten songs and at least one dedication, as follows:—

Craigieburn Wood (2 sets), p. 112-204	Lassie wi' the lint-white locks, p. 221
O wha is she that lo'es me? . 211	Sleep'st thou or wak'st thou? 221
O whistle, &c. (two sets), 196-314	Forlorn, my love, . . . 225
Long, long the night, . . 220	My Chloris, mark, &c., . . 330
Bonie was yon rosy brier, . 220	'Tis Friendship's Pledge, . 347

and perhaps some others, was born at Craigieburn, a mansion of most picturesque beauty near Moffat, where her father, Mr. William Lorimer, a prosperous farmer but a well-known smuggler, was tacksman for the time. Her own name was Jean or Jane. It was in this neighbourhood, it is said, the Poet was first introduced to her, at the house of her aunt, with whom she was then residing. The family afterwards removed to Kemis Hall, a farm on the opposite side of the Nith from Ellisland, and about two miles nearer Dumfries, where the visits of the Poet, in his official capacity, became much more frequent in consequence of Mr. Lorimer's persistent determination in many ways to defraud the excise. On this subject the reader may compare the Poet's letter to Findlater, Appendix, p. xxx. Miss Lorimer, remarkable for her personal beauty, and perhaps for her wilfulness, but wearied no doubt by unpleasant scenes at home, married, by elopement, at Gretna, according to one account, in her seventeenth year, 1793, a showy heartless impostor of the name of Whelpdale, from Cumberland, who had been for some time resident at Moffat, and to whom she was introduced by the Johnstons of Craigieburn at a public ball there. A few months after this inauspicious union, his true circumstances and character coming both to light, he absconded, and his half-widowed wife, in shame and poverty, returned to her father's roof. In 1816, twenty-three years after their separation, she discovered her husband a prisoner for debt in Carlisle Jail, and the wreck of dissipation and profligacy, unrecognisable almost in his degra-

dation. In these circumstances, she bestowed some affectionate care upon him whilst she remained in Carlisle; but no prospect of a reunion could ever be entertained by her. From this time they never met again. It is said that, by some indiscretion of her own subsequently, she lost the respect of society; but Mrs. Burns seems to think that these aspersions were unjust. [Compare Memoranda in Appendix, p. xxiv.] Certain it is, however, that after dragging out a miserable existence in the humblest situations, relieved occasionally by charity, gratefully and gracefully acknowledged by her, she died, September, 1831, "in a humble lodging in Middleton's Entry, Potterrow [Edinburgh], near the place where Burns first met Clarinda." The above details we gather partly from Chambers. On the other hand, we are informed by Mr. Carruthers of the *Inverness Courier*, that, in 1794, the lady still retained, or had resumed, her maiden name. Either, therefore, the date of her marriage must have been later than Mr. Chambers supposes, or she must have resumed her own name after being deserted by her husband. The evidence of this fact, adduced by Mr. Carruthers, is as follows:—"I have seen a copy of Collins' poems with this inscription, 'Jean Lorimer, a small but sincere mark of friendship from ROBERT BURNS.' The lady adds her own signature, 'JANE LORIMER, 1794.'"

Her name appears also as "Jean Lorimer, Kemyshall," underwritten with "John Gillespie," in the same hand, on a window-pane at Ellisland.—No date.

"CLARINDA,"—already sufficiently known to our readers, both by the correspondence addressed to her, and by occasional notices throughout, has been celebrated under the above designation, and also as "Nanie," "Lovely Nancy," and a "Lady," in the following songs or verses:—

Clarinda, mistress of my soul, p. 131	My Nanie's awa, . . p. 215
Ae fond kiss, ... 145	Behold the hour, . . . 223
O May, thy morn, . . . 156	Lovely Nancy, . . . 326
Anee mair I hail thee, . . 160	To a lady, with drinking-glasses, 370

Her history, as our readers are also aware, was sorrowful in the extreme; her personal prudence was questionable; but her influence over Burns's imagination at least, for a considerable time after her introduction to the Poet, is beyond doubt. Her maiden name was Agnes Craig. She was born in Glasgow, April, 1759, and was thus only three months younger than the Poet. Her father, Mr. Andrew Craig, was a surgeon of repute in Glasgow; and her uncle, Rev. William Craig, was one of the ministers of that city, and father of Lord Craig, a Judge of the Court of Session. Her mother was a daughter of Rev. John M'Laurin, minister first at Luss, and then of St. David's, Glasgow, a man of eloquence and piety; and his brother, Colin M'Laurin, was the celebrated mathematician, and friend of Sir Isaac Newton. Agnes Craig was, therefore, of most respectable birth. Mr. M'Lehose, her husband, was a young man of respectable connections also, and a member of the legal profession in Glasgow. He seems originally to have been much attracted by Miss Craig's beauty; insomuch that, despairing of an introduction otherwise, he engaged all the seats in a stagecoach by which she was to travel to Edinburgh, except the seat already taken for her. The result of this forced intro-

duction on his part was friendship and marriage. Mrs. M'Lehose, however, "soon discovered the mistaken estimate she had formed of her husband's character." Dissatisfaction, alienation, and separation finally took place, December, 1780, scarcely four years after their marriage. After many painful and abortive negotiations on the subject of their reunion, Mr. M'Lehose finally left this country for Jamaica, and devolved on his young wife the whole burden of supporting their surviving children. Mrs. M'Lehose was prevailed upon afterwards, at his own earnest entreaty, to repair to him in the West Indies. This voyage, from which happier results were expected, took place in 1792, by the very ship, "Roselle," in which Burns himself, a few years before, had intended to sail for the same destination. On arriving, however, the unfortunate lady found her husband surrounded by another family of his own; which, in addition to the cruelty of his treatment there, so overwhelmed her with mortification and pain, that she returned without a moment's delay to Scotland. It was both before and after this voyage that her acquaintance with our Author was maintained; and it is to the voyage itself that one or two of the most exquisite of the songs dedicated to her refer. She died at Edinburgh, October, 1841, aged eighty-two. The above facts we gather from a memoir of her life by her grandson, W. C. M'Lehose, Esq.

Agnes Craig, in happier circumstances, might have been a distinguished woman. She was acute, sensitive, vivacious, and poetically imaginative. In society she was attractive, but perhaps too much addicted to society, which may have been the occasion of jealousy at first on her husband's part. In her youth she was esteemed very beautiful; was of short stature, and had very small hands and feet. In Glasgow she was then known as the "Pretty Miss Nancy." In later life her figure inclined to stoutness; and her style, upon the whole, was perhaps not quite so attractive; but she cultivated society to the end. "I recollect," says a correspondent of our own, Thomas Thorburn, Esq., of Ryedale, "when I lived in Edinburgh, of being invited to meet the celebrated Clarinda at supper. She was the remains of a fine woman, was a splendid talker, made bad puns, and seemed to have forgotten the bad usage of her husband, for she was very happy."

Besides the songs in her honour, Burns is said to have addressed a poetical expostulation to this lady, beginning—

> Mild zephyrs waft thee to life's farthest shore,
> Nor think of me or my distresses more—
> Falsehood accurst! No! still I beg a place,
> Still near thy heart some little, little trace;
> For that dear trace the world I would resign,
> Oh let me live, and die, and think it mine, &c.—

The genuineness of this piece cannot, perhaps, be questioned; but the fact (which we have ascertained by the assistance of our esteemed friend, Mr. Manners) that the paper on which it is written was never folded as a letter, and scarcely folded at all, is sufficient evidence that it was *never* transmitted to Clarinda—which we thus publicly note for the satisfaction of all whom it may concern.

CRUIKSHANK, MISS JEANNY.—[Compare notes on "Lines to very Young Lady," p. 248, also on "Rosebud," p. 261.]

"ELIZA"—celebrated in song "From thee, Eliza, I must go," p. 73—one of our Author's earliest inspirers, identified by Mr. Chambers with "Miss Betty," one of the Mauchline Belles; but the evidence is not conclusive. Whoever this lady may have been, however, she is not to be confounded with the "Fair Eliza" of later date, nor the "Eliza" whose name was substituted for "Maria," Mrs. Riddel's name, at a moment when the use of that name might have given offence.

ELLISON BEGBIE, daughter of a small farmer at Galston, but resident for a while as servant in a family on the Cessnock Water, seems to have been a girl with many superior attractions, to whom our Author was manifestly most devoutly attached, but by whom his addresses were declined. His earliest love-letters are understood to have been addressed to Ellison, as Miss E.—Prose Works, p. 7;—and the verses "On Cessnock Banks," p. 374, in her own praise, were most probably recited by herself to Mr. Cromek after the Poet's death. To her also the "Lines written on a Copy of his Poems," p. 385, are understood to have been addressed by our Author.

"FAIR ELIZA," originally "Fair Rabina," p. 147, was a real personage, loved in vain by one of our Author's Dumfriesshire friends, but her name and history are now unknown. [Compare note on song, p. 270.]

FONTENELLE, MISS LOUISA—a member of Mr. Sutherland's corps dramatique at Dumfries, is described by Mr. Chambers as "a smart and pretty little creature." Two special Addresses were written for her by Burns—pp. 343, 344; and she has been celebrated also by him in an Epigram—p. 418. Of the letter addressed to her accompanying the prologue, "Rights of Woman," there seem to have been two copies by the Author. [Compare Prose Works, pp. 58, 206.]

FERRIER, MISS, eldest daughter of John Ferrier, Esq., W.S. Edinburgh. was sister of a lady more distinguished otherwise than herself—the authoress of "Marriage," "The Inheritance," &c. The Miss Ferrier to whom the lines, p. 402, are addressed became "afterwards Mrs. General Graham, now for some years deceased."—Chambers, 1836. She seems to have been a friend of Miss Grace Aiken's, in whose possession the original copy of the lines addressed to her was found.

"HANDSOME NELL." KILPATRICK, Burns's "partner" or companion on the hairst rig at Mount Oliphant, and the very earliest inspirer of his muse, a simple, sonsie, bonie lassie, was, according to Mrs. Begg's recollection, a daughter of the blacksmith in that neighbourhood who did work for the farmers around, and who first lent our Author the "Life of Wallace" to read—which had such an effect on his moral and imaginative nature. [Compare note on song, p. 282.]

ISABELLA M'LEOD, MISS, a daughter of the distinguished Hebridean family of that name (M'Leods of Raasay), sister to John M'Leod, Esq., whose death is commemorated, p. 124. [Compare note on song, "Raving Winds," &c., p. 260.]

"JEAN" ARMOUR, wife of the Poet, and chief inspirer of his muse, was the daughter of Mr. James Armour, a master builder, or practical architect, at Mauchline. She was born there on 27th February, 1767,* and was formally acknow-

* We quote from Register in the Poet's Family Bible. The date is elsewhere given as 1765; and it seems to have been so entered in the Register, as the reader may observe by consulting the fac-simile; but the figure 5, or whatever other figure it might be, has been erased, apparently after some discussion or inquiry on the subject, and the figure 7 distinctly subjoined. Mrs. Burns, therefore, must have been two years younger than is commonly supposed.

lodged as the wife of Robert Burns in 1787. Her parents seem to have been of the strictest sect in their religion; so that her education and upbringing must have been all that could be desired in that respect. But the rigidness of their domestic discipline, and the pride which sometimes accompanies too great austerity of morals and purity of creed combined, were undoubtedly the cause of much of the pain and humiliation which attended her marriage with the Poet. This lady, so celebrated in the world of song, and so justly entitled to her own high pre-eminence there, although a good-looking woman, does not seem, to judge of her by any pictures we now possess, to have been what men commonly call beautiful. But she was elegant, sprightly, piquant, and fascinating. She has been celebrated by her husband in at least sixteen different effusions, songs or poems, and possibly in some others. The entire list we need not now specify; but some of these—such as "Of a' Airts the Wind can Blaw," "O were I on Parnassus Hill," "I'll aye ca' in by yon town," &c., are unquestionably among the very finest lyrical compositions extant in any language. Yet it is remarkable that among the various epithets of admiration or endearment by which she is distinguished throughout, the distinctive appellation of "Bonie Jean," by which the world almost invariably now recognises her, does not occur once. The world, in this respect, seems to have fixed on a title for her, as it has also fixed on a likeness for her husband, neither of which is correct. Her "bonie sel," and her "bonie face," and her "lovely form," occur each once; and "my bonie Jean," which is a designation entirely different from "Bonie Jean," and implies the sacredness or exclusiveness of conjugal or betrothed love, occurs only in one song, "I'll aye ca' in by yon town," p. 182, where it reports, being in the last line of the chorus; and the same expression occurs also in the "Vision," p. 33, where, however, it was substituted, on second thoughts, for "Bess:" but all other epithets are different. She is "dear" repeatedly, and "dearer," and "doubly dear;" and "darling," and "sweet," and "young," and "artless," and "tempting," and most frequently of all, as it became a man sincerely and truly in love to call her—"My Jean." This very title, indeed, he even gives her expressly in prose, when referring to his marriage, letter (5) to Dr. Moore, as the title which really appertained to her most devoutly in his own heart; as also in the well-known lines—

> Miss Miller is fine, Miss Markland 's divine,
> Miss Smith she has wit, and Miss Betty is braw,
> There 's beauty and fortune to get wi' Miss Morton;
> But Armour 's the jewel for me o' them a'.

No reason whatever for this decided preference was, or philosophically could be, assigned by him. Burns's love for, and attachment to, his wife, therefore, seems to have originated in some peculiar attractions, or combination of attractions, in herself—which he could not, any more than other true lovers, if called upon, have specified—but by which, and not by the mere external aspect of countenance called beautiful, he was fascinated and enthralled.

For the particulars of Mrs. Burns's married life, the reader is referred to her own most interesting Memoranda, as given above—p. xxi. She survived her illustrious husband thirty-eight years; during which lengthened period she enjoyed the utmost respect everywhere, and exemplified the devotion and retirement of a "widow indeed," who had but one love in the world, and could never forget it. Towards the close of her life she had several shocks of paralysis, by the last of which she was deprived of speech, of hearing, and of motion. On her deathbed she could express her feelings of love and of anxiety for the relatives who surrounded her, only by "looks" the most eager and full of meaning, whilst the tears trickled down her cheeks; yet, "even if her salvation had depended on the exertion," she was incapable of "uttering a syllable, guiding a pen, or even making an intelligible sign." Consciousness itself at last forsook her; and at a late hour on Wednesday night, the 26th of March, 1834, she departed, having, according to the Family Register in her husband's Bible, just entered on her sixty-eighth year. Her interment took place in the Mausoleum on the 1st of April following.[*]

"JEANIE:" heroine of song, "O Poortith Cauld," p. 207, was a Miss Blackstock. [Compare note on song.]

"JESSY" LEWARS—pre-eminently the "Jessy" of Burns's poetry, although celebrated only in two songs and two or three epigrams, was the daughter of Mr. John Lewars, supervisor in Dumfries, and sister of Mr. John Lewars, Jun., fellow-exciseman with our Author in that district. [Compare letter (5) to Johnson.] She seems, among other accomplishments, to have been an excellent performer on the pianoforte, than raro, and to have entertained the Poet frequently with that music. But her characteristic excellence was that of an affectionate womanly nature, alive to sorrow, overflowing with sympathy, and ready for every office of kindness and humanity. She was the most intimate and esteemed friend of Mrs. Burns through many an affliction, and like an elder sister among the children of the Poet's household; above all, during those dark hours of approaching dissolution, she was, as Mr. Chambers truly says, "the ministering angel," not only in the household, but in the chamber and at the bed of death. Her father at this date was dead; but she resided with her brother in a house nearly opposite the Poet's, which enabled her more easily and frequently to assist in the family during his last illness. We learn, through Miss Begg, that Jessy Lewars, although constantly in attendance, had no exact recollection of such distressing utterances as are said to have escaped the Poet in his last hours; that she remembered he was occasionally delirious, and could not distinctly know what he himself was saying; and as for the approach of death, when that became certain, as regarded himself he was calm and resigned, but the thoughts of his wife and children occasioned great agony to him. Miss Lewars, according to Burns's own jocular prediction, married Mr. James Thomson, writer in Dumfries, to whom she had a family of five sons and two daughters. She survived her husband, and spent the years of her widowhood at Maxwelltown, in the neighbourhood of that burgh.

"LASS o' BALLOCHMYLE:" Miss Wilhelmina, sister of Claud Alexander, Esq., who became proprietor, by purchase, of the Ballochmyle estate, when that romantic property came

* It was on the night immediately preceding this interment that the cast of the Poet's skull was obtained.

to the market in consequence of Sir John Whitefoord's embarrassments in 1785. The interview occurred in the summer of 1786, at which date Miss Alexander, being a few years older than the Poet, would be about thirty years of age. The grounds of Ballochmyle being then interdicted to the public, the lady was naturally enough startled on encountering such a stranger, but immediately recovered her presence of mind, and passed on. The effect on Burns himself of this accidental interview, if interview it can be called, was also natural enough; although by what complicated motives he was induced not only to write the song in her praise, but to correspond with the lady herself and solicit her special permission to publish it, is not so easy to determine. Miss Alexander did not only not give such permission, but did not even reply to the youthful Poet's application. This silence, according to Mr. Chambers, was justified by the lady's friends on the grounds of propriety, partly because Burns was at that date a tenant of her brother's (who had acquired the property of Mossgiel), partly because certain rumours affecting his character had reached her ears, such as might deter a lady in her circumstances from opening a correspondence that might possibly be misconstrued, and partly because the difference in their respective stations in life would prevent any further intercourse. These apologies may be accepted, although the disparity of age between the parties might have obviated all scruples; but perhaps only a woman similarly situated with Miss Alexander, or who can correctly imagine such a situation, will be able to appreciate the difficulty of answering or not answering such a communication. Whatever her secret feelings at the moment, however, may have been, she had no difficulty at all about appreciating the compliment or vindicating her property in the manuscript. On this subject Mr. Chambers tells us, on the same unquestionable authority, there was but one decision—viz., that wherever she went there the precious documents must go also.

Miss Alexander afterwards resided for many years in Glasgow. The house she then occupied was on the east side of George Square, No. 60, being the house whose gable windows look into George Street. This house, in our own schoolboy days, we have often watched, in hopes of obtaining a glimpse of the celebrated beauty. On one occasion only had we that good fortune. Miss Alexander at the moment happened to be looking out from an open window into George Street. Her countenance, as we seem to remember it, was rather round and open; her complexion fair, contrasted on the cheeks with red; her hair, which was parted and curled, a lightish brown. She wore some head-dress fashionable at the day for ladies who had attained her years; and might present the remains of a beauty attractive enough, perhaps, at the age of twenty-five. Miss Alexander died unmarried, 1843, in the eighty-ninth year of her age. [Compare letters to Mrs. Stewart of Stair and Miss Alexander, pp. 9, 10; also note on song, p. 295, and on "Braes o' Ballochmyle," p. 138.] The spot where the interview took place was a few hundred yards beyond the point at which the female figure is seen in our engraving, and is now marked by a little rustic bower, where some lines from the song in Miss Alexander's honour were inscribed, by authority, in commemoration of the event.

LOGAN, Miss—to whom verses accompanying a copy of Beattie's poems were dedicated, p. 58—was sister to Major Logan of Ayr—"thairm-inspirin Willie"—and kept house for him. [Compare note on Epistle to Logan.]

"LOVELY DAVIES."—Miss Deborah Davies, celebrated in two songs, as "The Bonie Wee Thing," p. 145, and "Lovely Davies," p. 177; also in Epigram, p. 418, and honoured with the Poet's correspondence, was alike remarkable from her great beauty and the smallness of her stature. She was of English birth, but related to the Riddels of Friars-Carse, at whose residence, most probably, our Author might be introduced to her. According to Allan Cunningham, who obtained his information from her own nephew, she was betrothed in marriage to a Captain Delany, who, however, proved faithless to his engagement, went abroad with his regiment, and left her in his continued absence to droop and die.

"LOVELY POLLY" STEWART, heroine of the snatch, p. 158, was a daughter of the "Willie Stewart" whose convivial attractions were recorded on the tumbler, p. 419. Mr. Stewart at that time was factor on the Closeburn estates, and in that capacity occupied the castle, where the Poet was not unfrequently a visitor at his residence. On one of these occasions an acquaintance of Miss Polly's—Miss Agnes Yorstoun, whose uncle was then minister of the parish—happening to come in, was requested by Burns to favour him with a song or two. Among others, this young lady obligingly sang 'Roy's Wife,' the conclusion of which at the moment did not seem to satisfy the Poet, who immediately added the following stanza:—

> But Roy's years are three times mine,
> I'm sure his days can no be monie;
> And when that he is dead and gane,
> She may repent and tak her Johnnie.

These particulars we glean from an article in the *Dumfries Courier*, April 20, 1869; and we learn, from a farther notice on the same subject in the *Dumfries Herald* of a little later date, that the above lines were afterwards quoted, with some slight variation, into certain editions of the song. Polly Stewart herself, who was handsomely married, forfeited her own position in society, we lament to learn. After which, "she lived," says Mr. Chambers, "as 'a poor lavender' [or laundress] at Maxwelltown, Dumfries," and is said to have died in poverty in France.

"LUCY" JOHNSTON, celebrated in song "O wat ye wha's in yon town?" p. 208, and referred to in letter to Mr. Syme, was the daughter of Mr. Johnston of Hilton, and the wife of Richard Oswald, Esq., of Auchencruive. A person of the utmost elegance and beauty, of the highest accomplishments, and the greatest grace, she was also unfortunately of a very delicate constitution, and died prematurely at Lisbon, whither she had gone for the recovery of her health. The various encomiums which have been lavished on this lady's beauty are too numerous to be quoted. "According to Dryden," says Kirkpatrick Sharpe—

> "Whate'er she did was done with so much ease,
> In her alone 'twas natural to please;
> Her motions all accompanied with grace;
> And Paradise was open'd in her face."

None who ever had the delight of seeing her in the ballroom, giving double charms to a minuet, or dignifying a country dance, can question the truth of this feeble encomium." It is here, however, chiefly worthy of remark, that this accomplished woman was a musician also, and is said to have composed the air to which Burns's own celebrated ode, "To Mary in Heaven," is set. [Compare note on song, p. 296.]

"MALLY"—"Mally's meek," &c., p. 164—said to have been a simple country girl equipped for a journey, barefoot, who attracted the Poet's attention as she passed along the causeway of Dumfries. Name unknown.

"MARIA"—Lady Elizabeth Heron: Song, "Here is the Glen," p. 204. [Compare note on.]

"MARIA" WHITEFOORD: Song, "The Braes o' Ballochmyle," p. 138. [Compare note on.]

"MARIA" WOODLEY, otherwise Mrs. Walter Riddel, a lady of great beauty and spirit, with some fashionable foibles and perhaps follies incident to her sex, but many virtues, gifts, and accomplishments also—one of the most favoured correspondents and heroines of our Author, his friend, his adversary, and his eulogist—has been so frequently mentioned in the progress of this work that very few additional particulars require now to be stated concerning her. Maria Woodley seems to have been a creole; was the daughter of a Governor of Berbice; married very young to Mr. Walter Riddel of Antigua, a younger brother of Captain Riddel's, Friars-Carse; and came to Scotland with her husband, who nominally purchased the estate of Goldielea, which he named, in honour of his wife, Woodley Park, but of which the price was never paid, and which consequently reverted to its former proprietor. Here expensive festivities were frequent, and literary visitors were always welcome—Burns himself the most honoured and distinguished of the guests, till the unfortunate scene occurred which resulted in so painful an alienation. On Capt. Riddel's death, Mr. Walter Riddel succeeded to Friars-Carse, which, by the same extravagant course on his part, we believe, came also to the hammer. For some time after her husband's death Mrs. Riddel was an occasional resident with friends in the neighbourhood, particularly the Scots of Tinwald, but finally went to London, where she married a Mr. Fletcher from Ireland, and died in state apartments at Hampton Court, 1820. Before leaving Scotland, however, her last interview with our Author took place. Mrs. Riddel, July, 1796, was a convalescent at sea-bathing quarters at Brow, whither the Poet also, in the vain hope of restoring his own health, had gone. On hearing of his arrival she immediately invited him to dine, and sent her carriage to convey him. It was on this occasion, when entering the room "with the stamp of death imprinted on his features," that he addressed her with his usual spirit in the well-known words, "Well, Madam, have you any commands for the other world?" At this interview the reconciliation of these two gifted and really attached friends, which had been quietly proceeding in the meantime, was completed; all past offences seem to have been condoned, and something like a new friendship originated. "He lamented that he had written many epigrams on persons against whom he entertained no enmity, and whose characters he should be sorry to wound; and many indifferent poetical pieces, which he feared would now, with all their imperfections on their head, be thrust upon the world. . . . I had seldom seen his mind greater or more collected. . . . We parted about sunset on the evening of that day [the 5th of July, 1796]: the next day I saw him again, and we parted to meet no more." Shortly after his death Mrs. Riddel published, in the *Dumfries Journal*, a most eloquent, discriminating, and generous eulogy on his character, prophetic of his highest future fame; and attended by a young friend (son of Mr. Smellie, the printer, to whom Burns had introduced her), "the enthusiastic lady went that night," says Mr. Chambers, "at a late hour to St. Michael's Churchyard, and planted laurels over the Poet's new-made grave." The reader may compare correspondence with Mrs. Riddel; also songs—

Canst thou leave me thus, &c., p. 212	Impromptu, . . . p. 343
The last time I came, &c., . 328	Monody, &c., . . . 344
Farewell thou stream, &c., . 320	Epistle from Esopus to Maria, 309

with notes on; also note on the Sonnet on Death of Robert Riddel, Esq.; Letter to Smellie; and History of "Kerry Miniatures," Appendix, p. lxxiv.

A specimen of Mrs. Riddel's poetry may be found at p. 293.

"MARY," "HIGHLAND MARY"—Mary Campbell—"was of Highland parentage," says Mr. Chambers, "from the neighbourhood of Dunoon, on the firth of Clyde. Her father was a sailor in a revenue cutter, the station of which being at Campbelton in Kintyre, his family then resided there." Mary came to Ayrshire, it appears, to obtain a situation, where she was employed as child's-maid, in the summer of 1785, at Gavin Hamilton's in Mauchline; and as dairymaid, or byreswoman, in 1786, at Coilsfield, on the banks of the Fail, between Mauchline and Tarbolton—in the neighbourhood of which residence her betrothal to Robert Burns took place on Sabbath morning, 14th May of said year. That betrothal was made in very solemn circumstances, although some particulars, about the parties standing on opposite sides of a running brook, dipping their hands in the water, &c., as related by Cromek, are most probably apocryphal. The only thing most certain is, that Bibles were exchanged by the contracting parties; and that the copy of the Bible given by Burns to Mary was in two volumes, having the following inscriptions written on them by his own hand. On a blank leaf in the first volume—

"And ye shall not swear by my name falsely—I am the Lord."—Lever. xix. 12.

On the second volume—

"Thou shalt not forswear thyself, but shalt perform unto the Lord thine oaths."—Matt. v. 33.

On a blank leaf of the same his name had been inscribed, along with his *Mason mark.*[*]

Mary, after this engagement, revisited her friends at Campbeltown, to prepare for her marriage, or possibly even for leaving the country with her espoused lover, as he seems to have invited her to do, being then fully resolved to pursue his fortune in the West Indies. She returned again to Greenock, however, on her way to Glasgow—where she had accepted a situation in the meantime; but with the intention of taking farewell of Burns also, if she could not accompany him, on

---

[*] These volumes may be seen in Burns's Monument at Ayr.

his departure, in the month of October. She died of malignant fever at Greenock, caught by attending her brother on a sick-bed there, and was buried in the churchyard of that town in the end of said month—all which events took place within the space of six months, in the summer and autumn of 1786.*

All Mary's relatives, except her mother, seem to have been ignorant, superstitious, and narrow-minded people, and every way unlike herself. The Poet's letters to her have been all lost or destroyed; and " when Burns (after her death) wrote a moving letter, requesting some memorial of her he loved so dearly, the stern old man [her father] neither answered it, nor allowed any one to speak about it in his presence." Notwithstanding which neglect, Burns seems to have visited the country of her birth on his tour, in 1787, to Inverary. [See Prose Works, p. 205.] These particulars in the briefest form we thus record, as sufficient on the subject. For further details we refer our readers to notes on the songs in which this amiable and unfortunate young woman has been celebrated by our Author, as follows—

To Mary in Heaven,	. .	p. 138	Ye Banks, and Braes, &c.,	p. 214
Highland Lassie,	. . .	167	Will ye go to the Indies?	. 325
Mary!	. . . . .	121	Afton Water (doubted),	. 151

Our object here, more immediately, is to investigate the implied charge of cruelty or injustice towards Mary Campbell on Burns's part, which was suggested by Mr. William Douglas in an elaborate paper read by him (1850) before the Society of Scottish Antiquaries; and was subsequently adopted and confirmed by Mr. Chambers, and by almost all succeeding writers on the subject. According to this theory, Burns's engagement to Mary was a sort of heartless episode in his love for Jean; of which no honourable man, therefore, should have been capable, and of which nothing but moral injustice to one or the other of those two women could be the result. This view we have already [Biography, p. xxv.] denounced as unjust, and must now again, once for all, affirm to be not only unjust, but incomprehensible, and that for the following reasons:—

1. It is admitted by Mr. Chambers that Mary Campbell, being then resident at Mauchline, rejected Robert Burns's addresses as dangerous, in 1785.

2. The rupture with Jean Armour, and supposed dissolution of the Poet's marriage with her, took place in March of the following year, attended with so many circumstances of public scandal that Jean herself found it necessary to leave the neighbourhood, and visit Paisley. The marriage, it is true, was never dissolved, as we have now ascertained [Prose Works, p. 150]; but everybody at the time, Robert Burns himself included, and everybody since, all editors included, believed it to be practically dissolved.

3. Burns, in despair and anger at this treatment, betook himself again to Mary Campbell, who now accepted his offer, and was betrothed to him with the utmost solemnity in the month of May following.

These being the admitted facts of the case on her own side, we have simply to inquire whether those who charge Burns with levity or insincerity in this matter believe that a dairymaid who then lived at Coilsfield, and who had lately lived at

Mauchline, within an hour's walk, could be ignorant of what had taken place on the very streets of Mauchline in the meantime?—that she knew nothing of a scandal with which the whole country-side was ringing, in which her own former lover and successful rival were involved, and fell an unconscious dupe into the hands of a plausible deceiver? If this were so, then Mary Campbell must have been different from all other dairymaids in existence; and not only from dairymaids, but from all other women since the days of Paradise to the present moment. Clarinda, at the distance of eighty miles, did not long remain so ignorant. But that Mary Campbell knew all the talk of the country-side is just as certain as that she was within hearing; and knowing this, if she believed her lover to be guilty, she was herself more guilty in accepting him; and doubly guilty to do so in the name of God. But knowing the facts, if she believed him to be innocent, as he was, there was no harm, either to herself or to him, or to any one else; but a very great triumph for her, in competition with such a rival as Miss Armour. She was, in fact, the *Galatea victrix* of Ayrshire at that moment, and in virtue of that very engagement, with this supreme advantage, that her lover was an Apollo and not a Polyphemus. Her marriage was religiously provided for with the most gifted and attractive youth of the whole district, and she came unbidden, of her own accord, " across the sea," to take a last adieu of her betrothed lover. She was, in short, a satisfied and consenting party to the whole arrangement; and whilst she lived, he was faithful. Her own untimely death, among ignorant and vulgar relatives, was a cause of the profoundest agony to him, and seems to have had a saddening, perhaps a softening, effect on his whole remaining life. Certain at all events it is, that he had no further correspondence with Jean, on the subject of her broken promise, for many months after Mary's death—not till his return from Edinburgh in the summer of 1787. But by that accident of death, Mary herself entered on an immortality more beautiful than Beatrice' or Laura's, in which respect neither complaint as against Burns, nor sorrow as for her, should ever be obtruded on the world. It was enough for Mary and for mankind that Burns once loved her. Her name, her fame, her sweet bright womanly reputation, her existence itself, with all the honour and the glory, the tombstones, the monuments, the inscriptions, the pathetic paragraphs, the world of interest and inquiry connected with it, depend all absolutely and for ever upon him. How then has she been injured by such abundant love, or insulted by an apotheosis of melody that would have satisfied half the women in the world? Gentle, good, and true she no doubt was; blue-eyed, and yellow-haired, and comely, but never graceful; and born of such parents as Mr. Chambers describes, or educated apparently as she was, the probability is that she was not endowed with a tithe of the sweet indefinite attractions with which Burns alone has invested her. A lofty monument in Greenock churchyard, and an occasional paragraph of gallant tearful sympathy for her fate, are quite admissible in their place. But what did we know of her or of her virtues, except from Burns? All such monuments and paragraphs for her require to be countersigned by *him*. He is the sole respon-

---

* A monument was erected, by private subscription, to the memory of Mary Campbell in West Churchyard of Greenock, 25th January, 1842.

sible party; and on any other condition whatever they are sheer impertinences. On the whole, therefore, it may be found better to leave Highland Mary where she is, safe and beautiful, in the undivided custody of her immortal lover, who never sullied a hair of her head, or wronged her in the remotest degree by any indifference.

MARY MORISON: unless a relative of Mr. Morison, cabinet-maker, Mauchline, this type of feminine gentleness and beauty is unknown. p. 325.

MAXWELL, LADY WINIFRED: [Compare correspondence with; and Song of Welcome to, p. 146; with note on.]

M'LACHLAN, MRS., wife of an officer in the Indian army: "Musing on the Roaring Ocean," p. 152. [See note on.]

"MONTGOMERIE'S PEGGY,"—celebrated in song "Altho' my Bed were in yon Muir," p. 376—according to Mrs. Begg's authority, as quoted by Mr. Chambers, was an upper house-maid at Montgomery's of Coilsfield, and the Poet first became acquainted with her by sitting in the same seat at church. Peggy's affections, it should seem, were pre-engaged, and a temporary pang or two for him were the consequences.

"MY PEGGY."—Miss Margaret Chalmers, cousin to Miss Charlotte Hamilton by the mother's side, with whom she was residing at Harvieston at the time of our Author's visit there, and so an introduction was made which resulted in the warmest friendship. Miss Chalmers could hardly be said to be a beauty, but was a lady of great spirit and intelligence, as well as of the utmost frankness and cordiality—a combination of qualities which must have attracted Robert Burns, and which laid the foundation of a correspondence remarkable at once for its elegance, its vivacity, and its unreservedness on his part, and concerning which the only cause of regret now is that so large a portion of it was accidentally destroyed. [Compare note on correspondence; also on songs, "Braving Angry Winter's Storms, p. 261, and " My Peggy's Face, my Peggy's Form," p. 274.]

"NANIE O!" p. 75. The identity of this heroine has been much controverted. According to Gilbert Burns, she was an Agnes Fleming, daughter of a farmer in Tarbolton parish, and supposed to have been a servant at Gavin Hamilton's, Mauchline. This theory has been accepted by Thomson, Cunningham, and apparently by Chambers. According to Mrs. Begg, on the other hand, the girl has been identified with Peggy Thomson of Kirkoswald, who first captivated the Poet there, and the name altered to 'Nanie' for poetical purposes. This theory, we confess, does not seem so natural as the other, more especially as we know that although Agnes Fleming had no pretensions to be a beauty, she was certainly an object of the Poet's attention, and did herself declare that he had written some song in her honour.

"PEGGY, DEAR"—"Now Westlin Winds," &c., p. 75—the Margaret Thomson of Kirkoswald, above referred to.

"PHEMIE," Miss Euphemia Murray of Lintrose; celebrated in song, "Blythe was she," p. 133. [Compare note on.]

"PHILLIS," or "PHELY"—Miss Philadelphia M'Murdo, celebrated in the following beautiful songs :—

Adown Winding Nith, .	p. 310	O Phely, Happy be that Day,	p. 325
There was a Lass, &c., .	322	Phillis the Fair, . . .	327

daughter of Mr. M'Murdo, factor to his Grace the Duke of

Queensberry, and afterwards Mrs. Norman Lockhart of Carnwath, was the real poetical "Bonie Jean" of Burns's muse. Why such a designation should have been chosen for her, when "Phillis" had already been adopted, we are not expressly informed, and can only conjecture that it was by poetical caprice, as in many other cases, with some secret internal reference to his own experience and courtship as a lover. [Compare note on song "There was a lass," &c.]

"RONALDS OF BENNALS," p. 401—Jean and Anna, were daughters of a then prosperous farmer in the neighbourhood of Tarbolton, in whose family our Author, as a youth, was intimately acquainted. For further particulars the reader may refer to note on the "Holy Fair, p. 90, and Original Reminiscences, Part II., A, Appendix, p. xxxvi.

SCOTT, MRS.—"Gudewife of Wauchop."—See note on poetical Epistle to her, p. 430.

"SERAPH SISTER-BAND"—p. 55—daughters of Rev. George Lawrie, Manse of Newmilns.

STEWART, MRS. GENERAL, of Afton and Stair, one of the earliest friends and patrons of Burns—complimented by allusion to in "The Brigs of Ayr," and, as is supposed by some, in the song "Afton Water," p. 151. [Compare note on, at p. 271.] As some obscurity with respect to this lady's designations has hitherto prevailed, we give the following particulars from the best authority, that of Allason Cunningham, Esq., her grandson, to whose courtesy in this matter, through Sir J. Stuart-Menteth, we are indebted. Catharine Gordon was the only daughter of Thomas Gordon of Afton and Stair, son of Sir Thomas Gordon of Earlston, Bart. This lady had brothers, who died, and she therefore succeeded to the patrimonial estates. She married afterwards Major-General Alexander Stewart, and had a family of one son, who died, and four daughters. The oldest of these daughters became Mrs. Cunningham of Enterkine. [Compare note on "Fête Champetre."] At one time, the whole valley of the Afton, in Nithsdale, as also the estate of Dalleager, belonged to Mrs. Stewart's family; but she ultimately parted both with the Afton and the Stair estates, and purchased from Mr. Cunningham of Enterkine about forty acres of land, and built Afton Lodge upon it as a residence, that she might be nearer to her daughter, Mrs. Cunningham. At Afton Lodge her two unmarried daughters, the Misses Stewart, afterwards resided. The transfer of this name Afton Lodge to a newly-built mansion in another part of the country may have been the occasion of some confusion, as between it and Glen Afton, the hereditary possession of the same proprietress.

"TIBBIE, LASS"—Isabella Steven or Steen, afterwards Mrs. Allan. For particulars, see note on song, p. 261.

"YOUNG JESSY:" Miss Janet Staig—celebrated in song "True-hearted was he," p. 205. [Compare note on which.]

"YOUNG LADY"—with copy of Thomson's Collection, p. 346—Miss Graham of Fintra.

"YOUNG PEGGY" [KENNEDY]: A young lady of good birth and prospects, on whose betrayal and fall we need not now comment. The reader may refer to notes on the songs "Young Peggy," p. 259, and "The Banks o' Doon," p. 270, also to letter to Miss K——, p. 9.

Other Heroines are either traditional, fictitious, or unknown.

GLOSSARY:

FIRST, SECOND, AND THIRD COMBINED;

CAREFULLY REVISED AND SUPPLEMENTED.

A

A', all.
Aback, away, aloof, backwards.
Abeigh, or *abiegh*, at a shy distance.
Aboon, above, up.
Abread, abroad, in sight, published.
Abreed, in breadth.
Ae, one.
Aff, off.
Aff-loof, off-hand, unpremeditated.
Afore, before.
Aft, oft.
Aften, often.
Agee, on one side.
Agley, off the right line, wrong, awry.
Aiblins, perhaps.
Ain, own.
Airles, earnest money, hiring money.
Airl-penny, a silver penny given as airles.
Airn, iron, a mason's chisel.
Airt, region of the earth or sky.
Aith, an oath.
Aits, oats.
Aiver, an old horse.
Aizle, a hot cinder, an ember of wood.
Aheart, awkward, athwart.
Alake, alas.
Alane, alone.
Amaist, almost.
Amang, among.
An', and.
An, if.
Ance, once.
Ane, one.
Anent, concerning, about.
Anither, another.
Aqueesh, between.
Ase, ashes of wood, remains of a hearth fire.
Asteer, abroad, stirring in a lively manner.
Attour, moreover, beyond, besides.
Aught, eight; possession, as "in a' my aught," in all my possession.
Auld, old.
Auld-farran', or *auld-farrant*, sagacious, prudent, cunning.
Auld-shoon, old shoes, a discarded lover.
Aumous, gift to a beggar.
Aumous-dish, in which aumous is received.
Ava, at all.
Awa, away, begone.
Awfu', awful.
Awn, the beard of barley, oats, &c.
Awnie, bearded.
Ayont, beyond.

B

Ba', balls
Babie-clouts, child's first clothes.
Backets, boxes for removing ashes.
Backlins-comin, coming back, returning.
Back-yett, private gate.
Bad, did bid.
Baggie, the belly.
Baide, endured, did stay.
Bainie, with large bones, stout
Bairon, laying bare.
Bairn, a child.
Bairn-time, a family of children, a brood.
Baith, both.
Ballets, *ballants*, ballads.
Ban, to swear.
Bane, bone; *benie*, see *bainie*.
Bang, to drive, to excel; an effort.
Bannock, flat round soft cake.
Bardie, diminutive of bard.
Barefit, barefooted.
Barket, barked.
Barkin, barking.
Barley-bree, *barley-broo*, juice of barley, malt liquor.
Barmie, of or like barm, yeasty.
Batch, a crew, a gang.
Batts, botts, a disease in horses.
Bauckie-bird, the bat, *i.e.* balance-bird.
Baudrons, a cat.
Bauk, a cross beam.
Bauk-en', the end of a beam.
Bauld, bold.
Baws'nt, having a white stripe down the face—of horses, dogs, and cattle.
Be, or *bee*, to let be; give over, cease.
Bear, barley.
Bearded-bear, barley with its bristly head.
Beastie, diminutive of beast.
Beet, *beek*, to add fuel to a fire, to bask.
Befa', to befal, or happen.
Beld, bald.
Bellys, bellows.
Belyve, by and by, presently, quickly.
Ben, into the spence or parlour.
Benmost-bore, the inmost hole or corner.
Bent, the barn, open field.
Bethankit, or *bethankit*, grace after meat.
Beuk, a book.
Bicker, a wooden dish, a short rapid race.
Bickering, hurrying, quarrelling.
Biel', or *bield*, shelter, a sheltered place, the sunny nook of a field.
Bien, wealthy, plentiful.

Big, to build.
Biggin, building, a house.
Biggit, built.
Bill, a bull.
Billie, a brother, a young fellow, a companion.
Bing, a heap of grain, potatoes, &c.
Birdie-cocks, young cocks, still belonging to the brood.
Birk, birch.
Birkie, a clever, forward, conceited fellow.
Birnie, wiry, like burnt heather.
Birring, the noise of partridges, &c., when they rise.
Birses, bristles.
Bit, crisis, nick of time, place.
Bizz, a bustle, to buzz.
Black's the grun', as black as the ground.
Blastet, blasted, worthless.
Blastie, a shrivelled dwarf, a term of contempt, full of mischief.
Blate, bashful, sheepish.
Blather, bladder.
Blathrie, idle talk and nonsense.
Bland, a flat piece of anything; to slap.
Blawdin-shower, a heavy driving rain.
Blaw, to blow, to boast.
Bleer't, bedimmed, eyes hurt with weeping.
Bleer my een, dim my eyes.
Bleeze, flame; *bleezan*, flaming.
Blellum, idle talking fellow.
Blether, to talk idly.
Bleth'ran, or *bleth'rin*, talking idly.
Blink, a little while, a smiling look, to look kindly, to shine by fits.
Blinkan, smirking, smiling with the eyes.
Blinker, a term of contempt: it means, too, a lively engaging girl.
Blirt and blearie, outburst of grief, with wet eyes.
Blue-gown, one of those beggars who get annually, on the king's birth-day, a blue cloak or gown with a badge.
Bluid, or *blude*, blood.
Blype, a shred, a large piece.
Bobbit, the obeisance made by a lady.
Bock, to vomit, to gush intermittently.
Bocked, gushed, vomited.
Bodle, a copper coin of the value of two pennies Scots.
Bogie, a small morass.
Bonie, *bonnie*, *bonny*, handsome, beautiful.
Bonnock, a kind of thick cake of bread.
Boord, a board.

Boortree, the shrub elder, planted much of old in hedges of barnyards, &c.
Boost, behoved, must needs.
Bore, a hole in a wall, a cranny.
Botch, an angry tumour.
Bother, same as *buther*, to make a fuss, = to English *pother*; occurs only once in Burns—"Holy Fair."
Bousing, drinking, sitting to drink.
Bouk, or *bowk*, body.
Bow-hought, out-kneed.
Bow-kail, cabbage.
Bow't, bended, crooked.
Brackens, *brechens*, ferns.
Brae, a declivity, a precipice, the slope of a hill; = to *brie*, or *brow*.
Breid, bread.
Braik, a kind of harrow.
Brainge, to run rashly forward, to churn violently.
Brainge't, "*the horse brainge't*," plunged and fretted in the harness.
Brak, broke, became insolvent.
Brankie, gaudy.
Branks, a kind of wooden curb for horses.
Brash, a sudden illness.
Brats, coarse clothes, rags, children.
Brattle, a short race, hurry, fury.
Braw, fine, handsome.
Brawlys, or *brawlie*, very well, finely, heartily, bravely.
Braxies, diseased or *morkin* sheep.
Breastet, or *breastit*, sprung up or forward.
Breastie, diminutive of breast.
Brechame, a horse-collar.
Bree, juice, liquid.
Breef, an invulnerable or irresistible spell.
Breeks, breeches.
Brent, bright, clear.
Brewin, brewing, gathering.
Brig, a bridge.
Brisket, the breast, the bosom.
Brither, a brother.
Brock, a badger.
Brogue, a hum, a trick, an affront.
Broo, broth, liquid, water.
Broose, a race at country weddings; he who first reaches the bridegroom's house on returning from church wins the broose for bridegroom or bride.
Browst, ale, as much malt liquor as is brewed at a time.
Brugh, a burgh.
Bruilzie, a broil, combustion.
Brunstane, brimstone.
Brunt, did burn, burnt.
Brust, to burst, burst.
Buchan-bullers, the boiling of the sea among the rocks on the coast of Buchan.
Buckskin, an inhabitant of Virginia.
Buff our beef, thrash us soundly.
Buff and blue, the colours of the Whigs.
Buirdly, stout made, broad built.
Bum-clock, the humming beetle that flies in the summer evenings.
Bummun, humming as bees, buzzing.
Bummle, to blunder, to drone.
Bummler, a blunderer.
Bunker, a window-seat.
Bure, did bear.
Burn, *burnie*, water, rivulet, small stream.

Burn-e-win', burn the wind, the black-smith.
Burr-thistle, the thistle of Scotland.
Buskit, dressed.
But, without; *bot*, = to English *but*.
But and ben, the country kitchen and parlour, = to be out and be in.
By, beyond; "*by himself*," lunatic, distracted, beside himself.
Byke, a bee-hive, a wild bee-nest.
Byre, a cow-house, a sheep-pen.

C

Ca', to call, to name, to drive.
Ca't, or *ca'd*, called, driven, calved.
Cadger, a carrier.
Cadie, or *cuddie*, a person, a young fellow.
Caff, chaff.
Caird, a tinker, a maker of horn spoons.
Cairn, loose heap of stones on a grave.
Calf-ward, a small enclosure for calves.
Callimanco, a certain kind of cotton cloth worn by ladies.
Callan, a boy.
Caller, or *cauler*, fresh.
Callet, a loose woman, a follower of a camp.
Cam, came.
Canna, cannot.
Cannie, gentle, mild, dexterous.
Cannilie, dexterously, gently.
Cantharidian, made of cantharides.
Cantie, or *canty*, cheerful, merry.
Cantraip, a charm, a spell.
Cap-stane, cape-stone, key-stone.
Car, a rustic cart with or without wheels.
Careerin, moving cheerfully.
Caressin, caressing.
Cark, carking, painful anxiety, anxious.
Carl, an old man.
Carl-hemp, the male stalk of hemp, easily known by its superior strength and stature, and being without seed.
Carlin, or *carline*, a stout old woman.
Cartes, cards.
Custock, the stalk of a cabbage.
Cauldron, a cauldron.
Cauk and keel, chalk and red clay.
Cauld, cold.
Caup, a wooden drinking vessel, a cup.
Cavie, a hen-coop.
Chantan, or *chantin*, chanting.
Chanter, drone of a bagpipe.
Chap, a person, a fellow.
Champ, a stroke, a blow.
Checket, checked.
Cheek for chow, side by side, close and united, brotherly.
Cheep, a chirp, to chirp.
Chiel, *chield*, or *cheel*, a young fellow
Chimla, or *chimlie*, a fire-grate, fire-place.
Chimla-lug, the fire-side.
Chirps, cries of a young bird.
Chittering, shivering, trembling with cold.
Chockin, choking.
Chow, to chew.
Chuckie, a brood-hen, an old matron.
Chuffie, fat-faced.
Clachan, a small village about a church, a hamlet.
Claise, or *claes*, clothes.
Claith, cloth.

Claithing, clothing.
Clap, *clapper*, the clapper of a mill.
Clarkit, wrote.
Clartie, dirty, filthy.
Clash, an idle tale.
Clatter, to tell little idle stories, an idle story.
Claught, snatched at, laid hold of.
Claut, to clean, to scrape.
Clauted, scraped.
Claver, clover.
Clavers and havers, agreeable nonsense.
Claw, to scratch.
Cleckin, a brood of chickens, or ducks.
Cleed, to clothe.
Cleek, hook, snatch.
Clegs, the gad flies.
Clinkan, or *clinkin*, jerking, clinking; *clinkin down*, sitting down hastily.
Clinkum-bell, he who rings the church bell.
Clips, wool-shears.
Clishmaclaver, idle conversation.
Clock, to hatch, a beetle.
Clockin, hatchin.
Cloot, the hoof of a cow, sheep, &c.
Clootie, a familiar name for the devil.
Clour, a bump, or swelling, after a blow.
Clout, *cloutin*, to repair, repairing.
Clouds, clouds.
Clunk, the sound of drinking from a bottle.
Coaxin, wheedling.
Coble, a fishing-boat.
Cod, a pillow.
Coft, bought.
Cog, a wooden dish; *coggie*, dimin. of *cog*.
Coila, from Kyle, a district in Ayrshire, so called, saith tradition, from Coil, or Coilus, a Pictish monarch.
Collie, a general, and sometimes a particular, name for country curs.
Collie-shangie, a quarrel among dogs, an Irish row.
Comrin, or *comin*, coming.
Commaun, command.
Convoyed, accompanied lovingly.
Cood, the cud.
Coof, a blockhead, a ninny.
Cookit, appeared and disappeared by fits.
Cool'd in her linens, in her dead-clothes.
Cooser, a stallion.
Coost, did cast.
Coot, the ancle, a species of waterfowl.
Cootie, a wooden dish; rough-legged.
Corbies, carrion crows.
Core, corps, party. N.B.—This word is properly derived from *choir*, and not from *corps*.
Corn't, fed with oats.
Cotter, the inhabitant of a cot-house, or cottage.
Couthie, kind, loving.
Cove, a cave.
Cowe, to terrify, to keep under, to lop; a branch of whins or broom.
Coup, to barter, to tumble over.
Coupet, or *coupit*, tumbled.
Cowran, or *cowrin*, cowering.
Cowte, a colt.
Cozie, cosily, snug, snugly.
Crabbit, crabbed, fretful.
Crack, conversation, to converse.
Crackan, or *crackin*, conversing.

Craft, or *croft*, a field near a house, in old husbandry.
Craig, *craigie*, a high rock, the neck.
Craiks, cries or calls incessantly, a bird, the corn-rail.
Crambo-clink, or *crambo-jingle*, rhymes, doggrel verses.
Cramp, the noise of an ungreased wheel—metaphorically inharmonious verse.
Crankous, fretful, captious.
Crearuch, the hoar-frost.
Crap, a crop, to crop.
Craw, a crow of a cock, or rook.
Creel, a basket; "to have one's wits in a creel," to be crazed, to be fascinated.
Creeshie, greasy.
Cronie, a friend, a gossip.
Croud, or *croud*, to coo as a dove.
Croon, a hollow and continued moan; to make a noise like the low roar of a bull; to hum a tune.
Crooning, humming.
Croonie, crook-backed.
Crouse, cheerful, courageous.
Crousely, cheerfully, courageously.
Crowdie, a composition of oatmeal, boiled water, and butter; sometimes made from the broth of beef, mutton, &c.
Crowdie-time, breakfast-time.
Crowlan, crawling hatefully.
Crummie's wicks, marks on cows' horns.
Crummock, *crummie*, a cow with crooked horns.
Crummock, *to driddle on*, to walk slowly, leaning on a staff with a crooked head.
Crump-crumpin, hard and brittle, spoken of bread and of frozen snow.
Crunt, a blow on the head with a cudgel.
Cruskin, crushing.
Cuddle, to clasp and caress.
Cuif, see *coof*.
Cummock, a short staff with a crooked head.
Curch, a covering for the head, a kerchief.
Curchie, a curtsey, female obeisance.
Curler, a player at curling.
Curlie, curled, whose hair falls naturally in ringlets.
Curling, a well-known game on the ice.
Curmurring, murmuring, a slight rumbling noise.
Curpan, the crupper, the rump.
Curple, the rear.
Cushat, the dove, or wood-pigeon.
Cutty, short, a spoon broken in the middle.
Cutty-stool, or *creepie-chair*, the seat of shame, stool of repentance.

D

Dadie, or *daddie*, a father.
Daffin, merriment, foolishness.
Daft, merry, giddy, foolish.
Daft-buckie, mad fish.
Daimen, rare, now and then.
Daimen-icker, an ear of corn occasionally.
Dainty, pleasant, good-humoured, agreeable, rare.
Dancin, dancing.
Dandered, wandered.
Dappl'd, dappled.
Darklins, darkling, without light.

Dad, or *daud*, the noise of one falling flat; a large piece of bread, &c.; to thrash, to abuse.
Dawlie-showers, rain urged by wind.
Daur, to dare; *daur't*, dared; *daurna*, dare not.
Darg, or *dawrk*, a day's labour.
Daut, or *dawt*, to fondle, to caress.
Dautet, *dawtit*, fondled, caressed.
Davoc, diminutive of Davie, as Davie is of David.
Dawin, dawning of the day.
Dead-sweer, very loath, averse.
Dearies, diminutive of dears, sweethearts.
Dearthfu', dear, expensive.
Deave, to deafen.
Deil-ma-care, no matter for all that.
Delerit, delirious.
Descrive, to describe, to perceive.
Deuks, ducks.
Devle, a stunning blow.
Dight, to wipe, to clean corn from chaff.
Dimpl't, dimpled.
Ding, to worst, to push, to surpass, to excel.
Dink, neat, lady-like.
Dinna, do not.
Dirl, a slight tremulous stroke or pain.
Disrespecket, disrespected.
Distain, stain.
Dizzen, or *diz'n*, a dozen.
Dizzie, giddy.
Dochter, daughter.
Doited, stupefied, silly from age.
Doff, stupefied, crazed; also a fool.
Donsie, unlucky, affectedly neat and trim.
Doodle, to dandle.
Dool, sorrow; to "*sing dool*," to lament, to mourn.
Doos, doves, pigeons.
Dorty, saucy, nice.
Douse, or *douce*, sober, wise, prudent.
Doucely, soberly, prudently.
Dought, was or were able.
Doup, backside.
Doup-skelper, one that strikes the tail.
Dour and din, sullen and sallow.
Douser, more prudent.
Dow, am or are able, can.
Dowff, pithless, wanting force.
Dowie, worn with grief, fatigue, &c., half asleep.
Downa, am or are not able, cannot.
Doylt, or *doytte*, wearied, exhausted.
Doze, stupefied, the effects of age; to dozen, to benumb.
Drab, a young female beggar; to spot, to stain.
Drap, a drop, to drop.
Drapping, dropping.
Drawling, drawling, speaking with a sectarian tone.
Dreep, to ooze, to drop.
Dreigh, tedious, long about it, lingering.
Dribble, drizzling, slaver.
Driddle, the motion of one who tries to dance but moves the middle only.
Drift, a drove, snow moved by the wind.
Drinkin, drinking.
Droddum, the breech.
Drone, part of a bagpipe, the chanter.
Droop rumpl't, that droops at the crupper.
Droukt, or *droukit*, wet.

Drouth, thirst, drought.
Drucken, drunken, or *drukken*, drunken.
Drumly, muddy.
Drummock, or *drammock*, meal and water mixed, raw.
Drant, pet, sour humour.
Dryin, drying.
Dub, a small pond, a hollow filled with rain water.
Duds, rags, clothes.
Duddie, ragged.
Dung, *dang*, worsted, pushed, stricken.
Dunted, throbbed, beaten.
Dush, *dunsh*, to push, or butt as a ram.
Dusid, overcome with superstitious fear.
Dyvor, bankrupt, or about to become one: [So called from wearing *divers* coloured stockings, as anciently compelled by law.]

E

E'e, or *ee*, the eye.
Een, the eyes.
E'ebree, the eyebrow.
E'en, *e'enin*, the evening.
E'en, as; *e'en's*, even as.
Eerie, frighted, haunted, dreading spirits.
Eild, old age.
Elbuck, the elbow.
Eldritch, ghastly, frightful, elvish.
En', end.
Embrugh, or *Embrogh*, Edinburgh.
Eneugh, and *eneuch*, enough.
Ensuin, ensuing.
Especial, especially.
Ether-stone, stone formed by adders, an adder bead.
Ettle, to try, attempt, aim.
Eydent, diligent, constant, busy.

F

Fa', fall, lot, to fall, fate.
Fa' that, to enjoy, to try, to inherit.
Faddom't, fathomed; length of both arms.
Faes, foes.
Faem, foam of the sea.
Failet, forgiven or excused, on demand.
Fain, desirous of, overcome with joy.
Fairin, fairing, a present brought from a fair.
Fallow, fellow.
Fand, did find.
Fareweel, farewell, adieu.
Farl, a cake of bread; third part of a cake.
Fash, trouble, care; to trouble, to care for.
Fasheous, troublesome.
Fasht, troubled.
Fasten e'en, Fasten's even.
Fattrels, or *fatt'rels*, ribbon ends.
Faught, fight.
Fauld, and *fald*, a fold for sheep, to fold.
Faut, or *faute*, fault.
Fawsont, decent, seemly.
Feaefu', fearful, frightful.
Fear't, affrighted.
Feat, neat, spruce, clever.
Fecht, to fight.
Fechtin, or *fechtin*, fighting.
Feck, and *fek*, number, quantity.
Fecket, an under-waistcoat.

Feckfu', large, brawny, stout.
Feckless, puny, weak, silly.
Feckly, mostly.
Feg, a fig.
Fegs, faith, an exclamation.
Feide, feud, enmity.
Fell, keen, biting; the flesh immediately under the skin; level moor on a hill.
Felly, relentless.
Fend, *fen*, to make a shift, contrive to live.
Ferlie, or *ferley*, to wonder; a wonder, a term of contempt.
Fetch, to pull by fits.
Fetch't, pulled intermittently.
Fey, strange; one marked for death, predestined.
Fidge, to fidgit; *fidgin*, fidgeting.
Fidgin-fain, tickled with pleasure.
Fien-ma-care, the devil may care.
Fiend, fiend, a petty oath.
Fier, sound, healthy; a brother, a friend.
Fierrie, fiery, bustling, active.
Fissle, to make a rustling noise, a bustle.
Fit, foot.
Fittie-lan, the nearer horse of the hindmost pair in the plough.
Fizz, to make a hissing noise, fuss.
Flaffen, the motion of rags in the wind; of wings.
Floinen, flannel.
Flang, threw with violence.
Fleech, to supplicate in a flattering manner.
Fleechin, supplicating.
Fleesh, a fleece.
Fleg, a kick, a random blow, a fight.
Flether, to decoy by fair words.
Flethrin, flattering, wheedling words.
Fley, to scare, to frighten.
Fley'd, scared, frightened.
Flichter, *flichtering*, to flutter as young nestlings do when their dam approaches.
Flinders, shreds, broken pieces.
Flingin-tree, a piece of timber hung by way of partition between two horses in a stable; a flail.
Flisk, to fret at the yoke.
Flisket, fretted; *flisky*, skittish.
Flitter, to vibrate like the wings of small birds.
Flittering, fluttering, vibrating.
Flunkie, a servant in livery.
Flyte, *flyting*, scold, scolding.
Foor, hastened.
Foord, a ford.
Forbears, forefathers.
Forby, or *forbye*, besides.
Forfairn, distressed, worn out, jaded, forlorn, destitute.
Forgather, to meet, to encounter with.
Forgie, to forgive.
Forjesket, jaded with fatigue.
Forniaw'd, worn out.
Fou, full, drunk.
Foughten, *forfoughten*, troubled, fatigued.
Foul-thief, the devil, the arch-fiend.
Fouth, plenty, enough, or more than enough.
Fow, a measure, a bushel, also a pitchfork.
Frae, from.
Freath, froth, the frothing of ale in the tankard.

Frien', friend.
Fu', full.
Fud, the scut or tail of the hare, coney, &c.
Fuff, to blow intermittently.
Funnie, full of merriment.
Fur-ahin, the hindmost horse on the right hand when ploughing.
Furder, further, succeed.
Furm, a form, a bench.
Fusionless, spiritless, without sap or soul.
Fyfteen, fifteen.
Fyke, trifling cares, to be in a fuss about trifles.
Fyle, to soil, to dirty.
Fyl't, soiled, dirtied.

G

Gab, the mouth; to speak boldly or pertly.
Gaberlunzie, wallet-man, or tinker.
Gae, to go; *gaed*, went; *gane* or *gaen*, gone; *gaun*, going.
Gaet or *gate*, way, manner, road.
Gairs, parts of a lady's gown.
Gang, to go, to walk.
Gangrel, a wandering person.
Gar, to make, to force to; *gar't*, forced to.
Garten, a garter.
Gash, wise, sagacious, talkative; to converse.
Gatty, failing in body.
Gaucy, or *gawcie*, jolly, large, plump.
Gaud, and *gad*, a rod or goad.
Gaudsman, one who drives the horses at the plough.
Gaunted, yawned, longed.
Gawkie, a thoughtless person, and something weak.
Gawsie, see *gaucie*.
Gaylies, and *gaylie*, pretty well.
Gear, riches, goods of any kind.
Geck, to toss the head in wantonness or scorn.
Ged, a pike; *Ged's-hole*, a pool frequented by pike; metaphorically the grave.
Gentles, great folks.
Genty, elegant.
Geordie, George, a guinea, called Geordie from the head of King George.
Get, a child, a young one.
Ghaist, a ghost; *ghaistis*, ghosts.
Gie, to give; *gied*, gave; *gien*, given.
Giftie, diminutive of gift.
Giglets, laughing maidens.
Gillie, diminutive of gill; Gaelic for boy.
Gilpey, a half-grown boy or girl.
Gimmer, a ewe two years old.
Gin, if; *gif*—see "Scottish Language."
Gipsey, a young girl.
Girdle, a round iron plate on which oatcake is fired.
Girn, to grin, to twist the features in rage, agony, &c.; a snare for birds.
Girnaw, or *girnin*, grinning.
Girran, a "*pantherie girran*," a little vigorous animal; a horse rather old, but yet active when heated.
Gizz, a periwig, the face.
Glaikit, inattentive, foolish.
Glaive, a sword.
Glanzie, glittering, smooth, like glass.
Glaumed, grasped, snatched at eagerly.

Gled, a species of hawk.
Gleg, sharp, ready.
Gley, a squint, to squint.—See *A-gley*.
Gleyde, an old horse.
Glib-gabbit, that speaks smoothly and readily.
Glieb o' lan', a portion of ground. The ground belonging to a manse is called "the glieb," or portion.
Glint, to peep as light, quickly.
Glinton, or *glintin*, peeping.
Glinted by, went brightly past.
Gloamin, the twilight.
Gloamin-shot, twilight musing; a shot in the twilight.
Glow'r, to stare, to look; a stare, a look.
Glowran, amazed, looking suspiciously, gazing.
Glum, displeased.
Glunch, a frown; to frown.
Goavan, walking as if blind, or without an aim.
Gor-cocks, the red-game, or moor-cock.
Gowan, the flower of the daisy, dandelion, hawkweed, &c.
Gowany, covered with daisies.
Gowd, gold.
Gowff, the game of golf; to strike, as the bat does the ball at golf.
Gowk, term of contempt, the cuckoo.
Gowl, to howl; *gowling*, howling.
Graining, groaning.
Graip, a pronged instrument for cleaning cowhouses.
Graith, accoutrements, furniture, dress.
Graan, or *grain*, a groan; to groan.
Grannie, or *grannie*, grandmother.
Grape, to grope; *grapet*, groped.
Grat, past of *greet*, shed tears.
Great, *grit*, intimate, familiar.
Gree, to agree; "*to bear the gree*," to be decidedly victor; *gree't*, agreed.
Green-graff, green grave.
Greet, to shed tears, to weep.
Greetin, weeping.
Grey-neck-quill, a quill unfit for a pen.
Grieas, longs, desires.
Grieves, stewards.
Grippet, or *grippit*, seized, catched.
Grisle, gristle.
Groanin-maut, drink for the cummers at a lying-in.
Groat, "to get the whistle of one's groat," to play a losing game; to feel the consequences of one's folly.
Groset, a gooseberry.
Grousome, loathsome, grim.
Grumph, a grunt; to grunt.
Grumphie, a sow.
Grumphin, the snorting of an angry pig.
Grun', ground.
Grunstane, a grindstone.
Gruntle, the snout, a grunting noise.
Grunzie, a mouth which pokes out like that of a pig.
Grushie, thick, of thriving growth.
Gude, the Supreme Being.
Gude auld-has-been, was once excellent.
Guid, *guids*, good, goods.
Guid-e'en, good evening.
Guidfather, and *guidmother*, father-in-law and mother-in-law.

Guidman, and *guidwife,* the master and mistress of the house: *young guidman,* a man newly married.
Guid-mornin, good morning.
Gully, or *gullie,* a large knife.
Gulravage, joyous mischief.
Gumlie, muddy.
Gumption, discernment, knowledge, talent.
Gusty, gustfu', tasteful.
Gut-scraper, a fiddler.
Gutcher, grandsire.

H

Ha', hall.
Ha'-Bible, the great Bible that lies in the hall.
Haddin, house, home, dwelling-place, a possession.
Hae, to have, to accept.
Haen, had (the participle of *hae, i.e.* haven).
Haet, feint haet, a petty oath of negation, nothing, the fiend have it.
Haffet, the temple, the side of the head.
Haflins, nearly half, not fully grown.
Hag, a scar, a gulf in mosses and moors, moss-ground.
Haggis, a kind of pudding boiled in the stomach of a cow or sheep.
Hain, to spare, to save; *hain'd,* spared.
Hain'd gear, hoarded money.
Hairst, harvest.
Haith, a petty oath.
Haivers, speaking without thought, nonsense.
Hal', or *hald,* an abiding place.
Hale, or *haill,* whole, tight, healthy.
Hallan, a particular partition wall in a cottage.
Hallowmass, Hallow-eve, 31st October.
Haly, holy; "*haly-pool,*" holy well with healing qualities.
Hame, home; *hamely,* familiar.
Hammer'd, the noise of feet like the din of hammers.
Han's breed, hand's breadth.
Hanks, thread as it comes from the measuring reel, quantities, &c.
Hansel-throne, throne when first occupied.
Hap, an outer garment, mantle, plaid, &c., to wrap, to cover, to hap.
Hap-shackled, bound fore and hind foot.
Hap-step-an'-loup, hop, skip, and leap.
Happer, a hopper, the hopper of a mill.
Happing, hopping.
Harigals, heart, liver, and lights of an animal.
Harkit, hearkened.
Harn, a very coarse linen.
Hash, a fellow who knows not how to act with propriety, term of contempt.
Hastit, hastened.
Haud, to hold.
Haughs, low-lying, rich land, valleys.
Hausel, to drag, to pull violently.
Haurlin, tearing off, pulling roughly.
Haver-meal, oatmeal.
Haveril, haverel, a quarter-wit.
Havins, good manners, decorum, good sense.
Hawkie, a cow, properly one with a white face.

Healsome, healthful, wholesome.
Heapit, heaped.
Hear't, hear it.
Hearse, hoarse.
Heather, or *hether,* heath.
Hech, oh strange! a sigh of weariness.
Hecht, promised; to foretell, foretold.
Heckle, a board in which are fixed a number of sharp steel prongs upright for dressing hemp, flax, &c.
Hee balow, words used to soothe a child.
Heels-owre-gowdie, topsy-turvy, turned the bottom upwards.
Heeze, to elevate, to raise, to lift.
Helm, the rudder or helm.
Herd, to tend flocks; one who tends flocks.
Herrin, herring.
Herry, to plunder; most properly to plunder birds' nests.
Herryment, plundering, devastation.
Hersel, herself.
Het, hot, heated.
Heugh, a crag, a ravine; *coal-heugh,* a coal-pit; *lowan heugh,* a blazing pit.
Hilch, to halt; *hilchin,* halting.
Hiney, honey.
Hing, to hang; *hang,* hung.
Hirple, to walk crazily.
Hirplan, creeping.
Hirsel, so many cattle as one person can attend.
Histie, dry, chapt, barren.
Hitch, a loop, a stop, a knot.
Hizzie, hussy, a young girl.
Hoddin, the motion of a sage country farmer on an old horse, humble.
Hoddin-gray, woollen cloth of a coarse quality, made by mingling one black fleece with a dozen white ones.
Hoggie, a two-year-old sheep.
Hog-score, the distance-line in curling.
Hog-shouther, a kind of horse-play by justling with the shoulder; to justle.
Hoodie-craw, a carrion crow, corbie.
Hool, outer skin, nutshell or husk.
Hoolie, slowly, leisurely.
Hoord, a hoard, to hoard.
Hoordet, hoarded.
Horn, a spoon made of horn.
Horn-book, a sheet containing alphabet, &c., in large type, in wooden frame, glazed with horn to preserve it from injury by young scholars.
Hornie, one of the many names of the devil.
Hoste, or *host,* to cough.
Hostan, coughing.
Hotch'd, turned topsy-turvy, blended, ruined, moved.
Houghmagandie, loose behaviour.
Howlet, an owl.
Housie, diminutive of house.
Hove, hoved, to heave, to swell; swollen.
Howdie, a midwife.
Howe, hollow, a hollow or dell.
Howebackit, sunk in the back, spoken of a horse.
Howff, a house of resort.
Howk, to dig.
Howkan, or *howkin,* digging deep.
Howket, digged.
Hoy, hoy't, to urge, urged.
Hoyse, to pull upwards; a pull, &c.

Hoyte, motion between a trot and gallop.
Hughoc, diminutive of Hughie.
Hums and hawkers, mumbles and seeks to do what he cannot perform.
Hunkers, the hams.
Hurcheon, a hedgehog.
Hurdies, the loins, the crupper.
Hushion, a cushion, also a stocking wanting the foot.
Huchgoll'd, moving with a hilch.

I

I', in.
Icker, an ear of corn.
Ier-oe, a great-grandchild.
Ilk, or *ilka,* each, every.
Ill-deedie, mischievous.
Ill o't, awkward at it.
Ill-willie, malicious, unkind.
Indentin, indenting.
Ingine, genius, ingenuity.
Ingle, fire, fireplace.
Ingle-lowe, light from the fire, flame from the hearth.
I red ye, I advise ye, I warn ye.
I'se, I shall or will.
Ither, other, one another.

J

Jad, jade; also a familiar term among country folks for a giddy young girl.
Jauk, to dally at work, to trifle.
Jaukin, trifling, dallying.
Jawner, talking, and not to the purpose.
Jaup, a jerk of water; to jerk, as agitated water.
Jaw, coarse raillery; to pour out, to shut, to jerk as water.
Jillet, a jilt, a giddy girl.
Jimp, to jump; slender waisted, handsome.
Jinglan, jingling.
Jink, to dodge, to turn a corner; sudden turning of a corner.
Jinkus, or *jinkin,* dodging, the quick motion of the bow on the fiddle.
Jink an' diddle, moving to music; motion of a fiddler's elbow; here and there with a tremulous movement.
Jinker, that turns quickly, a gay sprightly girl; a wag.
Jirt, a jerk, to squirt.
Jocteleg, a kind of knife.
Jokin, joking.
Jouk, to stoop, to bow the head, to conceal.
Jow, to jow, a verb, which includes both the swinging motion and pealing sound of a large bell; also the undulation of water.
Jumpan, or *jumpin,* jumping.
Jundie, to justle; a push with the elbow.

K

Kae, a daw.
Kail, colewort, a kind of broth.
Kailrunt, the stem of colewort.
Kain, fowls, &c., paid as rent by a farmer.
Kebars, rafters.
Kebbuck, a cheese.
Keekle, joyous cry; to cackle as a hen.

Keek, a peep, a sly look; to peep.
Kelpies, a sort of mischievous water-spirit, said to haunt fords and ferries at night, especially in storms.
Ken, to know; *ken'd*, known; *ken't*, know.
Kennin, knowledge, a small matter.
Ket, a hairy, ragged fleece of wool.
Keugh, carking anxiety.
Kilt, to truss up the clothes.
Kimmer, a young girl, a gossip.
Kin, kindred.
Kin', kind; sort.
King's-hood, part of the entrails of an ox.
Kintra, *kintrie*, country.
Kirn, the harvest supper, a churn.
Kirsen, to christen, to baptize.
Kiss caups, to kiss caups, to pledge friendship.
Kist, chest, a shop counter.
Kitchen, anything that eats with bread.
Kittle, to tickle; ticklish, likely.
Kittlen, a young cat.
Kiuthen, cuddling, fondling.
Kiuthe, to cuddle.
Knaggie, like knags, or points of rocks.
Knap, to strike or break.
Knappin-hammer, a hammer for breaking stones.
Knots, see *mystic knots*.
Knurlin, crooked but strong, knotty.
Knowe, a small round hillock, a knoll.
Kye, cows.
Kyle, a district in Ayrshire.
Kyte, the belly.
Kythe, to discover, to show one's self.

L

Labor, or *labour*, toil; to thrash.
Laddie, diminutive of lad.
Laggen, the angle between the side and the bottom of a wooden dish.
Laigh, low.
Lairing, *lairie*, wading, and sinking in snow, mud, &c.; miry.
Laith, loath.
Laithfu', bashful, sheepish, abstemious.
Lallans, Scottish dialect, = Lowlands.
Lambie, diminutive of lamb.
Lammas moon, harvest moon.
Lampit, a kind of shell-fish, a limpet.
Lan', land, estate.
Lan'-afore, foremost horse in the plough.
Lan'-ahin, hindmost horse in the plough.
Lane, lone; *my lane*, *thy lane*, &c., myself alone, thyself alone.
Lanely, lonely.
Lang, long; *to think lang*, to long, to weary.
Lap, did leap.
Late and air, late and early.
Laughan, or *laughin*, laughing.
Lave, the rest, the remainder, the others.
Laverock, the lark.
Lawlan', lowland.
Lay my dead, attribute my death.
Lea [rig], unploughed land, = that which is left.
Lea'e, or *lea*, to leave.
Leal, loyal, true, faithful.
Lear (pronounce *lair*), learning, lore.
Lee-lang, live-long.
Leesome luve, happy, gladsome love.

Leeze me, a phrase of congratulatory endearment; I am happy in thee, &c.
Leister, a three-pronged and barbed dart for striking fish.
Leugh, did laugh.
Leuk, a look, to look.
Libbet, castrated.
Lick, to beat; *licket*, beaten.
Lift, sky, firmament.
Lightly, sneeringly; to sneer at.
Lilt, a ballad, a tune; to sing.
Limmer, a kept mistress, a strumpet.
Limp't, limped, hobbled.
Link, to trip along; *linkan*, tripping along.
Linn, a waterfall, a cascade.
Lint, flax; *lint i' the bell*, flax in flower.
Lint-white, a linnet, flaxen.
Livin, living.
Loan, the place of milking.
Loaning, lane.
Loof, the palm of the hand.
Loot, did let.
Looves, the plural of loof.
Losh, man! rustic exclamation modified from "Lord, man!"
Loun, a fellow, a ragamuffin, a woman of easy virtue.
Louper-like, *lan'-louper*, a stranger of a suspected character.
Lout, or *loot*, to stoop down.
Lowan, or *lowin*, flaming.
Lowan-drouth, burning desire for drink.
Lowe, a flame, to flame.
Lowrie, abbreviation of Lawrence; the fox.
Loose, to loose; *loosed*, unbound, loosed.
Lug, the ear.
Lug of the law, at the ear of the judge.
Lugget, having a handle.
Luggie, a small wooden dish with a handle.
Lum, chimney; *lum-head*, chimney-top.
Lunch, a large piece of cheese, flesh, &c.
Lunt, a column of smoke; to smoke, to walk quickly.
Lyart, of a mixed colour, gray.

M

Mae, and *mair*, more.
Maggot's-meat, food for the worms.
Mahoun, Satan—from *Mahomet*.
Mailen, a farm.
Maist, most, almost.
Maistly, mostly, for the greater part.
Mak, to make; *makin*, making.
Mally, Molly, Mary.
Mang, among.
Manse, the house of the parish minister.
Mantele, a mantle.
Mark, merks. This and several other nouns which in English require an *s* to form the plural, are in Scotch, like the words sheep, deer, the same in both numbers.
Mark, *merk*, a Scottish coin, value thirteen shillings and fourpence.
Marled, party-coloured.
Mar's year, the year 1715. Called Mar's year from the rebellion of Erskine, Earl of Mar.
Martial chuck, the soldier's camp-follower.
Mashlum, or *mashlam*, mixed corn.
Mask, to mash, as malt, &c., to infuse.

Mashie-pot, teapot.
Maukin, a hare.
Maun, must; *maunna*, must not.
Maut, malt.
Mavis, the thrush.
Maw, to mow.
Mawin, mowing; *mawn*, mowed.
Mawn, a small basket without a handle.
Meere, a mare.
Melancholious, mournful.
Melder, a load of corn, &c., sent to the mill to be ground.
Mell, to be intimate, to meddle; also a mallet for pounding barley in a stone trough.
Melvie, to soil with meal.
Men', to mend.
Mense, good manners, decorum.
Menseless, ill-bred, rude, impudent.
Merle, the blackbird.
Messan, a small dog.
Middin, a dunghill.
Middin-creels, panniers to carry manure in.
Middin-hole, a gutter at the bottom of a dunghill.
Milkin-shiel, a place where cows or ewes are brought to be milked.
Mim, prim, affectedly meek.
Mim-mou'd, gentle-mouthed.
Min', to remember.
Minawae, minuet.
Mind't, mind it; resolved, remembered.
Minnie, mother, dam.
Mirk, dark; darkness.
Misca', to abuse, to call names.
Misca'd, abused in wrong language.
Mischanter, accident.
Mislear'd, mischievous, unmannerly.
Misteuk, mistook.
Mither, mother.
Mixtie-maxtie, confusedly mixed.
Modewurk, a mole; otherwise *moudiwort*.
Moistify, to moisten, to soak.
Mons-meg, a large piece of ordnance, to be seen at the Castle of Edinburgh, composed of iron bars welded together and then hooped.
Mools, earth.
Mony, or *monie*, many.
Moop, to nibble as a sheep.
Moorlan', of, or belonging to moors.
Morn, the next day, to-morrow.
Mottie, full of motes.
Mou', the mouth.
Mousie, diminutive of mouse.
Muckle, or *meikle*, great, big, much.
Muses-stank, muses-rill, or fountain.
Musie, diminutive of muse.
Muslin-kail, broth composed simply of water, shelled barley, and greens.
Mutchkin, an English pint.
Mysel, myself.
"*Mystic-knots*," entanglements made by the bridesmaids on the bridal evening dress, so complicated as to seem the work of the Devil.—"Address to the Deil."

N

Na, no, not, nor.
Nae, or *no*, no, not any.

Naething, or *naithing*, nothing.
Naig, a horse, a nag.
Nane, none.
Nappy, ale; to be tipsy.
Neglecket, or *negleckit*, neglected.
Neebor, *niebor*, or *nibor*, a neighbour.
Neuk, nook.
Niest, nighest, next.
Nieve, *nief*, the fist.
Nierefu', handful.
Niffer, an exchange, to barter.
Niger, a negro.
Nine-tail'd cat, the hangman's whip.
Nit, a nut.
Norland, of, or belonging to the north.
Notic't, noticed.
Nowte, black cattle.

O

O', of.
O't, of it.
Ony, or *onie*, any.
Or, is often used for ere, before.
Orra-duddies, superfluous rags, old clothes.
Ourie, drooping, shivering.
Oursel, *oursels*, ourselves.
Outlers, outliers; cattle unhoused.
O'ergang, to trespass, to tread on.
O'erlay, an upper cravat.
Ower, *owre*, or *ow'r*, over.
Owre-hip, striking with a forehammer by bringing it with a swing over the hip.
Owsen, oxen.
Oxter'd, carried or supported under the arm.

P

Pack, intimate, familiar; twelve stone of wool.
Paidle, *paidlen*, to walk with difficulty, as if in water.
Painch, paunch.
Paitrick, a partridge.
Pang, to cram.
Parle, courtship.
Parishen, parish; pl. of parish.
Parritch, *pirratch*, or *porritch*, oatmeal pudding, a well-known Scotch dish.
Pat, did put; a pot.
Pattle, or *pettle*, a small spade to clean the plough.
Paughty, proud, haughty.
Paukie, cunning, sly.
Pay't, paid, beat.
Peat-reek, smoke of peats; a sort of whisky.
Pech, to fetch the breath short, as in asthma; *pechin*, breathing short.
Peghan, the crop, the stomach.
Pennie, riches; *penny-fee*, small money wages; *penny-wheep*, small beer.
Pet, a domesticated sheep, &c., a favourite.
Pettle, to cherish.
Philibeg, the kilt.
Phraise, fair speeches, flattery, to flatter.
Phraisin, flattering.
Pibroch, a martial air.
Pickle, a small quantity, one grain of corn.
Pigmy-scraper, little fiddler; term of contempt for a bad player.
Pine, pain, uneasiness.
Pingle, trouble, difficulty.

Pint-stoup, a two-quart measure.
Plack, an old Scotch coin, the third part of an English penny.
Plackless, pennyless, without money.
Plaidie, diminutive of plaid.
Platie, diminutive of plate.
Pleu, or *pleugh*, a plough.
Plinkie, a trick.
Plumrose, primrose.
Pock, a meal-bag.
Poind, to seize cattle, &c., for debt.
Poortith, poverty.
Posie, a nosegay, a garland.
Pou, to pull; *pou'd*, pulled.
Pouk, to pluck.
Pousie, a hare or cat.
Pout, a poult, a chick.
Pou't, did pull.
Poutherie, fiery, active.
Pouthery, like powder.
Pow, the head, the skull.
Pownie, a little horse, a pony.
Powther, or *pouther*, gunpowder.
Preclair, supereminent.
Preen, a pin.
Prent, printing, print.
Prie, to taste; *pri'd*, tasted.
Prief, proof.
Prig, to cheapen, to dispute.
Priggin, cheapening.
Primsie, demure, precise.
Propose, to lay down, to propose.
Pund, pound; *pund o' tow*, pound weight of the refuse of flax.
Pyet, a magpie.
Pyle, *a pyle o' caff*, a single grain of chaff.
Pystle, epistle.

Q

Quaick, cry of a duck.
Quat, quit; to quit.
Quauk, to quake; *quaukin*, quaking.
Queck, a drinking-cup made of wood.
Quey, a cow from one to two years old.
Quines, queans.

R

Ragweed, herb ragwort.
Raible, to rattle nonsense.
Rair, to roar; *rairan*, or *rowran*, roaring.
Raize, to madden, to inflame.
Ramfeezled, fatigued, overpowered.
Rampin, raging.
Ram-stam, thoughtless, forward.
Randie, a scolding sturdy beggar, a shrew.
Rantan, or *rantin*, joyous.
Raploch, properly a coarse cloth, but used for coarse.
Rarely, excellently, very well.
Rash, a rush; *rash-buss*, a bush of rushes.
Ratton, a rat.
Raucle, rash, stout, fearless, reckless.
Raught, reached.
Raw, a row.
Rax, to stretch, to reach out.
Ream, cream, to cream.
Reamin, brimful, frothing.
Reave, or *rieve*, take by force.
Rebute, to repulse, rebuke.
Reck, to heed.

Rede, counsel; to counsel, to discourse.
Red-peats, burning turfs.
Red-wat-shod, walking in blood over the shoe tops.
Red-wud, stark mad.
Ree, half drunk, fuddled, wild.
Reek, smoke.
Reekin, smoking; *reekit*, smoked.
Restit, stood restive; stunted, withered.
Remead, remedy.
Requite, requited.
Restricked, restricted.
Rew, to smile, look affectionately, tenderly.
Rickles, shocks of corn, stooks.
Riddle, instrument for purifying corn.
Rief-randies, men who take the property of others, accompanied by violence and rude words.
Rig, a ridge.
Rin, to run, to melt; *rinnin*, running.
Rink, the course of the stones, a term in curling on ice.
Rip, a handful of unthreshed corn.
Ripplin-kame, instrument for dressing flax.
Risket, a noise like the tearing of roots.
Rock, or *roke*, the distaff.
Rockin, friendly evening visit.—In former times young women met with their "rocks" during the winter evenings, to sing, and spin, and be merry; these were called "rockings."
Rood, stands likewise for the plural, roods.
Roon, a shred, selvage of woollen cloth.
Roose, to praise; *toom roose*, empty boast.
Roun', round, in circle of neighbourhood.
Roupet, hoarse, as with a cold.
Row, to roll, to wrap, to roll as water.
Row't, rolled, wrapped.
Rowtan, or *rowtin*, lowing.
Rowte, to low, to bellow.
Routh, plenty.
Roset, rosin.
Rowdie-gumption, rough common-sense.
Ran-deils, downright devils.
Rung, a cudgel.
Runkled, wrinkled.
Runt, the stem of colewort or cabbage.
Ruth, a woman's name, the Book so called; sorrow.
Ryke, reach; *raught*, reached.

S

Sae, so.
Saft, soft.
Sair, to serve, a sore; *sairie*, sorrowful.
Sairly, sorely; much.
Sair't, served.
Sang, a song.
Sark, a shirt; *sarkit*, provided in shirts.
Saugh, willow.
Saugh-woodies, withies made of willows.
Saul, soul.
Saumont, salmon.
Saunt, saint; *saunted*, dead and glorified.
Saut, salt; *sauted*, salted.
Saw, to sow; *sawin*, sowing.
Sax, six.
Scar, to scare; *scaur*, apt to be scared; a precipitous bank of earth which the stream has washed red.
Scaud, to scald.
Scauld, to scold.

Scawl, a scold.

Scone, a kind of bread.

Sconner, a loathing, to loath.

Scraich, to scream, as a hen or partridge.

Screed, to tear, a rent; *screedin*, tearing.

Scrieve, to glide swiftly, gleesomely along.

Scrievin, as adverb, gleesomely.

Scrimp, to scant; *scrimpet*, scant, scanty.

Scroggie, covered with underwood, bushy.

Seuldudrie, loose talk; fornication.

Seizan, seizing.

Sel, self; *a lady's sel*, one's self alone.

Sell't, did sell.

Sen', to send.

Servan', servant.

Sets, sets off, goes away.

Settlin, settling; *to get a settlin*, to be frighted into quietness.

Shaird, a shred, a shard.

Shangan, a stick cleft at one end for pulling the tail of a dog, &c., by way of mischief, or to frighten him away.

Shank-it, walk it; *shanks*, legs.

Shaucl't-feet, loose, ill-shaped feet.

Shaul, shallow.

Shaver, a humorous wag, a barber.

Shavie, to play a, to do an ill turn.

Shaw, to show; a small wood in a hollow place.

Sheen, bright, shining.

Sheep-shank, to think one's self nae sheep-shank, to be conceited.

Sherra-muir, Sherriff-Muir, the famous battle of, 1715.

Sheugh, a ditch, a trench, a sluice.

Shiel, shealing, a shepherd's cottage.

Shill, shrill; clear sharp sound.

Shog, a shock, a push off at one side.

Shool, a shovel.

Shoon, shoes.

Shore, to offer, to threaten.

Shor'd, half offered and threatened.

Shot, one traverse of the shuttle from side to side of the web.

Shouther, the shoulder.

Sic, such; *sic-like*, such as.

Sicker, sure, steady.

Sidelins, sidelong, slanting.

Silken-snood, a fillet of silk, a token of virginity.

Siller, silver, money, white.

Simmer, summer.

Sin, a son.

Sin', since; *sinsyne*, since then.

Skaith, to damage, to injure; injury.

Skellum, a noisy, reckless fellow.

Skelp, to strike, to slap; to walk with a smart tripping step; a smart stroke.

Skelpin, skelpin, striking, walking rapidly.

Skelpie-limmer, a technical term in female scolding.

Skiegh, proud, nice, saucy, mettled.

Skinklin, thin, gauzy, slatternly.

Skirl, to cry, to shriek shrilly.

Skirlin, shrieking, crying.

Skirl't, shrieked.

Sklent, slant, to run aslant, to deviate from truth.

Skiented, ran, or hit, in an oblique direction.

Skouth, vent, free action.

Skreigh, skriegh, a scream, to scream; the first cry uttered by a child.

Skyrin, party-coloured, the checks of the tartan.

Skyte, worthless fellow; to slide rapidly off.

Slade, did slide.

Slae, sloe.

Slap, a gate, a breach in a fence.

Slaw, slow.

Slee, sly; *slee'st*, slyest.

Sleeket, sleek, sly.

Sliddery, slippery.

Slip-shod, loose shod.

Sloken, to quench, to slake.

Slype, to fall over, as a wet furrow from the plough.

Slypet-o'er, fell over, as above.

Sma', small.

Smeddum, dust, powder, mettle, sense.

Smiddy, smithy.

Smirking, good-natured, smiling.

Smoor, to smother; *smoor'd*, smothered.

Smoutie, smutty, obscene; *smoutie phiz*, sooty aspect.

Smytrie, a numerous collection of small individuals.

Snapper, mistake in walking, &c.

Snash, abuse, Billingsgate, impertinence.

Snaw, snow, to snow.

Snaw-broo, melted snow.

Snawie, snowy.

Sned, to lop, to cut off.

Sned besoms, to cut brooms.

Sneeshin, snuff; *sneeshin-mill*, snuff-box.

Snell, and snelly, bitter, biting.

Snick, the latchet of a door.

Snick-drawin, trick-contriving.

Snirt, snirtle, concealed laughter.

Snool, one whose spirit is broken with oppressive slavery; to submit tamely, to sneak.

Snoove, to go smoothly and constantly, to sneak.

Snoran, snoring.

Snowk, to scent or snuff as a dog.

Snowket, scented, snuffed.

Sobbin, or sabbin, sobbing.

Sodger, a soldier.

Sonsie, having sweet, engaging looks; lucky, jolly.

Soom, to swim.

Souk, to suck, to drink long at a time.

Souple, flexible, swift; *soupled*, suppled.

Souter, a shoemaker.

Sowens, or so'ns, the fine flour remaining among the seeds of oatmeal made into an agreeable pudding.

Sowp, a spoonful, a small quantity of anything liquid.

Sooth, to try over a tune with a low whistle.

Sowther, to solder.

Spae, to prophesy, to divine.

Spails, chips, splinters.

Spairan, sparing.

Spairge, to dash, to soil, as with mire.

Spak, of speak, did speak.

Spaul, a limb.

Spates, speats, sudden floods after rain, &c.

Spaviet, having the spavin.

Speel, to climb.

Spence, the country parlour.

Spier, to ask, to inquire; *spier't*, inquired.

Spinnin-graith, wheel and roke and lint.

Splatter, to splutter; a splutter.

Spleuchan, a tobacco pouch.

Splore, a frolic, noise, riot.

Sprachled, scrambled.

Sprattle, to scramble.

Spreckled, or spriltt't, spotted, speckled.

Spring, quick air in music, Scottish reel.

Sprit, spret, a tough-rooted plant something like rushes, jointed-leaved rush.

Sprittie, full of sprits.

Spunk, fire, mettle, wit, spark.

Spunkie, mettlesome, fiery; will o' the wisp, or ignis fatuus; the devil.

Spurtle, a stick used in making porridge.

Squad, a crew or party, a squadron.

Squatter, to flutter in water, as a wild-duck, &c.

Squattle, to sprawl in the act of hiding.

Squeel, a scream, a screech; to scream.

Stacher, to stagger.

Stack, a rick of corn, hay, peats, &c.

Staggie, diminutive of stag.

Staig, a two-year-old horse.

Stalwart, stately, strong.

Stampan, stamping.

Stane, a stone; a weight of wool, &c.

Stang, sting, stung.

Stank, did stink; a pool of standing water, slow-moving water.

Stoo't, to stand, did stand.

Stap, stop, stave.

Stark, stout, potent.

Startle, to run as cattle stung by the gadfly.

Staukin, stalking, walking disdainfully, walking without an aim.

Staumrel, a blockhead, half-witted.

Staw, did steal, to surfeit.

Steek, to shut; a stitch.

Steer, to molest, to stir.

Steeve, firm, compacted.

Stegh, to cram the belly; *steghan*, cramming.

Stell, a still; commonly a smuggler's.

Sten, to rear as a horse, to leap suddenly.

Stents, tribute, dues of any kind.

Stey, steep, *steyest*, steepest.

Stibble, stubble; *stibble-rig*, the reaper in harvest who takes the lead.

Stick-an'-stow, totally, altogether.

Stilt, a crutch; to limp, to halt.

Stilts, poles for crossing a river.

Stimpart, the eighth part of a bushel.

Stinkan, foul smelling.

Stirk, a cow or bullock a year old.

Stock, a plant of colewort, cabbages.

Stockin, stocking; *throwing the stockin*, when the bride and bridegroom are put into bed, the former throws a stocking at random among the company, and the person whom it falls on is the next that will be married.

Stook, a shock of corn, twelve sheaves.

Stoor, hollow sounding, hoarse.

Stot, an ox.

Stound, sudden pang of the heart.

Stoup, or stowp, a kind of high narrow jug or dish with a handle, for holding liquids.

Stoure, or stowre, dust, more particularly dust in motion; *stoorie*, dusty.

Stown, stolen; *stownlins*, by stealth.

Stoyte, the walking of a drunken man.

Strack, did strike.

Strae, straw ; *to die a fair strae death*, to die in bed.
Straik, to stroke ; *straikit*, stroked.
Strappan, tall, handsome, vigorous.
Strath, low alluvial land, a holm.
Straught, straight.
Stravaig, wandering without an aim.
Streek, to stretch ; *streekit*, stretched.
Striddle, to straddle.
Strown't, spouted, pissed.
Stroup, the spout.
Strunt, spirituous liquor of any kind ; to walk sturdily, to be affronted.
Studdie, the anvil.
Stuff, corn or pulse of any kind.
Stumpie, diminutive of stump ; a grub pen.
Sturt, trouble ; *sturtan*, affrighted.
Styme, a glimmer.
Sucker, sugar.
Sud, shou'd, should.
Sugh, the continued rushing noise of wind or water.
Sumph, a pluckless fellow, with little heart or soul.
Suthron, Southern, an old name for the English nation.
Sward, sward ; the smooth grass.
Swall'd, swelled.
Swank, stately, jolly.
Swankie, or *swanker*, a tight strapping young fellow or girl.
Swap, an exchange ; to barter.
Swarf'd, swooned.
Swat, did sweat.
Swatch, a sample.
Swats, drink, good ale, new ale or wort.
Sweer, lazy, averse ; *dead-sweer*, extremely averse.
Swinge, to beat, to whip.
Swingein, a beating.
Swink, to labour hard.
Swirlie, knaggy, full of knots.
Swirl, a curve, an eddying blast or pool, a knot in wood.
Swith, or *swith awa*, get away.
Swither, to hesitate in choice ; an irresolute wavering in choice.
Swoor, or *swure*, swore, did swear.
Sword, a sword.
Sybow, a thick-necked onion.
Syne, since, ago, then.

T

Tackets, broad-headed nails for the heels of shoes.
Tae, a toe ; *three-taed*, having three prongs.
Tae, to ; only once so found in Burns—in Cunningham's edition of Epistle to Kennedy—a vulgarism.
Tait, a small quantity.
Tak, to take ; *takin*, taking.
Tangle, a sea-weed used as salad.
Tap, the top ; *tap-pickle*, highest on the ear of corn ; virginity.
Tapetless, heedless, foolish.
Targe, *targe them tightly*, cross-question them severely.
Tarrow, to murmur at one's allowance.
Tarry-breeks, a sailor.
Tassie, a small measure for liquor.
Tauld, or *tald*, told.

Tawpie, a foolish, thoughtless young person (spoken commonly of a girl).
Tawie, that allows itself peaceably to be handled (spoken of a cow, horse, &c.)
Tawted, or *tawtie*, matted together (spoken of hair and wool).
Teethless bawtie, toothless cur.
Teethless gab, a mouth wanting the teeth, an expression of scorn.
Ten-hours'-bite, a slight feed to the horse while in the yoke in the forenoon.
Tent, a field pulpit ; heed, caution ; *to tak tent*, to take heed.
Tentie, heedful, cautious.
Tentless, heedless, careless.
Teugh, tough.
Thack, thatch ; *thack an' rape*, all kinds of necessaries, particularly clothing.
Thae, those ; distinct from *they*.
Thairms, small guts, fiddle-strings.
Thankit, or *thankit*, thanked.
Thacket, thatched.
Thegither, together.
Themsel, themselves.
Thick, intimate, familiar.
Thigger, to crowd, to make a noise ; a seeker of alms, a sorner.
Thinkan, thinking.
Thir, these ; opposed to *thae*, those.
Thirl, to thrill ; to bind.
Thirl'd, thrilled, vibrated ; bound.
Thole, to suffer, to endure.
Thowe, a thaw, to thaw.
Thowless, slack, lazy.
Thrang, throng, busy ; a crowd.
Thrapple, throat, windpipe.
Thraw, a twist, a contradiction.
Thraw, to sprain, to twist, to contradict.
Thrawin, twisting ; *thrawn*, twisted, &c.
Threap, to maintain by dint of assertion.
Threshin, thrashing ; *threshin-tree*, a flail.
Thretteen, thirteen.
Thrissle, thistle.
Through, to go on with, to make out.
Throuther, i.e. *through-ither*, pell-mell, confusedly.
Thrum, sound of a spinning-wheel in motion ; thread at the end of a web.
Thud, to make a loud intermittent noise.
Thummart, foumart, polecat.
Thumpit, thumped ; did beat.
Thysel, thyself.
Till't, to it ; *fa' till't*, begin.
Timmer, timber ; a tree.
Timmer-propt, supported by timber.
Tine, to lose ; *tint*, lost.
Tinkler, a tinker.
Tip, a ram.
Tippence, twopence, money.
Tirl, to make a slight noise, to uncover.
Tirlin, uncovering ; *tirlit*, uncovered.
Tither, the other.
Tittlan, whispering and laughing.
Tittle, to whisper, to prate idly.
Tocher, marriage portion ; *tocher bands*, marriage bonds.
Tod, a fox ; *Tod i' the fauld*, fox in the fold.
Toddle, to totter, like the walk of a child ; *toddlan-dow*, toddling dove.
To-fa', a building added, a lean-to, a place of refuge ; *to-fa' o' the nicht*, when twilight darkens into night.

Toom, empty ; *toomed*, emptied.
Toop, a ram.
Toss, a toast.
Tosie, warm and ruddy with warmth ; good-looking ; intoxicating.
Tout, the blast of a horn or trumpet ; to blow a horn or trumpet.
Towzle, to ruffle in romping ; *towzling*, romping, ruffling the clothes.
Tow, a rope.
Towmond, a twelvemonth.
Town, or *toun*, a hamlet, a farmhouse.
Towsie, rough, shaggy.
Toy, a very old fashion of female head-dress.
Toyte, to totter like old age.
Trams, shafts ; *barrow trams*, the handles of a barrow.
Transmugrify'd, transmigrated, metamorphosed.
Trashtrie, trash, rubbish.
Trickie, or *trickie*, full of tricks.
Trig, spruce, neat.
Trimly, cleverly, excellently, in a seemly manner.
Trinle, the wheel of a barrow.
Trintle, to roll, to trundle.
Trinklin, trickling, as rain drops, or tears.
Troggers, wandering merchants.
Troggin, goods to truck or dispose of.
Trow, to believe, to trust to.
Trowth, truth ; a petty oath.
Trysts, or *trystes*, appointments, love meetings ; markets to which cattle are driven from a distance.
Tumbler-wheels, the wheels of a kind of low cart.
Twy, raw hide, of which in old time plough traces were frequently made.
Twy, or *tow*, either in leather or rope.
Tulzie, a quarrel ; to quarrel, to fight.
Twa, two ; *twa-fald*, twofold, bent.
Twa-three, a few, = to two or three.
'Twad, it would.
Twal, twelve ; *twal pennie worth*, a small quantity, a pennyworth. N.B.—One penny English is 12*d*. Scotch.
Twin, to part with ; to give up.
Twistle, twisting, the art of making a rope.
Tyke, a dog.
Tysday, Tuesday.

U

Unback'd filly, a young mare hitherto unsaddled.
Unco, strange, uncouth, very great, prodigious.
Unco, as an adverb, very ; "*unco pack an' thick thegither*," very intimate and friendly.
Uncos, news ; strange things ; strangers.
Undein, undoing, ruin.
Unfauld, unfold.
Unkenn'd, unknown.
Unsicker, uncertain, wavering, insecure.
Unskaith'd, undamaged, unhurt.
Upo', upon.

V

Vap'rin, vapouring, boasting idly.

Vauntie, joyous, with a delight which cannot contain itself.
Vera, very.
Virl, a ring round a column, &c.
Vogie, vain.

W

Wa', wall; *wa's*, walls.
Wabster, a weaver.
Wad, would; to bet; a bet, a pledge.
Wadna, would not.
Wadset, land on which money is lent, a mortgage.
Wae, woe; *waefu'*, sorrowful, wailing.
Waefu'-woodie, hangman's rope.
Waesucks! wae's me! alas! O the pity!
Wa'flower, wallflower.
Waft, woof; the cross thread that goes from the shuttle through the web.
Waifs an' crocks, stray sheep and old ewes past breeding.
Wair, or *ware*, to lay out, to expend.
Wair'd ew, spent upon, bestowed.
Wale, choice, to choose.
Wal'd, chose, chosen.
Walie, ample, large, jolly; also an exclamation of distress.
Wame, the belly.
Wamefu', a bellyful.
Wanchancie, unlucky
Wanrest, *wanrestfu'*, restless, unrestful.
Wark, work.
Wark-lume, a tool to work with.
Warl', or *warld*, the world.
Warld's-worm, a miser.
Warlock, a wizard; *warlock-knowe*, a knoll where warlocks once held tryste.
Warly, worldly, eager in amassing wealth.
Warran', a warrant; to warrant.
Warsle, or *warstle*, to wrestle.
Warsl'd, or *warstl'd*, wrestled.
Warst, worst.
Wastrie, prodigality.
Wat, or *weet*, wet.
Wat, I wat, I know, I wot.
Wat, a man's upper dress; a sort of mantle.
Water-brose, brose made simply of meal and water, without milk, butter, &c.
Wattle, a twig, a wand.
Wauble, to swing, to reel.
Waukt, thickened as fullers do cloth.
Waukin, waking, watching.
Waukrife, not apt to sleep.
Waur, worse, to worst; *waur't*, worsted.
Wean, or *weanie*, a child.
Wearie, exhausted; *many a wearie body*, many a different person.

Weary-widdle, toilsome contest of life.
Weason, weasand, windpipe.
Weaves the stockin, to knit stockings.
Wee, little; *wee things*, little ones; *wee bit*, a small matter.
Weeder-clips, instrument for removing weeds.
Weel, well; *weelfare*, welfare.
Weet, rain, wetness; to wet.
We'se, we shall.
Wha, who.
Wheezle, to wheeze.
Whelpet, whelped.
Whang, a leathern thong, a piece of cheese, bread, &c.
Whar, whare, where; *whare'er*, wherever.
Whase, whose; *wha's*, who is.
What-reck, nevertheless.
Wheep, to fly nimbly, to jerk, to toss over; *penny-wheep*, small-beer.
Whid, the motion of a hare running, but not frighted; a lie.
Whidden, running as a hare or coney.
Whigmaleeries, whims, fancies, crotchets.
Whilk, which.
Whingin, crying, complaining, fretting.
Whirligigums, useless ornaments, trifling appendages.
Whissle, a whistle, to whistle.
Whisht, silence; *to hold one's whisht*, to be silent.
Whisk, to sweep, to lash.
Whiskit, or *whiskit*, lashed; the motion of a horse's tail removing flies.
Whiskin beard, a beard like the whiskers of a cat.
Whitter, a hearty draught of liquor.
Whittle, a knife.
Whunstane, a whinstone.
Whyles, or *whiles*, sometimes.
Wi', with.
Wick, to strike a stone in an oblique direction, a term in curling.
Widdie, a rope, more properly one of withs or willows.
Widdifu', twisted like a withy, one who merits hanging.
Wiel, a small whirlpool.
Wifie, wifikie, a diminutive or endearing name for wife.
Wight, a man, a person; *fremit wight*, a stranger, or one estranged.
Wight, stout, enduring.
Wight an' wilfu', strong and obstinate.
Willyart-glower, a bewildered, dismayed stare.
Wimple, to meander, to enfold; *wimpl't*, meandered, enfolded.

Wimplin, waving, meandering.
Win', the wind.
Win', to wind, to winnow.
Win't, winded as a bottom of yarn.
Winna, will not.
Winnin thread, putting thread into hanks.
Winnock, a window.
Winsome, gay, hearty, attractive.
Wintle, a staggering motion; to stagger, to reel.
Winze, a curse or imprecation.
Wiss, to wish.
Withouten, without.
Wizen'd, hide-bound, dried, shrunk.
Woer-babs, the garter knitted below the knee with a couple of loops.
Wonner, a wonder; a contemptuous appellation.
Won, or *win*, to live.
Woo, to court, to make love to.
Woo', wool.
Wordy, worthy.
Worset, worsted.
Wrack, to teaze, to vex, to destroy.
Wraith, a spirit, a ghost, an apparition exactly like a living person, whose appearance is said to forebode the person's approaching death; wrath.
Wrang, wrong, to wrong.
Wreeth, a drifted heap of snow.
Wud, wild, mad; *red-wud*, see *supra*.
Wumble, a wimble.
Wyliecoat, a flannel vest.
Wyte, blame, to blame.

Y

Yaud, an old horse.
Ye, this pronoun is frequently used for thou.
Yealings, born in the same year, coevals.
Your, is used both for singular and plural, yours.
Yearns, eagles; otherwise, *earns*.
Yell, barren, that gives no milk.
Yerk, to lash, to jerk, to excite.
Yerkit, or *yerkit*, jerked, lashed, excited.
Yestreen, yesternight.
Yett, a gate.
Youks, itches.
Yill, ale.
Yird, earth; *yirded*, earthed, buried.
Yokin, yoking.
Yont, ayont, beyond.
Yirr, lively; a quick, startling sound.
Young guidman, a new married man.
Yowe, a ewe; *yowie*, diminutive of *yowe*.
Yule, Christmas.

END OF GLOSSARY.

To the following Correspondents, in addition to those whose names appear in the former list [Prose Works, p. 224], we are under special obligations for the courteous assistance they have afforded in contributing materials to our Appendix, as under:—

The following names should have been inserted in former list:

NEWSPAPER CORRESPONDENTS, &c.

To correct all the errors which from time to time occur in newspaper paragraphs, otherwise valuable, with respect to Robert Burns, would be a hopeless, perhaps a thankless, task; but the following is an instance in which, fortunately, one authority in that department of literature rectifies the inaccuracies of another.

DALSWINTON CORRESPONDENCE.—With reference to a newspaper notice quoted in our remarks on the Dalswinton Correspondence, p. 200, in so far as Lord Brougham's name is concerned, we must further quote from another newspaper, *Inverness Herald*, the subjoined letter which sometime ago appeared there, obtained from a correspondent of his Lordship's:—

          CANNES, FRANCE, May 6, 1865.

Lord Brougham presents his compliments to Mr. Aitken, and assures him that the account of his being with Burns at Dalswinton is a mere fable. He was only nine or ten years old in 1788, and he never was at Dalswinton till ten or eleven years after that time, and after the death of Burns.

[In newspaper report as quoted by us, p. 200, for (James Symington), read William Symington.]

NEW PSALMODY: Note on, p. 458. The following illustration of Lord Thurlow's profane swearing, which we find in Henry Crabb Robinson's Diary and Reminiscences, just published, seems to leave very little doubt that it is to him as

        The man that fears thy name

our Author alludes in that pasquinade.

  March 30th.—Dined with Messrs. Longman & Co. at one of their literary parties, ... The only one who said anything worth reporting was Dr. Rees, the well-known Arian, "Encyclopædia Rees." He related that when, in 1791, Beaufoy made his famous attempt to obtain the repeal of the Corporation and Test Act, a deputation waited on the Lord Chancellor Thurlow to obtain his support. The deputies were Drs. Kippis, Palmer [of Hackney], and Rees. The Chancellor heard them very civilly, and then said, "Gentlemen, I'm against you, by G——. I am for the Established Church, d——mee! Not that I have any more regard for the Established Church than for any other Church, but because it is established. And if you can get your d——d religion established, I'll be for that too!" Rees told this story with great glee.

After this, who shall say that Burns exaggerated, misrepresented, or too severely satirised the profanity of his day, in exposing it? or that he alone was inexcusable for occasional vehemence of language, or rudeness of expression? The truth is, he must have seen and heard, in company even with the most moderate and self-respecting men of the time, a thousand things more profane and gross than anything to be found in his own pages; and it seems one of the greatest miracles of his life that he should so far have escaped such contamination in his authorship. It is a curious fact worth noting, that the above-mentioned interview could not possibly have been known to Burns at the time, although the language employed by him with reference to Thurlow and the Church *of the very moment* so exactly corresponds to it.

DIRECTIONS TO BINDER.

INDEX:

WITH

ANALYSIS AND CLASSIFICATION OF WORKS.

DIRECTIONS TO BINDER.

INDEX:

WITH

ANALYSIS AND CLASSIFICATION OF WORKS.

Poetical Works.

AUTHOR'S FIRST EDITIONS—1786-1787.

POEMS, CHIEFLY SCOTTISH.

EPISTLES.

SONGS.

EPITAPHS.

Songs,

ACCORDING TO THEIR TITLES AND IN ORDER OF PUBLICATION.

JOHNSON'S MUSEUM, 1787-1803.

ORIGINALLY ACKNOWLEDGED BY THE AUTHOR.

THOMSON'S COLLECTION, 1793—1805,

AS HERE REPRESENTED.

[For remainder, see Currie's Edition, *infra.*]

From foregoing analysis of our Author's Lyrical Works, it appears that there were published by him Songs—

In Editions of his own,	14
In Johnson's Musical Museum—	
Originally acknowledged,	86
Not originally acknowledged,	57
Fragments, or Revisions almost entirely new productions,	35
In Thomson's Collection,	64
In Posthumous Works, by Currie and others,	43
Election Ballads, Fragments, &c., as songs,	17
Total number of Songs now known,	316

For the reader's convenience, the following Index of these, according to their first lines, with notice of all duplicates and variations, is added; and it is worthy of passing remark, that whereas in Johnson's Museum the Titles and the First Lines are often different, in Thomson's Collection they are almost always the same, a circumstance which goes far to establish the superior correctness of Johnson's Museum as a piece of editorial workmanship. What the Author's own titles for the songs which were edited by Thomson might be, can be determined now only by inference, or by external evidence, and in many cases may never be correctly ascertained at all.

Songs:

ARRANGED ALPHABETICALLY ACCORDING TO THEIR FIRST LINES.

In some editions of Burns we have seen, a considerable confusion may be observed in the use of the interjections "O" and "Oh!" as if the Author did not always understand the difference. By the above index of first lines, quoted as carefully as possible from his own recognised originals, the reader will perceive that no such confusion exists; but that on the contrary the nicest discrimination is observed in the use of said terms—"O" being employed only as a vocative, or as an exclamation of surprise or desire or joy; "Oh!" exclusively for the deepest pain or sorrow.

Posthumous Poetical Works.

CURRIE'S EDITION.

SONGS.

ELEGIES, ETC.

EPISTLES, ETC.

STEWART'S EDITION.

CROMEK'S EDITION.

EPISTLES, ETC.

SONGS.

LOCKHART'S EDITION.

CUNNINGHAM'S EDITION.

CHAMBERS'S EDITION.

PRESENT EDITION.

Fragments, Inscriptions, &c.

VARIOUS AUTHORITIES.

DOUBTFUL.

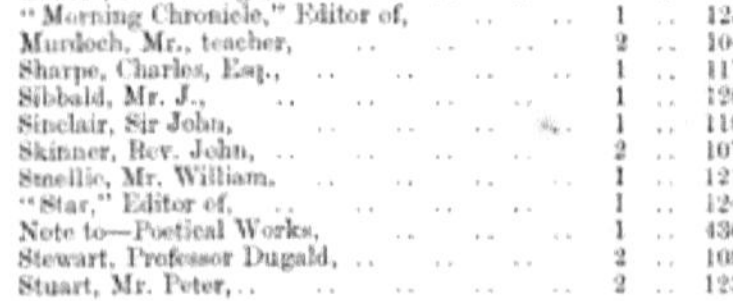

Prose Works.

SPECIAL CORRESPONDENCE.

LITERARY CORRESPONDENCE.

PRINCIPAL.

SUBORDINATE.

Appendix.

THE END.